Born in the London Borough of Islington, Victor Pemberton is a successful playwright and TV producer, as well as being the author of ten highly popular London sagas, all of which are published by Headline. His first novel, *Our Family*, was based on his highly successful trilogy of radio plays of the same name. Victor has worked with some of the great names of entertainment, including Benny Hill and Dodie Smith, had a long-standing correspondence with Stan Laurel, and scripted and produced many of the BBC's *Dr Who* series. In recent years he has worked as a producer for Jim Henson and set up his own production company, Saffron, whose first TV documentary won an Emmy award.

MY SISTER SARAH

NELLIE'S WAR

Victor Pemberton

headline

My Sister Sarah first published in Great Britain in 1999
by HEADLINE BOOK PUBLISHING

Nellie's War first published in Great Britain in 1998
by HEADLINE BOOK PUBLISHING

First published in this omnibus edition in 2004
by HEADLINE BOOK PUBLISHING

10 9 8 7 6 5 4 3 2 1

ISBN 0 7553 2263 0

Typeset by Palimpsest Book Production Limited,
Polmont, Stirlingshire
Printed and bound in Great Britain by
Mackays of Chatham plc, Chatham, Kent

Papers and cover board used by Headline are natural,
recyclable products made from wood grown in sustainable
forests. The manufacturing processes conform to the
environmental regulations of the country of origin.

HEADLINE BOOK PUBLISHING
A division of Hodder Headline
338 Euston Road
London NW1 3BH

www.headline.co.uk
www.hodderheadline.com

My Sister Sarah

For Ruth Messina, my dear friend,
and in memory of her husband Cedric,
who gave me so much encouragement

Part 1

1917 – 1921

Chapter 1

The Eaglet was Beattie's favourite pub. There was something about the place that appealed to her, the friendly atmosphere with the gang of regular customers who were always good for a laugh, and the warm welcome she always got from the landlord and his missus, who, unlike plenty of other publicans in the area, didn't object to an unaccompanied young girl propping up the counter of the public bar every Friday and Saturday night. Besides, these were the people she liked, not the stuck-up old buggers from her own part of Islington, up 'the Cally', but real flesh-and-blood working men, who knew how to give a girl a good time. Yes, The Eaglet's customers were the salt of the earth all right, or at least those remaining of them who had managed to get home on leave from the hellhole trenches of France after three years of savage hand-to-hand fighting with the army of Kaiser Bill.

Beattie was always popular with the male customers, especially the Tommies. To them, she was 'one of the lads', for she could join in with any bawdy song they sang, down a glass of bitter, smoke a fag, and play a game of darts with the best of them. One or two of them had enjoyed her company in more ways than one, for with her full bosom, rose complexion, shapely thighs and flashing blue-green eyes, she was more often than not the best-looking female customer in either the public or the saloon bar.

'Looks like the fleet's in port.'

The young bloke in naval uniform wasn't in the least surprised when Beattie approached him; they'd been eyeing each other up across the bar all evening through the thick haze of blue fag smoke.

'Anchor's down, and here I stay,' he replied with a knowing grin, and in an accent that was more public school than Islington. 'What'll you have to drink?'

Beattie sat down on the wooden bench seat he had vacated for her. 'Shandy,' she replied.

The young bloke pulled a face. 'Wasn't that a bitter you were drinking with the boys over there?'

Beattie smiled. 'They're my mates,' she replied, her accent an unnatural cockney. 'I only drink alcohol with people I know.'

'Then we'll have to do something about that, won't we?' The naval bloke offered her his hand. 'Edward. You can call me Ted.'

Beattie hesitated a brief moment, allowing herself time to look directly into his eyes, which were a bright, glowing pale blue. 'Beattie,' she replied, shaking his hand. 'You can call me Beattie.'

Edward laughed. He liked her. He liked her a lot. He had no way of knowing that he was not at all her type, for he was too clean-cut, too good-looking, and far too much like the family she had been born into.

'So you're an officer then?' she asked.

'Noncommissioned,' he replied.

Beattie looked puzzled.

'I'm a petty officer. A bit like a sergeant major in the army.'

'In other words, you're not just any old Jack Tar,' joked

Beattie, picking up his cap from the bench beside her, and trying it on. 'Nice uniform, though.' She watched him closely as he adjusted the cap on her head to a cocky angle.

Whilst he was making his way to the bar to order their drinks, Patch, a black and white mongrel dog, who was a firm favourite with The Eaglet's customers, was on his hind legs, swirling round and round in a dance, to the sound of 'See Me Dance the Polka' played on the pub upright piano by his loving owner, old Tubby Layton, a local rag-and-bone man. By the time Edward got back with the drinks, the customers were laughing, applauding, and cheering, which meant that Tubby's well-worn flat cap, placed on the piano lid, was soon tinkling with the sound of coins being dropped into it, and pints were being lined up beside it.

'Beattie?' Edward said, once the noise had died down. 'Must be short for Beatrice?'

Beattie, sipping her shandy, eyed him flirtatiously over the rim of her half-pint glass. 'You could be right.'

He drew closer, and stared straight into her eyes. 'But why do I think I've seen you somewhere before?'

'Oh, I get around,' was Beattie's only reply. For the time being, she had no intention of telling him that although they had never met, she knew Edward Lacey well. In fact she knew quite a lot about him.

A few minutes later, Patch had to sit guard on old Tubby, who was now the worse for all the booze that had been pumped into him by his fellow customers. A little later, everyone was reminded that there was a war on when the gaslamps on the walls began to flicker and lose their glow, plunging the pub into a gloomy half-light.

Beattie left The Eaglet with her petty officer. Behind them, with the blackout blinds firmly drawn, the pub, which nestled comfortably on the corner of the main Seven Sisters Road

5

and Hornsey Road, was nothing but a dark three-storey shape on a chilly late September evening. But from inside, they could hear the start of what promised to be a rowdy singsong, clearly intended to raise spirits and defy the war.

Beattie and her petty officer strolled hand in hand along the darkened Seven Sisters Road, heading in the direction of Finsbury Park, where Edward had lodgings. Apart from a tram with no interior lights, which clattered past them, the road was quiet.

A short time later, an eerie silence descended on the area. Even The Eaglet's customers had calmed down, exhausted by booze and song. Then a strange sound approached, whirring and throbbing.

In the distance maroons exploded into the air, giving a belated warning that an enemy aircraft was approaching.

A moment or so later, a barrage of anti-aircraft guns opened fire, sending out a profusion of shells with great puffs of white smoke into the low-lying clouds. This was followed by a crisscross of two searchlights, which scoured the sky for the intruder. Unfortunately, they were too late, for by the time they had picked up the great silver cigar-shaped Zeppelin in their beams, the deadly German war machine had deposited its high-explosive bomb on to the road below.

The bomb landed directly on to the roof of The Eaglet, tearing straight down three floors into the saloon bar, before exploding with a deafening blast in the cellar below.

In the sky, the great silver cigar disappeared into the protection of the dark evening clouds, engines whirring at full speed, heading back towards the Channel coast and home.

It was some hours later that they dug out those who had perished in the devastating explosion at The Eaglet.

The only survivor appeared to be a black and white

mongrel with a black patch over one eye. He was scraping frantically in the dust and debris of the ruined pub.

Sarah Melford polished the brass letterbox plate on the front door until she could see her face in it. This being a Tuesday, it was cleaning brass and silver day, and by the time she had got around to doing the letterbox, everything in the house, from the silver condiment set in the dining room to the brass fireguard and companion set in front of the sitting-room fireplace, had been restored to pristine condition. There was, of course, no need for her to do all this, nor in fact any of the house cleaning, for the Melford family could easily afford servants if they had wanted them. But Sarah hated servants, or at least the idea of them. Why should her father spend good money on getting people to clean the place when she herself had a perfectly good pair of hands, two good legs, and a healthy body that was perfectly capable of keeping the house in tiptop condition? And to Sarah, the family house, on Thornhill Road in the Barnsbury ward of Islington, was worth looking after. It was where she had been born nearly twenty-three years before, and she loved every single yellow brick it was built of, every window, and every room on all three floors. For that reason alone, she was perfectly happy to devote her daily life to its upkeep.

Once she had finished the letterbox, Sarah made her way to the closet room, where she tucked away the Brasso and cleaning cloths, and poured some water from a china jug into the washbasin. Whilst she was washing her hands, she took a passing glance at herself in the mirror above the washstand. Although she would never admit it, she was a lovely-looking girl, with a slightly pallid complexion, grey-green eyes, and long flaxen hair that was pinned up into a full bun behind her head. She looked more like her father

7

than her mother, for her face was marginally narrow, with a dimple right in the middle of a finely shaped chin. But because she was rather set in her ways, Sarah wore no makeup, and her daily wear usually consisted of a plain white blouse and a skirt that never rose up above her ankles. Her only concession to current fashion was the Royal Worcester Kidfitting corset she wore on special occasions, which helped to accentuate her already slender figure.

The smells of cooking that were coming from the kitchen at the back of the house finally persuaded her to join her mother. But not before she had wiped the washbasin round with a clean cloth, and tidied the few straggly hairs that had fallen over her forehead.

'Smells good,' Sarah called, as she joined her mother at the hob, where she was stirring a rabbit and onion stew. 'I can see why it's Father's favourite.'

'Well it won't be for much longer,' croaked her mother, Geraldine Melford, who was still recovering from one of her regular bouts of laryngitis. 'It says in *The Times* today the Government's going to ration meat and butter. But only in London and Southern England.'

'What?' snorted Sarah, outraged. The prospect of doing without meat stews, meat pies or the Sunday roast was, to her, quite unacceptable. 'Why should it always have to be us in the south who take the brunt of the war? We not only get bombed by Zeppelins and war planes, we also have to have our food on the ration.' Even though she was well-spoken, her voice, like her mother's, was often quite sharp. 'I tell you it's not fair. It's about time they picked on them up north for a change.'

'North, south – what does it matter? We're all the same country, Sarah. If we're going to bring this hateful war to an end, we're all going to have to do our bit.'

Sarah wasn't convinced. For a girl only in her twenties, she was curiously autocratic. She frowned on anything that hindered her own style of living. But she knew she'd been relatively lucky.

'I still can't stop thinking about those poor devils who got killed in the bomb blast at that public house a few months ago. How can their families ever recover from something like that?'

Geraldine sighed. 'I don't know, Sarah,' she said, going to the kitchen table to finish peeling potatoes. 'This war has been so ugly, so unnecessary. We've lost so many of our boys, young men who haven't even been given the chance to know what life is all about. Lord Kitchener has an awful lot to answer for.' She put on her rimless spectacles and picked up the peeler. Geraldine had a similar build to her daughter – tall, well-proportioned, and quite slender, especially for a middle-aged woman – but there the resemblance ended, for Geraldine had a full, rounded bust, and her face was rosy with high-boned cheeks. Like her daughter, she dressed older than her age, wearing a black lace bodice over a white blouse, lace cap to match, and a long dull grey skirt. 'Anyway, we must stop being so gloomy,' she said, as Sarah joined her at the table to start on the carrots. 'Now you've got a young man, you've got a whole exciting new life ahead of you.'

Sarah flinched. 'Oh, Mother,' she said, embarrassed. 'I've told you, I hardly know him.'

Geraldine looked up over her spectacles. 'You've been walking out for months now. It's time he asked your father if he can marry you.'

Sarah abruptly stopped peeling carrots. 'Mother! That's an absurd thing to say. How long was it before Father proposed to you? Three, four years?'

9

'That was different,' replied Geraldine, with just a hint of mischief in her voice. 'I was the only lady friend your father ever had. He was never sure whether I wanted him.'

Sarah felt a little reticent. 'This is the only man *I've* ever walked out with.'

Geraldine leaned across, and covered Sarah's hand with her own. 'All the more reason why you should grab the chance whilst it's there.' She continued with her peeling. 'So – when are you going to bring him home to meet us?'

'Oh, Mother!'

'For goodness' sake, child, why are you keeping so shy about him? You haven't even told us his name.'

Sarah put down her peeling knife, and smiled gently at her mother with a pleading look in her eyes. 'When I'm ready, Mother,' she said. 'When I'm ready.'

Samuel Melford was a lucky man. In fact, he told himself so every single day of his life. Samuel was never a person to take things for granted, and he was always grateful to the good Lord for giving him a loving wife and family, a well-paid job, and a home he could be proud of. Why then, he asked himself, as he made his way home on foot through the darkened streets of Barnsbury, was his mind these days so ill at ease?

'Evenin', guv'nor.'

On his way home on a Tuesday evening, Samuel never failed to make his ritual stop at Sid Perkins' hot chestnut stall on the corner of Richmond Avenue, where the warm glow of burning embers helped to soften the chill of a raw February evening. 'Good evening, Sid,' he replied, savouring the sweet woody smells that were wafting up from the hot chestnuts, whose hard brown skins had already split open over the intense heat. 'They smell good tonight.'

10

'That they do, sir,' sniffed Sid, who seemed to have a perpetual runny nose, which he only ever wiped on the cuff of his frayed jacket. 'Fresh from the Cally Market this mornin'. Same as usual, sir?'

'Two bags, please, Sid.'

Sid scooped up the blackened chestnuts, and filled two small paper bags with them. Then he wrapped them up in an old page of the *Islington Gazette*.

'Saw your youngest terday, sir,' he said, handing over the chestnuts. 'Reckon she was 'avin' 'erself a real good time.'

Samuel looked up with a start. 'Oh, really,' he said, guardedly. 'Where was that?'

'Up the Cattle Market. She was wiv a 'ole bunch of geezers. They was 'avin' a right ol' knees-up round Fred Kiley's barrel organ. Laugh a minute, it was. She's quite a gel. Chalk and cheese to your eldest.'

Samuel paid the twopence for the two bags of chestnuts, and after thanking Sid, went on his way. It was too dark for Sid to have noticed the pained expression on his customer's face.

After he left Gamages Department Store in Holborn each evening, where he was the General Manager, for Samuel the journey home seemed interminable. However, he always quickened his pace when he walked home to Thornhill Road from the tram stop in Liverpool Road, for the prospect of supper with the family, a pipe of good tobacco in front of a warm fire, and a chance to settle down with either *The Times* or *The Illustrated London News* was one of his few real pleasures in life. But tonight was different. Tonight, he walked slower than usual, for his mind was now preoccupied. '*Saw yer youngest terday, sir. Reckon she was 'avin' 'erself a real good time.*' Those words echoed through Samuel's mind as he strolled past the access to Lonsdale Square on his right, clutching the two bags of hot chestnuts in one hand and his briefcase in the other. At the corner of Richmond Avenue, he paused a moment or so before completing the last few steps home. Not a light was to be seen at the windows of any of the fine Georgian and Victorian houses, for the blackout regulations were strict, despite the fact that there had been no Zeppelin or aeroplane raids over the area for weeks. But the moon tantalised the rooftops as it sneaked in and out of the dark night clouds, enabling Samuel to take a lingering look at his own home, a sprawling Victorian building on three floors, and standing apart from all the other houses along Thornhill Road.

As he stood there, Sid's words were still ringing in his ears. '*Reckon she was 'avin' 'erself a real good time.*' What was it about his younger daughter that made her stand apart from the rest of the family? Why *was* she so different from her elder sister, who loved her parents, her home, and all the good things in life? Samuel rested his briefcase on the ground for a moment whilst he adjusted his homburg hat. Aware of its German origins, he had often felt guilty about wearing such a thing during wartime, but it was more comfortable and warmer than his usual trilbies.

At that moment, the moon emerged from behind the clouds again, and flooded the Melford house in a bright white glow. It also brought a warm, affectionate smile to Samuel's face. In some strange way, it encouraged him to think positive. Both his daughters were still very young, he said to himself. Both had a lot to learn about life and how to live it. Chalk and cheese they may be, but when it came to knowing what was right and wrong, neither would let her parents down. Not Sarah. Not even Beattie.

* * *

'They say the Bolsheviks are going to put the Tsar and his family on trial. I really think Mr Lloyd George should protest. It would be terrible if they tried to execute them or something.'

As she talked, Geraldine Melford set the large china casserole dish on the kitchen table, where it joined other hot dishes containing boiled potatoes, spiced white cabbage, and baby beetroot with chopped parsley. It was an odd custom that prompted the Melfords to use the kitchen for family meals, while the dining room was only used on high days and holidays.

'Well, it's their own fault,' sniffed Beattie, indifferently. 'They should have looked after their people more, the *real* people!'

'Beattie!' Her mother looked at her aghast. 'That's an awful thing to say. You can't blame the entire Russian royal family for all the things that have gone wrong in their country.'

'Well, it's true,' replied Beattie, provocatively. 'A royal family is no different to anyone else. They should be made to work for their livin'.'

'Just like you,' added Sarah, cuttingly, as she handed her mother a supper plate.

Beattie flicked a contemptuous glance at her elder sister, but decided to ignore her. 'If you ask me, I reckon our own King and Queen could do with a few lessons on what's goin' on in Russia.'

Samuel Melford broke his silence. 'King George and Queen Mary are only figureheads, Beattie,' he said gruffly. 'They have nothing to do with politics.'

Beattie took the first plateful of rabbit stew her mother had served, and handed it to her father. 'Then I don't see the point of having them,' she said, determined to have the last word.

13

Samuel saw no point in discussing the topic any further with his younger daughter. They had been down that road before, monarchy versus a republic, and as long as he lived, he would never understand how a girl from Beattie's privileged background could be such a champion of the working class, particularly when she herself had never done a day's work in her life. 'Please pass the potatoes,' he said to her vacantly. It was the safest way out of the conversation.

Once Geraldine had finished serving everyone with their share of the rabbit stew, supper continued in the same way that it did most evenings – in total silence. For almost an hour, the only sounds were of eating, knives and forks working hard on china plates, and the sipping of water from fine cut-crystal tumblers. To an outsider, it would seem hard to believe that this was a close-knit middle-class family gathered around the kitchen table for their evening meal. Occasionally Geraldine could be heard cooing, 'My angel!' to one of four cats, who ritually lined up on the floor beside her, waiting for a titbit of anything that might accidentally fall their way. The furry quartet were all strays that Geraldine had collected over the years and she adored them, much to the intense irritation of Beattie, who did not hesitate to give them a surreptitious sharp kick beneath the table.

Samuel Melford waited until the apple pudding had been served before bringing the silence to an end. At the best of times he was a man of few words, and his shyness often gave the false impression that he was moody. But he was a very thoughtful person who would often spend long hours in quiet contemplation and no decisions were ever taken until he had first considered them carefully and at some length. That was why his courtship of Geraldine had been for nearly four years, and even when he proposed to her he insisted that the actual wedding should not take place for a further year.

'Beattie,' he said, now without looking up at her, 'what was your business in the Cattle Market today?'

Beattie, clearly taken off guard, looked up with a start. She answered immediately, without swallowing the mouthful of apple pudding she had just taken. 'The market?' she replied, indignantly. 'Who told yer I was up the market?'

Her father glanced up at her. 'It doesn't matter who told me, Beattie,' he said gently. 'I merely ask what business you were engaged in.'

'Do I 'ave to 'ave business to go up the market?'

Samuel refused to be stonewalled. 'Yes, Beattie,' he replied, with quiet insistence. 'An unaccompanied young lady should only visit a market when she has a specific purpose for doing so.'

Beattie gave a bored sigh and slumped back into her chair. 'Oh really, Father. That's so old-fashioned.'

Samuel smiled politely at her. If it hadn't been for the fact that the only hair he had on his head was a thinly greying fringe over his ears, he and his youngest daughter were almost identical in appearance, with faces that were round and open, and blue-green eyes the colour of the glass lampshade dangling over the kitchen table. 'To be old-fashioned is no burden for me, my dear,' he said quietly, precisely. 'The welfare of my family is of far more importance to me than the fashion of the day.'

'I like the market, Father,' Beattie replied, irritated. 'I've got a lot of mates up there.'

'Ha!'

The sarcastic retort from Sarah only irritated Beattie even more. 'Oh yes,' she snapped, glaring at her sister. 'And what's it to you?'

15

Sarah wanted to answer, but an anxious look from her mother persuaded her otherwise.

'Listen to me, child,' said Samuel, distracting Beattie's attention from Sarah. 'No one is interrogating you. I just want you to be aware that some of the people in that market are not to be trusted.'

'That's not true!' Beattie snapped, sitting bolt upright in her chair. 'Costermongers are the salt of the earth. They're worth far more than some of the muvver's darlin's round this neck of the woods!'

Sarah was finding it hard to contain herself. Only her mother's hand covering her own on the table restrained her from speaking her mind. But she was heartily sick of hearing her young sister spouting on about her working-class 'mates'. She was sick to death of hearing her speak in an unnatural cockney accent, far removed from the way she had been brought up.

Beattie went on, 'It's not the officers who're fightin' this war, yer know. It's the Tommy, the poor old foot soldier. If it wasn't fer 'im, Kaiser Bill'd be sittin' in 10 Downing Street right now.'

'That's all I have to say on the matter, Beattie.' Samuel wiped his mouth on his damask napkin and rose from the table. Although he was only a moderately built man, he held himself straight, and his jacket, purchased at discount from the men's department of the store in which he worked, was well cut and styled. 'In future, if you have time to spare, use it wisely.' Samuel turned from the table, and quietly left the room.

As soon as he had gone, Beattie started again. 'It's ridiculous. He treats me like a child.' She got up from the table, folded her arms, and strode to the other side of the kitchen. 'People are important ter me, no matter where they come from. I want to mix wiv me own type.'

Her mother, still seated, clenched her fists angrily. 'Has it ever occurred to you, Beattie,' she said tersely, 'that *we* are your types – your own family?' Finding it difficult to control herself, she raised herself up from her chair, and glared at her youngest daughter, who watched her quite impassively from across the room. 'What happened to all the young people you used to know, your friends at school, in the Girl Guides, the church choir?'

'Oh please, Mother,' sighed Beattie, embarrassed and turning her back.

This only angered Geraldine even more. 'Don't you ever dismiss me, young lady!' she snapped, pointing her finger menacingly at the girl. 'Your father and I brought you into this world. You will *not* dismiss us!'

Sarah, already on her feet, quickly went to her mother. 'Don't be upset,' she said, putting a comforting arm around her. 'Beattie means no harm.' She said it unconvincingly, without so much as a glance at her sister. 'Why don't you go and join Father in the sitting room? I'll finish the washing-up, then bring you both a nice cup of tea.'

Her mother took a deep breath and, eager not to increase her anger, smiled gratefully at Sarah, and left the kitchen, closely followed by three of the four cats.

Sarah, now alone with her sister, turned to her. 'Why do you have to upset them like that?' she asked calmly. 'It's not fair, Beattie.'

To her credit, Beattie looked concerned. 'I'm twenty-one years of age. I'm entitled to a life of me own.' She returned to her place at the table, picked up her dessertspoon, and aimlessly scraped at the remainder of her apple pudding. 'I don't want to be spied on every time I step outside this house.'

Sarah started to collect the dirty dishes. 'Mother and

Father are not spying on you, Beattie. They're just concerned for your safety. There's a war on. There are so many dangerous people around.'

Beattie looked up with a start at her. 'Dangerous working-class people. Is that what you mean, Sarah?'

Sarah stopped what she was doing and looked at her young sister. In that brief moment, she thought she really didn't know her any more. Images of all their days of growing up together were flashing through her mind: their time at Barnsbury School just around the corner; sharing friends; outings to the seaside; the laughter, the tears, the disappointments. And yet, when she thought about those days carefully, she realised that even though she had always been Beattie's 'big' sister, they had never been close, and Beattie had never looked up to her. There were so many more memories of difficult times in their relationship than good ones. Why were their personalities so different in every conceivable way?

'Father goes to work, Beattie,' she said, without rising to her sister's bait. 'So do I, right here in this house. We're just as much working class as any of your friends in the Cattle Market.'

Beattie slammed her dish down on the table, and got up. 'I hate being told to do what's expected of me!' she growled, tossing back her straggly, unkempt auburn-coloured hair, like an unruly child.

Sarah said, 'Nobody expects you to do anything you don't want to do, Beattie.' She put down the pile of plates she was holding. 'Look, Beattie,' gently, she took hold of both her sister's hands, 'you're a beautiful girl. One day you'll find a man you want to settle down with.'

Beattie, irritated, tried to pull away, but Sarah held on to her.

'You'll have children of your own, children you care for, just like Mother and Father care for you and me.'

Beattie finally managed to break loose. 'I don't need anyone to care for me! I'm not a kid. I'm a grown woman!'

Sarah's expression hardened. 'Then start behaving like one, Beattie.'

Beattie smiled caustically, then made off towards the door. She paused briefly, and turned. 'Don't get too cocky, sister dear,' she said. 'You're not the only one with a classy boyfriend.'

Sarah watched her go. Beattie's remark had baffled her – in more ways than one.

The Islington Cattle Market positively bristled under the bright winter sun. Since the start of the war, the place had been used for many purposes other than the auction of cattle, for the costermongers down 'the Cally' had cashed in on the severe wartime shortages by setting up every type of stall from fruit and vegetables to household junk, and bric-a-brac concoctions of every shape and size. The air was filled with all kinds of sounds, from the vast crowd of chattering customers jammed around every market stall trying to bargain with the sharp local barrow boys, out-of-town farmers lining the cattle pens, inspecting the livestock before auction, the forlorn howls of domestic puppies and kittens waiting for sale, and, in the middle of it all, the whistling and chirping of hundreds of caged birds, resigned to their lifetime of captivity. Over the years, the old Cattle Market, situated between the main Caledonian Road and York Way, had gathered a reputation as a unique meeting place for rich and poor alike, and was nicknamed 'thieves' market' by local residents. Many a rich farmer and well-to-do lady had been relieved of their wallet or purse, and so there was always

19

a strong presence of 'foot bobbies'.

There had been a good inch of late February snow, which overnight had turned to ice, and it was so cold that many of the stall holders had lit braziers. This, of course, had the advantage of luring potential customers to the stall, to warm their hands over the fire, and view the goods on sale.

Despite her family's concerns, today Beattie was with her usual gang of 'roughs', most of them several years younger than herself and therefore not yet eligible for conscription. To her mother's despair, she had left the house that morning looking more like a gypsy than a girl from a well-heeled home in Barnsbury. Her cotton dress was more suitable for summer than winter, and much shorter than the austere fashion of the day allowed. Over her head she wore a brightly coloured shawl, which also covered her shoulders and body, and was her only concession to the cold. These days, Beattie was practically a fixture at the market; her raucous laugh alone was enough to turn heads. But despite this she was certainly not the queen of the castle in the market, for there were plenty around who could give as good as they got.

'Keep your bleedin' 'ands to yerself, Shiner, or you'll get my fist in yer face!'

Shiner was having none of this from no cut-glass moneybags from up Barnsbury. He was from the tough end of 'the Cally', and for most of his seventeen years he'd had to beg, borrow, and steal to survive. 'Don't give me no lip, Beat!' he croaked, his voice already hoarse from smoking too many nicked cheap fags. 'Yor gettin' too big fer yer boots these days.'

Beattie angrily shook off the tight clench of his hand from her arm. 'You touched me up, you dirty sod! Yer know yer did!'

Shiner, his ragged flat cap pushed back on his head, snapped back in a flash. 'So wot if I did? It's the first time *you've* ever complained!' He knew he was riling her, because he was a good-looking young bloke, and the rougher he was, the better she liked it. 'Wos up, Beat?' he said with a smirk, his dark mischievous eyes undressing her. 'Don't like the rough no more, is that it?'

Beattie, indignant, turned away from him.

'Prefer a bit of slap wiv the petty officer?' he called at her back. Beattie turned, and swung her fist at him. But he was there before her, and grabbed hold of her wrist. 'Wos 'e got that I ain't, Beat? Must be somefin' speshul?'

Although Beattie despised him, at the same time she was attracted to him. 'Why can't you leave me alone, Shine?' she said, pulling her arm away.

'D'yer want me to?' he replied, smiling. 'I mean – really?'

Beattie started to walk off. But he followed her.

'You've bin seein' this geezer for quite a time now,' he said, pursuing her. 'I fawt yer said la-di-das ain't yer type?'

She came to an abrupt halt, and turned to face him. 'Shine,' she said, completely ignoring what he had been saying to her, 'how can I get a job up here?'

Shiner looked taken aback. 'A job? You? In the market, yer mean?'

'That's what I mean,' she replied 'I want ter do somethin'. I want to earn some money of me own.'

Shiner sized her up for a moment. 'Wot kind er job?'

'Anythin'.'

'You're not cut out fer – anyfin'.'

Beattie stared him straight in the eye. 'I reckon I'm the best judge of that,' she said.

Shiner looked down at his filthy boots. 'I'll give it some fawt,' he said. At that moment, he caught sight of a couple of bobbies in the distance, slowly winding their way through the market crowds. He pulled his cap low over his forehead and was instantly gone.

Beattie turned back in the direction from which she had come. But as she did so, she came face to face with Nagger Mills, a young costermonger's daughter, who worked the tea urn for the farmers over in the cattle pen. 'Yer mustn't pay no 'eed ter Shiner, Beat,' she said. ''E's a stupid sod. Always puttin' people's backs up.' Nagger, whose real name was Lucy, but who got her nickname because she was always nagging her old man, took hold of Beattie's arm and gently strolled along with her. 'Did yer know 'e's 'ad 'is call-up papers?'

Beattie turned with a start. 'Shiner?'

Nagger nodded. ''E burned 'em. Now 'e really will 'ave the bobbies after 'im.'

As they walked, Beattie thought about Shiner, and how, if only he knew, he would be far better off in the army; at least he would get a couple of decent meals in his stomach each day. But then she remembered all the young blokes from the market who had been dragged off to those blood-filled trenches with Kitchener's army, and she felt ashamed even to have thought of such a thing.

'I'm lookin' for a job, Nags,' she said, pulling the shawl closer around her head and shoulders. 'D'yer know anyone round the market I could ask?'

Nagger came to a halt. She was shorter than Beattie, and younger. 'A job?' she said incredulously, briefly taking off her flat cloth cap and scratching her short mop of brown hair. 'You?'

In the background, a crowd of market customers were joining in with Fred Kiley's barrel organ as it played 'I Wouldn't Leave My Little Wooden Hut For You'. The sound they made seemed to defy the intense cold of the morning, for it drifted right up above the coloured stall awnings, and disappeared into the crisp blue sky.

'I'm getting desperate, Nags,' said Beattie. 'If I don't get a job of some sort soon, I'm going to land in real trouble.'

Nagger was baffled. 'But yer don't need ter work, Beat,' she said. 'Yer've always said so. Not in your situation – I mean, comin' from a good family an' all that, a roof over yer 'ead, and food in yer stomach.'

Beattie turned to her, looking unusually anxious. 'The thing is, Nags, the way things are goin', I may not 'ave that roof over me 'ead for much longer.'

Chapter 2

Sarah Melford longed to be a married woman. Ever since she was a child she had fantasised about the day when she would stand at the church altar, gaze into the eyes of the man she loved, and say 'I will'. And that was what she intended it to be: love – love real, love from the heart. It was perhaps every young girl's romantic illusion that love was all that was needed as the foundation of a long and happy marriage. After all, that was how it had been for her own parents; Geraldine and Samuel Melford had never had relationships with anyone else before they met, and they had now been married for almost twenty-five years. So if it had worked for them, Sarah was convinced that it would work for her too. She wanted to be married, she wanted to be able to walk into shops and be addressed as Mrs this or that, and talk to the other married women about mutual things such as children, and the kind of food she cooked for her husband when he came home from work in the evenings.

The trouble was that despite the fact that she was now twenty-three years of age, until recently she had never actually made the attempt to go out and try to meet a potential husband. But then she had met the man of her dreams quite by chance.

It had happened during the previous summer when she had paid a visit to a patriotic war exhibition which was being held in Gamages Department Store in Holborn. The exhibition, one of several organised by the War Ministry to bolster public confidence in the armed forces, was manned and operated by members of all three services. Months later, Sarah still could not believe how brazen she had been to ask the young naval officer questions about some photographs of warships she had been looking at on the display walls of the exhibition. But when she had overheard his well-spoken voice, so clear, articulate and manly, she felt compelled to speak to him. And when he called her 'miss' and she found herself staring straight into his pale blue eyes, she felt a strange surge flowing through her entire body, something that she had never experienced before. What's more, he was an officer and a gentleman, anyone could see that, even if he was only a noncommissioned officer.

'I'd better warn you,' said Sarah, as she clung on proudly to her petty officer's arm as they ambled along Whitehall, on a windswept Sunday afternoon, 'my mother's dropping hints that it's about time I brought you home to tea.'

Although the young petty officer had been expecting this sooner or later, he was still taken off guard. This was what he had been dreading. It was a step towards formalising their relationship. After a brief hesitation he turned to her and, with a weak smile, asked, 'How d'you feel about that?'

As he was a good head taller than she, Sarah had to look up at him when she replied gauchely, 'That's what I was going to ask you.'

The petty officer thought carefully before answering. 'It's up to you, Sarah,' he said, fidgeting uneasily with his uniform cap.

Sarah stiffened a little. 'It's not compulsory,' she said, her smile rather fixed. 'I just thought – well, since we've been walking out together for some time now, you might be a bit curious to know what kind of a family I come from.'

The petty officer managed to give her a forced smile without actually answering.

'They're not bad, once you get to know them.' Sarah was doing her best to reassure him. 'Except for Beattie, of course – my sister. She's quite a handful.'

At that moment, a gust of wind almost prised Sarah's large brown felt hat from her head, and in her desperation to hold on to it, she crushed the peacock feather attached to it. Most of the other Sunday afternoon strollers had the same problem, for March was living up to its reputation with an endless stream of gales and cold early-spring rain. In a gallant effort to shield Sarah from the wind, the petty officer put his arm around her shoulders. Sarah stiffened and pulled away.

'Not in public, Edward!' she said, looking around to make sure that no one had noticed.

Every time Sarah did something like that, Edward felt like shrivelling up inside. This girl was so set in her ways, so determined not to present the wrong type of image to everyone around her, that, even if he loved her, which he didn't, he found it difficult to see how they could possibly spend their future life together. So why, he asked himself on so many such occasions, was he incapable of just walking away from her and calling it a day? In fact, Petty Officer Edward Lacey had no idea how he had become so involved with someone like Sarah in the first place. What she was looking for was companionship, and a place in society. What he wanted was a woman who would give herself to him, in every meaning of the word. After all, she was a beautiful-looking girl, whose pallid complexion only enhanced the sparkle in her grey-green eyes. Oh how he longed to see that bun removed from the back of her head. How he longed to see that massive heap of flaxen hair tumble down over her shoulders. He wanted to see her, to feel her, to hold her close to his own body. But it was impossible. Sarah was untouchable; they never even held hands, or embraced. Each time they met, he hoped he might see the other Sarah, the one that was longing to be released.

'Everyone says it's hard to believe we come from the same family.'

Edward, still deep in thought, hadn't heard what Sarah had said. 'Er, I'm sorry. What did you say?'

Sarah sighed. 'Beattie. My sister. We've never been friends. Not *real* friends. When we were small children, our parents bought us so many beautiful things, lovely dolls, and so much else. Beattie hated dolls; she preferred to play in the street outside with some of the rough children of the neighbourhood.' For a brief moment, there was a wistful look in her eyes. 'Beattie doesn't like nice things. She doesn't like nice people. She just wants to be different.'

Edward felt a tight feeling in his stomach. He was aware that Sarah had turned to look at him, but he was too riddled with guilt to respond.

'Your cap, Petty Officer!'

Edward turned with an abrupt start to find an army captain just passing by. He immediately straightened up, adjusted his cap, and with a smart salute croaked back, 'Sir!'

'You're wearing the King's uniform, Petty Officer,' barked the army captain, without stopping. 'Don't forget it!'

'Sir!'

Before saying anything, Sarah waited for the captain to disappear amongst the crowds strolling along Whitehall. 'He's an army officer,' she sniffed indignantly. 'What's he doing giving you orders?'

'A commissioned officer is superior to me in any of the services, Sarah,' Edward replied rather gawkishly.

Sarah remained indignant, and after one last glare over her shoulder towards the army captain, she grabbed hold of Edward's arm, and led him off. As they passed Downing Street, a large crowd of pacifist demonstrators were being herded on to the pavement opposite Number 10, shouting loud protests at Prime Minister Lloyd George's refusal to enter into a compromise peace settlement with Germany. Sarah and Edward quickly eased their way through the sea of placards, and made off towards Parliament Square.

On their way to the tram stop on the Victoria Embankment, Edward had to tell Sarah that their Sunday afternoons together would have to be curtailed for the foreseeable future, as he was about to be transferred from his administrative position at the Admiralty, and posted to a crew-training job on board a warship being prepared for active duty in Portsmouth.

Sarah took the news far better than he had expected. 'The war has to be won,' she said bravely. 'But when it's all over, we shall have our whole lifetime together to look forward to.'

Sarah's confidence in the future weighed on Edward's conscience like a heavy lump of metal. As he helped her on to the Number 38 tram, and watched it disappear into the dark recess of the new Kingsway tunnel, the only thing his mind could take in was the feeling of betrayal and deceit.

Bob Sluggins had known the Melford girls since they were kids. In those days, he and his missus, Vera, were, for a brief period, landlords of the White Conduit public house on the corner of Dewey Road in Barnsbury. Although it was not exactly the most salubrious of pubs, Bob was well liked in the district, and, because he was quite a nifty handyman, he was often called upon by some of the locals, including the Melfords, to do an odd job of plumbing, or furniture repair. Some said he was also quite a hand at crochet work, which left him wide open to some pretty cryptic comments from his regulars down the pub. However, the same amiable feelings were rarely accorded to his missus, for to most people she was considered to be a bit of a bossy old slag, who was well known for giving short measures at the counter, especially on the shorts. Vera Sluggins couldn't bear the Melford family, especially the females – 'stuck-up bunch of cows' she used to call them – which made poor old Bob feel uncomfortable, for whenever he went to do a job for them, he really enjoyed their company.

But even in those days, he could tell the difference between the two girls, Sarah and Beattie. He was amazed how 'chalk and cheese' they were, one relishing the security of a comfortable family environment, and the other a creature of the streets – and the rough part of the streets at that.

When, some years before, Bob and Vera had given up the pub, they'd taken over a pawnbroker's business in the Holloway Road. Vera took to the work like a frog to water, but Bob found it depressing, dealing with the misery of folk from the highest to the low. But it did provide him and the 'old slag' with a respectable, if not lucrative, living, for there were many regular customers, including young Beattie Melford.

'One an' 'alf guineas, Miss Beattie. Top price.'

Beattie pulled a face. 'Come off it, Bob,' she groaned. 'My dad bought me that bracelet for my sixteenth. It's solid nine carat gold.'

Bob was still looking at Beattie's delicate, fine bracelet through his eyeglass. 'I can see wot it is, Miss Beattie. But

30

ter me, it's only worf its true value.'

Beattie looked desperate. It was bad enough having to come into such a tiny shop at all, with its oppressive smell of poverty, leather purses, belts, handbags, rolled gold, silver, brass, copper, threadbare fox furs riddled with moth-holes, second-hand boots and shoes, men's suits, women's dresses and coats, kid gloves, ships squeezed into bottles, stuffed animals and birds, and any amount of old pictures that might prove more valuable one day than they looked. 'Couldn't yer just make it a round two quid, Bob?' she pleaded. 'I've got ter get me 'ands on some ready cash – and soon. *Please!*'

Whilst Beattie was still pleading, Bob was shaking his prematurely grey head. 'I can't do it, Miss Beattie,' he insisted, removing his eyeglass and putting it in the lower pocket of his open waistcoat. 'Times in't good, yer know. There's no cash around 'cos of this ruddy war.'

Beattie's desperation was turning to irritation. 'Two quid ain't goin' ter break the bank, fer God's sake!'

'It may not break the bleedin' bank,' screamed Vera Sluggins from the back parlour, 'but it could break us!'

At the sight of the old slag approaching from the parlour, Beattie stiffened visibly.

'Let me see wot she's got there,' growled Vera, grabbing Beattie's bracelet from her old man's hand. She was a huge woman, with thinning hair dyed with henna, and a wisp of straggling hairs growing from her chin. 'Looks a bit of cheap old brass ter me,' she said provocatively. 'I fawt you Melfords was s'pposed ter be so loaded.'

'In case yer don't know, *Mrs* Sluggins,' snapped Beattie, furiously, 'that's a valuable piece of jewellery. An' if you're not interested in it, I'll take it elsewhere.'

The old slag grinned, and held out the bracelet to her. 'As yer wish.'

Before Beattie had the chance to take it back, Bob retrieved it from his wife. 'Wot say I split the difference wiv yer, gel? Firty-five bob?'

'Wot!' His missus, outraged, grabbed the bracelet from him, and thrust it back at Beattie. 'Wot d'yer take us for? Bleedin' millionaires?'

For the first time, Bob showed his anger. Before Beattie had the chance to take back her bracelet, he grabbed hold of his wife's hand, and retrieved the jewellery. 'Fank yer, my dear,' he growled, through clenched teeth. 'I can manage this transaction on me own.'

The old slag glared at him as if she was about to hit him. But something told her that she had better not push her luck too far, so, with a haughty shrug of the shoulders, she retreated back to the parlour whence she came, slamming the door behind her.

'So?' said Bob, undeterred. 'Do we 'ave a deal or not?'

Beattie sighed, and nodded.

Bob took the bracelet, and placed it carefully in one of his jewellery cases beneath the counter. 'I'll give yer a ticket,' he said, writing in his receipt book.

Whilst he was filling in the details, Beattie leaned across and, lowering her voice, said, 'I'm lookin' fer somewhere ter stay, Bob?'

Bob looked up with a start.

'Can yer 'elp me?'

Bob sized her up for a moment 'You leavin' 'ome?'

'I – might be,' said Beattie cagily. 'It's possible.'

'Your folks know about it?'

As usual, Beattie reacted by flaring up. 'That's my business, Bob.' But then she suddenly remembered that he was one of the few people she knew who had always been kind to her. 'Yer see, I've got a few fings ter work out fer meself. I'm twenty-one now. I need me independence.'

Bob stared at her for another brief moment, then continued filling in the receipt. 'You're lookin' fer somewhere round 'ere? Round 'Olloway?'

'Anywhere. I'm not fussy. I just need a room, that's all.'

''Ow much can yer afford ter pay?'

Beattie hesitated. 'Not much.'

She waited whilst Bob finished filling in the receipt. His silence before he spoke again seemed an eternity, and she felt that all the stuffed animals and birds in the shop were watching her every move. In fact, she was unaware that they were not alone. In a cluttered corner of the shop a tall, well-built young man was waiting to be served. He'd felt obliged to keep out of sight whilst Beattie had been haggling a price for her pawned bracelet.

Bob tore off the bottom half of the receipt, and gave it to Beattie. 'That's yer ticket. Don't lose it.'

Beattie took the ticket, and waited for him to hand over the thirty-five bob from the cashtill. 'Will yer keep yer eyes open for me, Bob?' she said with difficulty. 'Ter find a room?'

'Can't promise,' he replied. flicking his eyes up only briefly to meet hers. 'It ain't easy.'

She took the money from him and smiled awkwardly. 'Fanks a lot, Bob. I'll keep in touch.'

A moment later, Beattie was out on the Holloway Road. There was still plenty of snow on the ground, but over the past few days the bitterly cold wind had dropped, and with the milder temperature, a thaw had set in. The road was as busy as ever, with trams and omnibuses with open staircases chugging to and from the Archway in one direction, and Upper Street, Rosebery Avenue, and the Thames Embankment in the other. People were wrapped up well

33

against the cold – women in their long, ankle-length winter coats and, what men were left over from Lord Kitchener's army, in woollen hats, heavy top-coats and mittens. As food was now more scarce than at any time since the war started, shop windows were pretty bleak, and there were queues outside every butcher's shop for even the most basic available food, such as penny pig's trotters and hot saveloys and pease pudding.

Beattie pulled her shawl around her shoulders, and dipped her hands in her dress pocket to keep warm. As she did so, she could feel the thirty-five bob she had just received for her bracelet, which she clasped tightly in her hand where it felt cold and heartless to the touch. She decided to return home to Barnsbury by the same route she had come. This meant crossing over the main Holloway Road, cutting through Madras Place into Liverpool Road, then straight along to Barnsbury. On the way she passed by a terrace of Victorian houses which, earlier in the war, had been hit by a hand grenade, thrown from the control casket of a Zeppelin airship raider. Although there was little sign of any damage, she remembered reading in the *Islington Gazette* how an elderly man and his dog had both been killed when the small hand bomb had exploded right in front of them.

'If you're lookin' fer a place, I can 'elp yer.'

Beattie stopped dead. For a moment she resisted the temptation to turn and see who was addressing her, for, ever since crossing over the road from Bob's pawn shop, she had been aware that someone was following her. Finally, she turned around to find herself face to face with a tall young man, whose flat work cap was covering a head of ginger hair, and whose rough good looks were completely unsettling.

'Wot you after then, mate?' Beattie growled contemptuously.

'I'm not after nuffin', *mate,*' the man replied. 'But you are.'

Totally unafraid of the man, she strode right up to confront him. 'I never talk ter strange men,' she quipped.

The man grinned. 'Then 'ow yer goin' ter find this place you're lookin' for?'

Beattie's smirk became a look of steel. 'Where d'you 'ear that?' she demanded.

'The pawn shop does 'ave uvver customers, yer know.' He moved a step closer to her, and she could see that not only had he not shaved for a day or so, but the red choker tied around his throat was almost the same colour as his hair. 'Ever 'eard of the Bunk?' he asked.

'Who?'

'Yer mean yer don't know the Bunk – Campbell Road – up Finsbury Park, near Seven Sisters Road?' His face broke out into an even broader cheeky grin. 'Don't know much, do yer?'

'I don't know wot you're talkin' about.'

The man took a half-finished fag butt from behind his ear, fumbled around in his trousers pocket until he found a loose match, which he ignited by striking it against one of his fingernails, and then lit the fag. 'They got rooms up there,' he continued, after taking a deep puff. 'Goin' cheap.'

''Ow cheap?'

The man exhaled, then picked a strand of tobacco from the tip of his tongue. ''Alf a crown a week?'

Beattie's eyes widened. ''Alf a crown! Whose leg you pullin'?'

'If yer don't believe me, go an' ask fer yerself. Try Number 22. Yer can trust the ol' gel there. 'Art of gold.' He turned and started to stroll off.

Beattie was taken aback. 'Hey! Wait a minute!' she called.

35

The man stopped and, fag in mouth, turned to look back at her.

'Wot's in it fer you?'

The man took a deep pull of his fag, then exhaled. 'Nuffin' in it fer me, darlin'. I just don't like ter see a young gel taken fer a ride – if yer get my meanin'.' He turned and started to walk off again, calling back over his shoulder, 'Number 22. Tell 'er Jack Ridley sent yer.'

Beattie watched him disappear round the corner, back into Holloway Road. For a brief moment she couldn't believe the extraordinary encounter she had just had. Then she decided to take it all in her stride, shrugged her shoulders, and walked on.

But then, Beattie was like that.

Chapter 3

Sarah was sublimely happy. She had had the first letter from Edward since their last Sunday afternoon stroll together along Whitehall nearly three weeks before, and although it was a short letter, it contained enough for Sarah to know that he missed her as much as she missed him. Or at least, that is what she read into his words: 'When I get back to London, we'll have a lot to talk over, about us, about the future.' For Sarah, those words were a declaration of Edward's intent. After all, he had always said that as soon as the war was over they would be able to spend so much more time together, and if the news coming out of the war each day was any indication, the end could not now be that far away.

With all this in mind, Sarah started to make plans. First on her list was an absolute determination that Edward should meet her parents, so she wrote straight back to him, inviting him to come to tea on the first Sunday afternoon he was able to get leave from his new posting down at Portsmouth. To her delight, Edward wrote back immediately, accepting her invitation, and giving her a firm date on which he would be able to come.

The days leading up to this important tea party were the most exciting and nerve-racking of Sarah's life. She wanted everything to go so well, for all of them to get on together. She wanted to impress Edward; she wanted to show him that she was the kind of girl who was going to make him the best wife he could ever hope for.

At least a week before the big day, she chose the dress she intended to wear: her blue silk with the large bow fixed behind, and a hemline that was cut just on her ankles. For this one occasion she would comb out her bun, and tie her hair with a blue ribbon behind her head. As always, she would not indulge in make-up, which she stubbornly insisted was only intended for women of the street, but before Edward arrived, she would pinch her cheeks to try to disguise her pallid complexion. During a shopping expedition in Holloway Road, she stopped at the main window of James Selby and Sons, the large department store, where she spent several minutes staring at a 'new season's' wedding dress displayed there, with a confident, determined look in her eyes. As far as she was concerned, it was now only a matter of time before that wax model would become herself. The scene then was set. Everything was now prepared to make Edward's first meeting with his prospective in-laws as comfortable as possible. There was, however, one problem still remaining.

'Don't worry, sister dear,' gibed Beattie, in one of her mischievous moods. 'I wouldn't dream of barging in on your precious tea party. I've got better things to do with my time.'

Sarah was, as usual, having a hard time with her sister. It was only on very rare occasions that she ventured into Beattie's bedroom on the top floor of the house, but what she had to say to her was important enough for Sarah to risk being placed at a disadvantage. 'I don't think you understand, Beattie,' she said, refusing to rise to her sister's bait. 'I *want* you to be there at tea on Sunday, I *want* you to meet Edward. After all, you're my sister, you're part of the family.'

'Nice of you to say so,' replied Beattie, cuttingly.

'Sometimes I wonder.' She was sitting at her dressing table, which was so full of junk it was impossible to make out what anything was used for.

'You'll like him, Beattie, you really will.' Sarah moved behind her sister, and talked to her reflection in the mirror whilst Beattie gave an impression of trying to brush some sense into her tangled auburn locks. 'I've told him all about you, all sorts of things – like how when you and me were young, we used to chase the ducks in Finsbury Park. He thought that was hilarious!'

Beattie raised one eyebrow. 'I bet,' she said dryly.

In a desperate attempt to try to sell Edward to her, Sarah leaned over Beattie's shoulder, looking at both their faces in the mirror. 'I told him how you've always been the rebel in the family, but that it's never stopped us loving you.'

'Oh really?' was Beattie's bored response. 'And what about 'im?' she asked, carefully watching Sarah's reflection. ''Ow much d'yer know about 'im?'

'Oh, Edward comes from a very good family,' she said with mounting enthusiasm. 'They were in kitchen utensils.'

Beattie's face screwed up in disbelief.

'What I mean is, his mother ran a company that manufactured them. His father was in the navy. Unfortunately, he's a widower now. Mrs Lacey died several years ago.' In her enthusiasm, Sarah folded her arms around Beattie's shoulders and squeezed them. 'Edward lives with his father out in Suffolk. One day he's going to inherit a huge detached house.'

Beattie broke loose, got up, and moved away. 'Well 'e's got it all made for 'im, ain't 'e? You'll be able to clean 'is detached 'ouse till the cows come 'ome.'

Sarah waited a moment. She was trying so hard to make some kind of sisterly contact that she was prepared to compromise on anything Beattie said. 'I know he's not the kind of person you're interested in, Beattie,' she went on, knowing it was an uphill task trying to inject some kind of enthusiasm into her sister, 'but he's what I want. And I want him to like you too.'

'Well, you can but try,' Beattie said adroitly, as she sat down on the edge of her bed.

Sarah went across and sat beside her. 'You know, Beattie,' she said, 'things haven't always been – well – as they should be, between you and me. Somehow, we never seem to talk to each other, unless it's to criticise or squabble.' She put an arm around her sister's shoulders. 'I don't want to squabble with you, Beattie. You're my sister, my own flesh and blood. When I get married, I want us to be friends.'

Sitting so close to her young sister, Sarah could feel their two hearts beating, almost, it seemed, in unison. They were both from the same womb, they shared the same flesh and blood, and yet it was extraordinary that their hearts and souls were so different. She felt the urge to lean her head on Beattie's shoulder, and in one courageous move, that is what she did. It took all of Beattie's resilience not to react in the way that she really felt, so she just remained quite impassive.

Going through Sarah's mind were thoughts of what it had been like to have a young sister like Beattie. In those few quiet seconds she recalled times they had spent together as children – Beattie doing all the things they were told never to do, like trying to smoke one of their father's pipes whilst he was out, and feeling utterly sick as a result, and trying to get Sarah to play hookey from Sunday school, and go fishing down the Islington canal with some of the costermonger boys from the Cattle Market. And in one momentary flash, Sarah remembered the times when they used to go to the shop in Liverpool Road and buy their favourite sweet, sherbert powder with a liquorice bar bought for a penny, and served in a paper bag folded in the shape of a triangle. They were such vivid images, yet never seemed to reveal the true nature of the two sisters' relationship.

For her part, Beattie couldn't recall one single moment when she had actually enjoyed being in her sister's company. As far as she was concerned, Sarah was nothing more than a hindrance to her life, her freedom, her desperate attempts to express herself in her own abandoned way. Her sister's effort to create some type of bond between them only embarrassed her, making her feel hemmed in more than ever. To her mind, she and Sarah could never be friends. There never had been and never could be any kind of communication between them; to try would only end in tragedy. And yet, there *was* something that never ceased to trouble Beattie. What, she had asked herself on many occasions, would she feel if anything should ever happen to Sarah? What would she, Beattie, do? How would she react? She would never know that it was a question Sarah also had often asked herself about her young sister.

'What're yer afraid of, Sarah?'

Beattie's sudden question took Sarah by surprise. 'Afraid?'

Beattie got up, releasing Sarah's arm from around her shoulders. 'You didn't come up 'ere just ter tell me that yer want us ter be friends. Yer came 'ere because yer want ter make quite certain that I don't make a fool out of yer in front of yer fancy naval officer.'

Sarah, hurt, got up immediately. 'Beattie, that's not true. And in any case, Edward isn't an officer. He's—'

'I don't care wot 'e is!' snapped Beattie. 'I don't 'ave ter put on no airs an' graces for the likes of 'im!'

'No one's asking you to.'

41

Sarah used her handkerchief to wipe the small beads of perspiration that had formed on her forehead. Despite the cold outside, the room was stifling and smelled of soiled clothes, for Beattie would sooner die than open a window to let in some fresh air.

'Look, Beattie.' Sarah was determined not to be roused. 'I don't want – I don't expect you to be anything but what you are, not to me nor Mother and Father, nor anyone else. But I do want Edward to like my family. One day, you'll be doing exactly the same thing.'

Beattie threw her head back with a dismissive grunt. 'Ha!'

'Oh yes, you will,' persisted Sarah, as she watched her sister winding the handle of her one cherished possessions, a gramophone. 'And when you bring *your* young man home, whoever he is, wherever he comes from, you'll want us to like him too.'

Beattie was shaking her head. 'Yer don't understand, do yer?' she said, with a fixed, unsmiling expression. 'As long as yer live, you'll never understand. My life ain't about gettin' married, settlin' down an' 'avin' kids. If that's wot you want ter do, then that's fine. But don't expect me ter be the same – 'cos I'm not.'

Sarah felt crushed.

Beattie turned her back on her, and placed a record on the gramophone turntable. 'Don't worry,' she said, with just the faintest hint of remorse, 'I won't disgrace yer on Sunday.'

Sarah felt there was nothing more she could say, so she turned and made for the door. She paused there, then without turning to look back, said, 'How can two people be so close and yet so far apart?'

Closing the door behind her, for a brief moment she stood on the landing to recover from the stale air of Beattie's room.

Then in deep despair, she started to make her way down the stairs.

As she did so, she heard the wail of Beattie's gramophone record as the house echoed to the sound of the popular singer Gus Elen, lamenting on a forlorn hope, 'If You Were the Only Girl in the World'.

The steeple of St Andrew's church in Thornhill Crescent reached right up towards the bright blue spring sky like a hand stretching out towards the Almighty. During this gruelling time of war, the steeple, topped by its small cross, appeared to the residents of Barnsbury as a symbol of hope and defiance. Flanked on one side by the elegant curve of Thornhill Crescent, and on the other side by the rich splendour of Thornhill Square, the church was actually situated on Bridgeman Road, a quiet and pleasant back road that eventually led into the main Caledonian Road. Built of large quarried stone bricks, with a series of grey tiled roofs, St Andrew's doors were open night and day for all who wished to pray for the safe return from the front of their loved ones, and a speedy end to the war that had destroyed so much of the nation's family life. And, like so many other parts of Islington and beyond, Barnsbury had had its fair share of tragedy, so much so that during the early days of the war, the residents had organised the Barnsbury War Fund, which was one practical way in which people could help to relieve the suffering of the countless victims' dependants.

Samuel and Geraldine Melford, who were on the committee of the Barnsbury War Fund, tried never to miss Sunday morning service at St Andrew's and today their presence was especially important, for two more names were to be added to the endless list of local men who had been 'killed in action'.

'Private Harry Turner, nineteen years of age, 11th Battalion, London Rifle Brigade. Beloved son of Joseph and Laura Turner, Offord Road, and younger brother of Susan and Lizzie. Killed in action, Western Front, 25th March 1918. Rest in peace. And Lance-Corporal Ben Travis, nineteen years of age, Royal Army Medical Corps, 8th Field Ambulance, 2nd Division, beloved husband of Mary, and father of twins, Michael and Davey, Brooksby Street. Killed in action, Western Front, 4th April 1918. Rest in peace.'

Together with a hushed and crowded congregation, Sarah and her parents listened as the Reverend Cyril Wheatcroft concluded his litany of tragic news from the front. Despite the fact that news of the war had been improving day by day, it was inevitable that the Reverend's address had been a sombre affair, for even if the war were to end that very day, it was too late to save these two young men, whose families would probably never fully recover from their loss.

It was a difficult service for Sarah to attend, for although her heart was aching from the news of so much death and misery, her stomach was churning with excitement. This was the day that she had dreamed of, had planned for, the day when her family would meet the man that she had firmly decided to marry. But as she looked around the sea of sad faces, and heard the quiet sound of sobbing from the bereaved families of those two lost young Barnsbury boys, she felt churlish for even thinking of her own happiness at such a time. Even at her tender age the Reverend's sermon had brought home how brutal the war really was: 'In life, death is never far away.'

After the service, Samuel and Geraldine Melford stayed behind to offer their condolences to the bereaved families, so Sarah made her own way home. On the way, she passed fine houses, many built during the Georgian and Victorian period, though the war had taken its toll on all the elegant squares and terraces. With the lack of money, and superficial damage caused by enemy Zeppelin and aeroplane attacks, many properties had fallen into a sad state of disrepair, and the whole area had taken on an uncomfortable, seedy appearance.

'Sarah! Wait for me!'

Sarah was halfway along the wide and tree-lined Hemingford Road when she heard her friend, Winnie Carter, calling to her. She stopped to let Winnie, in Sunday best, and with her own copy of the Bible held firmly in one hand, catch up with her.

'I saw you in church,' Winnie said, out of breath, but displaying her cheeky, glowing smile, her pure white teeth seeming far too big for her mouth. 'I wanted to wave, but I thought, under the circumstances . . .'

'I saw you too,' replied Sarah, who had known Winnie since they were at Barnsbury School together. 'It was so sad.'

'I know,' said Winnie, her smile becoming more wistful. 'D'you remember Harry? Harry Turner? He used to walk me home from school. I can't bear to think what's happened to him. His poor mum and dad.'

As they walked, Winnie, who was much shorter than Sarah, had to take twice as many steps to keep up. 'You know,' she said, using one hand to hold on to her brown beret, 'when this war's over, there are going to be so many blokes we once knew who won't be coming home.' She sighed, but then broke into another of her huge smiles. 'I've got a terrible feeling I'm never going to find someone to marry me.'

'Don't be silly, Winnie,' said Sarah. 'It'll happen sooner or later, one day when you least expect it. There's always someone for someone.'

'It's all right for you,' Winnie said, quick as a flash. 'You've got someone for you already.'

Sarah came to a sudden halt. 'What do you mean?'

'Oh come off it, Sarah,' replied Winnie, cheekily. 'Everyone knows about you and your petty officer. Mr Wheatcroft was saying before the service that he was pretty sure he'd be putting up the banns for you any day now.'

Sarah was thunderstruck. Apart from her own mother and father, she hadn't told a soul about who she was walking out with. 'Just who told you all this, Winnie Carter?' she demanded.

Winnie's smile turned to a grin. 'Who d'you think?'

'Not – *Beattie*?'

'She stopped and talked to me in the Cattle Market the other day. She was with her usual gang, of course, so I didn't want to hang around for too long. But she told me all about your petty officer, what a good-looker he was.'

Sarah stiffened. How could Beattie possibly know what Edward Lacey looked like when she hadn't even met him?

Winnie was relishing every moment of the outrage she was causing. 'She said he was more your type than hers,' she continued mischievously. 'Speaks with too many plums in his mouth, *she* says.' Suddenly she became alarmed that Sarah was taking all this a bit too seriously. 'Oh, I wouldn't pay any heed to Beattie,' she said quickly. 'You know what she was like at school. Always making up things as she went along.'

Sarah was too deep in thought to respond.

Winnie's smile finally faded. 'It's nothing, Sarah,' she said, trying to reassure her friend. 'If you ask me, your sister's just jealous.'

Sarah perked up a little, and smiled weakly. She was determined to show Winnie that she was not nearly so concerned as she looked. But after Winnie had left her, as she made her way home, her mind was racing.

Beattie had never cared for Seven Sisters Road. For one thing, it was too long, stretching all the way from the Nags Head in Holloway and carrying on right up to Tottenham in North London. The part of this big main road that she hated most was between Holloway Road and Hornsey Road, for that was where all the shops were, and when she and Sarah were kids, their mother had dragged them around those shops, where they often had to spend what seemed like hours waiting for her whilst she dithered about how much cheese to buy, or take her place in a queue for two pounds of dried peas. No, if she had a preference for any part of that road, it was where it was flanked on one side by Finsbury Park, and on the other by a terrace of tall Edwardian houses, most of which were now used officially as cheap board-and-breakfast accommodation – and, unofficially, by servicemen for more dubious purposes. A typical 'pay-by-the-week-and-no-questions-asked' resident of one of these 'guest houses' was Petty Officer Edward Lacey.

'You're late.' After letting Beattie in the front door of the so-called Hazelville Hotel, he followed her up the stairs to his room on the third floor. 'I thought you said one o'clock?'

'I had fings ter do,' called Beattie, over her shoulder. 'I had ter go ter work.'

'Work!' called Lacey, his voice echoing down the well of the great barn of a house. 'Since when?'

'Needs must,' replied Beattie, breathless as they reached the second-floor landing. 'One of me mates got me a job up the Cattle Market. I'm goin' ter need all the cash I can get.'

As they made their way to the last flight of stairs, they passed another resident's door, which opened slightly. Watching them go, with a certain amount of titillation, were two pairs of eyes. It was that kind of establishment.

Once on the third floor, Beattie was relieved to be back inside Edward's room. She could never bear the smell of boiled cabbage and soiled underwear that hit her the moment she entered the downstairs hall.

'What do your parents think about all this?' Lacey asked, as he locked his bedroom door behind them.

Beattie threw off her shawl and swung around to look at him. 'About what?' she asked, puzzled.

'About you getting a job? Aren't they curious?'

Beattie ran her fingers through her rarely combed hair and shook it loose. 'What the eye doesn't see,' she said. 'But they'll know, sooner or later.'

Lacey, too impatient to wait any longer, went straight to her, threw his arms around her waist and pushed his lips against hers.

Beattie could tell he'd been drinking, for his breath smelled of whisky. 'Not so fast!' she snapped, prising him away. 'I've got a bone ter pick wiv you.'

Lacey looked at her in disbelief. This was the first time she had ever rejected his advances. Isn't this why she came here? 'What's up?' he asked.

'You didn't tell me yer'd written to 'er,' she said, her whole face bristling with irritation. 'Yer've said you'd come ter tea wiv 'er – back 'ome.' She pushed him away and looked him straight in the face. 'Wot's this all about?'

Lacey sighed, went across to the double bed, which was neatly made ready for the afternoon, and pulled out a Players Navy Cut cigarette from a packet on the small cupboard beside it. 'I've made up my mind, Beat,' he said, poking a

48

cigarette between his lips. 'I've decided to break it off with her.'

'Then why didn't yer tell 'er so in the letter?' she said, watching him light his cigarette.

Lacey's face emerged from a cloud of smoke that drifted around the small, claustrophobic room and settled on the wash jug and basin nearby. 'It's best I tell her face to face,' he said, sitting down on the edge of the bed.

Beattie came across to him. 'But 'ow can yer tell 'er if you're 'avin' tea wiv 'er, an' Mum an' Dad?'

Lacey inhaled deeply before looking up at her. 'Beattie, I have no intention of having tea with Sarah, or your parents.'

For a moment, Beattie just stared at him. This was the first time that she had actually *seen* him, for in that face and voice was now all that she hated most in her life. Why then had she got herself involved with someone like this? Yes, it was true that she had enjoyed making love with him in that bed every weekend he had been home on leave from his new posting down at Portsmouth, but the more she was with him the more she was aware of her reasons for taking up with him, and she hated herself for it.

'Wot're yer playin' at, Ed?' she asked tersely.

'I'm not playing at anything, Beat,' he replied. He got up, went across to the window, and stared out through the grubby lace curtains. 'The fact is, since I wrote that letter, I've done quite a lot of thinking.' He turned back to look at her. 'I don't love Sarah. I never have done. I blame myself. I should never have let it go on as long as it has done.' He went to stand in front of her. 'It's all been a farce, Beat,' he said. 'Sarah doesn't know how to live. She doesn't know what the world is all about – not the *real* world.' He tried to take hold of her hands, but she pulled them out of his way.

'And what is your *real* world, Ed?' she said, moving away

49

from him. For the first time, her eyes took in the tawdry surroundings: the poky little fireplace with only just a few pieces of coal there to keep the room from being ice-cold, the small, bare table with a chipped enamel kettle, brown china teapot, and a couple of stained white cups, and the two gas lamps on the wall that were never lit until it was almost dark. But most of all there was that double brass bedstead, where time and time again she had given herself to this man, not because he was what she wanted, but because she wanted to experience what Sarah wanted more than anything else in the whole wide world. 'If your world is all about tearin' somebody's life apart, then I don't want any part of you, mate.'

Lacey stiffened. 'You knew what you were getting into, Beat.'

For a brief moment, Beattie held her breath. Although she couldn't bear to agree with him, what he said was true. She turned, and slowly made for the door.

'I didn't mean it to be like this, Beat,' he said. 'I promise. I thought I loved her, but I was wrong. I want someone who doesn't flinch every time I touch her. I want someone who responds to me.' He finally went across to her, put his arms around her waist, and leaned his head on her shoulder. 'I want someone like you, Beat.'

It was a moment or so before Beattie spoke. When she did, she did not turn to look at him. 'You've got to meet her. You've got to tell her.' She turned around, and stared him straight in the eyes. 'If yer don't, I never want to see yer again.'

Lacey smiled at her with those pale blue eyes that had always so utterly defeated her. Then he nodded.

For the next hour they made love.

* * *

50

Sarah reached the tram stop in Liverpool Road almost half an hour early. She had made the arrangement to meet Edward there rather than have him come straight to the house because she wanted to arrive with him as a future married couple, arm in arm. Although it was only three thirty, the sky was so overcast it was obvious that it would soon be prematurely dark. Sarah didn't much like standing alone at a tram stop in a place like Liverpool Road, for there were many ruffians about, especially in the nearby Peabody Buildings, and as she was wearing her very best Sunday clothes, she worried that she might attract too much attention. Luckily, there weren't many people around.

By four o'clock, which was the time Sarah had arranged to meet Edward off the tram, her stomach was churning with a mixture of nerves and excitement. Her life was about to take on a whole new meaning; by the time the tea party at the house in Thornhill Road was over, her walking-out with Edward would be official, and her future assured.

As there was a Sunday service operating that day, only two trams came during the first half-hour that Sarah was standing there. Although she was well wrapped up against the cold, her thin kid gloves were not really warm enough, so every now and then she would rub her hands together to try to get the blood circulating. At one stage, an army Red Cross motorbus passed by, but she tried not to look at its passengers – young soldiers who had been injured at the front, on their way to the Army Hospital further along Liverpool Road.

Several times, Sarah looked at her watch pinned to the breast of her topcoat, but it was not until forty-five minutes had passed that she started to become anxious. Had she told Edward the right stop to get off? Was she sure it was four o'clock they had arranged to meet? Gradually, her mind was

51

becoming tormented by the possibility of her own fallibility. So many times she craned her neck to look as far as she could along Liverpool Road towards Holloway. She knew he had to change from a bus on to the tram somewhere, but couldn't remember exactly where. But what did it matter? He knew where she lived. She *must* have given him the right time, the right place. It was inconceivable that she, practical Sarah, could have been so negligent. Trying to dispel all negative thoughts from her mind, she transferred her gaze across to the other side of the tramlines where, with dusk drawing close, the residents of the long terrace of Georgian houses were beginning to draw their blinds for the evening blackout.

By a quarter to six, the sky had darkened even more, and it threatened to rain. Sarah decided to wait for just one more tram, and when it arrived, her heart nearly missed a beat, for as the tram approached, the first thing she saw was a man in naval uniform sitting in the front seat on the top deck. She waved frantically but as the tram screeched to a halt, she realised that, although the man was in naval uniform, it certainly wasn't Edward.

She watched the tram leave the stop, but waited until it had finally disappeared into the darkening gloom of the old road to the north. Once she could see it no more, she moved on.

It took her far longer than usual to walk the few minutes home. Somehow the distance seemed like an eternity.

52

Chapter 4

Under normal circumstances, the death of somebody called Manfred von Richthofen would have meant absolutely nothing to the residents of Barnsbury, but mention the Red Baron and it was a completely different story. In April, the Baron, one of Germany's most feared and skilled flying aces, was shot down and killed during aerial combat over the Western Front. Most of the newspapers couldn't make up their minds whether it was a Canadian fighter pilot who had shot him down, or an Australian army machine gun unit in the Allied lines, but Samuel Melford was convinced that none of this was true, and that the commander of the 'flying circus', who was credited with shooting down more than eighty British aeroplanes in little more than a year, was in fact brought down by 'one of our own courageous young fellows'. Whatever the truth, Barnsbury, like the rest of the nation, celebrated the event with renewed conviction that the end of the war was now surely in sight.

Unfortunately, the final flight of the Red Baron meant little to Sarah. The fact that her petty officer had failed to turn up for afternoon tea with her family two weeks before had left her feeling dejected and humiliated. The only explanation she could offer to her parents was that Edward must have been called away suddenly on active service, and that he was not the sort of person to do such a thing unless there was a pressing reason. Even though her parents appeared to have accepted her hollow explanation, Sarah felt sick inside. She hated lying. In her heart of hearts she knew only too well that her petty officer could not be trusted, for the letter that she had written to him in Portsmouth had not been answered, which led her to the conclusion that he had jilted her.

But there was something more worrying her, something that had been nagging inside ever since Winnie Carter had suggested that Beattie knew more about Edward Lacey than she, Sarah, had imagined. Until she knew exactly what it was that Beattie knew, she would be unable to dismiss it from her mind. However, since the day of that ill-fated tea party, Beattie had spent a great deal of her time away from the house, and on the rare occasions that she was actually there, she had made a point of keeping herself to herself.

On the day of Geraldine and Samuel's Silver Wedding Anniversary, things came to a head. The event started well, with members of both families coming to stay in the house for the weekend, and, to everyone's surprise, Beattie even gave up her own bedroom for her mother's elder sister, Dixie, who, like Beattie herself, was a bit of an outcast in the family, mainly because of the succession of 'amours' she had gone through since the second of her two divorces. On the whole, everyone got on well with each other, especially with Geraldine's mother, Bella, who was the biggest chatterbox in the world, and made a point of finding out all she could about her fellow guests even before the first cup of tea had been served. Both she and her husband, Ronnie, who had spent his working life in an insurance company, were really quite young for their age, which was in marked contrast to Samuel's father, Benedict, a widower, who must have been old the day he was born, for he never stopped complaining about rheumatism, and smoked cigars nearly all weekend, much to the disdain of Aunt Dixie, who constantly drew attention to the old boy's vice by coughing dramatically every time he lit up. One of the real problem relatives, however, was Terry, who was married to Geraldine's younger sister, Myra. Terry, who was a good bit older than his wife, was well known for his roaming eye, and as the weekend progressed, he was clearly beginning to get on Beattie's nerves, for he never stopped leering at her and twitching his pencil-thin moustache, which was apparently meant to overwhelm her with desire.

Several young cousins also turned up, whom Sarah adored and Beattie loathed, but apart from them, other guests, who were mainly the Melfords' friends from St Andrew's church and the Barnsbury War Fund, popped in from time to time to offer congratulations, and to sample Geraldine's home-made apple wine, together with a piece of Silver Wedding fruit cake made specially for the occasion by their neighbour, Bertha Stevens. So, all in all, it was a happy day.

The real problem came towards the end of the celebratory dinner on Saturday evening, which Geraldine herself had cooked with the help of Sarah, and Sarah's favourite cousin, Jenny, and which took place in the little-used dining room. Shortly after the speeches, in which various members of the family had praised the wonderful years of marriage of their hosts, Jenny's fourteen-year-old brother, Cecil, deliberately mocked his cousin Beattie by asking her when she was planning on getting married.

'If I was stupid enuff ter get married and 'ave a blockhead like you for a son,' snapped Beattie, vociferously, 'I'd go an' drown me bleedin' self!'

Aunt Dixie made no attempt to stifle her amusement, but the other guests showed their indignation by making up to

Cecil, who clearly revelled in the mischief he had instigated.

'I must ask you not to use that kind of language in front of your family, please, Beattie.' As usual, Samuel was convincing nobody how strict he was with his younger daughter, for even as he spoke the words he tried to soften their impact. 'I think it's fair to say that Beattie is no admirer of married life.'

Beattie was having none of this. 'I'm sorry, Farver,' she said, cuttingly, 'but marriage ter me ain't nothin' more than a 'ole lot er words on paper.'

'It takes more than words to make a marriage, dear,' said Geraldine's mother, Bella, doing her best to sound conciliatory.

'Marriage is an institution,' said Ronnie, her husband, who was already joining Samuel's father, Benedict, by smoking a cigar. 'It has to be worked at. But, my God –' he stretched out his hand to cover his wife's – 'it's worth it!'

Bella gave him an affectionate smile.

Nobody had noticed that two of Geraldine's cats were up on the sideboard, heads buried deep inside a large silver tureen, sipping the remains of the first-course vegetable soup.

Now it was Terry's turn to stir up some mischief. 'So what would it take for you to tread the path to the altar, Beattie?' he said, also puffing away at a cigar.

'A man,' retorted Beattie, without a blink. 'I mean – a *real* man.'

Terry nearly choked on his own cigar smoke.

'And what's *your* idea of a real man, Beattie?' It was the first time Sarah had said anything, but it carried far more significance than anyone at the table could have imagined.

Beattie paused for a moment before answering. Although she knew what her sister was getting at, she was going to take her time before she said what she really wanted to say.

In some perverse way, she was glad. She *wanted* to talk about men, she *wanted* to tell Sarah that she had been having a relationship with her fancy man. This was the opportunity she had been waiting for, the chance to expose the kind of person Sarah had always admired so much, someone from the same side of the fence as herself, who spoke and behaved well, and knew how to do all the right things in company. Yes, Edward Lacey was that kind of person all right, but he was also a liar and a cheat. What kind of a superior being was it that tried to have a relationship with two sisters at the same time, who broke promises, and left someone standing at a tram stop for the best part of two hours? All this she wanted to say to her sister, but for some reason, the words stuck in her throat. 'A real man is someone I could trust,' was all she was prepared to say – for the time being.

Sarah's eyes were lowered. She resisted the temptation to look at her sister.

At this stage, the two cats had finished off the remains of the soup and were now starting on the scraps left over on the serving dishes.

Aunt Dixie, who had been bored out of her mind from the very first moment that she had arrived for the weekend party, was at last enjoying herself. Much to the disdain of the male members of the family, she had already helped herself twice to the decanter of claret, and now she was reaching out for it again. 'You know, Beattie,' she said, 'I can't help agreeing with you. Men are such fickle creatures. You never know what they're going to get up to next.'

'Well, you couldn't have won this war without 'em,' sniffed Benedict, indignantly.

'We haven't won it yet!' insisted Dixie, gulping down her claret.

'Women ain't stupid, Grandfather,' Beattie said, leaning forward in her seat so that she could see Benedict at the far end of the table. 'We've got brains, and we oughta be given the chance ter use 'em.'

'Brains!' Old Benedict leaned back in his chair, refusing to meet his granddaughter's gaze. 'You mean like that damned Pankhurst woman, blowing up Lloyd George's house down at Walton just before the war? If you call that brains, I'd rather be without 'em!'

Beattie's hackles were rising. ''E asked fer it, the stupid old goat!'

'Beattie!' said Samuel, his voice raised just enough to be firm. 'That's enough now.'

'Well, it's true!' snapped Beattie, refusing to be silenced. 'That's the trouble wiv women. We've let blokes 'ave their way wiv us fer too long. We've got the right ter be 'eard!'

To everyone's surprise, Samuel thumped his fist on the table. 'I said – that is quite enough!'

Once again, there was a hushed silence.

Beattie flopped back on her chair, exasperated. After a moment she got up and made for the door. She turned and looked back at the hushed gathering around the table. 'Times're changin',' she said, quietly defiant. 'It won't always be like it is now.' With that, she left the room.

Samuel waited a moment before speaking. 'I'm sorry about all that,' he said, embarrassed. 'I'm afraid Beattie has a mind of her own.'

'It's to be expected given the type of people she mixes with.' Old Benedict snatched the claret decanter away from Dixie and topped up his own glass. 'You've only got to listen to her. Can't even speak the King's English. She's got a problem, that girl, and no mistake.'

Sarah's eyes remained lowered. She quietly got up from

the table, collected some of the dessert plates, and went out to the kitchen.

As she returned to the hall, Sarah noticed the sitting-room door partly open. Within, as she expected, she found Beattie stretched out on the sofa. Sarah closed the door quietly behind her. 'That was a pretty little scene,' she said, icily.

Beattie flicked her eyes up only briefly. 'Don't know wot you're talkin' about,' she replied indifferently.

'This is their night, not yours.'

'Oh, do shut up!' snapped Beattie, getting up quickly from the sofa, and going to look at herself in the large, ornate oval mirror hanging above the fireplace. 'I didn't ask ter spend me 'ole weekend wiv all that lot.'

'For God's sake, Beattie,' sighed Sarah. 'They've been married for twenty-five years. You may not approve of that, but at least you can help your own mother and father to celebrate on just one day of their lives.'

Beattie tried to pretend that she wasn't listening. She turned away from the mirror, went to a card table at the back of the sofa, and started aimlessly shuffling a pack of playing cards there.

Refusing to give way to Beattie's apparent indifference, Sarah went across to her. 'What do you know about Edward Lacey?'

Beattie's reaction was totally blank. '*Who?*'

'Don't play games with me, Beattie,' said Sarah, firmly. 'You know who he is, you know what he looks like. How?'

Beattie looked up only briefly from the playing cards she was setting out on the table. 'Are you talking about your petty officer?' she asked coyly. 'The one who jilted you?'

Sarah knew only too well that Beattie was taunting her. But she had to get to the bottom of it. 'How?' she demanded.

Beattie finally looked up. 'Coincidence really. We met

in a pub. He bought me a drink.'

Sarah was stony-faced.

From the dining room across the hall, they could hear the sound of laughter.

''E's quite a good looker,' continued Beattie, 'if yer like that kind of face. Can't say I do really.' She started to play Solo with the playing cards. ''E took a shine ter me. I couldn't do nuffin' about it, Sarah – honest.'

'I don't believe you.'

Beattie flicked her eyes up. They were as hard as steel. 'I'm not askin' yer to,' she said. 'I'm not asking you ter believe nuffin'. All I'm tellin' yer is that I've bin seein' 'im ever since.' She lined up a Jack of Diamonds. ''Is idea – not mine.'

On impulse, Sarah lunged forward, and with one hand swept the pack of carefully arranged cards on to the floor. 'You're a liar!'

'Oh yeah?' Beattie smirked and crossed her arms. She wasn't in the least bit intimidated. 'Why don't yer ask 'im? If yer can find 'im, of course.'

Sarah was much more unsure of herself than of Beattie. There was a time when she could tell whether Beattie was telling lies or not, but not any longer. Right from the time when she was a little girl, Beattie had loved to taunt people, to make them doubt themselves, to set one person against another. She had done it several times with their mother and father, and goodness knows how many times with Sarah herself. But this was different. It had to be a lie, it just had to be. How could it be possible that Beattie had been seeing a man who was so alien to the way she herself wanted to live? Now, face to face with Beattie, she was determined to find the truth. 'Where did you meet him?'

'I told yer, in a pub.'

'What pub? Where?'

'The Eaglet – in Seven Sisters Road.'

Sarah did a double take. 'The one that was bombed?'

Beattie smirked. 'The same night.'

'You're lying!'

Beattie shook her head slowly. 'It was a lucky escape, Sarah. A few minutes later an' I wouldn't've been standin' 'ere now.' She smirked again. 'Terrible fawt, ain't it?'

Sarah now had no intention of letting up. 'You've been seeing Edward ever since then?'

Beattie nodded.

'And in all that time, you never told him that I am your sister?'

Beattie did not answer. She seemed to be staring straight through her. 'I didn't 'ave ter tell 'im. 'E already knew.'

As she spoke, an old grandfather clock in the corner of the room chimed the hour.

Beattie waited for the chiming to stop, and then continued. 'It's me 'e wants, yer know – not you. And d'yer know why? Because I give 'im wot you never could, because you're incapable of it.' Sarah raised her hand as if to strike Beattie across the face, but Beattie quickly grabbed her wrist and held on to it. 'This is the kind of bloke you're dealin' wiv,' she said intensely. 'One of your *own* kind, who plays by the rules – providin' 'e's the one who makes 'em up.'

Sarah struggled to release her wrist, but Beattie's grip was hard and strong.

'D'yer know wot the joke is, Sarah?' said Beattie, her eyes making direct contact with Sarah's. 'The joke is, I can't bear the sight of your fancy man. He's wet an' weak an' everythin' I despise in a bloke. So as far as I'm concerned, yer can 'ave 'im. I 'ope I never set eyes on 'im again as long as I live.' She finally released Sarah's wrist.

Sarah felt quite empty inside. She turned and went to the large bow-shaped window, though the blackout curtains were already drawn. The shadow of her own image seemed to be dancing on the wall in the flickering of the gaslamps. So she just stood there, her back towards Beattie, not knowing what to do or say.

'If what you say is true,' she said eventually, her back still turned, her voice only barely audible, 'I want nothing more to do with you ever again.' She then turned to face Beattie. 'But I've known you too long, Beattie. I know how you like to hurt people. But you're not going to hurt me, because I don't believe a word you've said. Edward will write to me sooner or later, of that I'm sure. *He'll* tell me the truth, and then I'll never have to listen to any of your lies ever again.'

Sarah was about to turn and make her way to the door, when Beattie suddenly said, 'I'm pregnant, Sarah.'

Sarah stopped with a shocked start.

'Yes,' continued Beattie. 'It's 'is kid. But I don't want it.'

Sarah was shaking her head in disbelief.

'Oh it's true all right,' said Beattie. 'If yer don't want ter believe me, go up ter the clinic up Wells Terrace. Ask fer Dr Brooks. 'E'll tell yer.'

Sarah could bear no more. But as she rushed to leave the room, she found her way blocked by someone standing in the open doorway. It was their father.

'I want you out of this house first thing in the morning,' said Samuel, directing his look straight across the room towards his younger daughter.

With that, he left the room, closing the door quietly behind him.

* * *

62

Aunt Dixie was fast asleep when Beattie slipped into her room. It had been a long supper party, one that Dixie had thought would never end. But her salvation had been that decanter of claret, and by the time everyone had completed their day of congratulations to Geraldine and Samuel, Dixie had only just enough strength left in her legs to climb the three flights of stairs to Beattie's room.

After her lively encounter in the sitting room with her sister and father, Beattie made herself scarce. The first thing she did was to walk the darkened streets to give herself breathing space before she did what she knew she had to do. Then she went back to her bedroom and packed a suitcase. She hadn't really any idea where she was going to spend the night, but it didn't matter. All she wanted was to get away from that house, that family, and everything that had stifled her for so many years.

One last look back at the sleeping beauty, snoring away in a drunken stupor in her bed, and Beattie was gone.

The way she felt, it was very doubtful if she would ever see the house again.

Chapter 5

The summer of 1918 brought mixed blessings to the war-weary British people. On the Western Front the Germans launched an offensive near Compiegne, which was later repulsed with a massive Allied counteroffensive. The Allies also halted the German advance towards Paris, which raised hopes that the war was at last near an end. The news from Russia, however, brought an air of dark gloom as it was announced that the new Bolshevik regime had executed the former Tsar Nicholas II, together with his entire family. The shock waves spread throughout the entire British political arena, and prompted angry clashes between monarchist supporters and disaffected radicals. At home, Prime Minister Lloyd George and his coalition government were accused of giving misleading statements about military manpower to the House of Commons, and also criticised for abandoning Home Rule and conscription for the increasingly belligerent Ireland.

Like her father, Sarah followed the news of the day with passionate interest, and each evening, they analysed the day's copy of *The Times* together. During recent years, they had usually found that, in general, they were very much in agreement about the way the country should be run. But as the summer progressed, both Samuel and Geraldine began to notice a change in Sarah's attitude to life in general.

It had now been over three months since the events of that terrible Saturday evening, when Beattie had left home in the middle of the night. The news that Beattie was pregnant by Edward Lacey had devastated Sarah's vision of her own future, and turned her against her sister more than she would have thought possible. And yet, in some ways, Beattie had opened Sarah's eyes, for with the painful realisation that marriage on her terms was not to be, she had learned a cruel lesson about the type of person that Edward Lacey really was, and that out there in the wider world, there were plenty more Edward Laceys, just waiting to betray and deceive.

However, to everyone's surprise, Sarah had recovered remarkably well from the trauma of her experience. Instead of bitterness, she had gained strength, and she was determined to show that from now on, she would never allow a man to rob her of her dignity, her happiness, or her independence. Sarah's strength was in her resolve, and this, she was determined, would sustain her through the coming years.

The effect of Beattie's departure was felt mainly by Geraldine Melford. When she heard that Samuel had ordered their daughter out of the house, it prompted the first real quarrel they had had in their twenty-five years of married life.

'Whatever she's done,' insisted Geraldine, to her husband, on more than one occasion, 'she's still our own flesh and blood. How can we turn our back on her when, whether we like it or not, she's going to give us our first grandchild?'

But Samuel would have none of it. Thoroughly entrenched in his view that Beattie had brought shame and disgrace on the family, he absolutely forbade any contact with her, and made it quite clear that the girl would not be receiving a penny's allowance from him. As each day passed,

Geraldine felt more and more depressed that Beattie was out there alone in the world, disowned by her parents and with no one to support or guide her. The very thought was not only consuming Geraldine with guilt, it was making her ill.

The moment Beattie confronted her that fateful evening, Sarah made a conscious decision that she would never resume contact with her sister. But *never* was a long time, and when Sarah started to think more carefully about the situation, she wondered what she would do if she were to suddenly come across Beattie with her child walking along the pavement towards her. But that was still a long way off, at least another six months by Sarah's calculation.

In the meantime, one of the most difficult problems Sarah had to face during the summer months was her mother's persistent attempts to find a suitable replacement for Edward Lacey. Every time she and her parents went to church, her mother had carefully planned a chance meeting with a different young man. It was, of course, not only embarrassing for Sarah herself, but also for the intended suitors. Time and time again, Sarah tried to explain to her mother that she was no longer interested in finding someone to walk out with; as far as she was concerned, marriage in the foreseeable future was out of the question. But even though Geraldine had been just as shocked and outraged as her husband by Beattie's callous betrayal of her sister, she was convinced that it was her duty as a mother to stand by both of them. In her eyes, the real villain was Edward Lacey, who had brought such pain to her elder daughter, and shame to the Melford family. She was absolutely determined not to let this rogue destroy Sarah's life, so from now on she would concentrate all her efforts on helping Sarah to find the happiness the poor girl was entitled to.

At the end of July, however, Sarah's vision of a cosy future managing the day-to-day affairs of the family house in Thornhill Road began to feel worryingly insecure when, over supper one evening, her father had something to ask of her.

'Sarah, I want you and your mother to start looking round for a lodger.'

Sarah sat bolt upright in her chair. Was she hearing right? A stranger paying money to share the house with them, the Melfords' own house, which Sarah cherished more than anything else in the whole wide world? 'A lodger?'

Samuel, trying to make the announcement sound as unimportant as possible, continued eating whilst he talked. 'Both your mother and I feel that it is a waste to keep your sister's room vacant when it could be contributing to the expenses of running so large a house as this.'

Sarah swung a startled look at her mother, who was clearly doing her best to avert her gaze. 'A lodger? Here? In *this* house?' she asked. 'Is such a thing really necessary, Father?'

'Not necessary,' Samuel replied casually. 'But in the circumstances – appropriate.'

Sarah thought for a moment. She tried again to exchange a look with her mother, still without success. 'Do we need the money, Father?' she asked outright.

'This is wartime, my dear. Everything is expensive. We need to make as many savings as we can. And in any case, the running of a good household should always be backed with an adequate contingency.'

Adequate contingency? But here was the man who had always propounded the notion that 'the Englishman's home is his castle', and that it would be folly to bring strangers into such a place. The very idea of a lodger living in the house that she loved so much filled her with despair. She felt a sense of disquiet, and found it difficult to continue with her meal.

'Perhaps it would only need to be a temporary arrangement,' said Geraldine, rather feebly.

'That remains to be seen, my dear,' Samuel answered. 'We have the space, and we should put it to good use.'

Sarah looked straight across the table at her father. 'But what happens if Beattie comes home?'

Samuel quietly put down his knife and fork, and returned her gaze. 'That is not a situation that will arise, Sarah,' he replied, calmly but firmly. 'Your sister has already decided which course she wishes her life to take.'

Sarah couldn't believe this conversation was taking place. She sat back in her chair and glanced around the walls of the large kitchen, trying to imagine what it would be like if a lodger were to move in and use the place to cook his or her own meals. The whole idea offended her. This wasn't just a house, it was a home – the Melford home. One day it would belong to her, or Beattie, or both of them. It would be a sin to taint it with an outsider. But the more she thought about all this, the more anxious she became. Was her father experiencing some kind of money problems? If so, it was hard to believe, for not only did he have his well-paid job in the largest department store in London, but he owned one of the loveliest houses in Barnsbury. What *was* behind all this? 'Is there no other way, Father?' she asked.

Once again, Samuel briefly looked up from his plate. 'Needs must, my dear.'

'If there is a need, then why not let me help?'

'That's why I'm asking you to—'

'If it's money we need, then let me find a job.'

'Oh no, Sarah!' her mother said emphatically. 'Not you.'

Sarah was irritated. 'Why not?' she said sharply. 'I'm

not a child. I've got a good pair of hands, and I can think for myself. If we need to bring in some money, I see no reason whatsoever why I can't contribute.'

Samuel was shaking his head.

'Oh for goodness' sake, Father – why not?'

'Because you are my daughter,' he replied, 'and I do not expect a daughter of mine to go out to earn a living.'

For a brief moment, Sarah thought of Beattie. 'Forgive me for saying, Father, but that's very old-fashioned. You've kept me long enough. I can't just go on being a millstone around your neck.'

'Don't be silly, Sarah,' said Geraldine, agitated.

'Well, it's true, Mother.' Sarah stretched across, and covered her mother's hand with her own. 'You and Father have always been so wonderful to me. I've lived a life of luxury ever since I was born. It's time I did something for you, for this house.'

'That question does not and will not arise,' said her father, rather forcefully. 'You know very well that when your mother and I have gone, this house will be yours.'

'I am glad to say that that question will not arise for a very long time,' she said, spiritedly. 'I want to help, Father. If we have a problem, you *must* let me.'

Samuel put his knife and fork down on his plate, and dabbed his lips with his napkin. 'If you want to help, Sarah,' he said quietly, 'find a lodger.'

Gamages Department Store was quite an imposing building. Situated on the corner of Hatton Garden and Holborn Circus, the building reached up four floors, and overlooked a busy, bustling, and thriving community of newspaper offices, commercial buildings, and small shops that stretched all the way to the well-known half-timbered houses of Staple Inn on the main Gray's Inn Road. Although not in the same league as the more affluent Harrods in smart Knightsbridge, Gamages was considered by many to be the ideal family store, and, like its nearest competitor, Selfridges in Oxford Street, busy on nearly every day of the week. However, like many similar establishments in London, Gamages' fortunes had been severely hit by the austerity of war, and for this reason stocks were kept to a minimum and only replaced on demand. But all who passed through its doors could not help but warm to its friendly, welcoming atmosphere.

Samuel Melford had been appointed General Manager just before the war, and amongst the innovations he brought to the store were eye-catching displays, good discounts on all shop-soiled items, and a cafeteria that was the envy of every other big store. Samuel was, on the whole, quite popular with the staff, though some thought he was a little too strict and severe, and if there were any complaint at all about his management style, it was that he always played everything by the book.

Sarah's decision to seek an appointment with the personnel officer at Gamages was taken after a great deal of heart-searching. She knew that her action was likely to incur the wrath of her father, for she had not told him what she was doing, but with so much at stake, she was prepared to take that risk. She was determined at all costs not to advertise for a lodger, as her father had instructed. In spite of the despicable way in which Beattie had behaved to Sarah, it somehow seemed wrong to turn her room over to a stranger. After all, it was still just conceivable that Beattie would one day try to come home. Also, ever since Sarah had been jilted, the house in Thornhill Road had taken on a hugely increased significance for her. She'd always had a deep affection for the place, but now it was as though it was a part of her very soul. She adored every nook and cranny of the place from the red brick facade under the constant summer shade of a tall plane tree, with its fussy, straggling branches, to the large rooms inside, with high ceilings edged with white stucco mouldings; the wide staircase from the entrance hall to Samuel and Geraldine's and Sarah's rooms on the first floor, and Beattie's at the top. Above that staircase on the ground floor was a small length of exposed modern timber beam, which Sarah touched every morning as she came down the stairs with a bright 'Good morning, beam!' To Sarah the Melford house was a living thing, and she had absolutely no intention of sharing it with any stranger.

'You're not by any chance related to our General Manager, are you, Miss Melford?'

Sarah was prepared for the first question she was asked by Mrs Hetherington, Gamages' personnel officer. 'Oh goodness me, no,' she replied, without a trace of guilt. 'Is that his name too?'

Mrs Hetherington smiled. It was a warm smile, for she had a chubby face that looked as though it wouldn't know how to frown if it tried. 'A small world,' she said fleetingly.

The day had started well for Sarah, for on the way to Holborn, she had managed to find a front seat on the top of the open-air omnibus. It was now the first week in August and the weather was absolutely sweltering. As she passed along the sun-drenched streets, below her everyone was turned out in the minimum of clothing – women in short-sleeved dresses and summer bonnets, like herself, and she even saw men not wearing ties, although these were mainly manual workers. When she got to Gamages, the place was full, for she already knew that her father had supervised the August Bank Holiday week sales, which were clearly doing a roaring trade.

'I see on your application form that you've had no experience in selling.' Mrs Hetherington was peering at Sarah over the top of her pince-nez spectacles.

'No, I haven't,' replied Sarah, at her most businesslike. 'But I feel I have an aptitude for it, and I do learn very quickly.'

Mrs Hetherington smiled at Sarah's confidence, but it was obvious that she liked the girl. 'Well, to tell you the truth,' she said, 'if you'd applied for a job here just a couple of weeks ago I wouldn't have been able to help you. Things haven't been too good for the company of late. In fact we've had to lay off quite a lot of the staff, mainly in the storerooms. This war has taken its toll. I'm afraid. That, and all the troubles in the boardroom.'

Sarah was intrigued – and anxious. She wanted to ask more, but decided it was too risky to do so.

'Anyway,' said Mrs Hetherington, endorsing Sarah's application form in front of her, 'I'm sure we'll muddle through somehow. Once this war's over, things can only get better – *and* when we can get your namesake to pull himself together.'

Sarah was now really worried.

'Well, young lady,' said Mrs Hetherington, taking off her pince-nez and getting up from her desk, 'I'm going to try you out in Books. You've got a very nice speaking voice. You'll go down well with our reading customers.' She lowered her voice as though there was somebody else in the room listening. 'You can always tell breeding,' she said. 'Unlike some I could mention.'

A few minutes later, Sarah found herself being taken on a guided tour of the store. Mrs Hetherington was a very thorough guide, for she failed to omit one single department, from Ladies' Wear on the ground floor to the parlour games department on the top floor. For obvious reasons, Sarah couldn't tell her personnel officer that she had visited the store on many occasions, so she showed the necessary enthusiasm everywhere she was taken, though at any moment she quite expected to find herself confronted by her father. If this were to happen now Sarah knew it would be a disaster, for her whole plan depended on her getting the job on her own initiative, and not telling her father until he got home that evening. However, on every floor she was taken to, there was no sign of him.

'Heavens!' said Mr Lumley, who looked after the book department, and who had just been introduced to a Miss Melford, his new assistant. 'Not another one?'

Sarah and Mrs Hetherington laughed. 'No, Mr Lumley,' said Mrs Hetherington, reassuringly, 'you're quite safe. Miss Melford is no relation to our GM.'

Mr Lumley breathed a sigh of relief. 'Thank goodness for that,' he said. 'I couldn't cope with two of them.'

Sarah smiled weakly. 'Your General Manager sounds like a bit of a tartar,' she offered, trying to be as discreet as she could.

Mrs Hetherington answered, 'Not really. He's a bit too much to stomach, that's all. Poor man. He just can't seem to cope any more.'

Sarah felt all the hairs on her head bristling with concern. 'You mean he interferes a lot? He comes down here often?'

'Comes down here?' Mr Lumley exchanged a fairly cutting look with Mrs Hetherington. 'That'll be the day!'

Sarah looked puzzled.

'We don't see him at all, dear,' said Mrs Hetherington, again lowering her voice. 'No one sees him, not in any of the departments. In fact, Mr Melford hasn't been seen in the store, nor in his office, for six weeks.'

It was such a hot evening in Barnsbury that a lot of people were sitting at open windows or in their small front gardens, savouring the sweet, humid smells of summer. Samuel Melford had found it a stifling journey home on the tram. The lower deck had been jammed with people returning from work, and he had had to stand all the way. To make matters worse, the new starched collar that Geraldine had bought him for his previous birthday was cutting into his flesh and leaving a sore mark all the way round his neck, so he eagerly looked forward to removing it as soon as he possibly could.

He reached the corner of Richmond Road, where Sid Perkins' winter chestnut pitch had been taken over by Marco Rossini with his Italian water-ice van, which was little more than an ice box on wheels. As usual, there was a queue of small children and their mothers or fathers waiting there, for Marco's ice cream, which was made from flavoured frozen sugar syrup, had the reputation of being the best in Islington. Samuel shuffled past, for the humidity had slowed him down quite considerably, and made him look older than his years.

'Sorry to be late, dear,' Samuel said to his wife, who met him in the front hall. 'The heat seems to slow everyone down.'

After greeting him with a kiss on his cheek, Geraldine helped him off with his jacket. 'You poor thing,' she said, taking his briefcase and putting it down by the hall coat stand, 'you look exhausted. I'll go and pour you a nice glass of cool lemonade.'

As Geraldine dutifully rushed off into the kitchen, Samuel took his copy of the *Evening Standard*, and went into the sitting room. Sarah, who had been watching him from the top of the stairs, came down and followed him in.

Samuel went first to the mantelpiece and collected his favourite pipe. At the precise moment he was retrieving his jar of tobacco from the ornate, highly polished bookcase, he heard the sitting-room door close quietly behind him. Standing there was Sarah.

'My dear,' he said, as brightly as he was capable, 'I trust you've had a good day?'

'I have, Father, thank you,' Sarah said. Then she slowly strolled to the middle of the room, and waited whilst he filled his pipe. 'And you?'

'Busy, as usual,' he replied, packing the tobacco as tightly as he could into his pipe. 'There were so many people in the store today, our staff were almost literally dying of the heat.'

Sarah said nothing as she watched him make his way back to his favourite leather armchair in front of the fireplace. She waited for him to be seated before asking, 'Were you in your office the whole day then, Father?'

Lighting his pipe took Samuel quite some time. 'Every minute,' he replied, between puffs. 'Except for forty-five minutes during the lunch-break. I took a stroll in the sun along Farringdon Road. From there, you get such a splendid view of St Paul's Cathedral. That great big dome was absolutely bathed in sunshine.'

Sarah found it impossible to look directly at her father whilst he was saying such things, but she sat down on the sofa opposite him as calmly as she could, and clasped her hands together on her lap. 'Father,' she said eventually, and with some difficulty, 'I paid a visit to Gamages today.'

To her absolute astonishment, her father did not budge an eyelid. 'Oh really, my dear?' he said. 'And did what you saw please you?'

Sarah stared hard at her father, finding his behaviour increasingly strange. 'I went there to get a job. I've been

76

offered a place in the book department.'

This time there was a long pause. After a moment or so, Samuel emerged from behind a cloud of thick pipe smoke. 'I wish you hadn't done that,' he said in a very downbeat way. 'You know my feelings on that matter.'

'Father. Why did you say you were in your office today?' Sarah had now gone too far to turn back. 'I heard it said that you haven't been to work for the past six weeks.'

Samuel remained silent, staring down at the Persian rug, his pipe clenched tightly between his teeth.

Sarah leaned forward. 'Father, I don't understand. You've been leaving this house at the same time every morning, and returning at the same time every night, and yet you haven't been near your office. What is happening?'

Samuel suddenly sat quite upright, a bright look on his face. 'Happening? What's happening? Why nothing, my dear. I've just felt a little under the weather, that's all. But I'm much better now. I shall be going back to work on Monday.' He stood up, went to the fireplace and tapped the ash from his pipe.

Something was terribly wrong with her father, Sarah thought. He was trying to give the impression that life was perfectly normal, and yet it clearly wasn't. Something had happened to him, but she couldn't, as yet, detect what. She went across and gently put her arm on his shoulder. 'Father—'

He suddenly swung round to face her. 'It's very exciting, my dear,' he said, his eyes fixed but glowing. 'Just you wait and see. This is just the start. Once the war's over, the Melfords are going to be right on top again. Oh yes.'

Sarah watched him relight his pipe. She was devastated.

Chapter 6

Campbell Road had quite a reputation. Not only was it just about the roughest backstreet in Islington, but its residents, young and old, were considered to be nothing more than a bunch of wild animals. 'The Bunk', as the street was known, was just a stone's throw from the Seven Sisters Road at Finsbury Park, and nobody in their right mind ventured down there unless they had to, especially after dark. Gangs of adolescent and teenage thugs hung about on every street corner, pitching dice and intimidating anyone who dared to pass by. Cats and dogs were sought out and, as a matter of routine, strung up by their necks from lampposts until someone with a spark of humanity cut them down, usually only in the nick of time. There were so many fights, so many break-ins, so much mayhem in this lawless corner of the borough that the local copper station down at Hornsey Road assigned one particular flatfoot full time to pound the beat. The unlucky police constable, who had in fact volunteered for the job, was named Ben Fodder, and known by the locals as Big Ben. Big Ben was a huge man, weighing fifteen stone, who had once been a star amateur wrestler, which gave him a certain amount of notoriety, not to say respect, amongst the local troublemakers.

Beattie Melford moved in to Number 22 within a few days of walking out on her family. For the first night, she'd slept out rough, kipping with some of the down-and-outs beneath the railway arch opposite Holloway underground station. Then her friend, Nagger Mills, put her up for a day or so, although that was a bit of an ordeal as Nagger and her dad lived at the back of a cattle shed up the market, and the smell of cow dung kept her awake at night. Her break finally came, however, when she remembered the bloke she'd met that day after she'd been to pawn her bracelet at Bob Sluggins' place. Jack Ridley was his name, and she remembered how he had suggested a place up the Bunk. When she got there, she was none too sure; Number 22 was just about as seedy as you can get, with lace curtains hanging up at the windows that looked as though they'd never been cleaned, and the rest of the house, like all the other two-up two-downs along the grubby, litter-strewn street, was a run-down mess. If it hadn't been for the fact that the landlady, Ma Briggs, was standing at the street door, Beattie might have turned her back and made off. But Jack Ridley was right: Bunk or no Bunk, this was one old lady who did have a heart of gold, and, in complete contrast to the outside of the house, inside, from top to bottom, was spotless.

'Think of this as yer own 'ome, dearie,' she said, when Beattie said she'd take the room. 'Ol' Ma Briggs'll look after yer.' Beattie moved in at once, and had not once regretted it.

Come October, Beattie was over the worst of the morning sickness. Now it was just a question of waiting, which wasn't exactly easy, for she had had to take a job in a candle factory to help pay for her board and keep, and with a baby's feet now kicking quite regularly inside her stomach, working at a factory bench from seven in the morning to six in the evening was the type of initiation into working life that she had never anticipated.

As promised, Ma Briggs looked after Beattie as if she were her own daughter, for apart from giving her the best room in the house, she often had a meal waiting for her when she got back home from her day's work. However, the old lady was very concerned that Beattie's baby would arrive in this world without a father. 'Yer should write to 'im, dearie,' she said. 'Make 'im face up to 'is responsibilities.'

But Beattie had no intention of writing to Edward Lacey. Since the day he'd promised to tell Sarah that he didn't want to carry on with their relationship, and had broken that promise, she'd vowed never to see him again. And she was determined that Lacey would never see his child either. The more time she had had to think about the prospect of motherhood, the more she realised just how much it meant to her. In some strange way, her instinct told her that giving birth to a child was the one way she could come to terms with her own life. When the child was born, it would be hers, and hers alone, and she would never allow Lacey to be involved in bringing it up.

During the second week of October, Jack Ridley called to see Beattie. His visit was quite a surprise, for it was the first time she had seen him since the day he recommended Ma Briggs' place to her. She was immediately struck again by his dashing good looks, ginger hair and dark eyes, and thick, pouting lips. What she did remember from their previous meeting was the thick stubble on his cheeks and chin, but he had clearly recently shaved for his skin was now clear and smooth. However, for this initial meeting, Beattie did not yet feel confident enough to ask him up to her room, so she met him outside the house, where they perched side by side on the coping stone by the tiny front garden.

'I'm glad the old bird's takin' care of yer,' said Jack,

who was picking his teeth with a matchstick whilst he talked. 'Just as well – wiv the way fings are wiv you.'

'I'm very grateful to yer, Jack,' Beattie replied. 'I don't know wot I'd 'ave done if you 'adn't told me about this place. If there's ever anyfin' I can do fer you, just let me know.'

Jack grinned but only inwardly. 'So, who give yer the bun then?'

'It's a long story.'

'Army? Navy? Flyin'Corps?'

'Could we talk about somefin' else?' said Beattie, irritated.

Jack shrugged his shoulders. 'Suits me. I wos just wondrin' 'ow you're goin' ter cope, that's all.'

'I'll manage.' Beattie turned away to look along the road where a group of rowdy teenagers were kicking a milk bottle as though it were a football. 'What about you?' she asked, suddenly, turning back to Jack.

'Me?'

'I don't know nuffin' about yer. Where d'yer come from? Wot d'yer do?'

Jack flicked his matchstick into the kerb and pushed his cap to the back of his head. 'I come from anywhere I put me 'ead down, and I do anyfin' I'm asked ter do – brickie, bit of plasterin', chippie . . .'

Beattie was intrigued by his laid-back style. 'So you make a livin'?'

Jack turned to look at her with a smile. 'You could say that. Wiv a bit on the side, of course.'

Beattie was puzzled. 'What does that mean?'

Jack's mouth was curled up at the sides in a weird grin. 'I nick,' he replied quite unashamedly.

Beattie fixed him with a suspicious look. 'Nick? Yer don't mean – yer steal fings?'

Jack was quite surprised by her reaction. 'Why not?' he asked.

''Cos it's wrong,' she said.

'Wrong ter eat, yer mean?'

'There're uvver ways.'

'Tell me.'

Both turned to look off in different directions. For a moment or so, there was silence between them. Further down the road, the rogue teenagers had succeeded in smashing the milk bottle into pieces, and were now kicking bits of it at each other.

Jack was first to speak. 'I never knew my mum. She died when I was born. My ol' man brought me up. 'E 'ated my guts, beat me black an' blue, the sod. I did a bunk when I was seven. Never saw 'im again. Good riddance.'

Beattie couldn't understand why he was telling her all this. After all, she hardly knew him. And yet, there was something about him that fascinated her. It was to do with the way he talked without actually looking at her. He was a thinker. Beattie hadn't met many people like that.

'That's when I learnt 'ow ter nick. These geezers taught me, down the knackers' yard.' He flicked a quick glance at her. 'That's where they cut up the 'orse meat.'

He pulled one foot up, rested it on the coping stone, folded his arms, placed them on his knee, and rested his chin on them. 'They used ter get me ter nick from the drunks when they come out the boozers. It was easy money. I didn't get much of it, though. The geezers took most of it.' He paused only long enough to wipe his nose on his fingers. 'I come into me own later. Bigger fish. I didn't go 'ungry. Not no more.'

'Don't yer feel guilty, robbin' innocent people?' asked Beattie.

'Innocent?' said Jack, looking out at the teenagers on the rampage along the road. 'Who's the innocent – me, or them wiv the cash?'

After a moment, Beattie got up. 'I'd better be goin'. Fanks again, Jack.'

Jack grabbed hold of her arm, but he saw the surprise in her face, so he quickly released her. 'Wot yer goin' ter do when the kid arrives?' he asked.

Beattie shrugged her shoulders. 'Look after it, of course.'

'Wot d'yer do for cash in the meantime?'

Beattie thought about this for a moment 'I'll manage.'

'Well, if yer can't, yer know where to find me. Just ask Ma.'

He pulled his cap on straight again, put his hands in his pockets, and moved off.

Beattie watched him ambling down the road until he disappeared around the corner into the next street.

By this time, the rowdy teenagers were hurling as many milk bottles at each other as they could. In the distance, the burly figure of Big Ben was looming. Once again, the Bunk was on full alert.

Nagger Mills was turning out to be the kind of friend that everyone hopes to have, but rarely does. When Beattie left home, she was first to the rescue, taking Beattie back to share her room behind the cattle shed in the Caledonian Market; when Beattie moved into Ma Briggs' place in the Bunk, Nagger was first on the scene, bringing pots and pans to use on the gas ring in Beattie's room, an extra blanket and a feather pillow for her bed, a good supply of tea, sugar, a loaf of bread and a good lump of marge. She even treated her to a big pot of shrimps from Honest Harry's fresh fish stall up the market, and a pennyworth of Beattie's favourite peppermint-flavour bull's-eyes from Gert Snell's sweet shop. The fact was, Nagger was really quite concerned about her old mate, and felt very protective towards her. She was anxious that Beattie hadn't decided to get rid of the baby, and she wondered how she was going to cope once it arrived.

Nagger could be quite a firecracker, though, like the time when she overheard Shiner Fitch taking the piss out of Beattie by telling his mates down the market as how she'd got herself 'a bun in the oven'. Lashing out at Shiner, Nagger told him, 'If yer arse was as big as yer mouf, we could auction you off wiv the rest of the bulls!'

On the first evening in November, Nagger took Beattie to the Palace Cinematograph Theatre on the corner of Seven Sisters Road and Devonshire Road, which most people knew as Pyke's, after its former owner Montague Pyke. The theatre was only a few years old, and was very popular with the residents of Holloway, despite the fact that, as the audience filed in, a member of the staff was there to hand out cough sweets to counteract the pungent smell of fag smoke that filled the auditorium during every performance. The programme that evening was a very popular one, for it featured several two-reeler films, starring firm favourites such as Little Titch, Pola Negri, Buster Keaton, Tod Slaughter, and Charlie Chaplin.

Beattie and Naggs were joined by some of Beattie's workmates from the candle factory, including Ivy West and Marj Barker, who were always good for a laugh. And laugh they all did, especially when the piano accompanist, Doris Bell, better known to the regulars as 'good ol' Doll', lost her place on her music sheet during a tense moment in Pola Negri's latest melodrama, and got everything out of sync with the film.

After the show, Naggs walked Beattie home to the Bunk,

which gave her the chance to talk to Beattie about how she was going to cope once the baby was born. But there was one particular thing on her mind.

'Yer've gotta tell 'im, Beat,' she said, as they strolled arm in arm along Seven Sisters Road. 'Yer've gotta tell sailor boy about 'is kid.'

Beattie came to an abrupt halt. 'Now don't go fru all that again, Naggs,' she said, irritably. 'I've told yer, as far as I'm concerned, Ed Lacey don't even exist.'

'But 'e does, Beat,' insisted Naggs. 'Wot 'e's done is wrong, there's no two ways about that, and 'e's an absolute sod, but this kid is goin' ter be as much 'is as yours.'

Beattie tried to relieve the pressure on her bulging stomach by straightening her shoulders. 'What the eye don't see . . .' she said obstinately. 'I don't owe that man nuffin'.'

'That yer don't,' replied Naggs. 'But it's not right ter keep it from 'im. OK, so if yer do tell 'im, 'e could well decide ter take no notice and lay low. But if 'e wanted ter turn nasty – I mean, even more nasty – yer might end up in court.'

Until that moment, Beattie had only just realised that they had come to a halt on the corner of Hornsey Road, right opposite where the poor old Eaglet pub used to be. She stared hard at the shell of the building, and could still see herself and Edward Lacey standing at that bar. *Anchor's down, and here I stay.* His voice was echoing through her mind. *Edward. You can call me Ted.* A faint, wry smile came to Beattie's face.

'Look, Beat,' Naggs said, taking Beattie's arm again and moving on. 'Whatever yer fink of Edward bleedin' Lacey, it's not right ter take it out on the kid.'

Beattie was taken aback. 'The kid? Wot're yer talkin' about?'

'Yer could've got rid of it, Beat,' said Naggs, 'but yer

chose not to. In which case, a kid needs a farver.'

Beattie was indignant. 'Who says so?'

'It's obvious, Beat,' said Naggs, doing her best to sound reasonable. 'Yer 'ave ter fink of all the problems of bringin' a kid up on yer own. A kid costs money. Where yer goin' ter get it if yer can't go ter work?'

'I'll manage,' replied Beattie, defiantly. 'Ma Briggs said she'd 'elp. There won't be no problems.'

'There's somefin' else too, Beat,' said Naggs, once again bringing them to a halt. ''Ave yer fawt about what people are goin' ter say – I mean, you, a single woman wiv a baby?'

'Who cares what they fink?' snapped Beattie. 'It's nuffin' ter do wiv no one but me.'

'But it is, Beat.' Naggs turned Beattie around to look at her. 'People can be cruel. They can make your life hell. It's not only your dad that feels the way 'e does. If the same fing 'appened ter me, my ol' man'd beat the bleedin' daylights out of me.'

For a moment, Beattie said nothing. Her mind was full of what options, if any, she really had. What Naggs was saying was right, it was only too plain to see that. Even in the Bunk word had got around that she was in the family way, without a husband, without a man. As her stomach swelled more and more, people she passed in the street were noticing her. Their looks were disapproving; she knew, she could tell. It was amazing how small-minded people could be, no matter where, or which side of the fence, they came from. On the opposite side of the road, there was a right royal knees-up going on in The Medina Arms pub. They were all having a good time all right, and Beattie wished she could be there with them. But even there, they would know. They would see that bulge of hers, and they would know. And then the questions would come. '*How long ter go now, dear?' 'Where's yer hubby then?' 'In the army, is 'e?'* And when they knew, when they found out that there was no husband, they would just be like all the rest. A woman with a kid and no husband? Must be a tart. Beattie felt two small feet kicking inside her stomach. That tiny creature was trying to tell her something. But what?

'I just don't want *you* ter be in the wrong, Beat,' said Naggs, her arm affectionately hugging Beattie around the waist. 'I couldn't care a monkey's fer sailor boy, but I do care fer you.'

'If I do tell 'im, what 'appens if 'e says 'e wants ter come back an' live wiv me?'

Naggs thought about this for a moment. 'D'yer want 'im ter come back?' she asked.

'Yer've got ter be jokin'!'

'Regardless of wot people fink?'

In the frail light of an early winter's evening, Naggs could see that the look on Beattie's face was more determined than ever.

'Regardless of wot people fink,' replied Beattie.

Naggs broke into a broad smile. 'Then tell 'im ter get stuffed!'

Both of them roared with laughter.

Beattie crawled into bed and lay there, looking up at the grubby white ceiling which hadn't had a coat of paint since before the war. Although it was still only ten o'clock, or thereabouts, she felt drained. Two little feet inside her had shown her very little mercy during the day, and now she was resting on her back, that burgeoning life assured her that even if she was ready for sleep, *it* wasn't. Before getting undressed, she had turned off the gaslight on the wall without bothering to draw the blackout curtains. In any case, with rumours of an armistice at any time, many people had already discarded their blackout curtains, and as the residents of the Bunk cared little for decorum, at night it was now perfectly easy to peer into neighbours' front of house rooms as you passed by.

Even with no gaslight, the room was flooded with a bright, white glow, for the moon, although not full, was unhindered by any clouds. As Beattie lay there, her face bathed in the frosty rays of a cold November night, her mind was torn by indecision. Everything Naggs had told her was true; if nothing else, Edward Lacey was the father of the child she would bear. But when she dismissed him from her life, she did so in the knowledge that such a man was not fit enough to be a husband, let alone a father. Not that she would ever want to marry him or any other man, especially one from a world that was so different to everything she believed in.

And as she lay there, her mind slowly started to drift to other things. She wondered what was going on at home in Thornhill Road, and if what she had heard was true, that her father was unwell, and that Sarah had taken a job at Gamages. Since the early days of her pregnancy, she had thought a lot about her family, about her sister, Sarah, and all the years of lost opportunity – for both of them. She closed her eyes, and saw Sarah's face before her, smiling – that prim little smile – nodding her head graciously as if saying, 'It's wrong of you to do this, Beattie,' or 'It's wrong of you to do that.' A rare moment of guilt interrupted her thoughts. Who was to blame for their inability to get on? Was it Sarah, who was set in her ways and unable to compromise? Or was it Beattie herself, who could only see protest as a way to express herself. And then she thought of her mother, who tried so hard to retain the family in the traditional way. Poor, dear Mother. If there was any one person in the world who was likely to grieve over Beattie's absence, it would surely be her mother. Would she ever see them again? One day, would they recognise that she herself was a mother?

Just when the two small feet inside decided to stop kicking in the walls of her stomach, there was an almighty thumping on her bedroom door.

'Beattie! Wake up! Wake up! Beattie!' It was Ma Briggs calling from the landing outside.

Beattie's heart was thumping hard at the shock, but she managed to sit up, lower her feet on to the cold lino floor, and get across to the door to open it.

'Beattie!'

Beattie's tired eyes could hardly focus on the old dear, who was out there with a lighted candle, and wearing a pleated nightcap and tattered pink nightgown. 'Wot is it, Ma?' she spluttered. 'Wot's up?'

Ma Briggs could hardly contain herself. 'It's over, Beattie! It's all over!'

'Over? Wot's over?'

Ma was talking faster than her lips would allow. 'The war, Beattie! The war! They're signing the armistice next week. Can't yer 'ear 'em in the street? Everyone's goin' mad!'

Beattie suddenly woke right up. Forgetting about the bulge in her stomach, she rushed across to the window, rubbed her eyes, and looked out. It was true. There were groups of people rushing up and down the street, some of them leaping up and down, others shouting and singing, and others doing an impromptu knees-up. Yes, it really was true. It was over. This long, bloody war was over at last. How much had it cost in human life? Beattie wondered. Would what happened from now on really be worth those years of bitterness, anger, and hate?

She turned with a start. Ma Briggs was still standing in the open bedroom doorway. She was sobbing hard, the candlelight picking out the tears rolling down her cheeks.

'It's all right, Ma,' Beattie said, throwing her arms around the old lady and hugging her. 'It's all over. Now we can start ter live again.'

When Ma Briggs had gone back down to her room, Beattie turned up the gaslight, collected a pencil and some notepaper, and returned to bed.

Then she set about writing a note to Edward Lacey. She had decided to tell him that during the next three months, he would become a father.

The armistice between the Allies and Germany came into force at eleven o'clock on the morning of 11 November 1918. Two days prior to that Kaiser Wilhelm II fled to the Netherlands, where he immediately went into hiding. There was great rejoicing throughout the United Kingdom, and it was the one event that was approved by the people of both Barnsbury – and 'the Bunk'.

On that morning, Beattie put on her working clothes as usual, had a cup of tea, cut herself a thick chunk of bread, plastered it with marge and a big spoonful of strawberry jam, and devoured it as quickly as she could. Although it was after nine in the morning, it didn't worry her, for she imagined that the candle factory would be joining in the celebrations just as much as everyone else. So, after wrapping herself up in a warm topcoat, and with a large woollen scarf over her head, she made her way downstairs.

As usual, Ma Briggs was waiting for her in the hall. It was a ritual that was beginning to irritate Beattie, for to her mind it smelled a bit of regularity. However, today the old lady had a reason for being there. 'Somefin' in the post for yer, dearie. Looks important. I 'ope it's a windfall!' She roared with hoarse laughter, and handed over the envelope.

Beattie took a good look at it, and realised at once that it wasn't the reply she was waiting for from Edward Lacey. But in some perverted way, she was rather hoping that it wouldn't be. 'No windfall, Ma,' she said, despondently. 'More likely someone's after somefin'.'

Ma Briggs watched eagerly as Beattie ripped open the envelope and read the contents. She was surprised to see the lack of any kind of response on Beattie's face.

'Nuffin' important, Ma,' she said quite impassively. 'Do us a favour, will yer? Bung it in the bin for me?'

Ma Briggs took the letter and envelope from Beattie, then followed her to the door. 'We'll 'ave a little snifter tergevver ternight, dearie,' she called, as Beattie left the house. 'If yer feel like it, that is. We deserve a celebration.'

'Fanks, Ma!' called Beattie, as she made off down the street.

'See yer later!'

Ma stood in the open doorway, watching Beattie until she disappeared around the corner into neighbouring Fonthill Road. Then she went back into the house, closing the door behind her.

Still clutching Beattie's letter and envelope in her hand, she went into her front parlour and quickly searched for her wobbly, half-broken glasses. She found them on her breakfast tray, splattered with milk from her cup of tea. Quickly wiping them on her pinny, she cleared the tea tray to one side, and settled down at the table to read Beattie's letter, which was badly scrawled on plain notepaper, with no address.

Dear Miss Beattie (I regret you did not add your surname),

Your letter addressed to my son, Edward, and dated 1 November, has been forwarded to me by the Royal Naval Training Depot at Dartford . . .

Ma Briggs wasn't very good at reading words, especially words that weren't written very clearly. But even with her modest skills, it took very little time for her to discover that the grand-sounding Lieutenant-Commander Lacey had written to tell Beattie that her sailor boy petty officer, father of her future child, was dead.

Chapter 7

Parliament was dissolved a fortnight after the signing of the armistice, and the Labour Party became the official Opposition to the new Coalition Government headed by David Lloyd George. But the aftermath of the war was a tide of upheaval, brought about by widespread unemployment, the inevitable outcome of rapid demobilisation. The brief economic boom turned out to be a false dawn, and within months the soup kitchens were busier than ever, with long queues waiting for the most modest state handouts. Public disorder became the curse of the new government. At the forefront of this was the newly formed Women's Movement, which strongly objected to women being asked to vacate their jobs in favour of returning ex-servicemen. Then, to add to the country's burdens, a deadly influenza epidemic wrought havoc on the population, with more than fifteen thousand deaths in the London area alone.

Geraldine Melford succumbed to the epidemic in the spring of 1919, at a time when the worst of the crisis was finally coming to an end. With such a shortage of drugs to tackle the virus, Sarah buried her pride and sought out every old wives' remedy she could find. This involved everything from soaking her mother in a hot bath spiced with malt vinegar, to a five-day course of warm black treacle mixed with dried, crushed dandelion seeds. The taste was, to say the least, quite disgusting, but Geraldine's temperature had remained high for so long that she wasn't even aware of the physical torture she was being subjected to. Luckily, the influenza took its own course, and Geraldine eventually recovered.

The greatest problem facing Sarah at this time, however, was the mental state of her father. After weeks pretending to go to his office at Gamages each day, Samuel Melford had finally lost his job. It had been a difficult time for Sarah, for, despite her denials that she was not related to the former General Manager, word had soon got round to the contrary. Fortunately, Gamages' personnel officer, the down-to-earth Mrs Hetherington, had become a staunch ally of Sarah's, having suspected all along who the girl actually was. But then rumours had circulated around the store that the real reason her father had been forced to leave his job was because of some financial irregularities that had only come to light during the end-of-year audit of the company accounts. Matters were made worse when, much to Mrs Hetherington's regret, Sarah herself had lost her job in the book department, in order to make way for a former male member of the staff who was returning from active service on the Western Front.

Only too aware that the family's finances were now under severe strain, Sarah searched the Situations Vacant columns of the newspapers. Since she'd displayed such determination to do paid work rather than have a stranger live in the house, all question of finding a lodger had been dropped. But despite her rapid response to any likely-looking job, by the time she had applied in writing, there were at least fifty or sixty applications before her, and, owing to her lack of any real experience, she was turned down on every occasion. In desperation, she started to search for less ambitious work, which meant tramping the streets each day, joining queues of the unemployed outside shops and offices where Situations Vacant cards had appeared in the windows.

Sarah's fortunes, however, changed quite suddenly, and in the most unexpected way. It happened during one of her endless visits to the employment exchange in Upper Street, which, since the end of the war, had been under siege by thousands of desperate unemployed people, many of whom were living from hand to mouth. Like all the other employment exchanges, the queues were dominated by males, most of them young and middle-aged ex-servicemen, willing to do any menial job they were offered. Of the few young women who were there, most were looking for domestic positions, such as scullery or bed maids. On this particular day, Sarah found herself standing in the queue behind a very rough and irate young girl, who was involved in a slanging match with a male assistant at the counter.

'What d'yer take me for?' yelled the girl, bringing the usual morning crowd of unemployed to a hushed silence. 'I ain't workin' fer no bloody coon, an' that's fer sure!'

The girl's objectionable manner prompted the counter assistant, a restrained-looking middle-aged man with a neat grey quiff in his hair, and wearing a stiff white collar and tie, and rimless spectacles, to answer calmly, 'That's up to you, miss. Next, please!'

The girl was not taking that lying down. ''Ere you!' she screeched. 'Are you tellin' me that's the only job yer can offer me, workin' as a skivvy ter some black woman?'

'Next, please!' called the assistant, ignoring the girl, and looking past her to Sarah, who was behind her in the queue.

The girl reluctantly stood aside, but was now intent on stirring up trouble with the rest of the crowd. ''Ere! 'Ave

97

yer 'eard this then?' she yelled. 'All they can offer me is a job wiv a coon! Who won this bleedin' war then – us, or Kaiser Bill?'

In the present desperate climate of despair, her rabble-rousing did what the girl intended, provoking raised clenched fists, and yells of angry protests.

'It's time we stood up ter all this!' the girl continued. 'Stand up for our rights and demand decent jobs for a decent wage!'

This brought the crowd to a dangerous height of tension, with the prospect of a riot. But whilst everyone was busy giving support to the girl, two police constables appeared at the street entrance, and pushed their way through the crowd.

'Don't let 'em push us around, mates!' the girl yelled. 'A job fer every person in the country – man *an'* woman!'

This brought a mixed response, jeers from some of the men, cheers and applause from others, including the few women waiting in the queues.

During all the angry exchanges that had broken out behind her, Sarah, at the counter, remained quite still, too nervous to turn around to see what was going on.

The girl, her clenched fist now raised high to inflame the crowd even more, yelled, 'Demand yer rights!'

The crowd picked up her call, 'Demand our rights!'

At that point, the two police constables pounced on the rebellious young girl, each taking hold of an arm. Despite yells of protest from the crowd, she was led out of the exchange, closely followed by some of the more radical young unemployed men.

The counter assistant waited for the rumpus to die down, then returned to Sarah. 'Sorry about that,' he said, unmoved by what had been a potentially serious situation. 'Oh yes,' he said, adjusting his spectacles to look at Sarah's unemployment card, then he sighed. 'I'm sorry, Miss Melford. Nothing for you today, I'm afraid.'

Sarah looked crushed. 'Nothing at all?'

The assistant shook his head. 'It's not easy to find nice jobs for young ladies like you.'

Sarah was irritated. 'I'm not looking for a nice job,' she said. 'I'm looking for *any* job.'

The assistant gave her back her card. 'What can I say?' he replied, apologetically.

Sarah was about to turn away, when she suddenly remembered what had sparked the girl's protest. 'What about the job you offered to the girl before me?'

The assistant looked up with a start. 'I don't think that would be suitable, miss,' he said, lowering his voice. 'Not for someone like you.'

'May I at least know what the job is?' Sarah asked politely.

The assistant studied Sarah's face briefly, then referred to a piece of paper on the counter at his side. 'It's a vacancy for a companion – to an elderly coloured lady. She's from Ceylon.'

'Ceylon,' Sarah said, almost subconsciously.

'It's in Asia,' said the assistant, in a rather superior way. 'Somewhere near Asia, I believe.'

'Just off the southern tip of India,' Sarah said, in an equally superior tone. 'It's an island.'

The assistant was not amused to be put down and he slid the piece of paper to one side.

'What does the work involve?' Sarah asked, refusing to be dismissed.

'It's manual work, Miss Melford,' he replied. 'The lady is housebound. She can't get around. Unfortunately she has no relatives in this country, so she needs someone to look after her during the day. It's a question of cleaning, and cooking – that sort of thing. If you don't mind my saying, I think someone of your breeding might find that – well, a little degrading, shall we say?'

Once again Sarah stopped him from pushing the piece of paper to one side. 'As a matter of fact, I wouldn't,' she replied, quietly insistent. 'I'm perfectly used to such tasks, and I'd be very grateful if you'd give me an introduction.'

The weary assistant sized Sarah up. After all he'd gone through that morning, he didn't quite know what to make of her. 'Can you cook?' he asked with an exasperated sigh.

'I can.'

'Scrub floors?'

'Yes.'

'Clean windows?'

'Yes.'

'Polish brasswork? Sew?'

'Most certainly.'

The assistant was now at the end of his tether. 'And would you be sympathetic and patient with an elderly lady who can't get around on her own, who spends most of her day sitting in an armchair by the fire?'

'I would hope so.'

'Would you feel the same about an elderly *coloured* lady?'

Sarah smiled. 'The island of Ceylon is a part of the British Empire,' she replied serenely. 'I would have thought her colour was quite immaterial.'

It was said that the difference between a street and a road was that a street had buildings on either side, and a road didn't.

Considering that most of the streets *and* roads in Holloway had houses or buildings of some sort on either side, it made nonsense of the definition. Arthur Road had houses on either side, built in the Edwardian period very solidly of bricks and stone on four floors, with just the suggestion of a small front garden to each. Arthur Road was one of those rather elegant back roads (or streets) which nestled quite comfortably behind the big, main Holloway and Tollington Roads, and if you were lucky enough actually to own a house there, as opposed to the less elegant Roden, Hertslet, and Mayton Streets just around the corner, you were considered to be not hard up for a bob or two.

Sarah took to Arthur Road the moment she turned the corner from the more modest Annette Road. The thing that struck her most about the long, wide terrace on either side of her was that not all the houses were identical, like so many other terraces around Holloway. Also, a few of them were semi-detached, with little alleyways in between, and the windows of some of the houses were quite large, either bow-shaped, or with high French windows and balconies on the first floor. She had no idea who the road had been named after, but whoever Arthur was, Sarah thought that he certainly had good taste.

The house she was looking for was about halfway down on the right-hand side, and she could see that it had once been beautiful, built on three floors, with a plain cement stucco border along the top at roof level, stretching all the way down on either side of the house to the small front garden below. Surprisingly, the street door had recently been painted, which must have been something of a coup during the long period of wartime shortages, but the elegant navy-blue colour was not enough to deflect the heavy, tarnished brass door knocker. At the employment exchange before she came, Sarah had had to sign for the front door key of the house, for the elderly lady resident was not really capable of responding to callers.

After first ringing the bell, and then letting herself in, Sarah closed the door quietly behind her, as she had been instructed to do, and stood for a moment or so in the hall to acclimatise herself. The first thing she noticed was a strong, unfamiliar smell, which seemed to pervade the whole place. For such a large house, the hall was quite narrow, more like a carpeted passage. There was a room on either side, and at the far end of the passage were the stairs, also carpeted, behind which was the room she had been told to make for. This she duly did, and knocked gently and called lightly, 'Hello!'

To her surprise, there was an immediate response. 'Come in!'

The moment Sarah entered the room, which turned out to be the kitchen, that unfamiliar smell hit her full in the face.

'Hello? Who are you?' Sitting at the kitchen table was a fairly elderly woman, with swept-back dark hair that had only recently started to turn grey. She was wearing what Sarah thought was a wonderful, exotically coloured, full-length dress of fine silk. Her narrow face carried no make-up, and her thin eyes radiated humour and intelligence. The voice was a cultured one, but tinged with a slight, fascinating Asian accent. In front of her was a bowl of some kind of creamy mixture, which she had been beating with a large wooden spoon, and much to Sarah's surprise, a cigarette was burning in an ashtray on the table alongside.

'Mrs Ranasinghe?'

'That's right,' came the reply. 'You must have been sent by the agency.'

'The employment exchange,' replied Sarah. She held out her hand. 'My name is Sarah Melford,' she said, with a pleasant smile.

Mrs Ranasinghe stopped beating her creamy mixture. 'Sarah?' she said, more or less to herself. 'Yes. That's a good name.' She took Sarah's hand, and held on to it for a moment, as though trying to feel for the blood pumping through Sarah's veins. 'Twenty-two, twenty-three?'

Sarah was puzzled. 'I beg your pardon?'

'Your age.'

'Oh – yes, I'm twenty-four.'

Mrs Ranasinghe smiled and released Sarah's hand. 'So then, why don't you go and make us both a nice cup of tea? Kettle's on the stove. There's still some water left in it from my breakfast.'

Sarah couldn't get over how immediate and direct the old lady was, so much so that she found no difficulty in doing exactly what she was asked. Going straight to the gas cooker, which was tucked away in an alcove on the other side of the room, and on top of which a large saucepan of strong-smelling meat stew of some sort was bubbling away, she quickly checked that there was enough water in the kettle, found a box of Swan Vestas, and lit one of the gas rings.

'I can't tell you what a treat it is for someone to make me a cup of tea,' called the old lady. 'By the time I get out of bed in the morning, and wobble my way into this place, I'm so exhausted I feel like going straight back to bed again!'

Behind her, Sarah was having great success in finding a teapot, milk and sugar, and cups and saucers. She also found a pile of dirty plates and crockery in the washing-up bowl.

'Come and tell me about yourself, young lady,' said Mrs Ranasinghe. 'I want to know why you want to look after a broken-down old mess like me.'

Sarah returned to the table, and sat down on the chair that Mrs Ranasinghe had struggled to pull out for her. 'I can't believe you're anything of the sort,' she said.

'How do you know?' asked the old lady. 'You don't know me.'

Sarah had no real answer, but nevertheless, she tried. 'You're so wonderfully clear and bright,' she said. 'More than I could ever be.'

The old lady roared with laughter. 'You must want the job badly!'

Sarah laughed with her. As she looked at Mrs Ranasinghe's pale brown skin, she wondered why that unpleasant young girl at the employment exchange had created so much fuss. The old lady's skin seemed only a tone or so darker than her own.

Mrs Ranasinghe picked up the remaining part of her cigarette that was burning in the ashtray. Then she took a small, delicate puff, and quickly exhaled very little smoke. 'A terrible habit,' she said, 'but I love it. I never used to do this back in my own country, you know,' she said, almost apologetically. 'More's the pity. It gives me so much pleasure.' She took another puff, exhaled in exactly the same delicate way, then stubbed out the butt in the ashtray. 'Can you believe, I left Ceylon nearly ten years ago? Ten years! My husband died, and my family didn't like me. They said I was too "free-thinking"!' She roared with laughter again. 'So I decided to come to England. It's a good place to survive, England. And why not? After all, Ceylon *is* part of the British Empire!'

'What did they mean by "free thinking"?' asked Sarah.

'I apparently behave too young for a woman of my age. That's what they say, but what they really mean is that I am too independent. Ha! They should see me now.' She started to rub her kneecaps under the table; they were clearly giving her some pain. 'Riddled with every disease under the sun – if there ever was such a thing as sun in England. I have arthritis, bronchitis, a heart murmur, a spine disorder, and just about everything else. The doctors told me that if I didn't give up smoking, I'd kill myself. So what?' She stopped abruptly, and darted a quick look at Sarah. 'Do you think a woman should be independent, Sarah?' she enquired shrewdly.

Sarah thought for a moment before answering. 'As far as I'm aware, I've never been anything else.'

The old lady raised her eyebrows, then started a rapid cross-examination. 'Are you married?'

'No.'

'Never?'

'Never.'

'You live with your family?'

'My mother and father.'

'No brothers and sisters?'

Sarah thought for a moment before answering. 'None,' she replied.

The old lady sat back in her chair. Sarah clearly fascinated her. 'Don't you want to ask *me* some questions? About what work I would expect you to do?'

'I was told you needed looking after. They didn't mention that you were independent.'

'Does that worry you?'

Again, Sarah thought carefully before answering. 'If you wanted to employ me, I imagine my sole function would be to do only the things you want me to do. I presume that is why you have advertised this position.'

Now it was the old lady's turn to think carefully before continuing. 'I hate getting old. I don't like not knowing what is going to happen in the future.'

Sarah shrugged her shoulders. 'It can't be any worse than what's already happened.'

This time, there was a long pause. Sarah had no idea what the old lady was thinking. All she knew was that she was certainly a force to be reckoned with.

'I hope you can cook?' said Mrs Ranasinghe, quite suddenly.

'I do most of the cooking at home,' replied Sarah.

'I mean *real* cooking, not that terrible plain stuff you English eat.' The old lady started to beat her cream mixture in the bowl again. 'Egg hoppers, lamprais, fish curry, chilli sambol . . .'

Sarah was lost. 'I'm sorry?'

There was a broad but inquisitive grin on the old lady's face. 'Don't worry, you'll learn,' she said, with a mischievous twinkle in her eye. Then she paused only long enough to point to the kettle, which was now steaming furiously on the gas stove. 'Now can I please have my tea? Surely you can tell that I am absolutely parched?'

Sarah did as she was told. She had learned already that her new employer did not like to be kept waiting.

It was a source of great sadness to Sarah that her mother and father no longer slept together. In the old days, they were, of course, inseparable, and Sarah had always cherished the thought that, each night, her parents were lying together in their huge double bed with the brass head rail, snuggled up together in each other's arms. But Samuel's illness had changed all that, for there was rarely a night went by when the poor man was able to get more than a couple of hours' sleep. And so he moved into the spare room on the same floor, leaving his wife to sob her way to sleep in the huge bed that now seemed to be without heart or soul.

There was, however, a more urgent worry for Sarah, concerning the deterioration in her father's mental state.

106

Following Samuel's departure from his job at Gamages, Sarah had never tackled her father about the rumours circulating about the financial irregularities that had taken place during his final year as General Manager. As Samuel had never been visited by anyone from the police or the store itself, and as no charges had been levelled against him, she was willing to believe that the rumours were unfounded and spread by disgruntled members of his staff.

With so much time on his hands, Samuel now spent most of his days ambling along the towpath of the Islington Canal along Caledonian Road. When the weather was good, his favourite resting spot was an old cut-down treetrunk, which he perched on, enabling him to watch the coal barges on their way to the marshalling depots near King's Cross. But when it rained, he could usually be found crouched on the ground beneath the bridge over Caledonian Road, staring aimlessly down at his own reflection in the water for hours on end. At night, however, his behaviour was altogether more mysterious.

The grandfather clock in the sitting room had just struck eleven at night when, as regular as in his former commuting days travelling back and forth to Gamages, Samuel came quietly down the stairs, collected his jacket and homburg hat from the hall stand, and left the house. One night, though, he was not alone, for Sarah had been waiting for him, out of sight behind the kitchen door.

In the dark Thornhill Road outside, there was that kind of stillness that one only ever feels when the air is pure and the human race are in their beds. Spring had come and gone, and already the nights were showing the promise of a warm summer ahead. But Sarah was taking no chances, for even though her father was not wearing enough protection against the cool night air, she herself was well wrapped up in her favourite woollen topcoat with the rabbit fur collar.

Sarah only emerged from the shadow of the tree in the front garden when she was satisfied that her father was at a safe enough distance not to be aware of her presence. The moment she could see him heading off down Barnsbury Road, she stepped out, and carefully paced him. As she watched him shuffling off, head and shoulders stooped so low that it would have been impossible for him to see anything but the pavement at his feet, her heart was aching with the sight of this man, who only a few months earlier had been the perfect model of a husband and father, whose head was held high wherever he went. What had happened to bring him down to this level? Had it been shame or guilt at the realisation that he had cast his younger daughter out of his house without any recourse to balance or reason? What *was* going on in that tired mind, which had become so illogical, so detached from the realities of everyday life that nothing he said or did now made any sense whatsoever? Sarah felt a huge lump swelling in her throat, and she had to stifle her mouth with her hand to prevent the audible sound of the distress she felt.

Samuel and his daughter made slow but steady progress along Barnsbury Road, where the residents of the grand Georgian houses were long in bed, and where only the nightly gathering of stray dustbin cats were there to resent the human intrusion, their slinky eyes peering at them from the steps of every house basement along the road.

As Samuel approached the corner of Dewey Road, the mystery of his nightly foray gradually became more worrying and sinister. Across the road, standing in the shadows of the White Conduit pub, was a shadowy figure who waved to Samuel as he approached. Sarah held back for a moment or so, but managed to conceal herself close enough to see her father cross the road and meet up with the man.

'You're late, sir.'

It was a voice Sarah recognised immediately: old Sid Perkins, the hot chestnut seller, whom she had passed on the corner of Richmond Avenue many a winter's evening.

'I'm sorry, Sid,' returned Samuel. 'It's not easy to get out without notice.'

'They've bin waitin' fer nearly 'alf an 'our, sir,' the old chestnut seller croaked, in a tone that lacked his usual warm and friendly nature. 'Yer knows 'ow they 'ate ter be kept waitin'. It's a tricky business, wiv the law breavin' down their necks.'

On hearing this, Sarah's heart missed a beat. Her worst fears had been realised. Her father was mixed up in some kind of shady business. Oh God! What *had* he got himself involved in? She thought of everything, from a conspiracy to hold up a bank, to breaking into some wealthy person's house. Oh why hadn't she seen this coming? Why hadn't she got her father the care and medical attention he clearly needed?

Whilst she was agonising over all this, the old chestnut seller led her father into a yard at the side of the pub. Sarah waited a moment, then hurried across the road to follow them.

The pub itself had long since closed for the night and was in total darkness, but as the alleyway alongside came into view, Sarah could just make out a chink of light coming from what seemed to be some kind of large timber storage shed at the rear. She held back for as long as she could and watched whilst Sid Perkins tapped on the door of the shed, waited for someone to open it from inside, and then stood back to allow Samuel to enter ahead of him. The moment the door was closed and locked from inside, Sarah hurried along the alleyway, and tried to look in. Unfortunately, there was no hole big enough in the wood for her to see through. But as she moved slowly around the building, she eventually found a suitably safe spot to stop and put her ear to the outside wall. At first, all she could hear were men's voices. They seemed to be arguing angrily. Then she heard her father's voice, apologising profusely for keeping them all waiting. It seemed to take ages before the anger subsided. But then a different sound took over. It was a strange, brooding sound, which Sarah could not identify.

'Right!' called a heavily chesty-voiced man inside. 'This is yer last chance, Melford. Lose this one – and you're done!'

Sarah covered her mouth in horror. For as soon as the man spoke, there was a chorus of voices, ranting, shouting, and jeering.

But it was the other sounds that scared Sarah most of all. Sounds that she had unfortunately heard only too well – on more than one occasion.

Chapter 8

It was an irony that Young ed had been given his father's name. But Edward Lacey's death had somehow infused Beattie with such a sense of guilt that her conscience pressed her into giving the boy some lasting connection with the father he would never know. Young Ed was also a bit like his dad, especially his eyes, which were bright, glowing, and the palest blue. But he had his mum's jawline, there was no doubt about that, for it was firm and determined, obstinate to the core. Ma Briggs said that on the whole, he was a good little baby, much better than her two had been, for not once had she heard him crying in the night, which was pretty good for a child who wasn't yet six months old. But Beattie had had a hard time during the delivery, mainly because the midwife had been impatient and wanted to get home to her supper, but also because the new arrival had come out at an awkward angle, and was a tight fit, causing his mum to scream the place down. Young Ed had kicked and bawled his way right out into the midwife's hands, but the moment he'd been cleaned up and Ma Briggs held him, the little monkey shut right up, and for the next half an hour or so, no one heard so much as a peep out of him.

Beattie's greatest problem now was, as usual, money, or rather the lack of it. The paltry wage she was earning at the candle factory was only enough to cover the very basic day-to-day essentials, and with a young baby in tow, it was now a struggle to survive. Fortunately, Ma Briggs had turned out to be the most wonderful landlady anyone could wish to have, for not only did she charge Beattie the very minimum for her weekly lodgings, she also cared for Young Ed whilst Beattie went to work, from seven in the morning until six in the evening. This arrangement, however, did have its disadvantages, for Ma was a touch absent-minded, often forgetting what times she had fed the baby, as Beattie had requested. But she truly had a heart of gold, and there was no doubt that Beattie could not have coped without her help.

However, if ever there was a time when a daughter had need of her mum, this was it, and ever since the baby had arrived, Beattie had felt pangs of guilt that, apart from herself, her mother, the one other person in the world who had a right to be with the baby, knew nothing of him. And yet, every time she made up her mind to take the plunge and go back home to Thornhill Road to show off Young Ed to her family, she remembered what she had done to Sarah, and the hurt and pain she had caused her by robbing her of the child that should have been, by all rights, Sarah's own.

In recent months, a regular visitor to Beattie was Jack Ridley. At first she had been reluctant to become too involved with him, particularly knowing of his more nefarious activities. But as time went on, she found that she was attracted to him, for, despite his brash ways, he was the down-to-earth type of man she had always craved. However, kids were not part of Jack's plans, and he waited until the time was right when he would remind Beattie how much she owed him for the roof over her head. That time came one evening early in the summer, when young Ed was left in the care of Ma Briggs, whilst Beattie and Jack went for a drink at the Clarence pub, which was beneath the railway bridge in Seven Sisters Road.

'A job? What kind of job?'

Beattie's question brought a gleam to Jack's eyes. He leaned forward across the small corner table he had found for them, and gave her one of those intimate grins which made her fancy him like mad. 'One that yer get paid for,' he replied. As the Clarence was quite full that night, he had to raise his voice a little to be heard. 'Money that yer can do wiv right now.'

Beattie took one last drag on the half-finished fag she was smoking, then stubbed it out in the tin ashtray. Smoking was something that Jack had virtually forced on to her, and, as she really didn't care for the habit, she only did it when she was in his company. It also made her feel self-conscious, for like most other pubs in the area, the Clarence was a bastion of male companionship. 'If you're askin' me ter break the law,' she said, haughtily, 'yer can ferget it. I've got a kid ter bring up.'

'Precisely,' replied Jack. 'An' it costs money ter bring up kids. 'Speshully when they ain't got no farver.' He dragged his chair closer. 'The kind of job I've got in mind fer you, Beat,' he said, his mouth close to her ear, 'is just a bit of a lark really. It's somefin' you an' me could do tergevver.' Beattie attempted to interrupt him, but he talked over her. 'Before yer get all righteous wiv me, Beat, let me just ask yer somefin'. 'Ow much spondulix you got left in the kitty?'

Beattie, a sinking feeling in her stomach, tried to sit back in her chair, but Jack put his arm around her shoulders, and pulled her closer to him. As he talked, she could feel his warm breath in her ear. 'Kids cost money, Beat,' he said. 'There are easier ways of gettin' it wivout slavin' yer guts out ten or eleven hours in that bloody candle factory.'

113

'I make enuff, Jack,' Beattie managed to say. 'It's not much, but I can manage.'

'Manage now – oh yeah. But that's 'cos Ma looks after yer.' His lips were now practically touching the rim of her ear. 'But wot 'appens if Ma drops down dead termorrer?'

Shocked, Beattie swung round to glare at him.

'Oh, I'm not sayin' she will,' he said, with that tantalising grin on his face again, 'but yer never know. She ain't a youngster no more. She's 'ad a dicky 'art fer years.'

'Don't talk like this, Jack,' Beattie pleaded. 'I don't like it.'

'What *you* don't like, Beat, is facin' up ter the facts er life.'

'These chairs taken, mate?'

Jack and Beattie looked up to find a navvy type standing there, two glasses of beer in his hands, and a timid-looking girl at his side.

'Mind if we join yer?' the navvy asked.

'Piss off!' snapped Jack, giving the bloke a thunderous look.

The navvy was about to put down the two glasses of beer and take Jack on, but when Jack started to rise from his seat the girl pulled her mate away, leaving the two men to fight a scathing battle with their eyes.

Beattie was both horrified and excited by Jack's behaviour, but refused to show it. After a suitable moment of silence between them she downed the last of her shandy. 'I've 'ad enuff of this place,' she said.

A few minutes later, they were ambling at a leisurely pace down Campbell Road, Beattie with her arms crossed, and Jack, cap on the back of his head, fag in mouth, hands in trouser pockets. Neither of them spoke until they had almost reached Beattie's digs.

'This job,' Beattie said, trying to sound as casual as possible, 'is there any – danger?'

'Every job carries danger. Yer could set yerself on fire in the candle factory.'

For some perverse reason, this amused Beattie.

They came to a halt outside Ma Briggs' place. For a Saturday night, the Bunk was amazingly quiet, which made Beattie feel strangely ill at ease. 'Are you askin' me ter nick somefin'?' she asked.

Jack turned to face her. 'No,' he said. 'That's my department.'

Beattie was now intrigued. 'You scare me, Jack Ridley,' she said, watching the flicker of the street gaslight reflected in his eyes.

He drew a step closer to her. 'That's wot it's all about, in't it, Beat?'

After a brief pause, he put one arm around her neck, leaned closer to look at her lips, then, in one swift movement, he used the tip of his tongue very gently to caress her lips, before finally kissing her full on the mouth. This immediately aroused Beattie, and even though she had not set out to let this happen, there was clearly no way she could have prevented it.

It was only a short time later that Jack was seeing the inside of Beattie's room for the first time. He still had that smirking kind of grin on his face as he saw all the little things Beattie had done to brighten it up, to try to disguise the fact that it was really not much more than a dump. It was easy to see that Beattie was no housewife, for there were still dirty dishes in the china washbasin, left over not only from breakfast, but quite probably from the night before as well. There were also plenty of baby's dirty nappies around, which had clearly been there for a day or so and accounted for the sour smell pervading the room. But Jack acknowledged the trouble she had taken in putting coloured pictures of animals on the walls above the baby's basket, which nestled neatly in the corner of the room near the bed.

'Turned out ter be quite the little mum, ain't yer?' Jack said, with more than a hint of sarcasm. Beattie was only too aware that, for him, the flea in the ointment was young Ed.

Beattie tried to turn down the gaslamp whilst she was getting undressed, but Jack would have none of it. He wanted to watch her, to see every part of her body as each garment was removed. She played up to him well, using every sensuous movement she could think of. It had been more than a year since this kind of opportunity had come her way. And Jack relished every minute of Beattie's act – the full breasts, flushed complexion, blue-green eyes that sparkled in the gaslight, the bobbed auburn hair, and the shapely, milky-white curves of her thighs. Once she had finished, Beattie pulled back the bedclothes, and climbed in.

Then it was her turn to watch, for Jack started to remove his clothes, slowly, methodically, taking off each item and placing it carefully on a chair as though it was worth a fortune. And all the time he was playing out this game he never once lost eye contact with Beattie, always watching her reaction, to see if she liked what she saw. When he had finished, Jack stood for a moment, hovering over her. Beattie's eyes searched every corner of his body – the broad shoulders, firm waist, and heavy-muscled arms with a tattoo of a woman dancing down one of them. Every part of him seemed to be so much more perfect than young Ed's father; Jack Ridley was all man, she could see that now. And when he went across to turn down the gaslamps on the wall, she could see his fine, rounded buttocks moving together in perfect unison.

In his basket, young Ed, thumb in mouth, was in a deep sleep, completely oblivious to his mum's goings-on.

Jack Ridley climbed in alongside Beattie, and for a moment or so, they lay on their backs, staring up into the darkened room. After the erotic lead-up, their silence was curious, only broken when Jack finally turned towards Beattie.

'Yer still 'aven't told me what this job is,' she said, resisting his advance.

'This is 'ardly the time, now is it?' asked Jack.

'Wot're yer askin' me ter do, Jack?' persisted Beattie.

Jack's shadowy outline leaned closer to her. 'It's a minor job. Ready cash – not much, but enough for us ter split fifty-fifty. You wouldn't 'ave ter do nuffin' 'cept keep a lookout. I'll do the rest.'

There was a pause before Beattie responded. 'Wot sort er place?'

'A shop. A small shop.'

'*A shop?*'

'It's got a good cash-till, plus quite a lot of – interestin' loot.'

'Wot d'yer mean – interestin'?'

In the dark, she couldn't see the smirk on his face. 'Unusual.'

Beattie was getting irritated. 'Get ter the point, Jack!' she snapped. 'What kind of shop?'

Jack put his hand under the sheet and felt the warm flesh of her naked stomach. Then he started to raise himself on top of her.

'What kind of shop?'

Jack was now poised over her. 'A pawn shop.'

There was the briefest moment of delayed shock before Beattie gasped, 'Oh God – no!'

117

She tried to get up, but Jack had both her arms pinned down by the wrists. 'Relax, Beat! Relax!'

'No, Jack!' cried Beattie, struggling to sit up. 'Yer can't do it. Not Bob and Vera's place. Yer just can't!'

In his basket, young Ed sounded as though he was starting to wake.

'Why not, Beat?' growled Jack, who only had to use the minimum of strength to keep Beattie pinned to the bed. 'Yer need cash, don't yer? We boaf need cash. There's enuff in that till ter keep us going for a coupla weeks at least, maybe more. Then there's all that junk 'e's got stacked in those trays. Some of it could be worf a bob or two.' His face was now so close to hers that as he spoke he was practically spitting at her. 'There're some sparklers there, Beat.'

'No!'

'Some of it could be yours, yer stupid cow!' He was now having to fight with her as she tried to break loose. 'Don't yer want ter get that stuff back?'

'Bob Sluggins 'as bin good ter me!' gasped Beattie. ''E's 'elped me out of trouble time and time again.'

'An' wot about 'er – that ol' slag? Does she 'elp yer too?'

Beattie could now feel that Jack was fully aroused, which utterly confused her, because she was feeling exactly the same. 'Please, Jack,' she said in desperation, close to tears. 'I'll 'elp yer. I'll 'elp yer anywhere yer like. But not Bob. Not 'is place. Please don't do it, I beg yer . . .'

Jack gradually eased himself down on top of her, and she could feel the warmth of his naked body against her own. 'Now you listen to me,' he said. 'We're goin' ter do that pawn shop, boaf of us – you an' me tergevver. You owe me one, Beat.' His voice was almost a whisper. 'It's time ter settle up wiv me.'

He suddenly raised his body up again and, still pinning

Beattie down to the bed, he entered her.

For three consecutive nights, Sarah followed her father to the old timber shed behind the White Conduit pub, where he rendezvoused with Sid Perkins. But on each occasion she had been unable to summon up the courage to confront them, and although she had so far been unable to find any way of seeing what was going on inside the shed, those terrible sounds that sent such a chill through her entire body were evidence enough. Each time she set out on her father's tail on the dot of eleven, the most awful thoughts went through her mind. Why had her father kept this dark secret for so long, and what *was* he doing in the company of such a gang of murderous thugs? And what did that man with the chesty voice mean when he shouted at her father, 'This is yer last chance, Melford! Lose this one – and you're done!' Whatever the consequences, Sarah decided once and for all that she had to know what was going on.

'You're just in time, sir,' called Sid, voice low, the moment Samuel Melford crossed the road to meet him. 'They've 'ad a bit of a 'itch ternight, so they won't be startin' fer anuvver few minutes or so.'

Without saying a word, Samuel hurriedly joined him, and after Sid had taken a careful look round to make sure that the coast was clear, they scurried off into the timber shed.

Sarah waited until the guard on duty had closed the door, then she emerged from the shadows on the other side of the street and quietly made her way towards the shed. When she put her head to the outside wall, she could again hear voices inside, but, as yet, not the horrifying sound that had distressed her so much during the previous three evenings. But tonight, Sarah had a plan. It would be daring and dangerous, but action had now become inevitable.

Keeping well out of sight, she waited.

Her opportunity came no more than twenty minutes later. It was then that she heard those dreaded sounds again. It was time to move.

Coming out of the shadows, she made her way straight to the door of the shed. Then, pausing for a moment to summon up her courage, she took a deep breath, pulled back her shoulders and banged hard on the door.

Almost immediately, the door opened, and the guard peered out. But before he had time to register who was there, Sarah pulled at the door, and rushed straight in, where she was greeted by the most terrifying screeching sounds. 'Hey!' called the guard, as Sarah disappeared into the crowd of men gathered inside, but his voice was completely drowned by the shouting and jeering. 'Mr Rumbold!'

Sarah ignored the warning shouts, and pushed her way through the excited crowd, who were too involved in what was going on in the centre of the shed to notice that a woman had broken into their protected territory. Sarah's heart was pounding. But then she suddenly caught sight of the person she was desperately searching for. 'Father!' she yelled, over the roar of the crowd.

Samuel Melford turned with a start. He was standing right at the front of the crowd of onlookers, and when Sarah finally succeeded in pushing her way through to him, his face crunched up with distress, and he threw his arms around her.

'Oh, Father!' she said, her voice barely audible above the noise. But she was too overcome with horror to say anything more, for the spectacle before her was mounting to a climax, sending the spectators into a frenzy of excitement.

The chilling sounds Sarah had identified outside were now confirmed. Laid out before her was a circular cockpit, about twenty or so feet in diameter and scattered with sand, where two young cockerels were pitted against each other in a ferocious fight to the death. Sarah had arrived just at the point of kill, for the eye of one of the cockerels had been pecked out by its opponent, and its pure white feathers were splattered with blood. For Sarah it was a horrific sight, and her stomach retched with disgust and revulsion. It was not the first time she had witnessed the savage sport, for during her schooldays, she had twice come across teenagers pitting cocks against each other in a back street in the rougher part of 'the Cally', and the panicked screeching of those two poor doomed creatures was a sound that had lived with her ever since.

When the stronger cock had finally despatched its opponent, the crowd roared its approval, and the winners amongst them collected their cash.

'Oh, Father!' gasped Sarah, her arms holding him tight around his waist, her head buried in his shoulder. 'What are you doing here?' Then she looked up at him. 'How could you?'

Samuel was too confused to answer. All he could do was to stare back at her, and ask, 'Sarah?'

'Yer shouldn't've come 'ere, Miss Sarah!' said Sid Perkins, his eyes darting all round, looking out for trouble. 'Yer dad was on a winning ticket. It's the first time fer ages. 'E'll never pay off 'is debts if they know you're around.'

Sarah quickly pulled herself together, ignoring the men who were gathering round, glaring at her. 'You shouldn't have brought my father here, Sid,' she said sternly. 'You know how unwell he is.'

Sid was getting more and more nervous at the attention they were getting. ''E asked me, Miss Sarah. 'E begged me. Yer dad needs the lolly. This was the only way I fawt 'e'd

121

have a chance of gettin' some.'

'Well, well now,' called an approaching voice. 'And what 'ave we 'ere?'

Sarah turned, to see a large, rotund, middle-aged man making his way through the crowd, who cleared a path for him.

'Yer didn't tell me yer was 'avin a visitor ternight, Melford,' said the man, whose voice sounded so hoarse he must have suffered from asthma or bronchitis all his life. 'Yer know about the rules, Melford.' Menacingly, he leaned close to Sarah's bewildered father. 'Yer know, I really don't like people breakin' my rules.'

'If you have anything to say, sir,' said Sarah, defiantly, 'please address me, and not my father.'

The hoarse man turned his attention to her. 'Goodness grashush me,' he said, mockingly. 'Forgive me, miss. I was forgettin' we 'ad company – female company.' He took off his trilby and bowed. 'Allow me ter hintroduce myself. My name his—'

Sarah came back like a flash. 'I *know* who you are, Rumbold,' she snapped. 'Your reputation goes before you.'

Rumbold's face stiffened. 'Is that so?' he replied. 'I 'ad no idea I was so famous.' He turned with a false smile to Samuel. 'You didn't tell me yer 'ad such a lovely young gel, Melford. 'Ave yer told 'er that the female sex his not permitted in my establishment? 'Ave yer told 'er that when any of my customers lose at the game, I hexpect 'em ter pay out in full?' He leaned closer and stared straight into Samuel's weary, blank eyes. 'An hif they don't—'

'I would advise you not to threaten my father,' growled Sarah, pushing herself between Rumbold and Samuel. 'The law does not take at all kindly to blackmail.'

Rumbold reacted to Sarah's rebuff with a mixture of rage

and astonishment. 'Oh,' he said, 'so it's the law yer 'ave hin mind, his it?'

'It may well be,' returned Sarah. 'Unless, of course, you respond in a more businesslike manner.'

There were murmurs of astonishment from the gathered crowd.

'How much does my father owe you?'

Rumbold grinned. 'A small fortune, I'm afraid. Five quid.'

Sarah dipped into her coat pocket, took out her purse, and with all the startled crowd watching her, extracted a five-pound note and held it out to Rumbold. 'Five pounds!'

Rumbold hesitated for a moment, clearly taken aback. But he finally grabbed the note. 'Well, well now, gents,' he said, addressing the crowd. 'We appear ter 'ave a millionairess in our midst. We are indeed honoured.'

'Not a millionairess, Rumbold,' said Sarah, with firm clarity and defiance. 'Just one who takes care of one's hard-earned savings, and who does not spend them recklessly on out-and-out rogues!'

To Rumbold's humiliation and outrage, this provoked a roar of jeers and laughter from the crowd.

'You see, Rumbold,' continued Sarah, 'there are those in this life who do their best to live like decent, honest human beings. And there are others who feed off the misfortune of those who are incapable of defending themselves.' Now it was her turn to move a step closer to Rumbold. 'I would like to remind you of something, Rumbold,' she said, with complete abandon. 'You know as well as I do that cock-fighting – or whatever repugnant name you like to call these activities – is illegal.' She turned to the rest of the crowd. 'The government of this country abolished this odious business a long time ago. It would not go well if any of you people here tonight were caught betting and gambling on a fight to the death.'

At this point, Rumbold made a threatening gesture with his hand as if about to say something malicious to her. But Sarah was too quick for him.

'You may keep my five-pound note, Rumbold,' she said imperiously. 'But only on condition that I never set eyes on you or your "business activities" ever again.'

Rumbold again tried to speak.

'And if you think that I am intimidated by threats of physical violence,' she said, 'let me assure you that I do not scare easily.'

Apart from the cackling of some caged cockerels on the other side of the shed, there was complete silence.

For a brief moment, Sarah and Rumbold stared each other out. But Sarah was too overwhelmed by the stench of blood to stay any longer, so she took hold of her father's arm, and said, 'Come, Father. Let's go.' She started to lead Samuel through the crowd, who stood back to let her pass.

'Oh, miss? Miss Melford?'

Rumbold's voice calling to her brought Sarah to a halt. She turned, to find Rumbold coming slowly towards her. In his hands he was holding a beautiful white cockerel, with a full red mane, cackling and struggling to get away.

'Has a mark of my respect,' he said, with a bow, 'I'd like ter make you a little hofferin'.'

With Sarah, her father, and everyone watching, he held out the struggling cockerel, and then with both hands wrung the poor creature's neck.

Sarah, needing all her courage to hide her fear at the implied threat, clearly intended to scare her, stared at Rumbold in utter contempt. Then, without another word, she led her father out of the shed.

Chapter 9

For no apparent reason, Bob Sluggins' pawn shop usually did very little business on a Tuesday afternoon. This was also the time when Bob's wife, Vera, made her weekly shopping visit 'up west' with one of her mates from Crawford's hardware store along the road. It was for these very reasons that Jack Ridley had chosen such a day to carry out his plan, which he had laid out in meticulous detail to a very unwilling Beattie.

'Sorry, mate,' said Bob, as Beattie plonked an old handbag on his counter. 'I've got enuff women's 'andbags in my back room ter last me a lifetime. Can't 'elp yer, I'm afraid.'

Beattie sighed. She was doing her best not to show how her nerves were tearing her stomach apart. 'Surely yer can give me somefin' for it, Bob?' she pleaded. 'That bag's genuine cow 'ide. My mum bought that for me on my eighteenf birfday.'

Bob was still shaking his head. 'Makes no difference, Beat, gel,' he said. 'If I took in anuvver one of these, my old woman'd give me bleedin' 'ell.'

Beattie sniffed indignantly, and replied, 'That's funny. I always fawt this was *your* shop.'

Bob flicked a quick look up at her. Beattie hadn't changed a bit; she still had her old sharp tongue. 'I'll give yer 'alf a crown for it. Not a farvin' more. OK?'

Beattie sighed, and smiled weakly. 'Thanks, Bob,' she said. 'You're a toff.'

'I wish I was,' he replied. 'I wouldn't be runnin' this place.' He picked up Beattie's handbag, but as he did so, there was the sound of a thump coming from the back of the shop somewhere. 'Wot was that?' he said, with a start, turning to go into his back parlour.

Beattie was shaking with nerves. 'I didn't 'ear nuffin',' she said quickly. Unfortunately, she knew exactly what it was.

'That thumpin' sound out back.' Bob, still puzzled, started to move off. 'Wot the 'eck was it?'

'Yer couldn't give me my ticket and the money, could yer, Bob?' Beattie was doing everything in her power to distract his attention. 'I've got ter get back ter the baby.'

'Baby?' he said, taken aback. 'You got a kid?'

Beattie was relieved that she had inadvertently found a subject that would distract him long enough to let Jack get in through a back window of the shop. 'Yes,' she said, finding it difficult to look at him. 'Nearly six munffs now. 'Is name's Ed Junior.'

'After 'is dad, yer mean?' Bob was hooked, and slowly came back to the counter.

''Is dad was killed in the war. 'E was an officer – in the navy.'

Bob was suitably shocked and sympathetic. 'Blimey, Beat,' he said. 'I din't know nuffin' about that. I'm sorry ter 'ear it.'

Beattie, trying to look courageous, lowered her head.

''Ow long was yer married then?' asked Bob, who was already tying a tag on Beattie's handbag.

Beattie had to search for a quick reply, her eyes constantly flicking past Bob to see if she could see any sign of

126

movement in the back parlour. 'Not long,' she said. 'I didn't even get the chance to tell him the baby was on the way.'

'Wot a bit er bad luck,' he said. Then after a brief moment's pause added, 'Tell yer wot, I'll give yer five bob fer the bag. OK?'

Although Beattie had been getting tensed up, she breathed a sigh of relief. 'Oh fanks, Bob,' she said, her eyes still darting back and forth to the back parlour door. 'That'll be a real 'elp.'

Bob turned away, put Beattie's handbag into a box with dozens of others behind the counter, then returned to his cash-till, which was hidden behind a thin timber partition set apart from the counter. Whilst this was going on, Beattie felt her heart beating faster and faster. Behind Bob's back, she could see movement through the curtained back parlour door, which confirmed to her that Jack Ridley had successfully found his way in. What happened from there on she could only guess, and dread. All she wanted now was to do as Jack had told her to, once she had given him enough time to get in – leave the shop as soon as possible.

'There we are, gel,' said Bob, genially, returning with the two half-crown bits he was forking out for Beattie's handbag. 'You just make sure you get yerself somefin' decent ter eat, and that youngster of yours too.'

'You're a real good'un, Bob,' said Beattie, taking the two coins from him, and putting them into her dress pocket. 'I won't ferget it.'

'An' don't you ferget ter bring young Ed in ter see me sometime,' said Bob, as Beattie was about to leave.

'Who?' she asked, momentarily confused.

'That's 'is name, ain't it?' asked Bob, a bit puzzled. 'Ed? Ed Junior?'

Beattie suddenly came to. 'Oh – yes. Yes, that's 'is name.

127

I'll bring 'im in, that's fer sure.' She smiled, turned quickly, but as she made her way to the shop door her face brushed against the head of one of the many fox furs that were dangling down from a piece of rope across the shop ceiling. Taken by surprise, she gasped, but quickly recovered. Flustered, she called, 'Fanks again, Bob,' and as she reached the door: 'I can't fank yer enuff.' Before Bob had a chance to reply, she was gone.

In the street outside, Beattie felt quite sick, but she quickly took a deep breath, straightened up to regain her balance, and moved on. Her legs felt so heavy she wasn't sure how far they would take her, and as soon as she managed to turn the corner into Drayton Park, she stopped to compose herself. But she was just too agitated to relax, for the whole business of getting involved in Jack Ridley's plan was tearing her apart with guilt. All she could think about was how stupid she had been to let Jack talk her into it. It was one thing to help him to do a petty burglary at some rich person's house, but to do it to someone like Bob Sluggins was nothing less than a betrayal of everything she had ever believed in. Bob was a hard-working man who made only enough money to live on. Ever since she was a teenage girl, he had helped her by letting her pawn so much of her personal stuff that wouldn't have been worth a brass farthing anywhere else. As she stood there on the corner of two busy main roads, watching good, honest folk passing by on their way to their jobs or their homes, she kept asking herself time and time again how she could have allowed herself to be drawn into the world of someone like Jack Ridley. But the more she thought about him, the more she could see his face in front of her, and she knew only too well that it was not only sexual infatuation that was drawing her to him, but the sheer vibrant force of his personality.

Once she had cooled down, she felt brave enough to peer around the corner, and look down Holloway Road towards Bob's pawn shop. Fortunately, there was no sign of any disturbance, but she hoped that whatever Jack Ridley was doing, he would not harm Bob in any way. Beattie could tell by the clock on top of the furniture store opposite that it was over twenty minutes since she had entered Bob's shop, and so it was now rapidly approaching the time when she had arranged to meet up with Ridley, in the eel pie and mash café further along the road. But as she was about to move off, she was horrified to notice someone she recognised getting off a tram and making her way across the road to the pawn shop. It was the old slag herself, Bob's wife, Vera, whom Beattie had thought was 'up west' on her usual Tuesday afternoon shopping expedition. Beattie was now in a panic. What would happen if the old slag walked into the shop and found Jack Ridley going through the place? Beattie was beside herself, and for a moment didn't know whether to run or to hang around and see what happened. Then suddenly she knew what she must do.

''Ello, Mrs Sluggins!'

Vera Sluggins, struggling to carry a large woven bag of shopping, turned with a start to see Beattie hurrying towards her. 'Who's that?' she growled, squinting in the sunlight. 'Can't see yer.'

'It's me, Mrs Sluggins. Beattie. Beattie Melford. Can I give yer a 'and wiv yer bag?'

Vera pulled away when Beattie tried to take the bag from her. 'I can manage on me own, fank yer very much,' she replied haughtily. 'Just move ter one side, please. I want ter get 'ome.'

Beattie was standing directly between her and the front door of the shop. 'I've just bin ter see Bob,' she said, deliberately barring the old slag's way. 'I've pawned my 'andbag. The one me mum gave me when I was eighteen.'

'I'm not interested in wot yer mum gave yer,' complained Vera, trying to move past. But she suddenly came to a halt. ''Ow much d'e give yer?'

'Five bob.'

The old slag nearly had a heart attack. 'Five bob! For a bleedin' 'andbag?'

Beattie's heart was racing again. Her eyes were darting back and forth to the front window of the pawn shop. 'It's a very good one, Mrs Sluggins, honest it is. Best cow 'ide.'

'I don't care if it's made of bleedin' tiger skin!' roared the old slag. 'I'll give 'im 'ell when I see 'im! Out of my way!'

Beattie was now beside herself. If Vera walked in while Jack was holding up her old man, it could be really dangerous. 'Bob did me a good turn, Mrs Sluggins,' she spluttered desperately. 'Yer see, I've got a baby boy. 'E's nearly six munffs old.'

The old slag stopped dead in her tracks. 'Oh yes?' she replied cynically. 'An' who's the farver?'

Beattie lowered her eyes mournfully. ''E was in the navy. Got killed on the last day of the war.'

Vera paused only briefly to take this in, then remarked without any emotion, 'Oh well, yer'll 'ave ter find 'im anuvver old man, won't yer?'

Beattie was too taken aback to answer her. All she could do was to stand out of her way, and let her pass. Fortunately, at that moment she caught a glimpse of Jack Ridley, who was waving to her from along Holloway Road, so breathing a huge sigh of relief, she hurried off to join him in the eel pie and mash café.

* * *

Ma Briggs could hear the row going on upstairs, and she just hoped that it wouldn't wake up young Ed, who seemed to sleep more than any baby she had ever known. So she just quietly closed her parlour door, and hoped it wouldn't last too long.

'You're mad, Jack!' yelled Beattie, at the top of her voice. 'Stark ravin' mad! I told yer not ter touch 'im! I told yer I'd 'ave no part in it if yer laid one finger on Bob. 'E's my mate. 'E's bin good ter me!'

'Don't you shout at me, yer stupid cow!' warned Jack, who couldn't be bothered to raise his voice to Beattie. 'I told yer I'd do anythin' I 'ad ter do ter get that cash.'

'That didn't mean yer 'ad ter go an' tie 'im up and then knock 'im about. Wot 'appens if 'e's recognised yer?'

Jack was now getting really irritated with her. ''Ow many bleedin' times do I 'ave ter tell yer, I tied somefink round 'is eyes. 'E never 'ad a chance ter see me.'

'An' wot about *'er*? Wot about Vera?'

This time Jack bared his teeth as he replied. 'Ditto!'

Beattie wasn't satisfied. Pacing up and down her room, she felt as though she was going out of her mind. 'Bob knows me, so does she. I was talkin' to 'er just before she went into the shop. If they put two an' two tergevver, they're bound ter know I was mixed up in it wiv yer.'

Jack, who was stretched out on the bed, suddenly sat bolt upright, and yelled back at her angrily, 'Fer Chrissake, why don't yer just shut yer mouff? It's all over, I tell yer! It's done! It's finished!'

'Yes – and for wot? Fifteen quid and a couple of lousy bracelets that ain't worf nuffin'!'

Jack suddenly sprang up from the bed, rushed at her, and grabbed hold of her wrist. 'If you'd given me the right info about the old slag,' he said, pointing his finger menacingly at her, 'fings might've bin diff'rent!'

Beattie was recoiling from him in pain. 'Vera always goes up west on Tuesdays. 'Ow should I know she was gettin' back early?'

''Cos you're the one that's s'pposed to've known all about their movements, not me!'

Beattie was now on the verge of hysteria. 'I should never've let meself get involved wiv someone like you. I must've bin out of my bleedin' mind!' As she spoke, she was practically spitting. 'Why? Why? Why?'

Jack grinned and pulled her close to him. ''Cos yer love me, Beat. An' there's nuffin' yer can do about it.'

Now completely unable to control herself, Beattie spat straight into his face.

Jack was so angry, he cuffed her across the face with the back of his hand. The severity of the blow sent her reeling across the room, knocking over the washstand and ending up sprawled out on the floor. Jack went across, and stood over her. Then, wiping Beattie's spittle from his face with two fingers, he growled, 'Don't you ever do a fing like that ter me again, d'yer 'ear?'

Beattie, lying flat on her face on the floor, refused to look up at him. 'Get out,' she said, quietly.

Jack grinned at her again, picked up his jacket from a chair, and threw it idly across his shoulders. Then he moved to the door, collected his cap from the hook there, and put it on the back of his head. Before leaving, he turned to take one last look down at Beattie. 'Don't worry, Beat,' he said flippantly. 'The first time's always the worst. Fings can only get better.'

Beattie listened to his footsteps as he went down the stairs. As he left the house, he called out to Ma Briggs, and Beattie heard the front door slam behind him. She lay where she

132

was for several moments, her face pressed down on to the well-worn lino. Although she could feel blood trickling from her lip, and her right eye swelling up, she made no effort to get up. She felt no real physical pain from the blow Jack had given her, but what she did feel was torment and anguish. Was this really the life she had chosen to live? Were these people, whom she had admired for so long, fulfilling her in the way that she had always dreamed they would do? What *was* so special about Jack Ridley? How and why could she have abandoned one life, only to be knocked down flat on her face in another? She, who had always fought for her independence and the right to mix with what she called 'the real people', was now yearning for a part of her life that she had lost. Oh how she craved for someone to pick her up, and care for her, to understand her, to hold her close and say, 'This is what you should do, Beattie. This is how your life should be.'

Tears were welling up in her eyes as she eased herself on to her knees and slowly stared round the room. Everything suddenly looked so tawdry, so cluttered, and so unnecessary. She felt dazed, and although her body was now aching and she could feel a graze on her knee, she managed to get to her feet. Then she lumbered across the room and picked up the washbasin and jug, which, because they were made of thick, chunky china, had miraculously survived the onslaught of her body being thrown against them. But the floor was soaking wet, for the jug had been half full of water, and she wondered what Ma Briggs was going to say if any of it had soaked through the ceiling of the tenant in the room below. But remorse and apologies would have to come later. Her first thought was whether her face looked as bad as it felt, so she made her way to the small handmirror, which was propped up on the window behind the washstand. Her eye was bruised, and beginning to close, and there was indeed a small trickle of blood from her mouth, which she tried to wipe away with the back of her hand. Tears were streaming down her cheeks, a sure sign that she was feeling sorry for herself. For some reason that she couldn't understand, she began to think about the one person who would know what to do, how to face up to the first real crisis in her life. It was her mum, her dear, caring, loving mum. And then she even thought about her dad, obstinate and ungiving, and how wise he had been to throw her out of the house. But the strongest image of all was of the person whose face was haunting, accusing, overwhelming her with shame and guilt. Her sister, Sarah.

Geraldine Melford had made up her mind. The estrangement with her younger daughter had gone on long enough, and despite her husband's objections, she was now determined to end it.

'You're going to see Beattie?' Sarah asked her, with incredulity. 'But you can't. I told you what that friend of hers up the Cattle Market said. Beattie lives with the baby in that awful Campbell Road. It's not safe for any woman to walk around a place like that.'

'I don't care where Beattie lives,' replied Geraldine, defiantly. 'My mind is made up. I shall go on Sunday afternoon, whilst your father is having his sleep. I shall take the omnibus in Caledonian Road. It goes all the way along Seven Sisters Road to Finsbury Park.'

Sarah had joined her mother in the garden for it was a hot summer's evening, and despite opening all the windows in the house, it was impossible to keep cool there. It was quite a large garden for a town house, and because Geraldine and Sarah both had green fingers, there was a fine display of early summer flowers, with the prospect of a good showing of roses in the following weeks.

'And what will you say when you see her?' asked Sarah, in a voice that could not conceal her disapproval.

Geraldine had to think about this for a moment. But she was able to contemplate well, for she was lying back in a striped canvas deckchair, cooling herself with a lace fan, one large ginger cat on her lap, and her eyes staring aimlessly up at the deep blue evening sky. 'I shall tell her – that I've missed her.' She swung a look across to Sarah. 'I have, Sarah. I've missed her terribly.'

Sarah, seated on a wrought-iron garden chair alongside, could not find it in herself to respond to her mother, so she merely lowered her eyes, and remained silent.

'I blame myself for what happened,' said Geraldine, shaking her head miserably. 'Whatever Beattie's done, she is still my daughter, and I love her.' She was suddenly aware of Sarah's lack of response. 'I love you too, darling,' she said. 'I love both of you.'

Sarah finally looked up. 'Beattie doesn't want to know about family life, Mother. She's turned her back on us.'

'We turned our backs on her too,' replied Geraldine. 'That doesn't make it right. Beattie made a mistake, a huge mistake. But it was my duty to stand by her, and try to help her put things right. I failed her.'

'It was Father's decision,' Sarah reminded her.

'It was a wrong decision. I gave birth to Beattie. She's our own flesh and blood, and blood is thicker than water.' She turned away, and took a deep breath. 'How beautiful everything smells at this time of year,' she said. 'We're so lucky to have all this. Just think of that poor girl, being locked up in some terrible lodgings with a small baby and no fresh air.' She paused for a moment, then said, 'I long to see the

135

baby, Sarah. Can you understand that?'

Sarah couldn't help but meet her mother's eyes.

Geraldine said, 'Do you realise I'm a grandmother? It's very hard to explain what that's like. It's like having a child of one's own all over again – like turning back the clock. But I don't even know whether it's a boy or girl.'

Sarah waited a moment, then got up.

Geraldine did likewise, much to the disdain of the cat, who was immediately shoved off. 'Do you think you can ever forgive her, Sarah?'

Sarah was taken aback by this question. She wasn't really prepared for it. 'Forgive?' she replied, after a moment's thought. 'Oh, I can forgive. I just can't forget, that's all.'

Geraldine smiled gently, put her arm through Sarah's, and squeezed her affectionately.

'What about Father?' asked Sarah, after a pause. 'Have you thought about what he'll say if he knows you've been to see her?'

'Beattie is his daughter too,' she said almost guiltily. 'It's his duty to forgive. He'll never be at peace with himself until he does.'

Sarah tried to smile back at her mother. 'I'm going up to get ready for supper.' She kissed Geraldine on the cheek, and disappeared inside the house.

After Sarah had gone, Geraldine found herself being plagued by a large tabby, one of the more demanding of her cat quartet. 'Oh, Delilah!' she said, stooping down to pick her up. 'I'm sorry I didn't notice you. Yes, you are a beautiful girl.' Delilah broke into a loud purr the moment Geraldine started to stroke her. 'But, oh, Delilah,' she said, with a deep sigh, 'I hope for your sake you never become a mother. Children have such minds of their own. They think they know so much, but they actually know very little. Why can't they get on well with each other? They both come from the same place, and yet . . . and yet, they hardly know each other. You know, Delilah, it takes a great deal of love to keep a family together.'

She was suddenly distracted by a ring on the front doorbell, so she quickly lowered Delilah to the ground and made her way back into the house.

'It's all right, Sarah, I'm here!' she called as she hurried down the hall. She gave her hair a last-moment pat to make sure that it was tidy, then opened the door. Her shock was immediate.

Standing on the doorstep was Beattie, holding young Ed in her arms. 'Hello, Mother,' she said, her voice barely audible. 'This is Ed. He's your grandson.'

For a brief moment, Geraldine seemed to be suspended in time, for all she could do was to stare hard at Beattie and the small baby she clutched in her arms. Then her face started to crumple up, and the shaky pitch of her breathing indicated that she was about to burst into tears. Her arms outstretched, she virtually threw herself at the two of them, embracing them, and hugging them vigorously. Laughing, crying, and smothering them both with kisses, all she could gasp over and over again was, 'Oh, my baby, my dear little baby!'

Beattie was completely overwhelmed. As she and her mother exchanged hugs and kisses, she felt as though her heart was about to break. It was a moment she would never have thought possible, even just a few days before. So she closed her eyes tight, and did her best to stop the tears from rolling down her cheeks. But when she opened them again, she found herself peering over her mother's shoulder, straining to see the silhouette of the figure who was standing at the top of the stairs, watching the extraordinary reunion.

It was Sarah.

137

Chapter 10

Samuel Melford looked at his grandson, and then at his younger daughter. Yes, they were alike, in some ways; young Ed definitely had his mother's mouth, his full, pouting lips characteristic of her when she'd been his age. But Geraldine thought the baby had Samuel's eyes, dark and inquisitive, and she was certain that the moment she had him sitting on her lap at the kitchen table, he knew at once that she was his grandmother.

Much to Beattie's relief, her father had softened his opposition to her, and even allowed her to hug him. Young Ed had won over his grandfather completely, of course, first by making raspberry sounds at him, then by doing everything in his power to grab hold of the poor man's nose, which provoked gales of laughter from both Beattie and her mother. However, Beattie had been shocked to see how transformed her father was since the last time she had seen him, for his face was now white and drawn, and there was a vacant look in his eyes that she found strange and unsettling. There was no doubt how much her father had aged, and she felt nothing but guilt that this had probably been brought on by her own reckless behaviour.

Sarah's reaction to Beattie's sudden homecoming was, predictably, somewhat different to that of her parents. When she'd seen her young sister on the front doorstep, clutching a small baby in her arms, and witnessed the reunion with their mother, she'd retreated to her bedroom, and it was only the heartfelt pleas of Geraldine that finally persuaded her to join the family at supper in the kitchen. Beattie was only too aware that for Sarah to see Edward Lacey's child would be a painful experience, and she could hardly expect to be embraced by her sister after the way she had ruined her life. For her part, Sarah felt no pity for the predicament Beattie had got herself into, and when she listened to her sister's hard-luck tale of bringing up a child and trying to keep a job at the same time, she remained tight-lipped, her eyes lowered.

'Luckily, Ma Briggs is a treasure,' said Beattie, tucking into several slices of her mother's home-cooked ham. 'I don't know 'ow I'd cope if she din't look after Ed while I'm at the factory.'

Geraldine, cradling young Ed on her lap whilst Beattie ate, looked concerned, and asked, 'But, dear, how can you manage to pay this Ma Briggs woman on the small wages you earn?'

Beattie's mouth was full, but she spluttered, 'Oh, I don't pay 'er nuffin', fank Gord. If I 'ad ter do that, we'd boaf end up in the work'ouse.'

Geraldine shuddered. The thought of her daughter and grandson confined to a workhouse filled her with horror. 'Your father and I would never let that happen to you, Beattie,' she said quite resolutely. 'You must make us a promise that if you ever need money you'll come to us.'

Beattie looked up with what she hoped was a startled expression. 'Don't be silly, Muvver,' she said, swallowing the next mouthful of ham. 'I'd never ask yer fer money. I've made me own bed and I can lie in it.'

Sarah listened to all this, but did not react. Her silence throughout the meal told Beattie all she needed to know.

'D'you know what I admire most in a person?' Samuel's sudden question caused everyone to turn and look at him. 'Stillness,' he said. 'Most people only have it when they die.'

For a moment, no one said anything. Beattie was thoroughly taken aback by her father's sudden, extraordinary comment; it seemed to have no bearing on the conversation. And when she turned to look at her mother for some kind of explanation, Geraldine could only shake her head sadly, and concentrate on stroking young Ed's hair.

'I agree with you, Father,' said Sarah, covering Samuel's hand with her own. It was her first contribution to the conversation since the start of the meal. 'There's something beautiful about stillness. I wish I had it.'

Samuel nodded, but didn't really respond to Sarah, mainly because, these days, the moment he said anything, it usually slipped his mind.

'It's so good to have you home again, Beattie, my dear,' said Geraldine, quickly changing the mood. 'I've made up your room. It hasn't been touched since the day you left. Your father wanted us to take in a lodger, but –' she turned to look at Samuel – 'it wasn't really a very good idea, was it, dear?'

Samuel looked at her with a blank expression. He didn't really know what she was talking about.

'I can't stay, Muvver,' Beattie said awkwardly. 'I only come ter see yer, fer a visit. I've got an 'ome of me own ter go back to.'

Geraldine's whole expression changed to disappointment. 'But you've got a home – here,' she said. 'A home for you – and little Ed.'

Beattie shook her head slowly, guiltily.

'But why not?' asked Geraldine, holding on to young Ed as though she never wanted to let him go. 'I can look after him for you. He'll be safe with me, you know he will.'

'No, Muvver,' replied Beattie. 'It wouldn't be right. I 'ave ter do fings me own way. I only brought Ed up 'ere so's yer could see 'im. I wanted 'im ter see you.' Then she added poignantly, 'I did too.'

There was a moment's silence. Geraldine couldn't understand what was happening, why Beattie was so determined to continue her life of hardship. Then she looked down at young Ed and felt so upset, tears came to her eyes.

'It's getting late, Mum,' Beattie said. 'I'd better be gettin' 'im 'ome.' She stretched out, and took the baby into her arms, saying, 'Got ter get ter work in the mornin', ain't we?'

Young Ed gurgled.

A short time later, Beattie bid her mother and father a tearful farewell, with the promise that from now on she would pay them regular visits. Just before she left, Geraldine discreetly slipped two one-pound notes into the pocket of Beattie's flimsy cotton dress. Sarah saw, but pretended she hadn't.

Outside the house, Beattie put young Ed into a small, grubby pram. 'My landlady give it ter me,' she said. 'Apparently she used it fer both 'er own kids.'

Geraldine tried to smile, but it was an effort. 'Oh Beattie,' she said, anxiously, 'I can't bear the thought of you pushing the pram all that way. You'll be so exhausted by the time you get ho— by the time you get back to your lodgings.'

'There's no problem, Muvver, honest. It won't take long, no more than 'alf an hour. I'll be 'ome well before dark.'

The idea still tormented Geraldine, so she turned to Sarah, who was standing impassively behind them on the front doorstep. 'Sarah, dear, why don't you walk with Beattie for part of the way? It'll keep her company.'

Beattie had to smile at her mother's lack of judgement.

But when she briefly flicked a glance at Sarah, she thought it wasn't such a bad idea after all. 'Feel like a stroll, Sarah?' she asked, half joking.

Sarah hesitated. Then, without saying a word, she went to the garden gate and opened it.

Geraldine waited on the doorstep, waving madly, until both her daughters and grandson were out of sight. Only then did she reluctantly turn back into the house and close the door.

Once Sarah and Beattie had cleared Richmond Avenue, their pace slowed to a stroll. They didn't actually say a word until they were well into Liverpool Road, and never once did Sarah so much as glance down at young Ed, who was now fast asleep in his pram.

'Wot's 'appened ter Farver?' Beattie asked, quite out of the blue. ''As 'e 'ad some kind of breakdown?'

'Something like that,' replied Sarah, coolly. 'It was only to be expected.'

Beattie stiffened. 'Meanin', fanks ter me?'

'You're not the only problem in Father's life, Beattie,' said Sarah, pointedly. 'Just lately he's had rather a lot to cope with.' She turned to look at her. 'They have no money, you know. It's all gone. I've had to get a job.'

'I didn't come beggin', yer know,' Beattie replied, resenting the implication. 'An' I din't ask Muvver ter go an' put that money in me pocket.'

'I'm not suggesting that you did, Beattie,' Sarah said. 'But it's as well you know the situation.'

They walked on, Beattie pushing young Ed in his pram, and Sarah at her side, arms crossed nonchalantly as she walked. The sun had already set, and the red-brick mansion blocks along Liverpool Road were gradually dimming in the summer twilight. But it was still warm, and although it

143

would be dark within the next hour or so, there were plenty of people on the streets strolling aimlessly, and others sitting at their windows, watching the world go by.

On the corner of Offord Road, they paused a moment to let a horse and cart pass on its way to the coal merchant's in Brecknock Road. Whilst they were waiting, Beattie spoke, without turning to look at her sister. 'It ain't been easy, yer know,' she said, having to raise her voice to be heard over the sound of the horse's hoofs and the clatter of cartwheels. 'Fer me, I mean. These last few munffs.'

Sarah waited for the horse and cart to disappear before answering. 'What did you expect?' she asked, quite impassively.

Beattie looked at her. 'I shouldn't've done wot I did, Sarah,' she said. 'I was in the wrong, an' I admit it.'

'Then at least *something* has been achieved,' said Sarah, leading the way across the road.

When they got to the other side, Beattie brought the pram to a halt. 'I did yer a favour, yer know,' she said. 'If it 'adn't bin fer me, you'd 'ave bin lumbered wiv Edward Lacey fer the rest of your life. 'E wasn't worf it.'

'Is that why you had this child?' Sarah asked, cryptically.

Beattie lowered her eyes guiltily, and looked down into the pram. 'I know wot yer fink,' she said, doing her best to avoid Sarah's gaze. 'But it's not somefin' I wanted, or planned. I was careless, I know that. I 'ated wot I let that man do ter me. I didn't want 'is kid. I didn't want any part of 'im.' She sighed, then looked up again. 'But then, somefin' 'appened,' she said, aware that Sarah wasn't really looking at her. 'As soon as Ed was born, everyfin' seemed ter change. When I looked at 'im, 'e seemed so – ' she looked down at young Ed again, 'oh, I don't know – so small, so 'elpless. An' then I get ter finkin' – well, 'e din't ask ter be

144

brought into this world, did 'e?' She paused again. 'Maybe it was because of wot 'appened to 'is farver. Maybe it's because I felt guilty, I just don't know. But once I saw 'im – I knew I 'ad ter do me best for 'im.' She looked up at Sarah again. ''E should've bin yours. Yer know that, don't yer?'

Sarah swung back and glared at her. 'I was never given the opportunity,' she replied, sharply.

'The opportunity was there, Sarah. The trouble is, yer never took it. Edward Lacey wanted me fer one fing only.'

'And you were perfectly happy to give it to him.'

Beattie hesitated, then walked on. But after just a few steps, she came to an abrupt halt again. ''Ow're we goin' ter put fings right then?' she asked. 'I mean – between you an' me?'

Sarah thought for a moment, then replied, 'We could start by taking one day at a time.'

Beattie did not reply straight away. 'Be seein' yer,' she said eventually.

'Beattie?'

Beattie stopped and looked back.

'Why did you do it?' Sarah asked coldly. 'Why did you take him from me?'

Beattie shrugged her shoulders. 'Yer 'ad somefin' I wanted,' she replied. Then she continued on her way.

Sarah stood watching her for a moment, then turned and walked back towards home.

Mrs Ranasinghe was very pleased with the way Sarah was looking after her. The house was cleaner than it had been for quite some time, and the Ceylonese meals that the old lady had been teaching Sarah to cook were improving every day, although, to her mind, Sarah was still not putting enough chilli in the chicken curry. 'Chilli is for us Ceylonese as mustard is for you English,' she insisted, 'except that chilli is far more civilised!'

Sarah's one problem, however, was keeping the old lady from becoming too bored with her life. In many ways, Mrs Ranasinghe was unique, for she never complained about the pain she was suffering, and quite often made fun of her condition, calling herself 'the old bag of bones'. She had even taken to smoking through a long cigarette holder. 'The doctor told me to keep away from cigarettes,' she joked, 'so that's what I'm doing!' It was an old joke, but Sarah laughed every time the old lady told it. Without realising it, Sarah was becoming very fond of her employer, and when they sat down to eat together in the kitchen, she listened in awe to the old lady's tales of life on her native island. Until now, Sarah had only read about a place where pineapples grew and coconuts could be picked off the trees, where beaches were almost as white as snow, and where native workers from India picked the tea leaf that eventually found its way into the teapots of every home in England. But now, thanks to this spellbinding old lady, all of these pages from books had come to true and vivid life, and, listening to Mrs Ranasinghe, there were times when she felt as though she had been transported to the other side of the world.

But working as a companion for Mrs Ranasinghe was proving to be not only stimulating but also enlightening, for the old lady was turning out to be a mine of wisdom. This was never more evident than on one rainy afternoon in late September, when Sarah found herself being cross-questioned about her horoscope, which Mrs Ranasinghe had compiled, based on what she had learned about Sarah since she had come to work for her.

'I don't think there is any doubt in my mind,' said the old lady, with a sly twinkle in her eye, 'that romance for you, young lady, is just around the corner.'

Sarah tried to pretend that she was fascinated by this astounding piece of information, but she was more involved in trying to rinse the henna out of the old lady's hair, which she had just washed in the stone kitchen sink. 'I'm not really interested in romance,' she said. 'I think I'm getting too old for all that now.'

'Too old!' Mrs Ranasinghe pulled her head out of the sink so fast that streaks of black henna dye were running down her face. 'Too old at *your* age?' she spluttered, through her ill-fitting plate of false teeth. 'Ha! What is this thing that young people have about old age? Do you know what I said to my eldest daughter when she asked me why I couldn't grow old graciously? I told her I only wanted to grow old *un*graciously!'

Sarah laughed with her, then gently eased her head back into the sink.

Later, when the old lady was in bed ready for her afternoon sleep, Sarah tried to read her one chapter of Charles Dickens's *Old Curiosity Shop*. But Mrs Ranasinghe was in no mood to be read to, and wanted to talk.

'You must think it strange,' she said, reflectively, 'that a woman like me should want to leave her home and family, and all the things she loved most, to travel to the other side of the world where everything is so different – people, buildings, the weather, and religion. I came into this life as a Buddhist. I've remained so all my life. It gives me strength – oh not in the same way as in your churches, but in the way I've come to terms with myself. If it hadn't been for my faith, I think I would have thrown myself overboard from the boat on the way over to England.' Despite her efforts, her eyes were flickering for want of sleep, so she gradually slipped down beneath the sheets, rested her head on the pillow, and closed her eyes. But her mind was still wide awake. 'It's not

147

easy for a family to accept that one of them is different to the rest,' she said, her voice firm and strong. 'After my husband died, I never did any of the things my daughters expected of me, be a good mother, and devoted widow. I learned to ride a bicycle! It was wonderful.' Her eyes suddenly sprang open. 'Do you know, I only ever fell off once!'

By the time Sarah had smiled at her, the old lady's eyes had closed again.

'I bought a dog. Her name was Chuti. She was a beautiful little creature, so small and fluffy. My girls detested her. They said dogs were dirty and carried disease. But I loved her. I went on the train on my own, right up to the hills, to Kandy. It was – exhilarating. Everything looked so lush and green. Just me – and Chuti. Oh, I did lots of things on my own, things that ordinary people would not expect of a respectable Ceylonese widow.' Her eyes sprang open again. 'But I value my independence, Sarah. Without it, I would die. That's why I can never go home. I suppose it must be some kind of disease, because when I decide to do something, I just can't stop myself.'

The old lady's eyes closed again, but this time she fell into an immediate sleep. Sarah waited until she heard her snoring soundly. Then she gently covered the old lady's shoulders with the eiderdown, and left the room.

Sarah went into the sitting room, and flopped down on to the sofa. All around her were mementoes of Mrs Ranasinghe's extraordinary life: cushion covers embroidered with elephants, brass ornaments in the shape of temples, and a wooden head of the Buddha, which meant so much to this strange old lady. But more significant to Sarah were the vast array of family photographs scattered around the place, on small polished tables, on the wall, and on the mantelpiece. There were group pictures, portraits of her daughters and her grandchildren, all either laughing or taking their pose terribly seriously. Nothing out of the ordinary about them really. And yet, Sarah found it odd that someone as fiercely independent as Mrs Ranasinghe should want to be reminded of the life she had so readily abandoned, the members of her family who frowned on one of their own who had chosen to become an outsider. But then, was it really so strange to be different? She leaned her head back on the sofa, and stared up at the white plaster stucco design around the ceiling. And as she lay there, she began to think about Beattie, who, just like Mrs Ranasinghe, had forsaken so much to take that dangerous, uncharted road to independence.

Beattie knew there was something wrong the moment she got back from work that evening. Now that autumn was in the air, the nights were already beginning to draw in, so by the time she got home, it was practically dark. Usually even as she put her key in the street door, she could hear Ma Briggs playing with Ed Junior in her front parlour. But tonight, she could hear nothing.

'Ma!' she called, knocking on the parlour door. 'It's me. I'm home.'

'Come in, dear!' came Ma Briggs' voice from inside. But as soon as Beattie entered the room, she could see no sign of young Ed.

''Ad a good day, dear?' asked Ma, who seemed quite unruffled. 'Real autumn chill in the air now,' she said. 'Wot about a nice cuppa before yer go up?'

'Where is 'e, Ma?' Beattie asked quickly. 'Where's Ed?'

'Ed?' replied Ma, a bit taken aback. 'Why 'e's gone, dear. Like yer said.'

Beattie immediately panicked. 'Gone? Wot're yer talkin' about? Gone where?'

Ma was getting nervous. 'Jack took 'im. Over 'alf an hour ago.'

'Wot!'

Ma was now flustered. 'But – din't yer know? 'E told me yer asked 'im. 'E said yer asked 'im ter take little Ed fer a walk. Din't yer know? Yer must've—'

Beattie took hold of Ma's shoulders and shook her. 'Where, Ma?' she said over and over again. 'Where's 'e taken 'im?'

'I don't know, Beattie!' she cried, her face crumpling up with remorse and guilt. 'Honest ter Gord, I don't know. 'E just said—'

Before she could say anything more, Beattie had rushed from the room and out into the street.

The light outside was rapidly fading, and the street lamplighters were already lighting the gas mantles with their long poles.

In a wild frenzy Beattie looked all around her, from one end of the Bunk to the other. The street was deserted – no one to ask if they had seen a feller like Jack pushing a small baby in a pram. So, in desperation, she had to choose which way to go. She decided to try the Fonthill Road direction first, for that was where Jack usually made for when he used to leave her first thing in the morning.

'Jack!' she yelled, her voice echoing around the roofs and chimneypots as she went. 'Jack!'

So much was racing through her mind, for it had been some months since she had last seen Jack Ridley, the last time being when he had beaten her up for daring to criticise him. She was going crazy with fear. What was he up to? Was it possible that he was trying to kidnap little Ed as some kind of punishment because she had refused to have anything more to do with his ugly, unpalatable activities? Every time she thought about him, her flesh crept. Only by luck had she avoided being implicated in Jack's break-in at Bob Sluggins' pawn shop. It was bad enough to be questioned by the rozzers after the incident, but fortunately, no one had put two and two together, and that meant her and Jack Ridley.

'Jack!' She was now yelling hysterically. 'Jack Ridley, yer bleedin' sod! Where – are – yer . . .?'

Beattie's frantic yells had now brought people rushing to their windows and front doors, but no one wanted to get involved; no one came out to ask her what was wrong.

She finally reached the corner of Fonthill Road, but it was now so dark she could see very little. 'Jack . . .!' Her yells were now echoing along the entire length of the road. 'Don't . . . do . . . this . . . ter . . . me . . .!'

Standing alone on the corner of the darkened road, Beattie suddenly broke down into a fit of uncontrollable tears.

''Ere now, Beat,' said a voice, quietly, right behind her. 'Wot's all this then?'

Beattie swung round to find the dark shape of Jack Ridley, holding on to the handle of young Ed's pram. 'Yer sod!' she squealed, immediately trying to push him out of the way. ''Ow could yer? 'Ow could yer?'

Jack placed himself in between Beattie and the pram, preventing her from getting to little Ed. 'Not so fast now, Beat,' he said. 'Don't want yer wakin' up the poor little bleeder. 'E's bin 'avin' a really good kip.'

Beattie suddenly lost control and went for him, thumping at his chest with her fists. 'I'll kill yer, kill yer!'

Jack deflected her blows, and held on to her hands. 'Calm down now, yer silly cow,' he said quietly, and without fuss. 'No 'arm's come ter the kid. Go on – ask 'im,' he added, mocking her. Then he pulled her to him. 'I 'ad ter see yer, Beat,' he said, his face close to hers. 'Yer can't go on shuttin' me off – not all the time. This was the only way I could get to yer.'

Enraged, Beattie spat in his face.

Jack's immediate reaction was to cuff her, but he thought better of it and continued to restrain her. 'I love yer, Beat.'

Beattie was stopped dead in her tracks.

Jack moved close to her ear and whispered, 'I've never said that to anyone else in the 'ole wide world. Yer've got ter believe me.'

Beattie took a moment to calm herself, then said, 'Is that wot love's all about, Jack? Beatin' up people?'

Jack squeezed her wrists until they hurt. 'I swear ter Gord, I'll never lay an 'and on yer again.'

'Not till the next job, eh, Jack?'

Jack refused to be riled. 'That's all over, Beat,' he said reassuringly. 'I don't need it no more. But I do need you.'

He now felt confident enough to release her wrists.

'You're a nutcase, Jack Ridley,' she said. 'Yer know that, don't yer?'

'I make mistakes, Beat,' he said. 'But I'm not mad.'

'Yer 'ate the kid. Yer've told me a dozen times.'

'I was jealous of 'im. I still am. But I don't 'ate 'im. 'Ere. See fer yerself.'

He stood aside and allowed Beattie to go to little Ed. She found him fast asleep in the pram, sucking away quite contentedly on his dummy. Relieved, she started to sob again.

Jack took her in his arms, and held on to her. 'I've never met anyone like yer before, Beat,' he said softly. 'I knew that the first moment I saw yer.' He leaned in closer so that as he spoke his lips were virtually caressing her ear. 'Let me tell yer somefin'. You an' me tergevver could conquer the world. Gimme anuvver chance, an' I'll prove it.'

Chapter 11

It had been two years since the war had ended, and yet, during that time, it seemed as though the world had learnt nothing. In America, the US Senate had rejected the Versailles Treaty, which, under the all-embracing name of the League of Nations, was at least an attempt by the Allies to restore some kind of peace and unity in Europe. There was turmoil in Russia after the White Army leader had been executed by the Bolsheviks. In Syria, the French occupied Damascus. The Poles were at war with the Russians. In Italy there was serious industrial strife. Nearer to home, Sinn Fein supporters and Unionists were rioting in the streets in Belfast; there were the usual scandals involving accusations of corruption amongst members of Prime Minister Lloyd George's administration and, as unemployment continued to soar, labour organisations threatened strike action if the British Government declared war on Russia. Yes, the world had gone mad, and if only Samuel Melford had been in his right mind, he would have had quite a few comments of his own to make on the matter. Unfortunately, however, those times had now passed.

Samuel's illness, which had gradually deteriorated during the previous year, had been diagnosed by a hospital specialist as a form of premature senility. As each day passed, he seemed to know little of what was going on around him.

Sometimes, when Geraldine and Sarah were talking together, he would simply watch them as though they were strangers, and the bewildered look on his face suggested that their conversation had no meaning whatsoever, and merely consisted of two human mouths with lips moving at enormous speed. There was now, of course, no prospect of Samuel returning to any kind of job, which made the upkeep of the family house in Thornhill Road difficult. To make matters worse, during recent months, Beattie had been paying regular weekly visits to her parents, which were apparently arranged so that the couple could keep in touch with their grandson. But Sarah knew her sister well enough to be deeply suspicious of her motives. Her worries became more acute when she noticed that various objects that had been in the family for years were disappearing from their usual places around the house. These included fairly valuable items, such as a small silver snuff box, a set of Royal Albert finger bowls, two double brass candlesticks, a small Wedgwood fine bone china country maid figure, and even an early Victorian hand-embroidered beaded table cover.

'Got rid of them?' Sarah asked her mother, with incredulity. 'You got rid of *all* those things? All those beautiful things that you and Father have been collecting ever since you were married? But why, Mother?'

Geraldine had been dreading this moment. She knew it would be only a matter of time before Sarah noticed all the valuables that were missing, that she herself had been taking to Bob Sluggins' pawn shop in the Holloway Road. 'If you must know,' she replied, quite casually, whilst making heavy work of changing the sheets on her husband's bed, 'I was tired of them. In any case, we don't need all those silly things,' she said. 'They just clutter up the place and bring back memories.'

154

Sarah watched her mother with growing suspicion. There was a tense energy in Geraldine's behaviour, as though she was trying to make light of something that was in fact quite serious.

'Believe me,' Geraldine continued, as she pulled off the two soiled pillowcases and threw them on to the floor, 'when you've lived as long as your father and me, you learn that material things mean so very little.' She briefly flicked a glance over her shoulder at Sarah, without making eye contact with her. 'You'll know what I mean one day, when *you* get married and have a home of your own.'

These days, Geraldine was a changed person. Sarah had noticed it since they first became aware that Samuel's mind was drifting. As Sarah watched her mother each day, busying herself with unnecessary intensity over the most trifling housework, it distressed her to see the anguish in the poor woman's eyes. For Sarah, Geraldine had been the perfect mother, caring, loving, and always interested in anything her family was doing. But now, her whole life seemed to be obsessed by two things: the protection of her ailing husband, and a passionate need to spend as much time as she possibly could with her little grandson. It was so strange to see this once beautiful, lively woman so ill at ease with herself and everyone around her. Even her former immaculate dress sense had been abandoned, and these days she seemed quite prepared to meet any visitors to the house wearing her long, dull pinafore dress. And her hair, once so well groomed, now frequently fell into straggly locks across her forehead. Of course, it was hardly surprising that she seemed to care so little for her appearance, for she no longer had a husband to look nice for, no husband to hold her in his arms in bed at night. Sarah was convinced that she had to find some way of preventing her mother from just giving up, and, most

155

important of all, to stop Beattie taking advantage of her.

'Mother,' Sarah asked, as she helped her mother to make up her father's bed with clean sheets. 'What have you been doing with all the things you've got rid of?'

'What does it matter, dear?' Geraldine replied evasively. 'They've gone, and that's an end to it.'

'Have you sold them?'

'More or less.'

'What have you done with the money?'

This irritated Geraldine, and it showed in her voice. 'I really don't think that's any concern of yours, Sarah.'

Sarah stopped making the bed, and looked hard at her. 'Have you given it to Beattie?'

At this, Geraldine slammed down the sheet without tucking it in. 'I've given it to my grandson,' she snapped. '*My* own grandson, Sarah. Do you understand?'

Sarah felt chastened, but undeterred. 'You can't afford to spend your money like that, Mother,' she said. 'You and Father have little enough as it is.'

Geraldine angrily flicked away a lock of hair that had fallen over her eye. 'What sort of a person do you think I am if I can't even help my own flesh and blood?'

'But Mother, it isn't necessary for you to go and sell all your possessions like this. I know Beattie's not earning very much, but she certainly has enough to put a good meal inside her child's stomach.'

Geraldine came back at her immediately. 'When *you* were a child,' she snapped, 'you wanted for nothing – neither you nor your sister. You had food in your stomach – *good* food – clothes on your back, shoes on your feet, holidays down by the sea – all the things that a child needs in life. But this poor little mite has nothing, absolutely nothing.'

'With respect, Mother,' Beattie said, restrained, 'nobody

asked Beattie to have an illegitimate child.'

Geraldine was taken aback. 'How dare you?' she gasped, glaring across the bed at Sarah. 'Has it ever occurred to you that little Ed is your own nephew?'

Exasperated, Sarah turned away.

'That child has a right to our support,' Geraldine said, coming around the bed to confront her. 'When you have one of your own, you'll feel differently. Remember this, Sarah. Once a child is in the womb, it becomes a living thing, and from that moment on we all have a part to play in its future – whatever the circumstances.' Sarah turned to go, but Geraldine quickly took hold of her arm. 'Sarah, I love you,' she said. 'I love you *and* Beattie. And I love my grandson. You've no idea how much that little boy means to me. Especially now.' She released Sarah's arm and sighed. 'There's a huge, empty gap in my life, Sarah,' she said. 'I can't tell you how much I need to fill it.'

Sarah looked at her mother, and felt the emptiness that had engulfed the poor woman's life. Yes, it was true. Now that Geraldine had virtually lost Samuel into his strange, twilight world, having little Ed around the place was helping her to fill that awful gap. In fact, for Geraldine, at this traumatic time in her life, her grandson probably meant as much, perhaps even more, than her own two daughters. 'It's all right, Mother,' she said, going to Geraldine and putting her arms around her. 'Everything's going to be quite all right. I'll do anything I can to make you happy.'

Geraldine's eyes were doleful. 'Then make it up with your sister,' she pleaded. 'Then your father and I will know we still have a family.'

Much to Beattie's irritation, young Ed was beginning to look more like his father each day. Not that Beattie knew what

157

Edward Lacey looked like at eighteen months old, but there was no doubt that his son had the same glowing, pale blue eyes, and even at this age the boy had the same mischievous look that Beattie remembered when she first met Lacey in the Eaglet back in 1917.

There was also no doubt that young Ed was beginning to show signs of his own individual personality, such as a real appetite for picture books, which Ma Briggs bought for him every week when she picked up her ounce of pipe tobacco from the newsagent in Fonthill Road. Even when he was less than a year old, he was already identifying objects in the books, and always jumped up and down with excitement every time his mum or the old lady pointed out a cat or a rabbit or a cow. He also learned to pull himself up to his feet long before anyone had expected, despite his grandmother's warning that doing it so early could make the child bandy. But what was extraordinary was what a sensitive little boy Ed was developing into. When he was upset, it showed in his face. He never cried, but went immediately silent, lowering his eyes, and staring at his feet as though he was being punished. All this wasn't easy for Beattie, for she never wanted to have a baby, and, although she was turning out to be a protective mum, a feeling nagged inside her that she didn't really love the child.

Life for Beattie was not easy, especially with Jack Ridley around the place. Despite her initial forebodings, during the spring of that year Beattie allowed Jack Ridley to move in with her. It had been an unwise decision, for despite Ridley's assurances that he was now a changed man and that he would be good for her, within a few weeks he had virtually taken over the household, losing his temper every time little Ed opened his mouth, and using his fist on Beattie whenever he wanted his own way. Ma Briggs knew what was going on, for on those all-too-frequent mornings when she noticed Beattie trying to cover up a black eye or a cut lip, she wondered whether she had been right to give her blessing to Ridley moving in, which she had only agreed to because she had known Jack since he was a youngster, and felt that it was a wonderful chance for little Ed to have the father he had so far been denied.

There were times when Beattie was in total despair, for her resistance had become so low that she had no idea how to cope with a situation in which she not only hated Ridley for being such a sadistic bully to both her and her child, but she felt troubled and confused as to why she should want to hang on to a man for whom she had an inextricably fatal attraction. What Beattie needed, and needed desperately, was someone to make up her mind for her, to tell her what to do, and shoulder the burden of bringing up Edward Lacey's child.

In Beattie's mind, that opportunity finally came one morning in September 1920, when she opened a letter addressed to her, with a Suffolk postmark. Both the envelope and the letter were written by someone with a rather shaky hand, and Beattie found such difficulty in making it out that she could only make sense of it by reading out loud.

The Old Manor House
Stickley
Nr Sudbury
Suffolk
21 September 1920

Dear Miss Melford,

I am writing to you on the advice of my solicitor, Mr Albert Cordell of Cordell and Winters, No. 3A

Gainsborough Street, in Sudbury.

You will recall that I last wrote to you acquainting you with the death of my son, Petty Officer Edward John Lacey, who was killed in an unfortunate naval accident on the final day of the war in November 1918.

For his own reasons, prior to his death my son failed to notify me of his relationship with you. Had it not been for your letter to him, that came into my possession on his death, I would not have known of your existence. You will therefore understand the pain I suffered when my solicitor's enquiries revealed that you had given birth to my son's child. I am sure you can understand the devastating shock this news caused me, and the knowledge that somewhere in this troubled world there was a small child, who, despite the circumstances of his conception, was my grandchild, the offspring of my only son.

You will, no doubt, have many questions to ask as to why I have taken this amount of time to make contact with you, and it is in this regard that I am now writing.

After reading this, Beattie found it hard to concentrate. Oh yes, she had plenty of questions all right, such as why her son's own grandfather had waited so long before even bothering to find out how she was coping with a fatherless child. But then, she had no illusions about what he really thought about her – that she was a little tart, who couldn't wait to get her hands on some spare cash. But when she read on, she wasn't quite so sure.

When I was first notified about Edward's death, I was utterly bereft. Although he and I often clashed about the way he conducted his private life, the thought that he had been struck down at such an early age filled me with remorse and guilt. But when I discovered that he had been responsible for your pregnancy, that guilt quickly turned to anger. I just wanted to close my mind and tell myself that it simply wasn't true. But it *was* true, and despite the loss of my son, nothing in the world could change what had happened. With that thought in mind, I finally decided that there was no way that I could go on ignoring the fact that I had a duty towards my only grandchild, his future, and his rightful inheritance.

Beattie's eyes lit up. She now couldn't read on fast enough.

I would therefore like to invite you to the Old Manor House, where we can discuss in detail what I have outlined in more general terms above. The village of Stickley is just two miles outside the small town of Sudbury, which can be reached by taking a train from Liverpool Street. On arrival at Sudbury, you will be met by a member of my household. In acknowledging receipt of this letter, please be good enough to advise a suitable date of travel. Enclosed please find two one-pound notes to cover cost of journey for self and child.

    Yours faithfully,

    J.L. Lacey

    Lt. Comm. R.N. (Rtd)

Beattie put the letter down. Her hands were shaking; she could hardly contain herself. Despite the formal tone and the appalling presentation, she was convinced that this was the break she had been waiting for. Now she would be able to bring young Ed up in a civilised way instead of in the stifling atmosphere of her upstairs room. In her mind, she immediately started working out plans of how she and little Ed would move out of the Bunk into a flat of their own, or, if old Lacey offered her enough money, perhaps even into a small terraced house.

'We're movin' up in the world, Ed,' she called to the boy, who was stretched out on the floor using a black crayon to draw a big bushy moustache on a rabbit in one of his picture books. 'Wot d'yer fink about that then?'

Young Ed's response was to roar with excitable laughter. Beattie laughed with him, but for quite a different reason. She was thinking of how, with old Lacey's help, she would now have the chance to break with Jack Ridley once and for all. Or would she? As she sat down to write an immediate response to the letter, her mind was again plagued by indecision. Could she really go through with all this *without* telling Ridley? And if so, when he did eventually find out, what would he do to her then?

The Old Manor House wasn't nearly as grand as its name seemed to suggest. Beattie and young Ed's first glimpse of it came as the pony and trap they had been collected in at Sudbury railway station turned off the small country lanes outside the village of Stickley, and headed along what could only be described as an overgrown path lined on either side by tall elm trees. The member of Lacey's household, who turned out to be the old gardener, and not at all pleased to be leaving his vegetable beds for a trip to the station, remained virtually silent all the way, so if Beattie had imagined she was going to be able to pump the man for any kind of information about his employer, she was vastly mistaken.

When the house finally came into view, Beattie's first

impression was of an ancient building that had clearly once been quite beautiful, but which was now run down and sorely in need of repair. But as she and young Ed were helped out of the trap, the splendour of the old red bricks, leaded windows, and fine sculptured stucco work around the exterior walls presented a picture of elegant grandeur, and reflected the type of people who must have lived there for generations.

The heavy oak front door was opened by an elderly housekeeper. 'The Commander is waitin' for you in the hall, miss,' she announced, in a country burr that Beattie recognised from her childhood when she and Sarah had spent a summer holiday with their Aunt Dixie, who lived in another part of Suffolk.

Beattie, with young Ed clutching her hand, entered the front hall, which had a stone floor, wood panelling, and a huge open fireplace. Little Ed's eyes were as large as saucers as he noticed the head and horns of a shot deer placed on the wall above the fireplace.

''Ook!' he cried, pointing to the amazing spectacle.

'Don't point, Ed!' scolded his mum. 'It's rude!'

The housekeeper showed them straight into the sitting room, which looked more like a room in a hunting-lodge, for there were more heads of culled animals jutting out from the walls, and a smell of decay mixed with rotting timber. 'Here we are, Commander!' she called.

'Ah!' said the man, who was standing with his back to the fireplace. 'Miss Melford?'

Beattie took young Ed straight across to him. 'Please call me Beattie, Farver,' she said. 'After all, we're family.'

The Commander did not respond to this, but held out his hand for Beattie, who shook it. 'How do you do?' was all he said.

Beattie smiled and tried to identify some kind of resemblance between this man and his son, Edward, but, surprisingly, there was none. She was quite astonished that the retired naval officer didn't look at all old, in fact far younger than she had imagined, with dark blue vacant-looking eyes, short brown hair that showed not a trace of grey, and a moustache.

'This is yer grandson, Farver,' Beattie said, rather too well-rehearsed. She lifted up young Ed to show the Commander. 'Say 'ello ter Granddad, Ed,' she cooed.

''Ello.' Despite his mum's warnings, Ed Junior looked a little nervous as he offered his hand to the strange man.

Beattie was a little puzzled that the Commander failed to take the child's hand.

'Can I hold him?' asked the Commander.

''Course.'

Beattie readily handed the boy over, despite the fact that the poor little thing was wary and ill-at-ease.

The Commander took the boy and, for a moment, held him at arm's length, as though looking him over.

But once again, Beattie was puzzled to see that the Commander was not actually looking directly at the boy's face.

'What colour eyes does he have?'

Beattie was completely taken aback by this question. Only when she watched him gently feeling around the boy's eyes with the tips of his fingers did she realise that he was blind. It took her completely by surprise. 'Er – blue,' she replied awkwardly. 'A kind of light blue.'

The Commander's face broke into a broad smile for the first time. 'Ah!' he said, to the boy. 'Then you truly *are* your father's son, aren't you, Edward?' He put the boy down, and straightened up to face Beattie again. 'I'm sorry you weren't warned about my slight disability,' he said. 'I got it in an explosion on board my ship before the war. Stupid thing to happen. But you mustn't let it worry you. I can assure that I *can* see you – in a manner of speaking.'

Beattie was trying her best to cover up her awkwardness. 'I'm sorry,' she said. 'Edward never told me.'

The Commander gave her a wry smile. 'I don't expect he did,' he replied dryly.

The real purpose of the Commander's invitation to Beattie was not really addressed until all three had sat down to lunch at a long, highly polished table, where they were waited on by Mrs Routledge, the housekeeper, who served a meal of hot chicken broth, and cold beef and salad. Beattie knew that the only thing young Ed would eat was a slice of bread and butter, for even back home his eating was generally confined to things like minced scrag end of mutton and mashed potatoes. But his eyes did light up when the main course was followed by treacle tart and custard, which he polished off very quickly. After the meal, young Ed was allowed to leave the table, and with his mum and grandfather's permission, he was taken out into the garden by Mrs Routledge to look for frogs in the Old Manor House pond.

'As I wrote in my letter, Miss Melford,' said the Commander, once they were alone, 'or rather, as Mrs Routledge wrote for me, you must have been somewhat surprised to hear from me after such a long silence. And I wouldn't blame you for feeling angry at what I'm sure you must have felt was my complete indifference to the birth of my grandchild.'

Beattie tried her best not to show what she really felt about the way the old man had left her to struggle on, trying to bring up his son's child on her own for nearly two years.

But until she heard how he intended to put things right, she was prepared to give him the benefit of the doubt. 'I don't see no point in bein' angry,' she said, without bitterness. 'It won't bring Ed's dad back ter life again.'

The Commander was intrigued by Beattie's candour, and it persuaded him to be more open with her. 'I'm not proud of the way I've behaved, Miss Melford,' he said, his eyes flicking aimlessly. 'You see, I've always believed that children should only be born within the framework of family life. It was a shock to know that my own son had—' He stopped abruptly, and turned his eyes in Beattie's direction. 'Did you love my son, Miss Melford?' he asked.

Beattie was taken aback by this question. And yet she understood why he asked it. After thinking about it for a moment, she replied, 'No, I didn't.'

The Commander looked impressed. 'If he had lived,' he asked, 'would you have married him?'

Again, Beattie hesitated before replying. 'Only for the sake of my child.'

The Commander sat back in his chair. He seemed well satisfied. 'Thank you, Miss Melford,' he said.

Beattie watched him carefully, and was struck by the way he sat so erect in his chair, shoulders squared, and with those lifeless dark blue eyes staring past her. 'When was the last time yer saw Edward?' she asked tentatively. But then quickly correcting herself, she added awkwardly, 'Wot I mean is – when was the last time yer was tergevver wiv 'im?'

'Oh, we hardly ever met,' he replied, suddenly brushing away what seemed to be imaginary food crumbs from the arm of his dark blue blazer. 'Edward only ever came when he wanted something. Usually money.' He hesitated, and Beattie could see that he was deep in thought. 'We didn't

166

really get on well, you know. Chalk and cheese – that's what his mother always called us. She adored him, of course. Bit of a mother's boy, Edward.' He hesitated again before adding sadly, 'If I hadn't urged him to follow me into the navy, he'd be alive today.'

Beattie sensed his guilt, and for a brief moment, felt quite sorry for him.

'He once told me he'd never marry. Bit of a rogue, you know. I don't know what kind of a father he'd have made.'

'I'm sure 'e'd've bin marvellous,' said Beattie, reassuringly. She didn't believe a word she had said.

The Commander grunted. He didn't believe her either. 'So what are we going to do about this boy of his then?' he asked. 'Can't leave him to starve, can we?'

Although Beattie resented the implication that she was not somehow looking after his grandson, her heart started thumping at the prospect of some kind of financial offer of help. 'I'd never let Ed starve, Farver,' she said. 'Even if I 'ave ter go wivout meself, which I often do.'

The Commander ignored this, and carried straight on. 'Well, as the boy doesn't have a father, it's up to me to do what I can. He's part of my own flesh and blood, my own family. I'm the boy's grandfather. I won't let him down – nor his father.' He leaned forward in his chair, and directed his conversation straight towards where he could hear Beattie's movements. 'Tell you what I have in mind,' he said briskly. 'I've got quite a few nephews and nieces and godchildren littered around the world, so I can't go mad. And in any case, this house isn't worth as much as it used to be. Needs a lot doing to it.' He leaned back in his chair again. 'None the less, this boy is far closer to me than all the riffraff and hangers-on in my family, so I owe it to him to give him a good lift up in life. So I've instructed my solicitors to put him in my will.'

Beattie's heart was beating faster and faster.

'I want him to have a cut of the house, and five thousand pounds in cash. What d'you say about that, eh?'

Beattie clasped her hands so tightly together under the table that her knuckles went white. 'I – I fink that's – luvely of yer, Farver,' she replied, falteringly.

Both turned their heads towards the large leaded bow window, as they heard Ed Junior laughing and screeching in the garden outside.

The Commander smiled, raised himself up from his chair, and went to the window. 'I was tempted to leave him everything. But I believe a person should find his own way in life. If you make it too easy for them, they lose their energy and ambition.'

Beattie was biting her lip. To her mind, he was talking a load of old rubbish.

The Commander stood at the window, as though looking out into the garden, listening to the sound of Ed Junior giving poor Mrs Routledge quite a boisterous time. 'I want him to have something to fall back on,' he said, contemplatively. Then he turned his attention back to Beattie. 'But it'll be his, you know. Whatever my grandchild gets from me goes to him, no one else. D'you understand what I'm saying, Miss Melford?'

Beattie felt her back stiffen. 'Nat'rally,' she replied, coldly, but cautiously.

The Commander came back to the table, and leaned both his hands there. 'A child born out of wedlock,' he said, 'has a lot to bear for the rest of his life. He didn't ask to be brought into this world. And for all I know, it was not what his father wanted either.'

Indignant, Beattie sat bolt upright in her seat.

'Oh, I know how you feel, my dear,' said the Commander, fully aware of her outrage. 'But I would be deceiving myself if I thought I could trust you.'

Beattie slowly raised herself up from her chair. 'I fawt yer asked me 'ere to talk about yer grandson,' she snapped.

'Quite so, my dear,' he replied. 'But until I know what kind of sacrifices you are prepared to make as the boy's mother, in the event of my death, none of the inheritance I have mentioned will be made available until my grandson reaches the age of twenty-one.'

Chapter 12

These were hard times for the Melford family. The winter had been bad enough, with leaks appearing all over the roof of Number 14 after a week-long downpour during November, which was followed by a big freeze-up in December. Geraldine, in particular, hated the cold, and as there was very little money to buy coal for every fireplace in the house, she had to resort to wearing thick woollen underclothes, which was something she had shunned all her life. Samuel spent most of his days in his pyjamas and dressing gown, hunched up in front of the fire in his bedroom. But he seemed contented enough, especially when Sarah came back from work in the evenings and read him articles from the day's newspaper, which always seemed to stir something in his inner consciousness.

During the bad weather, Beattie's visits became less regular, but there was no doubt that whenever she called, little Ed's presence brought the house back to life. Despite her mother's pleas for her to 'make it up' with her sister, Sarah kept her distance, preferring to remain in her room whilst Beattie and her son entertained their parents downstairs. It was a painful experience for Sarah to hear the child romping around the place, laughing and yelling as he chased his grandmother's four outraged cats from one room to another. No matter how hard she tried, it was impossible for her to ignore that small, boisterous voice, the laughing eyes and podgy frame, a bundle of life and energy that should, in her mind, have belonged to her and her alone.

But Sarah's feelings towards her sister were to take a strange turn when, quite by chance, she and Beattie met each other in the Seven Sisters Road on the last full Saturday shopping day before Christmas.

'Didn't expect ter see you in my neck of the woods.'

Sarah always knew that it would only be a matter of time before she bumped into her sister whilst shopping for Mrs Ranasinghe, for these shops were only a stone's throw from Beattie's lodgings in the Bunk. But now it had actually happened, Sarah once again felt her whole body seizing up with tension. 'Hello, Beattie,' she said, without a glimmer of warmth.

'Ready fer Chris'mas, are yer?' Beattie asked, as she rested her large canvas shopping bag on the windowledge of Lipton's grocery shop. 'Got yer turkey yet?'

As Sarah had no intention of standing talking to Beattie for very long, she held on to her own small shopping bags. 'I'm afraid we can't afford a turkey this year, Beattie,' she replied, rather primly. 'We're having a chicken.'

'Roast chicken?' Beattie sighed wistfully. 'I reckon it's goin' ter be sausage an' onion rissoles for me an' Ed.'

Sarah was unmoved by what she considered to be Beattie's feeble attempt to gain sympathy. 'I seem to remember Mother telling you that you'd both be welcome to join us at home for a meal any time during Christmas.'

Beattie shook her head. 'I know,' she replied, pulling up her fake astrakhan coat collar as snowflakes began to flutter down from a darkening sky. 'But it wouldn't work. Not wiv the usual crowd, the family an' that, all disapprovin'. 'Cept

Aunt Dixie. She's always good fer a laugh.'

Sarah looked at her sister and thought what a fool she was. How could she even think about giving up so much for so little? How could she value independence more than the love and warmth of a good family, who were worth more than all her so-called working-class mates put together.

'I have to go, Beattie,' she said, starting to move off.

'I've just been ter see Bob Sluggins,' Beattie said suddenly and impetuously. 'Down the pawn shop.'

Sarah stopped.

Beattie took a step towards her. 'I saved up enough ter buy back Mum's silver snuff box. You know – that one Dad give 'er for 'er birfday a coupla years ago.'

Sarah looked at her, unsure how to react. For the first time in her life, she noticed that Beattie had a small mole at the base of her right cheek.

'I've bought back most of the uvver stuff she pawned,' Beattie said, her eyes showing the need she felt for Sarah's approval. 'I told 'er not ter do it, but she wouldn't listen. You know Mum. She always wants ter 'elp 'er kids.' She averted her gaze for a moment. Then: 'I've made up me mind, Sarah,' she said firmly. 'If I 'ave ter work twenty-four hours a day, seven days a week, I'm goin' ter get all those fings back for 'er. I'll give 'er the first lot back for a Christmas present. I know it's not the same, but at least it's somefink.'

Despite the heavy fall of snowflakes that were now settling on both women's heads and shoulders, Sarah felt a warm glow seeping through her entire body. As she looked at Beattie standing there in the ice-cold, she felt as though she hardly knew who this strange, vulnerable woman was. None the less, her face gradually loosened into a faint, appreciative smile. 'Thank you, Beattie,' she said, without the usual harshness in her voice. Then, after pausing briefly, she turned and moved off.

'Sarah!'

Again, Sarah stopped.

Beattie's eyes were glistening with the cold. 'Come back 'ome an' 'ave a cuppa tea wiv me.'

Sarah shook her head slowly. 'I don't think so, Beattie,' she replied, with some difficulty.

Beattie clutched Sarah's arm. '*Please*, Sarah,' she pleaded. 'I'm only a stone's throw from 'ere. I'd like ter talk ter yer. I *need* ter talk ter someone. I'll go out of my mind if I don't. Just 'alf an hour's chinwag, that's all. We ain't done that in a long time.'

'We don't know *how* to talk to each other, Beattie,' said Sarah. 'We never have.'

Beattie drew closer. 'Maybe we 'aven't tried 'ard enuff,' she replied.

It was a long trudge along Seven Sisters Road, for the snow was now falling thick and fast, and the earlier slight breeze had turned gusty, transforming the entire road into a dazzling carpet of white, where pavement, kerb and road were one. And even though it was a Saturday afternoon, in the middle of this great white blizzard a queue of men had formed outside the side entrance of a small copper works where, rumours had been circulating there were job vacancies. It was a forlorn hope, for the yard gates remained stubbornly closed, leaving the men outside to freeze in the snowstorm, which seemed to have turned the long, thin queue into a white-capped caterpillar, whose only comfort came from a nearby street accordion player entertaining them with a shaky rendition of 'Good King Wenceslas'.

By the time Beattie and Sarah had turned into Campbell Road, the blizzard had started to abate. The Bunk wasn't at all as Sarah had imagined it to be, for before her was a winter wonderland, flanked on either side by houses that, in their massive coat of white, looked positively beautiful. There was no sign of the tawdriness for which the Bunk was so famous – no rubbish bins turned on their sides, no broken milk bottles littering the pavements. For this one lingering moment, Sarah could see no more than a street like any other, serene and tranquil in the snow-white mist that was gradually engulfing it.

Ma Briggs was certainly relieved to see Beattie when she came through the front door. 'I was beginnin' ter fink you'd end up as a bleedin' snowman, gel!' she bellowed, laughing out loud at her own rusty humour. But as soon as she saw another young woman hurrying in behind Beattie, she quickly tried to make herself look presentable, wiping her usual dewdrop from the tip of her nose with the back of her hand. 'Sorry, mate,' she said. 'Din't know yer 'ad company.'

'Ma,' said Beattie, putting down her shopping bag and taking off her snow-covered headscarf, 'this is me sister, Sarah. She's the brains in the family.' Then turning to Sarah, she said, 'I couldn't manage wivout Ma, 'ere. She's a real life-saver.'

Sarah held out her hand to Ma. 'Pleased to meet you,' she said formally.

In one hearty movement, Ma grabbed hold of Sarah's hands and shook them hard with both her own hands. 'Our Beat's sister!' she cried jubilantly. 'Well, there's a turn-up fer the books!' Then the old girl completely unnerved Sarah by suddenly leaning forward close and giving her a good looking-over. 'Diff'rent as peas ter pods,' she sniffed airily. 'Looks don't run in *your* family, do they, mate? Still, looks ain't everyfin' in this world. It's wot's inside that counts.'

Sarah had no time to respond, for young Ed suddenly

came rushing out of Ma's front parlour, shouting and yelling, 'Mum! Mum! Mum!' ignoring everyone, and charging straight past them and up the stairs.

'Be careful, Ed!' Beattie yelled. ''Old on ter the banisters!'

'I lit yer fire about 'alf-hour ago,' said Ma. 'Should be nice an' warm up there by now. Nice ter meet yer, young lady,' she bellowed to Sarah. 'Looks like your mum 'ad a good time wiv the milkman!' Roaring with laugher at her own cheeky joke, she disappeared into her room.

Beattie's room was, as Ma Briggs had promised, nice and warm when they got there, so the first thing Beattie did was to fill a large blackened kettle with a jug of water, taken from a bucket in the corner. Then she lit one of the two gas rings on the portable hob, and put the kettle on to boil.

Sarah was somewhat surprised by the room, for, although it was in bad need of decoration, at least everything was neat and tidy, the large double bed covered with a plain pink eiderdown, and the brass bed rail polished. There were clean floral-patterned curtains at the windows, an old chest of drawers with a snapshot picture of Beattie holding young Ed in her arms when he was a baby, but, most surprising of all, no dirty dishes left in the china washbasin. Sarah thought it was all a far cry from the days when Beattie lived at home, with her bedroom constantly cluttered with clothes that had never been put away, and a bed that was never made until either their mother or Sarah herself had come in to do it. Sarah felt sad, however, to notice the open-sided cot that young Ed was still forced to sleep in, for it was obvious that he was rapidly outgrowing it.

'Not exactly a palace, is it?' called Beattie, as she bustled around looking for two enamel mugs for the tea.

'You've made it very nice,' replied Sarah, tactfully. 'It's – comfortable.'

'Not big enuff fer free of us, though.'

Although Sarah was quite aware that Beattie and young Ed shared their digs with a man, she did not react. She just looked across at the exuberant small boy, who was down on his hands and knees rolling a toy train engine across the cold lino floor. '*He* looks happy enough,' she said blandly.

Beattie pulled out a chair for Sarah to sit on, and they faced each other across the table. 'I share this place with my bloke,' Beattie said, stretching for a packet of Woodbines that were lying in an improvised tin-can ashtray on the other side of the table. 'Yer knew that, din't yer?'

Sarah sat up straight in her chair. 'It's none of my business, Beattie,' she replied, as she watched her light a cigarette. It was the first time she had seen Beattie smoking.

''E's got a temper like a ravin' loony,' said Beattie, resting her elbows on the table. 'Sometimes 'e knocks the livin' daylights out of me.'

Sarah stiffened and froze. 'Then why d'you stay with him?'

'Don't know really. Can't understand it.' Beattie took a deep puff of her fag, inhaled it down into her lungs, and exhaled less than half of it. 'I mean, it's not as though I love 'im,' she said, waving the smoke away with one hand. 'After wot 'appened wiv Ed Lacey, I vowed I'd never ever get 'ooked up wiv no more men. But then – along came Jack Ridley.' She flicked a quick glance at Sarah. 'Still, 'e's a good-looker, I'll say that fer 'im.'

'Is it enough?' asked Sarah, impassively.

Beattie thought about this for a moment. 'No. It's not enuff. But when yer don't know wot life's all about, it 'elps.' She held the fag between her fingers, rolling it over and over and staring at it as though it were a living thing. 'I owe a lot ter Jack. 'E's bin good ter me. If it 'adn't been fer 'im, I wouldn't have this place.'

Sarah continued to stare at her. She was not convinced.

'I don't know where I'm goin', Sarah,' Beattie said, looking and feeling thoroughly downcast. 'I've got a kid I never wanted, and a man who's capable of killin' me.'

Sarah was shocked. 'Killing you?'

Beattie was still playing with her fag. 'Oh, I'm not sayin' 'e'd actually do it, but when 'e loses 'is temper I get really scared.' She finally took a puff of her fag. 'A few weeks ago, 'e give me a real fourpenny one – right 'ere.' She touched her right-hand cheek with the tips of her fingers. 'It puffed up like a football, all blue and bruised. That's why I 'aven't been to visit Mum an' Dad fer a while. I din't want ter upset them.'

Sarah leaned forward and looked straight at her. 'Beattie, why don't you just tell him to go?'

'I can't.'

'Why not?'

'I need 'im.'

Sarah stared at her in disbelief. '*Need* a man who tries to kill you?'

Although Beattie hadn't finished her fag, she stubbed it out in the ashtray. 'Sarah,' she said, putting the unfinished stub in her dress pocket, 'yer don't understand. When yer need somebody, it's not just fer sex, or money, or even friendship, it's becos, becos – they're there. And when they're not there any longer, no matter 'ow bad they've been, yer feel lost and rejected. I know, 'cos 'e once did leave me – only fer a few days, mind yer. We 'ad a row, about nuffin' at all really, but 'e flared up and just walked out on me. I nearly went out of me mind, sittin' 'ere night after night wiv no one ter listen to me, no one ter put up wiv all me grumbles. So I went ter this buildin' site where 'e was workin', and I burst into tears. 'E was so embarrassed, 'e came back 'ome wiv me. It's stupid, ain't it? Night after night I lay at the side of 'im in that bed, and I keep prayin' that 'e'll get out of my life and leave me alone, and then, when 'e does, I want 'im back. I mean, it's not as though I love 'im, 'cos I don't. 'E even asked me ter marry 'im, and I said not on yer nelly!' She looked across the table at her sister. Tears were beginning to swell in her eyes. 'Who'd be a woman, eh, Sarah?'

For a moment or so, there was silence between them – Sarah sitting bolt upright in her chair, and Beattie with hands clenched together on the table in front of her, her head bowed low. Then Sarah tentatively reached out to cover Beattie's hand with her own. It was something she had never been able to do before. 'Beattie,' she said quietly, tenderly.

But Beattie flinched, and quickly removed her hand nervously. 'I've forgotten the milk,' she said, getting up from her chair and hurrying to the door. 'When the kettle boils, could you fill the pot for me? The tea's already in. Won't be long.' With that, she was gone.

For a moment, Sarah was too numb to move. She just sat there, slumped in her chair, casting her mind back over all she had heard during the past few minutes. *'Who'd be a woman, eh, Sarah?'* kept ringing in her ears. Who indeed? she asked herself. It was all so depressing. How could her sister, her own young sister, have allowed her life to get into such a mess? After all, out of the two of them, Beattie was the one who had been the very essence of independence, outgoing, strong, and wilful, able to take on anything and anybody. What had happened to her? Why had Beattie allowed this brute of a man to dominate her life, a man she claimed she didn't even love? Sarah sat back in her chair, covered her face with her hands, and sighed. She found it extremely hard to come to terms with all that had befallen the Melford family over the past few years. Was there no end to their run of ill fortune? Oh God, she thought, if only they could turn back the clock and start all over again.

'Will yer play trains wiv me?'

Sarah removed her hands from her face with a start to find young Ed standing right beside her, his face barely level with the top of the table. 'I – I . . .' She was so taken aback by the small boy's request that for a moment she didn't quite know how to respond.

'*Please*.' The small boy reached out, and tried to take hold of Sarah's hand.

Young Ed's pleas were irresistible, and Sarah knew that there was no way she could refuse. Taking hold of his tiny hand, she got up from her chair, and allowed him to lead her across the room to where his few pieces of train set were laid out on the floor. Both of them dropped to their knees, and within seconds, Sarah was joining him in making all the right train sounds, whistling, hooting, and being every inch the signalman. It was a very odd experience for Sarah, and she had to fight against her true instinct, which frequently reminded her who this small creature at her side really was. Every time she looked at the boy's face, she could see Edward Lacey, the same smile, the same pale blue eyes, even the way he tossed his head back when he laughed. Sarah couldn't explain the deep feeling of emotion that ran through her entire body. One part of her was so consumed with bitterness that she couldn't even bear to feel the boy's hand touching her own. But another part glowed with warmth and affection for him. It was as though their flesh was all from the same body. She suddenly felt an urge to take hold of the boy, and hug him. But she held back, afraid that she might be in danger of becoming fond of him. For a moment or so, she just watched the child, and gradually she saw her whole life flashing before her. Young Ed was what might have been, for her, and she for him. It was a daunting thought, and she agonised over it. She leaned forward, and gently stroked the boy's flaxen-coloured hair. It felt soft and fine in her fingers, and she caressed it affectionately. As she was doing so, she heard Beattie's footsteps coming back up the stairs, but when the door opened, another figure was standing there. It was Jack Ridley.

'Oh yeah?' he said, fixing his gaze on Sarah. 'An' who've we got 'ere then?'

Sarah glared at him only briefly. Then she turned away, as though he didn't even exist.

Christmas Day was a quiet affair for the Melfords. Because of the inclement weather, most of the usual family crowd decided not to turn out, and so, apart from Aunt Dixie, who would rather die than miss a whole day of food and drink, the party was a limited one. However, Geraldine's dream of bringing her two girls back together again under the same roof at last became a reality when, quite unexpectedly, Beattie turned up at the front door on Christmas morning. Jack Ridley, she said, had decided to go and spend Christmas Day with his brother in Stepney, although she wouldn't admit that the real reason was because Ridley couldn't bear to have the kid around his neck all day, and in any case, it would give him and his soak of a brother a chance to drink themselves into a coma for as long as they wanted.

Beattie and little Ed's presence transformed the atmosphere at the family home. Geraldine wept for joy as she watched her grandson playing with the decorations on the Christmas tree, and when they all sat down to open their presents, even Sarah was moved to see the smile on her mother's face. And when the boy climbed on to Samuel's lap, and started to sing 'Away in a Manger' to him, Aunt Dixie was so overcome with emotion that she had to retire to her bedroom for a while to pull herself together. After Christmas lunch of roast chicken, Brussels sprouts, parsnips, cauliflower and roast potatoes, followed by Geraldine's traditional home-made Christmas pudding, everyone gathered round Geraldine's old upright piano whilst she played for a family singsong, which, apart from Christmas carols, included such favourites as 'Early One Morning' and 'Come into the Garden, Maud'. But the highlight of the evening's entertainment was, as usual, Sarah reading a chapter from Charles Dickens's *A Christmas Carol*, during which little Ed fell fast asleep in his grandmother's arms. At the conclusion of the chapter, at the moment when Ebenezer Scrooge became transformed into a figure of goodness to wish Tiny Tim a 'Merry Christmas', something quite extraordinary happened. Until that moment, Samuel Melford had sat in his armchair by the sitting-room fire, his face blank, and his eyes transfixed on the glow from the burning embers. But quite suddenly, he sprang to his feet, and as if echoing what his daughter Sarah had just read out loud, he repeated the same greeting – 'Merry Christmas!' It was the first time for many weeks that he had responded to anything that had been going on around him, and it not only took everyone by surprise, but it was also the first real hope that perhaps a return to even a limited recovery was possible. Everyone sprang to their feet, and they all hugged him together.

Geraldine insisted that Beattie and little Ed stay the night, but as Aunt Dixie was using Beattie's old room, Beattie helped Sarah to make up the bed in the small spare room on the top floor. Little Ed slept through all the preparations, and hadn't even woken up enough to notice himself in a

182

strange bed. Geraldine took Samuel up to his room, and then, reluctantly, she went to bed in her own room.

Aunt Dixie sat up talking to Beattie and Sarah for as long as she could, but when she realised that the bottle of sherry she had been drinking from all evening was getting perilously low, she decided to retire.

Now alone together, Beattie took off her shoes and curled herself up on the sofa, whilst Sarah sat in her father's armchair, and rested her feet on his red velvet footstool. Although the fire was beginning to fade, the room was steeped in a sweet, rich smell of burning elmwood. Sarah had already lowered the flames from the gaslamps on the walls, so that what light remained from the fire cast dancing shadows, which bounced up and down as if part of a magic lantern show.

'I've taken your advice, Sarah.' Beattie's voice was low, but still cut through the calm of the room.

Sarah looked up with a start.

'I'm goin' ter tell Jack Ridley ter push off. It's the best thing fer Ed an' me, an' it's the best fing fer 'im. I should've done it a long time ago, but I couldn't see straight till you 'elped me make up me mind.'

'You mustn't listen to what *I* say, Beattie,' replied Sarah. 'It's your life, yours and Ed's. Only you can make decisions that affect your future.'

'It's not my future I care about,' said Beattie, the dying glow from the fire reflected in her eyes. 'It's the kid's. I don't want 'im ter grow up watchin' me bein' bashed all over the place. An' if I ever saw Jack lay a finger on the boy, I don't know wot I'd do.'

For a moment they both stared into the fire without speaking. Eventually, Sarah asked, 'What happens if this man refuses to go?'

Beattie answered without turning to look at her. 'Then I'll pack me bags and take the kid somewhere else.'

'Where will you go?'

'There's always somewhere. Ridley don't pay me a penny fer 'is keep, so I'm not losin' out on nuffin'. Only trouble is, I'd miss Ma's 'elp. I don't know 'ow I'm goin' ter keep a job wivout 'er.'

'You could always come home.' A few weeks before, Sarah would rather have died than suggest such a thing. But she now knew how vital it was that her young sister should get away from this sadistic man, and she was prepared to do anything in her power to help her.

'No, Sarah,' replied Beattie, putting her feet on the floor, and leaning back on the sofa. 'I've got to work this one out fer meself. All I know is, I've made up me mind,' she said firmly. 'I'm determined ter start the New Year by makin' sense of me life. Once I get rid of Jack Ridley, I never want ter see 'im again as long as I live.'

Sarah was relieved to hear her sister talking like this. Even if she didn't entirely believe her.

Geraldine lay in her bed in the dark, with her mind churning over all the things that had happened during the day. Most nights she couldn't sleep, and then she would lie awake reflecting on all the good times the family used to have, especially when Sarah and Beattie were children, and she and Samuel were able to enjoy all the love and comforts of married life together. But since Samuel's illness had first taken hold, she had spent so many nights in anguish and despair, fearing for her husband's state of mind, for her children, and for the future. Many a night she had cried herself to sleep, for there seemed to be no end to her problems, no future to look forward to. But tonight was different. She had seen her children get together under the same roof, sharing the delights of the family Christmas, her only grandchild laughing and romping around the house, and that restored her faith in what life was all about. For the first time in two years, she felt able to close her eyes, and fall asleep with a gentle smile on her face. It was all so perfect. If only Samuel was there to share the night with her, like he used to for so much of their married life – oh, how wonderful that would be. No more heartache, no more loneliness.

In her few moments of reflection, Geraldine had failed to notice the figure slipping quietly into her room. She couldn't see who it was sliding into her bed beneath the eiderdown, but she knew, and her heart started thumping with joy.

'I've come home.'

Samuel's voice was barely audible, but as Geraldine turned to greet her husband, they soon snuggled up together. It was just like old times.

As the New Year rolled in, the fortunes of the Melford family seemed to take a dramatic turn for the better. Not only were Sarah and Beattie making strenuous efforts to establish a relationship that they had both denied each other over the years, but Samuel's mind, although not as focused and logical as during his working life, was at least showing some signs of normality. However, although Beattie had always been Samuel's favourite, it was Sarah who gradually gave him the impetus to talk and take notice of life around him again.

One Sunday afternoon on the first weekend of the New Year, Sarah and her mother decided to try to reacquaint Samuel with the old towpath alongside the Islington Canal just beneath the Caledonian Bridge. For years this had been one of Samuel's most treasured spots, and when his illness became so severe that he was unable to go there alone, he sank into a state of abject despair. And so, with the blessing of his doctor, Samuel strolled with his wife and daughter to the bridge, and they made their way down the steps to the towpath, where, to their delight, a barge, towed by a magnificent long-haired black and white cart horse, was just coming into view. Samuel quickly took his place on his usual bench, and with Geraldine and Sarah at his side, he waited for the long, narrow, flat-bottomed boat to approach.

After the recent falls of snow, the towpath itself was still covered with a thin layer of slush that had turned to ice, and it was easy to see that the poor creature, who was attached to the forward section of the barge by a rope tied to its harness, had some difficulty in keeping its balance on the frozen grass.

'Wonderful! Wonderful!'

Samuel's excitement was a delight for Geraldine and Sarah to see, and as the barge drew closer and closer, they were thrilled by his enthusiasm, and his ability to recognise something that had meant so much to him in the past.

'This must be your New Year resolution, Father,' said Sarah, her arm around his shoulders. 'From now on, you must come to this favourite place of yours at least once a week.'

To Sarah's astonishment, he suddenly took hold of her hand and kissed it. Then he hugged his wife, who was seated beside him.

'Dear God,' said Geraldine, in soft, gentle prayer. 'Thank you for giving me back my Samuel. Thank you for giving me back my family.'

The old barge horse was now almost parallel with them, and for the first time, they could see that the cargo on the vessel was a pile of scrap iron, probably destined for a factory somewhere in the north of England. High above them, seagulls squawked, and, much to the disdain of the local sparrows, swooped low over the canal and skimmed the surface of the shimmering ice-cold water. By the time the horse and barge had reached the small party huddled together around the bench, the excitement proved too much for Samuel, and, to gales of laughter from his wife and daughter, he leaped up from the bench, and slowly followed the huge horse as it plodded its way along the path towards the bridge. Sarah and Geraldine also got up from the bench, and followed him.

'I mean what I said, Mother,' said Sarah, as they picked their way carefully along the icy path. 'We must bring him here as often as possible, get him used to things he did in the past. I'm convinced this is a new start for Father.'

Geraldine was clinging on to Sarah's arm as they walked. 'Oh, I do pray so, my dear. I do pray so.'

Samuel was now far ahead of them, following the barge horse as he gradually started to move along the towpath beneath the bridge. Then, delirious with the excitement of being back where he belonged, Samuel suddenly made a dash towards the old horse in what seemed to be an effort to pat it affectionately on the rump before it disappeared under the bridge. But in one swift movement, he tripped over the long towrope, and plunged head first into the icy waters of the canal.

Geraldine screamed out at the top of her voice, 'Samuel . . .!'

'Father . . .!'

Sarah couldn't believe what she had seen, for by the time she had reached the spot where her father had fallen in, he was struggling to keep afloat. She immediately fell to her

187

knees, and despite the slippery conditions on the ice, she stretched out her hand in a desperate effort to grab hold of him. But her father, whose face was only just visible above the surface of the water, seemed quite bewildered, as though he couldn't understand what was happening to him, and although Sarah briefly managed to cling on to the shoulder of his overcoat, he quickly slipped away out of sight.

'No, Father! No . . .!'

'Sam – uel . . .!'

The cries of panic and despair soon brought a crowd of people hurrying down from the bridge above, and the skipper of the barge immediately brought his horse to a halt. But it was all too late. Samuel had been sucked down into the muddy, ice-cold waters of the canal.

Part 2

1930 – 1931

Chapter 13

Ed Melford was no cissy. Thanks to Jack Ridley, he could rough and tumble with the rest of them, despite the fact that his body seemed to be no more than flesh and bones, held together with short trousers that were cut down from an old pair of Ridley's, and braces that didn't have enough buttons to cling on to. The trouble was that young Ed's passion was reading books – any books that he could lay his hands on, and newspapers too – and that, for an eleven-year-old from the wilder side of life meant that, to the gangs down the Bunk, he was his mum's darling, a number-one cissy. Ed, however, couldn't care less what any of the local 'spunks' felt about him, for what he lacked in brawn, he made up for with a brain that was constantly hungry for information. Mind you, it wasn't easy living with a mum who couldn't care less about what was going on in the world around her, and a stepfather who only ever read kids' comics such as the *Dandy*, and the *Beano*. Ed's interest was further roused by the fact that the country was going through one of the worst depressions of the century, with so many people out of work that, as a young, politically minded prodigy, he feared it would lead to riots in the streets.

Ever since she had taken the plunge and married Jack Ridley five years before, Beattie had spent most of her time either struggling, as the only wage-earner in the family, to

191

keep her job at the candle factory, or fighting with her neighbours down the Bunk, who considered her a 'stuck-up little cow' who should push off back to her own type on the other side of Islington.

That wasn't, of course, Beattie's only problem, for during the past nine years the state of her relationship with Sarah had swung back and forth like a yo-yo. When Beattie had opened her heart to Sarah during that eventful Christmas at the family home in Thornhill Road, it seemed as though they would finally be able to create a close bond, and after their father died both had made strenuous efforts to become friends, if only for their mother's sake. But personal and financial pressures burdened the whole family and all changes seemed to be for the worse.

Since then, the diabolical economic recession had overwhelmed the country, and despite Sarah's efforts to keep up with the seemingly endless bills, it was becoming an impossible task to maintain such a large house. The crunch came the year before when, after a long illness, their mother died of pneumonia. Geraldine had never really got over the untimely death of her husband, and when she succumbed again to flu, then developed pneumonia, she had neither the energy nor the will to survive.

To everyone's dismay, neither Samuel Melford nor his wife had made a will. It was therefore left to Sarah to sort out the mess, and the first thing she did was to put the house up for sale. During this period, relations between Sarah and Beattie had once again become strained. It was clear that Beattie's marriage to Jack Ridley, which she had vowed was something she would never do, had completely undermined the new-found confidence Sarah had in her young sister.

'How can you marry a man who tries to kill you?' Sarah

had asked, with incredulity. 'One minute he's everything you despise, and the next minute you're back in bed sleeping with him!'

Beattie had not taken Sarah's outburst lightly, especially when Sarah had accused Jack Ridley of frequently trying to 'touch' her whenever they had been left alone together.

'Yer'll never change, will yer, Sarah?' Beattie snapped back at her angrily. 'No wonder Edward bloody Lacey never laid 'ands on yer!'

After all the help and advice she had offered Beattie over recent years, this one remark had hurt Sarah most of all, and she vowed to herself that one day she would find a way to pay back her young sister for all the harm and pain she had caused her.

One day during the summer of 1930, Beattie discovered that she had yet another problem to cope with.

'Disappeared? The kid?' Ridley had only just got back home from another day job-hunting, and he was in no mood for any more bouts of Beattie's hysteria.

'I tell yer 'e should've bin 'ome from school nearly two hours ago!' snapped a near-panic-stricken Beattie, who had been waiting in desperation with Ma Briggs on the front doorstep of the house for Ridley's return. 'I went up the school, an' 'is teacher said 'e din't turn up all day.'

Exasperated, Ridley pulled off his flat cap, and scratched his head. 'So wot yer goin' on about then? Most kids 'is age do a bunk from school when they feel like it.'

Beattie came back at him like a flash. ''Ow would you know? You never 'ad a day's learnin' in yer life!'

Ridley wanted to cuff her, but with Ma there, he thought better of it. 'So wot d'yer want me ter do about it? Search the streets of bleedin' London?'

'See if yer can find Big Ben,' pleaded Beattie. "E'll know wot ter do.'

'Big Ben!' Ridley almost choked. 'If yer fink I'm goin' ter ask fer a bleedin' bluebottle's 'elp, yer've got anuvver fink comin'. 'Aven't yer 'eard? Me an' the law don't mix.'

'Ed's only a kid, Jack,' protested Beattie. "E's our son.'

'*Your* son,' retorted Ridley. 'Not mine.'

'Little monkey,' said Ma, whose eyes were anxiously scanning each end of the road. 'That's wot yer get fer too much book readin'. That boy's got too many fancy ideas in 'is 'ead.'

'This is no time ter keep goin' on about 'im!' spluttered Beattie, the palms of her hands pressed anxiously against her cheeks. 'Fer all we know 'e could be lying dead on some railway line. Remember that kid they found on the track at Canning Town the uvver week?'

Ma Briggs shook her head vigorously. 'Our Ed ain't lyin' on no railway line,' she said confidently. 'E's got too much sense ter do fings like that.'

'If yer looked after yer bleedin' kids, yer wouldn't 'ave so much trouble wiv 'em!' The woman's voice shrieking from an upstairs window a couple of doors away caused everyone to swing round and look up.

'You talkin' ter me, cow face?' yelled Beattie, unceremoniously.

'You ain't got cloff ear'oles!' came the terse reply.

Beattie immediately rushed along to the front door gate of her rowdy neighbour, and, shaking her fist, yelled, 'You come down 'ere, mate, an I'll show yer wot I've got!'

At that moment, an empty milk bottle came crashing down from another upstairs window in the same house, landing in pieces on the pavement just behind where Beattie was standing. This was followed by another woman's voice

yelling, 'Go back 'ome an' look after yer kids, loud mouff!'
This was followed by a man's voice yelling out to all of
them, 'Keep yer voices down! Wot d'yer fink this is, a
bleedin' circus?' Within seconds, people's heads were
peering out of their windows, shouting, yelling, waving, most
of their abuse directed at Beattie, who was taking them all
on. Pretty soon, bits of rubbish were being hurled at her by
some of the Bunk's teenage gangs, which prompted Ma
Briggs to take up the cudgel. 'If any of this stuff catches
me,' she bellowed, 'I'll 'ave yer guts fer garters!' Beattie
and Ridley had to duck as pieces of roof tiles came hurtling
towards them.

'All right then,' boomed a deep-throated voice from
nearby. 'Let's 'ave yer!'

Beattie turned with a start to find Big Ben, the burly PC
Ben Fodder, hurrying straight across the road towards them.

'It's about time you turned up,' Beattie yelled. 'They're
all bleedin' mad round 'ere!'

Big Ben's massive frame towered above her, and he
carried so much weight that one or two of his tunic buttons
were positively tugging at their holes. But his was a kind
face, completely round and podgy. 'So what's goin' on, Mrs
Ridley?' he asked, aware that at the precise moment of his
appearance, Jack Ridley had discreetly disappeared back
inside the house.

'My boy, Ed – 'e 'asn't come 'ome from school,' replied
Beattie, feverishly. 'Yer've got ter find 'im!'

'Take it easy now, missus,' said Big Ben. 'Let's get some
facts down first. Wot time was 'e supposed ter be back?'

'Over two hours ago,' chimed in Ma Briggs. ''E's usually
back dead on five past four every day.'

Big Ben passed only a brief, dismissive glance at Ma.
He'd known her for years. ''As 'e gone off wiv 'is pals, or

somefin'?' he suggested. 'Maybe they've gone off ter play football up Finsbury Park.'

'Yer don't understand,' said Beattie, urgently. ''E didn't turn up at school all day.'

Big Ben took a beat, and straightened up. 'Ah!' he exclaimed. 'Playin' 'ookey, is 'e?' He took out his notebook and pencil from a top pocket in his uniform. ''Asn't anyone round 'ere seen 'im all day then?'

'This lot?' snapped Beattie, scathingly. 'Just look at 'em – scum of the earth!' But when she turned round to glare back at her tormentors, the entire street was deserted, not a soul now at any of the windows.

To Beattie's irritation, Big Ben was busily scribbling in his notebook. 'I'll get this down to the station down 'Ornsey Road right away,' he said. 'If your lad's playin' truant again, our boys in blue'll find 'im.'

Beattie and Ma Briggs exchanged a puzzled look. 'What d'yer mean playing truant *again*?' Beattie asked. 'Are you sayin' 'e's done this before?'

Big Ben looked up from his notebook. 'Who – young Ed?' he answered with a wry smile. ''Course 'e 'as. Well, that's wot they told me down the school. I give the boy a good talkin'-to after the last time. I told 'im next time 'e did a bunk, I'd be on ter 'im faster than a dose of salts.' Then, aware of Beattie's pained expression, he added, 'Now don't you go worryin' yerself, Mrs Ridley. I'll find your boy if I 'ave ter scour every street in Islin'ton.'

Sarah got home late from work that day. Usually she left Mrs Ranasinghe round about four in the afternoon, but just lately the old Ceylonese lady had been in talkative mood, which was a sure sign that she was desperate for company, so by the time Sarah got on the bus in Tollington Road, it was already past six in the evening.

The bus journey home took less than ten minutes, and Sarah always used the opportunity to relax and look out of the downstairs window. The Caledonian Road looked particularly busy today, for Cattle Market day always brought a stream of visitors from outside the borough, which meant that the shops were full. Sarah wondered how, in a time of such poverty and depression, people managed to find the money to buy anything. None the less, every time she came on this journey, a faint, wistful smile came to her face, particularly when she passed the tobacconist's shop on the corner of Offord Road, where she could still visualise her dear late mother going to buy her husband one of his favourite brands of cigar. But the recession had taken a toll on so many small shops and businesses. Sarah's favourite chandler shop, where she could buy anything from candles to split peas, had been one of the first victims, closely followed by Peg's Wool Shop, Ernie White's China, overflowing with jugs and washbasins and commodes decorated with grass and poppies, the Cally Live Snake Market, and Mr Murphy's Funeral Parlour, where both Samuel and Geraldine Melford had been laid out in open coffins prior to their burial in the Islington Cemetery. As she looked out on to what was once a thriving shopping area, Sarah felt nothing but disdain for the endless stream of politicians who, over the years, had reduced the country to such a parlous state. The current offenders, Ramsay MacDonald and his Labour Government, had a lot to answer for.

Once she had got off the bus, Sarah stopped briefly to buy six pennyworth of sweet broken biscuits from Mrs Miller's, the baker on the corner of Richmond Avenue. Then she made her way home, passing St Andrew's Church on

197

the way, where she could hear the sound of choir practice taking place in preparation for the Harvest Festival service in a few weeks' time.

'Sarah!'

Sarah turned, to find her long-time friend Winnie Carter waving to her from across the road. Holding her hand was her four-year-old daughter, Melanie. Sarah waved back.

'I was beginning to think I'd never see you again,' Winnie called, as she led her little girl across the road to talk to Sarah. 'I thought you must have sold the house at last. You haven't, have you?'

Sarah shook her head. 'No such luck,' she sighed. 'I don't think I ever will.' She leaned down and smiled sweetly at Winnie's little girl. 'Hello, Melanie,' she said. 'And how are *you* today?'

'Say hello to Auntie Sarah,' urged Winnie. But the small child turned away and hid behind her mother's back. 'Don't be so silly, Mellie,' Winnie chided. 'You know Auntie Sarah. She's our friend.'

Sarah decided not to pressurise the child, who was prone to tears. But she was pleased to see Winnie again, if only for a few fleeting moments. Since her mother had died, Sarah seemed to have drifted apart from so many of her friends, mainly because the worry of trying to keep on the family house was weighing down on her.

'It seems so absurd that you haven't been able to find a buyer,' said Winnie. Marriage to Bank Manager Frederick Allsop clearly suited her well, for she had filled out immensely since the days when she and Sarah used to spend so much time together. 'How long is it now since you first put it on the market?'

Sarah shrugged her shoulders. 'I can't remember, Winnie,' she replied. 'It feels like years.'

'It's a crying shame,' asserted Winnie. 'It's such a beautiful house. If it wasn't for the fact that there's so little money around these days, I'm sure it would have been snapped up a long time ago.' She put her hand affectionately on Sarah's arm. 'You've had such rotten luck, Sarah.'

Sarah smiled at her. Dear Winnie, she thought. She must try to see her more often. 'Other people have more to put up with, Winnie,' she said. 'At least I have a roof over my head.'

'Well, as I've told you before, and I'll tell you again – ' Sarah could tell that Winnie was in one of her practical moods, for the shoulders of her small, ample frame were now pulled back firmly – 'if ever you need any help, you know where to come. Thank God, Frederick is still earning a good salary, and we can always loan you something till you get on your feet.'

Winnie's words really cheered Sarah, so she leaned forward and kissed her gently on the cheek. 'Thank you, Winnie,' she said warmly. 'You really are such a good friend.'

'And you're a good friend to me too,' insisted Winnie. 'You always have been, and always will – even after we've gone.'

Sarah looked at her with a start. 'Gone?' she asked.

'I haven't seen you to tell you, Sarah,' she said. 'Frederick's been told he has to take over a new branch. He can't say no, not the way jobs are at the moment. It's down in Kingston, in Surrey.'

Sarah put her hand to her mouth in dismay. 'In Surrey. Does that mean you'll be moving down there – to live?'

Winnie nodded. 'The house comes with the job. But it's not really all that far,' she said reassuringly. 'You must come down and see us – spend a Sunday with us all. It'll be like old times.'

Sarah smiled back bravely. 'Thank you, Winnie,' she said.

'I'd like that.' But as she took her leave of her friend, she found it difficult to disguise her dismay.

Clutching her modest bag of broken biscuits, Sarah made her way back home. She hardly noticed which street she was walking along, for her mind was too weighed down with the news she had just heard. It wasn't just the fact that Winnie was leaving the neighbourhood that hurt, but the pain she felt for the aimless direction of her own life. Now that she had passed thirty years of age, Sarah had begun to think of herself as an 'old maid'. Even if she had wanted to find a man and get married like Winnie, she saw no prospect of ever doing so. Between them, Beattie and Edward Lacey had thoroughly demoralised her, made her feel sexless and unattractive. But the main problem was that she wasn't yet self-sufficient enough emotionally to live a life without close friends like Winnie.

As she turned into Thornhill Road, she paused briefly to look up at the house that had been at the heart of the Melford family for so many years, and for one fleeting moment she wondered whether mere bricks and mortar were worth all the heartache she had had to endure since the death of her parents. The iron gates at the front garden entrance had still not been replaced since they'd been removed by the Borough Council to provide scrap for the war effort in 1915, and this somehow immediately presented an image of a house that had had its day, and was now only waiting for the winter of its life. But as she made her way up to the front door, Sarah refused to let her despair affect the deep sense of love she felt, and would always feel, for this very special place.

Inside, Sarah again had to face an intrinsically depressing atmosphere. With so much of the furniture sold to pay the bills, it was no longer the home it used to be. The rooms were barren and soulless, the walls were desperate for a coat of paint, there was a smell of emptiness and decay about the place, and as she moved from one room to another, her feet echoed on stone floors that no longer had any carpets. But despite her feelings of desolation, Sarah refused to feel sorry for herself. Life couldn't be like that, she thought. After all, the good Lord had only given every one of us a certain amount of time to live, so life had to be practical and uplifting. Striding across the hall that had once reverberated to the sounds of two small sisters rushing up and down the stairs, to her father arriving home at the front door after a busy day in his office at Gamages, and to the sweet, pervasive smells of her mother's home-cooking, Sarah made her way straight into the kitchen.

After placing the bag of broken biscuits on the kitchen table, she put the kettle on to make herself a cup of tea. As she took off her small summer hat and placed it on a chair, she was suddenly alarmed to hear a movement coming from the pantry. She wasn't quite sure what the sound was, for it was only slight, which led her to believe that a mouse had moved in. Warily, she approached the pantry, and in one swift, brave act, pulled open the door.

'Oh my God!' she gasped.

Curled up beneath the lower pantry shelf, doing his best to make himself as tiny as possible, was Beattie's boy, young Ed.

'Ed!' Sarah cried. 'What on earth are you doing here?'

Reluctantly, the boy crawled out, and allowed his aunt to help him to his feet. 'I came ter see yer,' he said awkwardly.

'Well, couldn't you just come to the front and knock on the door? How did you get in without a key?'

'Yer left the window open. Over there.' He pointed to a tiny window high up on the wall near the door, which was open, but hardly big enough for a cat to crawl through, let

201

alone a growing eleven-year-old boy.

Sarah shook her head in disbelief. 'Does your mother know you're here?'

The boy shook his head.

'You should have asked her first.'

Ed shrugged his shoulders.

It had been almost a year since Sarah had last seen her nephew, and she was dismayed at how thin he was, hardly enough flesh on his bones to make a meat stew, as her mother used to say. 'Are you hungry?' she asked.

He nodded vigorously.

Sarah led him across to the table. 'Come and sit here and have some biscuits. I'll make you a dripping sandwich.'

Ed did as he was told, and immediately started tucking in.

Sarah made him a sandwich of beef dripping. It was only a matter of minutes before he started gorging himself on what was, for him, a feast, the first meal he had had all day. Whilst she watched him eating, Sarah poured him a glass of ginger beer, and when he downed it without coming up for breath, she quickly poured him another. It was a curious experience for her to see the boy sitting at her own kitchen table, and it took all her self-control to discard all thoughts about the role his father had played in her life. She waited until he had practically demolished both the biscuits and the dripping sandwich before she started to question him.

'Why did you come here, Ed?' she asked.

Before answering, the boy wiped his mouth on the back of his hand. 'I told yer. I wanted ter see yer.'

Sarah removed her hat from the second chair, then sat opposite him at the table. 'You've never tried to see me before, Ed,' she said. 'What do you want with me?'

The boy burped, then pulled himself up, and sat cross-

202

legged on the chair. Sarah noticed how dirty he looked, but decided against forcing him to have a wash until he had had a chance to talk. ''Ave yer got any books?' the boy asked.

Sarah was puzzled. 'Books?'

'*Any* books,' continued the boy. 'I can read, yer know. I'm not so good at writin', but I can read anyfin' yer like.'

Sarah could hardly believe what she was hearing. 'You mean, you've come all the way up here to ask me for a book?'

Ed nodded.

Sarah scratched her head. 'Don't they give you books to read at school?'

The boy snapped back immediately, 'I don't like school, an' the books they give yer are stupid.'

'Stupid?'

'They're fer kids.'

Sarah found herself smiling. For some strange reason, she felt good. 'So – what kind of books do you *like* to read?'

Again the boy answered immediately. 'About foreign countries. About politics.'

Sarah was not sure if she was hearing right. Although she remembered how advanced at talking the boy had been at a very early age, it seemed incredible to her that at the age of eleven, he could possibly have an interest in such an absurdly grown-up topic as politics. 'Why haven't you asked your mother to get you some books like that?'

'Mum never talks ter me,' Ed replied, seemingly more interested in playing with his foot than concentrating on what his aunt was saying to him. 'All *she* ever says is that working-class people are the scum of the earth.'

Sarah's eyes opened wide in disbelief. Could it really be possible that, after all these years, Beattie was turning against the very type that had meant so much to her?

'She's stupid, my mum,' continued the boy. 'She don't

know nuffin' about the rich an' the poor.'

'And do *you* know?' asked Sarah.

'Poor people 'ave ter work fer their livin',' the boy replied, instantly. 'Rich people don't. They 'ave uvver people ter do the work for them.'

Sarah certainly found it illuminating to hear this from such a young mind. But in a strange kind of way, despite the simplicity of the boy's thinking, there was a sort of logic there somewhere. As she watched him sketching out imaginary figures on the tablecloth with his fingernail, she couldn't help imagining what the boy's father – his real father – would have thought about him. 'You know, Ed,' she said, trying to make eye contact with him, 'as you grow older, you'll discover that it takes all sorts to make a world. The poor need the rich, as much as the rich need the poor. In a sane world, there shouldn't be any poor. But what's really important is that we all talk to each other. Your grandfather used to say that if people ever stopped talking to each other, the world would come to an end.'

'Did you ever talk to *your* dad?' asked Ed.

The boy's question was so reasonable, but so direct, that it took Sarah by surprise. 'Yes,' she recalled. 'Your grandfather and I often used to talk together.'

'What about?'

'All kinds of things. We used to discuss what we read in the newspapers.'

'The only newspapers *I* read are the ones they let me 'ave down the chip shop.'

Sarah reached across the table, and was about to touch his hand. But then she thought better of it. 'It won't always be like that, Ed,' she said reassuringly. 'Some day you'll be able to afford a newspaper of your own.'

'Can I 'ave a book then?'

Sarah sighed. 'I'll see what I can find.' She got up from the table, but before she made for the door, said, 'If you want, you can come and see me again. When you come home from school.'

Ed replied, without looking up, 'I don't go ter school.'

'What do you mean?'

'I told yer. I don't like goin' ter school. The teachers don't know nuffin'. They're all stupid. Mum finks I go ter school, but I don't. I stay away lots of days.'

Sarah was horrified. 'Ed!' she snapped. 'Are you telling me you play truant?'

He merely shrugged his shoulders.

She rushed back to him, and made him sit up in his chair. 'Now listen to me. If you keep away from school, then you can keep away from me. Do you understand?'

He shrugged again.

'School may not be perfect, Ed,' she continued, 'but it's the best hope you have of learning all the things you want to know about. Now I'm going into the next room to see if I can find something for you amongst Grandfather's collection of books. If I let you have one, you must promise me that from now on, you won't miss one single day of school. And even more important, you won't lie to your mother. Is that clear?'

Again, the boy shrugged his shoulders.

Sarah shook her head in despair. Then she left him whilst she went off to look for a book in one of the large packing cases in the sitting room. She eventually came across a mammoth-looking thing called *The Class War – Struggle for Survival*, and was convinced that if that wasn't enough to put an eleven-year-old off politics for the rest of his life, nothing was. Hardly able to carry the monstrosity, she returned to the kitchen.

When she got there, Beattie's boy was curled up on the floor. He was fast asleep.

Chapter 14

At the beginning of September, Sarah had an unexpected offer for the family house in Thornhill Road that she couldn't refuse. It was a pretty paltry offer, almost half the real pre-war market value, but as she was desperate to pay off the mountain of bills outstanding on even the basic maintenance of the house, she had no alternative but to accept. It was a hard decision for her to take, especially as the buyer, a repellent character with the flowery name of Sebastian Plomley, was a property speculator, who clearly had no intention of using the place as a residence for himself, but was acquiring it purely as some kind of business investment. His spoiled young wife, Dora, was little better, for on first sight of the house her only comment was that it smelled like the place hadn't been lived in for years. Dealing with people like this had confirmed a feeling that had been growing steadily in Sarah's mind for some years, that people who had money generally lived their lives wanting more money. It had also not escaped her notice that, with the exception of Aunt Dixie, since the death of Sarah's parents, none of their families had offered any financial help, nor even consolation for the predicament Sarah had found herself in. Fair-weather friends, she told herself. There was no doubt that she was gradually becoming disillusioned by the so-called middle-class values she had been brought up with.

It was fortunate that, following her initial meeting with the unpalatable Mr Plomley and his spouse, Sarah had no need to deal directly with them. However, on the day that contracts on the sale were finally exchanged, Sarah had a quite different, though not entirely unexpected problem to deal with.

'No money left over? Who're *you* kiddin'?'

It was clear from the start that Beattie attached little importance to the day's events, for she had turned up at the house with not only young Ed in tow, but also Jack Ridley. It was an incongruous sight, for all three were togged up in their Sunday best, and Sarah was astonished to see Ridley wearing a tie, an accoutrement she had always firmly believed he did not possess.

'I'm afraid it's true, Beattie,' said Sarah, as she led the bizarre trio into a sitting room now stripped bare of everything but for two wooden stools, and a pouffe. 'If you remember, I warned you a long time ago that the expenses for maintaining this house far outweighed what I was able to afford out of my own modest income. However, it is just possible that once the legal costs of selling the place have been settled, there may be a little something left over for the two of us to divide between us.'

Beattie's eyes narrowed suspiciously. 'A little somefin'?' she pressed. ''Ow much?'

For a brief moment, Sarah stared directly into her sister's eyes. She found it hard to believe that those were the same eyes that had once pleaded with her for forgiveness. 'I don't know where I'm going,' Beattie had sobbed. 'Who'd be a woman, eh, Sarah?' It seemed a lifetime away. What she saw before her now was a self-confident, calculating little creature who had worked it out in her mind that she might be missing out on something. Or was it her? With someone like Jack Ridley at her side, Beattie was stripped of all sense of decency, and was quite capable of anything.

'A few pounds,' replied Sarah.

Beattie's eyes darted back at her. 'A few pounds? Does that mean 'undreds?'

'It means no more than a *few* pounds, Beattie.'

Beattie exchanged a quick, angry look with Ridley, then immediately turned back to Sarah. 'It's not possible,' she growled. 'Wot about all the furniture yer sold, an' all the rest of the stuff? That must've brought in a penny or two.'

'I sent you a list of everything I've sold. Every penny was put towards Father's debts.'

'You're not tellin' me that there wasn't enuff there ter cover the bills?' insisted Beattie.

Exasperated, Sarah went to the mantelpiece, picked up an old filing box, plunged her hand in, and pulled out a wad of bills. She thrust them at Beattie. 'Here!' she snapped. 'Take a look for yourself.'

Beattie, taken aback, had no alternative but to take the bills.

'You will find there a monthly account of all outstanding bills to date. Once payment of three thousand, two hundred pounds has been received for the sale of this house, the account will be in credit to the sum of approximately six hundred and twenty-four pounds.'

Beattie's face immediately lit up. 'There you are then! There *is* somefin' left over.'

'That, of course,' said Sarah, cutting straight through her sister's fatuous remark, 'is before the main outstanding debt has been accounted for.'

Beattie looked puzzled. 'Wot yer talkin' about?' she asked, half suspiciously but also warily.

Sarah, who had been waiting for this moment with Beattie

for a very long time, decided to make the most of it. 'Two years before he died,' she said, turning her back on Beattie, and strolling to the window with arms firmly crossed, 'Father took out a mortgage to cover the debt he had incurred through gambling.'

Beattie was now really shocked. 'Father – gambled?' she gasped.

Sarah, at the window, turned round to face her. Her figure was now little more than a silhouette. 'Everything – from horse racing to cock fighting. At the time of his death, he owed more than one thousand, seven hundred pounds.'

Beattie suddenly dropped the wad of bills to the floor. Young Ed rushed forward, and on hands and knees, scrabbled round to pick them up.

As she slowly strolled back to join her sister, Sarah could smell the smoke from Ridley's fag. Ever since they'd entered the room, she had been constantly aware of his presence, for although he kept silent throughout, she knew that he was taking in every word she said. 'Soon after Father died,' she continued, 'I went to see Mr Levinson, Father's bank manager. He told me that the debts were now the responsibility of our father's estate, and that his heirs would be expected to honour them. After careful persuasion, Mr Levinson agreed to let me take out a ten-year loan. I've been paying it back ever since.' She turned round to look at Beattie, who was now in such a state of shock that she had had to sit down on one of the stools. Satisfied that she had taken the wind out of Beattie's sails, Sarah concluded, 'At the current time, the outstanding balance stands at three hundred and ninety-two pounds, seven shillings, and seven pence.'

Young Ed finally succeeded in picking up the last of the bills, which he offered to his mother, who pushed them away. So instead he gave them back to his aunt, who put them straight away into the filing box.

'Why din't yer tell me about all this before?' asked Beattie, who looked shattered.

'You never asked me,' replied Sarah, acidly. 'In fact, as I recall, the only single thing you have ever asked me since our parents' death was in reference to what funds might legally be available to you – as your birthright, of course.'

'I fink that's bein' a bit 'ard on yer sister, Sarah,' said Ridley, as he strolled across to join them. 'I mean, she was only enquirin' about wot she's entitled to.'

'Really, Mr Ridley?' Sarah replied. Ever since she had first set eyes on the man, she had stubbornly resisted calling him by his first name. 'In that case, I'm sure your wife will be willing to share the responsibility of paying off the remainder of our father's debts. That would amount to the sum of one hundred and ninety-six pounds, three shillings, and ninepence halfpenny. Under the circumstances, I'll be willing to forego the rest of Father's debts that I myself have paid off over the past few years.'

Ridley had a wry smile on his face. ''Ow generous of yer.'

'Thank you,' Sarah replied, with her own wry smile.

For one very brief moment the two of them stared hard at each other. Both had wills and determination of their own, and though Ridley was a manipulator and Sarah a pragmatist, there was definitely a spark of mutual recognition.

'I fink we should go 'ome,' said Beattie, getting up wearily from her stool. 'No point in 'angin' round 'ere.' She looked round the cold, unwelcoming room, and for the first time, it suddenly dawned on her that she would never again see the place in which she had spent the formative years of her life.

''Ang on a minute, Beat,' said Ridley, who was still sizing up Sarah. 'Yer 'aven't asked yer sister wot 'appens to 'er

211

now she 'as ter move out of 'ere.'

Beattie shrugged her shoulders, and made for the door.

'Oh, you mustn't concern yourself about me, Mr Ridley,' replied Sarah, with false politeness. 'I've found myself some suitable accommodation – elsewhere. But thank you for your concern. It's much appreciated.'

Ridley now had a broad grin on his face. He liked, even admired Sarah's boldness. No one had ever played this kind of defiant game with him before, and it intrigued him. 'Well, if we can 'elp yer out any time,' he said, 'yer know where we live. Give us a shout.'

Sarah's expression was fixed as she watched Ridley put on his cap and follow Beattie to the door.

He turned to give a lingering look at Sarah. 'Be seein' yer then.'

Sarah watched him go without replying. All the time she had been in his presence, she had felt quite sick.

'Yer didn't sell Granddad's books, did yer?'

Until that moment, Sarah had forgotten about young Ed, who had spent most of the time sitting cross-legged on the bare floorboards in the corner of the room, mesmerised by a small brown cockroach, which had somehow toppled over on to its back, its tiny legs kicking helplessly in the air.

'No, Ed,' replied Sarah, going to him. 'I haven't sold any of Grandfather's books. I've kept plenty of them back for you.'

'Why did Granddad lose all 'is money?' asked the boy, quite innocently, whilst keeping his attention firmly fixed on the cockroach.

Sarah sighed. 'He made mistakes, Ed,' she replied, squatting down alongside him. 'It's something we are all capable of doing from time to time, but some people don't know how to put things right.'

'Was 'e a bad man?'

Sarah shook her head. 'No,' she replied. 'Your grandmother and grandfather were two of the kindest, most wonderful people who ever lived. When you were little, they loved you dearly.'

'I wish I was dead too,' said the boy. 'I could meet Granddad, an' we could talk about all sorts of fings – about 'is books an' fings.'

A cold shiver ran up and down Sarah's spine. For one brief moment, her young nephew's chilling remark had distressed and amazed her. But the more she thought about it, the more she realised what truth it had. Yes, young Ed and his granddad would have had a fine old time together talking about books – any books. In fact, Sarah reckoned that Samuel Melford would have found quite a lot in common with his grandson.

Beattie didn't sleep that night. She lay awake for hours thinking about her father's gambling, and the pile of debts he had incurred. Try as she may, she couldn't rid herself of the guilt she felt for letting Sarah take on the burden of paying back those debts, and for daring to imagine that she, Beattie, should be entitled to any kind of inheritance. Jack Ridley, of course, was no help. These days, their relationship hardly existed. They rarely slept together, and even when they did, it was usually when Ridley came home drunk and collapsed on to the bed. Night after night, Beattie asked herself why she had ever married such a man, for she knew for a fact that he was sleeping around with every whore in Islington, and he treated young Ed as though he was nothing more than a bit of horse dung. She had never worked out why he had married her either. At least, not until today. *'Yer stupid cow!'* he had ranted the moment they had left Thornhill Road after

213

Sarah had dashed their hopes of a windfall. 'Can't yer see, she's pulled a fast one on yer? She's made a bucket out of that house and you've let 'er get away wiv it!' Beattie turned restlessly from one side to the other. Yes, she was a stupid cow all right, for not realising before what Ridley was after when he practically frog-marched her to a five-shilling wedding up the registry office. If it wasn't for young Ed, she would be glad that there was no money from the sale of the old family home. But when she sat up in bed, and looked across at the boy, and saw him snuggled up on his pathetic second-hand mattress on the floor in the corner, she felt consumed with guilt and frustration that she had ever allowed herself to be dragged down by such a two-faced go-getter as Ridley. The only thing she did not regret was the time when she had secretly got rid of the baby he had forced inside her. 'Good riddance ter bad rubbish!' was all she felt now.

Her throat was parched with anxiety, so she got out of bed, found her enamel tea mug, and quietly got herself a drink of water from the bucket beneath the washstand. For a few minutes, she went to the window and just stood there, sipping her water, and staring down aimlessly into the barren street outside. The gaslamp just outside the house was still not working properly, for the mantle had a large hole in it which caused the light to flicker, and sent dancing shadows all along the fronts of the houses on one side of the street. The flickering light danced across Beattie's face too, and it showed exactly how she was feeling. How she hated that street. The Bunk was certainly the right name for it, not only for the filthy smell-hole of a place that it was, but also for the people who lived there. God, what a lesson she had learned! How could she ever have thought that all working-class people were the same, that they were the 'salt of the earth' and could do no wrong? They were just as bombastic, opinionated, and self-centred as any of that lot in Barnsbury. The only difference was that in the Bunk they'd tell you what they thought of you to your face; in select Barnsbury, they'd merely whisper it behind closed doors. As she stood there, turning things over in her mind, Beattie made a decision to do something to improve her lot in life. Somewhere, somehow, things *had* to change.

The following morning, Beattie turned up at Sedgwick's, the candle factory where she worked, to find her old mate Nagger Mills waiting for her.

'I'm gettin' married, Beat!' Nagger said, shaking with excitement. 'Taffy asked me last night. It's taken 'im bleedin' long enuff. We've been walking out fer nearly six years!'

Both women roared with laughter, as Beattie hugged her. These days they only got the chance to get together when Beattie was able to take a bus up 'the Cally', where Nagger still worked the tea urn for the farmers in the cattle pen. Although Beattie was quite jealous of how her old mate managed to look younger than her twenty-eight years, every time she was with her she felt as though she hadn't a care in the world. 'It's wonderful, Naggs,' said Beattie. 'Just fink of it, an honest woman at last!'

'Yer can say that again,' retorted Nagger, lowering her voice. 'I'll only just make it in time.'

Beattie gasped. 'You're jokin'?'

Nagger sighed deeply. 'I wish I was,' she said miserably. 'I only found out a coupla days ago. Fank Gord Taff din't fink twice about askin' me ter marry 'im.'

'An' so I should fink!' returned Beattie. ''E gave yer the bun, so 'e can pay for it!'

Again they laughed.

'Anyway,' continued Nagger, hurriedly, 'we're 'avin' a

booze-up ter celebrate down the Albion ternight. D'yer fink yer could make it?'

Beattie pulled a face. 'I don't know, Naggs. Young Ed's got an 'abit of slippin' out as soon as me back's turned.'

Nagger's normally sunny smile turned a bit sour. 'Wot about that bloke of yours?' she asked scornfully. 'Can't 'e keep an eye on the kid?'

Beattie was tight-lipped. Remembering how Ridley had practically knocked the daylights out of Ed on the evening he came home after calling on his Aunt Sarah when he should have been at school, she had no stomach to say what she really felt about Ridley – not even to her best mate. 'I'll find a way, Naggs,' was all she would say.

Ironically, the Albion pub was just a stone's throw from Number 14 Thornhill Road, which gave Beattie mixed feelings about accepting Nagger's invitation. But she told herself that her old mate's booze-up was far more important than what she felt about being so near to the old family home, so she turned up at about eight in the evening.

The Albion itself was one of the more pleasant pubs in the Barnsbury area; when it was first built in the nineteenth century, it was a fashionable tea garden, where the wives of rich businessmen passed their afternoons in hot gossip about their husbands' mistresses, and their own 'amours'. It was a very different establishment to the White Conduit pub just down the road, where Samuel Melford had spent so many of his latter years, drinking in the private bar, and in the cock-fighting shed in the back yard.

By the time Beattie arrived, Nagger's booze-up was in full swing in the public bar. As she expected, it was a pretty rowdy affair, for most of the menfolk present were already well oiled.

'So you're makin' an honest woman of 'er at last, are yer, Taff?' Beattie asked Nagger's intended.

'If yer ask me, I think it's the other way round,' replied the Welsh boy, who was a few years younger than Nagger, smaller, and decidedly plump. 'Got me under 'er thumb, and that's for sure,' he said, his accent thicker than a tin of treacle. 'Mind you, I'm a willin' party. At least I'll get my breakfast in bed every mornin'.'

This produced a roar of approval from all the men, and jeers from the women. 'Some 'opes!' roared Nagger.

In a matter of minutes, Beattie had a glass of bitter thrust into her hand. She didn't usually drink alcohol, but the way she was feeling these days, she was prepared to try anything. After all, this was a special occasion, and she was determined to enjoy herself. It felt so good to meet up again with so many of her old mates from the Cattle Market, and for a few fleeting moments it helped her to forget the disenchantment she felt for her neighbours up the Bunk.

''Allo, stranger.'

If it hadn't been that she felt his hand on her shoulder from behind, Beattie wouldn't have heard who was talking to her. But it didn't take her long to recognise Shiner, one of her gang from her days knocking around the streets up 'the Cally'. 'Blimey!' she said, half a pint of bitter in her hand, and a fag in her mouth. 'Where'd they dig you up from, Shine?'

'I've been around, mate,' he replied, with his usual gleam in his eye. 'Yer just 'aven't looked 'ard enuff fer me.'

Cheeky as he was, Beattie couldn't help liking him, though he was always taking liberties. She always knew how to handle Shiner, and he always knew how far he could go with her; it was a kind of mutual respect. And as she looked at his well-defined features, his dark eyes, and flat boxer's nose, it didn't escape her notice how much he had changed since she first knew him. Not only had he grown his hair so that it flopped over one eye, but he was dressed well in a black long-sleeved shirt, dark trousers, and a black trilby hat which was pushed to the back of his head. It was hard for her to believe that he was pushing thirty.

'Come up in the world a bit, ain't yer, Shine?' Beattie asked.

'When yer put yer mind ter somethin', yer can't lose,' he replied.

Beattie was impressed. 'So wot *'ave* yer been puttin' yer mind to?' she asked.

'Aw – you know – this an' that.' Shiner's appearance may have changed, but he was just as evasive as ever. 'Let's just say that me work involves – 'ow shall I say – lookin' after the public interest.'

Beattie didn't have to ask any more. He was clearly up to something that was *not* in the public interest.

'An' wot about you?' Shiner lit himself a fag, but he was watching Beattie all the time.

'Wot about me?' Beattie replied chirpily.

'No man in yer life yet?'

Beattie's reply was haughty. 'As a matter of fact, I'm married.'

Shiner grinned. 'Married? Wos that?'

'Sounds as though you 'aven't 'eard of such a fing.'

'Marriage?' retorted Shiner. 'Greatly overrated, Beat,' he assured her.

At that moment, the Guv'nor of the pub, George Beckwith, offered everyone in the bar a free drink to celebrate Nagger and Taff's forthcoming wedding. Shiner immediately collected two bitters – a half for Beattie, and a pint for himself. They had only just started to down them when the place suddenly erupted into a singsong, with Fred Gardner stomping out a string of current pub favourites on the old joanna, such as 'Daisy, Daisy', and 'Nellie Dean'. Most of Nagger's pals had a whale of a time, yelling their heads off and swaying back and forth to the music, and by the time they got to 'Knees up Muvver Brown', the place vibrated so much that the Guv'nor was beginning to think that his 'drinks on the house' was not such a good idea after all.

Shiner partnered Beattie in the knees-up, and she found herself enjoying herself for the first time since before she had young Ed.

'Yer know somefin', Beat?' yelled Shiner, above the roar of the party. 'I still fancy yer!'

Beattie tried half-heartedly to push him away. 'I told yer, I've got an 'usband.'

'So wot?' called Shiner. 'I'm not fussy.'

Beattie wanted to show her disapproval, but she just had to laugh. 'If your brain was as big as yer mouff,' she yelled, 'you'd make a fortune!'

'That's not very friendly,' replied Shiner.

''Ow friendly should I get?' asked Beattie.

Shiner didn't wait to be asked again. He just grabbed hold of her, and kissed her full on the lips.

Beattie struggled to pull away, but just when she had managed to do so, he kissed her again. This time, she did not try to resist.

Nagger, who was hard in the middle of the knees-up, gave an approving smile, seeing what her old mate and Shiner were up to.

Beattie and Shiner didn't wait until throw-out time. After saying their farewells and wishing Nagger and Taff their best for the future, they left the Albion and went back to Shiner's place in Leslie Street, just off 'the Cally'. They weren't bad digs, and Beattie was quite impressed to find that there was actually a lavatory on the landing halfway up the stairs. She hadn't anticipated having a fling with anyone that night, let alone Shiner, but now that she was there, she felt really good. At least somebody had shown that they wanted her, and that was something that hadn't happened to her in a long time.

As Ma Briggs was looking after young Ed that evening, Beattie could only stay with Shiner for a couple of hours. During that time she hardly thought once about Jack Ridley. She was also relieved when, just before she left, Shiner became a little more forthcoming about the nature of his work. It appeared he had just got himself a job as a recruitment officer for some kind of new political group.

The name of the bloke who was trying to get it up and running, he said, was some geezer called Mosley.

Towards the end of August, Sarah put the shutters up at the windows of her beloved house in Thornhill Road for the last time. It wasn't easy for her to say goodbye to so many years of memories, and as she turned the key in the lock of the street door, her hands tingled and her whole body felt empty and lost. No matter how hard she tried, she would never be able to think of the house as anything but a friend, whom she was deserting in its time of need. But she refused to look back, for if she did, she knew that the tears would come, and this was something she had promised herself she would not do. In her mind it would be a betrayal of her mother and father.

A taxi was waiting for her in the road outside, for she had already decided that when she left her home for the last time, she wanted to go quietly and quickly. She had no wish to imagine what the new owner would be doing to the place, but she hoped they would be kind.

The Melford house in Thornhill Road deserved nothing less.

Chapter 15

Mrs Ranasinghe brushed her thick black hair in front of the mirror. The henna dye, which helped to disguise her grey streaks, was holding up well, and the special oil she used kept her hair soft and moist. Despite her age and disabilities, she was determined not to lose her dignity, and so every morning she was up early to do her ablutions before Sarah arrived to start her day's work. Unfortunately, the old lady's arthritis was now so debilitating that most days she had to have help to get dressed, but she still made quite sure that she changed into a different sari each day. Today was to be rather special, so she chose the pale blue silk one, trimmed with gold, which, after a great deal of effort, she managed to swathe around her body with immense elegance. However, her feet remained stubbornly bare, which was a habit she had brought with her from Ceylon many years before, and which she had resolutely continued ever since. She also resisted any kind of make-up, calling it simply 'a western fad, which will never last'. The truth was that her face was strong and dramatic without any kind of embellishment.

That morning, Sarah arrived a little earlier than usual. Now that she had moved into a ground-floor flat just a few doors away, there was no worry about her having to wait for hours in a bus queue. In many ways, the old lady felt quite guilty that when Sarah was forced to leave her family home, she didn't offer to let her have a room in her own house. After all, there was plenty of room in the place, for the house was laid out on three floors, and the only occupant was herself. But Mrs Ranasinghe had always been very set in her ways, and as much as she had come to love and admire her young companion, she wanted no one to share the house with her. It wasn't something she was proud of. In fact, when she thought of how many homeless people there were around these days, she felt positively guilty. None the less, she was her own person, and she felt she had to follow her own instincts and fears.

'Mrs Ranasinghe! You look beautiful!'

The moment Sarah walked into her bedsitting room, the old lady shimmered with pride. 'It's nothing,' she said, failing miserably to sound modest. 'In Ceylon we wear things like this every day of the week.'

'Yes, I know,' replied Sarah, crouching down in front of the wheelchair to admire what the old lady was wearing. 'But this is so special, so colourful. What's the material?' she asked, delicately touching the gold rim of the sari between her fingers.

The old lady stiffened. 'Pure silk, of course!' she replied, haughtily, her accent still thick even after so many years in England. 'It's woven in a very exclusive shop I know in Kandy, in the hill country.'

Sarah continued to admire the sari, and the fact that the old lady had managed to wrap it around on her own. 'It really is beautiful,' she said. 'I'm quite envious.'

'English girls should wear English clothes,' said the old lady, imperiously. 'A sari is for we natives from the East.'

Sarah wanted to chuckle, but thought better of it. In any case, she thought, the idea of her wearing a sari would be quite bizarre.

'I think it's about time I made you a cup of tea,' she said, getting up from her crouching position.

The old lady straightened herself up in her chair. 'I'll wait until we get next door,' she said.

'Next door?'

The old lady leaned forward, and looked rather stern. 'It's over a week now since you moved into your flat,' she said. 'You still haven't invited me in.'

Sarah was taken by surprise. 'Goodness,' she said. 'I had no idea. Don't tell me you got dressed up just to pay me a visit?'

'Partly,' replied Mrs Ranasinghe. 'Partly not. As a matter of fact, I have one or two rather important things I want to discuss with you.'

A little later, Sarah was pushing the old lady in her wheelchair along the street outside. It was a fine summer's morning, and as they went, there were calls from the neighbours, such as ''Ello, ducks! You're lookin' rosy!' and 'You're lookin' marvellous, gel! Keep up the good work!' Mrs Ranasinghe waved back imperiously, like Queen Mary. She was very grateful that the people of Arthur Road appreciated her.

When they reached the rusty gate outside Sarah's new ground-floor flat, Sarah went ahead and opened the street door. Whilst she was doing so, Mrs Ranasinghe suddenly became hysterical when a ginger tomcat rushed past her feet. Sarah hurried back and quickly wheeled the old lady into the house. If there was one thing that was sure to give Mrs Ranasinghe nightmares, it was the sight of a cat. 'They should round them all up and drown them,' she had told Sarah on more than one occasion.

Sarah's bedsitter overlooked the street at the front, with the kitchen at the rear overlooking a small back garden. 'I'm going to try and plant a few roses,' she said, as she stood beside Mrs Ranasinghe, who was craning her head to look out at the garden through the kitchen window. 'But since I don't own the place, I don't really want to spend too much.'

The old lady agreed.

As the front room and the kitchen were all joined together as one, Sarah was able to make the tea whilst still talking to her employer. Mrs Ranasinghe liked the room, because it was very similar in shape and size to her own. But by her expression, she showed very clearly that she disapproved of the modern wallpaper design, which Sarah had inherited from the previous tenant, and which was a complete contrast to the old lady's plain white walls. However, she did approve of the few personal belongings Sarah had managed to bring with her from Thornhill Road, particularly the small round polished table, which was covered with a clean pastel lemon tablecloth, a couple of red velvet-covered dining chairs, and Sarah's own single brass-rail bedstead. The old lady's hawklike eyes soon picked out the framed family photographs on the mantelpiece above the small tiled-surround fireplace.

'Was *that* your mother?' she asked, rather jealously, pointing to a small oval-framed sepia photograph.

'Yes it was,' answered Sarah.

'Let me see.'

Sarah brought the photograph across to her.

The old lady studied it. 'Yes,' she said, looking back and forth from the photograph to Sarah. 'I can see the resemblance – the same rigid expression, same nose, that pale complexion. Yes – *very* English.'

Sarah stiffened. 'What's wrong with that?' she asked indignantly.

'Don't be stupid, girl!' retorted the old lady, pushing the

photograph back at her. 'That was meant to be a compliment.'

'Oh, I see,' Sarah said, humbly. 'Thank you.' Although she had been working for Mrs Ranasinghe now for over eleven years, she still often wondered what went on beneath that beautiful swath of dyed black hair.

'Was she a good mother?' asked the old lady.

'I've told you so many times,' replied Sarah. 'She was the best mother any daughter could ever have.'

The old lady grunted, and wheeled herself to the kitchen part of the room at the back. 'I'm a terrible mother,' she said. 'Always have been.'

'I'm sure that's not true,' said Sarah, preparing two cups and saucers for tea.

'Oh yes it is,' insisted the old lady. 'What would you say if your mother had walked out on you and the family, and ended up on the other side of the world?' She didn't wait for Sarah to answer. 'It was wrong. I was too busy thinking of myself. I had a responsibility to my two daughters, and I deserted them.' She began to light up one of her Capstan cigarettes in her long, thin holder.

'I think you're being too hard on yourself,' Sarah said.

Mrs Ranasinghe took a puff of her cigarette, and, as usual, coughed as she exhaled. 'No,' she said, shaking her head. 'I was wrong to leave them. My poor Michael, my dear husband. He must be turning in his grave.' She stared forlornly at her lap. Then she suddenly looked up. 'Did you know he died exactly twenty years ago today?'

'*Today?*' Sarah asked. 'Really?'

The old lady nodded. 'Now you know why I'm all togged up like this,' she said, her expression proud but not sad. 'It's a celebration of a life that was rich and wonderful.'

Sarah went to her, and gave her a hug.

'And now for the bad news,' Mrs Ranasinghe said. 'That letter you brought in from the postman yesterday, it was from my daughter, Marla. She's on her way over to see me.'

Sarah's face lit up. 'Mrs Ranasinghe!' she exclaimed. 'That's wonderful!'

'I doubt it,' returned the old lady. 'But since I wrote to her and asked her to come, I have to put up with it.'

'You asked her?'

The old lady put the cigarette holder into her mouth, turned her chair, and wheeled it back into the bedsitting room. Sarah followed her. 'I'd been thinking about asking her for a long time, ever since that doctor came to see me about my varicose veins. He said it was about time I started to think of putting my house in order.'

Sarah was puzzled. 'I don't understand,' she said. 'What does he mean?'

'He means that I'm not getting any younger, and I should be prepared if anything – should happen to me.'

Sarah was outraged. 'What nonsense! That doctor! How dare he say such a thing? He doesn't know what he's talking about!'

Mrs Ranasinghe smiled wryly. 'Perhaps,' she said, with that twinkle in her eye that told Sarah she was enjoying herself. 'But there are certain things I want done when I'm gone, and I want to make quite sure Marla does them.' With the cigarette holder clenched firmly between her teeth, she took a sly look at Sarah. 'And that's where you come in.'

'Yes?'

'I intend to tell Marla that if – when – something happens to me, I want to make quite sure that you are taken care of.'

Sarah turned away. 'I don't want to hear you talk like this,' she said dismissively. 'You have many years ahead of you—'

226

The old lady's determined voice carried loud and clear across the room. 'I intend to make quite sure that you are taken care of. And that's final!'

Sarah refused to listen. She went straight to the hob, removed the kettle which was boiling there, and briskly poured hot water into her mother's teapot. She couldn't bear to hear the old lady talking like this. Time enough to discuss such things when they happened, but not now, not when the old lady was still alive and fully alert. Just like her own mother, she said to herself, always planning and plotting things, so wretchedly practical. But then it occurred to her why she was feeling so upset. In the eleven years she had been working for this extraordinary old lady, she had actually grown fond of her. It seemed impossible to feel such warmth for someone whose background was so different in every way from her own, a woman from the other side of the world, who wore strange clothes, dyed her hair, and smoked cigarettes through a long holder. And yet, here she was, feeling in some strange, inexplicable way as close to this peculiar old woman as if she were her own mother.

'All this is quite unnecessary, Mrs Ranasinghe,' she said quite forcefully. 'I really am quite capable of taking care of myself.'

'That is the precise reason why I want to help you,' sniffed the old lady, on the verge of becoming tetchy. 'Oh, don't worry, I have no intention of telling you how. You'll have to wait for that until you hear from my solicitor, and *that*, by the will and grace of Lord Buddha, won't be until after my ashes have blown away in the wind.'

The soup queue outside the People's Mission Hall in Upper Street was longer than it had ever been. For most, it meant a wait of almost an hour just to get a bowl of chicken broth

227

and a lump of bread, and by the time the poor wretches at the end of the queue had reached the front, more times than not, supplies had run out, which often resulted in riots and fist-fighting. With unemployment now at an all-time record, people in the street were beginning to wonder whether it had been worth winning the war, for ever since 1918, the country seemed to have entered one recession after another. In the soup queues up and down the country, neither the Conservative Government of Stanley Baldwin, nor the succeeding Labour Government of Ramsay MacDonald offered any real help to those who were starving; they firmly believed that politics were for the rich and middle classes, not for the poor.

After waiting in the sweltering heat of a late September afternoon, Jack Ridley collected his pathetic lump of bread and mug of lukewarm chicken broth, and took it as far away from the queue as possible. He eventually settled down on some church steps, just around the corner in Almeida Street. He ate the meal, or whatever it was, as though he hadn't eaten for days, which, considering he hadn't been home for nearly a week, was more than likely. Then he took the empty chipped mug and pumped himself some water from the well just alongside a trough used by local cart horses. Although he was supposed to return the mug to the Mission Hall, once he had drunk down the water, he merely tossed it into the trough and left it floating there, until it finally filled with water laced with dead insects, and disappeared beneath the surface.

'You look like a bloke who could do wiv a decent meal.'

Ridley didn't have to look to see who was talking to him. It was 'Ritz' Coogan, one of the Dillon boys, a gang of former criminals who knocked around the Bunk. Ritz, who got his name after being sent down for eighteen months for a breaking and entering job at the Ritz Hotel in Piccadilly, was, at the age of twenty-four, already a hardened criminal, whose main aim in life was to make sure he never reformed.

'I never eat wiv strange men,' replied Ridley, dourly. He took the remains of a dog-end from behind his ear, shoved it into his mouth, and stretched out his hand to Ritz.

Ritz automatically handed him a book of matches. 'That's a pity, mate,' he said. ''Cos I know 'ow yer can afford a slap-up meal of yer choice.'

Ridley lit his dog-end, blew out the match, and tossed it on to the pavement. 'Oh yeah?' he replied, with just a passing glance.

Ritz moved closer and, making quite sure no one was watching them, said, 'Sedgwick's. They've got a lock-up round the back.'

'Sedgwick's?' said Ridley, sceptically. 'It's a candle factory.'

Ritz grinned. 'A bit more than that, mate,' he said, 'from wot *I* 'ear.' He leaned closer. 'Sounds ter me like they keep more than candles in their lock-up – at least fifty crates of 'igh-quality booze *I* was told – Johnnie Walker whisky.'

Ridley's eyes lit up. ''Ow much?'

'It's worf a bob or two.'

''Ow much in it fer *me*, yer knuckle 'ead?'

'Depends wot we can get under the counter,' replied Ritz, keeping a close watch all around as he talked. 'We'll cut it five ways.'

'Who else is in on it?'

'The usual. Me an' the boys. Wot d'yer say?'

Ridley thought for a moment. 'Depends.'

'On wot?'

''Ow yer intend ter get in.'

'Piece of cake,' replied Ritz, confidently. 'Mind you, we could use a bit of inside 'elp.'

'Meanin'?'

Ritz took a deep breath before he answered. 'Your missus works there, don't she?'

Ridley stiffened. 'No way!'

'All she needs to do is make sure the door's left open after work hours.'

Ridley pulled the dog-end out of his mouth, and threw it down hard on to the pavement. 'I said – no way!' he snapped, grinding the dog-end angrily into the ground with his boot.

'OK, OK! Keep yer 'air on!' pleaded Ritz, backing away a step or two, the palms of his hands held up as if to protect himself. 'I was just tryin' ter fink of a way ter make fings a bit easy for us.'

'Then forget about Beat,' Ridley growled angrily. 'She ain't fer sale.'

Ritz shrugged his shoulders apologetically, then waited a moment until he was quite sure Ridley wasn't going to hit him.

As they stood there, two small kids came running up to them, as though they were racing to see who could get there first. One was a boy, the other a girl, and both were dressed in tattered clothes, and looking more filthy than the pavement itself.

'Got a fag, mister?' asked the boy, cheekily.

'One each,' added the girl.

'Bugger off!' roared Ridley, raising the back of his hand as though he was about to lash out at them.

The two kids turned on their heels and ran for their lives, calling 'Stupid sod!' and 'Fat arse!' as they went. At the corner of the road, they even had enough gall to stop and make as many obscene gestures at Ridley as they could think of.

Ridley watched them go, but his anger quickly turned to apathy and frustration. Is this really where we've come to? he asked himself. This lousy, rotten world is turnin' us all into a bunch of bloody loonies! For Chrissake, how are we expected to survive without food in our stomachs and money in our pockets? 'Right!' he said, suddenly turning back to Ritz. 'I'm in. But no Beattie. Is that clear?'

Once again, Ritz held up his hands. 'Anyfin' yer say, Jack,' he sniffed. 'Anyfin' yer say.' Then he added, 'In any case, I agree wiv yer. It wouldn't be right ter bring Beat in on somefin' like this – oh no. I reckon she's got quite enuff ter keep her occupied as it is.'

Mick Wilson, the street lamplighter, had only just left the Bunk. He was late tonight, for he had had quite a lot of trouble with at least two or three of the gaslamps along the road, which were not working because someone had smashed the glass plates around the mantles. Mick didn't want to hang around in the dark for long; he knew the Bunk only too well, and if he didn't get out soon, he might not get out at all.

The moment Mick had scurried off into Seven Sisters Road, the Bunk fell into an eerie silence. The whole place looked as though it had died, and any moment now, great apparitions would spiral up from the sewers below, float across the rooftops, and gradually slither down the chimneypots. And yet there *was* life, if only the dancing shadows cast by that same faltering gas mantle right opposite the house where Beattie, Ed, and Ma Briggs lived.

Amongst the shadows that night was one that actually moved without the help of that faltering gas mantle. It was a

231

tall, elongated human image, that emerged from behind a front garden wall, where it had been hiding since twilight. Only now, as the thick darkness of night took over, did the image dare to move into the false white glare of that flickering gaslamp.

Jack Ridley's face was taut and grim. As he slowly crossed the road, his eyes remained firmly fixed on the upstairs window where Beattie and young Ed were, or should be, fast asleep. The room, on the second floor, was in darkness.

Ridley quietly let himself into the house using his own front door key. He closed the door behind him as softly as he had entered. As always, the only sounds he could hear were the distant snores of Ma Briggs, who slept in a back room on the ground floor. He knew only too well that even if the roof fell in, the old girl would probably sleep through it, so he had no worries about disturbing her.

Helped by a distorted filter of light beaming through the two frosted glass panels on the front door, Ridley slowly and silently found his way to the foot of the stairs and made his way up. As always, different smells competed with each other, from the remains of the gas from the extinguished wall lamp, to the pork trotters that had been boiling earlier in the kitchen, and finally to the pungent smell of the DDT disinfectant, which was helping to combat the nightly invasion of cockroaches.

It was only when he got to the first-floor landing that he heard a sound. He knew it wasn't old Rogers, Ma Briggs' new lodger on that floor, for he usually worked a night shift at the PO sorting office at Stroud Green. No, the sound he could hear, nothing more than a murmur at this stage, was coming from the upper floor.

Anyone who has ever tried to climb quietly up creaking stairs must know how impossible Ridley found it to make any progress without being discovered. None the less, he was gradually succeeding, and as he approached the final landing, the murmurs he heard earlier could be identified as two voices. Inch by inch, he crept his way towards the door of Beattie's room, then stopped, put his ear against the door, and listened. Beattie? Ed? He gently tried the door knob. The door was locked.

Without a moment's hesitation, he suddenly threw all his weight against the door, and burst into the room. From inside came a shriek and a gasp.

For a moment, standing in the dark in the open doorway, Ridley's silhouette appeared as a terrifying, menacing unidentified shape. But then he lit a match and cast a narrow ray of light on to the bed where two figures were sitting up, huddled in shock together.

It was Beattie and Shiner.

'Oh my God – Jack!'

In the dark, Ridley rushed across the room, and lunged straight at Shiner. Grabbing him by the throat, he yelled, 'I'll give yer exactly one minute ter get out of this room!'

Ridley's reputation had gone before him for years, and Shiner knew that he was in no position to argue with such a roughneck bruiser as this. Saying nothing, the moment Ridley released him, he leaped out of bed, made for his clothes, which were piled up on a kitchen chair, and rushed to the door. Although Ridley couldn't see him, he knew that the bloke was stark naked.

The moment Shiner had left the room and rushed down the stairs, Beattie got up and tried to go after him. 'Shine!' she yelled. 'Don't go . . .!'

Ridley barged straight in front of her, and slammed the door back on to its broken lock.

'Who gave you the right?' shrieked Beattie. 'Who gave

yer the bleedin' right ter come bargin' in 'ere . . .?'

Ridley smashed the back of his hand straight across her face. The blow sent her reeling to the floor.

As he reached down to feel for her, it was obvious that she too was naked.

Growling, sobbing, fighting for her breath, Beattie tried to slide away from him. But he caught hold of her hand, and dragged her back to him. 'Where's the boy?' he demanded.

'Yer can't touch 'im!' she yelled hysterically. ''E's wiv Ma! Yer can't touch 'im!'

Ridley dragged her up, turned her around, and pulled her arm up behind her. 'I'm goin' ter say this once, and once only,' he said quietly, but menacingly.

Beattie tried to scream, but he clamped the palm of his hand over her mouth.

'Wot's goin' on?' yelled a voice from the bottom of the stairs. It was Ma Briggs, who was clearly not as heavy a sleeper as Ridley had imagined.

'Once, and once only,' Ridley repeated to Beattie, whom he now held in a vicelike grip. 'If I ever catch you wiv anuvver man, I'll kill the bleedin' pair of yer. Do I make myself clear, Mrs Ridley? Do I?'

Chapter 16

Eunice Dobson had two things in common with her friend, Sarah. She was in her mid-thirties, and she was still unmarried. In some ways this was a blessing in disguise for both women, for when they got together they were able to pour out their hearts to each other about their inability to find the right kind of person to settle down with. Eunice was the younger of the two by six days, a fact of which she never stopped reminding her friend. But in other ways, the two of them were chalk and cheese. For a start, Eunice had come from a middle-working-class family from St Paul's Road up at Highbury, as opposed to Sarah, who was *pure* middle class. Eunice was also tall and lanky so that she towered over Sarah even without her shoes on, and she wore more make-up each day than Sarah would wear in a month of Sundays. But what they did share was the same sense of humour, which sometimes caused raised eyebrows, especially when they went out shopping together, or to an amateur variety show in the Emmanuel Church Hall in Hornsey Road. When Eunice laughed out loud, heads turned, and Sarah spent most of her time trying to keep her quiet.

There was no doubt that ever since they'd met at a church dance a few years before, they had formed a close bond. In fact it had been Eunice who had drawn Sarah out of her shell, warning her that unless she forgot about the past and concentrated on the future, she would end up on her own, bitter and twisted for the rest of her life. Consequently, despite her previous determination never to walk out with a man again, Sarah had in fact managed to have 'flings' with three or four different chaps, most of whom, to her surprise, she quite liked. One of them, a young man called Blake Courtenay, worked as a marine underwriter at Lloyd's, in the City and, despite the severe economic recession in the country, he clearly earned enough to offer her a secure lifestyle. But there was one factor against Blake – he was too young for her, in fact several years younger than Sarah, and after her experience with Edward Lacy, she was not prepared to get mixed up with someone simply because of their good looks. Whatever happened, however, she remained as determined as ever not to give herself physically to anyone unless she was quite certain that it was for love.

At the beginning of October, Eunice concocted a plan for Sarah to meet Freddie Hamwell, a barber from Upper Street, who was a friend of her elder brother, Ernie. Freddie, who had become a widower after just two years of married life, was in his forties, and considered by nearly all who knew him to be a thoroughly lovely man. For Eunice, however, it was a tricky business bringing Sarah and Freddie together, for Sarah was getting wise to her friend's endless attempts at matchmaking. On one occasion, she had arranged an 'accidental' meeting between Sarah and the manager of a local piano workshop, but when they discovered that the man was a confirmed bachelor, who preferred the company of his young male friends, Eunice burst into so many gales of raucous laughter that she and Sarah had been forced into a hasty retreat. However, an opportunity did finally arise, when Eunice arranged an evening on which her brother and Freddie Hamwell would, coincidentally, go to the cinema together at the same time as Sarah and herself.

The queue outside the Blue Hall cinema in Upper Street stretched almost to the Islington Angel. After the rip-roaring success of Al Jolson's first feature-length talking picture, *The Jazz Singer*, everyone wanted to *hear* what was going on up there on the screen as well as to see, and the follow-up musical drama, *The Singing Fool*, again with the inimitable Jolson, was clearly going to be as big a sensation as its predecessor.

Despite the fact that Sarah had no idea what had been planned for her, she looked wonderful. Gone were the days when she dressed practically for a night out; these days, she wore dresses that were shapely, tight-fitting, cut just above the knee, and colourful. What's more she now made all her clothes herself on an old Singer sewing machine Mrs Ranasinghe had given her, and they were stitched to perfection.

'Let yourself go!' was Eunice's motto, and Sarah took her advice, for she had now put the past behind her, and had started to live her life for herself and not just for others.

'Goodness!' cried Eunice, as she and Sarah arrived outside the cinema to find the long queue. As usual, it was a very badly acted reaction, for she knew very well that her brother, Ernie, and Freddie Hamwell were already queuing, and were very near the front. 'There's my brother!' she called unconvincingly. 'He'll get us in.'

As they quickly made their way to where the two men were standing in the queue, Sarah wasn't, at this point, quite sure whether it was a bit of luck, or yet another of Eunice's well-planned plots.

'Ernie!' squeaked Eunice, in that unmistakable high-pitched voice. 'How good of you to keep our places for us.'

The comment was clearly intended for the people queuing

up behind rather than for Ernie, and they knew it. 'Get ter the back, mate!' growled one angry man, 'No pushin' in!' grunted one of two elderly women who had come straight from their fish stall in Chapel Market, and smelled to high heaven.

'You'll pardon me,' said Eunice, haughtily, putting her arm through Sarah's, 'but my friend here is just getting over a very *nasty* illness, and my brother and his friend very kindly offered to queue up for us until we got here.' She turned to her bewildered brother. 'Isn't that right, dear?'

Ernie dutifully nodded his head. He'd gone through all this kind of thing with his sister before.

Sarah didn't know where to look. All she knew was that from this moment on, she had to act as though she was near death's door.

As far as Eunice was concerned, no more explanation to the rest of the queue was necessary. So she immediately turned to her brother's friend. 'Hello, Freddie!' she squealed, all wide-eyed innocence. 'What a lovely surprise to see you here.'

Freddie Hamwell was a pleasant, if not particularly handsome man. He sported a small dark brown moustache beneath a small nose, and because he was a bit short-sighted, it was difficult to see the colour of his eyes behind his thick, metal-framed spectacles.

'Nice ter see yer again, Eunice,' he said, raising his trilby politely.

Eunice hardly allowed him to finish. 'This is my friend, Sarah,' she said, gushingly, whilst practically pushing Sarah straight into his arms. 'Sarah. This is Freddie Hamwell.'

The barber raised his hat again, and offered his hand. 'Pleased ter meet yer, miss.'

Sarah smiled back, and shook hands. 'Hello, Mr

Hamwell,' she said, dutifully. Now perfectly aware that all this was yet another of Eunice's plots, she tried not to meet the barber's eyes for too long. But in the fraction of a second that she did, she thought that he looked quite ordinary – very ordinary in fact. He had beautiful manners, though, and she was impressed to see that he treated going to the pictures as an occasion, for he was dressed in a three-piece brown suit, with a gold watch and chain in his waistcoat pocket, and brown shoes that were well polished.

Eunice's manipulation of the queue worked wonders, and the shilling front-row seats in the circle they managed to get were certainly the best in the cinema. Ernie was furious when Eunice quietly insisted that he pay for them. Eunice immediately made sure that Sarah and Freddie sat next to each other, whilst poor Ernie was made to sit next to his sister, which meant being apart from his own best mate.

The Blue Hall, which some insisted was the first cinema in the country, had a beautiful Victorian auditorium, with a cream and gold décor. Tonight it was thick with cigarette smoke, for the audience from the previous two performances had hardly had time to clear before the place was filled up again. Ernie smoked, but although Freddie usually smoked a pipe, this evening he merely kept it unlit in his mouth. To Eunice's dismay, all during the commercial slides, not a word passed between Sarah and the barber. But hope came at the final moment, when just as the lights were going down, Freddie asked Sarah, ''Ave yer ever seen a talkin' picture before, Miss Sarah?'

'Yes, I have,' replied Sarah, brightly. 'Eunice and I came to see *The Jazz Singer*.'

The barber drew breath, like a cat hissing. 'T'rrific, wasn't it?' he said. 'D'yer know, I saw it five times. Cried like a bloomin' baby, I did.'

Sarah smiled back bravely. 'Yes. It was quite sad, wasn't it?'

Eunice listened to this fascinating conversation, convinced that she had finally found the perfect match for her best friend. As the auditorium was finally plunged into darkness, she crossed her fingers tight and hoped for the best.

The Singing Fool turned out to be just as much of a tear-jerker as its predecessor, and by the time Al Jolson came on to sing 'Sonny Boy' in that famous full-throated, powerful voice, there wasn't a dry eye in the house. Inevitably, the barber dabbed his eyes too, at the same time holding out a bag of sweets to Sarah. 'Bull's-eye?' he croaked. Sarah declined graciously, and did her best not to laugh. Eunice was unable to take one either. She was far too busy sobbing her heart out.

In the Angel pub after the picture show, Eunice tried to consolidate what she considered to be a good evening's matchmaking. 'Freddie's got a lovely barber shop just up the road,' she said eagerly. 'You must show it to her some time, Freddie.'

'Any time,' replied the barber directly to Sarah. 'It'll 'ave ter be outside workin' hours, though,' he added. 'I don't allow ladies in durin' the day, except when they bring in their youngsters.'

'Oh?' Sarah said, with raised eyebrows. 'And why's that?'

'A barber shop is a gentleman's sanctuary,' replied Freddie, rather stiffly. 'Ladies 'ave their own establishments fer 'airdressin'.'

Sarah's reaction was quite uppity. 'With respect, Mr Hamwell, that's absolute tosh.'

Eunice was quick to step in. 'Oh, I don't know, Sarah,' she said, quickly. 'Men have all sorts of things in a barber

240

shop that women shouldn't know about.'

'Really?' she asked mischievously. 'What kind of things?'

'Oh, don't be silly, Sarah,' Eunice replied, trying hard to keep her voice low. '*You* know.'

Ernie, who was already on his second pint of bitter, was nodding his head furiously. 'A woman's place is in the home, I always say,' was his contribution. 'I mean, just look at that suffragette woman, the one that threw herself under the King's horse.'

Sarah swung around with a start. 'What about her?' she asked, tersely.

'Bleedin' loony, that one,' insisted Ernie.

'Because she fought for something she believed in?'

Ernie was beginning to get riled. ''Cos she was a woman. Women've got no right to a say in how the country's run. That's a man's job.'

'Do you think a man has a right to a say in how his child is brought up?' asked Sarah, who was clearly in a combative mood.

'You'll fergive my sayin', Miss Sarah,' interrupted the barber, almost apologetically, 'but surely that's an entirely diff'rent question.'

'Is it?' retorted Sarah, swinging her attention back to him. 'But if a woman has a child who happens to be a boy, part of her is inside that boy when it grows up. What I'm saying is that a boy is influenced as much by his mother as by his father.'

Eunice was getting really worried now. This was not how she had imagined her matchmaking efforts would turn out. 'I don't vote meself,' she said, quickly trying to change the subject. 'I couldn't care less who runs the country.'

'Well, you should care, Eunice,' said Sarah, scoldingly.

'How could we bring down a corrupt government if we didn't exercise our right to vote?'

'That sounds a bit left wing, if you ask me,' sniffed Ernie, downing the last of his second pint of bitter.

'It has nothing to do with left or right wing, Ernie,' Sarah snapped. 'What we're talking about here is equality.'

The barber puffed on his pipe and said, 'Well, I still won't allow women ter come inter my shop – equality or no equality.'

For a brief moment, Sarah remained silent, then she smiled at the barber and said, 'That, Mr Hamwell, is your loss.'

Eunice slumped back in her chair. Once again, her matchmaking efforts had failed – miserably.

Beattie poured herself a large glass of Johnnie Walker whisky. For most of her life, she had carefully avoided alcohol because she just didn't like the taste, but these days, it was different. She could see no future for herself, so she could see no harm in taking an occasional glass of the hard stuff to dull the hopelessness. She still didn't like the taste, but the more she drank, the more she grew used to it – it helped her to forget things, to forget what a mess her life was in. It also helped her to cope with Jack Ridley, whose vicious threat still rang in her mind. She had no doubt, no doubt at all, that he *would* kill her if he found her with another man. Many a time in the last few weeks she had told herself that if it hadn't been for young Ed, she would have done the job for him. Thank God for Sedgwick's, she reckoned, and their under-the-counter discount whisky trade. Easy to nick, even for an amateur like her.

'You goin' ter go on boozin' all night?' asked Ed, as he watched his mother pour her second glass of whisky.

'If I do,' she replied, already beginning to slur her words, 'I shan't ask *your* permission – mate!'

Ed was squatting on his mattress on the floor, trying to read one of the books he had borrowed from his Aunt Sarah. But with his mother sipping booze and slamming around the place like a caged animal all the time, it wasn't easy. In fact, she had been hard to handle ever since the night Ridley had come home late and beat her up. She still had an unhealed cut above the eye, which clearly depressed her every time she had a wash and looked at herself in the mirror. At his young age, Ed had gone through many rough nights with Ridley living in the same room, but on that occasion, when Ridley had found his mum with Shiner, it had been like a nightmare.

'It's not fair, yer know,' he said, getting up from his mattress and going across to his mother. 'I'm not old enuff ter 'ave an old woman who's pissed every night.'

Beattie looked up from the table, where she was trying without success to wind some wool on her hands. 'Don't use language like that on me,' she said firmly, but slurring. 'I don't like it.'

Ed stood beside her at the table. 'Why won't yer tell me wot it's all about?' he asked. 'Maybe I could 'elp.'

Beattie gave a dismissive laugh. Her face was blotched, and puffed. 'Kids can't 'elp no one,' she replied. 'They only take. They never give.'

'If it's money you're worried about, I could get a newsround job. That shop in Fonthill Road's lookin' fer someone.'

'Ferget it.'

'They pay two or free bob a week. I'd give it all ter you.'

Beattie slammed down her tangled wool on the table. 'I said ferget it! Don't worry – you won't starve!'

243

The boy looked quite hurt. 'That's not wot I meant,' he said. He drew closer, but this time stood behind her looking at the back of her head. He could see several grey hairs there, which seemed wrong in a woman who was still only in her early thirties. For those few precious moments, he felt sorry for her. Suddenly he felt angry, really angry. His mother's life, and ultimately his own as well, was being torn apart by a man who couldn't care one twopenny-ha'penny for anything or anyone. 'Why don't yer just kick 'im out?' he asked.

Beattie slowly turned to look at him. It wasn't easy to focus. 'Wot're yer talkin' about?'

'Jack. We don't need 'im. Yer should kick 'im out.'

Beattie got up quickly from her chair, knocking it over as she did so. Without warning, she slapped the boy across the face. 'Don't you say fings like that ter me,' she barked, wavering back and forth shakily on her feet. 'Don't you *ever* say fings like that ter me, d'yer 'ear? Jack Ridley's your farver, an' 'e deserves respect. I don't want to ever 'ear you talkin' about 'im like that again!'

When his mother's hand struck him, Ed hardly flinched. His response was to look back at her with a mixture of cold anger and pity. Then he turned, moved away from her, and flopped down on his stomach on the mattress. He could hear the bedsprings as his mother climbed on to her bed. He tried to imagine what she was thinking, whether she regretted what she had just done. He tried to persuade himself that he didn't care – didn't care about his mother, and didn't care whether she lived or died. But that was hardly true, for the pillow on which he was resting his face was wet with tears.

Chapter 17

Sarah was none too pleased when her front doorbell rang at seven in the morning. Now that the long winter nights were setting in, she found it hard to get up at the best of times. Also, it was still dark outside and as her flat was freezing cold, the moment she got out of bed she quickly had to put on her warm fleece-lined dressing gown, which her mother had given her as a Christmas present soon after the war. She was halfway to the front door when the bell sounded impatiently again, and as she opened the door and peered outside, she was astonished to see a small, frozen figure on the doorstep.

'Ed!' she gasped, pulling the door wide open to let her young nephew in. 'What on earth are you doing here so early in the morning?'

The boy, trying to warm his hands under his arms, marched straight in. 'Got ter see yer,' he said, his teeth chattering with the cold. 'It's urgent.'

Sarah feared the worst. Putting her arm around his shoulders, she led him into her sitting room. 'Is it your mother?' she asked. 'Is she ill?'

The boy blew into his hands to warm them. 'I just want ter talk to yer,' he said.

Sarah quickly retrieved a box of matches from the mantelpiece, and lit the gas fire. 'Come and warm yourself,' she said, bringing the boy forward so that he could crouch on the rug in front of the fireplace. 'Would you like a nice hot cup of tea?'

'Don't drink tea,' replied Ed, warming his hands.

'I know what I'll make you,' she said busily. 'How about a cup of cocoa? That'll soon get rid of the cold. Just let me go and get the milk.'

Ed shrugged his shoulders.

Sarah disappeared for a moment, to collect the morning delivery of milk from her doorstep. When she returned, she made straight for the kitchen at the far end of the room, where she poured some milk into a saucepan. 'You poor thing,' she said, as she lit the gas. 'You must be frozen, walking all the way here in this weather.'

The boy, now huddled up in front of the fire, didn't reply.

'What's happened, Ed?' she asked, whilst mixing cocoa in two cups.

Ed stared into the fire as he replied. 'Mum's on the booze,' he said.

Sarah stopped what she was doing, and joined him. 'She doesn't drink alcohol,' she said. 'At least, she never used to.'

'Well, she does now,' he replied impassively, his eyes still focused on the fire.

It was pure luck that Beattie managed to wake up in time to go to work. Most mornings she got up around seven, had a wash, and a piece of bread and marge and a mug of tea for breakfast, then, after getting dressed, took a leisurely stroll to Sedgwick's candle factory, which was no more than five or six minutes' walk away. But just lately, things were different. These days, after a heavy night's drinking, she failed to wake up until there was only just enough time to get her clothes on and rush to work.

This morning, when she eased herself out of bed, it was no surprise for her to realise that she was still wearing her day clothes. She couldn't remember much about what had happened the evening before. All she knew was that it felt like someone had thumped her over the head with a sledgehammer. 'Go downstairs an' get the milk, Ed,' she called, rubbing her eyes and without actually looking to see if the boy was still lying in. When she eventually did manage to focus, the first thing she noticed was that the boy was not on his mattress. Her immediate reaction was to go to the door, open it, and call out, 'Ed! You down there?' There was no reply, so she called again. 'Ed? Can yer 'ear me?'

The reply from the bottom of the stairs came from Ma Briggs. ''E's gorn out, Beat!' she bellowed. 'Went first fing.'

'Where'd 'e go?' yelled Beattie.

''Aven't the faintest,' called Ma. ''E does wot 'e likes, that boy. In an' out like a dose of salts.'

Beattie heard Ma go back into her parlour and slam the door behind her. She closed her own door, and made her way to the washstand. It was only when she began to revive herself by dousing her face in cold water that it all came back to her.

The evening before, she had had yet another interminable bust-up with Ed. She remembered how, when he criticised her for her boozing, she went for him and accused him of being just as worthless as his real father. Oh God, what a shouting match! She looked at herself in the mirror above the washstand, water running down her cheeks, and couldn't recognise herself. Is this what I've become? she asked herself. How could she bring up a child, and let him see her like this? In that one moment of reflection, she decided that something had to be done. When the boy came home, she would tell him that from now on, things were going to change, that she would never touch booze again as long as she lived, and that she would start being a real mother to him. A new leaf, that's what it was going to be. At least she was lucky to have a job in times like this. At least there was *some* money coming in.

A few minutes later, she was on her way to work. Somehow, the day looked brighter than she had expected, even though there was no sun, and the sky was full of the usual dark grey clouds. Yes, as far as Beattie was concerned, this was going to be a new beginning: no more rows with Ed, no more Jack Ridley, no more booze. Last night had been the turning point. From now on, she had the chance to start all over again.

When she arrived at Sedgwick's to clock in, she found the foreman, Charlie Pearson, waiting to talk with her. Five minutes later, she was out on the street again. She had been given the sack for continuous bad time-keeping.

Sarah and Ed were sipping hot cocoa together, he squatting on the rug in front of the gas fire, and she sitting in the armchair at his side. In profile, she could see the shape of his young face, the slightly jutting jaw, pallid complexion, and ears that were more protruding than his father's. Sarah found it difficult to take in that this was Beattie's boy. A few years ago, she wanted to know nothing about the child that had ruined her future, but it was a strange act of fate that had brought the two of them together. The youngster had, for whatever reason, discovered in his aunt someone he could talk to, someone who could help him to sort out his problems. And in him, she recognised an enquiring mind, a thirst for knowledge, which, in her opinion, was at least a

248

ray of hope for a boy with his limited education and traumatic upbringing.

'Try to remember, Ed,' she said, as they both stared into the red glow of the gas fire. 'When was the first time you noticed she was drinking?'

Ed had his hands wrapped around the cup of cocoa to keep warm. 'Soon after *'e* found 'er wiv this bloke.'

Sarah lowered her eyes.

The boy suddenly turned to her. 'Ridley. 'E come 'ome in the middle of the night. I was downstairs wiv Ma, but I 'eard 'im bashin' the daylights out of 'er. If I'd've bin up there, I'd've killed 'im!'

Sarah felt herself tense inside. She could now envisage the whole situation. 'You said a few minutes ago that you hardly ever see your— you hardly ever see Jack Ridley?'

Ed looked back into the fire. 'Never see 'im, not from one week to anuvver. Then 'e suddenly walks in an' expects everyone to go runnin' after 'im.'

Sarah drained the last of her cocoa, got up, and put it on the small coffee table nearby. 'Does he have a job, Ed?' she asked.

'Who – Ridley? Ha! Don't make me larf !' The boy had a rim of cocoa around his mouth. 'The only job *'e* ever does is breakin' an enterin'.'

Sarah paused a moment, then turned back to him. 'Then how does your mother manage about money?'

'She don't,' he said bluntly, wiping his mouth on the back of his hand. 'We're broke.'

Sarah took the empty cup from him. 'Then how does she manage to buy alcohol?'

Again, the boy grinned. 'Nicks it, don't she?' he said. 'From up where she works. They don't only sell candles, I can tell yer.'

249

Sarah put the cup on the table, went to the window, and pulled back the heavy wooden shutters. It was now light outside, and when she pulled back the lace curtain she could see the pavement on the other side of the road glistening with early morning frost. 'I don't really know what to say to you, Ed,' she said with a sigh.

'Come an' see 'er,' the boy replied, immediately.

Sarah did a double take. 'What do you mean?'

'If yer talked to 'er, she might stop drinkin.' She might try an' pull 'erself tergevver. She'd listen ter you.'

Sarah shook her head. 'I doubt that, Ed,' she replied. 'Your mother and I haven't really talked properly to each other in a very long time.'

'Yer could try.'

Those pale blue eyes of his were so appealing, and yet so vulnerable, and it didn't seem natural to Sarah that a boy of his age should have dark rings beneath those eyes. 'I wish I could help you, Ed,' she said, 'but it wouldn't be right. You see, your mother and I don't see eye to eye with each other, and if I interfered, I might end up doing more harm than good.'

'If anyone could 'elp Mum, it's *you*.'

'What makes you think that?' Sarah asked, surprised.

''Cos you 'elp me,' Ed answered immediately. 'Yer talk ter me about books an' fings.'

'That's not help in the way you mean it, Ed,' Sarah replied. 'When we talk about a book, I'm merely sharing with you what I've got out of it myself. In that way, we can both learn an awful lot.'

'I learn much more from books than goin' ter school,' said the boy, now sitting cross-legged on the rug in front of her. 'I don't mean about addin' up, an' fings like that. I mean about 'ow people do fings, and why. When I read about the

250

people who run the country, I get really angry.'

Quite unexpectedly, this brought a smile to Sarah's face. 'Reading is not only about people who run the country, Ed,' she said, slightly teasing. 'It's about letting someone transport you to a world you may never know. It's about getting away from the harsh reality of life.'

'That's wot I mean,' said the boy. 'If you could talk ter Mum like that, if you could make 'er believe it, fings'd get better.'

Sarah looked hard at him. She couldn't believe that she was only talking to an eleven-year-old boy. But having a conversation like this with Ed was one thing, having the same thing with his mother was quite another.

Jack Ridley met up with Ritz Coogan and the Dillon boys in the Highbury Tavern, a seedy pub halfway between Finsbury Park and Highbury Grove. Nobody in their right mind set foot in the place after six in the evening, for the Tavern had a reputation for being the watering hole for some of the most hardened criminals in the neighbourhood. 'Snare' Riley, the pug-nosed Irish landlord, encouraged this type of clientele, for whenever they did a job, he usually got a cut for providing the right kind of cover. The cover tonight for the Dillon boys was Snare's back parlour.

'The week before Christmas. It'll be perfect timin', 'cos the place'll be jam full of booze for the 'oliday.' Charlie Dillon was not only the eldest of the three brothers, he was also the brains behind most of their jobs. There wasn't much of a resemblance between him and his two brothers, Phil and Joe, except that he dressed as though he was a City stockbroker, whilst the younger men stuck to flat caps and dungarees.

'Do we know yet wot kind of booze they're floggin'?' asked Ritz, whose Weights fag had almost burned down to his lips. 'Last time I 'eard, they said it was mainly Johnnie Walker.'

Charlie sat back in his chair, with a pint of Truman's brown ale in his hand. 'Far as I know, most of it is,' he replied. 'But by Chris'mas, there'll probably be plenty of uvver stuff.'

'Yeah,' said his younger brother, Joe. 'The number-one problem is, 'ow do we get it out?'

Charlie turned to the middle brother, Phil.

'Leave that ter me,' said Phil. 'I've got a Morris van. Once we've got into the place, I can back it through the rear yard.'

'Be a bit noisy, won't it?' warned Ritz.

'It'll be the middle of the night,' said Charlie. 'There's only one bloke on watch. We'll take care of 'im.'

Ritz looked a bit uneasy.

'So where do I come in?' asked Ridley.

'Good question, Jack,' replied the sharply dressed Charlie.

'We need some muscle,' said Joe. 'The way it's lookin', we're goin' ter 'ave ter move about an 'undred crates.'

'An 'undred!' gasped Ridley. ''Ow long's it goin' ter take us ter do that?'

The three brothers exchanged a knowing look. 'It can't take longer than fifteen minutes, Jack,' said Charlie.

'Maximum,' said Phil.

Ridley thought about this for a moment, and drew on his fag. This was the first time he'd worked with the Dillon boys, and he wasn't at all sure. Charlie Dillon had already done two years for a pretty heavy-handed break-in at Samuel's, the jeweller's shop in Holloway Road, in which

252

an assistant was badly injured. Petty larceny was one thing, a violent break-in was something quite different. 'Wot about the law?'

'The fuzz?' asked Joe. 'They couldn't care less what goes on around the Bunk. If they know wot's good fer them, they'll keep their noses clean.'

'Wot about Big Ben?' Ritz reminded them. ''Is nose can sniff out somefin' goin' on a mile away. I wouldn't want ter come up against *that* fifteen stone of fat in the dark,' he moaned, nervously gulping down the remains of his whisky.

'Don't underestimate Ben Fodder,' said Ridley, with a rare show of unease. 'That flatfoot's bin my shadow fer years. 'E's just waitin' fer a chance to send me down.'

Charlie smiled gently at Ridley. He didn't like him, he'd never liked him, but he was right for this job, because he was desperate for money. And anyone who was desperate for money would be willing to take chances. 'Yer know somefin', Jack? he said, putting his arm round Ridley's shoulder, and giving him an insincere hug. 'Yer worry too much. There's a lot in this fer you, fer all of us. All you've got ter do is ter trust us. Savvy?'

Ridley stubbed out his fag in an ashtray, and looked up at his new boss. Oh yes, he savvied all right. But he certainly didn't trust him.

Beattie left the labour exchange in Seven Sisters Road, and slowly made her way back home. It had been an agonising morning. First, the shock of getting the sack from that short-arsed little squirt at Sedgwick's, Charlie Pearson, and then hours of queuing up at the labour exchange to see if there was a job – any job – she could do that would keep her and Ed going until something better came along. There had been nothing for her.

Try as she may, she could not erase the deep feeling of bitterness she felt, not only for Charlie Pearson, but for just about every living person in the world. Only a few hours before, it seemed as though she was going to get a new lease of life, but suddenly, everything had collapsed around her. She was beside herself. Where would she get the money to pay Ma Briggs for her digs? Where was the money coming from to buy enough food just to keep her and Ed going for the next few days? It was an impossible situation, and, for the time being at least, she hadn't the faintest idea how she was going to cope.

'Yer've got a visitor,' announced Ma Briggs, the moment Beattie came through the front door. 'It's yer sister, Sarah.'

Beattie did a double take. 'Sarah – 'ere?'

'Young Ed brought 'er 'ome wiv 'im,' said the old girl, as Beattie left her and hurried up the stairs. 'I told 'im ter make 'er a cuppa tea!'

When she got to the top-floor landing, Beattie found the door to her room open. Inside, Sarah was at the kitchen table, sipping the cup of tea Ed had made. 'Wot you doin' 'ere?' Beattie said unceremoniously.

Sarah stood up immediately to greet her. 'Hello, Beattie,' she said, awkwardly.

'I asked Aunt Sarah ter come and see yer,' said Ed, also getting up. 'She said I ought ter ask you first, but I said yer wouldn't mind.'

'Did yer?' Beattie snapped, practically slamming the door behind her. 'Well next time – *ask*.'

The boy looked crushed, and Sarah went to put her arm around his shoulders. 'I'm sorry, Beattie,' she said. 'I told him it wouldn't be right—'

'Sit down and finish yer tea,' Beattie said, taking off her coat and hat, and hanging them behind the door.

Sarah exchanged an anxious glance with Ed, who begged her to sit down at the table again.

'So,' said Beattie, coming across. 'Wot's this all about?'

Sarah hesitated before answering, 'I wanted to see you, Beattie. It's been some time. I wanted to see – how you're getting on.'

'Why this sudden interest?'

'Mum!' protested Ed.

'I didn't ask *you*!' said Beattie, turning on him.

Already Sarah realised that it had been a mistake to come, though she'd wanted to help Beattie because the boy had asked her to. 'Ed tells me you've been having a bad time just lately.'

Beattie glared at the boy. 'Did 'e now?' Then, turning to Sarah, she quipped, 'Everyone's 'avin a bad time. Ain't you 'eard?' She pulled back the chair that Ed had vacated for her, and sat down facing Sarah across the table. 'I lost me job terday.'

Ed gasped. 'Mum!'

'I'm sorry, Beattie,' Sarah said, dismayed.

'I asked fer it,' said Beattie, eyes focussed on the table. 'I've bin goin' in late every mornin' fer weeks.' She looked up. 'Yer learn lessons the 'ard way.'

Sarah asked her, 'How will you manage?'

'Manage?' replied Beattie. She shrugged her shoulders. 'Why?'

'I'd like to help.'

Beattie narrowed her eyes suspiciously. ''Elp? Why should you 'elp *me*?'

'I don't know,' replied Sarah, nonchalantly. 'Perhaps it's because you're my sister.'

Beattie smiled wryly at her. 'And *'ow* would you intend to 'elp me, Sarah?' she asked.

Sarah thought for a moment. 'I could let you have some money. Not very much. But it might tide you over until things improve.'

Beattie tossed her head back and laughed. 'Improve!' she spluttered. 'That's a good one, that is!'

Ed couldn't bear to hear the way his mum was talking. 'Look, Mum,' he said. 'I asked Aunt Sarah ter come an' see yer 'cos she can fink straight. She can tell us some way we can get out of 'ere.'

'Get out of 'ere?' Wot d'yer mean, get out of 'ere? This is our 'ome. This is where we live. Just fink yerself bleedin' lucky yer've got a roof over yer 'ead, and food in yer stomach . . .' The words stuck in her throat, for at that moment she broke down.

Sarah immediately got up from her seat, and signalled to Ed to leave them alone. 'Beattie,' she said, tentatively putting her arms around Beattie's shoulders.

Beattie immediately stood up, went to the window, turned her back, and wiped her tears away with her hands.

Ed made as though he wanted to stay, but again Sarah signalled to him to leave the room, which he finally did.

Sarah waited a moment, then went across to Beattie. But this time she didn't attempt to touch her. 'Beattie,' she said quietly and without emotion. 'Let's for just a few minutes try to forget who we are, or where we came from. Let's try to pretend that we're two strangers who know absolutely nothing about each other.' She moved closer, so that she was now standing alongside Beattie, both of them looking out of the window into the street below. 'If we know nothing about each other, then we can be totally objective. What I mean is, we have no past to look back on, no memories of bad times together. It means that we can do things for each other without the past hanging around our necks.' She paused a moment before continuing, 'You know, Mother used to say that if you and I could only find time to stand still occasionally, and find out what each other actually looks like, we'd get on so much better.'

She slowly turned to look at her sister. Beattie also turned. Both stared hard at each other, Beattie with tears still glistening in her eyes, and Sarah trying desperately hard to elicit some kind of feeling from her.

It lasted only a brief moment, for Beattie suddenly broke away and went to sit on the edge of the bed. 'Why *did* yer come 'ere, Sarah?' she asked, taking out a small handkerchief from her dress pocket, and dabbing her eyes with it. 'Was it to 'elp me, or was it ter prove that you was right, and I was wrong?'

Realising that she was wasting her time, Sarah went back to pick up her gloves, then made for the door, but she stopped when Beattie called to her.

'Ed belongs ter me, Sarah – ter me, an' 'is farver. I'll never let yer take 'im away from me – never. I may not be the perfect muvver, but as long as I've got blood in me veins, I'll go on doin' me best for 'im.'

Sarah waited no longer. As she left, Beattie called out to her. 'Keep away from 'im, Sarah! Keep away from boaf of us!'

Chapter 18

Freddie Hamwell wiped the remnants of shaving foam from old Arthur's cheeks, and finished off the haircut and shave by puffing some talcum powder on to his customer's neck. This immediately caused the old boy to sneeze, and he was relieved when Freddie removed the towel from around his shoulders, so that he could lever himself up from the heavy leather-covered barber's chair. Freddie prided himself that he gave one of the smoothest shaves in Islington, mainly because he used the same cutthroat razor and strap that his late father had used during his long career as a gents' barber. Once the old boy was on his feet, Freddie used a small clothes brush to remove the surplus grey hairs from his tattered jacket. 'That'll be a tanner, please, Arfur,' he called. He had practically to shout into the old boy's left ear because he was as deaf as a post.

'A tanner!' protested Arthur, with a thunderous look. 'Don't nuffin' get cheaper round this place? 'Ighway bleedin' robbery, that's wot it is!'

Freddie grinned. He was used to the old boy's protest, for he made it every time he came in, which was usually once a month.

Arthur dug deep into his trouser pocket, came up with a handful of change, sorted through it as though it was all he had in the world, and handed over the sixpenny coin.

''Ighway bleedin' robbery!' he repeated, grudgingly.

''Urry up, Granddad!' called a small boy from one of the seats lined up along the wall behind. 'I'm getting' fed up 'angin' round 'ere.'

Arthur turned with a start, and growled back at the boy. 'Oy! Who d'yer fink *you're* talkin' to, 'Arry? You just keep yer tongue between yer teef, or I'll get yer dad on yer!'

Freddie laughed, as he put the old boy's tanner into his till. 'Next customer, if you please!' he called.

Harry, Arthur's eight-year-old grandson, got up from his seat, tugged at his braces, and went across to the big chair his granddad had just vacated. He was so small that Freddie had to lift him up into it.

'Wot'll it be terday, then, young man? Short back an' sides?'

The old boy answered for him. ''Is mum's asked fer the puddin' basin,' he rasped. 'Straight line all round.'

'Puddin' basin it is!' replied Freddie, tucking a towel into the boy's shirt neck.

Young Harry groaned and resigned himself to his fate.

Using comb and scissors, Freddie battled to untangle the snotty-nosed kid's blond locks. When he was satisfied that he had made progress, he collected a small porcelain pudding basin from a cupboard beneath the sink, and plonked it on to the child's head.

'Owch!' protested Harry. 'That 'urt!'

'Not 'alf so much as if I wallop yer!' called his granddad, flat cap on his head, and now settling back to read a copy of the *Daily Mirror* whilst he waited.

It was when Freddie got to the point where he was able to use his cutthroat razor on the line of hair beneath the pudding basin that he suddenly heard someone tapping on the shop window. He couldn't believe his eyes when he

260

recognised Sarah peering in and waving. He immediately rushed out to meet her.

'Miss Sarah!' he exclaimed, beaming.

'Hello, Mr Hamwell,' she returned, with a courteous but awkward smile. 'I hope I'm not disturbing you.'

'Not at all!' he replied instantly. 'Please, come in!'

'Oh no,' replied Sarah, holding up her hands in polite refusal. 'I wouldn't want to embarrass your customers.'

'You could never do that, Miss Sarah. Please come in . . . no, I insist!'

Reluctantly, Sarah allowed him to lead her into the shop.

'Blimey!' protested Arthur. 'A woman! Wot's the world comin' to?'

'It's all right, Arfur,' Freddie quickly explained. 'Miss Sarah's a friend of mine.'

'Oy!' called a small voice from the barber's chair. ''Ow much longer do I 'ave ter sit wiv this fing on me 'ead?'

'Comin'! Comin', 'Arry!' Freddie was now dithering between Sarah and his outraged young customer. 'Take a seat, Miss Sarah. I'll be wiv yer in just a tick.'

Sarah did as she was told, and sat in a chair at the side of Arthur.

The old boy glared at her, grunted, and moved on to the next chair along.

Whilst she waited, Sarah was like a child in a toy shop. Everything around was so new to her, so different from Martha's Ladies' Hairdressers in Caledonian Road, which she had visited regularly for so many years. There were two huge barber's chairs that swivelled around to enable Freddie to reach every hair of his customers' heads, an assortment of shaving brushes, sticks, and lethal-looking razors, and colourful displays that ran down the sides of the mirrors, advertising everything from Wright's Coal Tar Soap and

261

Player's Navy Cut cigarettes, to Doctor William's Rejuvenating Hair Lotion. She also noticed a certain small wall cabinet, which had an intriguing notice pinned on the door, marked 'FOR GENTLEMEN'. She imagined that this was what Eunice meant when she'd said, 'Men have all sorts of things in a barber shop that women shouldn't know about.'

Much to young Harry's relief, it took Freddie no more than a few minutes to finish off the kid's pudding-basin trim.

'There you are, young man,' announced the barber. 'You wait till yer gelfriend sees yer now!'

Harry treated Freddie's joke with complete contempt, waited for the towel to be removed from his shoulders, then jumped down from the chair.

''Ow much?' sniffed the kid's grandfather, rising from his seat, again dipping into his pocket for some coins. 'Five nicker fer kids, I s'ppose.'

Freddie laughed and wiped his hands on the towel. ''Ave this one on the 'ouse, Arfur,' he replied.

The old boy glared at him. 'Oh no yer don't!' he growled indignantly. 'I don't need no 'andouts just 'cos yer lady friend's wiv yer.' He sorted out a couple of penny coins, and practically pushed them into Freddie's hand. 'Twopence!' he cried. ''An that includes yer tip!' He turned, and made for the door. 'Come on you!' he called to his grandson.

Freddie quickly went ahead of him, and opened the shop door.

Arthur gave Sarah a scathing look as he passed. 'Next fing yer know, they'll be 'avin' lady barbers!'

He marched out of the shop, closely followed by the kid with his brand-new pudding-basin haircut, who acknowledged no one as he went.

Freddie closed the door behind him. 'I'm sorry about

that,' he said, turning back to Sarah. 'Old Arfur's a bit of a ranter when 'e wants ter be.'

'I'm the one who should apologise,' said Sarah, rising from her chair. 'It's just that I happened to be in Upper Street, and I remembered Eunice had said that your shop was in St Alban's Place—'

'Oh no,' said Freddie, quickly. 'No need ter apologise ter me. I'm really glad yer popped in.'

Sarah felt a bit embarrassed. 'What I mean is, I came to apologise for my behaviour the other evening – when we were in the public house with Eunice and Ernie.'

Freddie was puzzled.

'It was very rude of me to criticise you for not encouraging the opposite sex into your shop. Everyone has the right to make their own rules and regulations. I was extremely foolish.'

'Miss Sarah,' returned Freddie, who was clearly taken aback, 'there was nothing rude about your behaviour. Quite the reverse, in fact. I was the one who should've known better – I'm getting too set in me ways. I s'ppose I 'ave me dad ter blame fer that. 'E was very strict about keepin' ladies out of men's establishments.'

Sarah smiled gratefully at him. She wasn't going to let on that she had made the journey from the Nag's Head to Upper Street not by chance, but because she had a natural instinct to know about something that was denied her. But now that she was here, she was pleasantly surprised, not only by the shop, but by the barber himself. He somehow seemed different from when she had last seen him, not nearly so ordinary. In fact, whilst she had been watching him work on young Harry's pudding-basin trim, she had noticed what a fine head of hair he had himself. Whilst she had been talking to him in the pub, he had never once taken off his hat, so she was unable to see that his hair was dark brown with a neat quiff at the front, and a parting that was clear and straight enough to have been drawn. His moustache was also much thinner than she remembered, which made him, in her eyes, much more attractive. Attractive? As she had watched him at work, she pondered on this. Yes, she had to admit that, in a strange way, he *did* have quite a pleasant face, not nearly as ordinary as she had at first imagined.

'So, can I tempt you, Miss Sarah?'

The barber's voice brought her out of her momentary trance with a start. 'I – I beg your pardon?' she said nervously.

'I asked yer if yer'd care fer a cuppa tea,' said Freddie, apparently repeating the question she had not heard. 'It won't take a jiff ter boil the kettle.'

Saturday morning down the Bunk was a time when most of the young kids and teenage gangs would just hang around on the street, trying to work out what mischief they could get up to next. Weekends, however, were not popular with the people who lived in the neighbourhood, for it usually meant that fights broke out between rival gangs, or someone had fun throwing a milk bottle through a neighbour's window, or, for some really enjoyable entertainment, a stray cat or dog was tied to a railing whilst brave youngsters taunted it.

On this particular Saturday morning, young Ed was with one of the only mates he had anything in common with, a boy called Mick Cantor. The two of them spent most of their time aimlessly kicking an old corned beef tin up and down the kerb, much to the anger of a young unmarried woman in Number 27, who'd been trying to get her new baby off to sleep all morning. Ed's only reaction was to put two fingers up at the woman and yell obscenities back at her, and as he was something of a hero in his mate's eyes, Mick did likewise. What they hadn't noticed, however, was the approach of Constable Big Ben Fodder, who had Ed by the scruff of his neck before the boy had time to turn.

'Right then!' proclaimed the burly fuzz. 'I fink we've 'ad quite enuff of that, fank you, young man!'

'Get orff! Leave me alone!' yelled Ed, who, despite kicking and punching, hadn't a chance in hell of breaking loose from the firm grip around his neck. 'Mick!' he called. 'Get 'im orff!'

Mick, however, had other plans. He had already run for his life down the street, and disappeared into Seven Sisters Road.

''Old on now, old son, 'old on!' said Big Ben, as he finally brought young Ed under control. 'This is no way ter be'ave in front of yer visitor.'

Ed pulled himself away, and glared. 'You get away from me!' he growled. 'You got no right—' He stopped dead. He had not noticed that someone was standing with the constable.

'Hello, Edward,' said the tall, well-dressed stranger. 'That *is* your name, isn't it?'

'No, it ain't!' snarled the boy. 'It's Ed!'

The stranger resisted the temptation to move closer to the boy, just in case he ended up with a black eye. 'But you *do* have another name?' he said. 'A family name?'

Rubbing his neck after Big Ben's heavy-handed grip, the boy snapped back, 'Wot's it to yer, mate?'

'No lip now!' warned the constable. 'Answer the gent's question.'

The boy hesitated, then answered cockily, 'Melford. You can call me *Mister* Melford!'

The stranger exchanged a bemused smile with Big Ben.

'And where would I find your mother, Mister Melford?' he asked.

'She's at work.'

Big Ben butted in, 'She don't work at Sedgwick's no more.'

The boy sniffed dismissively at him. 'Know everyfin', don't yer? Well, she's got a different job now. A much better one.'

'And where is that, Edward?' asked the stranger.

The boy's bottom lip stiffened obstinately. 'Mind yer own!' he growled. 'I ain't tellin' *you* nuffin'!'

Beattie hated sweeping up the tunnel. She had done it five times during the past week, and every time she did it she felt sick from the smell of urine. But at least she had a job, even if it was only working part time as a temporary cleaner with London Transport. The tunnel in question was part of the entrance to Finsbury Park underground station, and was a popular haunt for drunks, who used it as a short cut from Seven Sisters Road to Wells Terrace, at the rear of the station. During the week or so that she had been there, she had seen two rats scampering along the stone floor, several cockroaches crawling over some discarded apple cores, and a long line of black ants marching in regiment down the white-tiled walls. It was a pathetic way to earn a few bob a week, she kept telling herself, but something was better than nothing at all.

Being a Saturday morning, the tube was busy with passengers going into the West End for the day to spend what little money the recession had left them for Christmas shopping, whilst others turned up for a half-day of work in offices, cafés, and shops in nearby Seven Sisters and Blackstock Roads. In other words, if there had been anyone she knew who was amongst the passing crowd of passengers, she wouldn't have noticed them. But she saw Ed the moment he came running down the tunnel from the Wells Terrace entrance.

'Mum!' he called several times, as Beattie strained to see his silhouette flanked by so many others against the daylight streaming in from the far end of the dimly lit tunnel.

'Ed?' she called, her voice echoing and bouncing off the walls. 'Wot yer doin'?'

The boy finally reached her. He was out of breath. 'This bloke wants ter talk to yer,' he said, very agitated.

'Hello, Mrs Melford,' the stranger said, as he approached. But when he offered to shake hands with Beattie, she pulled back.

'Wos this all about?' she rasped. 'Who're you?'

'My name is Johnson,' said the lanky stranger, who towered above her. 'I'm from a law firm who represent the late Lieutenant-Commander Lacey.'

Beattie wiped her face with the back of her hand. She looked bewildered. 'Who?' she croaked. But then she suddenly remembered. '*Him!*'

'Is there somewhere a little more private – where we can talk?' asked Mr Johnson.

'This is as private as I ever get,' Beattie replied wryly. 'Did you say "late"?' she asked. ''As Edward's old man snuffed it then?'

Johnson's expression became funereal. 'Yes,' he replied. 'I'm afraid he has. Just over a month ago.'

'Good riddance!' was Beattie's response. She never had any time for the old ratbag, and she showed it.

All three were now caught up in the crowd who had just come streaming up the stairs from a newly arrived train.

Johnson waited for them to clear before talking again.

'I'm sorry you feel that way, Mrs Melford,' he said, 'because your son is a beneficiary of the Lieutenant-Commander's will.'

'Oh yes, I know all that. A few bob when 'e gets ter twenty-one – right? An' stop callin' me Mrs Melford. Melford was me maiden name. Take it or leave it, me name's Ridley now.'

This was unexpected news for the law man. 'Oh, I see. You mean, you married again?'

Beattie gave a dismissive laugh. 'I was never married in the first place.'

As they stood there, one of the regular tube tramps came up to them. On his threadbare army tunic he wore a row of war medals. 'Anyone got a fag?' he asked with a chesty wheeze.

'Bugger off!' snapped Beattie.

Mr Johnson dug deep into his inside jacket pocket, took out a packet of cigarettes, pulled one out, and gave it to the man. The man took the fag, shoved it in his mouth without attempting to light it and, with an appreciative salute, scurried off. 'Do I take it then,' continued the law man to Beattie, 'that your financial situation is somewhat improved since you last saw the Lieutenant-Commander?'

Beattie roared out loud, her voice echoing along the tunnel. 'Oh yes, mate! Looks like it, don't it?'

Johnson was becoming increasingly ill at ease. 'Well, my instructions from the Lieutenant-Commander's executors are that you be notified of one of the codicils made by him just prior to his death.'

Now it was Beattie's turn to look baffled. 'Come again?'

The law man continued, 'As you know, some years ago our client notified you of his intention to bequeath a certain amount of money to your son, but not, as you rightly indicated, until he had attained the age of twenty-one.'

Beattie grunted.

'However,' continued Mr Johnson, who was eager to relieve himself of his duties as promptly as possible, 'our client decided that, if the period of time between him passing and the twenty-first birthday of your son should be in excess of five years, an interim sum should be paid to you for the continuation of his education and general welfare.'

Beattie was still not quite sure what the law man was going on about, but her eyes widened when she saw him unclip the leather briefcase he was carrying, and take out a long, buff-coloured envelope.

'You will find here a letter of intent, Mrs – er – Ridley,' said Johnson, very formally, handing her the envelope.

Before taking it, Beattie leaned her broom against the wall and wiped her hands on her coat. 'Wos it all about then?' she asked tentatively.

With the conclusion of his business close at hand, Johnson was already doing up the buttons of his overcoat. 'It gives you formal notice,' he said, 'that a cheque in the sum of one hundred pounds will be forwarded to you by post within seven calendar days of this meeting.'

Beattie's heart was thumping hard. Clasping the envelope to her chest, for once in her life, she was at a loss for words.

'Do you have any questions, Mrs – Ridley?' asked the law man.

Beattie was too stunned to answer. She merely shook her head.

'If by any chance you do not receive this bequest during the time stated,' Johnson added, 'please contact me at the address on my business card.' He gave her the card, which he had already taken from his briefcase. 'I am there most days of the week, Monday to Friday.' He clipped up his briefcase again, and offered his hand to Beattie.

This time, Beattie shook hands with him eagerly.

'I'll bid you good morning,' said the redoubtable Mr Johnson. And turning to Ed with a wry smile, he said, 'And to you too, Edw— young man.' With that, he made his way back out of the tunnel.

'Is it true, Mum?' Ed asked. 'Are we really getting' an 'undred quid?'

Beattie was still speechless. All she could do was to lean against the tunnel wall, look at the boy, and marvel at the way fate had decided to give them another chance in life, especially whilst they were stuck right here – in the middle of a urine-stinking tunnel.

It had been several days since Sarah had seen Freddie Hamwell. During her visit to his shop, she firmly believed that it would be the last time she would ever set foot in the place, but try as she may she couldn't get him out of her mind. Yes, she had heard several times from Eunice what a pleasant and kind man he was, and she certainly didn't doubt that. What she hadn't appreciated, however, was what an interesting person he was, for during that hour following young Harry's pudding-basin haircut, when, unusually, not another customer came into the barber's shop, she and Freddie had talked over a whole range of subjects from the negligence of the present Labour Government, to the heated subject of raising the school-leaving age to fifteen.

Gradually their talk turned to more personal matters, and Sarah was sad to hear how Freddie had lost his wife to a rare blood disease after only two years of married life. He also had much more of a sense of humour than she had at first imagined, especially when he poked fun at himself by referring to his shop as 'Sweeney Todd's of Upper Street'.

By the time they parted, she found she had promised to go out with him.

It was therefore a pleasant surprise when she arrived home one day from shopping to find a note from Mrs Ranasinghe pushed through her letterbox, informing her that a young man had called to see her, and that he would be returning that evening around eight.

With only a couple of hours to spare before Freddie was due to arrive, Sarah bustled around, tidying her small flat so much that, in her estimation, it was fit enough even for the King and Queen to visit. By a quarter to eight, she had changed into a long-sleeved navy-blue crushed-velvet dress, with a solitary small rhinestone in the shape of a cat pinned just below her left shoulder. She also brushed her hair back behind her ears, so that it was gathered together behind the head, and tied with a navy-blue ribbon to match her dress. As always, she wore only a minimum of make-up – a touch of pale red lipstick, a mere suggestion of face powder, and a very faint trace of eyeliner. She completed her outfit with a pair of half-heeled navy-blue suede shoes, which she'd bought herself for her birthday that year. By two minutes to eight, she was ready to entertain her caller.

The front street bell, however, did not ring until almost half-past. By that time, all her good thoughts about the barber were beginning to fade. But when she opened the street door, who was standing there, but Jack Ridley.

''Ello, Sarah,' he said, even touching his cap. 'Long time no see.'

'What are you doing here, Mr Ridley?' she asked tersely.

'Din't your old gel tell yer I was comin'?' he asked quite innocently. 'She wrote a note for yer, got me ter put it fru yer letterbox.'

'What do you want, please?' was Sarah's curt response.

271

'Wanna chat wiv yer.'

'What about?'

'Ain't yer goin' ter invite me in? I'm yer bruvver-in-law, remember?'

Sarah stared right through him for a moment, then reluctantly stood back to let him in. 'In there,' she said, closing the front door, and indicating the sitting room to him.

Ridley took his cap off, went in and looked around. 'Hm,' he commented with an approving nod. 'Not bad. Not bad at all.' He turned to look at her. 'Got *your* 'ead screwed on the right way, an' that's fer sure.'

'What do you want, Mr Ridley?' Sarah asked, uncompromisingly.

'The first fing I'd like,' he said, 'is fer you ter stop callin' me Mister Ridley. 'I 'ave got an 'andle to my door, yer know.'

Sarah's refusal to respond was indication enough to Ridley that she had no intention of warming to him.

'I come ter speak to yer about Beat,' he said. 'She's bin goin' fru a rough time, did yer know?'

Sarah crossed her arms. 'My sister and I are not in contact,' she replied, implacably.

Ridley sighed as though he were sorry. 'Yeah, I know,' he said. 'That's a real shame. 'Cos she's always goin' on about you.'

'Oh really?' replied Sarah, impassively.

'Oh yes. She reckons you ain't bin fair to 'er over the years. She reckons you've – misunderstood 'er.'

Sarah's arms were still crossed as she turned her back on him, and wandered off towards the fireplace. When she turned round to face him again, she was startled to see that he had sat down and made himself comfortable in her armchair.

272

'Mind if I smoke?' he asked mischievously.

'Get to the point, Mr Ridley,' Sarah replied, becoming irritated. 'I don't have the time to talk with you.'

Ridley took the fag from behind his ear and lit it, then looked around for an ashtray in which to deposit his matchstick. 'Yer know wot I fink?' he said. 'I fink it's about time you two got tergevver and sorted fings out. Your trouble is you're boaf so much like each uvver. Yer need yer 'eads bangin' tergevver.'

Sarah found an ashtray and put it in front of him. 'It's very touching that you appear to be so interested in the welfare of my sister and myself, but I can assure you that our differences are deep-rooted.'

Ridley took a puff of his fag and leaned back in the armchair. 'Yeah. I know wot yer mean,' he said. 'You've got so much more class than 'er.' He brought his head up suddenly. 'She's a whore, your sister. Did yer know?'

Sarah froze. 'I beg your pardon?' she said, icily.

'I come back one night and she was in bed wiv this bloke. Broke me 'art, I can tell yer. I mean, if yer can't trust yer own wife, then who can yer trust?'

Sarah's response was instant. 'I suppose it depends on how good a husband you are yourself.'

Ridley smiled back at her knowingly, took a puff of his fag, and got up. 'Well, when it comes down to it, I reckon life is fer livin'. Wot say you, Sarah?'

She just glared at him.

Ridley started to pace the room, giving the impression that he was interested in the place. 'You've got good taste, Sarah, anyone can see that. Worf a bob or two, some of this, eh?'

Sarah was watching his every movement, and when he came to stand in front of her, she refused to budge.

'I admire you, Sarah,' he said, looking directly into her eyes. 'I always 'ave. Yer know that, don't yer?'

'I think it's time you went,' she replied.

He stepped closer.

Sarah looked at him, and for one fleeting moment she could see why Beattie had been so devastated by him. His was quite simply a rugged, handsome face, a real man's face, that any woman would surely find hard to resist.

'Wot I like about you,' he continued, staring deep into her eyes, voice low, 'is yer've always bin yer own person. Not like Beat. She's like a kid. No sense, no feelin' . . .' He leaned forward, and made as though he was about to kiss her.

'Is that why you beat her up, Mr Ridley?' Sarah asked, as cold as ice.

Ridley hesitated and, moving his attention from her lips to her eyes, replied with a grunt and a smile. 'See wot I mean?' he said.

Sarah turned, and moved away from him. 'A whore doesn't need to have sense or feeling, Mr Ridley,' she said. 'A whore is just there for her body. But I'm sure I'm not telling you something you don't already know.'

Ridley casually followed her across to where she had her back to the shuttered window. 'It's not only your body I want ter know, Sarah,' he said, close to her again. 'It's *this*.' He pointed to his own forehead.

If she hadn't known by this time what Ridley had come for, she certainly knew now. She allowed him to look deep into her eyes, and could smell the aroma from the cheap soap he had used, could see the bristles on his face and chin that, given the chance, could scratch her flesh. Desire swept through her, and for one moment she felt that this could be her chance to get her own back for all the heartache and misery Beattie had caused her. As Ridley pressed closer and closer towards her, she thought of Edward Lacey, and all that he had ever wanted from her, but never got. She thought of love, hate, fear – and treachery. The time had come, and now that she had got this far, she would not lose her chance.

Ridley was now close enough to kiss her, and he closed his eyes for the final assault.

Suddenly Sarah stepped out of his way and struck him a thunderous slap across the face. 'Get out!' she growled. 'Get out – now!'

After the force of the blow, which caught him completely off guard, Ridley took a moment to recover himself. Then he looked at her. His face was grim and full of menace.

Although Sarah was convinced that he would now do to her what he had done to Beattie, she stood her ground and refused to be intimidated. 'If you ever try to do that to me again, *Mister* Ridley,' she warned, 'I won't be responsible for the consequences.'

Ridley's expression slowly changed, and menace gradually dissolved into a broad grin. Without another word, he collected his cap, silently made for the door, and left.

As soon as Sarah heard him in the passage outside, she called out, 'My sister is not a whore. And don't you forget it!'

There was a moment's silence. Then she heard the street door open and close, then the iron gate outside.

Sarah stood in the middle of the room. She could still smell Ridley's cigarette burning in the ashtray. She went across and stubbed it out. Her whole body was shaking.

Chapter 19

Beattie saw her opportunity, and she was now determined to take it. The cheque for a hundred pounds that she had received from the estate of Edward Lacey's father meant that she could not only pay Ma back the five pounds she owed her for rent, but she had the chance to move out of the Bunk for ever. With Christmas now only a week away, this was going to be an occasion that she would never forget.

Once she had discovered the way to cash the cheque at a bank, Beattie set two pounds aside for Christmas presents for both Ed and Ma. For Ed she found a second-hand book about life amongst the peasants in Spain, plus a new pair of shoes, which he had never had in his life. For Ma she bought a pink cotton petticoat from a stall in Chapel Market, which she knew would give the old girl immense pleasure and bring a tear or two to her eyes. Then she put thirty shillings away to buy a chicken, some vegetables, a small Christmas pudding (from another stall in the market), and a pound of liquorice allsorts to round off what was clearly going to be a slap-up Christmas dinner.

But despite all the elation, there was still the little matter of Jack Ridley to face up to, for once he found out that she was in the money, he would be down on her like a ton of hot bricks. But – how to keep it from him?

The solution came when Beattie heard of a place that

was going in Mitford Road, which was just off Hornsey Road, a district that was several cuts above the Bunk. When she and Ed went to look it over, they found that it consisted of three rooms on the ground floor of a terraced house that hadn't been occupied since the death, two years before, of the elderly couple who had lived there. It even had an inside lavatory, and, at the rear, a small back yard with just enough room for a few potted flowers. Despite the fact that the property was clearly in need of a coat of paint and some plasterwork, Ed thought it would be like a dream come true if they could live in such luxury.

'Oh Mum, please let's live 'ere,' he pleaded. 'I promise yer won't 'ave no more trouble from me ever again!' Beattie needed no persuading, but knew only too well that everything would depend on how much she would have to pay for rent. To her astonishment, however, she discovered that the place, which was being handled by the Borough Council, was, owing to the recession, going for a snip at thirty shillings a week.

'You're goin' – ter move?'

Beattie hadn't intended to tell Ma about the place in Mitford Road until after Christmas. But, having lived so close to the old girl for so many years, and having relied on her kindness, she wanted to prepare her before the actual move.

'We're not goin' till the New Year, Ma,' said Beattie, only too aware of the anguish she would be causing the poor old soul. 'An' me an' Ed wouldn't even fink about doin' it unless we was sure that yer could come and see us whenever yer want.'

Ma was in her kitchen making Ed a bread pudding when she was told the news, and was too upset to reply. But she was determined to put a brave face on it. 'We all 'ave ter do wot's fer the best,' she replied. 'Yer've boaf got yer lives ahead of yer. Yer can't go round finkin' of old gels like me.' Beattie put her arm around her, but Ma was not giving way to sentiment. There was plenty of time for tears after they'd gone. Practical as ever, she asked, 'So wot yer goin' ter do about Jack, then?'

This brought Beattie down to earth. 'I don't want 'im ter know, Ma,' she said, with a look that told Ma what she already knew.

Ma, her hands covered with soaked stale bread, looked up at her. 'If an' when I see 'im, 'e won't 'ear nuffin' from me,' she said reassuringly. 'I'll tell 'im yer just upped one night and did a moonlight flit.'

Beattie sighed with relief. 'Fanks, Ma,' she said.

'Don't fank me too soon,' she warned, grim-faced. 'You know Jack. If 'e finks 'e's missin' out on somefin', as sure as God made little apples – 'e'll find yer!'

Jack Ridley and Ritz Coogan met up in the Ton O' Feathers pub in Stepney High Street. It wasn't one of their favourite 'houses', but, as it was well away from their normal neck of the woods, they were less conspicuous.

'It's all set fer ternight,' croaked Ritz, who was sounding more chesty than ever after smoking too many of his rolled-up fags. 'Phil's got the van. If we play our cards right, we can pile the 'ole lot in the back.'

Both men were propped up with their pints on the end of the counter in the saloon bar, their backs turned to the other customers.

Ridley was shaking his head. 'I still say it's pushin' it ter get an 'undred crates of booze in the back of a van in fifteen minutes. If the fuzz get wind, we're done.'

As if to reassure him, Ritz put his hand on Ridley's arm.

'Look, Jack,' he said, voice low. 'This job's a cinch. We've got five pairs of 'ands ter pull it.'

'Yeah,' quipped Ridley, 'an' free knuckle 'eads ter make a piss-up.'

Ritz stiffened, and immediately looked over his shoulder, just in case any of the Dillon boys were around. 'Wot's up, Jack?' he asked. 'Don't yer trust Charlie?'

'Trust Charlie?' he said with a dismissive snort. 'Now yer *are* jokin'!' His face tensed. 'I wouldn't trust any of that lot ter take my missus on a day out ter Soufend.'

Somehow, this amused Ritz. 'Well if yer put it that way, Jack,' he croaked, with a grin, 'yer could 'ardly blame 'em, could yer?'

'Wot d'yer mean by that?'

Ritz shrugged his shoulders. 'Well, she's a good-looker, ain't she, your old woman?'

Ridley answered with a steely look in his eyes. 'I wouldn't know, Ritz,' he said. 'You obviously know more than I do.'

Ritz could have bitten his tongue. He'd known Ridley long enough to be wary of any comments about his private life. 'I din't mean nuffin', Jack,' he said defensively. 'It's just that I was finkin' 'ow useful she could've bin if we'd 'ad 'er in on this job. I mean, 'er workin' fer Sedgwick's on the inside an' all that.'

'Well, she ain't,' said Ridley, stubbing out his fag. 'So ferget 'er.'

'You're right, Jack, absolutely right,' said Ritz, eager to change the subject. 'Anyway, now she ain't there any more, it don't make no diff'rence.'

'Wot d'yer mean, she ain't there?'

Ritz looked surprised. 'Your missus,' he said. 'She's left Sedgwick's. Got the push fer bein' late, or so I 'eard. Got a job up Finsbury Park tube station. I fawt yer knew.'

Ridley thought about this for a moment, then drained his glass. 'I'm not interested,' he said acidly. 'Wot my missus gets up to is 'er own business. I've got far more important fings on me mind.'

Sarah had never been to a music hall before. When she and Beattie were young, they were only taken to places like museums or art galleries, which is what all middle-class children were expected to do. But what they were not encouraged to do was to visit places of entertainment that were, by and large, the preserve of the working classes. With this in mind, Freddie Hamwell decided to extend Sarah's education by taking her to Collins Music Hall on Islington Green, which was probably one of the most famous music halls in the country, maybe even the world.

It made no difference that during the week prior to Christmas, variety had given way to a thrilling melodrama entitled *Maria Marten or The Murder in the Red Barn*, for in one way, this was as much an entertainment as singers, jugglers, or even male impersonators. Starring Tod Slaughter, a great dramatic artist of his day, the story of a wicked squire who is haunted by the ghost of his pregnant mistress was ripely played, and brought chilling gasps from every audience.

Freddie sat through almost the entire performance with his eyes covered, but from the moment the curtain went up, Sarah was unconvinced by the whole thing, deciding that she had witnessed far more horror in real life than on the stage that night. What did enthral her, however, was the sheer magic of the theatre's ambience, rich in colour and atmosphere. She had never experienced anything quite like it, and tried to imagine what it would be like to be present during *Dick Whittington*, the pantomime that was due to

281

take over from the ghostly Maria Marten on Boxing Day.

Sarah was surprised how much she had taken to the 'demon barber of Upper Street', which was Freddie's own light-hearted nickname for himself. Although she had met him just a few weeks before , she felt she had known him all her life. Apart from his gentle manner, she was utterly won over by his courtesy. There was hardly ever a time when he allowed her to cross a road without first making quite sure that the way was clear, and on more than one occasion, he had taken out his handkerchief in a public place to wipe a chair that Sarah was about to sit down on. She was also very impressed at the way he treated his young teenage assistant, Tinker, always taking the trouble to show the lad the tricks of the trade, and giving him the opportunity to wash the hair of selected customers. But Sarah's great revelation about herself was the fact that she was now virtually walking out with someone who was so very positively from the working class.

After all the thrills of Miss Marten and her Red Barn, Freddie took the plunge and asked Sarah whether, as it was a reasonably mild night, she might like to walk back home to Arthur Road rather than take the tram. He was overjoyed when she replied that there was nothing she would like better.

It was indeed a mild evening, and hard to believe that in a couple of weeks' time they would be entering another New Year.

As they made their way along the widest stretch of Upper Street, Freddie found himself taking all sorts of risks. 'Sarah,' he said daringly, 'I 'ave a confession ter make.'

Sarah laughed. 'Don't be silly, Freddie,' she teased. 'I'm not a Roman Catholic priest. 'You don't have to confess things to me.'

'Oh, but I do,' insisted Freddie, deadly serious. 'I want to.'

Sarah was suddenly quite worried. Confession? What? Was this meek and mild man now going to reveal all sorts of skeletons in his cupboard? Did he have a mistress who was just waiting to blackmail him, or perhaps he had an illegitimate child languishing in an orphanage somewhere. Her curiosity was now well and truly aroused. 'Then tell me, Freddie.'

The moment he had her attention, Freddie regretted it. But after a moment's deep thought, he finally plucked up enough courage to say, 'I once killed a man.'

Sarah brought them to a halt and turned to look directly at him. 'You – killed someone?'

Freddie nodded. This confession was clearly going to be painful. 'It happened during the war. When I was in the army.'

Sarah sighed with relief. 'In the army?' she said. 'You mean you killed one of the enemy?'

Freddie shook his head sadly. He was consumed with guilt and anguish. 'Me own best mate.'

Sarah clasped her hand to her mouth. Her initial relief was short-lived. 'You killed – one of your fellow soldiers?' she asked timidly.

'Executed 'im,' replied Freddie. ''E was up on a court martial for tryin' ter make a run fer it. They found 'im guilty, an' we 'ad ter shoot 'im.'

Sarah felt total despair for him. 'Oh, Freddie,' she said, clutching his arm. 'How terrible.'

''Course, it may not have bin my bullet,' he continued, 'but one of 'em was. 'E 'ad ter be blindfolded. Fank God 'e never saw me. But 'e knew I was there. Oh yes.'

For a moment, there was silence between them, until quite spontaneously, they started slowly to move on.

'I never forgave the army fer wot they did,' said Freddie.

'Derek wasn't even eighteen. When 'e took the King's shillin', 'e lied about 'is age. But they still tied 'im to a post an' got us ter shoot 'im down. It was murder, Sarah, nuffin' short of cold-blooded murder. An' I was part of it.'

'It was a vile war, Freddie,' Sarah said, comfortingly. 'One day, they'll realise what they've done. All we can hope is that it never happens again, neither the war nor the killings.'

Once they'd passed Highbury Corner, Sarah took the initiative and put her arm through his. Until that moment, they had merely walked side by side, like mere acquaintances, but as they slowly strolled together down the good old reliable Holloway Road, they behaved like two people who had known each other all their lives. The more Sarah thought about Freddie's heart-felt 'confession', the more she realised how close they were becoming, and in so short a time. It seemed as though, during their few outings together, Sarah had heard practically the whole of Freddie's life history. She'd been told about his early days as the son of a local barber, and a mother who doted on him because he was the only child she was capable of bearing. She heard about all sorts of people – aunts, uncles, gran and granddad, cousins (especially cousin Lil, who'd had an affair with a man more than twice her age), friends, neighbours, and customers. She loved the way he described them all, and the obvious affection he felt for his family. How sad then that she was unable to respond with tales of her own happy family life. Listening to the way Freddie talked only convinced her more and more of the gulf that seemed to exist between the classes.

When they finally turned into Arthur Road, most houses seemed to be plunged into darkness, for it was now very close to midnight, and the unusually mild evening was already showing signs of giving way to a frost. As they passed, Sarah pointed out to Freddie the house where she worked for Mrs Ranasinghe, and even now, it seemed impossible not to notice the exotic smell of hot spiced curry that was still seeping out through the front street door.

When they stopped outside the gate of where Sarah lived, she asked Freddie whether he would like to come in and have a drink or a cup of tea. The moment she had suggested it, she could hardly believe how forward she had been. *She* of all people, asking a *man* into her flat late at night! No matter how innocent the offer, it showed how far she had come since those unnatural days with Edward Lacey. Fortunately or not, Freddie declined the invitation, either because he was nervous of being accused of taking advantage of someone he had become very attached to, or because he was just plain prudish. Either way, he thanked her for her company, and in what Sarah thought to be a wonderfully old-fashioned gesture, he took hold of her hand, and gently kissed it. But the moment he looked up at her again, she leaned forward, put her hands on his shoulders, and gave him a firm, but proper kiss. Once again, her own rash act took even her by surprise. When she pulled away, she said, 'Forgive me, Freddie.'

Freddie hesitated not a moment longer. Pulling her back to him again, he gave her a firm, lingering kiss.

When it finally came to an end, they continued to embrace, Sarah with her head resting on his shoulder, the taste of his pipe tobacco still fresh on her lips.

'My dearest Sarah,' he whispered, his soft breath warming her ear. 'I want you to know that this is the most wonderful night of my life.'

Sarah, eyes closed, heard his delightful old-fashioned words, and smiled to herself brighter than she had done for such a long time. 'Would you believe it, Freddie,' she replied, holding him tight, 'it is for me too?'

Sedgwick's candle factory had been established in Fonthill Road for a good many years. Nobody seemed to know for exactly how long, but it was certainly there before the start of the Great War, during which time it did a brisk business, thanks to the endless cut in power supplies for gas lighting. The founder of the firm, a man by the name of Bertram Sedgwick, was said by those who worked for him in those early days to have been a good and fair boss, but when, after his death, the firm passed into the hands of a local wide boy named Ricky Mercer, wages were no better than slave labour, and the business, quite literally, fell apart. Consequently, Mercer began to deal in other forms of activity, such as the illegal sale of discount booze. Most of the people employed there knew something of this bizarre trade, or how it worked, for most of the merchandise was kept locked up in a warehouse at the back of the premises, and supervised only by a carefully selected band of thugs. However, the business of making candles continued, and, because the endless recession was hitting hard, the law turned a blind eye.

Nob Koshak was on watch that night. The boss trusted him, because he got double time not just for night work but for keeping his mouth shut. Koshak, formerly a Jewish *émigré* from Bohemia, spent most of his nights playing cards in the back room of the warehouse. He rarely ventured out, for his room had the luxury of a wood-burning grate, which kept the place beautifully warm and cosy. Koshak had never been known to sleep on the job, which was why he was so highly thought of by the boss, but he did have a tendency to help himself to the odd bottle of Johnnie Walker from the pile of crates stacked high in the warehouse, and it was not unknown for him to go off duty first thing in the morning weaving from side to side as he walked.

By the time Jack Ridley and Ritz Coogan arrived outside Sedgwick's rear entrance, Joe Dillon had already used a pair of strong wire cutters to force a hole through the protective mesh fence. The whole area was virtually in darkness, the only light coming from a distant public gaslamp in nearby Wells Terrace. Joe, the youngest of the three Dillons, had dressed for the occasion, everything black – sweater, jacket, trousers, and cap – which made his face look absurdly conspicuous whenever the moon decided to make a brief appearance.

'Charlie's already inside,' he whispered. 'By now 'e's done the watcher.'

Ritz swallowed nervously. The one thing he wasn't looking for on this job was rough and tumble.

'Wot about the van?' asked Ridley. ''E was s'pposed ter be 'ere before us.'

'Keep yer 'air on,' replied Joe. 'Phil's parked it in the cul-de-sac at the back. There's no point in bringin' it across till we get the stuff out.' He suddenly ducked out of sight. 'Wotch it!' he cracked. 'Someone comin'!'

Ridley and Ritz dropped to their knees and took refuge in the shadows. A dark figure came out through the rear door of the warehouse. Not until it approached the fence did they see that it was Charlie Dillon.

'Right!' he called, voice low. 'We're clear. Joe, tell Phil ter bring the van.' He suddenly caught sight of Ridley and Ritz. 'You two,' he snapped. 'Let's get goin'!'

Inside the warehouse, Ritz was relieved to see that, apart from being blindfolded, gagged, and hands and feet tied together, no real physical harm had come to Koshak.

Using his own flashlight, Ridley took a good look at the stacks of crates, each containing bottles of good-quality

Johnnie Walker whisky. It was only when he lifted one of the crates that he realised how heavy it was. 'Fifteen minutes fer this lot?' he called, his voice so low it was straining to be heard. 'You're bleedin' loony!'

Ridley's comment irritated Charlie. 'You're bein' paid for yer muscles, Ridley,' he snapped, 'not yer brains!'

Ridley gritted his teeth; he wanted to smash Charlie's face in but he thought better of it, and went to meet the van as soon as he heard it pulling up at the rear door.

Within moments, the place was a hive of activity, with the beams from flashlights crisscrossing the dark roof and walls of the warehouse, and lighting the way for the frenzied convoy of crates being rushed into the Morris van at the rear door. Every so often, Charlie would shout in muted voice, 'Move it!' and it took every bit of brute force the five men could muster to do just that.

At the end of ten minutes, only half the crates were in the van, but the pace was visibly slowing. Ritz was fit to drop, and even the younger Dillon boys were feeling the strain.

But just as Charlie was trying to make the all-important decision whether to carry on moving as much of the stuff as possible, or to cut their losses and take what they had already, the whole place suddenly echoed to the sound of a voice booming from the yard outside: 'Stay where yer are! The 'ole lot of yer! You're under arrest!'

Everyone froze.

'It's Ben!' gasped Ridley.

'Christ!' croaked Ritz.

'Don't move!' ordered Charlie. 'There's too many of us. 'E can't take us all!'

Ritz was first to break. He made straight for the watcher's room at the rear of the factory, closely followed by Ridley.

Charlie and his brothers were less fearful. The first thing

they did was to arm themselves with anything they could lay their hands on. Joe ripped off a lump of wood from one of the crates, Phil found a long metal spanner in a tool box, but Charlie's vicious-looking crowbar was the most lethal weapon of all.

As all three made a dash out to the van, the sound of Big Ben's shrill police whistle pierced the night air.

'Stay where yer are!' Ben repeated. 'No one moves!' But by the time he had reached the van, the Dillon boys were already inside, with the doors locked.

The van moved off at speed, with Ben chasing after them. But the constable's heavy frame prevented him from keeping up with them, and his only recourse was to blow his whistle again and again.

Back inside the warehouse, Ridley and Ritz had succeeded in climbing through the window into the factory, where they were able to find a way out into Fonthill Road. Ritz was in a state of terror and confusion.

'Bloody fuzz!' he yelled.

'I told yer!' Ridley panted, as the two of them made off as fast as they could down the road. 'I told yer Ben'd be on to us!'

As they spoke, the Morris van came roaring out from the rear of the building, and with brakes screeching, skidded round the corner into Fonthill Road. Following laboriously on foot was Big Ben, still furiously blowing his police whistle.

The van picked up speed, and rapidly approached the corner of the Bunk. But Phil suddenly turned the steering wheel too sharply, and before anyone could do anything, the van skidded again, shook from side to side, and toppled over.

Whilst the three Dillon boys were scrambling out, Big Ben came puffing round the corner in hot pursuit. The worst hurt was Joe, who had blood streaming down the side of his face from a cut on his forehead, though Charlie and his younger brother, Phil, seemed to have escaped reasonably unhurt. But when his two brothers started to make a dash for it, Charlie, flaming with anger, called them back. 'Stay where yer are!' he ordered.

'No, Charlie!' pleaded Joe. ''E's right be'ind us!'

'We've gotta get out of 'ere!' insisted Phil.

'I said – stay where you are!'

Charlie's voice boomed along the road, where faces were now beginning to peer from behind the curtains of windows on both sides.

With the sound of Big Ben's boots rushing towards them, Charlie stood his ground. 'We can't let 'im get away wiv this!' growled the eldest, and most dangerous of the Dillon boys. ''E knows who we are. They'll root us out, an' they'll frow the book at us.'

'Charlie!' pleaded Joe.

'Let's go!' begged Phil.

Charlie refused to move. He glared angrily as the heavyweight flatfoot came charging along the road.

Within moments, Ben, truncheon drawn, and panting heavily, was upon them. But for a moment, he kept a wary distance. 'Done it this time, ain't yer, boys?' he called. 'Looks like you're not goin' ter enjoy yer Christmas this year, mates!'

Much to the disbelief of his brothers, Charlie strolled up quite fearlessly to the constable. 'Yer know somefin', Ben?' he said, calmly. 'You're becomin' a bloody nuisance.'

'Really, Charlie?' replied Ben, with a satisfied grin. 'Well, I must say, I'm glad ter 'ear that.' He came forward slowly. 'Now please do me the honour of lyin' down flat on yer stomachs – all of yer!'

290

For a moment, nobody moved.

Charlie stared at him, a faint wry smile on his face. Then, almost in slow motion, he started to fall to his knees. But just at the point when it seemed as though he was fully complying with Ben's command, he suddenly sprang back up, and, producing the crowbar from behind his neck, crashed it down on the constable's head.

Ben yelled out, and tried to protect himself with his hands, but it was too late. The blow struck him on the side of the head so hard that, despite any protection he might have had from his helmet, he crunched up and dropped heavily to the ground.

Simultaneously, Joe and Phil started to make a run for it, but once again, Charlie yelled at them. 'No! Get back 'ere!'

'Fer Chrissake, Charlie!' cried Joe.

'Let's get out of 'ere!' called Phil.

'No!' growled Charlie. 'If we leave 'im now, we're done for! We've got ter finish 'im off!'

Joe and Phil exchanged a look of disbelief. Even in their fast and furious world of petty street crime, they had never anticipated anything like this.

Charlie's eyes were scanning the kerb. He found what he was looking for. 'Get 'old of 'is feet,' he barked. The two brothers hesitated. 'Now!'

With blood streaming from a vicious cut at the side of his forehead, Big Ben was groaning, and only half-conscious. Reluctantly, Joe and Phil took one foot each.

'Get 'im over 'ere!' commanded Charlie with urgency.

The two boys did as they were told, and with great effort managed to drag the badly injured police constable to the edge of the kerb. With horror and incredulity, they watched whilst their elder brother struggled to pull off the metal grate of the water drain. Once he had accomplished this, he turned to the others, and rasped, 'Get 'is 'ead down there!'

The two brothers looked thunderstruck.

'D'yer wanna be topped?' he snarled.

The brothers were in anguish.

'Then get 'im down there!'

Charlie bent down, pulled off Big Ben's helmet, and with his reluctant brothers pushing from behind, gradually eased the head of the massive human frame down into the drain. It was a difficult job, and Ben's shoulders had to be forced and wedged into the restricted space. But then, with Charlie urging them on, between them they all finally managed to upend Ben's huge body, and submerge his head beneath the water line halfway down the drain.

From a distance came a shrill cacophony of police whistles.

'Let's get the 'ell out of 'ere!' yelled Charlie.

The Dillon brothers made off as fast as they could, leaving Big Ben's body upended in the drain.

From the corner at the end of the road, Jack Ridley looked on in abject horror. Then he turned, and fled for his life.

Chapter 20

The brutal murder of Police Constable 'Big Ben' Fodder sent shock waves throughout the entire community. Even by the low standards of the residents of Campbell Road, it confirmed the Bunk as a bastion of wild criminal activity, and the Metropolitan Police were castigated by both the local and national press for their inability to control the situation. And, as if to enhance their reputation as one of the most dangerous areas in London in which to live, the residents of the Bunk built their own wall of silence around the grim events that had taken place in their very midst on that dark, cold night, only one week prior to Christmas. Despite exhaustive police investigations, it appeared that no one in the entire street witnessed anything other than some kind of fight amongst a gang of youths, the kind of thing they had grown used to over the years. But when anyone was asked if they could identify any of the youths present, their replies were identical, that it was a dark night, and that they knew what could happen to them if they poked their noses into things that didn't concern them. Even Sedgwick's watcher had been of no help. Bound, gagged, and blindfolded, he could recognise no one, and even if he could, Rick Mercer, his boss, was, for obvious reasons, determined to keep the events of what happened that night as low key as possible.

Sarah read about the Bunk murder in the newspaper the

following day. Although she was not altogether surprised at anything that went on in such a place, her immediate thoughts were of Beattie. Despite the fact that she had no time for the way her young sister was living her life, her natural instinct was concern, and she wondered how much longer Beattie would be able to bring up young Ed in such an unsavoury environment.

When Beattie heard the news, she felt quite sick. Both she and Ed had heard the rumpus going on in the street the previous night, but it was too far along the road for them to see what exactly was going on. But there was no doubt that the savage murder of the burly flatfoot had left even her in a state of shock. It seemed such a cruel, mindless act that anyone could hate a person so much that they would resort to something so horrific.

'Wicked sods, that's wot they are!' growled Ma Briggs, tears in her eyes, and voice cracking with anger. ''Ow could anyone do such a fing? I mean, I never cared much fer the man, the way 'e strutted up an' down the place like 'e owned it, but fer Gord's sake, 'e was a 'uman bein'! Just fink wot sort of a Christmas 'is poor missus an' kids are in for next week.'

Beattie and Ma were standing in the open front doorway, watching all the activity going on in the road outside, the place quite literally crawling with flatfoots. 'Wot're we goin' ter say ter the flatties when they come round askin' questions?' asked Beattie, anxiously.

'Well, I can't tell 'em nuffin',' replied the old girl. 'I slept fru it all, din't 'ear a fing. Sometimes it pays ter be deaf. I tell yer this much though.' She wiped her eyes, and then her nose, on her pinny. 'I 'ate this bleedin' road. I 'ate everyfin' about it. I only wish ter Christ I could get out of the place, an' never set eyes on it again.'

'Then why don't yer, Ma?' Beattie said impetuously.

'Wot d'yer mean?'

'Come an' live wiv me an' Ed. There's a spare room upstairs. We could offer the Council five bob a week extra for it, an' you could come an' go as yer please.'

Ma was slowly shaking her head.

'Why not?' asked Beattie. 'You're like a second mum ter me. An' ter Ed too.'

The old girl's face crumpled up. 'It wouldn't be right. You're a married woman. Now that Ed's gettin' older, you're entitled to a life of yer own. And anyway, yer've got quite enough problems ter cope wiv.'

'Such as?' asked Beattie.

'Wot about Jack boy?'

Beattie's expression changed immediately. Yes, she thought, suddenly tense and anxious, what about Jack Ridley? What would *he* say once he knew that his loving wife and her son had disappeared out of sight, and taken Ma Briggs with them? But there was more on her mind than that. Where, she wondered, was Ridley during the time Big Ben was being shoved down the drain just along the road? Even as the thought occurred to her, two men were approaching her and Ma, one in plain clothes, the other in police uniform.

'Pardon me, madam,' said the uniformed flatfoot. 'We're looking for a Mrs Ridley.'

On Christmas Eve, Beattie finished her cleaning job early, and she and Ed joined the crowd of carol singers who had gathered round a huge Christmas tree just outside the entrance to Finsbury Park. It had now become bitterly cold, and although there was as yet no sign of a white Christmas, during the past twenty-four hours the temperature had fallen dramatically, and the danger now was of ice patches forming on all the side roads. None the less, the seasonal atmosphere was in full swing, and as everyone rushed about to do their last few hours of shopping, it was hard to resist the temptation to join the throng of carol singers who were filling the twilight air with the uplifting sounds of 'Good King Wenceslas' and 'Silent Night'.

The sound of voices joined together in harmony and Christmas cheer helped Beattie in some part to cope with the feeling of total despair that had overtaken her since the murder of Big Ben just a few days before. And, young though he was, Ed was sensitive enough to know how his mum was feeling, and uncharacteristically, whilst they stood there, joining in the communal singing together, he had put a comforting arm around her waist. Much to his surprise, Beattie responded by putting her arm around the boy's shoulders. However, the brief moment of lost care came to an abrupt halt when Beattie suddenly felt someone's chin resting on her own shoulder, and a familiar voice close to her ear saying her name. 'Beattie.'

Beattie, immediately panicked by Jack Ridley's voice, tried to turn.

'Don't move!' he demanded. 'Carry on singin'!'

Beattie did as she was told, but Ed refused to co-operate. 'Leave us alone!' the boy snapped.

Ridley, clearly tensed up, dug his knuckle into the boy's back.

Beattie pulled Ed back towards her.

'I need ter talk to yer,' came the voice from behind. 'I'll see yer in the park in five minutes, on the bridge. I'll go first.' He paused a moment, then added, 'Leave 'im 'ere!' To show who he meant, he again dug his knuckle into Ed's back.

A few minutes later, Beattie made her way through the park entrance, and headed off towards the railway bridge close to the football pitch. The light was now fading, and Beattie was afraid the park would soon be closing. But she pressed on regardless, and pulled her long woollen scarf around her head and shoulders to protect her from the first signs of a biting cold drizzle. When she got to the metal steps leading up on to the bridge, she felt her heart thumping, for as she climbed the steps, Ridley came into view. He was waiting for her, his cap pulled down close over his eyes, the collar of his jacket pulled up in a pathetic attempt to keep his neck warm, and his hands tucked beneath his arms. As usual, there was a lighted dog-end in his mouth, and the smoke from it curled through the metal railings of the bridge.

The moment she reached him, she was astonished to see how pale and drawn he looked. 'Wot 'ave yer done, Jack?' she asked, directly.

Ridley pulled his shoulders back, and stared straight at her. It seemed as though he was about to square up to her. But quite suddenly, his whole appearance changed, for his face crumpled up, and he burst into tears. 'I didn't do it!' he spluttered, pulling the dog-end from his lips and tossing it over the bridge on to the line below. 'I didn't bleedin' do it!'

Beattie couldn't believe what she was seeing. Never in all her time with Jack Ridley had she seen him go to pieces like this, blubbering like a baby. Although her instinct was to rush forward and throw her arms around him, she knew why this was happening, and, for the moment at least, there was no way she could respond.

'The law,' she said, grim-faced, 'they've bin round askin' questions. They've bin askin' everyone. They asked me – and Ed.'

Ridley, who had been covering his eyes with one hand, slowly looked up at her.

'We told 'em we 'adn't seen yer,' Beattie continued. 'We told 'em yer ain't part of our family any more.'

'I didn't do it, Beat,' said Ridley, wiping his eyes with the back of his hand. 'I saw 'em do it, I saw wot they did to 'im. But I 'ad no part in it. I swear ter God I din't!'

What a pathetic sight, Beattie thought to herself. What happened to the big, tough bully who would sooner use his fists on a woman or a kid than find a decent way to survive this hell of a life? 'There's a rumour goin' round the Bunk it was you an' the Dillon boys.'

Ridley shook his head strenuously.

'Oh, don't worry,' Beattie assured him, 'nobody's goin' ter split on yer. Unless, of course, there's somefin' in it for 'em.'

As she spoke, a railway train approached at full speed making its way north, leaving a trail of thick black smoke behind to engulf the bridge above. When it had cleared, Ridley drew closer, glanced all around, then lowered his voice. 'Listen ter me, Beat,' he said, with almost a look of begging in his eyes. 'I was in at the job at Sedgwick's, but I split the moment I 'eard Ben comin'. The boys – they did the rest. I was round the corner at the time, at the end of the Bunk. There was nuffin' I could do.'

'Really, Jack?' replied Beattie, staring coldly at him. 'Yer mean yer couldn't've stopped the cold-blooded murder of a man whose 'ead was pushed down a drain just because 'e was doin' 'is job?'

Ridley took hold of her arms. 'You don't know the Dillon boys, Beat,' he said earnestly. 'If I'd've put one foot out of place, they'd've topped me too.'

Beattie was quite impervious to his plea. 'D'yer know

'ow many kids Ben has?' she said. 'Five. The eldest is seventeen, the youngest is two. They took 'is missus off ter the 'ospital when she 'eard. Merry Christmas – eh?'

Ridley again shook his head in anguish. ''Elp me, Beat,' he pleaded. 'Please 'elp me.'

'Wot d'yer expect *me* ter do?' she asked, acidly.

'I've got ter get away. I need some cash.'

Beattie turned, and started to move away.

Ridley went after her, and held her back. '*Please*, Beat!' he begged. 'If I turn meself in, they'll top me.'

'If yer din't 'ave anyfin' ter do wiv it, then why should they top yer?'

Ridley stared hard at her. ''Cos they 'aven't an 'ope in 'ell of findin' the Dillon boys. The Dillons 've got their contacts; they can vamoose wivout any trouble at all. This is a flatfoot killin', Beat. The fuzz are goin' ter want ter get someone, even if it ain't the right man.'

Beattie thought about this for a moment, and she saw that what Ridley was saying made sense. A police killing was one of the worst crimes anyone could commit. Ben's pals in the fuzz would never rest until they took their revenge on anyone who was even remotely involved. 'Where are yer making for?' she asked reluctantly.

'I don't know,' he replied. 'Somewhere – anywhere. But I've got ter find some way of gettin' out of the country. Maybe go ter Ireland or somefin'. But I need some cash. I ain't got a farvin' in the world.'

''Ow much?'

Ridley shrugged his shoulders.

Beattie sighed and moved a short way from him. Through the narrow metal grille of the bridge, she could just see the tiny figure of young Ed, who was waiting for her on the deserted football pitch down below. And then she thought

299

about all the plans she and the boy had made about moving into their new home, their hopes, their aspirations. How could she betray the boy by giving up the best part of a hundred pounds to a man who had abused both her and the son that she had brought into this world? Ed deserved the right to a new start in life, she was telling herself. He was a kid with a good brain, who deserved to be given a good education, a good home to live in, and a chance to show what he could do. But then she thought about what would happen if Jack Ridley were to turn himself in. Like it or not, he was still legally her husband, even though he had never treated her like a wife, in or out of bed. And how would it be if her son went through life branded with the stigma of having a stepfather who was hanged for murder? The dilemma was tearing her apart. After a moment, however, she turned back to Ridley. 'All right, Jack,' she said firmly. 'I'll give yer wot I've got.'

Ridley breathed a sigh of relief.

'But on condition,' added Beattie, 'that neivver me nor Ed ever 'ave ter set eyes on yer again. 'Cos if we do, I swear ter God – I'll turn yer in.'

Being a Buddhist, Mrs Ranasinghe didn't recognise Christmas as the most important festive season of the year. However, she always celebrated it, even if devilled chicken, vegetable curry and rice, and seeni sambol were her preferred Ceylonese favourites to roast turkey and Christmas pudding. This being a special year, because her married daughter Marla was visiting her in England for the first time, her small annual dinner party was held on Boxing Day. Although Sarah was in the strict sense an employee, the old lady now considered her to be more of a friend, so after helping Marla in the kitchen, Sarah took her place at the dining-table alongside her 'gentleman friend, the barber', who had also been invited. The only other guest was Mrs Elsa de Silva, an old friend of Mrs Ranasinghe, who had left her husband in Colombo over twenty years before, and had lived in London ever since.

Despite the old lady's constant carping about how old-fashioned her daughter was, the moment Marla had arrived, Sarah took a liking to her. Unlike her mother, Marla was quite a tubby little woman, who, oddly enough, preferred to wear western-style clothes to the traditional Ceylonese sari. But she had a great sense of humour, and knew exactly how to keep both her mother and Mrs de Silva in check.

Sarah loved the way the two old ladies had built their relationship on one-upmanship. Several times during the evening she had listened to them reminiscing about their childhood days in Kandy, and she frequently had to suppress a giggle when the two of them nearly came to blows over their different versions of events.

There was also a tricky moment when Mrs de Silva asked everyone, 'Tell me, does anyone know why the English insist on calling today Boxing Day?'

To everyone's surprise, Freddie immediately came up with more or less the right answer. 'Actually, Mrs de Silva,' he said, with gentle courtesy, 'my gran once told me that in the old days, employers usually gave their Christmas boxes to their employees on the day after Christmas Day. I s'ppose that's where the name came from. Of course, it's all changed now.'

Mrs Ranasinghe looked very smug. 'You're quite right, Mr Hamwell,' she said. Then, turning to her old friend, added, 'After all the years you've been in England, Elsa, I'm surprised you didn't know that.'

Mrs de Silva grunted, and turned to look the other way.

'Actually,' said Marla, interrupting like a mediator, 'I

heard that Boxing Day had something to do with taking a collection in church for the poor.'

'You're probably right, Marla,' said Sarah. 'We could do with some of that today. After all these years, this country is still plagued with poverty.'

'Well, you only have Ramsay MacDonald and this damned Labour Government to blame for that!' Mrs de Silva sniffed.

Mrs Ranasinghe sat bolt upright in her wheelchair. 'Come now, Elsa,' she said touchily. 'What makes you think Baldwin and the Conservatives would do any better?'

'The Conservatives are a better class of person,' returned Mrs de Silva. 'They know how to handle business.'

'Poppycock!' spluttered Mrs Ranasinghe, indignantly. 'Anyway, it's very rude of you to discuss political matters when you're not entitled to the vote!'

Marla exchanged a resigned sigh with Sarah.

'It's not only in England where there's trouble with business and the economy,' said Freddie, quickly diffusing the situation. 'Just look at other countries – unemployment, rows and fights, people on the dole everywhere. I'm afraid it's goin' ter get worse before it gets better.'

'I think it's time I did the washing-up,' said Sarah, quickly rising from the table.

'I'll come and help you,' said Marla, also rising, and collecting the dishes as she went.

As they made for the kitchen, both Sarah and Marla took one last wicked look back at Freddie, who was clearly quite concerned at being left alone with the two old warhorses.

'Actually, I've been wanting to talk to you, Sarah,' said Marla, drying the dishes as Sarah washed them. 'Mother got her appointment to see the specialist the other day. Did she tell you?'

Sarah shook her head. 'Anything concerning her health she usually keeps from me,' she replied, with a smile. 'It's nothing serious, though, is it?'

'I hope not,' said Marla. 'But I've been a bit worried about these pains she's been getting in her chest.'

Sarah turned with a start. 'Pains in her chest?' she asked anxiously. 'She didn't tell me about that.'

'I don't think it's anything to worry about,' said Marla. 'As you know, she likes her food a lot, so it may be indigestion. But I think it's best to be on the safe side. Anyway, we shall find out definitely in the New Year.' She started to pile the dry dishes on the kitchen table. 'But one thing I must say,' she said, 'is how wonderful you've been to my mother. I don't know how she would have coped without you all these years.'

'Oh, it has nothing to do with me,' replied Sarah. 'Your mother is a very determined lady. She knows what she wants, and she knows how to get it – regardless of anything I do.'

They both laughed gently at this.

'Mother thinks highly of you, you know,' said Marla, whose firm and cut-glass accent sounded as though it came straight out of an English public school. 'I think she'll miss you a great deal when she has to go back home.'

'You mean, that's a possibility?' Sarah asked, tentatively.

'I think it's inevitable sooner or later,' replied Marla. 'If anything should happen to her, it would be better for her, and for us, if she was home amongst her own family. Despite what she may have told you, we all love her very much.'

Sarah smiled, but she couldn't help feeling a little sad inside. They were interrupted by a ring on the doorbell.

'Who on earth is that at this time of night?' asked Marla. 'I thought the carol singing was all over now.'

'It's probably one of the neighbours coming in to cadge a

drink from your mother,' Sarah said lightly. 'Don't worry, I'll take care of it.'

'No,' said Marla, making for the door. 'One look at me, and they'll run for their lives!'

Sarah laughed. She carried on washing up, concerned by what she had heard about her employer. Although she had tried to dismiss the thought from her mind, over the past few weeks the old lady had indeed been less lively than in the past, and even more disturbing was the way she had stopped talking about the plans she was making for the house, something she had done since the first day Sarah had come to work for her.

'You have a visitor,' announced Marla, as she returned.

Sarah was astonished to see who Marla had brought in with her. 'Ed!' she cried, drying her hands on the wiping-up cloth, and going to him. 'What are you doing here?'

The boy hung his head low, and didn't reply. He looked not only cold, but thoroughly miserable.

Sarah exchanged a concerned look with Marla. 'I'm sorry, Marla,' she explained. 'This is my nephew, Ed. Say hello, Ed.'

Ed could only manage a quiet grunt.

Marla held up her hand to Sarah. 'I'll leave you two together,' she said with an understanding smile as she made for the door. 'Take your time.'

After she had gone, Sarah took the boy's flat cap off, and led him to the table. 'What is it, Ed?' she asked, sitting him down. 'What's happened?'

The boy looked up slowly at her. His eyes were raw from crying. 'It's Jack Ridley,' he said. ''E's stopped us from movin'.'

'Ridley? Stopped you?' said Sarah. 'But I thought you told me it was all arranged. You were supposed to be moving

304

to Mitford Road some time in—'

'I tell yer, 'e's stopped it. We ain't goin' – not now, not ever!'

'But why?'

The boy looked slowly up at her. His eyes were now once again swelling with tears. 'She's given 'im the money, the money we got from Granddad. She's given 'im the money. 'E's a killer, an' I 'ate 'im! An' she's given 'im the money!'

Chapter 21

The year of 1931 was already turning out to be even more of a mess for the country politically than the dark years of the General Strike. In February, Oswald Mosley resigned from the Labour Party in protest at the parlous state of the economy. This was followed by his forming his own radical 'New Party', which fomented as much trouble as it possibly could on the streets, particularly in the poorer districts of London. With unemployment now more than three million, the long-term unemployed were enraged when they were asked to submit to a means test before receiving any further relief from public funds, and their grievances, on top of everything else they had endured over the years, threatened to turn into another full-scale showdown with the government.

The situation abroad was little better. In Spain there was the real prospect of a civil war when the government of General Berenguer was forced to resign and King Alfonso XIII had to flee the country. In Germany too, the years of crisis since the end of the war were taking their toll on the population. With unemployment there also at record levels, there were signs that a thuggish type of political uprising was becoming a very real threat.

For Beattie and Ed the year had started better than they had anticipated. The great life-saver was, of course, being able to move into the new property in Mitford Road after all. The bonus was Ma Briggs, who had been persuaded to give up living in the grime and hate of the Bunk, and who had immediately taken it upon herself to make sure that the new premises were scrubbed out thoroughly with DDT from top to bottom, so that by the time she had finished there wasn't a cockroach in sight. She had also helped Beattie and Ed to put up wallpaper, which was a new experience for all of them. But both women were surprised to see what a dab hand Ed was at painting the woodwork. His joy at moving into such a place, with his own bedroom, an inside lavatory, and a yard out back, had clearly given him a new lease of life.

For Beattie also, moving away from the Bunk and all its implications was a gift from heaven, or rather from Jack Ridley. She had never stopped thanking God for the day that Ridley had waited for Ed outside his school, and handed back the eighty pounds Beattie had given him to help him get out of the country. Although Ridley's apparent change of mind didn't make him any better a person, at least it showed that he had some degree of conscience.

Beattie's main preoccupation now was to put the events of the week before Christmas behind her. She hoped that, three months since the callous murder of Big Ben Fodder, the residents of the Bunk might have come to their senses and at least made an effort to restore some kind of decency to their tarnished community.

Beattie's priority now was Ed. The moment she left the Bunk, she was determined that with the prospect of the school-leaving age now being raised to fifteen, the boy was to be given all the support he needed to catch up on his lost education – no more truancy, no more kicking tin cans around the street. She had been given full-time work as a cleaner at Finsbury Park tube station, and she was able to give Ed a small weekly allowance with which to buy the books he craved.

She rarely thought about Sarah, whom she hadn't seen since the morning she flew into a rage at her for what she suspected was an attempt by her sister to turn the boy against her. But she held no malice against Sarah, and in some ways even regretted the fact that they were no longer in contact. With her new attitude of mind, Beattie decided that, when the time was ripe, she would make the effort to improve the atmosphere between them. Unfortunately, even the best intentions go awry.

On one fine spring morning in March, Beattie found herself sitting just a seat away from Sarah on a number 38 tram, heading up Holloway Road and Upper Street towards the Angel, Islington. At first, their contact was no more than a double take, but after they had established full eye contact, Beattie had no alternative but to move into the seat next to her sister. 'Long time, no see,' said Beattie, which was her usual greeting when she was taken by surprise.

'Hello, Beattie,' replied Sarah, stiffly, moving up as much as she could to give Beattie more room.

The lower deck of the tram was jammed, and every so often the standing passengers swayed to and fro as they struggled to hold on to the overhead straps.

'So where yer off to then?' asked Beattie, who was surprised to see her sister with a new hairstyle, and looking far younger and more radiant than she'd hoped.

'I'm going to see a friend of mine,' replied Sarah, who thought that Beattie was looking tidier, and wearing more suitable clothes then she could ever remember. 'He's a barber. He has a shop near the Angel.'

'Oh yes,' replied Beattie, who wasn't too interested. 'That's nice.'

'So how've you been?'

Beattie perked up immediately. 'Oh,' she said, 'fings couldn't be better. When Lacey's farver died, 'e left us – I mean, 'e left Ed – a nice little nest egg. 'E probably told yer about it.'

'If he did, I don't remember,' replied Sarah, carefully. 'I don't see Ed very much these days,' she said, tactfully.

Beattie was in a quandary. The moment she saw Sarah, she wanted to put things right, she wanted to tell her that they should bury the hatchet and try to become friends again. But then, before she could do anything about it, she found herself wanting to make an impression, to make Sarah jealous that things were actually going well for her. 'Me an' Ed 'ave moved into a nice little place up Mitford Road,' she said, proudly.

'That's wonderful, Beattie,' replied Sarah, genuinely pleased. 'I'm so happy for you both.'

'Oh yes,' Beattie continued, trying hard not to show that she was boasting, even though she obviously was. 'We've got a room each, an' a kitchen/diner. We've got our own lav – toilet – an' a lovely little garden at the back. Yer must come an' visit us some time.' Even as she said it, she wished she hadn't.

'That's very kind of you, Beattie,' said Sarah. 'Some time.'

The tram rattled its way along the Holloway Road, and when it reached Highbury Corner, it was a relief for both sisters to see so many people getting off. But once the last of them had cleared the platform, a queue of new passengers filed on board.

'So what's happened to your husband?' asked Sarah, as casually as she could manage. 'Has he moved in with you?'

Beattie hesitated only briefly. 'Oh no,' she replied, cagily.

'Jack's gone abroad. He's got a job.'

'Oh really? That's nice.' Sarah didn't sound at all convincing.

'Me an' Jack are not really tergevver now,' said Beattie, who kept fidgeting and tidying her dress uneasily as she talked. 'These fings 'appen, though.'

'Of course.'

'But 'e's bin good about our new place,' she added, again trying to impress Sarah. 'Oh yes. In fact we 'ave 'im ter fank fer us gettin' most of the cash. It's just that 'e ain't cut out ter be a family man, that's all.'

Sarah smiled, without giving anything away. 'I'm so pleased to hear that things are going so well for you, Beattie,' she said. 'Especially after the terrible time you must have gone through at Christmas.' She paused only long enough to think what she was going to say. 'I hear the police are looking for some local men who were involved.'

Beattie was quick off the mark once more. 'Oh, those bruvvers, yer mean?' Her reaction was again accompanied by fidgeting. 'If it's the lot I remember, they deserve everyfin' they get. They used ter play dice an' fings down our road. Poor old Ben was always after 'em. They gave 'im an 'ell of a lot of lip.' Then she added as an afterthought, 'Jack was always tellin' 'em ter leave the poor man alone.'

Sarah nodded, her smile fixed. 'That was brave of him,' she replied. Her remark carried more meaning than Beattie would ever know. 'But then, he was always a man of many surprises, wasn't he?'

Tinker Murdoch swept the barber shop floor. It had been quite a busy morning, for Freddie had done eight haircuts without a break. The hair left over on the floor was a wonderful kaleidoscope of colours, curls, and just plain

311

straight. There were three different shades of brown, two greys, a couple of blondes, and even a bright ginger. Young Tinker had a broad grin on his face as he swept it all up into a pile, because every selection of discarded hair reminded him of the head that it had come from. And what a collection it was! One or two of them were casual customers, but the regulars, such as Mr Mooney from the flower shop in Upper Street, and Mr Pyle, the commissionaire from the Blue Hall cinema, had the most wonderful habits, which were a gift to a mimic such as Freddie's young apprentice. For instance, Mr Mooney often quite unconsciously picked his nose, which always ended up in his sneezing his head off, and Mr Pyle's face never failed to stop twitching with anticipation when he knew that he was the next customer to be attended to. There was also a young chap who came in every fortnight, whose girlfriend always waited outside, peering in the window and waving at him, which somehow made the chap feel quite good, as though everyone was envious of his undoubted attraction to the female sex. Whenever she came into the shop during the lunch hour, Sarah loved Tinker's impersonations; she was always telling him that he should be on the stage.

Sarah arrived at the shop at exactly one o'clock, but as the last customer before lunch had already left, Tinker had put up the 'CLOSED FOR LUNCH' sign on the inside of the shop door. The moment he saw Sarah, Freddie went to meet her. Tinker covered his eyes when they embraced and kissed, saying he was far too young to witness such goings-on. He never, of course, referred to his own girlfriend, who was waiting for him in the caff just down the road, but before he went off to join her, he did manage to get in one quick impersonation of one of the morning's customers, who spent the whole time whilst Freddie was cutting his thinning hair admiring himself in the mirror facing him. As usual, Sarah absolutely loved Tinker's turn and was in fits of laughter.

Once Tinker had left, Sarah noticed that there was something different about Freddie. 'You're looking awfully smug today, Mr Hamwell,' she chided.

'I'm glad yer noticed, miss,' he quipped, before suddenly disappearing into his back room, to re-emerge almost immediately clutching a huge bunch of daffodils. 'Compliments of the management!' he announced grandly. 'Mr Mooney in the flower shop chose 'em 'imself.'

Sarah was taken aback as Freddie passed them to her. 'But – why, Freddie?' she asked.

'Do I 'ave ter 'ave a reason?' he asked.

'Well, no, no of course not,' she replied. 'But—'

'They're a celebration,' he said.

'Celebration?'

'It's the anniversary of our first meetin', when yer came up 'ere ter see me. Five munffs this week.'

Sarah laughed. 'Thank you, Freddie,' she said, giving him a gentle kiss. 'But you've got it all wrong. The first time we met was in the queue outside the Blue Hall, with Eunice and Ernie.'

'Yeah, but that was diff'rent,' said Freddie. 'When yer first saw me, yer 'ated the sight of me.'

Sarah's expression changed immediately to concern. 'Oh, Freddie, that's not true. I could never hate anyone like you. You're one of the sweetest people I've ever known in my entire life.'

Freddie beamed. 'Then your old lady was right.'

Sarah was puzzled, as he put his arm around her waist and led her to the row of customers' chairs along one side of the shop. 'Old lady?' she asked. 'Who are you talking about?'

Freddie eased her down on to one of the chairs, and then sat alongside her. 'Your boss. Mrs Rana-thing.' He was thoroughly enjoying the game he was playing. 'She told me, long ago, if I din't ask yer ter marry me, I'd be the biggest chump in the 'ole world.'

Sarah's mouth dropped. 'Freddie!' she gasped.

'Wot about it, Sarah?' he asked, with a begging, longing look in his eyes. 'I want ter marry you, an' I want us ter live tergevver fer the rest of our lives.'

Sarah was half-laughing, half-crying. 'Freddie, I don't know what to say.'

'Just say yes,' he replied quickly. 'If yer like . . .' He suddenly dropped to his knees in front of her, and in a mock attempt at the old-fashioned proposal ritual, took hold of both her hands and looked up at her . . . 'I can do it the proper way.'

Sarah was laughing. 'Don't be so silly,' she said.

'Well, will yer – or won't yer?'

Sarah was at a loss for words. If someone had told her a few years ago that she would be sitting in a men's barber shop, with a funny little working-class man proposing to her, she would have laughed in their face. But Freddie Hamwell was different. What he lacked in sophistication, he made up for in warmth, care, and understanding. And what he didn't understand, he made it a point to find out. There was nothing dark or mysterious about Freddie, and though he had his weak points, like sulking when someone contradicted him, or refusing to let other people do things for him, he was basically honest and open, a man of immense compassion. But could she marry him? Was he the one man she would want to share the rest of her life with? Could she be sure? Could she be absolutely sure? Whatever her doubts, her mind was made up. 'If you really want me, Freddie,' she said, staring into his eyes, 'I'd be very proud to be your wife.'

The wide beam on Freddie's face told it all. He immediately got to his feet, eased Sarah up from the chair, threw his arms around her and hugged her. Over his shoulder, he could see an eager face peering through the shop window. He gave the thumbs-up sign.

Tinker's cheeky face lit up. Then he pulled off his cap, and threw it straight up into the air.

'Married?' barked Mrs Ranasinghe, who had reacted to Sarah's news as though it had come as a complete surprise. 'Who to?'

'You know perfectly well who to!' chided Sarah. 'In fact, you put him up to it, you know you did.'

The old lady had a mischievous twinkle in her eye. 'Oh, if you're talking about that barber fellow, then it's all right.' Having made her approval obvious, she held out her hands to Sarah, took them, and pulled her down so that she could give her a kiss on the cheek. 'I shall miss you, young lady,' she said with hidden significance.

'Miss me?' Sarah returned, immediately. 'Well, don't think you're getting rid of me as quickly as that. Freddie and I won't be able to get married until next spring at the earliest. We've got so many things to do, and plans to make.' She was so breathless with excitement, she was practically tumbling over her words. 'We're going to live in Freddie's room above the shop – just for a while, until we find somewhere bigger and more permanent. Freddie's got all sorts of ideas where he wants us to go. I'm leaving it all up to him.'

Marla then came over to her. 'It's wonderful, Sarah,' she said, hugging her. 'I'm so happy for you. We both are, aren't we, Mother?'

315

The old lady sniffed. 'I suppose so,' she said, clearly determined not to show how thrilled she was. 'At least you won't have to pay to have your hair done any more!'

Sarah and Marla laughed. But despite the old lady's apparent happiness, Sarah could sense that both Mrs Ranasinghe and her daughter were trying to put on brave faces. It was this thought, and the odd exchange of looks that passed between Marla and her mother, that gradually changed Sarah's expression to one of concern.

'Is anything wrong?' she asked, addressing her question to both of them.

Marla hesitated, then looked at the old lady. 'I think, Mother,' she said awkwardly, 'you have something you want to say to Sarah.'

Sarah switched her look from Marla to her mother.

Mrs Ranasinghe was looking very pale and drawn. Sarah hadn't really noticed before now that the old lady was developing lines to the sides of her mouth and beneath her eyes, on what had been until recently a beautiful, clear pale brown face. 'It seems my family want me to go back home,' she said. 'My other home, that is.'

Sarah felt her stomach tense. 'Oh, I see,' were the only words she could find.

The old lady settled herself back in her wheelchair. 'I fear they want to keep an eye on me, just in case something should happen when they're not around.' There was just a suggestion of that wry smile on her face that Sarah had come to know and love so well. 'It's all poppycock, of course. I intend to live for at least another twenty years – if not more!'

'Indeed you will, dear lady,' said Sarah, brightly. She could feel Marla's eyes searching for hers. They clearly had a different story to tell. 'So – when are you planning to leave?' she asked, stoically.

Marla answered. 'If we get things cleared up here in time, there's a boat from Tilbury on the twenty-ninth of next month.'

Sarah felt a sense of despair. 'Goodness. That's less than a month. We'll have quite a lot to do before then.'

Marla was looking at her. There was a pained expression on her face. She wanted to say something, to explain, to make it all sound as though there really wasn't anything to worry about. But the words just wouldn't come. 'Why don't I leave you two to have a chat?' she said, tactfully. 'You've got a lot to talk through.' She smiled gratefully at Sarah, and then left the room.

The old lady wheeled herself to the window. It was a glorious day outside, and the spring sunshine was streaming through the lace curtains, casting weblike patterns across her face. 'I can't remember the number of times I've sat at this window on my own, staring out at the same old things, same people, big dogs, little dogs, awful cats, the milkman, the baker, the postman. And yet, one way or another, they're all different. You know, I often wonder what your God or mine was thinking about when He made the human race.' She turned briefly to throw a look at Sarah. 'I mean, we really are a peculiar lot, aren't we?'

Sarah came across to her and placed her hands gently on the old lady's shoulders. 'Not all of us,' she said. 'People like you are quite special.'

The old lady chuckled. 'Oh yes, I know,' she said, with a wave of her hand. 'I bet you say that to all your old ladies.'

Sarah laughed with her. Then, for a moment or so, they both remained silent, their faces streaked with patterns of light.

It was finally Mrs Ranasinghe who broke the silence. 'I want you to promise me something,' she said. 'I want you

317

to promise that you'll keep in touch with Marla. She likes you, respects you. I hope one day you and your husband will come to visit her out in Ceylon. I won't be there to greet you, but I'll certainly be there in spirit.'

Sarah increased the loving pressure of her hands on the old lady's shoulders. She knew what she was trying to tell her, but she was making quite sure that she would not betray the unspoken understanding they had between them.

'You would like it out there,' continued the old lady, eyes still fixed firmly on the street outside. 'We're a very close-knit community, always conniving against each other. But it's all part of the game, you see. We're actually quite nice, quite harmless.' She reached up for one of Sarah's hands, and then covered it. 'You'll have a lot of new things to experience in life, Sarah, so many exciting, wonderful things. One day, you will wake up and find that everything is suddenly in focus. You will finally know where you are, where you are going.' Again she paused briefly to look up at Sarah. 'That's how it happened to me,' she continued. 'The time came when I knew that I had a family, a family who needed me, and who I needed myself. One day, it'll be like that with you and your sister. Not that blood is thicker than water, but that you will both realise that you have a need to be part of each other again. One day, your Beattie will also wake up and wonder what has happened to her sister, Sarah. And when that day comes, that need will bring you closer together than you have ever been before.'

She spun the wheelchair around to face Sarah. 'When you walked through that door for the first time, with the awful smell of Yorkshire pudding and Brussels sprouts all over you, I was absolutely convinced that, by bringing you into my home, I was making the biggest mistake of my life.' She paused, and swallowed hard. 'I want you to know, young lady, that I couldn't have been more wrong.'

Sarah's eyes swelled with tears. She leaned down, and hugged the old lady as hard as she could.

There was never a dull moment at Liverpool Street Station. During the war its platforms had been invaded by British troops on their way to and from their training camps in the East of England en route to the battlefront in France, and during peacetime, it had been destined to become the heartbeat of office workers who were forced to commute every morning and every evening in a relentless circle of drudgery. It was also the hub of cross-Channel activity, for, together with Victoria and Waterloo Stations, it handled many of the ferry services to the European continent. This grandly built station was also used for the boat train service to Tilbury, where ocean liners took passengers to far-distant destinations such as Australia, the Far East, and South East Asia.

The boat train service for the Orient Line *Orion* ocean liner was scheduled to leave at eleven o'clock, and it was rare for it to depart late. With that fact in mind, Mrs Ranasinghe, Marla, and Sarah arrived at least half an hour early for the service, for it was obviously going to take quite a time for the old lady's wheelchair to negotiate both platform and railway carriage steps. Mrs Ranasinghe's huge trunks, together with Marla's four suitcases, and vast collection of goods that had been bought in London to take back to Ceylon, had already been sent on in advance by road to the docks at Tilbury, which made the prospect of the rail journey far less cumbersome.

As soon as she arrived at the platform, Sarah was astonished to see such a vast mixture of brown and white faces. In all the years she had been working for Mrs

319

Ranasinghe, it had never really occurred to her that there might be other people like her boss and Mrs de Silva living in this country. She was also fascinated to see the exotic colours of the ladies' saris, and the formal white tropical suits of the male passengers, which all seemed a little incongruous in the winds and drizzle of London in April. This, coupled with the rising hum of excited chatter, and tearful farewells, presented a picture that could have come straight out of a painting in an art gallery, so alive, and so full of emotion.

'If they call this first class, I dread to think what the poor devils in third class are suffering!' Mrs Ranasinghe was not amused by what she considered to be a less than inferior railway carriage, for there were grease marks on the windows, and particles of black coal dust on the off-white head rests. It was, however, at Marla's insistence that her mother was to travel first class back to Colombo, for, as had become only too clear to Sarah since she was first informed about the reasons for her employer's hasty return home, the least she was entitled to for this one last journey was a little luxury.

Sarah took out her own handkerchief, and tried to rub off the grease from the carriage window, but the more she tried, the worse it got. After a while, she gave up. At least the irritation of having it there would keep the old lady's mind occupied for the duration of the journey to Tilbury.

Once she was satisfied that Mrs Ranasinghe was comfortable, Sarah prepared herself for the moment that she had been dreading. 'I must say, I envy you,' she said, bravely. 'How wonderful to cruise along the Mediterranean, and then through the Suez Canal. Six weeks at sea is such a splendid prospect.'

'It is if you don't get seasick!' complained the old lady. 'You don't, do you?'

'Not Mother,' said Marla, who looked so anxious, it was as though she was already about to plough through the choppy seas of the Indian Ocean. 'I'm the one who suffers. On the way out, I spent nearly the entire journey lying in my bunk in the cabin. I just wanted to be left to die!'

Sarah laughed sympathetically.

'Write to me!' the old lady suddenly demanded.

Sarah smiled, and covered the old lady's hand with her own. 'Of course.' Until this moment, she had tried to avoid making direct eye contact with Mrs Ranasinghe. She had tried to forget that Marla had told her about the doctor's fears that her mother's heart condition would probably kill her within a year. She tried to forget that this was going to be the last time that she would ever see this remarkable woman. 'I think you should write to me too, though,' she said.

'You know I hate writing,' replied the old lady, her Ceylonese accent already more pronounced after hearing her fellow passengers jabbering away in Sinhala. 'But I won't forget you.'

Their eyes finally met. There was recognition there, a complete understanding of what both were feeling.

'And if there are any more wars,' said the old lady, trying to conceal her feelings, 'you and your husband are to get on the first boat and come out to us!'

'There won't be any more wars,' replied Sarah, with a smile. 'After what happened last time, the world has to come to its senses.' Her eyes momentarily flicked up to a railway travel advertisement on the wall just above the old lady's head. It read: 'FRANCE, LAND OF PEACE AND BEAUTY'.

The first shrill guard whistle filled the air. There was an immediate hustle amongst the crowds milling around the

321

railway carriages, and the slamming of doors all along the platform.

Sarah felt quite chilled. She knew that if she spoke one more word to Mrs Ranasinghe, she would make a fool of herself. So she turned first to Marla, and they embraced. Then, finally, she returned to the old lady, bent down to her, and quickly hugged her. 'I'll never forget you,' she said. Then she rushed off the train.

As she reached the platform outside, the final whistle echoed. The excited chatter amongst the well-wishers subsided instantly. Even before the train's departure, loved ones were standing at the carriage windows, waving frantically, and trying desperately to touch the hands of those they were leaving behind, perhaps for the last time.

Gradually, the train started to move, and with it moved the platform crowds, all trying to keep up with it as it went.

Sarah walked with them. All she could do now was to place her hand on the carriage window, where Mrs Ranasinghe was doing her best to take one last look at her. And then, just as the tips of Sarah's fingers were pressing hard against the glass, the old lady leaned as close as she could manage, and, placing her lips against the window, kissed Sarah's fingers through the glass.

Within moments, the train had twisted its way along the platform, its thick dark smoke curling up into the glass and metal roof of the station as it went, until it finally disappeared out of sight.

Suddenly, there was silence. Excitement had turned to emptiness, laughter to tears.

Sarah watched the train until she could neither see nor hear it any more. Then she turned, and started to make her way slowly back along the platform towards the gates. She passed through them, and found herself on the vast station concourse. She was too numb, too disoriented to know where she was going, and it took her several minutes to work out which exit would lead her to her bus stop.

Eventually, she found her way to the main station entrance, and then to the street outside. For Sarah, bidding farewell to Mrs Ranasinghe was like a chapter of her life coming to an end. And yet, in another sense, it was only just beginning.

As she ran for her bus, which was just leaving the stop, she failed to notice a news vendor's placard board nearby, which had been poorly scrawled with the words: 'GERMANY: THE NEW REVOLUTION'.

Part 3

1940 – 1941

Chapter 22

Ma Briggs was convinced that her time had come. Three times in the past week, the house in Mitford Road had been shaken from top to bottom, and on one occasion, when she and Beattie had got back from the Anderson shelter in the back yard, she found that part of the ceiling in her room had collapsed on to her freshly ironed clothes. The language she had used then was not exactly that which was becoming of a lady, but then, as Ma had never considered herself to be one, it didn't really seem to matter. None the less, it was obvious from the name she frequently called Herr Hitler, Goering, and that rat-voiced Lord Haw-Haw that she considered they had the misfortune to be fatherless.

The country was now at war with Germany for the second time this century, and there was hardly a family in the land that had not been affected by it. After nearly ten years of rebuilding her life, Beattie was now having to cope with a new kind of hardship, such as the rationing of everything from food to clothes. Just over a year before, when war had been declared, it seemed as though life was carrying on more or less the same as it had done for years. But in September 1940, the so-called phoney war came to a dramatic end, when the German Luftwaffe began their massive daily onslaught on the civilian population of London and the Home Counties. Since then, Beattie had divided her time between her job as a clippie on the buses, and getting herself and Ma safely down the air-raid shelter.

Despite the war, Beattie seemed to have found a new purpose in life. With the turmoil and horrors of the Bunk long behind her, she had settled down to a much more coherent routine, which gave her the will and the energy to survive even the most difficult situations. In many ways, she had returned to her roots, embracing many of the middle-class values that, as a young woman, she had spurned with such disdain. This was especially reflected in her home. It wasn't exactly a palace, but with the regular wage she had been earning since she had got her job on the buses, and the modest wage Ed had earned working in the Islington Central Library after leaving Holloway Grammar School, the house in Mitford Road had been transformed into a comfortable, lower-middle-class home. With Ma's help, Beattie had learned how to wash clothes properly in an aluminium bath, and to mangle, and then iron. She had even learnt how to sew on buttons, and darn Ed's socks when they sprouted holes in the heels. Domestication, which had once been an anathema to her, had now transformed the young rebel into an organised woman, who was progressing towards middle-age with a new-found confidence.

These days, Beattie was also more responsible about her own personal appearance. When she was not in her bus conductress uniform, she always managed to look good in smart, belted dresses, or a stylish blouse and skirt that she had bought in either Selby's department store in Holloway Road, or the North London Drapery Store in Seven Sisters Road. She even took trouble with her hair, which she spent time in the mornings combing up into a bunch of curls on the top of her head, a style currently so fashionable in Betty Grable musical films. And if ever she went out for the evening with any of her clippie mates, she sometimes donned a small pillbox hat, which she wore at a cheeky angle, with hair piled up all around it.

Another extraordinary change in Beattie was that, despite the fact that her job brought her into contact with working-class people, the cockney slang she had affected for so long in her younger days had gradually given way to a more gentle North London way of talking.

'Jairmany calling! Jairmany calling!'

The phoney upper-class English voice of William Joyce, better known as 'Lord Haw-Haw', the Nazis' chief English-language propagandist broadcaster, echoed out of Ma Briggs' wireless set, crackling with static and false information. His nightly commentaries on how Britain was losing the war infuriated anyone who was foolish enough to tune in to him. ''Ere 'e comes agin, the snotty-nosed git.' Ma was in good form, for Lord Haw-Haw was the one she most loved to hate. 'Goin' ter tell us that we're done for, are yer?' she barked, at the wireless set.

'Poor little Englanders,' sneered the assumed cut-glass voice, 'time is running out for you all, I fear.'

'There yer are!' protested Ma, angrily. 'Wot'd I tell yer?'

'Soon,' continued Ma's sworn enemy, 'the powerful boots of the Führer's troops will be leaving their glorious mark all over the faded white cliffs of Dover . . .'

'Some 'opes!' yelled Ma, shaking her fist at the wireless. 'Just wait till we get our rope round your neck, mate. We'll separate yer from yer bleedin' breff!'

'Ma!' called Beattie, who was half-laughing whilst ironing at the kitchen table. 'Why d'you always listen to that stupid man? You *know* he only does it to work us all up.'

''Cos I like ter work out in me mind wot an 'orrible

329

bleedin' fissog 'e's got, an' 'ow I'd like ter get my 'ands round 'is froat an' wring the bleedin' daylights out of 'im!' Ma had her hands stretched out towards the wireless set as though she was about to strangle the creature sheltering inside it.

Beattie was getting used to Ma's nightly ritual. One minute the old girl was laughing her head off at Tommy Handley in *ITMA*, and the next, she was lambasting Winston Churchill and the entire government for not sending out a raid party to capture her pet hate in the wireless set.

Even so, in time of war Ma was an inspiration, a real morale booster. Now a sprightly eighty-two-year-old, she had more energy and drive than many people half her age, so much so that she still insisted on washing her own hair in the kitchen sink every week, and putting in the same curlers she'd kept in her old mum's 'vanity box' for what seemed like a hundred years. And, despite the wartime rations, she had managed to fill out to nearly twice the size she'd been when she'd run her boarding house back in the Bunk.

'Of course,' continued Ma, relentlessly, 'yer know this git used ter be in the Fascist Party, wiv ol' Mosley?'

Beattie didn't reply. Ma told her the same information every night she listened to Lord Haw-Haw, so there was really very little she could say. But every time Ma mentioned it, Beattie thought of Shiner, whom Jack Ridley had once threatened to kill if he ever tried to sleep with his wife again. Like the dangerous Fascist agitator himself, he had been detained in prison for the duration of the war.

'I tell yer this much though,' Ma whined, still glaring with venom at the wireless set, 'the way 'e reads that stuff, yer can tell that 'e ain't got a bleedin' brain in 'is—'

'Ma – quiet!' Beattie suddenly shut her up.

'Wos up?'

'Listen!' said Beattie, going to the wireless. 'I want to hear what he's saying.' To Ma's astonishment, she turned up the volume.

The plummy voice of the Nazi collaborator now filled the room. '. . . and after the invasion of Egypt by the brave forces of our victorious Italian ally, Marshal Benito Mussolini, the totally demoralised men of your English 8th Army are now being chased through the Western Desert, in one of the greatest humiliations in British military history.'

'Lyin' sod!' yelled Ma.

Beattie turned off the set abruptly.

Ma was no fool. She knew at once why Beattie had reacted in such a way. Struggling to her feet, she went straight to her, and put her arms around her. 'Don't listen to 'im, Beat,' she said comfortingly. 'No 'arm'll come to our Ed. 'E's far too clever.'

Beattie smiled weakly. 'Of course, Ma,' she said. 'I know.'

At that moment, they were distracted by the distant wail of the air-raid siren.

'Oh blimey!' groaned Ma. ''Ere we go again!'

'You go ahead,' said Beattie, quickly shunting the old girl towards the back yard door. 'I'll join you down the shelter as soon as I've put the ironing away.'

Ma left, grunting and groaning. 'Take no notice!' she called, as she went. ''E's a lyin' sod!'

After the old girl had gone, Beattie closed the door, and drew the blackout curtain across. For a moment or so, she stood in the pitch-dark, listening to the distant anti-aircraft gunfire. But her mind was occupied with something far more important than the start of yet another night's aerial bombardment. She was thinking of Ed, and how the worst moment of the war had been when he had volunteered for military service. Every time she thought about it, she ached

331

inside. God knows, it had been hard enough to accept that her only son had been taken from her, but to know that his life would be in constant danger was just too much to take.

Her mind drifted back to the day when the boy tried to find a way of getting to Spain to fight against the Falangists in the Civil War, despite the fact that he was no more than seventeen years of age at the time. Then, when he was barely twenty-one, going straight into the army, to be sent within weeks to fight in France with the British Expeditionary Forces, only to return shell-shocked and traumatised from the horrifying retreat at Dunkirk. And if that wasn't enough, active duty again 'somewhere in North Africa'. It didn't make sense, rhyme, or reason. Oh yes, Ed had guts all right, but he was still her son, and he was only made of flesh and bones. Damn Lord Haw-Haw, she thought.

The droning of enemy aircraft grew closer and closer, and the house shook beneath the barrage of ack-ack fire that greeted them. Damn Lord Haw-Haw, Beattie fumed again. Damn him and all those who made him possible.

She opened the door, and went down to join Ma in the shelter.

Sarah swept the glass on the pavement from Freddie's barber shop window, and piled it into the kerb, to await, along with all the other bomb damage debris, the Borough Council collection. It had been another night of intense bombing by Jerry, in which poor old Essex Road nearby had copped a high-explosive bomb on a sweet shop, which had caused considerable damage throughout the neighbourhood right up to the Angel.

'Well, we've been lucky so far,' said Freddie, who was already fixing a 'BUSINESS AS USUAL' sign on his front door, now boarded up with strong timber planks. 'It was bound ter be our lot sooner or later.'

Sarah had just finished the clearing up when it started to rain. 'It's those poor devils in Maynards I'm thinking about,' she said, coming back inside with Freddie. 'They say it was a direct hit, nothing left of the sweet shop. I don't see how anybody could survive that.'

'Yer mustn't upset yerself, dear,' said Freddie, closing the shop door behind him. 'I'm afraid it's goin' ter get worse before it gets better. This could well be Jerry softenin' us up before 'e pays us a visit.'

Sarah was alarmed. 'Oh God, Freddie,' she said. 'D'you really think there *will* be an invasion?'

Freddie immediately wished he hadn't said that, so he put his arms around her. 'No, of course I don't, yer silly fing,' he said, holding her to him. 'If Jerry ever tries ter set foot on Blighty, we an' the gang'll be waitin' for 'im.'

Sarah pulled back, and looked at him. After eight years of married life, she had grown terribly protective of him. 'I don't want to hear you talk like that, Freddie,' she said, deadly serious. 'You're fifty-four years of age now. Fighting should be done by young men.'

'Wot young men?' asked Freddie.

Sarah thought about this. It was true. Most young men, just on the threshold of life itself, had been called up, taken away, and plunged into a useless exercise to prop up the retreating French troops whose positions had collapsed before the advancing German military machine. Young men like Tinker, Freddie's former apprentice, barely twenty-five years of age, killed in action in France after stepping on a landmine. It was cruel, so very cruel. 'Please don't take chances, Freddie,' she said with pleading eyes. 'I couldn't bear anything to happen to you.'

Freddie kissed her lightly. 'The 'Ome Guard don't take

chances, Sarah,' he said, with a comforting smile. 'We're just around in *case* of trouble.'

Until the start of the Second World War, life had been good for Mr and Mrs Freddie Hamwell. They were married in the spring of 1932 at St Mary's Church in Upper Street, with Sarah looking beautiful in a modest three-quarter-length wedding dress of white organza set off at her neck by a fluted lace collar, and a thin, half-length cotton veil topped by a small cluster of spring flowers – all made by herself. Both families were there, but Freddie's side far exceeded Sarah's, except that Aunt Dixie made up for all those who weren't there, by drinking as much gin as she could lay her hands on at the wedding reception afterwards at the Freemasons Hall in Clerkenwell Road. Against her instinct, Sarah did invite Beattie to the wedding, but was much relieved when she declined, 'owing to a prior commitment'. However, young Ed did turn up, and created a big impression amongst the two families by talking with great intelligence about such things as the danger of Oswald Mosley and his New Party, and the suppression of the peasants in Spain. Despite his opinions, the reception was a huge success.

Since then, there had been two major disappointments in Sarah and Freddie's marriage. The first was that, despite Freddie's early promises, they had still not moved from his cramped two rooms and a kitchen above the shop, which made life very difficult whenever Sarah wanted to invite family or friends over for tea. But the greatest sadness had been for Sarah to discover from a gynaecologist that she was unable to have children. For a time, this gave her a terrible complex, for she felt guilty, blaming herself for betraying Freddie, and denying him one last chance of becoming a father. But when Freddie told her, 'Having you as me wife is the most precious thing I have,' she realised what a special

334

man he really was, and why she loved him more than anything or anybody else in the whole wide world.

Within an hour or so, Sarah and Freddie between them had cleaned up the shop, so that by their normal opening time of half-past eight, business could resume – despite Jerry's determination that it should do otherwise. And sure enough, at exactly half-past eight, the first customer arrived. It was old Arthur Ballard, who some years before had regularly brought his young grandson into the shop for a pudding-basin haircut. But the boy was now a teenager, and, according to Arthur, would soon be getting a free haircut, courtesy of the army barber. Now pushing ninety, the old boy had the most wonderful shock of white hair.

'Reckon it's about time 'e give yer double time fer this job,' quipped the old boy, taking his seat in the barber's chair. 'Mind you, I still don't 'old wiv wives workin' fer their 'usbands.'

Sarah smiled, and put a clean towel around his neck. 'I'm not working *for* him, Arthur,' she said. 'I'm working *with* him.'

'That's right, Arfur,' said Freddie, combing back the old boy's hair. 'There ain't no lads around these days. They're eivver called up, or makin' some fast cash in better-paid jobs.'

'This bleedin' war!' growled the old boy, as Freddie trimmed his hair. 'It's breakin' up families all over the place. Yer can't tell if the kids're alive or dead!'

Sarah shuddered as she thought of Ed, and wondered if she would ever see him, or Beattie, again.

'Business as usual! That's wot I like ter see!' The bright and cheery voice calling from the shop door was Frank, the postman. In his outstretched hand he was clutching just one letter. 'Lucky ter get somefin' terday, mate!' he called. 'They got the sortin' office last night. 'Ole lot went up in smoke.'

Freddie reluctantly took the letter from him. 'If it's a bill, yer can stick it!'

Frank laughed. 'Don't expect me ter pay it!' he joked as he left.

Freddie looked at the letter. 'Fer you, dear,' he said. 'Don't worry, it don't look like a bill.'

Sarah took the plain white envelope from him. The address was written by hand, but all in capital letters. She tried to read the postmark, but it was none too clear. When she slit open the envelope with one finger, she looked straight to the end of the hand-written letter to see who had sent it.

Fortunately, it wasn't a bill. It was from Beattie.

Beattie had only been a clippie on the trolleybus for a couple of months. Before that, she had been operating on the number 14 route, which was a good old-fashioned double-decker petrol bus that crossed London all the way from Hornsey Rise in the north, to Putney in the west. But although the trolleys were clearly the transport of the future, Beattie didn't care for them, mainly because they worked off overhead power lines, and whenever the two connecting poles came off, and started to flap around in midair, it was her job to slide out the long, cumbersome pole from underneath the bus and get the overhead connection working again. But at least it was a smooth ride, and one advantage the trolleys had over the petrol buses was that they were wider and easier to move around in.

On the morning after the Essex Road sweet shop bomb, Beattie was on duty on the 609 route to Moorgate. There were, as always, plenty of passengers, and Beattie found herself going up and down the stairs continually. On the upper deck, she could hardly see through the thick haze of

336

cigarette smoke, and as no passenger ever seemed to want to open a window, the atmosphere was stifling. None the less, her ticket machine was kept busy, punching out tickets at a penny, twopence, and threepence. Very few passengers were travelling the entire journey, and some of those who did, tried to insist that they had only got on at the previous bus stop.

As the bus reached Highbury Corner, Beattie tried to peer through the protective gauze-covered windows, where it was obvious there was quite a lot of activity after the bomb blast the previous night. Shopkeepers were sweeping up broken glass from their windows, and others were busily boarding up the devastated shop fronts. All along Upper Street, fire engines were racing past heading off to the worst-affected areas where water mains had burst and electric power lines had come down. It was a scene of utter chaos everywhere, and one that was becoming more and more familiar as the aerial onslaught continued.

'Wanna a pair of nylons, mate?' one of the younger male passengers asked Beattie as she punched him out a twopenny ticket. 'Goin' cheap. You've got the legs ter fill 'em!'

Beattie gave him his ticket, and wanted to tell him where to stuff his black-market nylons. But she thought better of it, took the bloke's coins, gave him the ticket, and with a stern, disapproving look, moved on.

Her next customer was an elderly lady, who had a large mongrel dog wedged in between her feet. 'One adult and one dog to City Road, please, dear,' she said.

Beattie took one of the coins from the palm of the old lady's hand. 'Let's forget about the dog, shall we?' she replied, with a grin. 'He's not a seat-paying passenger!' She put the coin in her satchel, took a penny ticket from her machine, punched it, and handed it over.

The old lady winked at her, and mouthed a silent 'Thank you.'

'I'm not a seat-payin' passenger eivver,' said the man sitting at the window, just in front of the old lady. 'Can I go free too?'

Beattie was just about to give him one of the pat answers she always kept in reserve for passengers who were too fresh, but when she looked at the man, she did a double take. Not only had she recognised the voice, but, despite the fact that he had lost his moustache, and had grey hair sprouting over both ears, there was no doubting who he was. 'Christ!' she said.

It was Jack Ridley.

29A Mitford Road
N.7
26 Oct. 1940

Dear Sarah

I know this will seem strange to you, my writing to you after so long, but just lately I've been thinking a lot about you.

Freddie Hamwell listened with rapt attention as Sarah read aloud the contents of the letter she had just received from her sister.

This war has brought home to me so many things that I've never really thought about before. I often think about the times when we were kids together, how you were always the one who knew how to play games or put things together, and how furious I was when I couldn't do anything myself. I also remember how many times we argued, how many times I sulked if I didn't get my own way. When you think about it, and I'm sure you have lots of times, I've been quite a failure as a sister. I'm not much good at being a mother either, but, in spite of everything, I *have* tried.

What I'm getting at is, I'd really like to see you again. I know you're married now, and Ed told me what a lovely man your Freddie is, but I would like to see you. You could, if you wanted, come here to tea, or even for a meal if you like. But I know you probably wouldn't like that. So, if you can bring yourself to forgive your sister for all the stupid things I've done in my time, maybe we could meet up on 'neutral territory' or something. I promise you, I'd sleep better at night if we could.

I miss you, Sarah. Sounds ridiculous, doesn't it, especially after all these years of distance between us. But I *do* miss you. There's a gap I can't fill, and I don't know why.

Please write. I would appreciate it. And please give my best to your Freddie. I'd love to meet him some time.

Love

Your sister, Beattie

Sarah put down the letter. She found it hard to take in what she had just read. 'Why?' she asked

Freddie removed his spectacles, and ran his fingers through his greying hair. 'She misses yer.'

Sarah slowly shook her head. 'It's not possible. Every time we've met, she's been aggressive and unpleasant. She's never liked me.'

'She's older now,' said Freddie. 'So are you.'

'You mean, older and wiser?' asked Sarah.

'Yer never know.' Freddie, with his arm around Sarah's shoulders, was sitting next to her on the customers' row of chairs. 'Sounds like she needs you,' he said.

'It would be the first time.'

Freddie squeezed her shoulders. 'There's always a first time for everyfin',' he said. 'Who knows? P'raps you need her too?'

Chapter 23

'I'm a changed man, Beat.'

Despite the fact that his physical appearance had mellowed, Jack Ridley's words seemed as hollow as ever. The good looks were still there all right, but now that he was in his mid-forties, his rugged build had surrendered to a paunch, which suggested a period of good living. And if some of the aggression he had as a young man had been knocked out of him, he had certainly not lost the quick tongue, nor the flashing dark eyes, that had so captivated Beattie in her young days.

'They say travel broadens yer mind,' Ridley continued. 'Well, I've certainly 'ad me share of that. Been all over Ireland, from norf ter souf. It's a wonder I 'aven't turned into a bleedin' leprechaun!'

Ridley's humour failed to impress Beattie. She just sized him up over a mug of tea in the London Transport caff at the Moorgate turnaround.

'Got a lot ter tell yer, though, Beat,' Ridley said, rolling his own fag. 'Got meself a bob or two in Dublin. The war don't mean much ter the Paddys. No bombs over there.' He licked the ends of the fag paper, then stuck it between his lips. 'I managed ter set up me own business,' he said enthusiastically. 'You know – plasterin', brickie, that sort of fing. Mind you, I 'ad ter lay low fer a while. The fuzz never give up after wot 'appened ter old Ben.'

Beattie was doing her best to find some compassion for this man, but as she watched him lighting his fag, all bright and full of himself, she couldn't help casting her mind back to the last time she had seen him, his face crumpled up and crying like a baby, pleading to her to help him get away.

"Course, yer must've 'eard wot 'appened ter the Dillon boys – ter Phil and Joe?' He didn't wait for an answer, but carried right on talking. 'Caught their lot in a nicked car crash, up in Liverpool or some such place, or so I 'eard. At least they won't 'ave ter swing fer wot they did.'

Beattie watched him take a deep, uneasy draw on his fag.

'Not so wiv Charlie, though,' he continued. 'Ritz told me 'e got out ter Australia just before the war started. 'E's probably leadin' a 'ighly respectable life as a sheep farmer or somefin', wiv a wife an' six kids!' He flicked a quick glance up at Beattie, who had hardly spoken since they'd sat down at the table. 'Yer look good, Beat – not a day older. Must be almost ten years. Time flies.'

Beattie finally broke her silence. 'What d'you want from me, Jack?' she asked.

Jack hesitated before answering. 'I want yer back, Beat.'

Beattie sighed, and sat back in her chair.

'I'm not all bad, yer know,' said Ridley. 'Oh, I know I've got me faults—'

'Faults!' Beattie spluttered, in disbelief. 'You treat me like an animal, you beat up me – and my son – you get yourself involved with a gang of murderous thugs, then you run off and leave me to take the can back for ten years. And you tell me you have *faults*?'

Aware that the other bus crews in the canteen were watching them, Ridley stretched across the table and covered her hand with his own. 'I know I've made mistakes, Beat,'

342

he said, voice low. 'But deep down inside, I've always 'ad a soft spot for yer.'

Beattie snatched her hand away. 'Don't talk to me like that, Jack!' she growled. 'I'm not a child. I'm not one of your pick-ups from the pubs down Stepney High Street.' She leaned across the table and faced him eye to eye. 'I've moved on, Jack. I'm not only older, but I've also come to my senses. You walked out of my life ten years ago, and that's an end to it!'

Ridley's expression hardened. He was far too vain to have expected this kind of response. 'So wot d'yer want ter do about our marriage then, Beat?' he asked, his face set firm. 'In case yer've fergotten, you're still me wife.'

Beattie couldn't believe that she was having this conversation with him. It had been sex, not love, that had brought them together, but as she looked at him now, with his square, obstinate jawline and dramatic but shifty eyes, she found him to be just about the most unappealing creature she had ever known. 'I want a divorce, Jack,' she said firmly.

For a moment, Ridley was stung. But then, as he sat back in his chair and took another drag of his fag, his face broke into that old, familiar grin. 'Do yer now?' he replied. 'An' wot if I say no?'

'You won't, Jack,' she replied. Then, after a perfectly timed pause, added, 'Because I know too much.'

Having sized her up in silence, Ridley finally leaned forward, stubbed his fag out in the tin top ashtray, and said, 'Yor'll 'ave ter find me first.'

But as he started to rise from the table, Beattie said: 'There is one thing I have to thank you for, Jack. If you hadn't returned that money, Ed and I would never have been able to get away from the Bunk. I shall be grateful to you for that for the rest of my life.'

Ridley looked at her as if she was mad. 'Wot're yer talkin' about?'

'That eighty pounds I gave you – after Big Ben's murder, the money you needed to get away. Ed told me what you'd done, how you'd given it to him, and told him to return it to me. I think it was very noble of you to go it alone.'

Ridley hesitated, then burst out laughing. 'Me – *noble*?' He laughed even more. 'Let me tell yer somefin', darlin',' he said. 'I don't know an' I don't care wot your son told yer. *I'm* tellin' yer that that money came in 'andy. An' I would never've given it back if yer come crawlin' on 'ands an' knees!'

With that he was gone.

Ma Briggs was none too pleased about her bloomers. Two pairs she'd lost when that last bomb fell. As it was, she only possessed four pairs in the entire world, and to lose two of her warmest flannelette ones, which Beattie had bought her for her birthday, was too much to bear. How would she ever be able to get a boyfriend now? she wondered, chuckling to herself.

Ma never stopped thanking the good Lord for giving her Beattie. Whatever good deeds the old girl had done for her had been more than repaid since they moved into Mitford Road, and since she hadn't seen any member of her own so-called family for years, Beattie and Ed were the nearest she had to a daughter and grandson. Even so, she worried continually about Beattie. It seemed to Ma that a young woman had no right to be all alone in this world. She needed a man about the place to spoil her and look after her

Ha! she thought. A man – look after her, look after anyone. No hope! They're only out for themselves, for what they can get, not for what they're prepared to give – you only have to look at Jack Ridley for that, and her own late husband too. Bleedin' stupid old sod, killin' 'imself with booze before he was even fifty. It's not easy being a widow for over thirty years. But that Beattie, she's different. She should find herself a nice man, not over good-looking, but just a nice down-to-earth hard worker, who can give her all she wants in life – and a bit more besides.

Ma was suddenly jolted out of her daily afternoon snooze in the armchair in front of the gas fire in her bedroom. Someone was banging on the front door, but with her rheumatism, it was going to take her some time to get there.

'All right! All right!' she yelled, as she carefully lowered herself heavily down each of the seemingly endless stairs that she counted every time she went up and down them. The heavy thumping on the street door continued, which only made Ma more and more tetchy. 'Wot's up wiv yer?' she yelled. 'Who d'yer fink I am – an Olympic bleedin' runner?' When she finally reached the door and opened it, she was surprised to see a teenage telegram boy waiting there on the doorstep.

'Afternoon, dear old lady!' the boy said brightly, holding up an orange-coloured telegram envelope. 'One telegram for a Mrs Ridley.'

Ma snatched the envelope from him. 'None of your bleedin' cheek,' she said, about to close the door.

'Wot – no tip?' asked the boy, mischievously.

'Yes!' snapped Ma, irritably. 'Tip of my boot!'

She slammed the door in the boy's face, unaware that he had put two fingers up at her after she had done so.

Once the door was closed behind her, Ma's confidence disappeared immediately. A telegram! Oh Gord in Heaven, she thought. No one gets a telegram these days unless someone's died – or been killed in action. With shaking hands, she made her way into the kitchen. She couldn't see what was written on the front of the envelope, for she hadn't got her glasses on, so she quickly found them, took the envelope over to the table where the light was better, and read out what it said. IMPERIAL TELEGRAM. MRS B. RIDLEY.

Torn by worry and fear, Ma pondered on what to do next. Should she open the telegram herself right away, or wait until Beattie came home that evening? But then, she asked herself, if it was bad news about Ed, wouldn't it be better if she herself broke it gently to Beattie? For several minutes, she stood there, trying to decide what to do. She finally decided on the solution. Going to the gas hob, she put on a kettle of water to boil. When the steam started to appear at the spout, she held the sealed side of the telegram envelope over the steam and gradually prised it open. With fear and trepidation, she carefully unravelled the telegram and read it:

HOORAY! STOP. I'M COMING HOME ON LEAVE. STOP. LOTS OF LOVE. STOP. ED. STOP.

Ma, overjoyed, felt her heart miss a beat. Then she quickly put the telegram back into the envelope, and sealed it down.

Sarah looked wonderful in her sari. Freddie told her so the moment she came out of the bedroom and gave him a fashion show all to himself. Although Sarah had been left the sari by Mrs Ranasinghe, after the old lady's death eight years before, she had kept it locked up in her bottom drawer. She had always considered it to be far too precious actually to wear, and in any case, she still had such fond memories of her former employer wearing it on the anniversary of her husband's passing. She also never forgot the wonderful letter Mrs Ranasinghe's daughter Marla had written to her at the time, in which she mentioned her mother's last wishes, which consisted of one thousand pounds in cash, together with the sari 'which my dear girl liked so much, and who will wear it with dignity and charm'. It was a poignant departure, and one that Sarah would never forget. The thousand pounds had immediately been put into a savings account, ready for the day when she and Freddie were able to afford to move into their first real home, and the pale blue sari with the gold trim was wrapped up in tissue paper, and stored safely. But today was a special occasion, Freddie's birthday, and Sarah felt that this was the time when that wonderful old Ceylonese lady would want her to wear her very special bequest.

That evening, Sarah cooked a birthday meal for Freddie unlike anything he had had before. In keeping with her appearance, and as a tribute to the memory of Mrs Ranasinghe, she cooked a full Ceylonese meal of rice and curry, dried vegetables, and fruit chutney. Freddie was a bit suspicious of it all at first, but once he'd got the taste, he was a convert. 'Best birfday I've ever had,' he said, 'even if there weren't no Yorkshire pud!'

A little later, Sarah gave him his birthday present: a pair of gold-plated cufflinks, each in the shape of a pair of scissors. But there was a shock in store for Sarah when Freddie told her that he had a present for her too.

'I've put a down payment on a house,' he announced, quite suddenly.

Sarah was totally taken aback. 'Freddie!' she exclaimed. 'Wot? Where?'

'For the time bein', yer'll just 'ave ter be patient,' he said, clearly enjoying the game he was playing.

'But Freddie,' said Sarah, who was initially excited, but was now nagged by doubt, 'why didn't you talk it over with me first? After all, if we're both going to live there, we should choose it together.'

Freddie looked hurt. Suddenly, the 'gift' he had planned so carefully seemed to have gone sour. 'I couldn't really tell yer, dear,' he said, sheepishly. 'I wanted it ter be a surprise. Yer see, it's very special.'

'Even more reason why you should have discussed it with me.'

Freddie looked worried, as Sarah collected the dishes and took them to the sink. He could tell that she was upset with him. Going across to her, and putting his arm around her waist, he said meekly, 'Don't be angry wiv me, dear. I did it 'cos I love yer.'

Sarah wanted to say that everything was quite all right, but there was something inside her that wanted to sulk, to show her disapproval. In nearly nine years of marriage, this was the first time she had ever shown any real irritation with him. She also showed irritation with herself as well, for she knew she was being inflexible and selfish. But after a moment or so, she was willing to try. 'Can you at least tell me where it is?' she asked.

Freddie was concerned. 'If I did that,' he said mournfully, 'it wouldn't be a surprise any more, would it?'

Sarah put the last of the dishes to soak in the sink, then wiped her hands on the drying-up cloth. Then she turned to face him. 'Don't let us ever keep secrets from each other, Freddie,' she pleaded. 'Because secrets between married people can only lead to – problems.'

'Do you have any secrets, Sarah?'

Freddie's extraordinary question came like a bolt out of the blue. 'What do you mean?' she asked.

'Oh, I don't know,' he replied. 'I suppose everyone 'as a dark secret in their life at one time or anuvver. All I mean is that if yer did, yer would tell me, wouldn't you?'

'Of course,' she replied with some surprise. 'I would never keep anything from you.'

'Nuffin'?' he asked. 'Nuffin' at all?'

Sarah was now quite unnerved by the way he was putting her on the defensive. 'Freddie,' she said, uneasily, 'I don't know what you're getting at.'

Freddie put his arms around her waist, and pulled her close, her head resting on his shoulder. 'I was just wonderin',' he said, 'who that man was who come in lookin' for yer terday.'

Beattie got home from her day shift on the Moorgate route at about seven in the evening. She was dog-tired, and the first thing she did was to go straight into her bedroom and kick off her shoes. Then she pulled off her uniform beret, and threw it on to the armchair by the fireplace, followed by her uniform jacket, which she hung on a hook behind the door. Absolutely dead on her feet after running up and down bus stairs all day long, she quite literally flung herself on to the bed, and lay spread-eagled there.

After a moment, there was a tiny tap on the door. 'Come in, Ma!' she called, wearily.

'Sorry, Beat,' said the old girl. 'I 'eard yer come in, and wondered if yer'd like a nice cup of tea.'

Beattie sighed hard, sat up, and rubbed her eyes. 'You're a dear, Ma,' she replied. 'But I think I'd just like to have a wash before we have to get down the shelter again.'

Ma looked anxious. 'Come on, dear,' she said, trying to coax Beattie, 'it won't take long. I've got it all ready. It's on the table.'

Beattie felt quite sick inside. She didn't want to hurt Ma's feelings, because she knew the trouble she always took to look after her. 'Just five minutes then.'

Ma beamed, and left her to it.

A few minutes later, Beattie came down the stairs, but she was curious to know why Ma seemed to be waiting for her in the passage. 'Anything wrong, Ma?' she asked.

'Wrong?' asked Ma. ''Course not!' she replied. 'Tea's on the table. I'll leave yer to it.'

Beattie watched the old girl disappear into the kitchen, then wrapping her winceyette dressing gown around her, she went into the front room. Her face was a picture, as she immediately saw someone standing by the fireplace, his back turned towards her. He was quite a tall, skinny young man, with a short back and sides haircut that made his ears protrude far more than they would if his hair had been longer. But when he smiled at her, there were no guesses as to who this young man in army uniform was.

'Oh Christ – Ed!'

'Hello, Mum!' he said, beaming.

With that, she ran straight into his arms.

Even in his wildest imagination, Ed had never guessed that he would be spending his first night home on leave in an Anderson air-raid shelter in the back yard. Not that he wasn't used to life in a dugout, but that was on the front line, where soldiers were expected to keep their heads low, and try to protect themselves against enemy shells and sniper bullets. This was different. This was a hole in the ground for civilians, with a cold, unfriendly, sloping roof made out of corrugated iron, which, if you were tall like Ed, dared you to stand up and not bang your head. And the noise of ack-ack gunfire was just like the chaos at the front, relentless, night and day,

day and night. He found it hard to believe that his own mother was having to survive this kind of life; in many ways, he found it far more frightening down in this particular English hole than in any old mud-filled dugout in France.

'I had my heart in my mouth when I heard Lord Haw-Haw boasting about the destruction of the British forces in Egypt.' Beattie was half-dozing in an old wicker armchair with Ed at her side, an affectionate arm around her shoulders. 'After your last letter, I was convinced they'd sent you out to the desert. I had no idea you were in Greece.'

'We were part of an advance party,' said Ed, trying to be heard above the racket going on outside. 'Everyone knows Jerry and the dagos are going to invade sooner or later. We were there to help the Greeks set up their defences.'

'It's all so frightening,' said Beattie.

'Not really,' Ed assured her. 'Yer can't just let the Fascists take over the world. There has to be a time when you say, "That's it, mate. That's as far as you go!"'

In the lower bunk behind, Ma was snoring so loud, it sounded as though she was trying to compete with the constant drone of enemy aircraft overhead.

Beattie leaned her head against Ed, and she felt the surge of warm blood rushing through his body. This was the child she never wanted, and yet she felt sick every time she knew he was in danger. 'What I can't get over,' she said, 'is why they brought you home? I mean, if it's as bad as you say it is out there, surely they need all the men they can get?'

'Good point, Mum,' he replied with a knowing grin. 'But I wasn't really much good to them with my wound.'

Beattie sat bolt upright. 'Wound?' she gasped. 'You mean, you've been injured?'

Ed laughed, and gently kissed her on the forehead. Now that he had outgrown that snotty-nosed kid in the Bunk, he was much closer to his mother than he had ever been during those days. 'Nothing to worry about, Mum,' he said reassuringly. 'Someone dropped a shell on my foot, broke two bones. I had to spend two weeks in the field hospital. They said I wouldn't be much use if I suddenly had to make a break for it.'

Beattie almost looked relieved. 'Does that mean you won't have to go back?' she asked, hopefully.

Ed smiled. 'I wouldn't bank on it,' he replied, gingerly.

For the next few moments, they just sat there deep in thought, thinking about the past, the present, and what the future was likely to hold for not only them, but for the whole of the human race.

'I saw Ridley,' Beattie said, quite suddenly.

'Oh?' Although Ed was shocked, he tried not to show it. 'So they haven't caught up with him?'

'I doubt they ever will,' replied Beattie. 'He's too clever by half. But if they do . . .'

'If they do,' said Ed, carrying on where she'd left off, 'God help him.' He pulled himself up, took a cigarette out of a packet in his uniform trousers pocket, and lit it. 'Has he changed much?' he asked.

'Ridley will never change,' replied Beattie. 'He wouldn't know what to do if he did.' She paused for a moment, then said, 'He wanted me to get back with him again.'

Ed laughed, and practically choked on his cigarette. 'That's a joke!' he spluttered.

'No, he meant it,' said Beattie. 'The thought of it practically gave me a nightmare.'

'I'm not surprised.'

For a brief moment, the barrage of ack-ack fire seemed to cut out, to be replaced by an ominous silence, but for the deafening chorus of Ma's snores.

Then, quite out of the blue, Beattie asked, 'D'you remember all those years ago, just before Ridley skipped the country, how you told me that he'd given you back the money I'd given to him? D'you remember that time, Ed?'

Ed drew on his fag. 'I remember,' he replied, quietly.

'Well, a funny thing happened,' she said. 'He told me he never gave you any money at all. And yet, when you came back that day, you had that eighty pounds. Where did it come from, Ed?'

Ed leaned back in his vastly uncomfortable wooden upright chair. With his cigarette in his mouth, his eyes were transfixed on the sloping ceiling of the shelter, where condensation was running down slowly, then gathering speed down the walls. He was now a one-pip lieutenant in the Royal Fusiliers, and his training as a commissioned officer had prepared him for just a situation such as this – decision, tact, and truth in the face of all adversity. 'Does it really matter now, Mum?' he asked. 'It was a long time ago.'

Beattie turned to look at him. 'It matters to me, Ed.'

Without holding the fag between his fingers, Ed blew out smoke from it. 'It came from Aunt Sarah.'

'Sarah?' Beattie gasped, in absolute astonishment. 'My sister?'

'*My* aunt,' replied Ed. 'I went to see her. When there was a chance that we'd lose this house, I asked her to help. No, I begged her.'

'Oh God, Ed!' she groaned. 'You didn't?'

'She took the money out of her savings, then told me what I should tell you. She wanted you to think that Jack had paid it back. She never wanted you to know the money came from her.'

'Ed, how could you have done such a thing?'

After a brief moment's thought, Ed turned to look at her.

353

'I did it because I wanted to, because I *had* to. Aunt Sarah needed to do it, Mum. Because *she* needs you, as much as *you* need her. Sooner or later you're both going to realise that.'

The barrage of ack-ack gunfire opened up again. By then, both Ed and his mother were looking hard at each other.

It was almost daybreak. They'd been talking all night.

Chapter 24

If the first few days of November were not exactly an Indian summer, they were certainly milder than usual for the time of year. But what with the combination of the early blackout, the dreary long nights, and regular nightly air raids that began at dusk and continued until dawn, the weather was no real help to the morale of the thousands of people who had to spend their nights in an air-raid shelter. But there was certainly no doubt that since the unexpected success in September of the RAF's campaign to combat the German Luftwaffe, there had been a decisive turnaround in the nature and scale of the London Blitz, as it was now called. For a start, so many enemy aircraft had been shot down or destroyed in midair that the German pilots now found it far too dangerous to carry out bombing missions over London and the Home Counties during daylight hours. Subsequently, the strategy changed to massive air strikes against civilian targets under cover of dark, which inevitably caused widespread damage. But there was one element of night-time raids that even the superior power of the Luftwaffe could not cope with.

Sarah hated fog. It scared and disoriented her. Once, when she was a child, she had got lost in the fog in the garden of the old family home in Thornhill Road, and she'd screamed so loud that her mother had had to come out to rescue her.

To Sarah, fog was sinister and threatening, and whenever it came down, she tried to make sure that she was safely at home. This evening was a real pea-souper, and she had been caught out in it, as it had come down quite suddenly as she made her way home from collecting the bagwash in Upper Street. She immediately began to panic, for the blanket of thick, choking fog seemed to engulf her, forcing her to lose all sense of direction. Although she could hear voices in the distance, all traffic seemed to have come to a standstill, and she couldn't make out whether she was still on the main road, or hadn't inadvertently turned a corner into a side street. She cursed herself for not having brought her torch, even though it would have been no use in such conditions, as the beam would only have produced a blinding glare. So her only solution was to ease her way towards the shop fronts, and quite literally feel her way to the corner of St Alban's Place, where she would find it easier to locate the barber shop. Her task was made more difficult for, as it had already passed blackout time, there were no lights in the shop windows. Fortunately, she did bump into a young couple, who were having as many problems as herself in finding their way about, but their only response when she asked if they knew where they were was, 'Sorry, missus. 'Aven't the foggiest!' She cursed them too, as their silly giggles disappeared into the murky grey blanket behind her.

Her spirits were raised, however, when her hand suddenly identified the rolled timber shutters over the shop window of her neighbour, Mr Timmins, the tobacconist. All she had to do now was to feel her way past the walls of the other few houses along the quiet side street. She was just a few doors away from the barber shop when she heard a movement directly in front of her. She stopped dead, and called, 'Is someone there? Freddie? Is that you?'

There was no response. In the claustrophobic box she was enclosed in, her voice sounded dull and blank, and she was almost overpowered by the smell of coal fires, pumping out thick black dust from chimneys all over London. Again, she heard something, or rather sensed it.

'Please,' she begged, nervously, 'if there *is* someone there, say something.'

'Sarah.' She was answered by a man's voice, little more than a loud whisper.

Sarah took a step backwards. She was frightened. 'Wh-who are you?' she asked anxiously.

The eerie outline of a man slowly materialised, but as the fog was now dense, there was no way he could be identified. 'Don't worry,' he said. 'I'm not going to 'urt yer.' He moved closer. 'It's yer bruvver-in-law, Sarah, yer long-lost bruvver-in-law.'

It took Sarah a moment to take it in, and then it dawned on her that it was Jack Ridley's voice. 'You!' she gasped, no longer nervous, but angry. 'What the devil d'you think you're doing?'

'I come ter see yer, Sarah,' he said, trying to sound as though he was hurt. 'I'm sorry I din't choose the right time.'

'There's never a right time to see you, Ridley!' she snapped. 'How dare you call on my husband and tell him we're close old friends?'

'Ah!' replied Ridley, a grin in his voice. 'So 'e told yer, did 'e? 'Ow d'yer know it was me?'

'Oh, I knew!' replied Sarah, scathingly.

'Even after all these years?'

'Oh yes,' she said. 'Even after all these years. The moment he described you, I didn't have to think twice.'

'I'm flattered.'

Sarah thought about making a run for it, but she was so

357

disoriented she just didn't have the nerve. 'What do you want, Ridley?' she asked.

'I could do wiv some 'elp, Sarah,' he said, his outline distorted by the drifting fog. 'I need some – respectability, shall I say?'

'What the devil are you talking about?'

Voices were heard in the distance, distraught passers-by on Chapel Street, trying to work out which way they were heading.

Ridley waited a moment until they had gone, then withdrew his shadowy outline back into the fog. 'I want a wife, an 'ome, a family,' his voice coming from nowhere. 'I want *my* wife, *my* 'ome, and *my* family.' He had now moved into a position somewhere at her side. 'In uvver words, I want ter get back wiv your sister again.'

'Why?'

Ridley was stung by her question. ''Cos I love 'er, of course.'

'Don't talk nonsense, Ridley,' she said. 'What have you ever done to love my sister?'

'I married 'er, din't I?' he snapped. 'In't that enuff?'

Sarah paused. 'No, *Mister* Ridley,' she replied. 'That is not enough.'

There was an unnerving pause from Ridley whilst he gathered his thoughts. During the years he had been lying low in Ireland, in his mind he had often rehearsed this moment with Sarah, gaining her support to help reinstate him. Despite what he had told Beattie, for the past ten years his life hiding away in Ireland had been a hell on earth. From one day to the next, he never knew whether someone would turn up at his room in the middle of the night and take him back to England, to gaol, and the real possibility of a walk to the gallows. 'Sarah,' he said, finally, 'I don't want ter run any more.'

'You should have thought about that before you killed that poor man.'

'I din't 'ave nuffin' ter do wiv wot 'appened ter Ben!' he insisted firmly, though in a low voice. 'I 'ad no part in it!'

'Then go to the police and tell them so.'

'It's all in the past, I tell yer,' Ridley pleaded, his voice cracking with frustration. 'Nobody cares wot 'appened nearly ten years ago!'

'His wife and five children do,' replied Sarah.

She started to move on, but Ridley suddenly appeared from behind, clutched her arms, and held her. 'Look. All I want is a chance ter get a job and settle down. Talk ter Beat for me. She'd listen ter you. Tell 'er that I'm not the man I used ter be. Tell 'er I'll do anyfin' I can ter make 'er 'appy.'

Sarah hesitated, then said, 'Go away, Ridley. Leave us alone – all of us.'

She started to move again, but Ridley suddenly increased his hold on her arms. 'Tell me somefin', Mrs barber shop lady,' he said, his voice more like his old self. 'Wot d'yer fink your lovin' 'usband'd say if 'e knew about – you an' me?'

Sarah swung round. 'I beg your pardon?' she snapped indignantly.

'If I wanted to, I reckon I could tell 'im a fing or two – wouldn't you say? I mean, 'e'd 'ave ter draw 'is own conclusions about whevver it's the truth or not. But it ain't easy, is it? There's never no smoke wivout fire, is there?'

Ma Briggs had lost her false teeth. She distinctly remembered taking them out before she went to bed in the air-raid shelter the previous night, so there was absolutely no doubt in her mind that that's where they were. But Ed took a different view. He was just as sure that before Ma went down to the

359

shelter the previous night, she hadn't had her teeth in. Whatever the truth, both his mum and himself had searched the house from top to bottom without success, but the elusive pearly whites were still missing.

'Don't worry, Ma,' said Ed, 'I'll buy you a new pair.' Then added teasingly, 'We'll leave your old pair to scare the mice away!'

Ma was not amused. She was very sensitive about talking to people without her teeth in, so from now on when she did so, she would have to cover her mouth discreetly with her hand.

Ed's teasing did not, however, lessen the great affection she had for the boy. Practically the moment he walked through the door, she had thrust one of her home-made bread puddings, his all-time favourite, into his hands. Over the years, their relationship had developed into a deeply loving one, and in spite of the fact that he still called her Ma, he really thought of her as his grandma. When Ed was a small boy, they would sit alone together and discuss his mum, and all the problems they had to face up to, especially Jack Ridley. ''E's not all bad,' Ma would often say, 'but 'e can be a real pain in the arse.' Now Ed was all grown up, if ever there was anything he needed to know about his mum, it was always Ma he turned to. But on his second day home on leave there was something he particularly wanted to ask her.

'Boyfriends? Yer mum? Ha! That's a larff, that is!' Ma was taking full advantage of having Ed all to herself whilst Beattie was doing her day shift on the buses. 'Well,' she said, correcting herself, 'that's not altergevver true. There is this bloke in 'Ornsey Road she's quite keen on – 'e's a schoolteacher or somefin'. But every time she finks 'e's gettin' serious, she backs orf. If yer ask me, she's worried about once bitten, twice shy, if yer know what I mean.'

Ed did know what the old girl meant. His mum's experience of men had been none too happy, and she had now fallen into a style of life that seemed to suit her best of all. Or did it? He was now adult enough to know that, for whatever reason, people need people, and his mum was too young and too good-looking a woman to be wasted on a solitary existence. 'But doesn't she ever go out anywhere?' he asked. 'I mean, to have an evening out with anyone?'

Ma stopped peeling the spuds, and shook her head. 'Only wiv her old mate, Nagger Mills. But Nagger's got an 'usband an' family of 'er own ter look after. She don't 'ave much time for gallivantin'.' She plopped a spud into a saucepan of water in front of her. 'Mind you,' she said, wistfully, 'it's a pity yer mum don't keep in touch wiv 'er sister, Sarah. I mean, look at 'er. She's 'appy as a sandboy that one, good 'usband, good 'ome. I often wonder why they don't just bury the 'atchet and get tergevver. I know yer mum'd like to. Gord knows, she's always goin' on ter me about it.'

Ed was astonished. 'Mum says she'd like to get back together with Aunt Sarah?'

'Oh yes,' replied Ma. 'She's always goin' on ter me about 'ow badly she treated 'er sister Sarah, and 'ow, if only fer the sake of yer gran and granddad, she'd like ter put fings right.'

Ed was fascinated to hear all this. Only a couple of nights before, when he'd told his mum about the eighty pounds Aunt Sarah had taken from her savings, his mum had more or less indicated that she didn't really care if she ever saw her sister again.

'Does Mum still never try to make contact with Aunt Sarah?' he asked.

'Just once,' replied the old lady. 'She wrote to 'er, coupla weeks ago. She asked if they could meet up, an' talk fings over. I mean, when yer fink 'ow proud yer mum is, that took quite a bit of doin'.'

'Well, what did Aunt Sarah say?' asked Ed.

'Not a word.'

Ed was puzzled. 'You mean, she didn't reply?'

The old girl shook her head. The ordeal of talking without her precious pearly whites had been too much for her.

Freddie Hamwell finished getting into his Home Guard uniform. All he needed now was his khaki topcoat, his gasbag, and his rifle. Sarah didn't like him doing night duty, for it meant that as she had herself volunteered for civil defence work in the Women's Voluntary Service, they had been forced to spend many nights apart. At the moment, this was even more worrying, for ever since his birthday supper, when he'd casually asked Sarah who the man was that had been into the shop enquiring after her, he had remained stubbornly uncommunicative.

'Why are you sulking, Freddie?' asked Sarah, with concern, handing him his gasbag.

'Don't know wot yer mean,' he replied, awkardly, and coldly.

'You know very well what I mean. You've hardly spoken to me since your birthday. Why can't we talk about it?'

'Nuffin' ter talk about,' he said, putting his gasbag over his shoulder.

Sarah was rapidly losing her patience. She knew what was nagging at him, and she was determined to have it out with him. 'Freddie Hamwell, I won't have you treating me like this. I'm your wife and you're my husband. If something is wrong, we should bring it out into the open.'

'I've got ter go, Sarah,' he said, edging his way towards

the bedroom door. 'I don't want to be late on duty.'

She took hold of his arm, and yanked him back. 'Don't be so silly, Freddie,' she said, scolding him. 'I know very well that you're not on duty until seven o'clock, and it's not yet even six. What's this all about?'

'Please, Sarah,' he said, trying to pull away. 'Let me go.'

'D'you think I'm having an affair with another man?' she asked, point-blank.

'Couldn't tell yer,' he replied, indifferently.

'Oh really, Freddie,' she said, straightening his khaki tie. 'After nearly nine years, I honestly thought you knew me better than that. I'm a married woman. It's ridiculous to think that I go around having secret liaisons.'

'Why not?' replied Freddie, sulkily. 'You're an attractive woman.'

'Sit down, Freddie,' Sarah said calmly.

'I've got to go.'

'For God's sake!' she snapped. 'Sit down and let's discuss this like rational human beings.'

Freddie hesitated then, like a naughty schoolchild, he went back to their bed and perched himself on the edge.

'I know what this is all about,' she said, going to him. 'I know you think that the man who came into the shop looking for me was – well, what you think he was.' She perched on the bed beside him. 'You've got it all wrong, Freddie. I want to tell you about it. I *have* to tell you about it.' She took his hand and gently cupped it in her own. 'The man you saw was my sister's husband.'

Freddie swung a look at her. 'Jack Ridley?'

'Yes.'

'But you told me they didn't live together, that he'd run off to Ireland or some such place.'

363

'All that's true,' she said. 'But what I've never told you is *why* he ran off.'

Freddie looked at her in bewilderment as he listened to her harrowing account of the murder of Big Ben Fodder in the Bunk, of Ridley's involvement with the Dillon boys, and the way he had beaten up Beattie ever since the day they married. She also told him about her relationship with Edward Lacey, how he had jilted her, and why. It wasn't easy for her to open her heart to him, for her involvement with Lacey had left a permanent scar on her pride and dignity. But she knew that she owed it to Freddie to tell the truth, especially since he not only knew young Ed, but he liked him a great deal. In the period before the boy joined the army, every time the two of them met, Ed often talked enthusiastically to Freddie about books, and all the things he had learned from them. Although Freddie himself hadn't been very well educated, he was a wonderful listener, and this gave the boy the most tremendous encouragement.

When Sarah had finished pouring her heart out to him, Freddie took off his gasbag, laid it on the bed behind him, and put his arm around her waist. 'Why din't yer tell me all this before, yer silly gel?'

Sarah leaned her head on his shoulder, and sighed. 'I didn't want to lose you,' she said.

'Yer won't lose me that easy, Mrs 'Amwell,' he said, hugging her.

But a sudden thought occurred to her. 'Freddie,' she asked anxiously. 'What are we going to do about Ridley? He frightens me.' She sat up straight and faced him. 'Years ago – he tried to take advantage of me. And last night . . .'

Freddie lowered his eyes.

Sarah continued with difficulty. 'Last night, he was waiting for me outside, in the fog. He tried to get me to persuade Beattie to have him back. He said if I didn't, he'd tell you that his advances towards me all those years ago – had not been rejected.'

Freddie still couldn't look at her. 'An' were they, Sarah?' he asked, grim-faced.

Sarah put her hand underneath his chin and gently raised it. She was now looking straight into his eyes. 'What do you think, Freddie?' she asked.

Freddie took her hand and held it.

After a pause, Sarah continued, 'In some ways it's not his fault. Ridley is a victim of his own upbringing. He's like so many of his kind who've cut themselves off from their families. Beattie once told me his was a lost childhood, a childhood without hope, without any form of direction. Unfortunately for everyone else, however,' she said, with an anxious sigh, 'Ridley *is* dangerous. He could do Beattie a lot of harm. He could do us all a lot of harm.'

As she spoke, the shrill call of the air-raid siren pierced the air outside.

Chapter 25

London was now in the grip of an intense campaign by the German Luftwaffe to bomb the daylights out of it. But it was night after night that they came, one great aerial armada after another, engines droning like a dragon's roar, and hundreds of high-explosive bombs raining down on the homes, businesses, and places of worship of the rich and poor alike. But if the intention of Herr Goering was to bomb the spirit out of the civilian population, it clearly wasn't working.

'Show me the way ter go home!' Wave after wave of people's voices belted out the words of a popular morale-raising song, and the magnificent sound they made echoed out loud across the River Thames at the Victoria Embankment, right in the heart of London Town. Further up river, the flickering glow of massive fires surrounded the mighty dome of St Paul's Cathedral, turning the waters of the river into an inferno. There was frantic activity everywhere, with mere handfuls of exhausted firemen desperately trying to tackle major incidents with the most limited resources, and women from the civil defence units and auxiliary emergency services there to give all the support they could, from medical aid to life-saving cups o' char. On the other side of the river, there was competition from a Salvation Army band, who were determined to obliterate the whining sound of high explosives and Molotov cocktail incendiary bombs, with the strains of 'Yes, Jesus Loves Me!' in words, song, drums, and tambourines.

Sarah and her old friend Eunice Dobson were on WVS mobile canteen duty just near the Embankment entrance to the Kingsway tram tunnel. After a hard night pouring endless cups of tea for the exhausted teams tackling the persistent fires around Charing Cross and Northumberland Avenue, it was now approaching daybreak. But, weary though they were, the two women joined in the rousing song, Eunice's squeaky voice piping above the rest.

Despite the fact that she was now a married woman with three kids of her own, Eunice always defied regulations by leaving the top buttons of her uniform tunic open, which left very little to the imagination of the firemen. 'Poor sods!' she squeaked to Sarah, usually after yet another admirer had given her a lustful grin, 'they've got ter 'ave a little somefin' ter look forward to, 'aven't they?'

Amongst the usual nightly crowd of firemen and rescue workers, there was always a fair number of special reserve police constables, and members of the armed forces. Many a night the two women had been told by soldiers just back from the front somewhere that they felt safer where they'd come from than taking their chances on the streets of London. There was always someone to chat to, someone to comfort, or someone to tell that they were perfectly safe and that no harm would come to them. But whilst Sarah was in the middle of trying to serve a small animated group of servicemen, who had all descended on her in a mad rush, she suddenly picked out a face that took her totally by surprise.

'Oh my God!' she cried. 'Ed!'

Her young nephew beamed. 'Hello, Aunt Sarah!' he

called from the seething crowd, his hands trying to reach out to her. 'How are you?'

Sarah couldn't hear what he was trying to say, and in any case she dare not stop pouring cuppas for the crowd that was besieging her and Eunice. 'See you after the all clear!' she mouthed.

'Can't hear you!'

'She said, she'll see yer after the all clear!' answered one of the firemen, standing at the front of the queue. 'Wot's up wiv yer, mate?' he quipped, amidst weary laughter from the others. 'Got cloff ears or somefin'?'

It was half an hour later that the all clear siren wailed out across the river. By then, the rescue workers were moving on to reinforce their embattled colleagues in the City of London, where scores of fires were still raging out of control. With the night's events now at an end, Eunice told Sarah that she would wash and clear up the cups to enable Sarah to go off for a chat with her nephew.

It was strangely quiet along the Embankment at six o'clock in the morning, for, after the frenzied activities of the night, most of the clearing-up operations seemed to be confined to the areas that had had direct high-explosive hits. As they strolled down Northumberland Avenue, Sarah and Ed had to step carefully over the last of the dozens of hose pipes, which had snaked all the way back to Trafalgar Square.

As they strolled, Ed told his aunt about all that had happened to him since they last met, careful not to alarm her too much about the dangerous missions he had been involved in. At the Embankment, they crossed the road, and made for Cleopatra's Needle. Here, Sarah and Ed perched on the riverbank wall and looked out at the mighty London river, now just beginning to shed its thin layer of early morning November mist. To their left, they looked out on to the City skyline, with numerous pockets of thick dark smoke still curling up into the murky grey clouds from the night's savage firebomb onslaught. And to the right stood the great clocktower of Big Ben, impervious to all the provocation, standing proud and contemptuous to the overhead intruders, a true inspiration to the 'Mother of all Parliaments', which had itself been damaged in an air raid during the autumn.

'I never thought I'd live to see this day,' said Sarah, taking off her tin helmet and shaking out her hair. 'Bombs on so much of this lovely city – it's a crime.'

'Not only London,' said Ed. 'Just think what they did to poor old Coventry the other night. Practically destroyed the whole city. God knows how many were killed.'

'They can destroy our cities,' said Sarah, 'but they'll never destroy the people's spirit.'

Ed lit a cigarette, and for a moment or so they both just sat there, unwinding from the night's traumatic events, staring out along the river, undaunted in the early morning light.

'I thank God you're safe,' said Sarah. 'I've often told Freddie how concerned I am for you.'

'I've been concerned for you too, Aunt Sarah,' replied the boy.

Sarah gave him an affectionate look. 'Thank you, Ed,' she replied gratefully.

There was again a moment of silence, of deep thought between them. Their eyes glistened in the weak winter sunlight. A gentle breeze carried the smoke from Ed's cigarette down river.

'I was looking at a photograph I keep of you the other day,' he said, quite out of the blue.

'Really?'

'It was of you and Mum when you were small kids

together. She said it was taken when Grandma and Granddad took you on holiday to the Isle of Wight.'

'Oh yes,' she said with a faint smile. 'It was a glorious fortnight. I think I only quarrelled once with your mother.'

They both chuckled. Their eyes, however, remained turned towards the river, which was now swelling in the oncoming tide.

'I'm very flattered that you keep a photograph of me, Ed,' said Sarah. 'It's a sweet thought.'

'It's not the only photo I keep,' he continued. 'I've got a whole lot of them in my wallet. Every time I think I might not get back from a pretty dicey mission or something, I always take them out first and have a look. It never fails. I'm still here.'

Sarah felt quite sick inside. She knew that if she turned to look at him she would cry, so she merely felt for his hand and gave it a loving squeeze.

'You know, Aunt Sarah,' he said reflectively, 'you've given me so much in my life. I don't know how I'd have done what I have if it hadn't been for you.'

Sarah was embarrassed. 'That's not true, Ed,' she said. 'What you've achieved, you've done all on your own.'

'Oh no,' he insisted. 'I remember those days back in the Bunk. It was like being locked up in a prison. When I came to see you, I could talk to you about all the things inside me that were trying to get out. I learned so much from Granddad's books that you gave me.'

'He would have liked that,' replied Sarah.

'I learned about people, the way they talk, the way they think, the way they can make you happy or inflict pain. I learned about the gulf between the rich and the poor, and about inequality. It was thanks to you that I started to think things out for myself, to use my own mind, to have opinions and make decisions. It was the reason I wanted to go to Spain, to help the weak in their struggle against the powerful. It was the reason I joined up at the start of the war. I can't bear the Fascists. I can't bear injustice.' He tossed his cigarette into the river and turned to her. 'As much as I love Mum,' he said, 'she couldn't give me what you've given me.'

Before Sarah could answer, he gently put his fingers over her lips. 'If you could do all that for me,' he said, 'why couldn't you do it for her?'

Sarah lowered her eyes. 'You're a young man, Ed,' she said. Then she raised her eyes again. 'One day you'll know a lot more about your mother and me.'

'I know more than you think,' he said. 'I know that she loves you. And she needs you now more than ever before.'

Ritz Coogan hadn't changed a bit. In ten years, he still looked as dumpy as ever, and there was hardly a line on his chubby little face. His only concession to advancing years, however, was his hair, which had once been dark and wavy, but which was now pure white, due no doubt to the fright he got when he heard how the Dillon boys had dealt with Big Ben. Since those days, he had spent most of his time in Belgium, making as much money as he could doing casual labour. He never remained in one place long enough for anyone to get to know him properly, which was just as well, for Scotland Yard, back in the home country, had never closed their investigation into the murder of one of their own.

Over the years, there had been very little contact between Ritz and Jack Ridley. Their paths only crossed occasionally once Ritz had found the place in Ireland that Jack had mentioned as being the perfect backwater to hide out in. Since then, although they kept their distance, they agreed to stay in touch, just in case of unwelcome developments.

These days, the two men kept away from the pubs, not only because they would be the first place they would be recognised, but because some of the old clientele would only be too glad to shop them. And so, when Ridley decided that he had something he needed to talk over with his former criminal sidekick, he chose as a meeting place the back row of the stalls in the Marlborough cinema in Holloway Road.

The good old 'bug-hutch' was fairly empty that afternoon, with no more than a handful of regular elderly patrons there to watch Gary Cooper and Ray Milland in *Beau Geste*, a stirring tale of courage and cowardice in the French Foreign Legion. The cinema was a perfect place to meet, for the lighting was very poor, with the only real light coming from the picture screen itself.

'Got a little job for yer, Ritz,' said Ridley, careful to keep his voice down. 'No risk involved. Just a little visit to my lovin' wife.'

After the last job he was involved in with Ridley and the Dillon boys, Ritz was a bit cagey. 'I dunno, Jack,' he replied, whilst digging into a tub of synthetic ice cream. 'I've 'ung up my gloves these days. As far as I know, the fuzz still don't know fer sure that I was involved wiv the Dillon boys. I don't wanna take no chances.'

Even in the old days, Ritz had always irritated Ridley. But he knew that, on this occasion, he needed him to help him do a job that had – immense possibilities. 'I told yer, Ritz, there's no risk involved,' he said. 'An' if yer keep yer cool, there's a grand in it for yer.'

Ritz's eyes widened. 'A grand!'

'No 'olds barred,' continued Ridley. 'Let me tell yer.' He leaned his head sideways, drawing close to Ritz. 'Yer see, my wife is sittin' on a real little nest egg – or at least 'er boy is.'

'Ed, yer mean?'

'The very same.' He quickly sat up straight again, when the beam from an usherette's torch flashed across the seats further down the aisle. He waited whilst she showed two old ladies to their seats, turned off her torch, and disappeared again through the back exit. 'It would appear,' he continued, leaning his head back to meet Ritz's, 'that my young stepson is on the verge of inheriting – shall we say – a considerable sum of money. In uvver words, 'e's sittin' on a bleedin' fortune!'

Ritz, thunderstruck, bent down, as though picking something up from the floor. ''Ow come?'

Ridley joined him, so that they were now both out of sight below the seats. ''Is ol' man's farver – rich as a row of bean poles – died years ago, but 'e left the kid everyfin'—'

'What!'

'On one condition,' continued Ridley. 'The kid can't get 'is 'ands on it till he reaches the ripe ol' age of twenty-one.'

'An' when's that?'

'Next Friday week.'

Ritz's teeth nearly fell out from his dropped jaw. 'Christ!'

'Precisely.'

'But 'ow d'yer know all this?'

Again, Ridley was irritated by Ritz's naïve questions. 'Let's just say I know a geezer who knows a geezer – who *knows*.'

Ridley raised himself up in his seat again. Ritz did likewise.

On the screen, a pitched battle was taking place between the heroic Legionnaires and the marauding Arabs. As if the gab Ridley was giving him was not riveting enough, the sound of frenetic gunshots was unnerving the daylights out of Ritz.

'But wot's this got ter do wiv yer wife?' he said, trying to be logical. 'If the cash 'as bin left to the kid, wot's in it fer 'er?'

'Fer Chrissake, Ritz,' Ridley snapped. 'She's 'is own flesh an' blood, ain't she?'

Ritz cowered against Ridley's outburst. 'All I was sayin' was, she may be 'is muvver, but surely the cash belongs to 'im?'

Ridley calmed down. 'Good point, Ritz. A very good point. 'Cos that's where we come in.' He leaned close to whisper directly into Ritz's ear. 'Yer see, my wife ought ter be able to advise 'er son on wot ter do wiv such a large amount of cash. Ter do that, she needs advice 'erself; she needs a man about the place. An' who better fer that than 'er own lovin' 'usband?'

Beattie's front room had never looked so good. She was now on night shifts, and every day, before she started work, she made a point of cleaning everything in sight. The linoleum was swept, washed, and polished, rugs beaten with a shovel in the back yard, fire grate freshened with stove paint, brass ornaments polished with Brasso, and any cobwebs removed with a long feather duster. On the day before the special occasion, she had even got Ed to help her put up clean white lace curtains at the windows, whilst Ma was given the job of polishing the cutlery, which used to adorn the Melfords' more formal dining table back home in Thornhill Road.

'You know, you don't have to go to all this trouble, Mum,' said Ed, as his mother laid the table with her best china. 'Aunt Sarah and Uncle Freddie are only coming to tea. They're not coming to inspect the place.'

'It matters to me,' replied Beattie, who was setting out

linen napkins beside each tea plate on the table, something Ed hadn't seen her do in a long time.

'I 'ope all this is worf it,' said Ma, grumpily. She was getting just a bit fed up with all the fuss. 'Gord knows, I've used up all our week's food rations ter make the fruit cake!'

'It'll be worth it, Ma,' Beattie assured her.

Ma grunted, and disappeared into the kitchen.

After she had gone, Ed went to his mother, who was polishing the mirror over the fireplace. 'Come here, you!' he said, taking her hand and plonking her down on the sofa. 'You're getting yourself all worked up for nothing. You know that, don't you?'

'Do let me go, son,' Beattie said, trying to get up again. 'They'll be here soon.'

Ed pulled her back again, and sat beside her on the sofa. 'Relax, Mum,' he said, comforting her.

'I'm nervous, Ed,' she replied. 'I'm not sure this is a good idea.'

'But you invited them,' said Ed, holding her hand. 'At least Aunt Sarah replied to your letter. You didn't think she ever would.'

'She waited nearly three weeks.'

'Better late than never.'

Beattie sighed. 'I *am* nervous.'

'Let me tell you something,' Ed said, putting his arm around her shoulder. 'Aunt Sarah is probably just as nervous about this meeting as you are. You've had a stormy relationship over the years, but now you're older it's worth the effort to find new ground. And in any case, you'll like Uncle Freddie. He's a very genuine man. It's hard to believe that, after all these years, you've never even met your own brother-in-law.'

Beattie leaned her head back on the sofa. 'What happens

if it all goes terribly wrong?' she asked. 'The last time Sarah and I met, we were at each other's throats. I was absolutely awful to her.'

'That was a long time ago,' said Ed. 'Don't look back. Just think of a new beginning.'

'I'm trying to, son,' Beattie replied. 'God knows, I'm trying to.'

They were interrupted by a ring on the front doorbell. In a panic, Beattie sprang to her feet. 'Oh my God! They're here!'

Ed tried to calm her. 'I'll go and bring them in. Just take it easy, and try to enjoy yourself.'

'Enjoy myself!' Beattie took a deep breath.

Ed went to the front room door, then turned and called back to her, 'Remember. A new beginning.'

During the few seconds that Ed was gone, Beattie felt her stomach churn with anxiety. Although she had written that conciliatory letter to Sarah, she had never thought through the consequences of what might happen if she accepted her invitation to meet up. But then she tried to remember that since the last time they had met, she and her sister, Sarah, had changed. A little more than ten years ago, she, Beattie, had been a reckless young woman, with no thought for anyone but herself, a rebel who imagined that the world owed her something, something that she was not prepared to earn. And Sarah, what of her? She was now a married woman, and had settled for a way of life that, until their parents had died, no one would have thought possible.

Oh God, thought Beattie, I do so want to like Sarah. I do so want her to like me. But what if it doesn't happen like that?

Despite Ed's efforts to bring them back together, it could all end in disaster, and this would be the last time: they would probably die without ever meeting again. She tried to imagine what Sarah would be like when she walked through that door. Would she look older, be just as set in her ways, formal, unyielding, critical? Or would she have mellowed with the passing of time?

'Hello, Beattie.'

Beattie turned with a start. She was there. Her sister, Sarah, was standing in the doorway. And suddenly Beattie was only five or six years old again. 'Sarah,' she replied nervously, apprehensively. 'Thank you for coming.'

The two sisters warily approached each other. For a brief moment, they hesitated as though not knowing what to do next. Then, watched by Ed, Ma, and Freddie, they embraced, kissing each other gently on each cheek.

'Some people have all the luck,' said Beattie, nervously. 'Just look at you.' She stood back to look at Sarah. 'You're younger than the last time I saw you.'

Sarah, embarrassed, shook her head. 'Oh no,' she replied with a friendly smile. 'I can assure you I feel every day of *my* age.

Behind Freddie at the door, Ma dabbed her eyes and blew her nose. It was all too much for her.

'Uncle Freddie,' said Ed. 'Come and meet Mum.'

As her brother-in-law approached, Beattie squeezed her eyelids together to try to avert her tears. 'Hello, Freddie,' she said, holding out her hand. What she saw was a greying middle-aged man with kindly eyes and a beaming smile that could melt anyone's heart. 'I'm pleased to meet you.'

''Ello, Beattie,' Freddie replied warmly. 'I'm pleased ter meet you too.' He ignored the hand she was offering him, and leaning gently forward, he kissed her on the cheek.

Beattie had really gone to town on the tea, which turned out to be more like a feast. Despite the rationing, she had managed to get some veal and ham pie, cold pork trotters, fresh bread with a small pat of *real* butter, a pint of whelks, some shrimps, and sugar with the tea instead of the usual saccharin tablets. She had also prepared the most delicious trifle, with apples, and tinned fruit, and the custard layer on top was made with powdered milk. Freddie and Ma got on like a house on fire, and they both tucked into the grub as though they hadn't eaten since the start of the war. Ed smoked all the way through the meal, for he was far too intent on observing how his mum and his aunt were getting on to eat. In fact, tea time turned out to be a real eye-opener, for everyone seemed determined to get on well with each other, all talking at the same time, recounting memories from their days in Thornhill Road, the Bunk, Mitford Road, and St Alban's Place. There was no doubt that looking back was helping to break the ice.

The turning point, however, came when Ed made a conscious decision to draw his mum and his aunt closer together. Until that moment, they seemed to have been nervous of having a one-to-one conversation, and had merely joined in the light-hearted banter around the table. Ed knew that the time had come to move the two women on to a more productive relationship, but to do that, he felt he needed to pick their brains about the past.

'It must have been peculiar living in that house in Thornhill Road,' he said provocatively. 'I mean, what I remember was that it was quite a barn of a place.'

Inevitably, Sarah took the bait. 'I don't know how you can say that, Ed,' she said, firmly. 'It was a wonderful house. It was big, but it had an atmosphere all its own.'

'Atmosphere, yes,' replied Ed, mischievously, 'but freezing cold in winter and hot as hell in summer.'

Surprisingly, Beattie came to her sister's defence. 'Oh,

our house was never cold, Ed,' she chided. 'During the winter we had coal fires in nearly every room. It was so snug and warm. You were just too young to appreciate it.' At this point, she turned to Sarah, who was sitting alongside her. 'Sarah, d'you remember the time when we were both small kids, when Mother bathed us in front of the wood stove in the kitchen?'

'Oh yes,' replied Sarah, with a broad smile. 'I remember how you made such a mess, Mother's cats fled for their lives!'

Everyone joined in with their laughter.

'Sounds like your poor mum 'ad a 'ell of a time wiv yer!' said Ma, her mouth full of trifle. 'I'd've given yer boaf a clip round the bleedin' ear'ole!'

'We weren't that bad, Ma,' said Beattie.

'Oh yes we were!' said Sarah, lightly.

Now Freddie joined in. 'Wot about that time yer told me about, Sarah? You know, when you an' Beattie played merry 'ell wiv yer dad – 'idin' 'is cigars an' all that.'

Both Sarah and Beattie burst into laughter.

'It was wonderful!' cried Sarah. 'Beattie hid them under the rug in the drawing room.'

Beattie continued the story. 'And when Father came into the room, he trod on them! He was furious!'

She and Sarah roared with laughter.

Freddie turned to Ma at his side. 'Wot would yer do wiv kids like that, eh, Ma?' he asked.

'Strangle the little buggers!' Ma growled.

This only produced more laughter from around the table.

Ed waited for the laughter to settle down, then said, 'Sounds like you two had quite a childhood.'

For a second, neither his mother nor his aunt answered.

'It had its moments,' said Sarah, with a sideways glance at her sister.

Ed exchanged a bit of a grin with Freddie.

After tea, Ed's plan was complete. Packing Ma off to have her customary afternoon doze, he then enrolled Freddie to help him do the washing-up, which left his mother and his aunt free to have a chat alone together.

It was by now beginning to get dark, so Beattie went to the window and drew the blackout curtains.

'I must say, you've got a wonderful memory,' said Sarah, when Beattie came back to join her in front of the fire. 'I'd completely forgotten all about that bath Mother gave us. And that telling-off we got from Father about the cigars.'

'I can remember things that happened a long time ago,' Beattie replied, 'but I couldn't tell you a thing about last week. Must be a sign of old age.'

Sarah watched her carefully. 'You'll never age, Beattie,' she said kindly. 'Even when you reach a hundred.'

Beattie gave a dismissive laugh. 'A hundred!' she gasped. 'I can't imagine me at a hundred years old. In fact, I wouldn't want to live to that kind of age.'

'It's easy to say that now,' said Sarah. 'But when it comes to it, I fancy we might think differently.'

Beattie sighed deeply. 'Maybe,' she replied.

Even in those few quiet moments, it was clear that there was a special kind of atmosphere developing between them, quite unlike anything they had experienced before. Usually, five minutes in each other's company would have been turbulent and unyielding, but in some extraordinary way, a calm had descended upon them.

'Thank you for coming, Sarah,' Beattie said, breaking the silence. 'I can't tell you how grateful I am.'

Sarah lowered her eyes guiltily. 'You don't have to thank

me, Beattie,' she said. 'It's something I've wanted to do for a long time.'

Beattie was puzzled. 'Then why did it take you so long to answer?' she said.

Sarah thought hard. It wasn't easy to explain how she'd felt when she'd received Beattie's letter. It wasn't easy to tell her, after their last meeting so long ago, that she had dreaded ever coming into contact with her again. 'I wanted to be sure,' she replied. 'I wanted to be sure that this time we had a real chance of understanding each other.'

'Oh God,' sighed Beattie. 'I've hurt you so many times. I don't deserve to be forgiven.'

Sarah leaned forward on the sofa where she was sitting. 'It's not a question of being forgiven, Beattie,' she said. 'We've both made so many mistakes. I suppose it happens in families. Everyone's looking for something different. Everyone thinks theirs is the only way. You made up your mind long ago what you wanted from life. I did too.'

'I was wrong.'

'I was too.'

Beattie sat with her hands in her lap, back straight. 'I just wanted my independence,' she said, painfully. 'I wanted to be free. I didn't want to do all the things that were expected of me. I thought the only real people were those who had to work to survive.'

Sarah leaned across and put her hand on Beattie's. 'It doesn't matter where or what you come from, Beattie,' she said, 'everyone has to work to survive. Where you went wrong, where we both went wrong, was that we judge people for what they seem to be, not for what they are. Sometimes we forget that, whatever class we come from, there is good and bad in all of us.' She rose up from the sofa, went to Beattie, and kneeled beside her chair. 'In your letter to me,' she continued, 'you wrote that, as a sister, you've been a failure. Well, if that's true, then I've been a failure too.'

'It's not the same, Sarah,' Beattie said. 'When I think of you and Lacey, and all the pain I caused you. Blood is supposed to be thicker than water, and yet I treated you worse than any trash in the streets. And I was so jealous of the way Ed adored you so much more than me . . .' With a wave of the hand, Sarah tried to dismiss this. But Beattie would have none of it. 'No,' she insisted, 'it's true. You gave him so much more than me. You told him about all the things in life he needed to know, things that I've turned my back on all my life.' She hesitated only long enough to compose herself. 'During these past few years I've often asked myself why it was that I could never bring myself to get on with you. It took Ed to help me find the reason why. He told me that I need you, that I've always needed you.' Her eyes swelled with tears. 'He's right,' she said.

Sarah put her arms around Beattie, and hugged her. 'I need you too, Beattie,' she said. 'The only trouble is that I've always been too proud to admit it.' She held on tight to Beattie. 'I'm not afraid to admit it now,' she said.

Tears now also swelled in Sarah's eyes. It was the first time that had happened in a very long time.

Chapter 26

Sarah just couldn't make out why Freddie had decided to close the shop early that day. Half-day closing was, and always had been, on a Thursday, and the fact that this was only Tuesday worried her greatly.

'But where are we going, dear?' she asked, as she put on her thick winter coat and warm woollen beret. 'It always makes me nervous when you behave like this.'

From the moment they'd got up that morning, Freddie had behaved in a very mysterious way. He'd started by singing out loud as he shaved, which was most peculiar, because when he shaved he nearly always whistled. Then, at breakfast, he lit his pipe, which made Sarah's porridge taste like wallpaper paste. But it was the final straw when, the moment he put the 'CLOSED' sign on the shop door, he went immediately to the back parlour and combed his hair. Extraordinary! Sarah was convinced that he was about to go down with the flu or something.

But the plot thickened even deeper when, as they left the shop and Freddie locked up, a taxi was waiting for them at the kerb outside.

'Freddie?' Sarah asked, all at sixes and sevens. 'What's all this about? Where are we going?'

Freddie opened the taxi door for her. 'Step in, and you'll find out.'

A few minutes later, they were heading off along Upper Street, but before they reached the Angel, the taxi turned off right into Liverpool Road.

Sarah was now so bewildered, she was beginning to get worried. Closing his shop early, spending good money on a taxi – it was all beyond her. As they passed all the streets that were so familiar to her, she felt a deep sense of sadness to see great gaps in the rows of lovely terraced houses, which had been devastated during the relentless air raids. She wondered what had happened to the people who lived there, people that she must have passed in the street a hundred times when she was young, or stood next to in a queue at the greengrocer's. No, even her beloved Barnsbury had not escaped the savagery of the war. In one way, it was a blessing that her parents were not alive to see it all.

When they suddenly turned into Richmond Avenue, and pulled up outside the Melfords' old family house, she was totally confused.

'Freddie!' she pleaded. 'What are we doing here?'

Freddie ignored her pleas, helped her out of the taxi, and paid the driver. The taxi pulled away.

'Freddie,' she asked again, 'what are we doing here?'

Freddie had a smug look on his face. 'I told yer I was lookin' fer a place ter buy yer,' he said, turning his gaze towards the house. 'Well – *this* is it.'

Sarah clamped a hand to her mouth. She was shocked. 'Oh my God!' she gasped. Then she turned to look up at the house where she was born. 'You haven't – you can't!'

'Oh yes I can!' he boasted. 'An' I 'ave!'

'You – you've bought it?' she asked, with incredulity.

'Well, not exactly,' he replied. 'I've just put the deposit down. But it's in a bit of a state. Nuffin's bin done to the place fer years. We won't be able to move in fer quite a time yet, I'm afraid.'

Sarah thought she was dreaming. Freddie took hold of her hand and gently led her through the open brick fence, where once the iron gates had been positioned with such grandeur. Only when they moved into the front garden, however, was the full extent of the negligence really noticeable. They had to step over a pile of rubble to get to the front door, for bomb blast from nearby Liverpool Road had caused considerable damage, which had not been attended to. There were cracked bricks and grey slates from the roof, broken glass, drain pipes dangling out from the walls, and bits of discarded and partly burned furniture scattered all over the place.

For Sarah, it was a deeply depressing sight, and thrilled though she was by what Freddie had done, she had a sinking feeling. 'It's – tragic to see it looking like this,' she said, her eyes scanning the outside of the building from top to bottom. 'It's such a beautiful house. It needs love and attention.' She turned to Freddie, and linked her arm with his. 'Oh, Freddie, it's heartbreaking.'

'Well, we 'ave ter fank the previous owners fer that.'

'What happened to that awful man I sold it to?' she asked. 'I can't even remember his name.'

''Aven't the faintest,' replied Freddie. 'The agent says it's 'ad six or seven occupants in the last few years alone.'

Sarah couldn't believe her ears. 'Six or seven!' she cried. 'What's the matter with people? Don't they recognise a beautiful home when they see one?'

Freddie put his arm around her. 'It's just a 'ouse ter most people, Sarah,' he said sympathetically. 'Ter *you*, it's a 'ome.'

He had great difficulty in opening the front door, for it

had warped, and when he finally did succeed it very nearly came off its hinges.

Sarah stepped through the entrance, and despite the unbelievable mess she found there, she immediately sensed the atmosphere of her younger years. In her mind, she could smell her mother's cooking, and she could hear the sound of Beattie's roller skates down the passage leading out into the back garden. From the hall, she could see the drawing-room door half open, and somehow she expected at any moment to see her father coming out to meet her, with his usual cigar stuck firmly in the side of his lips. The place was most surely full of ghosts, she thought, but friendly ones.

''Fraid we can't go upstairs,' said Freddie. 'The stairs are a bit rickety, and so are the floorboards up in the bedrooms. But we'll soon put it all right. It's goin' ter take time, dear,' he warned, still holding her hand. 'We shan't be able to move in till next summer at the earliest.'

They strolled into the drawing room. It was a depressing sight, for, as the windows had been blown in by bomb blast, it was freezing cold, and there were broken tiles around the fireplace, and a terrible smell of decay everywhere. For a moment or so, they just stood in the middle of the room, staring all around them.

'Where are we going to find the money to do it all?' she asked, apprehensively. 'It's going to cost a fortune.'

'We'll manage,' Freddie assured her, his arm around her shoulders. 'For obvious reasons, I got the place fer a snip. My old mate Charlie Stumper – 'e's a builder – 'e's promised to do it up for us. It'll take time, but we'll do it.'

'Why?' asked Sarah, turning to look at him.

'Why will it take time?'

'No,' said Sarah. 'Why did you do this for me?'

Freddie smiled. 'Because I knew that this is where yer

'art is. I knew that, no matter where we went, this is the one place you'd always fink about most. Did I do right, Mrs 'Amwell?'

Sarah sighed deeply then, after a quick, loving look around the room, replied, 'Yes, Mr Hamwell. You did right. My God, you did right!'

Beattie and Ed picked their way over the debris that was scattered all along the streets of Holborn. Fortunately, the tube was still working after the heavy air raid of the night before, so they'd been able to get out at Holborn tube station. However, the Kingsway route was temporarily closed off, as quite a bit of masonry had apparently tumbled down on to the entrance of the tram tunnel, so they had to take the long way round via High Holborn, Chancery Lane, and Fleet Street. Although things were not much better there, they were at least able to take a short cut to their destination, a solicitor's office in St Clement's Inn, just behind the Law Courts.

Mr Johnson, whom Beattie had first met many years before, was now the senior partner in the firm of Silkin, Silkin and Johnson. These days he sported just the suggestion of a moustache, which was all the current rage for men, who all wanted to look like Rhett Butler, played by Clark Gable in a massive new hit film, *Gone With the Wind*. But time was catching up with even him, for wisps of grey were gradually appearing in that moustache, his sideburns, and even his eyebrows.

'May I first of all offer you my warm congratulations on your coming of age,' proclaimed the legal man, immaculately dressed in a dark three-piece pin-striped suit. Admiring the officer's uniform Ed was wearing, he added, 'If I may say so, your grandfather would have been proud of your commission.'

Ed acknowledged the compliment with a polite nod. 'Thank you, Mr Johnson.'

Whilst discreetly searching for his tortoiseshell spectacles, which were trapped somewhere beneath a pile of documents on his desk, Johnson began his customary recitation. 'As I'm sure your mother has already told you, on attaining the age of twenty-one, in his last will and testament, your grandfather, the late Lieutenant-Commander Lacey, made you one of the prime beneficiaries of his estate.' He finally recovered his spectacles, put them on, and picked up the original copy of the will he was referring to. 'However,' he said, viewing both Ed and his mother over the top of his spectacles, 'there is some good news for you in this bequest – and some bad.'

Ed exchanged a discreet, but puzzled look with his mother.

'Let us deal with the bad news first,' continued the legal man, turning over a page of the will. 'I gather that when my client first approached you back in . . .' he referred to some notes on his desk, '. . . September 1920, he indicated his intention to you that, on his demise, your son would inherit a part share of the sale of the Old Manor House, together with a cash lump sum of five thousand pounds. Is that correct?'

Beattie leaned forward in her chair opposite him, and answered, 'Yes it is.'

'Yes, indeed,' said Johnson, 'that was the amount specified in the Lieutenant-Commander's will. However,' he took off his spectacles, 'I'm afraid that part has been declared null and void.'

Beattie could feel her hackles rising. 'What on earth for?' she demanded.

'For the simple reason that, after death duties, there

weren't enough funds left over.'

Beattie sighed, and sat back in her chair.

'Yes, it is unfortunate,' said the legal man, now switching his gaze back to Ed. 'But I'm afraid your grandfather was quite a chap. In his latter years, he was quite generous to – shall we say, one or two lady friends.'

'Like father, like son,' Beattie muttered under her breath.

'I beg your pardon?' asked Johnson.

'Nothing,' replied Beattie, with a wry smile.

'However,' continued the legal man, 'all is not lost. The good news is that on the sale of the Old Manor House back in 1931, a sum of five thousand pounds was realised from a purchaser in Norfolk.'

Beattie sat up again.

'But,' said Johnson, shrugging his shoulders apologetically, 'I'm sure you are aware that apart from yourself, Lieutenant, there were two other beneficiaries to your grandfather's will. In effect, that means that you are entitled to a one-third share of the sale of the Old Manor House, and that amounts to . . .' he put on his spectacles again, and read from some more notes, '. : . the grand sum of one thousand, six hundred and sixty-six pounds, six shillings, and six pence – give or take a penny or two.' He took off his spectacles again, and gave Ed an ingratiating smile. 'That was, of course, the gross amount. Naturally, we had to deduct our standard company fee.'

'Naturally,' said Beattie, cryptically.

Johnson smiled weakly. 'Which leaves an amount in your favour, including some modest interest, of one thousand, two hundred and thirty-one pounds, four shillings, and seven pence.' He searched around on his desk, found the cheque and held it out to Ed. 'Made out in your name, Lieutenant.'

Ed stared at the cheque for a moment, then took it. Then,

to the legal man's astonishment, he dropped it back on to the desk without even looking at it. 'No thank you, Mr Johnson,' he said, politely, but firmly.

Beattie sat up with a start. 'Ed!'

'It's no good, Mum,' he said, turning round in his chair to look directly at her. 'If I took that money, it would be a betrayal of everything I believe in. I don't want people leaving things to me. I want to earn my own way in life.'

Johnson couldn't believe what he was hearing. This was the first time in his experience that a beneficiary to a will had actually *refused* a bequest. 'But the Lieutenant-Commander was your own grandfather, sir,' he said.

'All the more reason for me not to take it,' replied Ed. 'I'm sorry, Mum, ' he added, turning to Beattie.

Contrary to what Ed had expected, Beattie was smiling in admiration at him. 'You know, it's a funny thing,' she said. 'On the only occasion that I ever met your grandfather, I couldn't bear the sight of him. To me, he was nothing but a selfish, arrogant, grasping old goat.'

The legal man leaned back in his chair with disbelief.

'But there was one thing he said that has now made me think how alike you are. He said, "A person should find his own way in life. If you make it too easy for them, they lose their energy and ambition." You've never lost your energy nor your ambition, Ed. You never will.'

They smiled knowingly at each other.

'That's all very well,' said the exasperated legal man, 'but would somebody please tell me what I am supposed to do with this cheque?'

Ed turned back to him. 'I'd like you to issue another one, please, Mr Johnson. Made out to my mother—'

'No.' Beattie's interruption was firm and adamant. 'If my son doesn't need it, then neither do I.'

The harassed Mr Johnson shook his head in despair. Suddenly, his overcrowded, musty office seemed to be desperate for some fresh air.

Having thoroughly enjoyed what they had done, Ed and his mother exchanged another warm, knowing look. They were in no doubt that the dutiful Mr Johnson would soon find some poor deserving soul to relieve him of that bequest.

Freddie hadn't cut this particular customer's hair before. But, whoever the man was, for his age, he had a beautiful head of thick, manageable pure white hair, so different from the wisps of barbed wire that Freddie had to tackle with monotonous regularity. He certainly seemed like a nice enough little bloke, even if he did tend to talk the hind legs off a donkey. East Ender, that's what he was, Freddie decided. You could always tell a genuine cockney by his mischievous grin and his cheeky banter. Mile End, Freddie reckoned, or even Bow itself. But when his unfamiliar customer dropped a bombshell, Freddie couldn't have cared less where he came from.

'I'm a pal of Jack Ridley,' said Ritz. 'Or at least, I *was* until I stepped fru that door.' He carefully watched Freddie's reaction in the mirror in front of him. 'Guess yer've 'eard of *'im*, Mr 'Amwell. Am I right?'

Freddie's attitude towards the man changed at once. He had already finished cutting his hair, and was starting to lather his face ready for a shave. Swinging a glare at him in the mirror, he growled, 'Who *are* you?'

Ritz trod carefully. He didn't like the look of that cutthroat razor Freddie was brandishing. 'It don't matter who I am, mate,' he replied. 'It's what I come ter tell yer that counts.'

Freddie swung the barber's chair round so that Ritz was facing him. 'What about Ridley?'

''E wants somefin' – from your sister-in-law.'

Freddie hesitated a moment, then he went to the parlour door at the back of the shop, and called up the stairs. 'Sarah! Can yer come down 'ere, please. Quick as yer can.'

Sarah's voice called from the rooms upstairs, 'Be right with you!'

Freddie turned back to Ritz, who had got up from the chair and was using the towel around his neck to wipe the shaving foam off his face. Fortunately, there were no other customers in the shop so he was able to talk freely. 'I don't know what you're up to, mate,' Freddie warned, 'but this'd better be good.'

Ritz dropped the towel back on to the chair behind him. 'It's nuffin' good wot I 'ave ter tell yer, Mr 'Amwell,' he said, provocatively, 'but it's somefin' yer need ter know.'

Sarah suddenly came into the shop. 'Yes, dear?' she asked. But when she saw him with a customer, she smiled brightly and said, 'Good morning, sir.'

'This "gentleman" 'as somefin' ter say to yer, Sarah.'

As she saw the look on both men's faces, her smile faded. 'What's the matter?' she asked with concern, switching her attention from Freddie to the customer.

Ritz took a step towards her. 'I'm an acquaintance of your bruvver-in-law, Mrs 'Amwell. I come 'ere ter warn you.'

Sarah stiffened.

'I've known 'im a long time,' Ritz continued. 'We've done – quite a few jobs tergevver.'

Sarah watched Freddie as he went to the shop door, pulled the blind, turned the 'CLOSED' sign round, and locked the door.

Ritz made sure he kept his distance from both of them. ''E wants somefin', Mrs 'Amwell,' he said, voice lowered as though Ridley was in the shop, 'an' 'e wants it bad. Not from you. From yer sister.'

'Get ter the point!' growled Freddie, simmering with mistrust.

''E wants ter get back wiv 'er – yer sister, I mean.'

'I'm aware of that,' replied Sarah, coldly.

'Yeah,' Ritz said, quickly. 'But wot yer don't know is – *why*.' For one reckless moment, he dared to take a step towards her, but Freddie moved forward to stand beside his wife. 'It's not 'er 'e wants,' he said. 'It's the money.'

Sarah did a double take. 'Money?' she said. 'What money? My sister doesn't have a penny to her name.'

'Not 'er money, Mrs 'Amwell,' said Ritz, nervously. ''Er boy's.'

Sarah exchanged a puzzled, astonished glance with Freddie. 'I don't know what you're talking about,' she replied.

Ritz pressed on. 'Ed's 'is name, in't it?' he said. 'See, I know everyfin'. Twenty-one terday? Right? Got the key ter the door? Right?'

'My nephew has no more money than his mother,' insisted Sarah. 'I don't know what you're getting at, but you've got it all wrong.'

Ritz sized Sarah up. Ridley had often talked about her. She was the one with the brains, he'd always said, she's the one who's got it all going for her. If things had been different . . . 'Ten years ago, 'is grandfarver – 'is farver's farver that is – well, 'e died an' accordin' ter Jack, 'e left everfin' 'e 'ad to 'is only grandchild. That's where Ed comes in, if I'm not mistaken.'

Sarah found it hard to take this in. Over the years she had had many a conversation with Ed about his mother, even his father, but never once had she ever heard him mention his paternal grandfather.

Ritz went to the coat stand and collected his jacket. 'From all Jack tells me,' he continued, 'that boy could've bin worf a fortune years ago. The only snag was that he couldn't lay 'is 'ands on it till 'e was – wait for it – twenty-one years of age. Savvy?'

Sarah covered her mouth with her hand. Suddenly she felt quite weak.

'I don't see the connection,' said Freddie, who was still brandishing that razor. 'If the money was left to the boy, 'ow could Ridley possibly get 'is 'ands on it?'

'Oh, 'e'd find a way, don't you worry about that. 'E's a slippery one, is our Jack.' He put on his jacket, then took his overcoat from the coat stand.

'Beattie wouldn't have anything to do with him,' insisted Sarah. 'She told me that herself.'

Ritz chuckled to himself. 'I'm afraid yer don't know 'ow persuasive 'e is, Mrs 'Amwell,' he said, with a sigh. ''E wants me ter go an' chat 'er up, ter tell 'er wot a good bloke 'e is. He also wants me ter tell 'er that 'e's dyin' of cancer or somefin', an' that 'e's only got a while ter live.' He chuckled again, whilst struggling into his overcoat. 'I don't know 'ow your sister would take ter that kind of story, Mrs 'Amwell,' he said, 'if she was made ter fink it was true.'

Trying to take everything in, Sarah went to the row of customers' chairs and sat down. She was thinking about Beattie, and whether she could – or would – ever feel sorry enough for Ridley to take him back.

'I don't know who you are,' she said, looking across at Ritz, 'but if what you say is true, why are you telling us all this?'

Ritz took his trilby off the coat stand and plonked it on

his head. 'I dunno really,' he replied. 'Maybe it's 'cos there ain't no honour amongst fieves no more.'

Beattie walked at a brisk pace down Hornsey Road, past the old Star bug-hutch cinema, where years before hordes of kids queued to get in to the Saturday morning blood-an'-thunder shows, and endless cowboy serials with Tom Mix and Gene Autry. It was a pleasant enough afternoon, for the winter drizzle, which had settled overnight and turned to ice, had very quickly melted, the moment the sun had established itself.

On her way past Hornsey Road baths, she recognised one or two of her neighbours from Mitford Road, waiting with their bits of scrubbing soap and towels to pay twopence to have a public bath. So she hurried past, for if anyone recognised her, they would be bound to ask where she was going, and that was the last thing she wanted. Once past the police station, she felt safe, so by the time she had crossed the main Seven Sisters Road at the traffic lights, she felt confident enough not to have to rush.

As she walked, she wondered about all that had taken place in the offices of Silkin, Silkin and Johnson that morning. She thought of Ed, and how proud she had felt to know that she had brought a son into the world who had principles that he believed in and fought for. She wondered what sort of life was ahead for him, and what he would make of it, providing, of course, that he survived this nightmare of a war.

Like a lot of people who miss so much when they walk along a road staring at their feet, she didn't take in the terraced shops on either side of the road, many of their windows now boarded up after bomb blast, and roofs temporarily covered over with tarpaulins. Thankfully the back of

Pakeman Street School appeared to be intact, although most of the windows were covered over with protective strips of sticky tape. She didn't slow down until she had almost reached the railway arch, which stretched high above the road, for her destination was very close.

The house, which was set on three floors, was like all the others in the terrace, in bad need of a coat of paint. Even here, several of the windows were boarded up, which must have meant that the interior was desperately short of natural daylight. Using her own key, Beattie let herself in at the front door. Then, after wiping her feet on the passage rug, she quietly made her way up the stairs. The room she was looking for was on the second-floor landing, and when she got there, she tapped as softly on the door as she could.

The door opened and a man peered out. His was a young, pleasant face, with a pasty complexion, blue eyes, and light brown hair that fell over one eye. As soon as he saw Beattie, his face lit up. Beattie went straight in.

When the door was closed, they kissed passionately, and then they embraced. The man was several years younger than Beattie, probably about thirty years old. He wasn't particularly good-looking, but he had an intensity that was more emotional than physical. 'Oh God, I've looked forward to seeing you,' he said, breathlessly. 'I've missed you so much, Beattie.'

Beattie looked into his eyes and stroked his hair. 'Come off it, Chris,' she said with a teasing smile. 'It's only been a week.'

'Is it only that long?' he replied.

A few minutes later, they had undressed and were making love in the young man's modest single bed. It was fortunate that the boards up at the windows prevented not only daylight from streaming in, but also the prying eyes of neighbours on the other side of the road.

When they had finished, they lay side by side, snuggled up as tight as they could to one another. 'How much longer do we have to go on like this?' said Chris, his voice low and intimate. 'I love you, and you love me. So why do we have to keep it such a secret?'

'Because this is not the right time, Chris,' she replied, her tone equally intimate. 'One of these days, it will be. But not now, not just yet.'

Chapter 27

At his own request, Ed's twenty-first birthday was a very low-key affair, which consisted mainly of having a Sunday midday drink in the Hornsey Arms pub with some of his civvy pals, followed by a special meal at his Aunt Sarah and Uncle Freddie's place above the barber shop, to which his mum and Ma Briggs were also invited. As it happened, the occasion turned out to be tinged with sadness, for it also marked the conclusion of Ed's sick leave. In fact, as soon as the meal was over, he had to leave for Charing Cross Station, but the only person he allowed to go with him to see him off was Freddie. It was, inevitably, a poignant departure, and would have been absolutely unbearable if Ed hadn't remained so optimistic and so completely confident that it wouldn't be long before he was back home safe and sound again with his family.

After Ed and Freddie had left for the station, Sarah, Beattie, and Ma did the washing-up together in empty silence. Then Sarah suggested that Ma go into the bedroom to have her usual afternoon doze, an invitation which the old girl readily accepted. As there was an hour or so to pass until Freddie's return, Sarah asked Beattie if she would like to take a walk and get some fresh air, which would also help to take Beattie's mind off the fact that Ed would not be there when she and Ma got home that evening. Sarah knew that a casual stroll out in the cold winter frost would not only be an ideal way to clear their heads, but would also help them to build on their new-found relationship.

For a Sunday afternoon, there were a surprising number of people strolling along Upper Street. Some of them were young couples, holding each other's hands and getting to know each other, others were there to see how the clearing-up was going on after the recent heavy week of air raids. Most people were impressed to see that nearly all the rubble had been cleared away from the severely damaged Lloyds Bank building. In front of the site itself, a small group of people had even stopped to talk over what had happened, and to speculate about whether the bank would be totally demolished or rebuilt.

As the sisters turned into Liverpool Road, it seemed as though the years behind them were once again flashing before their eyes. This was their neck of the woods, where they had played together, walked together, and then moved on into their different lives.

'It's all changed so much since our day,' said Sarah. 'The war has made such a difference. Nobody has the heart to take care of their property; they never know from one day to the next whether the place will still be there when they step out of their shelters in the morning.'

'Oh, I don't know,' said Beattie, whose eyes were scanning the long rows of Georgian terraced houses. 'It all looks pretty much the same to me, a little worse for wear, perhaps, but that's all.'

About ten minutes later, they had reached as far as Richmond Avenue, but when Sarah turned the corner, Beattie came to a halt. 'Do we really want to go any further, Sarah?' she asked. 'I'm not sure I want to go back.'

Sarah returned to her. 'What are you afraid of, Beattie?'

'I'm not sure,' she replied. 'I don't think I'm afraid. But I do feel guilty.'

Sarah was puzzled. 'Guilty? About what?'

'The way I treated it,' replied Beattie, uneasily. 'The way I treated you, and all my family.'

Sarah smiled and put her arm around Beattie's waist. 'Trust me, Beattie,' she said affectionately. 'I brought you here deliberately. There's a very special reason why I want you to come back to the house.'

A few minutes later, to Beattie's absolute astonishment, Sarah used her own key to open the front door of the house. Sarah ushered Beattie in first.

As she came into the hall, Beattie felt a sudden cold chill. 'Oh God!' she cried, her voice echoing round the large empty space. 'It's hard to believe. This is home, *our* home.' She took a few steps further, looking up to the ceiling, then all round her. 'I never thought I'd ever be standing here again.' She crossed her arms and squeezed them tight. She felt pain and anguish. 'You're right, Sarah,' she said. 'I *am* afraid.'

'There's no need to be, Beattie,' said Sarah, strolling over to her, 'because from now on, this place is back in the family, where it belongs.'

Beattie turned with a start. Had she heard right?

'Freddie's put down a deposit on the place,' Sarah said. 'We're going to do it up bit by bit, and, if the house survives the air raids, we'll move back in a few months' time.'

Beattie's eyes were wide with astonishment and bewilderment. 'Oh, Sarah!' she breathed.

'And both Freddie and I want you to know,' Sarah said, tenderly, 'that the door of this house will always be open to you and Ed. That's the way Mother and Father would have wanted it.'

Beattie, her eyes glistening with tears, threw her arms

403

around her sister and they hugged each other.

They then strolled together into what was once the kitchen. Like the rest of the place, it was a depressing sight, for the old gas cooker was black and filthy, the Ascot heater broken and hanging from the wall, the stone sink had split in two and was lying in separate halves on the floor, there was no glass in the windows, and what was left of the linoleum was covered with huge scorch marks.

'It's hard to believe we used to have most of our meals in here,' Beattie said, trying to take it all in. 'Mother and Father must be turning in their graves.'

'Don't worry,' assured Sarah. 'It'll look different in a few months. All this dear old house needs now is some love.'

Sarah's remark triggered something in Beattie's mind. It was something she had been keeping from everyone for so long, but which she realised now had to come out into the open. Sadly, she had always found that there were very few people in life that she could trust, *really* trust. It was strange, but even during her young years, if ever she had something that was troubling her, or needed someone to take her side, there was only one person she could turn to. It was neither her mother nor her father, but her sister, Sarah. And so it was all over again. Her new-found relationship with Sarah was the opportunity she had been waiting for to discuss something so intimate that she could not talk about it with Ed, or even Ma Briggs.

'I need someone to love me too,' she said, quite suddenly, and unexpectedly. 'And I think I've found him.'

Sarah swung her a startled look. 'Beattie!' she said, beaming.

'I've been meeting someone for over a year,' Beattie continued. 'His name's Chris Wilkins. He's a schoolteacher. He wants me to marry him.'

404

Sarah was overjoyed. 'Oh – Beattie!' she gasped, throwing her arms around her and embracing her. 'How absolutely wonderful! We must meet him,' she said, quickly, eagerly, pulling away from Beattie and looking at her. 'You must invite him over to tea. Freddie and I would love to meet him. He'll be absolutely thrilled. *I'm* thrilled! I'll help you, Beattie. I'll help you in any way I can. Oh, what's he like? After all you've been through, you deserve a good man to look after you—'

'There's a snag,' said Beattie, cutting straight through her sister's excited response. 'He's a good deal younger than me.'

Sarah stopped abruptly. For a brief moment, her joy was overtaken by concern. 'How much younger?' she asked, apprehensively.

'About fifteen years.'

Sarah breathed a sigh of relief. 'Oh, that's all,' she replied. 'For one moment I thought you were going to say he was still in his pram!'

They both laughed.

'I'm not that bad!' quipped Beattie. 'But there's another problem. He's been married before.'

'Oh.' Sarah bit her lip anxiously.

'They married when they were both only eighteen. They were too young. It never worked. They split up within a year and got a divorce soon after. He hasn't seen her since.'

Sarah thought about this carefully for a moment before asking, 'Does the fact that he's been married before – worry you?'

If Beattie had doubts, she wasn't showing them. 'No,' she said, shaking her head firmly. 'But I'd be untruthful to myself if I wasn't just a little uneasy that he'd spent at least part of his life with another woman. But then, with me –'

she perched herself on the remains of a wooden trestle table – 'there *was* Edward Lacey. Not to mention Jack Ridley.'

Sarah shrugged her shoulders in agreement. 'The main point is, do you love this man?'

Beattie hesitated. 'More than I ever thought possible. It's ridiculous, isn't it,' she said, with a sigh, 'falling in love at my age?'

'Love can come at any age, Beattie,' replied Sarah. 'It's not the preserve of the young.'

Beattie smiled appreciatively. 'I wonder what *they* would have thought about all this?' she said, her eyes scanning the rack and ruin of the poor old kitchen. 'Mum and Dad.'

Sarah came to her, put her arm around her waist, and joined her in reflective contemplation. 'I think they're very proud of you, Beattie,' she said with great affection. 'Something tells me they're going to approve of their new son-in-law.'

'I was actually referring to you and me, Sarah,' said Beattie. 'Please don't ever let us part again. I couldn't bear it.'

The two of them held each other tight.

'Now we only have one small problem to deal with,' said Sarah, whose mind was already concentrating on a more pressing matter. 'What are we going to do about Jack Ridley?'

Throughout his life, Jack Ridley had seldom stayed in any one place long enough to unpack his clothes. Not that he had many clothes to worry about, for it seemed to be his style to live from hand to mouth. But in his humble opinion, things were about to look up. Once Ritz had done his bit with Beattie, he would be able to move back into the fold, and work on his next move, which would be how to get his hands on part, if not all, of the small fortune left to Ed by his grandfather.

Jack's latest 'abode' was a room above a bombed-out toy shop in Duckworth Mews, just off the Mile End Road in East London. It wasn't much of a place, but he had got the rent for a song from a bloke who was half pissed at the time, whom he had met in a pub called the Bow Arms, just near the tube station. The room itself consisted of nothing more than a single bed, a table and two chairs, a gas ring to make a cup of char, and a cold tap and washbasin in the corner, which was, for some absurd reason, hidden behind a tatty cloth screen.

But for Ridley, the one great asset of the room was the second door, which was situated at the rear, and a very handy device for making a quick exit to the back yard below, if and when it should be required.

Today, Ridley was in a very happy mood. Ritz was due to report back to him about his meeting in Mitford Road with Beattie. He tried to imagine how Beattie would react when she heard how Ridley was embarking on the final years of his life, struck down by a deadly illness, with no one to look after him during the winter of his life. As he lay back on his bed, smoking his usual rolled fag, he grinned to himself, amazed at the sheer genius of his idea. The only flea in the ointment was, however, Ritz himself. Ridley had never fully trusted the little pile of pig dung, mainly because his brains were about as big as a peapod. He began to have doubts about how Ritz would handle the situation. Would Beattie believe his story? Would Ritz be so convincing that she wouldn't fail to welcome Ridley back with open arms? Or would Ritz make a complete bungle of the job, just like he always had done, especially when he'd got him, Ridley, involved with the Dillon boys. Even as he was contemplating all the worst possibilities, there was a thumping on the door downstairs, followed by a voice calling out to him. 'Ridley! Are you there? Open up!'

Ridley leaped up from his bed and rushed straight to the small window at the front of the room. Peering from behind the curtain, he could see Sarah looking up at him from the cobbled mews below. 'Open up, Ridley!' she called. 'I want to talk to you.'

Ridley was about to panic. What's *she* doing here? he thought to himself. Why isn't it Beattie down there? He cursed Ritz. What had he done? This wasn't what he expected at all.

'Come on, Ridley!' came Sarah, again. 'I know you're up there. I need to talk to you. Open up!'

Ridley stood back from the window and thought hard. The last time he'd approached this woman, he'd warned her what would happen if she didn't speak up for him to Beattie. His whole attitude changed. This was good, this was very good. This is just what he wanted. Beattie's sister was there to help him. She had clearly decided that speaking up for him was far better than him ruining her own marriage. In one swift, impulsive movement, he rushed out of the room.

'Well now,' said Ridley, as he opened the front door downstairs. ''Ere's a pleasant surprise.'

'Are you going to let me in,' asked Sarah, 'or do I have to wait on the doorstep all day?'

Ridley grimaced, and let her in. 'Welcome to my 'umble abode!' he said. He liked this woman's nerve.

'Leave the door open, if you please,' she said firmly as she came in.

'Wot's up?' he asked, cheekily. 'Don't yer trust me?'

'How did you guess?' she answered, tersely.

The passage was full of broken toys and old cardboard

408

boxes. There was junk everywhere. As she followed him up a small flight of stairs, Sarah covered her mouth with her hand; the smell of cat's pee was overpowering.

'So?' asked Ridley, once they were inside his room. 'And wot do I owe for the pleasure of your company?'

'You owe me nothing,' replied Sarah. 'And I certainly owe you nothing.'

Ridley's smile disappeared. 'Who told yer where ter find me?' he demanded, icily.

'That doesn't matter,' said Sarah. 'What does matter is the proposition you made me.'

Ridley's face lit up again. 'Ah!' he beamed. 'Now we're talkin'. Wot about a little snifter?'

'I didn't come to drink with you, Mr Ridley,' she replied. 'I came to ask you a few questions.'

'Fire away,' said Ridley, going across to the small cabinet at the side of his bed to pour a drink.

Sarah made sure that she kept her back as close to the main bedroom door as possible. She felt stifled by the smell of stale beer and rolled fag smoke. 'I want to know, if I speak on your behalf to my sister, what you intend to do if you go back to live with her again?'

Ridley was puzzled. *'Do?'* he asked, whilst pouring himself a glass of dark brown bitter from a quart bottle. 'I intend ter take up where I left off, ter look after me wife, and be a good 'usband to 'er.'

'Are you sure you'll be well enough to do that?'

Ridley swung a look at her. 'Wot's that s'pposed ter mean?' he growled.

Sarah shrugged her shoulders. 'I gather you're almost at death's door,' she replied.

'Ah!' said Ridley. 'So Beattie's 'eard, 'as she?'

Sarah was now on the attack. 'In all the years you've

409

been married to my sister, you've never once treated her like a proper wife. So what makes you think you can do so now?'

'That's not fair, Sarah ol' gel,' replied Ridley, taking down a huge gulp of bitter. 'I've always been fond of my little missus.'

'Is that why you beat her?'

'Is that wot she told yer?'

Sarah squared up to him. 'It's what Ma Briggs told me, and plenty of those ghastly neighbours of yours in the Bunk.' She moved further into the room. 'Ma Briggs said there were times when my sister had so many bruises and black eyes that she was tempted to call in the police.'

Ridley was angry. 'That stupid ol' cow!' he barked, wiping the beer foam from his lips with the back of his hand. 'She was always tryin' ter make trouble, always takin' Beat's side whenever we disagreed about anyfin'!'

'What do you really want from my sister, Mr Ridley?' asked Sarah.

Ridley came across to her, and angrily slammed his glass down on the table. 'Are yer goin' ter speak to 'er for me,' he rasped, 'or would yer prefer me ter 'ave a little word wiv your 'usband?'

'I ask again,' insisted Sarah, refusing to be intimidated by him. 'What do you want from my sister? Or should I say – from her son?'

Ridley froze, and stared her out. Gradually, his face broke into a huge grin. 'Ah!' he replied. 'I see we talk the same language after all.' He picked up his glass of bitter again. ''E's goin' ter be a very rich boy, your nephew,' he said, strolling back to his bed, and perching on the side of it. 'I fink the least 'e can do is ter take care of 'is poor ol' stepfarver.'

410

'I don't think that's very likely, Jack.'

Ridley leaped up from the bed to see Beattie, who had entered the room from behind Sarah.

'I'm afraid you won't get much out of him,' said Beattie, joining Sarah. 'Or me.'

'Wot the 'ell's goin' on 'ere?' snapped Ridley, rushing straight across to confront her. 'Where's Ritz? Did 'e bring you 'ere?'

'No, Jack,' replied Beattie, with cool calm. 'Sarah and I came all on our own.' She stood side by side with her sister. 'We wanted to have a little chat with you.'

Ridley eyed them both with deep suspicion.

'I'm afraid Ed had quite a disappointment,' said Sarah. 'Isn't that so, Beattie?'

'That's right,' replied Beattie, who, like her sister, was directing her words straight at Ridley. 'You see, his grandfather turned out to be not quite as generous as we all first thought.'

'It appears the old chap was a bit of a philanderer,' said Sarah.

'He went through his money like a hot knife through butter,' said Beattie.

'Which means,' continued Sarah, 'that there was nothing left for a twenty-first birthday present for the stepson who you adore so much.'

'Sad – isn't it, Jack?' contributed Beattie. 'But you can still come back and live with me, if you like.'

'Provided, of course,' said Sarah, 'that you'll be well enough to live that long.'

The two sisters exchanged wry smiles.

Ridley looked from one to the other. 'Ritz!' he barked. ''E's put yer up ter this! Just wait till I get me 'ands on 'im. I'll kill the sod!'

'The saving grace in all of this, Mr Ridley,' replied Sarah, 'is that your friend appears to have a conscience. It's something you might consider yourself some time.'

'Get out of 'ere!' He rushed over to the door and pulled it wide open. 'Go on – boaf of yer! Out!'

'No, Jack,' said Beattie, going to a chair at the table, and calmly sitting there. 'You're the one that's leaving, not us.'

'You see, Mr Ridley,' said Sarah, continuing where Beattie had left off, 'my sister and I are tired of your constant intimidation. We want to see the back of you – once and for all.'

'And I want a divorce, Jack,' added Beattie. 'Since you've disappeared without trace for so long, I don't think the Courts will have too many problems granting it. Do you?'

'Do we make ourselves quite clear, Mr Ridley?' added Sarah.

Ridley's hand seemed to have frozen on the door knob. He still hadn't quite taken in what had hit him. He gently closed the door, went back to the bed, and perched there. Suddenly, he felt like a man drowning; his whole life was floating before him. Throughout his lifetime, he had mixed with criminals and nefarious characters of all types, and always he had somehow managed to cope with them. But this was the first time he had come up against two women who were using their brains against him rather than their fists. As he looked across at the two of them, he found it hard to believe that they had been distant with each other for so long. There seemed to be a bond, a union between them that was hard to define. But, physically strong as he was, they unnerved him. No, there was no going back now, he told himself. This was the end of the road for him, and he had no alternative but to go along with what they wanted. But, being Jack Ridley, he would not give up without one last attempt.

'And what would you say,' he said, looking as menacing as he could, 'if I told yer ter go ter 'ell?'

Sarah walked slowly across to him. 'I don't think you'd do that, Mr Ridley,' she said, in a cool, businesslike voice.

'As I told you once before, Jack,' added Beattie, 'I'd hate to be the one who shops you.'

Perched uneasily on the edge of his bed, Ridley sat staring aimlessly at the linoleum on the floor beneath his feet.

'We want you to pack your things, Mr Ridley.'

Ridley looked up to see Sarah standing over him.

'If you ever try to approach either me or my sister again,' she said, uncompromisingly, 'we'll make it our business to inform the police about your part in the murder of a police constable.'

Jack looked long and hard at her, and then at Beattie. It was the last time he would ever do so.

Ma Briggs didn't much care for the schoolteacher. Not that it was anything personal – his looks, his appearance, or his manner. No, nothing like that. It was the disruption he was about to cause to her life that she objected to. In fact, although she was overjoyed in one way for Beattie, the prospect of Beattie getting married again thoroughly depressed her, for it meant that she would most probably have to pack her bags and leave for an old people's home or something. At least, that's what she thought. But on the evening that Beattie first introduced her to her schoolteacher friend, Mr Wilkins, all was not what she had been dreading.

'We want you to come and live with us, Ma,' Beattie said, during five o'clock tea time.

'We're going to look for a place outside London,' said Chris, the schoolteacher. 'In the country somewhere, probably Surrey.'

'In the country?' replied the old girl in disbelief. 'Outside London?'

'As much as we love Mitford Road, Ma,' added Beattie, 'don't you think it would be nice to find somewhere away from the smells of city streets, with fresh air, and cows and sheep in fields?'

'I like the smell of city streets,' Ma snapped, grumpily. 'An' I 'ate fresh air and cows and sheep.'

Beattie and Chris exchanged gentle laughs. 'But you like me,' said Beattie. 'And Ed.'

'I don't like yer,' replied the old girl, 'I love yer. But I still don't like cows and sheep. Stupid ol' fresh air!'

The moment she had told Ma about Chris, Beattie knew she had a problem on her hands. The poor old girl was now at an age when she was thoroughly set in her ways. But Beattie was determined that after all Ma had done for her and Ed, she would never dump her in an old people's home.

'I'll tell you something, Ma,' said the quiet-spoken schoolteacher. 'I was born in the countryside, a little village in Norfolk, a place called Swaffham. It was so small, hardly anyone seemed to live there except me and my mum and dad and two brothers. It was so peaceful, so peaceful in fact that it bored the pants off me. Then, after I'd done my teacher's training, I was sent to a school in the East End. God, what a difference! Talk about rowdy. And all that traffic going down the Mile End Road and Stratford. But I loved it – at least, I did for the first few years. It was a novelty, so different from everything I'd ever known. But I tell you something, after a while the novelty wore off, and pretty soon I became just as bored living in London as I was in the country. In fact, I longed to get back home again. But I'm glad I came here. Otherwise, the only kind of life I'd have ever experienced would have been in a tiny village in Norfolk. And most of all

– ' he turned to Beattie, who was sitting at his side on the sofa – 'I'd never have met Beattie – or you.'

Ma, whose indomitable curlers were dangling down from the few hairs she had left on her head, listened to all the schoolteacher had to say with rapt attention. All the time he was talking, she was sucking her gums, for those elusive pearly whites of hers had still not been recovered. But she did hear everything he said, and it made her feel guilty.

'I didn't mean ter sound ungrateful, Beat,' she said. 'It's just that, well, I fink I'm too old ter change now, too old ter up me roots an' go dancin' around the cows and the sheep in the country.'

'Listen to me, Ma,' said Beattie, stretching across for Ma's hand. 'As long as you live, you'll never be too old for anything. Of all the people I've ever known in my life, you're the one who adapts to change more than any other. I remember when me and Ed asked you to leave the Bunk, to come and live with us in this road. I remember how, from the first moment you arrived, you gave us all the drive and the energy to make this place what it is today. If you did it then, Ma,' she said, 'you can do it again.'

As usual with Ma when she had just been given what she always considered was a lecture from Beattie, she sat with her hands on her lap, staring into the coal fire. After what seemed to Beattie and Chris to be an interminable silence, the old girl finally looked straight at Chris. 'It's nuffin' personal, yer understand,' she said sheepishly.

Chris gave her a great big smile. 'I know that, Ma,' he said.

Shortly after, the old girl went to bed in her usual place down in the air-raid shelter. Now left alone, Beattie stretched out on the sofa, with her head resting on Chris's lap. She was miles away.

'Penny for your thoughts?' he asked, smoothing her forehead gently with his fingers.

Beattie thought for a moment before replying. 'Oh, I was just thinking how lucky I am.'

'Lucky?'

'To have Ma, to have Ed, to have my sister, Sarah, but most of all, to have you.'

'I'm pretty lucky too.' As he looked down into her eyes, he took off his thick-lensed spectacles, which had been the reason why he had been turned down for military service. Then he leaned his head down and kissed her tenderly on the lips.

Beattie sighed. 'I feel strange,' she said. 'As though I'm coming to the end of an era.'

'That's a funny thing to say,' he replied. 'I would have thought we're just starting one.'

'No, but you know what I mean,' she explained. 'The past and the future seem to be coming together all at once, coming together in the most wonderful way. God knows, Ma's ancient, but at least we've still got her. And Ed – oh, Chris, I can't wait for you to meet him. You two are going to get on like a house on fire. I just pray he survives this awful war. It's odd. All those years ago when he was first born, I'd have taken any opportunity to throw him straight into the Regent's Canal, but now—' She sighed despondently. 'If anything happened to him, I don't know what I'd do.'

'Nothing's going to happen to him, darling,' said Chris, reassuringly. 'After the war, he's going to come home, and he and me are going to make your life hell!'

Beattie laughed, because she wanted to believe him. 'I can't wait for you to meet my sister, Sarah, either,' she said. 'These past few weeks have been – extraordinary. It's as though the two of us have been born all over again. Every

416

time I think about it, I find it so amazing that we never held on to each other. But in some strange way, it's not just about flesh and blood – it's something deeper than that. There are times when I'm alone, when I feel she's such a part of me, I know where she is, and what she's doing.' She moved her eyes, and gazed lovingly up at Chris. 'For the first time in my life,' she said, 'I feel I know her. And I think she knows me too.'

She sat up and faced him. 'I just hope we're never parted again.'

'You won't be,' he answered, confidently.

'How can you be so sure?'

Chris thought about it for a moment. 'Because you don't want to be,' he replied.

She fell into his arms, and they started to make love. But the wail of the air-raid siren soon put a stop to that.

Chapter 28

The aerial onslaught on London came to a climax on the night of 29 December 1940, when practically the whole city was ablaze. Street after street, office blocks, restaurants, railway stations, hospitals, churches – all were left either in a pile of rubble, or consumed with flames in an inferno. Although the Royal Air Force courageously diminished the fire power of the marauding Luftwaffe, during the first few months of the following year, other cities such as Plymouth, Portsmouth, Coventry, Manchester, Leeds, and Liverpool all came under attack. It was, of course, a concentrated effort by Reichsmarshal Goering and his Nazi hierarchy to undermine the morale of the British people, but that morale was far more determined and indomitable than they had anticipated. Despite the constant day and night air raids, life went on as near normal as was humanly possible. The fish and chip shops did a roaring trade, so did the pubs, and even though food supplies were short, the British housewife queued outside any shop that could offer even a suggestion of something palatable. Whale and horsemeat, spurned as cruel and barbaric in times of peace, were, despite their foul taste, a necessary replacement for other foods that were simply unobtainable. People were also constantly forced to clear up each morning after the bomb blasts of the night before, and when it was impossible to find any more glass for their windows in the hardware shops, they settled for timber boards, which often had a huge 'V' for Victory chalk-marked on them. Everywhere else, the 'BUSINESS AS USUAL' signs sprouted like mushrooms. If this was to be the People's War, then this is how they would fight it.

During the early spring of 1941, Beattie married her schoolteacher boyfriend, Chris Wilkins. She desperately wanted a white wedding, but as the vicar of the local church was a bit puritanical about divorced couples, she had to settle for a straightforward registry office ceremony in Islington Town Hall. Even so, part of her wish was granted, for, undaunted by the vicar, Sarah took it upon herself to make a wedding dress for her sister, made from a white synthetic taffeta material, which Freddie managed to get for her on the black market. Very few guests were invited for the occasion, as several eyebrows had already been raised when it was known that Beattie was marrying someone who was fifteen years younger than herself. Sadly, Ed couldn't be there either, for at the last moment, his compassionate leave had been cancelled owing to the fact that he was about to join his unit for an 'undisclosed destination'. Chris's family turned out to be a lovely bunch, and everyone on Beattie's side, including Aunt Dixie, Aunt Myra and Uncle Terry, got on splendidly with them. During the wedding reception afterwards, which was held in a large hired room above a furniture store in Lower Holloway Road, Sarah and Freddie had a wonderful time chatting with Chris's mother and father, warm, charming people, who had apparently taken to their future daughter-in-law the moment they laid eyes on her.

Ma Briggs, however, was the big success of the evening. Despite her years, she did a tango with Chris's father, who was a bit of an expert in ballroom dancing, and they were applauded so loudly that the record of Victor Sylvester and his Ballroom Orchestra playing 'Green Eyes' was played so many times, the grooves were nearly worn out.

Just before Christmas, Sarah's first meeting with Chris had at first been a little uneasy, mainly because she had grown very protective towards her younger sister, and didn't want her to get hurt any more. In many ways, Sarah was still quite old-fashioned in her outlook on life, and on that first meeting with her future brother-in-law, she treated him with a certain amount of suspicion. It was therefore not until several weeks after the wedding that she really got to know, and like him.

It was almost closing time at the barber's shop when Chris turned up to have Freddie give him his usual haircut. He was the last customer of the day, so, as soon as he came in, Sarah lowered the door blind, and reversed the 'OPEN' sign to 'CLOSED'. Then she went out into the back parlour and made all three of them a cup of tea. By the time she came back, Freddie was just finishing off Chris's comb-and-scissors trim.

'I was just asking Freddie,' said Chris, as Sarah put his cup of tea at the side of the hairwash sink. 'You must have wondered why Beattie should've got mixed up with a younger bloke like me.'

'Those sort of matters are not our concern, Chris,' said Sarah, rather primly. 'They're personal to you and Beattie, not us.'

'I know,' said Chris. 'But you must have heard the tongues wag. I have. So has Beattie.'

Sarah put Freddie's cup on the ledge by the sink. 'If you love each other,' she said, 'what business is it of anyone else?'

'Precisely!' answered Chris. 'I tell Beattie that all the time. But she still worries about it. She also worries about the fact that she's too old to give me a family of our own. I can't seem to make her understand that, as much as I love children, I love her more. I told her that right from the start, long before we decided to get married.'

'There we are then!' said Freddie, removing the towel from around Chris's shoulders. Then he collected the hand mirror, and showed him the cut from all angles.

'Excellent! Thanks, Freddie!' Chris said, swivelling himself round in the barber's chair. 'You're an artist!'

Freddie laughed, collected his tea, and went across to join Sarah, who was sitting on one of the customers' chairs.

'In any case,' continued Chris, 'if we want children all that badly, we can always adopt them. But there are other things I want to do first.' He turned around briefly, and picked up his cup of tea. 'I want to make Beattie happy,' he said. 'She's very special to me.' He paused a moment. 'D'you know she's the only woman in my life I've ever cared for. I often tell her how much I love her, and I've never told anyone that before, not even my first wife – especially my first wife!'

Sarah and Freddie exchanged tactful smiles.

Chris sipped his tea. 'But truthfully, there's so much I want to do for her. I have so many plans. So has she. D'you know, when we're down the air-raid shelter sometimes, we plan all the things we're going to do after the war. We talk about everything, from where we want to live, the kind of school I'd like to end up teaching in, the kind of people we'd like to get to know, even the colour of the walls in our bedroom! Poor old Ma. She must be sick to death of listening to all our drivel by now. It's a good thing she sleeps soundly!'

They all laughed.

'I'm a lucky bloke, that's for sure!'

They were interrupted by a tapping sound on the shop door. Freddie put his tea down and went to see who it was.

422

Beattie was peering in and waving through the window. Freddie opened the door for her.

'I thought he'd be lurking in here!' she said, going straight across and giving Chris a kiss. Then, ruffling his hair, she said, 'I hope you've paid my brother-in-law for that haircut?'

'It's all in the family!' quipped Freddie.

'Hello, Sarah dear,' Beattie said, giving her sister a kiss on the cheek. 'I hope my husband's been behaving himself?'

'He's been a model customer,' replied Sarah, with a smile. 'So where've you been?'

'To see Mr Ogden,' she said, 'the dentist down the road. He's making a new pair of dentures for Ma. They won't be ready for another week.'

'Oh God!' groaned Chris. 'She'll go out of her mind!'

'Poor Ma,' said Sarah. 'She does so hate to be without her teeth.'

'So would you if you didn't have any!' quipped Chris, to gales of laughter from the others.

'We have to go, Chris,' said Beattie, with some urgency. 'It'll be the siren any minute. I don't want to get caught out in the ack-ack.'

'Right,' said Chris, turning then to Freddie and Sarah. 'Thanks a lot then, Fred. And for the tea, Sarah.'

'Byebye Chris,' replied Sarah, kissing him lightly on the cheek.

'Come on then,' said Freddie. 'I'll see yer out.'

Freddie led Chris to the door, leaving Beattie alone for a moment with Sarah.

'Thanks for everything, Sarah,' said Beattie, embracing her sister. 'As usual.'

'Come and see us soon,' replied Sarah. 'We've got a lot of gossip to catch up with. And by the way, I think you've got a very nice husband.'

Beattie's face lit up. 'Oh, Sarah, d'you really think so?'

'He's madly in love with you. Did you know that?'

Beattie giggled. These days, she seemed so much younger than her age. 'I'm pretty mad about him too,' she confessed. 'But it means a lot to me that you like him. When we got married, I had my doubts.'

'Well just remember this,' said Sarah, putting her arm around Beattie's shoulder, and leading her towards the door. 'Whenever you feel you're at your lowest ebb, just think how much you've got to look forward to. A new husband, a wonderful son, and a promising new life. So make the most of it.'

They stopped at the door, and paused. Beattie was radiant, and beaming. 'The next time I see you, I want to hear all that gossip you keep promising me.'

'I won't forget.'

'Promise?'

'Promise.'

They embraced, then Beattie went out to join Chris, who was waiting with Freddie outside. After final farewells, Beattie and Chris made off at a brisk pace down St Alban's Place to catch their bus back home from Upper Street. It was now getting dark quite quickly, and along the main road people were hurrying to get home before the air-raid siren heralded the start of yet another night's bombing.

Freddie put his arm around Sarah's shoulders as they watched Beattie and Chris head off towards the end of the quiet side street. 'I fink she's done all right there, don't you?' said Freddie.

'So has he,' replied Sarah. 'I don't think I have to worry about Beattie any more. She's happy now.'

'Yes,' said Freddie. 'But all these plans 'e keeps goin' on about, I wish 'e'd 'urry up an' get on wiv 'em.'

424

'Don't be silly, dear,' replied Sarah. 'They're still young. They've got all their lives ahead of them.'

Beattie and Chris stopped briefly, and waved back to Sarah and Freddie. And then they turned the corner, and were gone.

'Jairmany calling! Jairmany calling!'

Ma Briggs was clearly a glutton for punishment. When Beattie and Chris arrived back home, there she was, listening to the man with the sneer up his nose again, cursing and blinding, and ready to smash up the poor wireless set with her bare fists. Lord Haw-Haw's subject tonight was the great success of the German invasion of Greece, and the ultimate surrender of the ancient city of Salonika. But when he got on to the continuation of the London Blitz, and how the population was gradually weakening beneath the pressure of the superior German air power, Ma was fighting mad. 'Lyin' sod!' she yelled at the pseudo-aristocratic voice. 'We should string 'im up an' be done wiv it!'

'We've got to capture him first, Ma,' said Chris, who liked nothing better than to wind up the old girl. 'When they do, I think you should be given first chance to get at him. What do you say?'

'Stop it, Chris,' scolded Beattie. 'Things are bad enough as they are. When you think how they nearly burned down the whole of the city last December, it gives you the creeps when you listen to what he says.'

'Don't be frightened, Beattie,' Chris replied. Sometimes he took it for granted that her nerves were made of steel, but in fact, she was just as nervous and vulnerable as anyone else. 'Why don't we play a game of Monopoly?' he said. 'It'll help to calm our nerves.'

'Calm our nerves?' barked the old girl. 'Buyin' an' sellin'' uvver people's property? It's enuff ter give yer a 'art attack.'

'I don't think we should, Chris,' said Beattie, anxiously. 'The siren went nearly half an hour ago. We should get down the shelter before they start coming over.'

'They usually come over within a few minutes of the siren,' replied Chris. 'I haven't heard a thing. I don't think it's going to be much tonight.' He went to the sideboard. 'Come on,' he said. 'Let's make it a short one, and I'll show you how I can buy Mayfair and Piccadilly Circus all in a few minutes.'

Whilst Chris was getting out the Monopoly board, money, and cards, Ma reluctantly turned off the wireless set, but not before raising two fingers to her 'Jairman' collaborator friend.

A few minutes later, all three of them were hunched over the Monopoly board, engaged in the crucial business of takeovers, bank loans, and the buying and selling of valuable property. To Chris's intense irritation, tonight, as on all nights, it was obvious that Ma was going to be the triumphant player, for she was cunning enough, and observant enough to know every single move before it was even contemplated. But although Beattie loved seeing Chris get rattled, her ears were constantly listening out for the familiar droning sound of enemy aircraft. But the encouraging sign was that there was, as yet, no ack-ack anti-aircraft fire, and so, without being too complacent, she carried on with the game. Even so, her mind was on other things. 'I hope it won't be long before we hear from Ed,' she said, quite out of the blue. 'I haven't heard anything from him since before the wedding.'

'I doubt you will,' said Chris. 'If Jerry's going to try an invasion here, every bloke in khaki's going to be sitting around waiting for him.'

'It's so unfair,' protested Beattie. 'He's only a boy, and

he's already been involved in some of the worst fighting of the war. Thank God he survived Dunkirk, and then all this business in Greece. He should be given a break, and let the others do some of the dirty work.'

'Unfortunately, there aren't enough "others" to go round,' said Chris. 'If there was any justice in this world, I should be out there with them.'

Beattie turned on him. 'No, Chris!' she snapped. 'You can't help your eye problems. And in any case, you do your bit in the ARP. That's quite enough.'

'You don't 'ave ter worry about Ed,' said Ma, confidently. 'If anyone knows 'ow ter take care of 'imself, that one does. Hey!' She had suddenly advanced her car token around the board so that it had landed on a prize property. 'Park Lane!' she bellowed. 'I'll buy it!'

Chris clutched his forehead in frustration. 'Oh no!' he sighed. 'Not another one!'

'Be quiet!'

Chris and Ma suddenly looked up at Beattie, who could obviously hear something, for her eyes were turned upwards towards the ceiling.

'What is it?' asked Chris.

'Listen!'

After a few seconds, they could hear the approach of what sounded like a single aircraft, its engines droning monotonously. It came from the far distance, and seemed to take a long time to establish itself, but there was no doubt that it was there.

'Must be one of ours,' suggested Chris, whose eyes were also turned towards the ceiling. 'Can't hear any ack-ack.'

Even as he spoke, all hell broke loose, as the air was lambasted by the deafening crack of anti-aircraft fire.

'Everyone under the table!' yelled Chris, as he leaped

up, and quite literally yanked both Ma and Beattie off their chairs, and helped them under the table they had been playing on.

But Ma was not as agile as the others, and she had a job to squeeze herself under the table. 'Bloody 'Itler!' she yelled, furiously. 'I'll get yer fer this!'

As the barrage of ack-ack fire pounded the night sky, all three finally managed to huddle together beneath the table. But it was a nerve-racking experience, and Chris had to use his arms to protect and comfort the two women.

The barrage continued for quite a while, with the house being rocked to its very foundations by the deafening sounds, and the tinkling of shrapnel on the pavement outside. And then, quite suddenly, the guns stopped firing. What followed was an intense silence, with only the distant shouting of people along the road outside.

After a moment or so, the three heads beneath the table felt confident enough to look up. 'Sounds like it's all over,' said Ma, who hardly dared to speak.

'That plane,' whispered Beattie. 'What happened to it? Did they shoot it down?'

'Hard to say,' said Chris, who felt more confident than the others to speak in a normal voice. 'I certainly can't hear it.'

They waited a moment or so longer, until they finally decided that it was safe enough to emerge from their makeshift shelter.

'Oh God!' said Beattie. 'We should have gone down the shelter. It's too dangerous to stay in the house once the siren's gone.'

'Well, I don't know about you,' complained Ma, bitterly, as both Chris and Beattie helped her up on to her feet. 'I'm goin' straight down there now. It's way past my kip time . . .'

'Out! Out! Out! Out! Out!'

The terrifying yells that suddenly pierced the air were coming from the road outside.

'Oh Christ!' called Beattie. 'What now?'

'Down!' barked Chris. 'Down!'

But by the time all three of them had thrown themselves to the floor again, another voice was yelling, 'Para – chute . . . !'

The word had hardly been completed when there was a sudden, deafening explosion, followed by a blinding blue flash. In one horrifying moment of unreality, as if in slow motion, the entire house came tumbling down, bricks and mortar, glass, plaster, furniture, and personal possessions. The thick black smoke was dense, and by the time it had settled, nothing could be seen but a pile of rubble.

In the unnatural silence that followed, there was only the distant sound of a dog barking.

It was nearly two o'clock in the morning when Sarah and Freddie reached the Royal Northern Hospital in Holloway Road. Had it not been for the police constables who had brought them in their car, the only way to get there would have been to walk. The knock on the front door of the barber shop had given them quite a shock. At first, they didn't hear it for they had taken shelter in their Morrison, which had been erected in the back parlour. As soon as they heard the news about Beattie, they got dressed quickly, and were given a lift.

The air raid was still in full swing as they made their way to the emergency wing of the hospital through the Manor Gardens entrance. The place was jam-packed with ambulances bringing casualties from bombed-out buildings all over the borough, and in the waiting area of the wing itself, there were so many seriously injured patients waiting to be attended to that there was hardly enough room to move.

The moment they arrived, they were immediately sent to a temporary emergency ward on the ground floor that had been set up to deal with bomb blast casualties. The sound of people groaning was soul-destroying, and it took all Sarah's strength to take in what was going on.

'I think you should both come straight in,' said a harassed ward sister with a soft Irish voice. 'I'm afraid there's not much time.'

Sarah's heart sank, and Freddie had to keep a comforting arm around her for support. Before they reached the last bed at the end of the ward, Sarah asked the nurse if she knew what had happened to the other occupants of her sister's house. But there appeared to be no information, other than that the house itself had been right next door to the house where a parachute bomb had been dangling from a roof top, until it finally exploded.

Beattie was in a bed behind screens. Sarah had to steel herself to go in, but when she did, she was still horrified to see the state her younger sister was in. Swathed in bandages that were blotched with leaking blood, and with tubes coming out from all parts of her body, it was obvious that she was fighting for her life.

'She had an operation to try to save her lung,' said the nurse, softly. 'There was so much heavy debris on her, it just crushed her entire body.'

'Can she survive?' This was the only question that Sarah now wanted answering.

The nurse responded by lowering her eyes.

After the nurse had gone, Sarah went to the side of the bed and searched for Beattie's hand beneath the bedclothes. She took hold of it, and gently squeezed it. To her astonishment, Beattie responded by slowly opening her eyes. 'Beattie,' Sarah called. 'I'm here. It's Sarah, darling. You're not alone.'

Beattie's torn and scratched face tried hard to smile. Then she tried to open her mouth. She was thirsty. Sarah immediately found a glass of water on the cabinet at her side, and using a spoon, eased a few drops of water between her lips. 'Is that better, darling?' she asked.

Beattie's head nodded just enough to notice. 'Sa-rah.' Her voice was only just audible.

'Yes, Beattie,' answered Sarah, leaning as close as she could. 'I can hear you, my darling.'

'Fred-die?' she was trying to ask.

'Yes, he's here,' said Sarah. 'Freddie's here.'

Freddie came round to the other side of the bed, and leaned down over her. ''Ello, mate,' he said, his voice cracking. 'Don't worry, I'm 'ere. You're doin' fine, mate, just fine.'

Beattie tried a smile again. It was as if she knew about the game that was being played, and it somehow gave her at least a moment or so of renewed strength. 'For-give me – Sarah,' she said, fighting for breath. 'For-give me for all I did.'

Sarah was struggling to keep back tears. 'There's nothing to forgive, Beattie. Nothing.'

'You – were always so – strong. I was – weak.'

Sarah was shaking her head. 'No, Beattie, no.'

'I remember . . .' Beattie swallowed hard, then coughed. But she quickly controlled herself. 'I . . . remember,' she continued, 'when we – had our picture taken – together – hand in hand.' She closed her eyes, but continued to talk. 'I put my tongue out . . .' A faint smile came to her face.

'Yes, Beattie,' said Sarah, softly. 'I remember.'

'When we saw – the picture – we laughed. We both laughed.'

'I remember, Beattie,' said Sarah, again. 'And I remember how angry Father was because he was the one who took it. He said we were two of a kind.'

Beattie was still smiling. But then she went silent. For one terrible moment, Sarah thought she had gone. But she was relieved when Beattie half opened her eyes again.

'Ed – yours now.' As she spoke now, Beattie's words seemed to be totally unconnected to anything she had indicated before. 'Ed – my boy – yours now. He's – always – been yours.'

Tears were now swelling hard and fast into Sarah's eyes. As she looked down at the frail features of her young sister, all she could think of were the wasted years, the angry years of distance between them, the missed opportunities, and the sharing of life and experience. Until just a few hours before, Beattie and her new young husband had all their life ahead of them. They were about to discover the joys of a true marriage together, to learn how to respect and grow old together. But now, all Sarah could see was a life slipping away, a life that had endured so much pain and suffering, so many failed hopes. 'No, Beattie,' she said, feeling the warmth of Beattie's blood as she held her hand. 'Ed belongs to you, he always has. He loves you. He'll always love you.'

Beattie tried to raise her head. 'Your boy – Sarah,' she struggled to say. 'I – took him – from you. Stand – by him. Guide him. Love him.' Her head flopped back on to the pillow. She was silent for a moment, then she only had barely enough strength to whisper. 'Sarah . . .'

Sarah leaned close, and put her ear to Beattie's mouth.

'My . . . sister . . . Sarah . . .'

Sarah felt Beattie's warm breath gush into her ear, then

432

stop. At the same time, her hand quivered, and went limp. She was gone.

Sarah sat there for a moment or so, unable, and not wanting to move.

Freddie let go of Beattie's other hand. Then he came round to comfort Sarah. Tears were streaming down his cheeks.

'She asked me to forgive her,' said Sarah, numbed, and still caressing her sister's hand with her fingers. 'But there was nothing to forgive.' She took Beattie's hand out from beneath the bedclothes and gently kissed it. Then she stood, and took one last look at her face. Despite the gashes and the complexion that now seemed to be drained of all blood, she thought her younger sister looked just as lovely as she always had done. But she would remember her not as she was now, but as she was in the picture they had posed for together – side by side.

Sarah turned, and with Freddie's comforting arm to support her, slowly made her way out along the ward.

A week later, Beattie's son, Ed, arrived home on compassionate leave. Unfortunately, he had been too far away to get back home in time to attend the funerals of his mother, her husband, Chris, and Ma Briggs, all of whom had perished in the parachute bomb explosion that night. But he was determined to say his own personal farewell to his mother, by paying one last visit to what had once been his home.

Mitford Road had quite literally disappeared. The entire road had been obliterated by the bomb, leaving just a pile of rubble.

As Ed approached the utter devastation that had once been his home, the numb feeling in his stomach almost made him turn back. But something made him go on, and when he eventually reached the front brick wall of the house, which, amazingly, was still standing, he paused just long enough to contemplate what had really happened on the night of the explosion. Then he moved on and, climbing over the mass of half-burned timbers, broken roof tiles, crumbled plaster, and fallen masonry, he made his way up what was left of the passage stairs. He had gone only a short way when something caught his eye, gleaming in the bright glow of the April sun. He crouched down and started to retrieve the object from a pile of rubble that had once been part of Ma Briggs' room on the first floor. He finally succeeded, but it was only when he managed to clean off the mud from the object that he was able to recognise it.

It was a set of pearly white false teeth.

Chapter 29

August was a funny old month. No matter how hard it tried, it just couldn't make up its mind whether it was to be the height of summer, or a reminder that autumn was on the way. In the end, however, it made its decision known by having a very positive heatwave. For several days at least, London and the south-east took the full brunt of the soaring temperatures, which sent thousands of people flocking into the parks wherever, and whenever, they could. Now that the Spitfires and Hurricanes of the Royal Air Force had finally stemmed the tide of the Luftwaffe blitz on London, there was an easing of tensions on the streets, and just a hint that perhaps the tide of the war was beginning to turn. And the news that Prime Minister Churchill had met with President Roosevelt on board the cruiser HMS *Prince of Wales* somewhere at sea was also a sign that perhaps at last the people of the United States of America were about to stand shoulder to shoulder with their British counterparts in their epic struggle against the Nazi tyrants.

It was therefore significant that Sarah and Freddie should have chosen a day during the heatwave to move into their newly restored house in Thornhill Road. From the time they stepped out of the taxi ahead of the furniture removals van, the house was bathed in hot, brilliant sunshine, and even the pavement outside was like walking on hot coals.

As most of the iron railings in London had been confiscated to help make weapons for the war effort, there was still a gap in the brick wall, but at least the front garden had been cleared of all the rubble and rubbish that had been accumulating there over the years.

When they stopped at the front door, Freddie paused, and turned to face Sarah. 'I've been waitin' fer this day fer a very long time,' he said. Then he formally handed her the key.

Sarah took it, and embraced him. 'Thank you, my dear, dear Freddie,' she said, holding him tight. Then, with a sigh, she put the key in the lock. This time, the front door opened effortlessly.

Inside, everything had been transformed. Despite the fact that they had both visited the house several times whilst Freddie's builder mate and his team had worked on the seemingly endless restoration, it was the first time that Sarah had actually had the feeling of coming home. Everything she saw reminded her of the old days, when the Melford family scurried about the place, taking everything in its stride. At one moment, it was almost as though she could see her mother disappearing into the kitchen, and then calling back, 'Supper's on the table! If you don't come soon, don't blame me if it gets cold!' The sights and sounds may not have been there in reality, but they were certainly in Sarah's mind, and she hoped they always would be.

'I'm going to walk round ter the dairy ter see if I can get some milk,' said Freddie. 'The removal blokes are bound ter want a cuppa when they get 'ere.'

'If not,' called Sarah, 'I've got some powdered milk!'

'Right!' Freddie called, as he left. 'I'll be right back!'

Sarah was now alone. She looked around the hall, and even though the place was still bare whilst waiting for the furniture that would make it a home again, she was astonished what had been achieved since Freddie first brought her there on that surprise visit so many months before. Most of all, she was impressed how Freddie's mate, Charlie Stumper, had managed to get enough paint on the black market to brighten the place up, especially as there was such a shortage of all building materials during a time when so many of London's homes and businesses had been damaged or destroyed by bomb blast. Even in the drawing room, all the holes and cracks in the walls and ceilings had been freshly plastered, and the green and gold wallpaper she had chosen weeks before was now giving new life and elegance to the room.

Going up the stairs on her own, however, was turning out to be more of an ordeal than she had imagined. In her mind, she could hear voices calling to her, beckoning, urging her on. But there was nothing threatening in the voices, or menacing; ghosts they may have been, but they were embracing her, and gently reminding her of the past. She could hear her father saying, 'I want you and your mother to start looking around for a lodger,' and Beattie throwing one of her tantrums about her relationship with Edward Lacey: 'It's me 'e wants, yer know – not you. And d'yer know why? Because I give 'im wot you never could, because you're incapable of it!' Sarah tried to dismiss the voices by hurrying up the stairs. But they pursued her right up to the first landing. 'Do you realise I'm a grandmother?' came the slightly deep-throated sound of her mother's voice, floating along the empty first floor. 'It's like having a child all over again – like turning back the clock.'

Her mother and father's room was bathed in the bright glow of summer sunshine pouring through the freshly painted windows. She remembered when she and Beattie were very small, and how on Christmas morning, at crack of dawn, they always invaded the room, and begged their parents to let them open their presents before breakfast. Without being aware of the fact, she had a huge smile on her face. Further along the landing, she went into what had once been her own room, and again, pictures of her early days there came flooding back – favourite dolls, a miniature teddy bear, and books – books everywhere.

The most difficult part of her exploration was yet to come, for as she climbed the stairs to what was once Beattie's room, her mind was crowded with horrifying pictures of Mitford Road on that last evening of Beattie's life. She opened the door of the room, and immediately felt Beattie's presence there. She could almost hear her saying, 'It's good to be back, Sarah – despite everything.' And then she recalled those last few moments she had spent with Beattie in that wretched hospital bed. 'For-give me, Sarah. Forgive me . . .' Those words would haunt Sarah for the rest of her life.

She walked across to the far side of the room, and stooped down, looking to see if there was still something there that she remembered from long ago. To her astonishment, the wainscoting around the bottom of the wall still bore the initial 'B' that Beattie had carved into it with a coin when she was a rebellious adolescent. As Sarah got up again, the voices returned: 'Your sister has already decided on which course she wishes to take . . . take . . . take . . .' This time, her father's voice disturbed her. 'Beattie made a mistake,' said her mother, whose voice intermingled with all the others. 'I failed her . . . failed . . . failed . . . She gave you so much pain . . .'

'For-give me . . .'

Sarah shook the voices from her head, and, arms crossed, strolled to the window and looked out. But for a moment, she could see nothing, for Beattie's voice persisted: 'Ed – my boy – yours now . . . He's – always – been yours . . .'

Sarah closed her eyes. Hearing Beattie's quiet, gentle voice was tearing into her; the pain of losing her was more than she could bear.

'. . . Always . . . been . . . yours . . .' Finally with indescribable sweetness, Beattie's voice whispered, 'Sarah . . . my sister . . . Sarah . . .'

And then there were no more voices, only silence – and peace. At last, Sarah knew that she and her sister would never be parted again.

Even though her eyes were tightly closed, tears were struggling out of them. When she opened them again, she found herself trying to look at something in the front garden down below. With the back of her hand, she wiped away the tears, and focused on the tall, lanky figure who was standing down there, face turned up towards the window.

It was Beattie's boy. And now he was *her* boy, Sarah's boy. It was – Ed.

Nellie's War

For Peter and Josephine, my dear friends.

Dedicated to that great little dancing duo, Les Street and Jose, and all the wonderful troupers of the British Music Hall, who kept a smile on our faces during those dark days of the Second World War.

Chapter 1

Thick black smoke spluttered up from the wreckage of the old Victorian building and was gradually swallowed by the brooding mist of a dark November night. The ferocious glow of endless fires cast sinister dancing shadows across the surface of the huge mound of red bricks and masonry, and the crackling sound of burning timbers competed with the frantic clanging of ambulance and fire-engine bells and the constant overhead roar of enemy planes discharging their deadly cargo of high-explosive bombs. Soon the place would be crawling with people from the emergency services, desperately searching the debris for any survivors. But this 'incident' was just one of many in the surrounding area that night, and it would have to wait its turn for attention.

It was several minutes before the first sign of life appeared – tiny pink fingertips, pushing their way through several layers of cement dust, desperately searching for an escape. Finally, the fingers forged enough passage for a hand. It was a small hand, connected to a thin, white, delicate arm, streaked with bleeding scratches. But it was an obstinate hand, for it suddenly tensed and formed into a clenched fist which pushed and shoved until it had cleared a way for a shoulder, then the other shoulder, and finally the head itself. It was a young head, with a face covered in white dust, and straggly, mousey-coloured hair that was gritty with chips of red brick and broken glass. It was only when the raw fingertips managed to clear the eyes of thick white dust that the outline of a face began to emerge. It was a girl, a teenager of about fifteen or sixteen, whose eyes were brown and oval-shaped, and glistening with the reflection of the fires raging around her.

After a hard struggle, she managed to release herself from the rubble she was pinned beneath. But when she tried to move her right foot, she found it obstinately wedged between a shattered chest of drawers and a pile of bricks. It took supreme effort to free herself completely, and when she finally did, she was engulfed by a burning pain from a long gash in her left leg, from which blood was seeping through the white dust that covered it. Using her elbows for support, she eased herself up, and, once she was confident enough to move, she gradually began to pick her way cautiously across the rubble. But when she tried to stand upright, it was with great difficulty, for not only was her injured leg stiff and painful, but she discovered that she had lost her shoes.

A few minutes later, the whole place was flooded with bright white lights, and Alsatian tracker dogs were sniffing out the rubble for any signs of human life. By the time the emergency services arrived, the teenage survivor was already making her way along a wide main road. She had to tread carefully in order to avoid the broken glass from shattered shop windows all along the street. It wasn't easy, for she was in a daze, not knowing who or where she was, or what had happened to her. All around, people were rushing past, desperate to get to the devastation of the latest bomb blast, unaware of the small teenage girl who had just pulled herself out of the debris. Sirens wailed, ambulance bells clanged, anti-aircraft shells exploded in the dark sky above, and in between all this was the sound of anxious voices calling out the names of friends, relatives or neighbours who might be buried beneath

2

the wreckage. The year was 1940. And this was the ugly face of war.

Several hours later, the teenage girl was still wandering the streets aimlessly. The constant barrage of anti-aircraft guns had gradually come to a halt, and the air was once again relatively silent. But it was still pitch dark, and her flimsy cotton dress was no protection against the biting cold. She couldn't feel the cold, however, perhaps because she was too dazed, or because the pain from the gash in her leg was distracting her from any discomfort. Her mind was unable to take anything in; she had not even noticed that she had found her way into a narrow, unlit back street that had seemingly been untouched by the night's air raid. After a while she found herself at the bottom of a small flight of stone steps. Her ice-cold feet were unable to walk any further, so she started to climb the steps, with difficulty, one at a time. At the top, a large arch-shaped door was partly open. It was quite heavy to move and she had to use all the little strength she had left to squeeze herself inside.

She found herself in a strange, unfamiliar place. It was like a large, narrow hall, with high stone walls and stained-glass windows, and carved stone faces and coloured pictures. At the front of the hall to one side was a tall statue of a woman with what seemed like a scarf over her head. Her eyes looked almost real. Two tall candles burning brightly nearby cast eerie shadows on the high ceiling above. Rows and rows of long wooden benches led into the gloom. This place was unlike anything the girl had ever seen before. Exhausted, she stretched out on one of the benches. It was only a few moments before her eyes closed, and in her sleep she saw so much. Young people of her own age, laughing, chasing each other mischievously in a playground. She could even see herself . . .

* * *

3

Toff had never robbed a church before. The idea had always given him an uncomfortable feeling, especially as he was brought up in the Jewish faith which condemned stealing as a major sin. But he had heard rumours that the doors of St Mary Magdalene's Roman Catholic Church in Bedale Street were never locked, and that there were always a few coins lying in the collection plate just by the main door. So his mind was made up. Funds were getting low. This was no time for a guilty conscience.

'But what 'appens if we get nicked?' asked Nutty who, at fourteen, was the youngest of this gang of vacs, or evacuees, who had returned to live on the streets of London in preference to the safety of country homes belonging to unfriendly strangers. 'The cops'll frow the book at us for doin' over a church.'

'We're not doing over a church,' replied Toff. He was already quite tall for his sixteen years and, unlike the others, spoke with no trace of East End Cockney, which was why they called him Toff. 'In any case, we've never been nicked before, and we're not going to be this time either.'

The others agreed. There were only eight of them in all, and they'd had a busy night doing over people's houses during one of the fiercest air raids of the Blitz so far.

Toff blew out the candle, leaving only the flickering light from the embers of a dying fire. There was nothing left in what was once the back parlour of Dicks' Hardware Shop, for an oil bomb two weeks before had virtually gutted the place, leaving only a charred table, a few chairs, and the remains of a floral patterned sofa. 'Anyway, we don't all have to go to the church,' Toff said, tying a heavy woollen scarf over his head and round his neck. 'Rats and Bonkers, you can come with me. The rest of you can carry on doing Dalston.'

4

Nutty, for one, looked relieved. During air raids, he much preferred doing 'safe' houses, where he was quite sure the occupants were taking cover in an outside shelter.

Rats and Bonkers were uneasy. Since joining the gang, they had become something of a double act. They were both aged fifteen and not only thought alike, they had so many similar features that some people thought they were brothers, which they weren't. They both wore nicked men's overcoats that were far too big for them, but they didn't at all mind how weird they looked; at least the coats kept them warm during their nightly winter forays into other people's homes.

'Is it really worf doin' a church?' asked Bonkers, who was an inch taller than his other half and wore a battered old RAF cap halfway down his forehead. 'I mean, they don't get much in them collection plates.'

'A quid at the most,' added Rats, whose trilby covered his ears.

Toff tensed. 'A quid is a quid!' he snapped. 'We've got hardly nothing left in the kitty, and if we don't do something about it pretty soon, we're going to have to spend every night looking for grub.'

'But what about the Clapton Road vacs?' called Shortso from the doorway; he got his nickname because of his short back-and-sides haircut.

'What about them?' Toff growled without bothering to look at Shortso.

'I hear they work the Bedale Road area,' said Nutty, whose voice was squeaky and several octaves higher than the others'. 'If we muscle in on their territory, there'll be trouble.'

Toff swung round to address all the shadowy faces surrounding him. 'Look, if there's trouble, we'll give as good as we get!' He pushed his way to the door. 'If anyone wants to come with me,' he said as he went, 'they can come. The rest of you can please yourselves.'

For a moment, no one moved. Rats and Bonkers were the first to follow. Although they didn't fancy the idea of a punch-up with the Clapton Road vacs, they knew only too well that without Toff they hadn't a chance in hell of surviving life out on the streets.

From the outside, St Mary Magdalene's Church wasn't a very imposing building. It was built around the turn of the century to establish a Roman Catholic presence in this part of the East End and had had to rely mainly on public contributions to keep it in good repair. The war had already taken its toll on the place; the exterior red bricks and stucco were pitted with holes and abrasions from a bomb blast at a nearby secret ammunitions factory. But St Mary Magdalene's had retained its dignity, and prided itself on never locking its doors; anyone, rich or poor, could take spiritual respite from the nightly air raids.

By the time Toff, Rats, and Bonkers reached the seedy back street, all hell had broken loose again overhead and the sky was vibrating to a barrage of ack-ack fire. The three of them eased their way silently through the half-open church door without touching it.

Toff signalled to his companions not to speak until they had checked the place out, so for a while they stood in silence in the shadows watching the light from the two huge flickering candles cast eerie shadows across the tall stone walls right up to the eaves of the plain arched ceiling.

'The collection plate's over there,' Toff whispered, indicating the font. 'See what you can find. I'll have a quick look to see if there's anything we can flog.'

Rats and Bonkers were both wearing old army boots,

so their efforts to tiptoe quietly to the collection plate were not entirely successful.

Toff used the torch he had taken from someone's bicycle to make his way cautiously down the central aisle. There wasn't too much life left in the battery but there was enough to pick out the seemingly endless rows of stark wooden pews on each side as he went. When he finally reached the two wide steps which led up to the area in front of the altar, he paused for a moment, taking in the strange objects and tall candles that were picked out in the fading beam of his torchlight. He felt strange standing here, almost as though he was smaller in size than he actually was. It was the same feeling that he had had before the war, when he was a small boy standing with his father before the holy tabernacle in the synagogue, with its altar of incense and golden candlestick. As his torchlight picked out the plain, simple cross on the wall behind the altar, he felt uneasy, for if he were to steal from this holy place, it would be like stealing from his father's own place of worship. He quickly moved on until he reached the statue of the Madonna, beneath which were two lit candles and various scraps of paper which he discovered were notes left by worshippers. 'Dear Mother Mary,' read one, 'please protect my family against the bombs.' 'Dear Mother Mary,' read another, 'please end the war.' Toff could read no more. He turned off the torch.

'There's nuffink 'ere!' came a strangulated whisper from behind.

Toff turned, to find Rats making his way up the aisle.

'A tanner and two farvin's,' he complained. 'It weren't worf the effort.'

'Sixpence is better than nothing at all,' Toff replied, holding out one hand. 'It'll buy us a couple of loaves and some milk.'

7

Rats reluctantly dropped the sixpence into the palm of Toff's hand.

'Toff!'

Toff and Rats turned with a start. Bonkers was rushing up the aisle towards them, the steel tips of his boots echoing on the stone floors as he came.

'There's someone 'ere!' he spluttered, his voice only just audible. 'Up the back!'

Toff immediately put a finger to his mouth, warning the other two to keep quiet. Then he slowly moved along one of the pews to the far aisle, keeping in the shadows as much as possible. Rats and Bonkers followed him. When they reached the back of the church, Bonkers pointed silently in the direction from which he had heard the movement. In one swift action, Toff turned on his bicycle torch and shone the beam along the last but one pew from the back. As he did so, there was a groaning sound. Bonkers gasped.

The beam from Toff's torch quickly passed along the pew until it picked out the tattered figure of a young teenage girl, curled up and fast asleep.

'It's a gel!' squealed Rats, suddenly scared by the echo his own voice was making.

Toff edged his way along the pew until his torch beam finally rested on the face of the girl. He was shocked by her appearance, the cuts on her face and arms, and the white dust and small pieces of rubble still embedded in her hair. But the real shock was when his torch beam found the long gash in her leg, which was oozing blood, and her feet which were also cut and bleeding.

'Blimey!' was all Bonkers could say as he and Rats peered at the girl from the pew just in front.

'Is she dead?' asked Rats nervously.

'Take the torch,' instructed Toff, handing the torch to Rats who directed the beam straight at the girl's face.

Toff bent down and gently prodded her shoulder

with his hand. 'Are you all right, miss?' he asked softly. 'Miss?'

There was no response from the girl.

'She *is* dead!' gulped Rats.

Toff tried again. 'Miss?' he called, carefully using one finger to clear away some of the girl's dust-filled hair from her eyes. 'Miss? Are you all r—?'

The girl's eyes suddenly sprang open, and with a startled yell she sat bolt upright.

Rats and Bonkers immediately ducked for cover.

Toff grabbed hold of her shoulders and held on to them. 'It's all right! It's all right. I won't hurt you.'

By now the girl was almost hysterical, and struggling to get up. 'Leave me alone!' she yelled over and over again, her voice echoing up to the high ceiling.

'What's happened to you?' Toff said, trying to restrain her. 'You're bleeding all over.'

'Leave me alone! Leave me alone!'

'You're injured,' yelled Toff as he struggled to hold on to her. 'You're badly injured. You need help!'

Suddenly the girl slumped into his arms.

Rats and Bonkers were horrified. 'Crikey,' gulped Rats. 'She's dead!'

'She's not dead,' snapped Toff. 'Get round here quick. Give me a hand.'

The two boys climbed over the pew and helped Toff lower the girl gently back on to the bench.

'Rats,' Toff said urgently. 'Give me your scarf, and one of your bootlaces. You too, Bonkers.'

'What?' protested Rats.

'What for?' squealed Bonkers indignantly.

'Don't ask questions! Just do it!'

Rats and Bonkers took off their long woollen scarves and reluctantly handed them over to Toff. Then they sat down and began the arduous task of untying a lace from one each of their boots. Toff propped the bicycle torch on the pew in front of the bench where the girl was lying. He took out a handkerchief from his trouser pocket, which he used to wrap round the gash on the girl's injured leg. Then he took off his own cotton scarf and wrapped that round the wound as well.

'What are we doin' all this for?' complained Bonkers miserably as he held out his bootlace. 'She oughta be in an 'ospital or somefin'.'

Toff was now carefully wrapping one of the girl's badly lacerated feet in Rats' scarf. 'She's not going to a hospital. She's coming back with us.'

'What?' gasped Rats. 'Yer can't do that.'

'Why not?'

''Cos she's a gel,' replied Rats as he finished untying his own bootlace. 'We don't 'ave no gels wiv us.'

'Anyway, 'ow we gonna move 'er?' added Bonkers. 'Look at 'er. She's out fer the count.'

'We'll use the pram, the big one,' said Toff, who was now wrapping the girl's other foot in Bonkers' scarf.

'Yer don't mean the one we use fer carryin' the goods around?' asked Rats indignantly. 'We'll never get her in there!'

'Stop griping, Rats!' snapped Toff. He used the two boys' bootlaces to tie the scarves round the girl's bloody feet. 'Both of you get back to the shop and bring that pram here as fast as you can. It'll be daylight in another couple of hours. We've got to get her back before the All Clear.'

Rats and Bonkers knew better than to try to argue with Toff. Although he hadn't been brought up on the streets like they had, he was still the boss of the outfit, and it was his brains that were keeping them and all the others from starving. So they did as they were told and hurried out of the church.

After they had gone, Toff took off his duffel coat and covered the girl with it. He picked up his torch

10

and directed the beam straight on to her face. He was intrigued to know who this mysterious creature was, and how she had received her terrible injuries. As he bent down to take a closer look at her soft but badly drawn and scratched face, he told himself he ought to do what Bonkers had suggested, and just take her to the nearest hospital to be looked after by those who knew how. But no. There was something about that face, the expression, the high cheek bones, and the almost white complexion and full lips, something quite sensual and hypnotic.

He couldn't let her go. Not now.

It was a dazzling white light. Her eyes couldn't really cope with it, not for a few moments anyway. But gradually she felt adventurous enough to open them again, and when she did, it wasn't too difficult to see the paraffin lamp suspended from a piece of wire dangling from the ceiling just above her. When she tried to sit up, a sharp pain shot across her neck and down her spine. She felt as though she had been dragged through a hedge backwards; her entire body seemed to be a mass of bruises. And when she put her fingers up to her face, the cuts and scratches there seemed to be wide open. Her injured leg and both her feet were burning hot, as though she was lying on a bed of hot ashes. Only then did she realise that she was in fact lying on something quite different – a rather smelly mattress laid out on the stone floor of a totally bare room. For a moment, she panicked. She had no idea what had happened to her, where she was, or where she came from.

'How are you feeling?'

The male voice came from the other side of the room, but when she turned to look, all she could see was a shadowy figure in the corner.

'Who are yer?' she asked tentatively, her throat

parched from the amount of dust she had swallowed beneath the debris of the bomb blast. 'W-where am I?'

The figure slowly came across to her. 'My name's Martin. But nobody calls me that round here.' As he leaned down towards her, the bright paraffin light picked out the strong features of a good-looking teenage boy. 'They call me Toff,' he said with a wry smile. 'Apparently I talk posh.' He drew a little closer, so that his face seemed almost larger than life. 'How about you?' he asked. 'What's your name?'

The girl didn't reply. Her mind was confused, and all she could do was look at him.

'What's your name?' Toff asked again. 'Aren't you going to tell me?'

'Dunno.'

'Don't know your own name?'

She shook her head.

'Where d'you come from?'

Again, she shook her head.

'Don't you know what happened to you?'

The girl was becoming irritated. 'Why all the questions?' she snapped.

Toff wasn't offended. He was only too aware that she was still suffering from shock. 'You've had a bad time,' he said. 'When we found you, we thought you were going to die. Anyway, you're going to be all right. I managed to patch up your leg and feet.'

The girl immediately threw back the eiderdown and duffel coat that covered her. Her right leg and both feet were swathed in bandages. The smell of disinfectant was overpowering. 'What have you done to me?' she wailed. 'I can't move my legs!'

Toff tried to calm her. 'There's nothing to worry about,' he said reassuringly. 'I cleaned up the gash on your leg with some disinfectant. Your feet too. They were in a terrible state. I remember how my father used to clean up wounds. He's a doctor in casualty at the Royal Northern.'

The girl looked devastated. 'What happened to me?'

Toff knelt beside her. 'That's what we'd all like to know. Don't you remember anything? Anything at all?'

She shook her head slowly. 'I don't remember nuffin'.'

'Not even your name?'

Again, the girl shook her head.

Toff gave her a huge, comforting smile. 'Then we'll have to give you one, won't we? Until you get your memory back, that is.' He bent his head down lower to try to get her to look at him. 'OK?'

She looked up, and found herself staring straight into Toff's eyes. They were dark eyes, almost as dark as his jet-black hair. And, if he hadn't spoken in such a posh voice, she would have been convinced that he was a foreigner.

'Where did you find me?' she asked.

'In Saint Mary Magdalene's,' Toff replied, getting to his feet.

The girl looked puzzled.

'The Catholic church in Bedale Street,' explained Toff. 'You must have gone in there to shelter from the air raid.' He looked at her. 'Unless you went there to pray.'

'Is that why *you* were there? To pray?'

Toff went to the paraffin lamp, raised the glass, turned down the wick, and blew out the flame. 'I don't pray any more. I used to, when my father took me to the synagogue. But not any more.'

Daylight was filtering through an old blanket hanging across what was once the back door. Toff went across and drew it to one side. Dull morning light indicated the start of a new day. For a moment, Toff just stood there, looking out solemnly at the grey November mist and the ruins of what had once been a row of shops. Then he reached under his pullover and retrieved a half-smoked cigarette from the top pocket of his shirt.

'Are you old enough to smoke?' he asked.

The girl thought about this for a moment, then answered, 'I dunno.'

In the dim light, Toff turned to smile at her. 'You really have got a lot of catching up to do, haven't you?' He found a match in his trouser pocket, struck it against the cement pointing between the bricks on the wall, and lit his cigarette.

The smell of cigarette smoke drifted towards her. 'How did you get me here?' she asked.

Toff leaned his head against the wall and inhaled deeply. 'We had our own transport,' he said loftily.

The large baby's pram, covered with a pink eiderdown and pushed by three teenage boys through the streets of Dalston only a couple of hours ago, would have raised more than a few eyebrows if anybody had been about to see them. As it was, most people were taking cover from an air raid.

'You'll find out a lot about us, when you get to know us,' Toff said, taking one last puff of his cigarette before throwing it on to the stone floor and grinding his heel on it. Then he turned and made his way back to the girl, exhaling a spiral of smoke as he came. 'It's beginning to get light. I'd get some sleep if I were you. When you wake up, we'll see if we can get you some breakfast.'

The girl did in fact feel drowsy enough to lay her head back on the embroidered cushion.

Toff stood over her. 'You've got nothing to worry about now. I don't care what the others say. We're going to take care of you even if you are a girl.'

When she closed her eyes, Toff turned away. From the open doorway he said, 'How about Nellie? That

14

was my gran's name. Nellie Esther Rabinovitz. Yes. Sounds good. Anyway, if it was good enough for my gran, it should be good enough for you. What d'you think?'

She didn't hear him. Nellie was already fast asleep.

Chapter 2

It was one of those mornings when the sun was absolutely determined to poke through the clouds. As it was November, it was quite a struggle, for the clouds were in reality dirty grey banks of fog, caused mainly by the endless coal fires belching up thick black smoke from chimneys all over North London. Fires caused by the previous night's air raid, one of the worst of the war so far, added to the smoke; a trail of havoc and destruction stretched from one side of the capital to the other.

Of all the worst hit targets of the night, none distressed the local community more than the bombing of Barratts' Orphanage in the Islington part of New North Road. Founded in 1902 by the late Louisa Barratt and her husband, Clarence, the Victorian building had originally been the site of the Islington Workhouse, a hellhole of a place that had been closed down at the turn of the century because it was infested with rats and cockroaches. When Louisa and Clarence took over, they cleaned up the place with their own hands, converted the old building into living quarters for children, and opened their doors to any abandoned child or homeless waif the authorities decided to send to them. When the place was full, more than forty children of varying ages were given food, board, and loving care and attention there. When Louisa died in 1936, her husband decided he could no longer cope with the stress and strain of running the orphanage on his own, so he handed it over to a much younger woman there, Ethel Ackroyd, from Yorkshire, who immediately embraced the young boarders in her charge as her own family. Both staff and orphans adored her, for she treated everyone the same, with absolutely no favourites – with one possible exception.

The destruction of Barratts' Orphanage by a high-explosive bomb was a tragedy. By the grace of God no one was killed; at the time of the explosion, all the staff and boarders were sheltering in the vaults beneath the old workhouse building – all, that is, except one.

'If she's under that rubble,' warned Fire Brigade Officer Mick Jenkins, 'she wouldn't have stood a chance.' He and his men had been working all night searching for even the faintest sign of life beneath the debris, but now grim reality had to be faced. 'She's gone, I'm afraid.'

Ethel Ackroyd looked as though all the blood had drained from her body. 'Don't give up. Please don't give up,' she said, her tired pale blue eyes pleading. 'We can't just abandon Vicky. She's got so much to live for.'

The group of orphanage staff with Ethel lowered their heads sadly. They knew how guilty she was feeling, but it was unjustified guilt. Vicky Hobson was a rebel. If she had got herself killed, then it was her own fault.

Ethel pulled up the collar of her camelhair overcoat and tried to wrap it closer round her neck. Although she appeared tough, it was well known that she was very emotional, and when anything happened to one of her flock, she felt as though her insides had been torn apart. 'I should never have gone down that shelter knowing she wasn't there,' she said, her Yorkshire accent now only very slight after years of living and working in London. 'Oh, why wouldn't she ever do what she was told? Where was she when the air raid started? She must have heard the siren.'

Before her were the ruins of the old Barratts' building,

the timber beams still smouldering from the fire that had raged through it. It was a truly tragic sight, with the remains of toys and teddy bears and articles of children's clothing scattered everywhere. The scene was now calmer than the previous night but there was an air of deep despondency among the rescue workers, a mixture of frustration and anger that an orphanage could be the victim of such wanton, mindless destruction. It was a miracle that there was apparently only one fatality. If the staff had not herded the youngsters into the shelter as quickly as they had, it would have been a very different story.

'It's no use hanging around here now, dearie,' said grim-faced Mrs Hare, the orphanage cook. She put her arm round Ethel's waist as they watched the weary rescue workers clambering over what was left of the old building. 'It's all over now. We can't bring back what's gone for ever.'

Well-intentioned though it was meant, Mrs Hare's remark irritated Ethel. 'You're wrong, Mrs Hare,' she replied firmly, climbing up on to a lump of masonry. 'This is not the end of Barratts'. It'll take more than Hitler to destroy a lifetime's work.'

Mrs Hare brushed away a tear. The kindly, plump old woman had always been a mother figure to the children, and she found it hard to come to terms with the fact that 'the family' had been broken up in such a way. 'I can't bear the thought that we'll never see young Vicky again,' she sniffed, dabbing her eyes with her tear-drenched ball of handkerchief. 'She was a handful all right, even though she was only an 'alf-pint. But I'll miss 'er. Oh yes. I'll miss that real stubborn streak, that's fer sure.'

Ethel refused to give in to her own feelings of total emptiness. Despite being the rebel of the orphanage, Vicky Hobson, or 'Half-Pint' as she was known because of her below-average height for her sixteen years, was

Ethel's favourite. The girl had character, guts and determination, which had helped her to survive her life as an orphan. As she stood there, Ethel could see the girl in front of her, with her mousey-brown hair, oval-shaped eyes, and sallow complexion. But behind that frail look was a steel-like obstinacy that reminded Ethel of what she used to be like when she was that age back home in rural Yorkshire. 'We don't give up till we know, Mrs Hare,' she said, her face grim and determined as her eyes scanned the remains of the orphanage. 'As far as I'm concerned, Vicky's still alive until they find – until they find her.'

A few minutes later, a large crane appeared on the back of a lorry to start the arduous task of removing pile after pile of bricks and rubble. If Half-Pint was buried beneath the remains of the orphanage, the determined emergency workers would find her. So it was a depressing moment when, several hours later, they unearthed something of significance from beneath the rubble of what had once been the girls' dormitory.

It was one of Half-Pint's shoes.

Nellie had no intention of lying flat on her back on a smelly, flea-infested mattress all day, shut up in the grubby, bombed-out remains of Dicks' Hardware Shop. She wasn't dying, she kept saying to herself, she wasn't ill, so why should she take orders from this toffee-nosed knuckle-head with the plum in his mouth? But when she threw back the pink eiderdown and tried to stand up, it was a different story. Despite the fact that her feet were swathed in bandages and smelt like a hospital, they hurt like mad. And the gash on her leg was throbbing, and the scratches on her face were smarting. If only she could remember what had happened last night. How had she reached that church? She must have got caught in an air raid, but where? And who

20

was she? What was her real name, and where did she come from?

Daylight was now streaming into the dark room through the partially covered doorway. The fire in the grate had been allowed to go out and the room was freezing. Nellie picked up the eiderdown and wrapped it round her shoulders. The rough floor hurt her feet and she found it difficult to walk. Then she noticed that a large pair of women's warm indoor slippers had been left beside her mattress, so she carefully put them on. They fitted comfortably over her bandaged feet and she managed to shuffle towards the doorway.

Outside, Nellie found a scene of devastation. She had been brought to a bomb site. Four or five shops had been reduced to rubble, and the surrounding area of old terraced houses and a pub was pitted with blast damage, the windows boarded up with crude pieces of wood. She stared in horror at it all, shivering with cold.

'Feeling better?'

Nellie turned with a start to find Toff and a sea of cold red faces staring at her. 'What you lot gawpin' at?' she squawked, quick as a flash.

Toff grinned. 'Yes,' he said, 'you *are* better. We were very concerned about you.' He made a few steps towards her.

'Don't you come near me!' snapped Nellie, nearly tripping over her eiderdown as she backed away. 'Who are you lot?' She eyed them all up suspiciously. 'Why ain't you all in yer own 'omes?'

There was complete silence from the group. As well as Toff, Nutty, Shortso, Rats and Bonkers, there were several other teenage boys, all wearing a weird assortment of winter clothes that were either too big or too small for them.

'We don't have homes, Nell,' said Toff, who looked positively normal compared to his companions.

21

'Not since we got kicked out,' squealed Nutty, who was barely visible behind some of the taller boys.

Nellie was curious. 'What d'yer mean, kicked out?'

Toff looked around his pals then back to Nellie again. 'We're all evacuees, Nell,' he explained. 'Most of us were sent away from our homes as soon as war broke out. It was supposed to be for our own protection, because of the Blitz.'

'Ter get rid of us, more like!' yelled Shortso, digging his hands angrily into the pockets of his raincoat.

'The fact is,' continued Toff, 'none of us wanted to go. Well, not us lot anyway. They bunged us into all sorts of places out in the country, places like Hertfordshire, Surrey, Wales, Somerset – everywhere.'

'Yeah!' piped Nutty. 'And wiv people we'd never met in our lives.'

'People who'd clack yer 'round the ear'ole if yer even opened yer mouf!' This from one of the boys at the back.

The others responded with a disapproving chorus of, 'Yeah!'

'Mind you,' said Toff, 'some were lucky. They found themselves a real cushy number, in far better homes than they'd come from. But not us,' he said.

Nellie looked at the faces in front of her, all of them young but disillusioned with life as they had lived it so far. 'So why don't yer just go back 'ome to yer mums and dads an' 'ave it out wiv 'em?' she asked.

'Because they wouldn't listen to us!' came the reply from a tall, thin boy of about fourteen, who looked as if he was in need of a decent meal.

'Once parents have made up their minds that what they're doing is good for their kids,' said Toff, in sadness rather than in anger, 'nothing will change them. That's how it was with my mother and father. They know best, and nothing in the whole wide world will ever change them.'

'S'pose they *are* right?' Nellie was now so cold she pulled the eiderdown right up over her head. 'S'pose they *did* send yer away fer yer own good?'

'It isn't true, Nell,' replied Toff, who had crossed his arms and put his hands under them to keep warm. 'Sending us off to live with other people was just an excuse to get us out of the way. Not for everyone, mind. But it was with us.' He twisted his head to look at his companions. 'That's how we came to meet up. That's why we decided to stick together.' He turned back to Nellie. 'That's the reason we live the way we do. We can't go home because they'd send us right back to where we came from.'

One or two of the boys decided they'd hung around long enough and wandered off. Nellie watched them go in bewilderment.

'Yer mean you're livin' out rough like this, in the streets?' she asked.

Toff smiled. 'It's not so bad, once you get used to it.'

'In this sorta wevver? 'Ow d'yer keep warm? 'Ow d'yer get grub?'

'We nick it,' said Rats. 'Durin' the air raids.'

'When they've all gone down the shelter,' added Bonkers.

Nellie was horrified and took a step back. 'You *nick* from people's 'ouses?'

'Only food and clothes,' said Toff quickly, trying to sound reassuring. 'We only take money as a last resort.'

'But that's breakin' the law!' Nellie's eyes were bulging with disapproval. 'Wot 'appens if the rozzers catch up wiv yer?'

The boys laughed. 'Rozzers can't catch us!' yelled

Shortso who was perched on top of a pile of bricks. 'We're too clever by 'alf!'

Nellie's eyes scanned the bleak scene around her. Pile upon pile of rubble everywhere. Across the road, two drunken men came out of the pub; clearly its boarded-up windows were no hindrance to trade. As the door opened briefly, the sound of someone tinkling on a tinny piano inside was audible. The pianist had no ear for music, for it was a tuneless sound, but at least it lifted the gloomy atmosphere; it was like an act of defiance in the unrelenting grind of war.

'So does this mean yer'll never go 'ome?' Nellie asked, her nose now red and numb with cold.

'We'll go 'ome when the war's over,' said Shortso. 'When they can't send us away no more.'

'Livin' in the country ain't like livin' round 'ere,' squeaked Nutty forlornly. 'It's too quiet.'

The others agreed.

Nellie was beginning to feel the strain of the extraordinary situation she found herself in. What was she doing with this wild bunch who were willing to forsake the comfort of their own homes to live rough in the streets of North London? Her head was thumping with pain and confusion. She wished she could remember who she was and where she came from.

'If you want, you can join us,' Toff said suddenly.

There was a gasp from some of the boys behind him.

'No!' protested Rats.

'She's a gel!' complained Bonkers.

'Yer remember wot we said, Toff,' grumbled Shortso. 'No gels!'

Toff paused briefly before turning to face the group. 'Listen, you lot,' he said calmly. 'Nell went through a hell of a time last night. Just look at her. She might have died if we hadn't got to her when we did.'

'No gels, Toff!' yelled one of the boys. 'Yer promised!'

Toff refused to be intimidated. 'It doesn't matter whether she's a girl or a bloke. What sort of people d'you think we are if we let her go off and live out rough on the streets? If Nell needs our help, we're going to give it. It's our duty to look after her.'

This angered Nellie. ''Ang on a mo!' she said. 'Who said anyfin' about me needin' anyone ter look after me?' In her anger, she threw the eiderdown from her shoulders to the ground. She was dressed in nothing more than the thin, tattered cotton frock she had been wearing when she clambered out of the ruins of the orphanage. 'I know 'ow ter take of meself, see! I got me own family ter go to, me own mum an' dad ter look after me. If you fink I'm goin' ter knock around the streets wiv the likes of you lot, yer've got anuvver fink comin'! Oh no. Me? I'm goin' straight back ter me own 'ome!'

She turned and started to climb over the rubble towards the street.

Toff watched her for a moment, then called, 'What home is that, Nell?'

Nellie came to an abrupt halt. She turned slowly and gazed helplessly at the young faces staring at her.

Ethel Ackroyd spent the day with her staff, caring for the youngsters in her charge, trying to help them come to terms with the traumatic events of the night before. Thanks to the intervention of Islington Borough Council, Barratts' Orphanage had been given temporary accommodation in a local school which had been closed since the start of the Blitz. But there was no heating in the old building, and it was left to the voluntary services to provide food, clothes, and beds for the indefinite stay. The children were still in a state of shock after being

25

rescued from their underground shelter, but most of them adapted pretty well to their new surroundings. At least they were all alive – except one.

'The last time I checked the top-floor dormitory,' said Martha Driscoll, who taught sewing and dress making to some of the older girls in the orphanage, 'Vicky was listening to *Variety Bandbox* on the wireless. She was the only one there. The others were downstairs playing table tennis.'

'What time was that?' asked Ethel, who hadn't touched the piping hot tomato soup that she and the rest of the staff were eating at a makeshift dinner table.

'Must have been soon after eight,' replied Martha. Her eyes were red and sore from crying. 'I blame myself,' she said, after trying unsuccessfully to swallow a mouthful of soup. 'If only I'd gone up to the dormitory as soon as I heard that siren, Vicky would still be alive.'

'Don't talk like that, please, Martha,' said Ethel firmly. 'Vicky's not dead until we know – officially.'

'I think the chances are not good, Miss Ackroyd,' said Arthur Driscoll, Martha's husband, who helped out with sports and handicraft activities for the boys at Barratts'. 'I mean, let's face it, we've spent most of the day out there on the site but they still haven't found her.'

'They found her shoe,' replied Ethel, whose eyes were firmly fixed on the youngsters eating at tables around the bare old school hall.

Arthur exchanged a grim look with his wife. Only a few hours before, the chief fire officer at the scene had told him that there was not a chance in hell of finding Vicky alive. And even if they did, there would be very little left of her, for the dormitory on the top floor of the building would have taken the full brunt of the explosion. Arthur twisted the end of his thick moustache, trying to fight his own feelings of guilt about

26

Vicky Hobson, for in his heart of hearts he knew that he had never liked her. Many a time he had heard the girl giving lip to his wife, and he had often wanted to give her a piece of his mind. Vicky was a real firecracker with a mind of her own. If anyone was going to get into trouble, it was inevitable that it should be her. And at a time like this – especially at a time like this – he felt nothing but a deep sense of guilt for even thinking of such things.

'It's so unfair,' said Martha, trying to keep her voice low in the sombre, unnatural atmosphere of children eating in virtual silence. 'Vicky wasn't a beautiful child, but she had such character. It's amazing when you think that she was barely five feet tall.' Once again she dabbed her eyes with her handkerchief. 'I remember once, when she was in knitting class, she asked me what it was like being married. I thought it was such an odd question from a girl who was no more than fifteen at the time. But she wanted to know. She really wanted to know. I don't think Vicky was ever a child. She was always a woman.'

The conversation was too maudlin for Ethel. 'If you'll excuse me,' she said, rising from the table, 'I must get some fresh air.'

By the time Ethel reached the bombed orphanage, the watery sun had already set, and the nightly November mist was undulating eerily around the narrow North London back streets. A small group of local manual workers had taken over from the emergency services at the bomb site. Ethel stared at the pitiful heap of personal belongings and children's toys that had been retrieved from the rubble. She had come here still clinging to a vestige of hope that the one missing youngster in her charge had been found alive, but the look on everyone's faces soon told her otherwise. Despite an all-day search, no trace had been found of Vicky Hobson. As mist and darkness descended on the sombre pile of bricks and stones, the search was abandoned until the next morning.

After the last workers had gone, Ethel climbed up a flight of stone steps which had miraculously survived intact. They had led from the courtyard at the back of the orphanage up to one of the first-floor classrooms. As she stood on the top step, she sought solace in memories of the much-loved institution which only a few hours before had been her domain, her world, her kingdom. She could hear the sound of her children's voices, lining up for morning roll call or hurrying into the dining room for their midday meal. She could hear the little ones reciting the alphabet and multiplication tables, laughing, singing, and playing in the back courtyard. She could hear the babies crying in the nursery, those poor little unwanted creatures left abandoned on the orphanage doorstep by wayward mothers and uncaring fathers. Her mind was echoing to the sounds from her past. But no sound registered more than that of Vicky Hobson.

Standing alone on those steps in the dark, a tall but slight figure silhouetted against the final light of day, Ethel recalled the time when Vicky was first brought to Barratts'. It was sixteen or so years ago, soon after her father had been killed accidentally in a fall from scaffolding on a building site, and her mother, bereft and unable to cope, had thrown herself into the path of a train at Stepney Green Underground Station. Even then, Vicky had shown a determined, free-willed spirit. Like so many of the other young orphans at Barratts', she had grown up never knowing the love of real parents and, despite the efforts of so many, she had always been determined to live life her own way.

'*When I leave this place, I ain't never goin' ter come back.*' Ethel could hear Vicky's voice ringing in her mind as clearly as though she was standing in front of her right now. And she could see her face, pallid

28

but defiant, lips curled and stiff, eyes staring straight through her – those wonderful brown, perfectly shaped eyes. *'I'm sick of bein' shut up in a prison. I'm sick of people lookin' down at me.'*

Ethel turned the words over and over in her mind. Why was the child so concerned about how small she was? Why did she think that such things were important? What Vicky lacked in height she made up for in personality. She was the most vivacious child Ethel had ever known, and when she wanted to, Vicky had the ability to make so many people laugh. Oh, how she yearned to see that face and to hear that defiant voice again. She refused to believe that the child had just vanished into thin air. She refused to believe that somewhere beneath those ruins Vicky Hobson wasn't mischievously hiding, just waiting to be found, waiting to get on with her life and make something of herself. And if she wasn't beneath the ruins, where was she?

Ethel pulled up the collar of her coat, adjusted her headscarf, and dug her hands deep into her pockets. And as she stood there, she vowed that, whatever happened, she would never allow Vicky to leave her. If that extraordinary girl was still alive, then Ethel Ackroyd would make it her mission in life to find her.

Suddenly the air was pierced by the wailing sound of the air-raid warning siren. Another night of horror was about to begin.

Chapter 3

It took Nellie several weeks before she plucked up enough courage to do her first 'job'. By then the swelling in her lacerated feet had subsided and, thanks to Toff's expert medical attention, learnt from his father, the gash in her leg had healed. In fact, Nellie had a lot to be grateful for. Toff had been wonderful to her, dressing her wounds, getting her warm clothes to wear and hot food to eat. Most admirable of all was the way he protected her from the boys in the gang. Since Nellie still had no idea who she was or where she came from, she had decided to take the plunge and join them. But being part of a street gang was one thing, breaking into someone's house in the middle of an air raid was something quite different.

'You don't have to do it if you don't want to,' said Toff reassuringly. 'This is really a boy's job. I know that.'

Nellie took umbrage at this. She was already dressed for the night's work, tucked up in a warm, newly stolen coat, with woollen gloves and a knitted hat. 'What d'yer mean, a boy's job?' she scowled indignantly. 'Yer fink I'm made of jelly or somefin'?'

'That's not what I'm saying, Nell.' Toff offered her a cup of tea that he had just stewed up in an old aluminium kettle over a makeshift fire indoors. 'I just don't want you to think we're forcing you to do something.'

Nellie grabbed the chipped cup. 'Let me be the judge of that, mate!'

Toff shrugged his shoulders and smiled.

When she saw his smile, Nellie suddenly felt guilty. The fact was that although she was getting a bit fed up with this boy looking after her like an old nanny, every time he looked at her, she was beginning to feel a bit funny inside. So she did her best to make sure that whenever he did smile at her, she averted her gaze.

Nellie warmed her hands round the cup and blew on the hot tea. 'Just tell me wot I'm s'posed ter do.'

Toff finished pouring a cup of tea for himself, then put a teaspoonful of dried milk into it. 'You don't have to do anything until we hear the siren,' he said. 'Then we'll take you down to this place near Highbury.'

Nellie was beginning to get nervous. ''Ighbury? Where's that?'

Toff looked at her. 'Don't you remember anything about anywhere?' he asked.

Nellie thought hard for a moment, then slowly shook her head.

Toff took his cup and crouched down on Nellie's mattress which had been laid on the floor just in front of the fire. For a moment he said nothing and just sipped his tea, staring into the flames of burning timber taken from the bombed buildings outside. The room was cosier since Nellie had first arrived; it was full of loot and supplies of food taken from people's houses during the nightly air raids. In one corner, tins of Spam, dried eggs, packets of tea, and bottles of Camp coffee were stuffed untidily into wooden fruit boxes; warm coats, hats, and several pairs of shoes were stacked in a neat pile along one wall, together with several blankets and pillows. There was also a prize possession: a paraffin stove. Unfortunately it contained no paraffin.

'One of the boys has been watching this house we found,' Toff said. 'Two old women live there. I think they must be sisters or something. Anyway, they go down Highbury Tube every night at five on the dot. People shelter down there during the air raid. They never come back till the morning, till the All Clear.'

Nellie now felt easy enough in Toff's company to join him in front of the fire.

'It's a nice house,' Toff continued. 'Three or four storeys high. In a terrace.' He turned to look at Nellie. 'They must be well-stacked.'

Nellie became aware that her heart was beating faster than normal. 'What do I 'ave ter do?' she said, the flickering flames of the fire reflected in her eyes.

Toff smiled. 'Nothing to it, really,' he said reassuringly. 'We'll get you in there. Just make your way to the kitchen, grab some food – fresh stuff if you can – then get the hell out of the place.' As they knelt there, Toff could almost hear Nellie's heart thumping. 'You really don't have to do it, Nell,' he said softly, sympathetically. 'It's not expected.'

Nellie looked up at him, but when her eyes met his, she quickly averted her gaze. 'I'm not scared or nuffin',' she said. 'It's just that I don't like the idea of takin' fings that don't belong ter me.'

Toff smiled again, then raised her chin so that she had to look at him. 'Sounds like you've been brought up the right way,' he said.

Nellie did a puzzled double take, and suddenly felt a cold chill down her spine.

And then came the wail of the air-raid siren.

Dolly and Mabel Gresham were late for the shelter that night. This was unlike them, for every day, immediately after they had had their afternoon nap and tea, they always made early preparations for their nightly trip to the shelter. It took them about twenty minutes to walk from their house in Highbury New Park to the Tube station, for Mabel suffered from bad rheumatism in one of her thighs and their progress was slow, especially as they carried a deck chair each, together with a blanket and a flask of hot cocoa.

The tall, elegant, Edwardian house had been in the Gresham family for many years, and after their parents died, Dolly and Mabel, who had never married, lived there alone together. People in the neighbourhood knew very little about them for they kept themselves to themselves and never asked for help, even when some of their windows were blown in by a bomb which landed in a road close by. The house was a gem, with large rooms and a spacious kitchen and hall, and a long back garden where the sisters spent much of their time pruning and weeding during the summer months.

When the sisters came out through the front door and locked up, the air-raid siren had already sounded but enemy planes had not yet begun buzzing overhead. The sun had set and blackout curtains were firmly drawn. The wide tree-lined street was very dark, concealing Nellie, Toff, Shortso, and Nuts while they waited in silence until the two elderly sisters were well on their way to the Tube station.

'Go after them, Shortso,' whispered Toff, emerging from behind a tall elm tree. 'Whatever you do, don't let them out of your sight. If they change their mind and come back, get back here soon as you can.'

Shortso didn't have to be told twice. He hurried off into the darkness after the sisters.

'Wait out here, Nuts,' Toff instructed. 'We're going round the back. If there's any sign of anyone at all, you know what to do.'

Nuts didn't answer. He was well used to the routine.

'This way, Nell,' said Toff, gently pinching Nellie's arm and leading her off.

Nellie felt quite sick as she followed him across the street. It was pitch dark, and all she could see was

34

a dim outline of the terrace. She could hear distant voices singing Christmas carols, and it made her realise just how close Christmas was. How she wished she was sitting in some nice warm room sharing it with just about anybody other than this wild bunch of vacs.

Toff avoided the front door and led Nellie to an iron gate which gave access to the back garden. Once they had got that far, Toff decided it was safe enough to use his torch. But he played safe and kept the bright beam partially covered with one hand. 'There,' he whispered, directing the beam on to the upper part of a back window. 'The old girls always leave that window open. There's not much room to get in, but if you can get your head and shoulders through, I reckon you can make it. Now you know why we wanted you for this job.'

Nellie looked up at the small space she was expected to crawl through. 'I'll never get through that,' she protested, forgetting to whisper. Toff clamped his hand over her mouth to keep her quiet.

'There's nothing of you, Nell,' he whispered. 'You'll get through easy. I wish I was your size,' he added to spare her feelings.

Nellie didn't notice. She was feeling far too queasy about the whole thing.

'Here, take the torch,' Toff continued, giving it to her. 'I'll give you a bunk up. When you get inside, make your way down to the street door and let me in. OK?'

'I'll try,' was all Nellie could reply. Although her heart was racing, a sense of excitement was building in her. She watched Toff quietly roll an old water tub under the open window and carefully tip out the rainwater it contained. He turned it upside down and helped Nellie climb on to it. 'Wot 'appens if someone comes while I'm in there?' she asked anxiously.

'You'll have plenty of time,' whispered Toff. 'Nuts is on lookout. He'll give us a signal.'

Not at all reassured, Nellie turned off the torch, put it into her topcoat pocket, and with surprisingly little effort climbed up to the small open window. But even with her height and build, it was a struggle to squeeze through.

She dropped quietly on to the floor inside and froze, too nervous to turn on the torch. She could make nothing out in the darkness and had no idea what part of the house she was in. When she did finally turn on the torch, the beam picked out a single bed, a chair, and a washbasin on a pedestal table. The bedroom was small and cramped but to Nellie it seemed the height of luxury, and for a few seconds she looked all around her, and even tried lying down briefly on the bed to feel how comfortable it was. Then she made her way to the door.

It opened on to what was obviously the main hall. A number of doors led off it, but she had no way of telling which one would take her to the kitchen. She began to shake all over as realisation hit her that she was actually standing in the middle of somebody else's house without their knowledge or permission. And what a house it was, so unlike anything she had experienced before, or if she had, she just couldn't remember it. It was all so different from the life she was living now, a cast-off in the streets in the company of a wild bunch of mixed-up teenage boys. She spent so long shining her torch around the elegant hallway, with its Victorian coat rack and tall flight of narrow carpeted stairs, that she forgot all about Toff who was on the front doorstep outside waiting for her to open the door.

She took a deep breath to calm her nerves and moved on. She peered into one ground-floor room and then another, only briefly stopping to admire the old period furniture, delicate lace curtains, and fine colourful rugs. As she went she picked up small knick-knacks that took her fancy, old snuffboxes and china ornaments, and quickly stuffed them into her coat pockets. To live in such a beautiful place with so many fine and wonderful things would be like a dream come true. And it was all so cosy and warm, with the dying embers of a fire still glowing in the grate. Who were these lucky old ladies who lived here? she wondered. What had they ever done to deserve such luck?

Out in the hallway again, Nellie suddenly heard Toff rattling the front door letterbox. 'Nell!' he called in as loud a whisper as he dared. 'Nell, are you in there? Open up!'

Nellie made for the door. Then she changed her mind and stopped. She knew it was irrational but quite suddenly she wanted to do something on her own, and for herself. Impetuously she turned and went off to look for the kitchen.

She eventually found it at the end of a small passage, at the back of the house. Even before she reached the door, she knew it had to be the kitchen, for the smell of cooking earlier in the day still drifted out into the passage, making her stomach yearn for whatever it was. As she reached for the doorknob, she desperately hoped that she was about to find some succulent leftovers of fried sausages or Spam fritters or perhaps even a meat stew. Slowly, she turned the doorknob and went in. What greeted her was a shock that turned her blood to ice.

Glaring at her in the beam of her torchlight was the huge face of a large, savage-looking dog, eyes red, teeth bared, growling menacingly. Nellie's first instinct was to turn and run. But she knew that if she made even the slightest move, the beast would leap straight at her. So she remained as still as her paralysed body would allow, her back pinned against the open door. For a moment, she and the dog were quite motionless, just poised there sizing each other up. Desperately, Nellie tried to think of a way of getting out into the hall to call to Toff. But then a change seemed to come over her. She had already taken her decision and settled for doing this job without Toff's help. Fear was gradually replaced by a need for power, and without moving a muscle, she found herself talking to the dog.

'Sit!' she said, quite calmly.

The dog refused her order. His lips continued to quiver angrily.

Nellie took a deep breath. 'Sit!' This time her voice was stronger, more decisive.

Again, the dog refused her order.

Regardless of the risk, Nellie shouted at him. 'I said *sit*, you ugly great monster! *Sit*, or I'll knock yer bleedin' 'ead orf!'

To her utter amazement, the dog stopped growling, and after a moment of indecision he sat down with a thud.

Nellie summoned up enough courage to draw closer to him. Without faltering, she put out her hand and stroked his head. 'That's better, mate,' she said, somewhat breathlessly. 'Now s'pose yer tell me where I can find the grub.'

Toff was still outside on the front doorstep anxiously rattling the letterbox. His concern increased when he heard the drone of approaching aircraft, quickly followed by the first ack-ack fire of the night. 'Nell!' he yelled through the letterbox. 'What the hell are you up to?'

The street door promptly opened and Nellie appeared. 'Two pork trotters, two sausage rolls, some cheese, and a bottle of pickled onions,' she said triumphantly, holding up a bulging paper bag. ''Ow's that for a beginner?'

As the first wave of enemy aircraft thundered across the sky above and bombs whistled down in the distance, Nellie and Toff ran down the front steps of the house and were immediately joined by Nuts. All three made a wild dash for the main road in Highbury Grove, which was lit up by searchlights criss-crossing the sky and the flash of ack-ack shells as they exploded high above the protective net of barrage balloons. With debris now tinkling down on to the pavements around them, it was time to take cover.

'This way!' yelled Shortso, who was beckoning to them from outside a pub in the Balls Pond Road. 'There's a place round the back!'

They hurried towards him, but before they had gone more than a few steps, there was a gigantic white flash that produced a myriad of sparks that set fire to a nearby tree. The three teenagers immediately threw themselves to the ground. When they eventually looked up they were horrified to see Shortso rolling himself over and over on the wet pavement, trying desperately to put out the flames which had engulfed his clothes.

Chapter 4

Christmas 1940 was a miserable time for the people of London. The festive spirit which had always existed at this time of year was completely absent, for during the last two months the Blitz had taken its toll, and in December alone thousands had been killed. On top of that, food rationing was biting hard, and the little luxuries that people had come to expect just weren't there any more. In some of the poorer parts of North London and the East End, a Christmas meal consisted of nothing more than the usual bowl of soup and some vegetables, and even in the more fortunate working-class areas it was almost impossible to get all the ingredients for a Christmas pudding. The air raids were relentless and people spent most of their time either in an underground shelter or risking their lives in their blacked-out homes. The only consolation was that Christmas Day itself was free of air raids.

Nellie spent much of the day following up a clue to her real identity. She had had a dream a couple of nights before, in which she saw herself with a whole lot of children and young people, running down some steps inside an old large building. When she woke up she remembered the dream but she didn't understand it. She wondered whether it was about when she was at school, and she tried very hard to make sense of where it might have been. But it was a casual remark from Toff that gave her a clue. He mentioned an orphanage in New North Road that had been bombed just a few weeks before. So on Christmas morning, Nellie left the gang's latest hideout in a bombed-out furniture store just behind Essex Road and made her way to the site of the old orphanage. When she got there, all she saw was yet another pile of rubble, which for the first few moments meant absolutely nothing to her. As she started to clamber over some charred timbers, which were now covered with a thin layer of cold white frost, she came across what looked like a noticeboard which was partly concealed beneath a frozen puddle of mud. She stooped down, and with some difficulty managed to pull the board free. It had one word printed on it: BARRATTS'.

'Does it mean anything to you?'

Nellie turned with a start, to find Toff perched on some bricks just behind her. 'What you doin' 'ere?' she asked irritably. 'Did you foller me?'

'As a matter of fact, I did,' Toff replied cheekily. 'D'you mind?'

Nellie felt self-conscious. He was smiling that smile at her again, and she didn't really want to respond. 'What d'yer want?' she asked.

'To see if you've found yourself,' Toff replied, hands dug deep into his overcoat pocket, looking at the noticeboard Nellie had just retrieved. 'Barratts',' he read. 'Does it ring any bells?'

Nellie's puzzled eyes searched the bleak scene around her. 'I *feel* somefin',' she replied, obliquely. 'Somefin' inside.' It was true. The sight of that noticeboard had triggered something; she could hear laughter, shouting, just like in her dream.

Toff kicked a piece of broken brick which went tumbling down the debris he was standing on to join another pile of rubble below. 'An orphanage is a place where kids come because they have no parents.' He paused, then turned to look at her. 'D'you reckon this is where you came from, Nell?' he asked gently.

Nellie suddenly felt quite numb. She was trying so hard to remember something, anything, that she wondered if she was just imagining the sound of children's voices, of being part of such a place. She stared hard at the broken bricks and mortar, the charred timbers, the arched windows in isolated walls that still stood. Then her gaze moved to the stone steps that had clearly once led up to the front door of the building. She jumped across to them, and stood there, trying to remember, trying to bring her life into focus and to know if she had ever been part of this strange, tragic place. Then, without turning to look at Toff, she said, 'If I did come from 'ere, then I don't want ter know. I want ter belong ter someone. I want ter be part of someone's family.'

Toff picked his way carefully across the rubble and joined her on top of the steps. 'You do belong to someone, Nell,' he said, staring into her eyes and putting both his hands on her shoulders. 'You're part of *our* family now. Me and the gang.'

Nellie lowered her head, but Toff's hand reached down and gently raised her chin. When he looked into her eyes this time, he saw that they were filling with tears. 'Merry Christmas, Nell,' he said with a smile.

'Merry Christmas, Toff,' Nellie replied.

'Martin,' Toff said firmly. He wanted her to call him by his real name.

'Martin,' replied Nellie, at last managing a smile.

Ethel Ackroyd was beginning to regret that she had never married. It was something she had thought about lots of times, especially since the start of the war, but not when she was of the right marrying age back home in the Yorkshire Dales. In those days she had known a lot of boys and could have had her pick of them in the

43

village where she was brought up. She had had many a fling, but never with the right person, never with a boy she felt she could spend the rest of her life with. Now, unfortunately, it was too late. She was in her late forties, time had passed her by – or at least that was how she felt. Her work at Barratts' Orphanage was a kind of compensation. As far as she was concerned, all the unwanted children there were her own children, and she was able to share their problems and help them to sort out their lives. But there were one or two of them who refused to share their problems. Like Vicky Hobson. She was such a rebel, such a misfit, so like Ethel herself when she was the same age, which was perhaps why the girl had fascinated her so much.

'Penny for your thoughts,' said Mrs Hare. She and Ethel were watching the children playing musical chairs in the assembly hall of the school in which they had been given temporary accommodation. 'Bet you it's that young Vicky.'

Ethel looked at her and smiled. The old lady was a good soul, and a shrewd observer. 'She's out there somewhere, Mrs Hare,' she said. 'I won't rest till I find her.'

Mrs Hare sighed, and shook her head despondently. Since the bombing of the orphanage, she knew only too well how obsessed Ethel had become about losing Vicky Hobson. She also knew that Ethel was the only person who was convinced that the girl was still alive. 'I wouldn't hold out your hopes, dearie,' she said. 'Even if she did survive that bomb, why wouldn't she just've found her way back to us?'

Ethel turned to look at her with a pained expression. 'Because she didn't want to, Mrs Hare,' she replied despairingly.

At that moment there was an almighty cheer, followed by shrieks of laughter, as the piano playing stopped and two children fought for the last musical chair. This provoked shouts and jeers, and some of the younger children called out excitedly, 'Cheat! Cheat!' Finally, Arthur Driscoll, who had been playing the piano, came down from the platform and, to prolonged cheers, triumphantly declared one of the children the winner. After that, the forty or so orphans filed into the dining hall for their Christmas afternoon tea party, most of which had been provided by contributions from various charitable organisations, and local people.

It was not until the early evening when the children were playing party games that Mrs Hare was able to continue her chat with Ethel. The two women were taking a breather from the festivities with a stroll around the school playground.

'What did you mean?' asked Mrs Hare, her puffy cheeks red from the cold. 'About young Vicky not wanting to come back to us.'

Ethel was reluctant to answer. She had her reasons for not wanting to talk about that afternoon, the afternoon before the air raid. But if she didn't talk about it to someone, she would go out of her mind. The guilt was just too much to bear. 'We had – a quarrel,' she said, with difficulty. 'Just a few hours before the bomb. I hit her, Mrs Hare. I slapped her face. She said she'd run away. She said she hoped I'd die.'

'What?' gasped Mrs Hare, clasping her hand over her mouth in shock.

'It happened when I started talking to her about the future. About what she wanted to do when she was old enough to leave Barratts', when she found herself a husband to settle down with and start a family. For some reason she flew into a rage and accused me of poking my nose into her private business. I told her that as I'd known her since she was a baby, I had every right to talk to her as her own mother might have done.

45

But she wouldn't listen to me. She said I just wanted to know if she had any boyfriends, and what she got up to when she was out of sight. She called me an interfering old hag, an old maid.'

'The little vixen!' Mrs Hare said angrily. 'Didn't I always tell you what a packet of trouble she was? We all knew it.'

'You don't understand, Mrs Hare,' Ethel said, in anguish. 'Vicky was only telling me what I've been thinking about myself all these years. I know nothing about life outside the walls of the orphanage.'

Mrs Hare was fuming. 'You're a good woman, Ethel, and don't you ever think otherwise. What you've done for these children is nothing short of a miracle. There's not a person who knows you that doesn't love you.'

'Except a man,' replied Ethel.

Mrs Hare ignored this. 'Vicky was a wicked girl, my dear. Mark my words.'

Ethel laid her hand on the old lady's arm. 'No, Mrs Hare. What Vicky told me is the truth. I was trying to live out my own life through her. And she knew it. That's why she wanted to get away from Barratts', away from me.'

The old lady's knuckles were white with tension. 'May God forgive me, but I say it's a good thing He took her.'

'Don't ever say such a thing, Mrs Hare!' Ethel cried, almost in panic. 'They never found Vicky, so as far as I'm concerned she's still alive. There are children running wild all over this city, children who've run away from home, children who ran away from evacuation. She could be out there with them – anywhere. If she is, I'm going to find her.'

From inside the school hall, the two women could hear the children singing 'Away In a Manger'. They stood there in the cold, frosty, evening air, their faces turned towards the blacked-out windows, listening.

★　　★　　★

The best part of Christmas for Nellie was to see Shortso sitting with her and the other boys eating Christmas dinner. She had been horrified to see him rolling about on the pavement trying to put out his burning clothes. He had been lucky to escape with only minor burns on his neck, hands, and legs. Anything more serious and they would have had no alternative but to get him straight to the hospital. And that could have meant all sorts of questions being asked. It brought home to Nellie more forcefully than anything how tenuous her life on the streets with these boys was.

Their Christmas meal consisted of a piece of roast leg of chicken, some carrots, boiled onions, and a slice of fried bread. It wasn't the most traditional of Christmas meals, but beggars – and thieves – could not be choosers. At least it was all hot food. They had built a fire right in the middle of the gutted furniture store and cooked the food in an assortment of pots and pans that they had acquired since living out on the streets. There was no Christmas pudding but Rats and Bonkers had delighted everyone by producing two dozen mince pies which they had found in cardboard boxes in the storage room of a baker's shop. All in all, the meal was an unqualified success and much more fun than Nellie had ever imagined it would be. Nuts set the mood by appearing at the meal as a waiter, his hair greased down with lard and parted in the middle, a thin moustache created with soot, and a white towel draped professionally over one arm.

After the meal, everyone sat around squat-legged on the floor and told stories about Christmas from the time when they lived at home. Some of it Nellie found a bit childish, but she had to laugh when Nuts told of the Christmas when his dad dressed up as Santa Claus, crept into Nuts' bedroom late at night, and then tripped over the cat. It was all a welcome relief from the usual nightly routine of life on the streets, sneaking in and out of people's homes during the air raids and making off with their measly food rations. Nellie had come to accept that if they were to survive, there was no other way. But she didn't enjoy this false way of life. What she wanted, what she craved was a family of her own, a real family, whom she could be proud of and tell funny stories about too. And yet she couldn't shake that dragging sense that perhaps she had never had a family at all, and that if ever she did remember who she was and where she came from, the truth would hurt.

The last part of Christmas evening did, however, cheer Nellie up no end. Shortso, the back of his hands and face discoloured by dark red blotches from his burns, revealed a hidden talent. For the best part of an hour and a half, he played a mouth organ while Nellie and the gang joined in with some of the popular songs of the war, such as 'Run, Rabbit, Run', 'You Are My Sunshine', and 'She'll Be Coming Round the Mountain'. To Nellie's surprise and delight, everyone got up to dance, and the boys acted the fool by bowing and then dancing with each other. Their antics made Nellie roar with laughter, and for a precious hour or so she and the others simply enjoyed themselves and forgot all about the tensions they had to live with each day. The most touching moment came when Toff stood up and gallantly offered his hand to Nellie to dance. At first she refused, but after a great deal of cajoling and calls of, 'Come on, Nell!' she took hold of Toff's hand and allowed him to help her up. Shortso played a tune that was regularly bashed out on pub pianos. It was called 'Always', and it was perfect for a nice, smoochy dance. Nellie couldn't remember ever having danced before but she followed Toff's steps as best she could. After a moment or so, the space between them grew less, and it was not very long before their bodies were pressed very firmly against each other. The only light came from the old paraffin lamp, but somehow this only added to the atmosphere, so much so that some of the boys, either jealous of Toff's growing fondness for Nellie or grieved that a girl was intruding too much on their close bond of friendship, decided to call it a day, and one by one they left. Nellie and Toff seemed oblivious of this and continued to move to the poignant wail of the mouth organ. Finally, Shortso came to the end of the song, but Nellie and Toff kept on with their dance, locked in an intimate embrace. Shortso and the few boys still there decided it was time they left too, and they quietly retreated to the coal bunkers where they slept.

Nellie and Toff continued to sway to and fro to the evocative song that was now only a memory.

No matter how hard she tried, Ethel Ackroyd had never liked Lizzie Morris. The fact was that the child was sly, and whenever she was able to tell tales about any of the other orphans at Barratts', she would do so. It was a pity, because Lizzie was a pretty child, with a round, almost doll-like complexion, and long auburn hair that draped beautifully over her shoulders. She was a little on the plump side, which was unusual considering the wartime rations, but as she was only fifteen years old, most people put this down to puppy fat. Ethel tried to make allowances for the fact that she was the victim of a broken marriage – her parents had separated when she was at the vulnerable age of eleven. Unfortunately the child had used her situation to cause trouble for just about everyone. And that included her worst enemy, Vicky Hobson.

'I bet I know where she's gone,' Lizzie cooed mischievously, her large blue eyes slyly watching for Ethel's reaction. She and some of the orphans and staff were taking a Boxing Day afternoon stroll across Highbury

Fields, and Lizzie had deliberately attached herself to Ethel. 'She's wiv one of those gangs who've run away from being evacuated. Vicky always liked bein' wiv boys.'

'How would you know such a thing, Lizzie?' asked Ethel, trying to sound as nonchalant as possible.

'Because Vicky told me she was going,' answered Lizzie.

Ethel stopped abruptly. 'She *told* you she was going to join the evacuees?'

Lizzie, delighted that her remark had had the desired effect, came to a halt too. 'Why yes, Miss Ackroyd,' she said demurely. 'I thought everyone knew how much Vicky liked being in boys' company.'

Ethel was irritated. 'She told you she was going to run away?'

'Yes, Miss Ackroyd.'

'When was this?

'Just a few days before the bomb dropped.'

Despite Lizzie's reputation as an inveterate liar, Ethel was alarmed enough to question her further. She took hold of Lizzie's hand and led her to the nearest park bench. 'Now I want the truth, Lizzie,' Ethel said, pulling the girl down beside her on the damp bench. 'None of your usual made-up stories, just the truth.' Grimly she looked the child straight in the eye and asked, 'Are you telling me that Vicky had been planning to run away from Barratts'?'

Lizzie shrugged her shoulders. 'I suppose so.' Her attention was drawn to a grey squirrel which was sitting up on its hind legs just in front of them. 'Oh look!' she squealed excitedly.

Ethel refused to be diverted. She took hold of Lizzie's arm and asked sternly, 'Did Vicky Hobson talk about being – unhappy at Barratts'?'

Lizzie squirmed. 'You're hurting my arm!'

Ethel persisted. 'Did she?'

'Yes!' howled the child. 'She never liked Barratts'. She said so over and over again. You can ask the others. They'll tell you. They'll tell you that as soon as Vicky got the chance, she was going to get as far away from you as she could!'

Ethel gasped, and released the girl's arm.

The rest of the party had gone on ahead but Martha Driscoll spotted Ethel and Lizzie on the bench. Suspecting that something was wrong, she left the others and began to make her way back.

Ethel tried to compose herself, and after a long, deep breath, asked calmly, 'Are you telling me the truth, Lizzie?'

By this time, Lizzie was giving the impression that she was terrified of Ethel questioning her. 'Yes, miss! Honest, miss!'

The squirrel quickly sensed the atmosphere and made a hasty retreat up into the huge chestnut tree from where he had come. An elderly couple walking their Scots terrier dog had to restrain the creature when, barking furiously, he slipped his leash and tried to make after the squirrel.

Ethel, undeterred by the commotion, continued to cross-examine Lizzie. 'What makes you so sure that Vicky is still alive?' she asked as calmly as she could.

Lizzie thought carefully before answering. 'Because that's the reason she never came down the shelter that night,' she said, flicking her long hair away from her face. 'I could tell that was the night she was goin' ter do it. I could tell that was the time she was goin' ter make a run fer it.'

Ethel stared at her.

'By the time the bomb come down,' Lizzie went on with an unpleasant smirk, 'she was more than likely already on 'er way.'

51

Ethel felt nothing but contempt for her. 'And yet,' she said icily, 'you didn't tell me or any other member of staff. Why, Lizzie? Why?'

The girl fixed her with a hollow smile. 'I'd never do that, miss,' she replied. 'You might've changed your mind.'

Without a moment's thought, Ethel allowed all her feelings of loathing for the girl to surface. Rising quickly from the bench, she slapped Lizzie across the face.

Lizzie screamed and tried to run away, but Ethel grabbed both her arms and started to shake her.

The elderly couple with the dog stared in horror.

'Ethel!' Martha Driscoll rushed forward and managed to prevent Ethel from slapping the girl again. 'No, Ethel! No!'

Lizzie quickly became hysterical, more for effect than actual pain. Sobbing out loud, she yelled, 'I hate you! I hate you!'

Ethel, her face blood-red with uncontrolled anger, suddenly found her arms pinned behind her back by Martha's husband, Arthur, who had rushed to his wife's help.

'Get back to the others,' said Martha to the girl.

Lizzie, her eyes glistening with tears, hurried off, sobbing loudly.

But when she had gone some distance along the path, she looked back briefly over her shoulder to see Ethel, Martha, and Arthur Driscoll in tense conversation.

And the tears very quickly gave way to a satisfied smile.

The night after Boxing Day, it was business as usual for the Luftwaffe. Once again the skies echoed to the wail of the air-raid siren, the drone of enemy aircraft, ack-ack fire, fire and ambulance bells, and once again everyone rushed off to keep their nightly rendezvous in the air-raid shelters. This also meant business as usual for the evacuee gangs.

Toff had decided to concentrate their efforts on the back streets around the Nag's Head in Holloway, where the terraces of three-storey Victorian houses provided rich pickings for the intruder. From earlier recces, Toff had discovered that during an air raid most of the working-class people who lived there retreated to the corrugated-iron Anderson shelters in their small back gardens, leaving the house unprotected. Unfortunately, break-ins were not without risk, for the area contained at least one air-raid precaution post to co-ordinate fire-fighting operations, with plenty of wardens and Special Constables patrolling the streets.

After her near disastrous encounter with the guard dog, Nellie had decided that she was no longer interested in taking part in any more jobs. It didn't matter to her that she had given in to jibes from the boys that breaking into people's homes was not for girls; as far as she was concerned, her own safety was far more important than personal pride. So on the evening of the gang's first post-Christmas job, she decided to take herself off to the pictures at the Rink Cinema in Finsbury Park.

Nellie chose the Rink because its rear exit door was easy to open, mainly because people leaving from earlier performances never bothered to close the door properly behind them. Toff had shown her the knack of getting into the place without paying and, more importantly, how not to be caught once inside. This involved finding her way to a row of empty seats in the upper circle and lying flat on the floor until the lights went down and the programme started. Everything went according to plan, except that when she lay face downwards on the cold lino floor between the seats, something wet and sticky attached itself to her nose. It was a piece of used chewing gum and it positively refused to detach itself completely from the end of her nose. When the lights went down, she was at last able to sit up in a seat, although she kept a constant lookout for the beam of light from the usherette's torch when she approached.

Nellie couldn't remember ever having been inside a cinema before, and she was overawed by the vastness of the long, narrow auditorium, visible in the flickering projected light from the screen. The cinema had once been an old tramway with a roller-skating rink at the rear. And the smell! It was so strange, a mixture of damp rot, sweet perfume, and cigarette smoke. But it was when the film itself came on that she discovered how entrancing it was to come to such a place. The names of the stars – Katharine Hepburn, Joan Bennett, Frances Dee – that came up on the screen at the beginning meant nothing to her, but the tale of four young girls growing up in America before the Civil War captivated her.

The film, which was called *Little Women*, had quite an impact on Nellie, for it was about a family, and it prompted all sorts of questions within her, such as why couldn't she have a mum and dad of her own, and brothers and sisters, like those lucky girls down there on the screen? Why did she have to live a rough life out on the streets with a bunch of misfits? And then she got to wondering why she just didn't go to the nearest police station and tell them her story, how she had lost her memory, and ask who she was and where she had come from. But what if she *did* find out who she was? What if she discovered that she came from that bombed-out orphanage and that she'd never had a mother and father or brothers and sisters? What would be worse, to know that she really did have a family of her own and didn't remember them, or that her whole life had been spent inside a dingy old institution?

At that moment a message appeared along the bottom of the screen, telling the audience that the air-raid siren had sounded but that the film would continue. Nellie was too engrossed in the film, in the story of that family, to let any more bombs ruin her life.

On the way back to the burned-out furniture store, the air raid was in full swing and the whole sky was bright red with the glow of burning fires. No buses were running so Nellie made her way on foot along Blackstock Road to Highbury and then to Essex Road. It was quite a long walk, but in the middle of an air raid it was definitely the safest way to get around, for whenever the fall of shrapnel was too great she was always able to take cover in a shop doorway. There was one scary moment, however, when she had to throw herself flat on her stomach after a bomb whistled down in the distance on to one of the streets near the Arsenal football stadium. The sound of glass shattering all around unnerved Nellie, and it was several minutes before she recovered enough to continue her journey.

When she eventually turned into Essex Road and reached the furniture store, there had apparently been a direct hit on a pet shop on the main road, which caused chaos and pandemonium as distressed local people tried to rescue the puppies, kittens, birds, and other helpless creatures who were trapped, screeching in panic.

'We're in trouble!' called Nuts, out of breath as he ran to catch up with Nellie who was just about to take cover in the gang's own makeshift shelter. 'When I left Toff about 'alf an 'our ago, the rozzers were on to 'im. Fer all I know, 'e's already locked up in the clink.'

At that moment, there was another explosion just a couple of streets away, so both of them practically threw themselves into the bowels of the dark shelter.

Nellie's heart had missed a beat when she heard about Toff. Not that she was surprised that the law had caught up with him; it was inevitable that it would happen sooner or later. But she hated the stupidity of it all, the mad way in which this bunch of outcasts put their lives at risk every night. 'Well, wot're yer goin' ter do about it?' she snapped. 'There must be somefin' yer can do!'

'We can't do nuffin', Nell,' squealed Nuts in the dark. 'Just leave it ter Toff, that's all. 'E can talk 'is way out of a cast-iron box, that one!'

Both of them ducked as the place vibrated from a volley of ack-ack fire in the sky above them. This was followed within seconds by a hail of shrapnel raining down.

When the explosions were replaced by the incessant clanging of fire and ambulance bells, Nell could hear Nuts breathing hard. 'Nuts?' she called in the dark. 'Nuts? Are you all right?'

Nuts hesitated before replying. 'I d-dunno 'ow m-much longer I can g-go on like this,' he stuttered in a barely audible voice. 'One of these days, I'm goin' ter cop my lot.'

Nellie was taken aback. Until this moment, she had been under the impression that Nuts, like all the rest of the boys in the gang, was quite fearless of the air raids. It came as a shock to hear Nuts shivering as he talked. 'Then why d'you carry on livin' like this?' she asked, raising her voice over the chaotic sounds outside. 'Why don't yer all just give up and go back to yer own 'omes?'

Nuts thought for a moment before answering. ''Cos they don't really want us back. My lot don't, anyway.'

''Ow can yer say that?' replied Nellie, irritated. ''Ow can yer say that when yer don't even talk to them? Why don't yer just go back, sit down an' talk to them?'

'Yer don't know my mum, or me dad. *They* do the talkin'. *I* do the listenin'.'

There was another loud explosion. This time Nellie yelled out, for it was too close for comfort. As she did so, someone threw himself down into the shelter, almost flattening her.

'Anyone at home?' he called out.

'Toff!' Nellie felt a surge of excitement. 'Where've yer been?'

'I fawt they'd nabbed yer!' spluttered Nuts.

'They nearly did,' growled Toff, 'thanks to you and Shortso. If you'd done something to divert them, I'd have made a better break. Stupid nerds!'

'You're the stupid nerd!' barked Nellie, more out of relief than anger. 'Why d'yer 'ave ter take risks? Why d'yer 'ave ter go on wiv this stupid nickin' all the time?'

'Come off it, Nell,' replied Toff, trying to make light of it. 'We've got to eat, haven't we?' But when he tried to take hold of her hand, she pulled away.

'Why can't yer learn that this ain't worf it! None of this is worf it!' Nell was letting off the steam that had been building up within her ever since she was asked to do her first job. 'Yer livin' like animals! When yer goin' ter give up and be yer age?'

Nell would have been even more furious with Toff if she'd known he was grinning at her in the dark. 'Sorry you feel like that, Nell,' he said mischievously, 'because I've brought you a present.'

Nellie didn't reply. But she was curious.

'Well, don't you want to know what it is?'

Nellie remained silent.

'Hold out your hand, Nell. Come on now. I went to a lot of trouble to nick this for you.'

Nellie waited a second or so, then decided to do as he asked.

Toff felt around for her outstretched hand, then dropped a small metal object into her palm.

Nellie had no idea what it was.

Toff leaned forward and whispered into her ear, 'It's a lipstick. Just your colour. You're going to look sensational.'

Chapter 5

Despite the severity of the Blitz, that stalwart of British entertainment, the music hall, remained in business. At the start of the war, the government closed most of the theatres, cinemas, concert halls, and football stadiums, but as time went on, the civilian population was in dire need of having their spirits raised, and everything sprang back into life, albeit under strict wartime conditions. Among the greatest saviours of the day in London were places like the Shepherd's Bush Empire, the Wood Green Empire, the Chiswick Empire, and the Finsbury Park Empire. Here, fun-starved audiences were given the chance to forget the air raids for a couple of hours, and to be cheered by a performance of song, dance, laughter, mystery and illusion, and above all a wonderful line-up of character comedians. During the war, there was nothing quite like the music hall to get you into a party spirit and to help you forget the horror and reality of the bombed streets outside.

The Hackney Empire, in East London's Mare Street, was one such place, and even though it was late January, the Christmas pantomime season was still in full swing. Ever since Nellie had started to use the lipstick he had nicked for her, Toff had waited for an opportunity to show her off to people other than the gang, and a visit to the Hackney panto turned out to be just such an opportunity.

The panto this year was the good old favourite

Cinderella. Owing to the blackout, most performances had to be in the afternoon. Nellie and Toff had no money to pay the admission charge, but needless to say Toff had a plan of campaign. This involved mingling with the audience filing up the stone steps to the gallery, and if the usherette asked them for their tickets, they would point to some unsuspecting man and woman ahead of them and reply indignantly that their mum and dad had the tickets, and had already shown them. Then all they had to do was either find two spare seats that weren't booked, or wedge themselves among the overflow audience standing at the back. The plan worked perfectly, and they even found two seats in the front row at the side. They watched anxiously when anybody came near them, just in case they were there to claim their booked seats, but when the house lights finally went down, they knew they were safe.

Nellie was as excited as the rest of the audience, which included quite a lot of children. The theatre, with its crimson stage curtains and gold tassels, seemed to her to be like a kind of fairy wonderland, albeit one that stank of Zubes cough drops, which were the only real substitute for rationed sweets. When the orchestra started to play a rousing popular tune and the curtains swung back to reveal a whole lot of people in brightly coloured costumes and make-up, singing and dancing, she felt her stomach turn over with excitement and exhilaration.

Toff was more excited to see Nellie so happy, and throughout the first half of the show he couldn't take his eyes off her. He thought she looked so sexy. The lipstick really suited her, and she had combed her usually straggly hair and pinned it back over her ears, which gave her a much more grown-up look. He was determined that at the right moment he would tell her he thought she looked sensational, that what she lacked in height she made up a hundredfold in personality and sex appeal.

While Cinderella was sitting alone in her kitchen, singing of her despair at being left to do the chores while her ugly sisters went to the Prince's ball, Nellie and Toff took a peek between the brass protective rails, down into the circle and stalls below. There was a party of excited children there, most of them with adults. After the interval, when they all filed back into their seats, Nellie noticed one young teenage girl gazing up towards the gods, apparently at her and Toff. Just before the lights went down again, the girl seemed to be jumping up and down in her seat, pointing up towards where Nellie and Toff were sitting, trying hard to get some of the adults with her to look. This worried Nellie, and she quickly slumped down into her seat. To her relief, the performance began again, and the girl in the circle just beneath them was forced to sit down and keep quiet.

Nellie soon forgot about her as she became caught up in the colour, costumes, and glittering set of the Prince's ball. But despite the spectacle and romance of the story and the popular songs, Nellie was impressed most of all with what was called in the programme, '*A Speciality Act*'. This turned out to be a tall, skinny middle-aged man with a funny foreign accent, who used different coloured lights and handkerchiefs to create all sorts of strange illusions. He even had a cupboard on the stage in which he made his young lady assistant disappear, and then made her reappear in one of the stage boxes. He was a wonderful character, with his pencil-thin black moustache, and constant exclamations of "*Ere iz my miracle!*", and Nellie thought him an absolute revelation. Toff enjoyed it all too, but as he puffed on his fag and blew circles of smoke up into the hot, sticky atmosphere, he was far more amused by the youngsters along the front row of the gods who were mischievously pelting people in the circle below with dried peas.

At the climax of the show, when the Prince named

Cinderella as the girl he would marry, the whole theatre burst into cheers and tumultuous applause. And when the show was finally over, the performers took a bow on stage and invited the audience to sing one last popular song with them, followed by 'God Save the King'. This brought the curtain down, and the lights up. As the audience rose from their seats to leave the theatre, Nellie turned to look down at the circle below, and once again she saw the young teenage girl calling out and pointing up at her. She nervously ducked out of sight, unaware who Lizzie Morris was, or why she was desperately trying to point her out to the principal of Barratts' Orphanage, Ethel Ackroyd.

It was only a matter of minutes after the audience had streamed out of the Hackney Empire that the wail of the air-raid siren echoed along the length of Mare Street. Everyone raced to get home to the safety of their shelters; queues of theatre-goers quickly formed at bus stops on either side of the busy main street, while others chose to make their way as fast as they could on foot.

One of the last people to leave the theatre was Ethel Ackroyd. She struggled to push her way through the crowds to get to the exit used by the gallery audience. It was a futile effort, for by the time she got there a male attendant was already bolting up for the night.

'Excuse me,' she said breathlessly to the man, 'did you notice a young girl coming out just a moment or so ago? She was about this high, with mousey-coloured hair, and—'

''Ang on, missus,' he said, looking at Ethel as though she was mad. ''Ow many people d'yer fink we 'ave up there?'

'But you'd know this one,' she said, holding on to the door he was trying to bolt. 'She's really quite small – and pretty.'

'Is she now?' replied the attendant tetchily. 'Well, believe it or not, I ain't got eyes in the back of me blinkin' 'ead, yer know!' Then he pulled the door from her grip. 'You better get down the shelters. Don't yer know there's an air raid on!' With that, he slammed the door with a loud thud and locked and bolted it from inside.

For several moments, Ethel stood there in a state of anguish and confusion, her eyes anxiously searching the last remaining members of the audience as they hurried out of the front entrance of the theatre. She didn't really know whether to believe what Lizzie Morris had said about catching sight of Vicky Hobson up in the front row of the Hackney Empire gallery. But it was just possible that Vicky had been there, and if she was, Ethel felt devastated that she could have missed her after being so close. On the other side of the road she could see the charabanc waiting for her to join the party of children she and the Driscolls had brought to the pantomime. Once she was quite sure that there were no more stragglers left inside the theatre, she reluctantly moved off, trying hard not to be angry with the hordes of careless young couples who bumped into her as she went.

She was much too fraught and preoccupied to notice that one of those couples was Nellie and Toff.

It was about half an hour before the first wave of enemy aircraft was heard, droning in from an easterly direction along the River Thames. In the distance, Nellie and Toff could hear the first bombs whistling down, and the angry barrage of ack-ack fire that was doing its best to bring down as many of the raiders as possible before they reached central London.

'Looks like it's Stratford way,' called Toff, arm round Nellie's waist as they hurried along Balls Pond Road. He had to shout to be heard. 'We'd better make a dash for it!'

Nellie broke into a run, not only because it was dangerous to be on the streets in the middle of an air raid, but also to put some distance between herself and Toff. She wished he would stop treating her like a precious flower. In fact, she was becoming more and more anxious with the attention he was always showing her; it was almost a fixation. Not that she didn't appreciate Toff's concern for her. In many ways, she felt flattered. But she wanted to be her own person, to think things out for herself, and make her own decisions. She was also concerned that Toff was becoming too moony about her, and although she did feel something inside for him, it was all too complicated for her to understand, and the only solution she had was not to respond.

By the time they got back to the old furniture store in Essex Road, the bombardment was in full swing. Most of the gang were out on jobs, with the exception of Rats and Bonkers who were waiting in the underground shelter, still wearing the tin helmets they'd nicked from a local ARP post. Nellie was at least grateful that there was a candle burning in the shelter; there was nothing worse than sitting in the dark listening to all hell breaking loose in the skies above. But the place still smelt heavily of cat's piddle, and there was at least an inch of rainwater seeping up through the muddy floor from last night's downpour.

'We got two buckets of shrapnel terday,' Bonkers announced proudly.

'We took it up the post,' added Rats. 'This ARP geezer give us a tanner fer the lot.'

'We din't ask fer nuffin',' Bonkers continued, his outsize tin helmet wobbling on his head as he talked. 'We told 'em it was fer the war effort.'

''E told us our mums and dads oughta be proud of us,' said Rats. 'Much better than the tykes who nicked 'is 'elmets!'

Both of them burst into laughter.

'What was that?' Nellie's voice cut through the sound of the ack-ack gunfire outside.

'Nothing to worry about, Nell,' said Toff reassuringly. 'It's pretty busy up there tonight.'

'No, not that,' replied Nellie. 'Something else.' The sound of a kitten mewing was just audible. 'There!' she said.

Rats and Bonkers exchanged a guilty look.

'It's nuffin',' said Rats, shrugging his shoulders dismissively. 'Yer get a lot of mogs down 'ere.'

'Where is it?' Toff demanded firmly.

'It's nuffin', Toff, 'onest,' Bonkers said quickly.

'I've told you two, no cats, dogs, or any other pets! We don't have enough to feed ourselves, let alone strays.'

'But this one's different,' pleaded Rats. 'We found 'im on a site down Dalston. 'Is mum was dead.'

Bonkers added his own plea. ''E was buried under all this debris. 'Is bruvvers an' sisters too.'

'Where is it?' demanded Toff. 'Come on. Get it out of here!'

Rats and Bonkers exchanged another guilty glance, then Bonkers shrugged his shoulders and dug deep into his pocket. He pulled out a tiny ginger kitten which immediately let out a wail.

Nellie's face lit up immediately. She reached across and gently took hold of the small creature. It had so little fur on it, it could not have been born more than a week before. 'It's beautiful!' she gasped.

'Maybe,' growled Toff, 'but it still has to go.'

Nellie swung an angry look at him. 'Why?' she asked. 'It's only a kitten.'

'Please, Nell,' Toff said. 'They know the rules. We have to have some rules. No pets.' He turned to Bonkers and said firmly, 'Get it out of here, now!'

Bonkers knew from experience that it was no use arguing with Toff, so he quickly snatched the kitten from Nellie and made for the curtain covering the open entrance.

'Wait!' Nellie stood up quickly. 'Can't we at least wait till morning? It's cruel to put it out there on a night like this.'

Toff suddenly became angry. 'Give me that thing!' he raged, grabbing the small creature from Bonkers' hand. The kitten started to screech.

This show of temper from Toff took Nellie by surprise. It was the first time she had seen him in a mood like this, and it was a side to his character that she did not like. 'No!' she yelled, suddenly barring Toff's way. 'Why der *you* always 'ave ter 'ave the last say about *everyfin*'?'

'Because I'm in charge, Nell!' Toff roared back. 'Someone has to take some responsibility around here.'

'That doesn't mean yer 'ave ter yell at people and be cruel ter dumb animals.'

'Don't be so stupid, Nell!' snapped Toff, trying to push his way past her.

Nellie refused to budge. 'It strikes me, you're the stupid one 'round 'ere, mate!' she said angrily, staring straight at him in the dim candlelight. 'If you're in charge, then yer shouldn't allow this lot to carry on livin' like this. Yer shouldn't allow them to sleep rough in smell-'oles like this, livin' on uvver people's rations and hard-earned pickin's!'

Toff wasn't prepared to take this kind of talk, not even from Nellie. 'I seem to remember that *you* didn't object too much when we took you in and looked after you!'

This remark infuriated Nellie even more, and her eyes were now sharp with rage. 'Look 'ere, mate,' she spluttered. 'I din't ask no one ter look after me. I'm capable of takin' care of meself, see! If you're so 'igh an' mighty, why can't yer go back ter yer own 'ome and try bossin' yer own folks around?'

Rats and Bonkers stood back in the shadows, dumbfounded by this angry exchange between Nellie and Toff.

Toff was clearly stung by what he considered to be Nellie's ingratitude. In a slightly cooler voice, he replied, 'You're not a prisoner here, Nell. No one's forcing you to stay. If you don't like the way we do things around here, you're at liberty to go.'

'That suits me fine, mate,' she replied haughtily. ''Cos that's wot I've bin wantin' ter do ever since I got 'ere!' She turned and made a move to leave. But as she did so, there was a powerful explosion just a few streets away. The force of the bomb knocked her off her feet, and as she and the others fell to the muddy floor, dust came tumbling down on to them from the makeshift ceiling. At the same time, the kitten Toff was holding tore into his hand with its tiny claws and bolted.

'Bloody thing!' Toff yelled, his hand bleeding.

'Come back!'

'Don't let 'im go!'

Rats and Bonkers were immediately up on their feet and making a dash for the door.

'You stupid idiots!' yelled Toff as the two boys rushed out after the kitten. 'You'll get yourselves killed! Get back here!' Then he turned and quickly pulled Nellie to her feet. 'Look what you've done!' he growled.

Outside the shelter, the whole world looked as though it was on fire. As far as the eye could see, sheets of flame crackled up into the dark night clouds, and every so often small puffs of menacing black smoke were punched into the sky by exploding ack-ack shells. In all directions, from Victoria Park in Hackney, Clissold Park in Stoke Newington, and Finsbury Park in Islington, magnificent great silver barrage balloons were bursting into flame, ignited by machine-gun fire from enemy aircraft. Rats and Bonkers went sprinting across this desolate landscape, their movements illuminated by the flames and the white light from a winter's moon as it dodged in and out of the clouds.

'Over here!' yelled Rats, as he caught sight of the elusive kitten who was scampering off towards the shell of an old furniture warehouse.

Bonkers was right behind him, and between them they tried to head off the small creature.

'Get back here, you idiots!' Toff yelled, trying to make himself heard above the sound of clanging fire and ambulance bells and distant bomb explosions. 'Leave the bloody cat!' he roared, now having to compete with someone else's voice booming out through a loud-hailer across the street, where a terrace of single-storey houses had just received a direct hit. 'You're mad! Let the thing go!'

Nellie watched in alarm as the two young boys clambered over the debris, calling out to the small kitten, stretching out their hands to try to retrieve it from a pile of fallen masonry. As she watched, she became aware of a new sound, a strange rat-a-tat-tat, like someone tapping their fingers on a drum, fast and furiously. Her blood froze. Toff stared up into the sky behind him, where a sinister dark shape was descending at speed from the sky, swooping low over the burnt-out shells of the furniture store and warehouse.

'Rats! Bonkers!' Toff's voice was now close to hysteria. 'Get down! Get—'

His voice was drowned by the deadly sound of machine-gun fire which cut into the debris in two advancing columns directly towards Rats and Bonkers.

'Rats! Bonkers!'

It was too late. The young German pilot of the enemy Messerschmitt fighter plane had found his targets and very quickly brought the two boys down in a hail of machine-gun bullets.

'No . . . !' Toff's anguish was immense.

Nellie was horrified by what she had seen. She was too scared to scream, and could only turn away and press her body against the outer wall of the burnt-out furniture store. She was shaking from head to foot, and was so cold she felt numb. When she was finally able to turn and look, she saw Toff crouched over the slumped, blood-stained figures of Rats and Bonkers.

He raised his head and saw Nellie watching him. The tears running down his cheeks glistened in the moonlight. 'I hope you're satisfied?' he called, his voice cracking with emotion.

Nellie clamped her hand across her mouth. She was too shocked and distressed to answer. In one swift movement, she disappeared into the furniture store, made straight for her sleeping quarters, and collected the large shopping bag containing the few belongings she had acquired since joining the gang.

A few minutes later, shopping bag strapped across her shoulder, she made a discreet exit through the back of the old store and headed off on her own along Essex Road, which was rumbling to the sounds of yet another aerial onslaught.

The boiler and storage rooms in the bowels of Melbourne Road School were not the perfect places for forty or so orphans and staff to shelter in during an air raid, but as all the school's regular pupils had been evacuated at the start of the war, no proper shelters had been prepared. The basement rooms had been made as comfortable as possible, with mattresses and bedding taken from beds in the upstairs classrooms/dormitories. There were no separate rooms for the staff, and this had meant a great deal of organisation to ensure privacy for the male and female staff. Under normal circumstances, the children would have found it a great adventure to sleep in such unusual surroundings, but after their traumatic experience in the

69

bombed orphanage, the sound of the nightly air raids was an unsettling experience for them all.

Tonight, however, the children had come back from the Hackney Empire in a happy mood, their spirits raised by the sight of the grotesque ugly sisters being chased by Connie the Cow, the sing-song with the principal boy, Buttons, and the spectacle of the Prince's wedding to Cinderella. But as Ethel watched them all chatting excitedly and laughing about their treat, her mind was obsessed with the thought that Vicky Hobson had been in that theatre at the same time as all the other Barratts' orphans.

It wasn't until lights out that Ethel had the chance to relax and turn things over in her mind. Although the air raid was still rumbling on in the streets above, most of the children and staff were now asleep, and in the far corner of the main room, Ethel could hear the loudest snores of all coming from Mrs Hare. It was dark in the basement except for two paraffin lamps turned down very low. Ethel sat in a chair beside her bed, finishing a lukewarm cup of cocoa which Mrs Hare had made for her at least twenty minutes before. Then she leaned her head back against the chair, and closed her eyes. Her mind was racing. Could she believe that wretched child, Lizzie Morris? Had Vicky really been in that panto audience, and if so, why did no one else see her? Oh, why was Vicky doing this to her? What had she, Ethel, done to provoke such hate? Guilt. Guilt. Guilt.

''Scuse me, miss.'

Ethel's eyes sprang open. In the half-light, she could just make out a child's figure standing in front of her. 'Who is it?' she asked.

'It's me, miss.' The girl's squeaky voice was unmistakable.

'What do you want, Lizzie? Why aren't you asleep?'

Lizzie paused before answering. 'I couldn't sleep, miss.

70

Not until I'd said sorry – for what 'appened this after-noon.'

Ethel stiffened, and her stomach went quite tense. 'What are you talking about?' she asked.

'About seein' Vicky, miss.'

Ethel felt the anger rising in her. Ever since she had come back from the theatre she had been tormented by the thought that Vicky had been there too. It would be absolutely contemptible if this child had been lying. 'Are you telling me that you *didn't* see her?'

'I'm not sure, miss,' replied Lizzie.

'Not sure?'

'Well, it looked like 'er, it really did. But there were lights shinin' in me eyes from the balcony upstairs and, well, I might 'ave been mistaken. It looked like Vicky, but then again, p'raps it wasn't.'

Ethel hated the way she felt about Lizzie. Every time she heard her weak, simpering voice, she felt like taking her by the shoulders and giving her a good shake. And as the child stood there in the dark, Ethel could imagine what she looked like, her tiny sharp eyes darting all over the place, her feigned look of innocence. It took all Ethel's strength to control her feelings of distaste, to keep herself cool and calm, and to remember that whatever she thought about her, Lizzie, like all the other children, depended on the orphanage for love and care. 'At the time you seemed quite sure,' she said. 'What changed your mind, Lizzie?'

Ethel could almost hear the mechanism in the child's brain working to think of an answer. ''Cos I knew 'ow upset you were, miss,' she replied. 'I'm not sayin' Vicky wasn't there, just that I'm not an 'undred per cent sure that she was.'

This time Ethel paused before answering. 'Thank you, Lizzie. I appreciate what you've said. Now go to bed, please.'

'Yes, miss.' Lizzie turned to go, then stopped. 'Miss,' she said, competing with Mrs Hare's snores.

'Yes?'

'I love yer, miss,' said the child, in her most unctuous voice. 'We all do. 'Onest we do.' Then lowering her voice to what was almost a sinister whisper, she added, 'If anyfin' ever 'appened to you, I'd be ever so upset.' Lizzie didn't wait for a reply. She scuttled off as silently as she had come. A few moments later, Ethel heard the rustle of bedclothes as the child tucked herself up in her eiderdown on the floor.

Ethel decided to go to bed too, but after that sickening declaration of love, she didn't think she would get much sleep.

Nellie had no idea where she was, or how far she had come. All she knew was that she had finally broken away from her extraordinary life with the vacs gang, and never wanted to know anything about them ever again. But the sight of Rats and Bonkers being mown down by machine-gun fire would haunt her for the rest of her life. And Toff was right, in a way she was responsible for what had happened to them. If only she hadn't argued with him about the kitten, if only she had accepted that what he had said about not keeping pets was common sense, perhaps those two boys would still be alive. Every time she thought about it, the skin all over her body went taut. She was consumed with guilt, and she had no idea how she was going to live with it. The large shopping bag containing her belongings seemed very heavy now, and as she struggled on her way, she was practically dragging it along the pavement.

Although the air raid was still in progress, during the past half-hour or so the intensity had subsided, and by the time she had made her way along Canonbury Road and reached Highbury Corner, the rumble of gunfire seemed to be confined to the far distance, probably somewhere over the London docks. Her only moment of panic came when she was approached by a Special Constable who asked why she was out all alone in the middle of an air raid. But after she had explained that she was on her way to join her mum and the rest of the family down the Tube, she was allowed to proceed unhindered.

Nellie didn't know why she had chosen to go down the main Holloway Road, for she could have gone in a southerly direction along Upper Street towards the Angel, Islington. But the road seemed to be very wide, and it gave her the chance to meander rather than to walk in a straight line.

Once she had got past the Highbury Picture Theatre, she found herself passing the Salvation Army Hall, the Central Library, and then a whole cluster of small shops that seemed to go on for ever. But the cold realisation dawned on her that she really had no idea where she was going, or how she was going to survive without food or somewhere to sleep. She might not have liked living rough with the boys up at Essex Road, but at least they had looked after her, at least she had felt safe in their company. And she could trust them, trust them all. Especially Toff.

She passed another cinema, the Regent, then made her way beneath the railway arch opposite Holloway Road Tube Station. As she passed yet another cinema, the Savoy, she could hear the rumble of gunfire getting closer again. Despite the weight of her cumbersome carrier bag, she began to trot, and when the sky was once again lit up by searchlights, she knew it would be only a matter of minutes before the first enemy raider was caught in the middle of them, like a fly caught in a spider's web.

She soon found herself running past a department store called Jones Brothers. There were no lights in the windows, and the large glass panes were patterned with sticky protective tape. Without warning, there was an angry barrage of ack-ack fire which was immediately followed by an open truck racing past her. It carried a multi-barrelled anti-aircraft gun on the back and a man was firing a rapid succession of small shells up into the sky. Now she was frightened, really frightened, and her first thoughts were of Toff. She found it hard to believe that at a moment like this he was the one person that she actually missed.

She ran across the road and took shelter in the doorway of what seemed to be a large restaurant right on the corner of Holloway and Tollington Roads. By now she was so exhausted, all she could do was to flop down on to the cold tiles and wait for the air raid to pass.

As she lay there, propped up against the glass door criss-crossed with protective tape, her mind was dominated by thoughts of Toff and the gang, and the night's events which had so shattered her life. And then, for one fleeting moment, she thought about herself, about who and where she was, and what she was going to do with herself now that she was out here on her own – truly on her own. How would she live? How would she survive?

Dazed with tiredness, eyes closed, her head slowly drooped and came to rest on her right shoulder. When she opened her eyes again, she saw a small hand-scrawled notice stuck to the restaurant window. It read:

'WANTED: Waitress. Must be prepared to work long hours. Good wages, food, and (if required) accommodation. Apply within.'

Chapter 6

Monsieur Pierre came out of his front door in Tufnell Park Road and took a deep breath of warm summer air. It was such a glorious June day that for the first time this year he was wearing his lightweight fawn summer suit, which perfectly matched his cream-coloured shirt and light-brown patterned Tootal tie. His shoes, which he had miraculously preserved since before the war, were dark brown and set off his brown trilby hat, which he always wore at a rakish angle. His sartorial elegance marked him out as a gentleman – of the theatre. Wherever he went he was noticed, for at six feet two inches tall, he towered over most people, but he was so painfully thin that anyone who met him for the first time felt like offering him some of their ration coupons to get himself a good meal.

His wife, referred to by Monsieur's legion of admirers as simply 'Madame', was quite different. Small and dumpy, she wore the same clothes day in and day out. They usually comprised a Woolworth's cotton dress, a long-sleeved black velvet jacket (a gift from her ancient mother), and a moth-eaten cotton hat with a green cockatoo feather stuck in the side. But now that it was early summer, she too had opted for a cooler, more seasonal look. She had discarded the velvet jacket. Although completely different in shape and size, this stylish pair were the perfect foreign couple – except that their real names were Albert and Doris Beckwith, and they came from Stepney in East London.

For the past three months or so there had been a lull in the air raids, and with the start of summer, there was cautious optimism everywhere. Not that anyone was complacent, for only the previous month there had been a terrifying all-night air raid with a heavy death toll, and only a few days before, the Prime Minister Mr Churchill had warned the British nation to be vigilant. However, the sun knew how to bring out the best in people and the streets were bustling with activity, with all the shop windows doing their best not to look too austere. It was a perfect day for 'Monsieur and Madame Pierre' to take their regular morning walk to their favourite Holloway restaurant, Beales.

In the winter the journey from Tufnell Park Road to the corner of Holloway and Tollington Roads took a laborious eight minutes, but in the summer, with the aid of his black ebony cane (a personal gift from the Maharaja of Jaipur), Monsieur set a brisk pace, and they always arrived in six and a half minutes precisely.

For a midweek morning, Beales was quite full today. Most of the people there were shoppers, for Jones Brothers department store was just across the road, and Holloway Road contained Woolworth's, Marks and Spencer, Selby's, and a veritable treasure chest of small shops such as Liptons, Sainsbury's, Lavells the sweet shop, Hicks the greengrocers, and the North London Drapery Stores around the corner in Seven Sisters Road. As it was only ten thirty in the morning, lunch was still an hour or so away, so Monsieur and Madame Pierre had plenty of time to have their usual cups of Lipton's tea, and whatever biscuits were available.

'Mornin', Pierre, Mrs Pierre,' said Nellie, looking as pretty as a picture in a waitress's cap stuck on top of her neatly permed head of tight brown curls, a black dress, and white apron. 'The usual?' she asked, waiting to memorise the order as she was still unable to read or write.

'But of course, ducks,' replied Monsieur in a broad Cockney accent that hardly matched his classy foreign appearance. 'Got any new bickies terday?'

''Fraid not,' she replied, shaking her head sadly. 'Lincolns or crackers.'

Monsieur sighed. He hated Lincolns and crackers. So dry, so bland, and not sweet. Oh, how he longed for the good old days before the war, the time of digestives, petit beurres and chocolate fingers.

'Never mind, Nellie dear,' said Madame, who had a lovely smile and an attractive mole on her right cheek with two dark hairs growing out of it. 'We're lucky ter 'ave anyfin' in these 'ard times.'

Nellie smiled, did a brief curtsy, then scuttled off to the kitchen.

'She's such a luvely gel,' said Madame, watching Nellie disappear. 'She shouldn't be workin' in a place like this. She should be 'ome wiv 'er mum an' dad, bein' looked after.'

'You 'eard wot she told us,' replied Monsieur, resting both his hands on top of his cane as he took in the other customers, in the hope that at least one of them would recognise him as the great music hall illusionist. 'She's got no family. That's why she 'as ter live in accommodation next door.'

Although Monsieur and Madame had been regular customers at Beales since they got back from their provincial tour up north, they had only actually been waited on by Nellie three or four times. But the moment they saw her, they were impressed by her good manners and the way she kept her back straight and erect as she went in and out of the kitchen balancing trays of tea on the fingers of one hand. When they did eventually get talking to her, they liked her so much that they had asked the restaurant supervisor, Mrs Wiggins, to make Nellie their 'regular'. And today they had quite a treat for her.

When Nellie went into the kitchen, Mrs Wiggins was helping the chef peel potatoes for lunch. She was a kindly woman. When Nellie had first approached her for the job back in January, she had overlooked the fact that the girl had neither an identity card nor a National Security number, and taken her on without hesitation, saying that a girl of sixteen was hardly likely to be a Nazi spy! Nellie was the youngest person on the staff, for the three other waitresses were all middle-aged. They all got on well together, and once or twice Nellie had been invited back to the women's homes to meet the rest of their families. Nonetheless, Nellie was finding it a hard life, on her feet from eight in the morning until closing time at five thirty in the evening. But at least her room in the hostel next door to the restaurant was comfortable, and as the job included two good meals a day, she had no complaints.

'I want you to be extra nice to the gentleman and his wife today, Nellie,' said Mrs Wiggins, who had a rather elegant face which gave the impression that she should be above peeling potatoes. 'Mr Beckwith is going to allow us to put his photograph up on the wall,' she whispered, even though Hubert the chef had already heard the news. 'And he's also agreed to sign it. Don't you think that's wonderful, Nellie? It'll be so good for business to have a music hall star's photograph on our wall.'

'Won'erful,' replied Nellie, who was just as excited as Mrs Wiggins.

'We need some more spuds!' yelled Hubert.

'Coming up!' returned another male voice in the scullery adjoining the kitchen.

Nellie quickly prepared a tray of tea and biscuits for Monsieur and Madame. She poured boiling water from a kettle into the white teapot and collected two white cups and saucers and a small jug of powdered milk.

Behind her, Mrs Wiggins produced two Chelsea buns from a cardboard box that was tucked underneath the work counter. 'I want you to give these to the gentleman and lady. Tell them they're with the compliments of the management.'

Nellie took the buns and put them on to two small tea plates. Then she picked up the tray, balanced it on one hand as she had been trained by Mrs Wiggins, and wound her way back through the kitchen mayhem to the swing doors.

'Oh, and Nellie!'

Nellie stopped and turned.

'Tell them we've got no marg,' said Mrs Wiggins. 'Apologise.'

Nellie nodded, and went into the restaurant.

When she reached their table, she found Monsieur smoking an Abdullah cigarette through a long cigarette holder and Madame reading an article in the *News Chronicle* about how the Germans had invaded the Greek island of Crete, and how many good British soldiers had died trying to protect their mates during the subsequent evacuation.

'I 'ate the war,' sighed Madame, putting her newspaper down to make room for the tea tray. 'I 'ate the Germans. All they can fink about is killin' and more killin'.' She looked up at Nellie. There was despair in the poor woman's eyes. 'Sometimes I fear fer the future. Not fer me, but fer the likes of young fings like you, and me own two kids.'

'Stop bein' so gloomy, Doris,' said Monsieur. 'The war won't last for ever. And anyway, we have some exciting times to look forward to.'

Madame smiled affectionately at her husband. He was such an escapist, but she loved him dearly.

'The supervisor told me to give you these buns,' said Nellie. 'Compliments of the management.' She put them on the table in front of Madame.

''Ow smashin'!' she said.

79

'Marvellous!' he said.

'Sorry there's no marg, though,' added Nellie. 'Nor any sugar.'

Madame shook her head. 'Don't worry about that, dear.' She bent her head forward to savour the smell of her bun. 'We're very lucky people, aren't we, Albert?'

Monsieur drew on his cigarette holder and exhaled a long thin trail of blue-grey smoke. 'That we are,' he agreed.

Nellie bowed briefly and turned to leave.

''Ang on a moment, love,' Monsieur said quickly. 'Got somefin' ter give yer before yer go.'

Nellie watched Monsieur hold the cigarette holder between his teeth, dig into his inside jacket pocket, and produce what looked like a small piece of paper.

'A little present from us ter you,' he announced with a flourish.

Nellie looked at the piece of paper in his hand as though it was something dangerous. 'What is it?'

'Take it, dear,' said Madame with a broad, friendly grin. 'It'll bring yer luck.'

Nellie took the piece of paper, looked at it, but was none the wiser. She asked again, 'What is it?'

Monsieur pulled himself up in his chair to his full height. 'That, me dear,' he said, taking the cigarette holder out of his mouth, 'is a ticket to a star performance.'

Nellie's eyes widened.

Madame leaned forward and rested her hand on Nellie's arm. 'It's a ticket fer our next bookin', dear,' she said, voice low. 'Finsbury Park Empire. First 'ouse, Monday. Max Miller's top of the bill, but Albert's closin' the first 'alf.'

Nellie looked back at the piece of paper she was holding between her thumb and first finger. Suddenly it seemed like magic. 'Fer me? A ticket – fer the feater? *Free?*'

'As free as air, darlin',' exclaimed Monsieur loudly.

'It's our way of sayin' fank yer fer the nice way yer treat us when we come 'ere,' said Madame. 'It's a nice, comfy seat in the stalls, third row from the front, right in the middle.' She leaned closer again. 'You'll be sittin' wiv our two boys,' she whispered. 'You'll get on like an 'ouse on fire.'

Nellie was overwhelmed and didn't know what to say. 'F-fank yer,' she spluttered. 'Fank yer very much.'

Madame was delighted to see such a smile come to Nellie's face, and she squeezed her arm affectionately. 'Somefin' ter look forward to, dear,' she said.

Monsieur looked pleased with himself. No, more than that. He was over the moon. This was mainly because a young couple at the corner table had recognised him and sent their small son across to ask him to sign the back of an empty cigarette packet.

When Nellie got back to the staff hostel each evening, she was usually dead on her feet. The hours were indeed long, and for the best part of the day she spent her time going backwards and forwards between the restaurant and kitchen balancing a whole weight of dishes on a large metal tray. Not that her height or slight build in any way restricted her from doing what the rest of the staff did – in fact Mrs Wiggins had often remarked how sturdy Nellie was – but it was a soulless job that never seemed to get anywhere. It did have its compensations, however, like meeting different people such as Monsieur and Madame, and having a little money in her pocket to go to the pictures or take a bus up to Finsbury Park. And one of her great joys was that her room had a wind-up gramophone on which she could hear all the latest records by such popular performers as Bing Crosby, the Andrews Sisters, Anne Shelton, Donald Peers, and Harry Roy and his Band. In the staff sitting room there was also a wireless set, but it was always tuned to the news. Nellie absolutely hated the news because it was all about the war, and war to her brought back so many horrific memories.

Because most of the staff were middle-aged, in the five months or so since she had been at Beales, Nellie had made very few friends of her own age. She had met no one like Toff, and whenever she was at her lowest, she always thought of him. She was still tormented by the feeling that she was responsible for what had happened to Rats and Bonkers. The painful memory was worst at night as she lay in bed before going to sleep. But Toff's face was always there before her, with those gleaming dark eyes, jet-black hair greased back over his slightly protruding ears, and a swarthy complexion that gave Nellie a tingling sensation every time she thought about him. But Toff was in the past, and nothing in this world was going to persuade her to look for him.

Nellie's best friend at the restaurant was Hubert the chef. He was a funny little bloke, not much taller than Nellie herself, and his constant grumbling about the customers made Nellie laugh, mainly because she agreed with practically everything he said. Even his face made her laugh. It was small and round and Nellie often told him that he looked like a rabbit because even when his mouth was closed she could see the tips of his teeth. Hubert was in fact quite a sad character. Ever since he left school it had been his ambition to become a policeman, but his height and the fact that he wore spectacles put paid to that. It was also the reason why he had been turned down for conscription. But whenever Nellie was feeling fed up, it was usually Hubert she turned to. He was a real stay-at-home; he spent most evenings alone in his room, endlessly reading the sports pages of the *Daily Sketch* and smoking himself to death with foul Woodbine cigarettes. Tonight, however, Nellie was determined to get him out of his room.

'Come on, Hube!' she called, thumping on his bedroom door soon after she'd had her supper in the staff dining room. 'Don't be such a lazy ole git! It's a luvely evenin'. Put yer shoes on an' let's go out an' 'ave a walk.'

Hubert's door suddenly opened and a pall of choking cigarette smoke wafted out. 'Walk?' he bellowed, fag in mouth, coughing his lungs out. 'Wot do we wanna walk for? I've bin on me plates of meat all day!'

Nellie laughed and fanned away the smoke with her hand. 'There's somefin' outside called fresh air,' she jeered. 'Why don't you an' me sample it?'

Despite Hubert's objections, a few minutes later they were strolling idly along Tollington Road. After a long hard winter stuck down the air raid shelters, many people were taking advantage of the warm weather to sit on chairs in their small front yards or chat amiably with their neighbours at the gate. The war seemed a long way away this evening. Not that anyone was under the illusion that it was all over; this was only a temporary lull and everyone knew it. But it was good to feel the evening sun on their faces and watch the sparrows and pigeons preening themselves on the leafy branches of elm and poplar trees.

Nellie enjoyed living in this part of Islington. It wasn't nearly as snooty as some of the boys in the gang used to tell her; she put down their resentment to the divide between North Londoners and those living in the East End, who considered themselves, quite rightly, to be the real London Cockneys. She admired the tall Edwardian houses on either side of the busy Tollington Road. Small back streets led to Seven Sisters Road on her left and the red-brick Shelburne Road School on her right, which was now being used by the Auxiliary Fire Service.

'Tell me about yerself, Hube,' Nellie said brightly as they crossed Hornsey Road.

'Wot yer talkin' about?'

'Tell me about yerself,' Nellie said again. 'You know,

83

about where yer come from, yer mum an' dad an' all that.'

Hubert scratched his head. His stroll was more of a shuffle, and he never once took the fag from his lips. 'I 'ad a mum an' dad once. That I do know.'

'Of course yer 'ave a mum an' dad, yer twerp!' said Nellie. 'Everyone does. Wot I mean is, where are they now?'

''Ow should I know?' replied Hubert, whose fag was now almost burning his lips. 'Down Romford, I reckon. That's where they live.'

'Don't yer ever see them?'

Hubert turned with a start to look at her. 'Wot do I wanna do that for? I don't like 'em. They don't like me.'

Nellie stopped, shook her head, and sighed. 'Yer know, I don't understand boys,' she said. 'None of 'em seem ter get on wiv their folks at 'ome.'

Hubert shrugged his shoulders, pulled the fag butt from his lips and threw it to the pavement. 'Wot's so special about 'ome?' he asked.

Hubert's response bewildered Nellie, and then she asked herself, what *is* so special about home? Well, for one thing it meant being part of a family, your own family, with a mum and dad who cared for you, who took the trouble to talk to you when you were in trouble, who allowed you to be yourself and didn't keep questioning you about where you went and what you did. Home was about love, and being loyal and faithful, and thinking about other people and not just yourself. 'I wouldn't mind one of me own,' she said with a glance at Hubert. 'They say what yer've never 'ad, yer never miss,' she added wistfully. 'Not in my case, it ain't.'

They moved on past the Globe pub where Bessie, the regular tinkler, was already bashing out a favourite song on the old joanna. Although it was only eight o'clock in the evening, the customers were in boisterous mood, belting out a spirited rendering of 'Boiled Beef and Carrots'. Further along the road, Nellie and Hubert stopped for a few moments to watch a team of workmen, stripped to the waist, pulling down the remains of some houses that had recently been devastated by a high-explosive bomb.

'The fing is,' said Hubert, who was lighting up another Woodbine, 'we all 'ave ter make our own way in this life. Take me, fer instance. I'm a square peg in a round 'ole, that's me. I coulda bin workin' down the Ritz if it weren't fer me old man. When I told 'im I couldn't get in the police force 'cos I wasn't tall enough, 'e practically told me I was a liar. An' yer should've 'eard 'im when I said I was goin' ter work as a cook. Called me all the bloody pansies under the sun.' He took a deep drag of his Woodbine and nearly choked. 'So don't talk ter me about 'ome. Ter me, it's all overrated.'

Nellie only half heard what Hubert said, her attention was focused on the workmen. 'Yer know, it's a funny feelin' not knowin' who yer mum an' dad was,' she said, 'or if yer 'ad any bruvvers or sisters or aunts an' uncles. There are times when I feel – empty, as though I've got no stomach. Take the people who lived in those 'ouses over there,' she said, indicating the bomb site. 'I wonder 'ow many of them were families.'

Hubert was concerned that she was getting maudlin about her lack of identity. He moved round to stand in front of her. 'It's not important, Nell, believe me. It's not who yer are that matters, but what yer are.'

Nellie, eyes glazed, appeared to be looking straight through him. 'That's not what Miss Ackroyd says,' she answered.

Hubert scratched his head again. 'Who's Miss Ackroyd?'

Nellie blinked. 'Wot d'yer say, Hube?'

'I said, who's Miss Ackroyd?'

Nellie looked totally nonplussed. 'Who? I don't know wot you're talkin' about.'

Chapter 7

A few days later, Hitler committed what Winston Churchill later described as one of the greatest blunders in history: the Nazi leader invaded Soviet Russia. For the people of London, this meant a continuation of the lull in air raids, as it was obvious that from now on, the Luftwaffe would need to deploy much of their aggressive air power to a second front. And so the pubs were packed again, parks were crowded with people enjoying the hot summer sunshine, and places of entertainment such as cinemas were gradually reverting to their normal opening hours.

The Monday first house performance at the Finsbury Park Empire was full to capacity, not a seat was empty. This was unusual for a first house, for most people didn't get home from work until six o'clock or so, which made getting to a six fifteen first house show almost impossible. But this particular week there was a good reason for the great demand for tickets, for top of the bill was one of the great stand-up comedians of the music hall, the 'Cheeky Chappie' himself, the one and only Max Miller. This ribald entertainer was a star wherever he went, despite the fact that on occasions he had been in trouble with the authorities for his blue jokes and outrageous humour. Nonetheless he was an idol for countless millions of music hall and wireless fans, and an appearance on the Moss Empires circuit meant the clicking of cash tills all over the country. And if a performance by this famous London comedian wasn't enough, the lead supporting act of Monsieur Pierre, 'Illusionist Extraordinaire', made the whole evening irresistible.

Nellie arrived at the theatre before the doors had even opened. The fact that she was able to get there so early was due to Mrs Wiggins who, thrilled to know that Nellie was to be Monsieur's guest at the show, let her off work the moment she had done the three o'clock afternoon tea shift. When she got there, there was an aura of excitement in the foyer, a real buzz that this was not only the start of a new week's shows but the first night of a 'special'.

The moment she got inside, she was thrilled to be given a programme of her own, which had been thoughtfully organised by Monsieur and Madame. Her very own programme! And when the usherette showed her personally to her seat, she felt as though she was Lady Muck herself! Waiting for her in row C, third row centre stalls, were Monsieur and Madame's two sons, Sid and Lenny. Sid, at thirteen, was the older of the two brothers and looked like a carbon copy of his dad, except that he had a mole on his right cheek, just like his mum. Young Lenny was two years younger than his brother, and looked nothing like either his mum or dad. In fact he was quite plain, with a perpetually sulky expression, tight blond curls, small metal-rimmed spectacles, and two large upper front teeth which, according to his brother, made him look like Count Dracula. 'Bet you're lucky to have a famous star for a dad, ain't yer?' was one of the first questions Nellie asked her companions. But as the only response she got was a bored shrug, she decided to look around the theatre and look at her programme until curtain up.

To Nellie, the auditorium of this lovely music hall was truly beautiful to look at. Like the Hackney Empire, where she had seen *Cinderella*, the curtains were scarlet plush and gold, and looked dazzling in the glare of the spotlights. She swivelled round in her seat to look at the upper circle and the gods, where she would have been sitting if she hadn't been given a free ticket. The atmosphere was quite unlike anything she had ever experienced. It was a hot night, and everywhere she looked she could see a mass of faces gazing down towards the stage, all fanning themselves with their programmes, and even in the posh seats in the four boxes bordering each side of the stage, men had removed their jackets and ladies were in short-sleeved summer frocks, wiping their foreheads with their handkerchiefs. Nellie herself, however, was as cool as a cucumber. She was wearing a second-hand cotton summer dress she had bought from a market stall in the Caledonian Road the previous Saturday afternoon. In fact, although the two sons of Monsieur and Madame made it only too obvious that they couldn't care less what their companion for the evening was wearing, Nellie looked radiant with her hair tied behind her head with a piece of blue ribbon, and a thin layer of dark red lipstick which she had picked up from a jumble stall in the same market.

When the lights finally went down, Nellie was in such a high state of excited anticipation, she thought she would never last until the interval before having to go out to the Ladies. But as soon as a bright white spotlight picked out the arrival of the orchestra conductor in his long black tails, bow tie, and white carnation, her worry vanished. Suddenly, the orchestra was playing a riotous overture of 'Here We Are, Here We Are, Here We Are Again!' and as one the whole audience joined in the chorus.

The first half of the show consisted of five acts. Nellie couldn't read, so her programme was only good as a souvenir to cherish, and every time the secondary stage curtains parted, each new act was, for her, a delightful surprise. First came some chorus girls dancing in a line. This made Nellie snigger, for the girls' costumes were very scant and provoked quite a few wolf whistles from some servicemen in the audience, and also Nellie's two young companions. This was followed by a strong lady who tore up telephone directories, a wonderful ventriloquist named Albert Saveen with a saucy but lovable dummy called Daisy, and a crooner who also did impersonations of Arthur Askey, Sir Harry Lauder, and Winston Churchill. But the moment Nellie, and presumably her two companions, had been waiting for finally arrived as a booming voice announced over the theatre's tannoy system, 'And now, ladies and gentlemen, the Finsbury Park Empire is proud to present, straight from his success at the Grand Theatre, Leeds, the irrepressible, the incorrigible, the master of mystery and imagination, the man who can work miracles, the Illusionist Extraordinaire, Monsieur Pierre!'

The theatre erupted in applause and cheers, with Nellie clapping her hands so hard they began to sting. The house lights went out, and as the curtains slowly began to part, a small spotlight picked out what looked like a toy snake which gradually began to rise and waver to and fro towards the audience. It was such a creepy image that Nellie began to sink down into her seat, but she sat bolt upright when, with a clash of cymbals, the snake suddenly vanished and in its place appeared a skeleton! Some of the female members of the audience screamed, including Nellie, but when the lights were suddenly turned up again, the skeleton disappeared, to be replaced by the extraordinary figure of Monsieur Pierre himself. When Nellie had recovered from her shock, she was thrilled to see her friend Monsieur bowing to the audience, who were giving him a rapturous reception. She stared goggle-eyed at the stage setting. Question-mark motifs hung all over the drapes, and different coloured lights flashed on and off, eerily illuminating the upright coffin-like cabinet centre stage. The biggest surprise for Nellie was to see Madame sitting at a grand piano to the side of the stage. She looked so different in her black evening dress, trimmed with black fur round the neck, and her hair neatly permed into tight black curls. When Monsieur started his act, she played music which perfectly matched the mood of the mysterious illusions created by the star.

The act itself lasted almost twenty minutes, and consisted of Monsieur Pierre, with the help of a young female assistant, performing a series of tricks which gave the audience the impression that they were watching something that was not really there at all. Nellie was fascinated by it all, but when she turned to comment on the act to her two companions, both of them were leaning back in their seats, eyes closed, obviously bored, chewing toffees that their dad had managed to get them on the black market.

Monsieur Pierre, immaculate in a one-piece suit of black satin, a green sash draped across his chest, an ultra tall top hat perched on his head, and with his eyes made up with thick pencil lines and mascara to match his black moustache, performed his illusions with flair, panache, and extraordinarily agile movements. He appeared as light and nimble on his feet as a ballet dancer, and his frequent heavily-accented calls of 'See me! I am invincible!' and ''Ere is my miracle!' were made with a theatrical flourish that would have impressed even the most sceptical of onlookers. Once or twice Madame glanced briefly at Nellie in the stalls, which brought a blush to her cheeks because she had the feeling that the whole audience was looking to see who and where she was – which of course they weren't.

Monsieur's *pièce de résistance* was accomplished with the aid of his female assistant, who had spent most of the time with a fixed grin on her face, gesticulating towards the 'Master' as though she herself had performed all the tricks. The final illusion consisted of putting the female assistant inside the upright wooden coffin and making her disappear, to reappear instantly from the wings of the stage. 'Now you zee 'er – now you don't!' proclaimed Monsieur, triumphantly, and with great humour. The audience burst into thunderous applause, which went on for several minutes, before the red plush curtains came down, then opened just wide enough for Monsieur to take a bow. Then he called on Madame and the young assistant, and all three joined hands, took a bow together, then disappeared into the wings.

During the interval, whilst the Safety Curtain came down to allow projected advertisements for local shops and services, Nellie did her best to make conversation with her two companions. 'Wasn't yer dad marvellous!' she enthused as the lights went up.

Sid sat up in his seat and shrugged his shoulders. 'He was OK,' he replied dourly. 'I've seen him before.'

'Lots of times,' chimed in Lenny. It was more or less the first time the two of them had opened their mouths all evening.

'If *I* 'ad a dad like that,' said Nellie, a touch irritated with them, 'I'd be really proud.'

'Yeah, I bet,' sneered Lenny with a smirk. 'Just fink wot 'e could do ter you if 'e put *you* inside that coffin.' He and his brother sniggered.

'Just fink wot *I* could do ter you two if I put *you* in there!' Nellie retaliated.

The two boys stopped sniggering.

'Don't worry,' she added mischievously. 'I'd make sure yer was dead first!'

When the show was over, Nellie, the two boys, and

92

the rest of the audience filed out through the main foyer where the second house crowds were lined up waiting for admittance. For Nellie, the evening had been wonderful, what with seeing Monsieur perform his own act on the stage and then rolling with laughter at Max Miller's dirty jokes at the end of the second half. In fact just being inside the theatre had somehow inspired her; it had such an aura, an atmosphere that was so different from anywhere else. And that persistent pungent smell of sweet perfume and cigarette smoke. It was intoxicating!

Nellie had promised to go backstage to visit Monsieur and Madame after the show. As she accompanied the boys to the stage door, they passed the entrance to the gods where a long queue had formed waiting for entrance and any return tickets.

'Straight in, miss!' called the stage door keeper without even inquiring who she was. It was obvious that he had seen Monsieur and Madame's boys many times, and as she was with them, he had no need to waste time asking questions. 'Dressin' room number two.'

Nellie followed the two boys through the stage door and found herself in a narrow corridor with plain green plaster walls. After going down some stone steps, they turned into another narrow corridor. As they did so, a door opened suddenly, and a man's head peered out.

''Arry!' he yelled. 'Get us a bottle of Guinness, will yer?'

Nellie stopped dead. It was the great man himself, Max Miller.

''Allo, 'allo, 'allo then,' he said, still removing his make-up with a piece of cotton wool smothered in cold cream. 'Back fer some more punishment, eh, lads?'

''Allo, Mr Miller,' the two boys said in unison.

'This gel's wiv us,' groaned Lenny. ''Er name's Nellie.'

'Is it now?' replied Miller. 'Pleased ter meet you, young lady,' he said to Nellie with a nod of the head.

Nellie's mouth dried up, and when she replied it was more of a croak. 'Fank yer, sir,' she said. 'I fawt you was marvellous ternight, sir. I larffed ever so much.'

Max Miller's face lit up. 'Hey!' he said brightly. 'That's really nice of yer ter say so, duckie. Yer must come again – soon.' With that, he returned to his dressing room, where voices inside indicated that he had visitors waiting for him.

Nellie watched him close the door before following the two boys, who had already disappeared into their parents' dressing room further down the corridor.

'Come on in, darlin'!' Monsieur's voice boomed out from inside the dressing room. The door was wide open.

Nellie peered in and saw Monsieur at his dressing table, also removing make-up with cold cream. But when she saw his reflection in the dressing-table mirror, it took her some time to bring the Monsieur she was used to into focus, for his head was bald, with just a fringe of greying hair over his ears and around the lower part of his head. Not that she thought his lack of hair made him any less striking, but his appearance was so different from the well-coiffured look she was used to.

'Come in, Nellie dear! We're just goin' ter 'ave a nice cup of tea.'

Nellie turned her attention to Madame, who had just finished boiling up a kettle of water on a small gas ring in the corner of the room.

'We always 'ave our tea in between first an' second 'ouse,' Madame said with her usual comfortable smile. 'Gives us a chance ter rest an' unwind.'

Nellie smiled back. Sid and Lenny, she noticed, were occupying the only armchair in the room, and were tucking into a plate of cheese and pickle and Spam sandwiches.

'So wot d'yer fink, Nellie?' asked Monsieur, talking to her reflection in the mirror while he continued to remove his make-up. ''Ow d'yer like the act?'

'I fawt yer was t'rrific, sir,' she answered timidly, quite overcome by the strange room she was in, with the blinding lightbulbs round the dressing-table mirror dazzling her eyes. 'Fanks ever so much fer givin' me the ticket.'

'Pleasure, darlin'!' he said, taking a deep drag on an Abdullah fag through his cigarette holder. 'Now yer know 'ow we feater folk really live.'

Yer can say that again! Nellie thought to herself, her eyes watering in the smoke-filled room. She was fascinated by the weird paraphernalia stacked around the place. The room itself was quite small and bare, with plain green distempered walls, but Monsieur and Madame's different costumes draped on hangers on various hooks and the props from the act made everything seem exotic and glamorous. Even the coloured handkerchiefs and the magic lantern Monsieur had used looked as though they were alive, and Madame's black velvet costume and fur collar made her look not only slimmer but also quite mysterious.

'I must say, you were a lovely audience, dear,' Madame said from the washbasin where she was adding water to some powdered milk. 'Very appreciative.'

'You was too slow on the lantern trick,' sniffed Lenny, his mouth stuffed full of Spam sandwich.

'Bull!' snapped Monsieur. He was combing his jet-black wig which was mounted on a stand. 'It was dead on!'

'Lenny's right, Dad,' said Sid, less sourly than his brother. 'The kaleidoscope effect got held up 'cos you was a bit late.'

As usual when her sons criticised the act, Madame intervened. 'I must say,' she said sweetly, only too aware that as the two boys had seen the act so many times, they were picking holes in it, 'I didn't notice it, dear. From where I was sitting, it looked wonderful.'

Such a perfect wife, thought Nellie.

''Ow would *you* know?' snapped Lenny. 'You can't see nuffin' from where *you* sit.'

Nellie felt as though she could have strangled the boy. Both children were clearly spoilt brats, although Sid, the older one, was slightly less objectionable than his brother.

Just then, there was a knock on the door and without being asked to come in, Monsieur's young girl assistant poked her head in. 'Mind if I go an' 'ave a breaver, Albert?' she rasped. She was a brassy looking girl, with long blonde hair piled on top of her head, held down with a gawdy rhinestone coronet. 'Eddie Sparks 'as asked me ter go 'an 'ave a cuppa wiv 'im at the tea stall outside the park gates.'

'Off yer go,' replied Monsieur, who was already applying fresh make-up ready for the second house show. 'Make sure you're back by the 'alf.'

'Righto.'

The girl was about to close the door and go, when Madame called to her. 'Ange, dear, before you go, come an' say 'ello to a friend of ours. Nellie, this is our Ange. She's a foreigner,' she said jokingly. 'From down Streatham way. Ange, this is Nellie.'

Ange, who was still wearing her rather skimpy stage costume, came into the room and offered her hand. 'Pleased ter meet yer.' Her voice was more like a squeak.

'Me too.' Nellie took her hand, which was limp and sweaty, a bit like a wet kipper, she thought. As Ange turned to go, Nellie noticed that her costume was too tight for her; her rather large bum looked, to say the least, somewhat constricted.

'An' put some clothes on,' said Monsieur, watching his assistant's reflection in the mirror. 'You go out like that an' you'll 'ave 'alf the British Army after yer!'

The girl slammed the door behind her as she left.

'I know wot she's after,' growled Lenny, downing a glass of Tizer.

'Don't be rude, Lenny,' said his mum handing Nellie a cup of tea. 'It's none of your business, son.'

'Who cares?' remarked Monsieur. 'As long as she don't get boozed before the 'alf. I don't want 'er fallin' about all over the place.'

'Before the 'alf?' said Nellie, looking puzzled.

''Alf an 'our before the act goes on,' explained Madame. 'We 'ave a lotta funny slang in the feater.'

For the next half hour, Nellie had tea and some sandwiches with Madame while Monsieur drank brown ale, poured from a quart bottle which he kept on one side of his dressing table. For Nellie it was not only a fascinating experience to be in the dressing room of a famous music hall performer, but a comforting feeling to know that she was in the presence of a family, a *real* family. Monsieur and Madame obviously cared for each other and, lousy brats though they were, they cared for their kids too. It sent pangs of longing through Nellie's veins, and maybe because of this, it gave her the feeling that somewhere in her former life she too had been part of a family. For call them what you will – Monsieur Pierre and Madame, or just plain Albert and Doris Beckwith – to Nellie they were a true inspiration.

'Oh, by the way, Doris, me darlin',' said Monsieur from the ensuite toilet where he was washing his hands in the chipped enamel sink, 'after the show ternight, yer'd better go on 'ome wiv the boys. I've got a meetin' wiv Charlie 'Orton.'

Madame turned with a start. 'Oh Albert,' she said, clearly taken by surprise. 'Not ternight. Not the first night.'

Monsieur was now wiping his hands on the towel in the toilet. 'Can't be 'elped, darlin',' he said, sounding apologetic. 'Business is business. Eddie reckons there's a chance of gettin' a spot in the new show at the Palladium. Can't miss out on that.'

Madame looked thoroughly downcast. But she quickly composed herself and smiled bravely. 'It's all right, dear. I quite understand.'

Even though Madame had clearly had to cope with this kind of disappointment before, after such an unblemished happy evening, for Nellie it was a strangely disturbing moment.

By the time Nellie left the Finsbury Park Empire, the second house had already begun. As she passed the gods entrance, she could hear the happy chorus of 'Here we are, here we are, here we are again!' bursting forth from the orchestra pit and auditorium, and even as she made her way beneath the railway arch in Seven Sisters Road, in her mind's eye she could still see the stage and everything that had taken place on it.

As she passed the vast white tiled frontage of the magnificent Astoria Cinema and started to make her way back along Isledon Road towards the hostel, her mind was dominated not by Monsieur Pierre's performance but by Albert and Doris Beckwith and their two young sons. For some inexplicable reason they had focused her attention on something that had been on her mind since she and Hubert had gone for their evening stroll just a few days before. Who *was* Miss Ackroyd? Where did the name come from when she had no recollection of any such person in her life? She wondered if Miss Ackroyd might perhaps be her *own* name. Maybe the memory of her former life was at last beginning to filter back. Perhaps, after all, she hadn't come from that orphanage. Perhaps she did have a family of her own, and the bombing of Barratts' Orphanage that same night was pure coincidence. Suddenly her spirits were raised, and she started to imagine a whole new scenario, a mum and dad of her own, maybe brothers and sisters. From there, she imagined all sorts of things, that the Ackroyd family were probably at that very moment trying to find her, that she was on a missing persons list at the local police station. Or did they believe that she had been blown to pieces by a bomb somewhere? Would they have simply accepted her death as inevitable, in view of her disappearance? Whoever the Ackroyd family were, wherever they were, they must be heartbroken. What should she do? What *could* she do? And once again the answer came to her. Nothing. She would do nothing because the truth scared her. If what she had imagined was not true, how would she ever be able to face up to the future?

As she climbed the stone steps leading to the hostel, one of two terraced houses next door to Beales Restaurant, a light summer drizzle began. She found her keys, opened the front door, and hurried in.

Inside her room, she opened the blackout curtains which she had drawn before she went to the theatre. It was still light outside, but dull and grey, so she decided to go to the sitting room. As she expected, no one was there, which gave her the chance to turn on the wireless in the hope that there was something more than the boring old news bulletin. Unfortunately she had missed *Monday Night at Eight* on the Home Service, and the nine o'clock news had indeed already started. She quickly re-tuned to the forces station and immediately recognised one of her favourite singers, Anne Shelton, who was the main guest on a variety programme called *Northern Music Hall*.

Settling back in a rather austere armchair, she was soon carried away by the sweet sounds of 'You'll Never Know', sung in those characteristic velvet tones that had made Anne Shelton such a popular wartime singer. After a few moments, the door opened and in walked Hubert.

'Wotcha!' he called. 'So 'ow'd it go?'

Nellie turned to look at him. ''Ow'd *what* go?' she asked.

'The Empire, yer nut! Finsbury Park. 'Ow was the show?'

Nellie knew she was no longer going to be able to listen to Anne Shelton, so she got up and switched off the wireless. 'It was smashin'. Specially Monsewer Pierre.'

Although there was no fire in the grate, Hubert went and stood with his back to it, took out one of his dreaded Woodbines, lit up, and started coughing, as usual. 'Wot about old Maxie Miller?' he asked. 'Plenty of dirty jokes, I bet.'

Nellie grinned. 'Oh yes,' she replied.

Hubert waited a moment. 'Well, come on then. Let's 'ear some.'

'Don't be daft,' said Nellie, curling up side-legged on the sofa. 'I can't remember jokes. They all sound the same ter me.'

'Gels!' Hubert spluttered, disappointed. 'Yer miss all the best parts.'

''Ad a good time wiv Mr Beckwiff. An' 'is missus. I really like 'em.' Even as she spoke, Nellie felt a nagging feeling inside. She couldn't exactly understand why, only that she had been concerned by Madame's expression when her husband told her he had to go out on business after the show that night. 'As a matter of fact, they've asked me over ter 'ave tea wiv 'em on Sunday afternoon. They're playin' at Chiswick Empire all next week.'

Hubert flopped down into the armchair that Nellie had just vacated, put his feet up unceremoniously on to a small highly polished coffee table in front of him, leaned his head back, and smoked his cigarette. 'Looks like you're well in there,' he said, again coughing and spluttering. 'Unless they 'ave ter close down the 'alls and picture 'ouses again.'

Nellie turned with a start. 'Close them down again? Why should they?'

'Churchill's warned we might get some more air raids. It was on the six o'clock news. Could be worse than ever.'

'Oh no,' groaned Nellie. 'Not again. I fawt it was all over.'

After a moment's pause, Hubert looked across at her. 'Ever fawt about gettin' out of this place, Nell?' he asked gingerly.

'Wot d'yer mean? Leave Beales?'

'I mean leave London. Go somewhere safe. Out in the country. We could go down Guildford way. That's in Surrey. I 'eard they're lookin' fer staff at this 'otel down there. I could cook, you could do wot you're doin' now.'

Nellie looked puzzled. She wasn't sure she'd heard right. 'Yer mean leave 'ere an' get a job in the country? You an' me, tergevver?'

Hubert looked quite hurt. 'Well, don't make it sound like I'm tryin' ter kidnap yer!' He sat up in the armchair. His feet only barely touched the floor. 'I just fawt yer wouldn't wanna stay 'round 'ere no more if fings start 'ottin' up again.'

Nellie suddenly felt guilty. She had never suspected that Hubert had felt anything for her before, and his consideration for her welfare touched her. 'You're smashin', Hube,' she said, smiling affectionately at him. 'You're probably right. I'd 'ate it if fings did get – well, bad.' Then added, 'I've 'ad enough of this war.'

'Then wot's stoppin' yer?'

Nellie lowered her eyes. 'Instinct,' she said.

Hubert looked slightly embarrassed. He got up and stubbed out his cigarette in the nearest ashtray. 'Just an idea, that's all,' he said, shrugging his shoulders. He made for the door. 'If yer change yer mind . . .' he said brightly as he went.

'Fanks, Hube,' Nellie replied. 'You're the tops.'

'It's nuffin',' said Hubert, opening the door. 'Oh, by the way. Your pal turned up terday. The famous Miss Ackroyd.'

Nellie's eyes widened; she felt a tingling sensation up and down her spine.

'Seems she ain't a ghost after all,' Hubert said with a grin.

Chapter 8

Nellie had never been into Finsbury Park before. Under normal circumstances she would have felt happy at the prospect of a stroll beside the few remaining flower beds and those that had been turned into vegetable allotments to help the war effort. But her reason for being there on such a sunny and warm Tuesday evening filled her with deep apprehension. Who was this Miss Ackroyd who, until the night before, had only been a name which had suddenly sprung to life from out of her subconscious? And why had she agreed to meet her, a woman about whom she knew nothing whatsoever? As she made her way through the main park gates and headed off in the direction of the old boating lake, she knew that her past, which she had so far carefully avoided, was about to catch up with her.

It was now almost six o'clock in the evening, and most of the people there were families enjoying the last few hours of a perfect summer's evening. Nellie's legs felt quite shaky, for they were trying to move faster than she really wanted them to, and when the boating lake finally came into sight, she thought they would collapse beneath her.

There was only another hour or so left before the last of the rowing boats had to be called in, but with the absence of air raids there was a relaxed atmosphere everywhere. People were strolling on the path round the lake or having sparse picnics on the grass verges. Children ran up and down playing tag while their mothers watched and dreamed of the day when their servicemen husbands would be back from the war and able to see their own children growing up.

Which one of all those faces out there was Miss Ackroyd's? Nellie's legs, which now felt like lead, came to a halt, and she slowly looked around, waiting for one of those people to come up to her.

'Hello, Vicky.'

The voice came from behind, but as the name meant nothing to her, Nellie did not turn immediately. When she did, she saw a tall, thin but sturdy woman, and for a split second, no more, she thought she recognised her short auburn hair, large soulful eyes, and gaunt face. But the recognition disappeared as quickly as it came. 'Miss Ackroyd?' she asked timidly.

The woman stretched out her hands. Her face crumpled up, and there were tears in her eyes. 'Oh, Vicky. I knew I'd find you one day. I always knew.' But when she moved forwards to embrace her, Nellie stepped back.

'I don't know who yer are,' she protested. 'Me name's not Vicky.'

Briefly, Ethel Ackroyd looked hurt. But realising that she had moved too quickly, she composed herself, lowered her arms, and remained still. 'Don't you remember me, Vicky? I'm Miss Ackroyd. From Barratts'. From the orphanage.'

Nellie's expression turned to stone.

Ethel waited a moment before continuing. 'I've been searching for you, ever since it happened. That night. That terrible night.' There was pleading in her eyes. 'I never gave up. I never would give up.'

If the truth of her past was gradually unfolding before her, Nellie was still unwilling to acknowledge it. 'I – I don't know wot yer talkin' about,' she said, staring up into Ethel's eyes.

Ethel paused again before answering. 'Will you come and sit with me for a few minutes, and let me tell you?'

They made an odd pair, one tall, the other pint-sized, Ethel in a clean white blouse and dark brown skirt, and Nellie in her Sunday best cotton dress. But when they sat on a bench seat beneath a huge chestnut tree overlooking the lake, they became more equal, both in size and character.

'On the night the orphanage was bombed,' Ethel began, in her soft Yorkshire voice, 'everyone told me you were dead. But I refused to believe them.' She turned to look at Nellie with a warm smile, her eyes still moist. 'I didn't know why. I still don't. It's just something I felt – here.' She placed her hand against her heart. 'You've always been very special to me, Vicky.'

Nellie was puzzled and uneasy.

Ethel smiled reassuringly at her. 'Oh, I know how difficult all this must be for you to take in. But from that first day you were brought to the orphanage, I knew that you were different from the other children.'

Nellie continued to look blank.

'You don't know what I'm talking about, do you?'

Nellie shook her head.

'Don't you remember anything? Anything at all about your time with us at Barratts'?'

Nellie shrugged her shoulders. 'I'm not sure,' she said.

'You were quite a handful. No worse than many of the others really, but you certainly had a mind of your own. A sharp tongue, too. Mrs Hare, our cook, got very cross with you at times. Do you remember Mrs Hare, Vicky?'

'I'm not sure,' she said again.

'I had to take your part against her quite a few times, I can tell you. But I didn't mind. I admired your spirit.'

'Who am I, Miss Ackroyd? I want ter know about me mum an' dad. Where are they? *Who* are they? Why did they put me in an orphanage?'

105

The sudden intensity of Nellie's questions took Ethel aback. Gently taking hold of her hand, she started to tell her all she wanted to know. For the next hour or so, the two of them sat there as the evening sun became more crimson and began to caress the ripple of waves drifting lazily across the lake.

Ethel told Nellie everything about the tragic circumstances of her parents' death, how, soon after she was born, her dad had died in an accident working on a building site, and how her mum had been so distraught that she had thrown herself into the path of an oncoming Tube train.

As she listened, Nellie stared forlornly out at the lake. For a few brief moments, she felt as though she could see two faces reflected in the water out there, the faces of those two tragic people who had brought her into the world. For Nellie, it was a moment of deep despair. It was as though she had entered a long dark tunnel with two other people and emerged alone.

Ethel watched her carefully. She wanted to tell the child that everything was all right, that once she had accepted what had happened to her parents, she would forget all about them. But Ethel knew only too well that it wasn't like that. She had had to tell so many children the awful truth about why they had been put away in an orphanage. It was never easy. It was painful, and always would be. 'I can tell you this much though,' she said softly. 'Your parents would have been very proud of you.'

Nellie's eyes flickered, as though she had just woken up. Then she slowly turned to look at Ethel. 'Proud?'

'You have some remarkable qualities, Vicky. I recognised that even when you were a small child.'

Nellie stared at her in disbelief. 'A few minutes ago yer was tellin' me I was quite an 'andful.'

Ethel smiled at her. 'That's right. But for those who

took the trouble to understand you, you had quite a lot to offer.'

Nellie was puzzled.

'Listen to me, Nellie. There's a lot more to a person than what she knows. It's what she *is* that counts. Yes, it's true, you were a handful. In fact you were a troublemaker. At times I was very angry with you. But for all your worst qualities, there was always something to compensate.' She relaxed her body and leaned back on the bench. 'You know, Vicky, when I was your age, I was a bit like you, a mind of my own, full of myself. I really thought I was the cat's whiskers and that everyone admired whatever I said.' She paused a moment. 'I only learnt the truth about myself as I got older. I discovered that being the centre of attention only turned people away from me. I lost friends, and made enemies.'

Nellie was embarrassed. 'I'm sorry, Miss Ackroyd,' she said. 'I don't know wot this's got ter do wiv me.'

Ethel hesitated before replying. 'You were my friend, Vicky.'

Nellie was lost. 'Me?'

'Whenever I was at my lowest, the one person I could talk to was you. Not the staff, nor the other children, but *you*. Oh, you were pretty hopeless with your school studies, that's why you could hardly read or write. But you had other qualities. You had an instinctive knowledge about people, about their weaknesses, and how they think. You were the only person I knew who could see right through me. Even when you were a child, when you were behaving like a monster, you knew what I was thinking, how I was feeling. You had a way of talking to me, of listening to me. Whenever I was down in the dumps, whether it was about lack of money for the orphanage or something personal, like the way I looked, you were the one who always knew, who always understood. You were also the only one who knew how to hurt me.'

Nellie stared hard at her. 'Hurt you?'

Ethel turned and smiled. 'You once called me an old hag, a spinster who wouldn't know how to find a man if she tried.'

Nellie's face crumpled up and she turned away.

'Oh, you mustn't be upset, Vicky,' said Ethel. 'What you said was true. You were always perceptive enough to know more about me than I ever knew myself. That's why I admired you. That's why I was distraught when I thought I'd lost you.'

For a brief moment, there was silence between them.

Nellie was first to speak. ''Ow did yer manage ter find me?' she asked.

Ethel straightened up and stretched her neck. 'I searched everywhere for you, all over Islington, Hackney, Stoke Newington – everywhere. I finally followed a lead to a pub in Essex Road. They told me there about a gang of evacuees who were living rough out on the streets. I managed to track down one of them.'

Nellie's look was an inquiring one.

'A boy called Martin. Martin Hecht.'

Nellie's eyes widened. 'Toff! You talked ter Toff?'

'It took quite a time to find him. He'd gone back home to his parents in Highgate.' Ethel lowered her eyes as she continued. 'He told me quite a lot about you, and where I could find you.' When she looked up, Nellie was staring hard at her.

'Toff knew I was workin' at Beales?'

'Yes. Apparently his father is a doctor at the Royal Northern Hospital just down the road from the restaurant. You may not have realised it, but you often waited on his table.'

It took Nellie a moment to take this in. Then she looked up suddenly. 'If Toff knew where I was, why didn't 'e come ter see me?' she asked, indignantly.

Ethel briefly lowered her eyes. When she looked up

again, she found Nellie glaring straight at her. 'I gather he felt guilty about some of the things he said when he last saw you. But he seemed very concerned about you, Vicky. That much I do know.'

'Toff concerned about *me*?' Nellie said acidly. 'That's a larff, that is!' Even as she spoke, she thought how false her words sounded. The very mention of Toff's name had sent a longing through her veins. So many nights she had lain awake thinking about him. So many times in her dreams her mind had recalled that special Christmas night when Shortso played 'Always' on his mouth organ while she and Toff smooched around the muddy floor of the old gutted furniture store. Why did the very mention of his name fill her with such longing?

'Martin is a very sensible young man, Vicky,' Ethel said, breaking Nellie's line of thought. 'He said you'd been through a terrible ordeal, and that you needed love and attention.'

Nellie sprang to her feet, crossed her arms, and glared angrily into the water. 'Yeah, well, I don't need 'is advice, fanks all the same!' Now quite agitated without really knowing why, she turned to Ethel and said, almost apologetically, 'Look, Miss Ackroyd, if it's all the same ter you, me name's not – well, wotever it was I used ter be called. I don't want a name that reminds me of the past, especially *my* past. I want ter be the person I am now, the person I'm goin' ter be in the future.'

Ethel waited a moment, then got up and joined Nellie at the water's edge. 'Nellie's a good name. I like it,' she said calmly, and with complete understanding. Still looking into the water, she added, 'I'd like you to come home, Nellie.'

Nellie swung a look at her. ''Ome?' she asked. 'Yer mean go back ter the orphanage?'

'You wouldn't have to stay there for ever. I'm sure

109

we could soon find foster parents for you. A nice family who'd take care of you.'

'I can take care of myself,' Nellie said firmly, avoiding eye contact with Ethel.

'You're only sixteen years old, Vicky.'

'Stop calling me that name!' she snapped. 'Once an' fer all, me name's Nellie!'

Ethel tried to calm her down. 'I'm sorry, Nellie. I'm just worried about you, that's all. You shouldn't have to be fending for yourself at your age.'

'If I'm old enough to work fer me livin', I'm old enough ter fend fer meself.' She stooped down to pick up a chestnut leaf that had fallen from the branch of the tree above them. Without realising what she was doing, she started to pick the leaf to pieces. 'I'm sorry, Miss Ackroyd,' she said guiltily. 'I don't want yer ter think I'm ungrateful, but I've got the right to a life of me own. I don't want ter go back ter the orphanage. I want a 'ome of me own, a mum an' dad, an' a family I can call me own.'

Ethel was becoming desperate. 'But we can help you to do that, Vick— we can help you to do that, Nellie.'

Nellie turned and stared at her. 'I don't want yer ter do that, Miss Ackroyd. I want ter do it meself.' She opened her hand and released the remains of the chestnut leaf.

Ethel realised that she could go no further. After a brief moment of hesitation, she returned to the bench and collected her handbag. 'I'll send along your identity card and ration cards,' she said, trying hard not to sound anxious. 'Now I know where you are, I won't worry so much.' Despite a sinking feeling in her stomach, she tried a weak smile. 'In the next few weeks, the orphanage is moving out into the country. As soon as we get settled, I'll send you the address.' She paused. 'If you ever need help – anything, no matter how big or small – I want you to promise that you'll get in touch with me. Will you do that for me, please, Vicky?'

Nellie resisted the urge to be annoyed at being called by her real name again, and merely nodded her head.

Ethel took just one step towards her and offered her hand. 'Then I won't trouble you any more. From now on, you're on your own, Vicky. Just you and the wide, wide world. As far as everyone else in my world is concerned, you no longer exist.'

Nellie took Ethel's hand and shook it. For a brief moment, she felt a sense of guilt.

Ethel smiled affectionately. She wanted to cry but was determined not to. Then she turned, and started to go. But after a few steps, she stopped and looked back.

'You're a remarkable girl – Nellie,' she said. 'I'll never forget you.' And then she was gone.

Sunday was Monsieur Pierre's favourite day of the week. This was so for many reasons, but most of all because after the end of the second house Saturday show, for at least twenty-four hours he could discard the mystery and panache of his stage persona and revert to his everyday plain and simple Mr Albert Beckwith. Therefore, to Albert, Sunday morning was always known as his 'bliss morning', which meant that he could lie in bed, have tea and two pieces of toast brought up to him by his ever loving wife Doris, and scour the pages of the *Sunday Pictorial* from start to finish. Doris herself had her own way of relaxing. For her, just being at home with her family was bliss enough, and there was nothing she adored more than preparing Sunday lunch which, despite the rationing, always consisted of a roast, followed by baked rice pudding or apple pie (sweetened with saccharin tablets) or just occasionally a nice jam roly-poly. Sid and Lenny also enjoyed Sundays, for by then they had usually finished their homework, which left them free either to go out with their mates around Tufnell Park Road where they lived, or to have them all

111

in to play table tennis in the conservatory at the back of the house.

It had been a triumphant week for Monsieur Pierre at the Finsbury Park Empire. The show had been a complete sell-out and more bookings were coming in for not only the Moss Empires circuit but also other provincial theatres and several one-night stands. After a depressing and unproductive time during the height of the Blitz, things were certainly looking up. But although Sunday in the Beckwith household was always a day of rest, it was also a time to prepare for the next date, which in this case was a week's engagement at the Chiswick Empire in West London, starting the following day.

'Got ter do somefin' about that gel, yer know,' yawned Albert, who had just got up and was still in his patched silk dressing gown, his bald head not yet covered with his toupee, which his two boys invariably referred to as their dad's 'rug'.

'Which gel's that, dear?' asked Doris, who was at the kitchen table, scraping potatoes.

'That little tart, Ange. D'yer know she 'ad the cheek ter ask me fer a raise last night? Bloody nerve.'

As she scraped the new potatoes, Doris's glasses were splashed with water from the saucepan in front of her. 'Well, she's probably right, dear,' she said, peering at Albert over the top of her specs. 'She's been in the act for the best part of a year now. P'raps we ought ter up 'er anuvver 'alf-crown or so.'

Albert nearly had palpitations. ''Alf a crown! Yer expect me ter give that – that little – you expect me ter give 'er anuvver 'alf a crown? She's already on a quid a week! An' fer wot? Fer tartin' round the stage in the altergevver, doin' absolutely bugger all!'

'Watch yer language, Albert!' whispered Doris, turning to look over her shoulder into the conservatory to make sure the two boys hadn't heard. 'Ange only does wot

112

yer ask her. After all, she's only s'posed ter be there ter assist you.'

'Oh yes,' growled Albert as he searched for his packet of Abdullahs in the kitchen dresser drawer. 'Then why does she carry on as though she's the star of the bleedin' act?'

Once again Doris took a sly look over her shoulder into the conservatory. 'You mustn't keep goin' on like that about Ange, dear. She's only young. She means well.'

Albert found his Abdullahs, took one out, and lit it. In the seclusion of his own home, he never used a cigarette holder.

'Is that why you was late last night, dear?' Doris asked suddenly, but casually.

Albert stopped what he was doing but did not turn to look at her. 'Wot d'yer mean?'

'Yer didn't get in till well after one o'clock,' said Doris, still concentrating on the spuds. 'Was it Ange who kept you back? Or Eddie?'

Albert was taken slightly off guard but he managed to keep his composure. 'Actually,' he replied, 'I went fer a drink wiv Max. If yer remember, I told yer I might do. It *was* the end of the run, yer know.'

Even though Albert had his back towards her, Doris looked across at him with an affectionate smile. 'Of course it was, dear,' she said benevolently. 'But I'm surprised you went drinkin' with Max. Let's face it, good ol' Max Miller ain't known fer dippin' inter 'is own pocket, now is 'e?'

Doris chuckled to herself. But Albert was not amused. Well, not entirely.

Nellie had not enjoyed her week. It had started well enough, with her free visit to the Finsbury Park Empire and tea with the famous Monsieur and Madame in their dressing room after the show. But from Tuesday onwards, after her traumatic meeting with Miss Ackroyd in the park, it was downhill all the way. Hubert was the first to notice it. He always knew when Nellie was down in the dumps because she virtually dried up and didn't talk to him more than she had to. And since Tuesday, she had gone off to her room after work each afternoon and hardly emerged until breakfast the following morning.

Nellie had indeed spent a great deal of time in her own room. She had a lot on her mind, so much to think about and churn over. An orphan, no mum or dad, no family, no one she could call her own . . . She kept telling herself that she wished she'd never been told about her former life. Why couldn't she go on living a lie? Why couldn't she just go on being Nellie and never know one lousy thing about a person called Vicky? Each night, as she lay in bed in the dark, staring up into a void, she tried desperately hard to cry but somehow the tears just wouldn't come despite the fact that she couldn't stop feeling sorry for herself. The crunch came on Saturday evening. It happened quite suddenly when, after hours of lying around doing nothing all day, she felt a strong urge to visit a certain place that she had not been to for some time.

The interior of St Mary Magdalene's Church in Bedale Street looked much the same as the last time Nellie had been there, shortly after the bombing of the orphanage. The only difference now was that it was not biting cold, for it was a summer's evening, and there were several people there, some of them kneeling in prayer in the pews, one or two waiting outside the confessional box in the side aisle.

Nellie entered quietly through the main entrance which was wide open. But before she could get inside, she had to pull back a large curtain which was hanging in front of the doors, screening off the interior of the church from the street outside.

The first thing she noticed was the intense feeling of

peace, for although there was a hum of worshippers quietly saying the rosary or offering up prayers to the statue of Mother Mary just in front of the first row of pews, the air seemed so pure and untarnished. For a moment Nellie felt as though she was intruding, especially when an elderly woman, accompanied by what looked like her young grandson, turned round to glance at her. But when the woman gave her a warm smile, she felt reassured.

She made her way silently to a pew near the back of the church. It was the same pew where she had sought refuge the night she had strayed into the building more dead than alive. She had no intention of doing what everyone else was doing, for she had never prayed before, and even the idea embarrassed her. So she just sat there, hardly moving, staring straight ahead at the altar, which seemed miles away. Then she closed her eyes. Alone now with her thoughts, she began to see herself, on that night, that horrifying night, her face and arms bruised, feet lacerated, blood seeping out of the deep cut in her leg. She could see herself stretched out on the same bench she was sitting on now. But what she saw more clearly than anything was that she was alive – bruised, cut, dazed, but alive. And then she could see Rats and Bonkers – and Toff. There they were, standing over her, whispering, peering down at her anxiously. She could almost hear Rats' voice: 'She's a gel. We don't 'ave no gels wiv us!' The image brought a smile to Nellie's face. She was alive! Nothing in the whole wide world could change that. She was alive! And her whole life was ahead of her.

Her eyes were still closed as tears gradually began to trickle down her cheeks.

Tufnell Park Road was quite an affluent part of Holloway. It was a fairly wide, long side road leading off the main Holloway Road, and the terraced Edwardian houses in it were three or four storeys high. Even though some people in the adjoining streets thought there was a certain air of 'kippers and curtains' about the place, there was no doubt that quite a few of the residents there were not short of a bob or two.

It took Nellie only a few minutes to reach number 147A, for Tufnell Park Road was a short walk from Beales Restaurant and her hostel. It was a good walk, because that's how Nellie felt. The traumas of the past few days had given way to a new determination to get on with her life, and see what she could make of it. That's why she was really looking forward to having tea at the home of Monsieur and Madame.

'Oh, we're just a couple of silly ol' Cockneys who've struck lucky in the world,' said Madame, soon after she had shown Nellie into the front room.

'Not so lucky!' protested Monsieur as he joined them. 'We've 'ad ter work darn 'ard fer our livin'.'

The moment Monsieur entered the room, Nellie was immediately in awe of him. He was wearing his toupee and after a hearty Sunday roast followed by an hour's nap, he was as bright as ever, looking very dapper in his casual cream-coloured trousers, striped short-sleeved summer shirt, and a green polka-dot cravat. As ever, Madame had not tried to compete, but she did look rather pretty in a simple pale blue cotton dress cut just below the knees.

Nellie adored the front room, for it was so unusual. A huge aspidistra plant was climbing up as far as it could in front of the lace window curtains, and there seemed to be masses of ornaments scattered all over the room – snuff boxes, a little Dutch china boy and girl in traditional clothes, and lots of novel items such as a miniature brass theatre programme cover, inscribed 'Theatre Royal, Drury Lane'. The furniture was very ornate, and it seemed to Nellie to be more for show than for practical use. The floor of the room was covered with a multi-coloured Persian carpet which was just beginning to show its age. Nellie was particularly fascinated by the array of framed photographs adorning the walls. It seemed that every space had been taken up with portraits of famous music hall entertainers, some of them signed. It was a wonderful gallery of Monsieur and Madame's fellow artistes and friends, and to Nellie at least a sign that this house was quite unlike any other in Tufnell Park Road.

Monsieur and Madame told Nellie stories about their travels around the country and their performances in places like Huddersfield, Bristol, Birmingham, Manchester, Liverpool, Leeds, Sunderland, and even as far away as Glasgow and Aberdeen in Scotland. They brought out some scrapbooks of the different shows they had been in, leaving Nellie quite overwhelmed with the sheer magic of it all.

It was not until they sat down to tea that Nellie was persuaded by her hosts to talk a bit about herself. 'Nuffin' much ter tell really,' she said lightly. She was far more interested in the kitchen where they were having tea, for it was so well equipped, with a beautiful gas cooker, a large oak dresser, and a round table which had been set with a lovely blue lace tablecloth and a china tea set that Nellie thought must have cost a bomb.

'Come on now, Nellie dear,' insisted Madame. 'Tell us about yer mum and dad. 'Ow many bruvvers an' sisters 'ave yer got?'

''Ope ter Gawd they ain't as bad as our pair!' growled Monsieur, glaring at Sid and Lenny who were sitting opposite Nellie at the table and who hadn't waited to be asked before pouncing on the fish paste sandwiches.

'Ain't got no mum, nor dad,' Nellie finally admitted. Somehow she felt less self-conscious about saying it than she had expected.

Monsieur and Madame exchanged looks.

'No mum or dad?' said Madame.

117

'Nor bruvvers or sisters,' added Nellie. 'I was the only one. Me mum and dad died soon after I was born. I lived in an orphanage up New Norf Road.'

For a moment there was a shocked silence apart from the sound of munching coming from the two boys.

It was eventually Madame who spoke. 'I'm so sorry, dear,' she said with the utmost sincerity. 'Wot a terrible fing, not 'avin' people of yer own ter care for yer.'

Nellie shrugged her shoulders. 'Just one of those fings.'

'Are yer sure they din't kick yer out or nuffin'?' quipped Lenny.

'Lenny!' snapped his mum. 'Don't say fings like that!'

Nellie took no notice of the boy, merely pulled a face at him and replied, 'No. They din't kick me out. The only person who could do that was 'Itler.'

Again, Madame and Monsieur exchanged a glance.

Nellie realised that it was better for her to tell the whole story, and so during much of teatime that is what she did.

Monsieur and Madame listened with rapt attention, interrupting every so often to ask questions about how she had managed to survive on the bombed streets, and with such a bunch of juvenile delinquents. Nellie found herself constantly defending her old mates, despite the fact that they had never really accepted her as one of their own. Even Sid and Lenny were quiet throughout; at times they seemed almost inspired by the sheer adventure of it all.

When Nellie had finished telling all she could tell, Madame asked her about the future. 'Surely yer can't go on living in one room in an 'ostel for the rest of your life,' she said. 'It ain't natural.'

Nellie shrugged. 'I'll stay there till the war's over. Then I'll look around for somefin' more permanent.'

When tea was over, Nellie and the family sat out in the garden. It wasn't a very big garden, for the Anderson shelter took up quite a bit of it, but it was more than Nellie had ever experienced and she felt very grand lounging back in a striped canvas deck chair, staring up into the evening sky as the light gradually faded. For a time, she and Monsieur played darts with the two boys, who cheated like mad and created a fuss every time their dart missed its target. When both of them had gone to bed, the three adults stayed outside, watching day turn to night, and the sky gradually filling with a galaxy of bright, shining stars. It wasn't long before Nellie could smell the pungent aroma of Monsieur's Abdullah cigarette. Because of the blackout, she couldn't see either him or his wife, but she could feel their presence so much.

'Yer know,' came Madame's voice in the dark, close by, 'I don't know 'ow I could 'ave coped if I'd bin in your shoes. Sometimes I don't fink we realise 'ow lucky we are. Wot say you, Albert?'

Monsieur didn't answer immediately. But Nellie heard him inhale, then blow out a lungful of smoke. 'Everybody should 'ave someone in this world,' he said in a solemn voice, which was rare for him. 'Sometimes life can be bleedin' unfair.'

On the garden wall, two moggies were locked in mortal combat, growling and hissing and claiming every inch of territory for themselves.

'D'yer ever get lonely, Nellie?' Madame asked, quite out of the blue.

Nellie thought about it for a moment. Strangely enough, the worst pangs of loneliness she had had for a long time had been during tea at the kitchen table. Watching the family together had only made her realise how much she had missed out on. 'Sometimes,' she replied. 'But then I reckon most people do from time ter time.'

There was a long pause. The two moggies finally gave up the struggle and went their separate ways.

'Yer know, Nellie,' Madame said, 'I know I ain't yer

mum, and never could be, but if – just *if* yer ever need someone, well, someone ter talk to, I'm never really far away, yer know.'

In the dark, Nellie felt Madame's hand take hers and squeeze it.

'Wot I mean is,' Madame continued, 'I've always wanted a daughter of me own. Someone ter talk to, ter listen to. That's somefin' I've never 'ad. D'yer know wot I mean, Nellie?'

'Let's not beat about the bush,' came Monsieur's crisp East End voice. 'Wot she means, wot we boaf mean is, when yer want a 'ome ter come to, yer've got one – right 'ere.'

Chapter 9

The summer of 1941 was a glorious time for Nellie. The evenings were long and hot, and apart from an occasional Luftwaffe intruder, the lull in the air raids continued.

Nellie had come to enjoy living in the Holloway part of Islington. Although it was quite a busy area, sometimes it seemed like a village. As well as her regulars in the restaurant, she got to know all sorts of people in the shops, they were so friendly and full of good humour. Sometimes she and Hubert would go to the pictures, for there were at least five cinemas within walking distance, and other times they would just stroll for miles, exploring the maze of little back streets behind Holloway Road all the way up to Archway in one direction, or to Camden Town in another, or up to Highbury Corner and the Angel. And when they went on bus rides, there was always something new to discover. On August Bank Holiday Monday, they even went on a number 14 bus to Piccadilly Circus and strolled around the West End. For Nellie it was a wonderful experience, for although she was disappointed to find that the statue of Eros had been removed to a safe place for the duration of the war, she had the chance to see Nelson's Column in Trafalgar Square for the first time in her life, and feed the flocks of pigeons there. When she and Hubert passed the National Gallery on the north side of the square, Nellie was amazed to see so many people queuing up to get inside for a lunchtime piano recital given by someone called Myra Hess. Despite the war, everyone was doing their best to go about their lives in as normal a way as they could.

On 14 September, Nellie was surprised to receive a birthday card from Miss Ackroyd, which told her she was seventeen years old that day. So, for a special treat, Hubert took her 'up West' to see a musical revue at the London Palladium. The star was a comedian called Tommy Trinder who brought the house down with his hilarious routines, and the show itself was a dazzling spectacle. The Palladium was a much bigger place than the Finsbury Park Empire, but being inside a theatre once again made Nellie think of Monsieur and Madame, whom she had not seen since they went off to fulfil a series of engagements in the provinces.

Over the previous few weeks, Hubert had become a really close friend of Nellie's. She found him good company, for they spoke the same language and both loved a good gossip about people. They spent most of their spare time together. It helped that Hubert was physically the same height as Nellie; she frequently had to use her finger to lift stray strands of his straight brown hair out of his eyes. Of course he smoked too much, chain-smoked in fact, and it worried her that he often burst into uncontrollable fits of coughing. Hubert was becoming an important part of her life, so much so that she began to rely on him. And it was not long before that, too, started to worry her. It was her fault, not his, for Hubert was just as independent as she was and never showed that he was in the least romantically inclined towards her. Nonetheless, she felt the time had come to start looking for other friends.

The opportunity came one Saturday afternoon when she was in Saville's Record Shop in Holloway Road, sorting through some of the latest gramophone records. As usual there were plenty of teenagers in the booths, listening to a variety of songs such as Bing Crosby and the Andrews Sisters singing 'Don't Fence Me In', and Glenn Miller and his Band playing 'Little Brown Jug'. In the next booth to where Nellie was trying to listen to the latest hit record of Spike Jones and his City Slickers, there was a boy listening to an orchestra playing some noisy classical music which he was pretending to conduct. This really irritated Nellie, so she banged on the window and mimed to him to turn the sound down. The boy shrugged his shoulders and ignored her. Furious, she took off her own record, marched straight into his booth, and turned off the gramophone he was using.

'Wot's up wiv you, mate?' Nellie snarled. 'You deaf or somefink?'

The boy, who looked about a year older than Nellie, looked astounded. 'Here!' he gasped, in a faintly Irish accent. 'What the hell d'yer think you're doin'!'

'I can't 'ear myself breave in there!' snapped Nellie. 'There's me tryin' ter listen ter Spike Jones, an' all I can 'ear is that muck!'

The boy crossed his arms angrily and glared at her. 'That is not muck! It happens ter be Rachmaninoff!'

'Well, 'e's too loud, whoever 'e is. So just turn 'im down, or else!'

'Or else?' The boy put his hands on his hips defiantly. 'Or else *what*, may I ask?'

'Or else I'll break the bleedin' record over yer bleedin' 'ead!' Nellie shouted.

The angry exchange was causing the other customers in the shop to stare at them. Nellie was aware of this, so she quickly strode back to her own booth and put on her Spike Jones record again, this time turning it up full blast.

In the next booth, the boy glared at her, put on his record, and also turned up the volume.

The combination of Spike Jones and Rachmaninoff's second piano concerto was formidable, and half the customers in the shop left.

Eventually, the challenge was too much for Nellie, so once again she flung open the door of her booth and went next door, where the boy was waiting for her.

''Scuse me!' called a voice from behind.

Nellie turned, to find the harassed middle-aged shop-keeper glaring at her. 'In't it about time you two lovebirds kissed an' made up?' he asked.

The wail of the air-raid siren was totally unexpected. It had only been heard a few times since the disastrous raid on London on the night of 10 May, and nobody seemed to be prepared.

Nellie was fast asleep in bed. At first she thought she was dreaming the sound, but when her eyes sprang open in the dark and the siren's wail continued, she leapt out of bed and rushed to the window. She pulled back the blackout curtain and looked out.

In Tollington Road below, she could see people rushing to and fro all over the place. ARP wardens were hurrying to their post in nearby Shelburne Road School, and several families were emerging from Hertslet Road just round the corner, some of them still wearing their night clothes under their coats, making for the nearest air-raid shelter alongside the Savoy Cinema in Loraine Road.

Nellie was still at the window when the siren stopped wailing. She quickly got dressed and rushed along the passage to knock up Hubert. She thumped on the door and called out, 'Hube! Are yer in there, Hube? We've got ter get ter the shelter!' There was no response. In desperation, she tried the door handle. To her surprise, the door opened.

'Hube?' she called again. 'Are yer in 'ere, Hube?'

As she peered inside, the first thing she heard was someone groaning. The blackout curtains had not been drawn, and by the light of the full moon she saw Hubert stretched out face down on the floor.

'Hube!' she cried in alarm. Quickly crouching down beside him, she tried to turn him over. But he was a dead weight, and almost impossible to move. He also stank of booze. 'Hube!' she cried again. 'Wot's 'appened to yer? Wot 'ave yer bin up ter, yer stupid twerp!'

Hubert's only response was to groan again.

At that moment came the first salvo of anti-aircraft gunfire. The whole house shook.

'Hube!' Nellie tried to shake some life into him, but it was no good. Desperate, she looked around the room for something she could use to sober him up. She spotted a jug of water on the washstand. She rushed across, lifted it out of the china basin and struggled back to Hubert with it. Without another thought, she poured the water over his head.

There was an almighty explosion somewhere outside, which shook the very foundations of the place. Nellie leapt up with a loud yell and dropped the water jug.

'Hube!' she yelled, again crouching down and trying to help him up. 'We've got ter get out of 'ere! There's an air raid. We've got ter get ter the shelter.'

To her relief, Hubert stirred, and turned over. 'W-wot's goin' on?' he groaned, slurring his words. 'Wot's g-goin' on?'

'Give me yer arm,' yelled Nellie over the sound of ack-ack fire and emergency service bells clanging out along Holloway Road outside. ''Ang on ter me!'

Hubert put his arm round Nellie's neck and with her help managed to get to his feet. But he was very wobbly, and he had to grab on to her to keep his balance.

''Old on!' she said. But even as she spoke, he collapsed on to the floor again.

Nellie knew there was no way she could get him to the shelter. The next best thing was to try to get him and herself under the bed. She grabbed hold of his arm and using all her strength started pulling. 'Come

125

on now, Hube!' she yelled. 'Give us a bit of 'elp, fer Gawd's sake!'

Hubert groaned again and tried to lever himself out of the pool of water he was lying in and along the floor. It was a slow, laborious process.

With the sound of enemy aircraft droning overhead, ack-ack gunfire intensifying outside, and the emergency services racing along both Holloway and Tollington Roads outside, Nellie finally succeeded in getting Hubert under his own bed. There was barely enough room for them under there, but Nellie was convinced that this was their best chance of shelter.

It was almost daybreak when the siren sounded the All Clear. By that time, both Hubert and Nellie, still wedged hard under the bed, were fast asleep.

Luckily, the Saturday night air raid was not as serious as it had seemed while it was taking place. The explosion that had shaken the entire area turned out to be a magnesium bomb which had come down somewhere around Manor House, more than a mile away, and the majority of damage elsewhere was superficial, mainly caused by jagged fragments of anti-aircraft shells. But there was no denying that the sudden attack had caused great alarm around Holloway and beyond, and many people feared that this might be the start of a new Blitz.

When Nellie opened her eyes on Sunday morning, the room was flooded with bright sunlight. Her entire body ached, for she was still wedged under Hubert's bed, and her feet were prickling with pins and needles. 'Fanks fer nuffin', Hube!' she groaned, turning over and trying to pull herself out from under the bed. But when she looked, Hubert had already gone.

By the time she had managed to stand up, the door opened and in walked Hubert, carrying two cups of tea.

''Ere yer go then, Nell,' he said rather sheepishly.

'Somefin' ter wet yer whistle wiv. Sorry fer last night. Must've mixed me drinks or somefin'. Reckon I owe yer one, eh?'

Nellie rubbed her eyes, then glared at him. ''Onestly, Hube,' she croaked hoarsely, 'wot d'yer fink yer was up ter? Yer was boozed out of yer mind!'

Hubert went to his bed, sat on the edge of it, and put his cup and saucer down on the small bedside cabinet. 'I went round the corner, ter the Eaglet,' he said, taking out a fag. 'There was this darts match. Din't know no one, but I got dragged in.'

'Sounds like it,' said Nellie, propping herself on the windowsill, sipping her tea. 'When did you start boozin' then? I've never seen yer sloshed before.'

Hubert lit up his Woodbine and spoke through the smoke. 'Just one of those fings,' he replied.

Nellie shook her head disapprovingly. 'Yeah, well, you're lucky we din't get our 'eads blown off. Did yer 'ear that racket goin' on last night?'

'Din't 'ear nuffink,' Hubert replied, adding, 'You was a brick, Nell. I don't know wot I'd 'ave done wivout yer.'

Nellie shrugged her shoulders. She didn't mind Hubert having a drink if he wanted one. After all, he worked damned hard in that kitchen from Monday to Saturday. But she was curious about his odd behaviour over the last week or so. She had always accepted that Hubert was a very self-contained individual who seemed to have no hobbies except smoking Woodbines and reading kids' comics and the sports pages of the newspapers. But just lately he had been more withdrawn than ever, keeping himself to himself, and going out on his own in the evening.

'By the way,' Hubert said, after taking a mouthful of tea without exhaling the smoke he had just inhaled, 'did I tell yer I've given in me notice?'

'Wot!' gasped Nellie.

'Remember the job down at that 'otel I told yer about? The one near Guildford. I've decided ter take it.'

Nellie took a moment before answering. 'Hube,' she said, suddenly feeling all let down inside, 'why din't yer tell me?'

'I did ask you ter come wiv me. Remember?'

'Yeah, I know, but,' she took a quick gulp of tea to steady her nerves, 'why all the rush? Yer din't mention anyfin' about it durin' the week.'

Hubert drew hard on his fag. 'Once yer've made up yer mind ter do somefin', I say yer should get on wiv it.'

Nellie noticed that he seemed to be addressing the floor rather than her. She went across to him. 'Hube, I don't understand. I fawt yer liked it 'ere. A room of yer own, free grub . . .'

'Well, I don't!' he snapped, suddenly springing up from the bed and moving away from her. 'Anyway, why d'yer 'ave ter keep askin' me questions? If you like it 'ere, that's OK by me, but just stop askin' me questions all the time. Right?'

Nellie was taken aback. 'Right.' Her reply was more startled than angry. She put down her cup and went to the door. 'Fanks fer the tea,' she said and quietly left the room.

Later on in the morning Nellie heard a rumpus. She was spread out on a tiny patch of grass in the hostel's small back yard, alone, but only too aware that every so often Hubert was taking crafty looks at her from his bedroom window on the first floor. After the scene she had endured no more than an hour before with him, her mind was racing. Why had he spoken to her like that? What had she done to offend him? Did this mean that they were no longer friends? She was deeply depressed by it all. But most of all, she was bewildered by the fact that he was leaving his job at Beales at such short notice.

The rumpus in the next-door back yard of the restaurant suddenly snapped her out of her soul-searching. There were men's voices, voices she hadn't heard before, the sound of dustbins being moved around, then a door opening and closing. Since the restaurant wasn't open on a Sunday, Nellie was intrigued and worried, so she got up, went back into the house, and made her way quickly to the street outside.

She was shocked to see a police car parked in Tollington Road near the front entrance of the restaurant, and when she went to investigate, she found the front door wide open. She went inside to see what was going on.

'It's all right, dear,' a voice called the moment Nellie entered the dining room. It was Sarah Wiggins, the supervisor. With her was a uniformed policeman. 'There's been a little – problem,' she said rather cagily as she came across to Nellie. 'There's nothing for you to worry about.'

On the other side of the dining room, Nellie could see two of the kitchen girls talking to a second policeman. They were Molly Clarke and Brenda Kitson, both of whom lived in the hostel accommodation next door, but whom Nellie rarely saw. They looked fraught and anxious. 'Wot's 'appened?' Nellie asked. 'Wot're the rozzers doin' 'ere?'

Mrs Wiggins sighed deeply. 'Somebody got into my office last night, Nellie,' she replied, voice low. 'They broke into the safe and took last week's takings.' She shook her head despairingly. 'I blame myself,' she said. 'I should have banked it all on Friday. It was so careless of me.'

Nellie looked around. 'But 'ow did they get in? They must've done it durin' the air raid last night.'

'No, Nellie,' Mrs Wiggins said, slowly shaking her head. 'Nobody broke in.'

Nellie was puzzled.

Mrs Wiggins sighed. 'The police think it's an inside job.'

The Savoy Cinema in Holloway Road was not the most attractive cinema, but at least it was brand new. It had opened only the year before, in February 1940, at the height of the 'phoney war', that strange period when the idea of air raids seemed nothing more than bluff. However, it did not arrive without controversy, for to accommodate it, part of Jones Brothers department store had had to be demolished. Nellie quite liked the place because it was just a few minutes' walk from the hostel, and the pastel colour of the interior made her feel that she was in very contemporary surroundings. This being Sunday, there were just two separate performances, afternoon and evening. After the drama of the day's events, it had come as a bit of a godsend for Nellie when Brenda and Molly, the two kitchen girls from the restaurant, asked her to accompany them to the afternoon show.

Today's film was showing Peter Lorre as the notorious Japanese detective Mr Moto, but as Brenda and Molly chatted incessantly, Nellie feared she would not be hearing very much of Peter Lorre's performance.

'So what did they ask you, Nell?' Brenda was quite a pretty girl, with lovely blue eyes and light blonde hair that was permed into tight curls. But her voice was so high-pitched, Nellie felt the whole audience could hear her. 'The two flatfoots. Did they ask yer where you were last night an' all that?'

Nellie had to lean forward to reply, because Brenda was sitting on the other side of Molly, to her right. 'I just told 'em I was back at the 'ostel, listenin' ter the wireless.'

'Bet they asked yer wot the programmes were,' said Molly.

'I remembered most of them,' replied Nellie, her voice

130

much lower than her two companions'. '*In Town Ternight*, *Music 'All*, then *Saturday Night Feater*. Wot about you two?'

'We was at the dance down the Irish Club,' said Brenda.

'Din't get back till after midnight,' sniggered Molly, which sent both her and Molly into hoots of laughter.

Nellie was glad she wasn't sitting between them. ''Ow much did they take from the safe then?' she asked. 'Anyone know?'

'That younger flattie told me it was over forty quid,' squeaked Brenda, leaning forward to answer Nellie.

'That ought ter buy someone a few bottles of gin on the black market!' sniggered Molly.

Once again both girls burst into laughter.

Nellie was relieved when the house lights began to dim and the beautiful new cream-coloured stage curtains curled up to give way to Pathé News.

The news was all about the meeting at sea between Winston Churchill and President Roosevelt the previous month, and then lots of awful newsreel film of the war between Russia and Finland. Nellie couldn't bear to watch the screen; news about the war was something she never wanted to hear or see. In any case, her mind was still on the break-in. What did Mrs Wiggins mean about it being an 'inside job'? Did she mean a member of the staff? And if so, who did they suspect? If the burglary took place during the evening, as the flatties said it did, then she knew for a fact that, apart from herself, all the staff staying in the hostel had gone out for the night. If it was a member of the staff who'd nicked the forty quid, they must've been either pretty desperate or boozed half out of their mind. Then she remembered Hubert, stretched out blind drunk on the floor of his bedroom.

The crowing cockerel brought Pathé News to an end. When the house lights went up again, Brenda and Molly were surprised to see Nellie sitting bolt upright in her seat, her face ashen, eyes staring in a cold fix.

'Nell!' said Molly anxiously. 'Is anyfin' wrong?'

Nellie turned quickly to look at both her companions. 'Did they mention anybody?' she asked breathlessly. 'Did they mention a name?'

Molly and Brenda exchanged a puzzled look.

'Did *who* mention a name?' asked Brenda.

'Wot yer talkin' about, Nell?' asked Molly.

Without saying another word, Nellie sprang up from her seat and started to leave.

'Nell!' called Brenda.

'Wot's wrong, Nell?' called Molly. 'Come back!'

As the house lights started to dim again, Nellie had already pushed her way past the irritated people sitting in the same row and was heading for the exit.

Although she had only been inside the picture house for less than an hour, Nellie had to adjust to the bright sunlight as she came out. As the feature film hadn't yet started, there were still a few people filing in, and when she pushed her way through them, there were some angry calls of, 'Wot's yer 'urry, mate!'

Nellie's feet couldn't carry her fast enough. She ran all the way along the Holloway Road, straight past Jones Brothers, and in a few minutes she was within sight of Beales. At once, her worst fears were realised.

The police car that she had seen earlier in the day was now parked directly outside the front door of the staff hostel, and before she reached it she caught a glimpse of someone being led down the outside steps of the hostel, accompanied by two grim-faced policemen. 'Hube!' she yelled from the other side of Tollington Road.

Hubert, arms held firmly by the two officers, paused briefly and looked across the road towards Nellie. But before Nellie could reach him, he was quickly hustled into the car.

'Hube!' she yelled again, almost walking straight under a motorbike as it rushed past to beat the traffic lights.

But the police car was already on its way along Tollington Road, making for Hornsey Road Police Station. As it went, Hubert, wedged in the back seat between the two policemen, turned half-heartedly and Nellie caught a glimpse of his face before the vehicle disappeared round the corner of Hertslet Road.

Nellie, distraught, stood helplessly on the pavement. She couldn't believe it. She couldn't believe that Hubert, ordinary, harmless Hubert, was a thief.

'There's nothing we can do now, my dear.'

Nellie turned, to see Mrs Wiggins standing just behind her. She looked crushed and miserable.

'Wot're they doin'?' Nellie croaked, her voice breaking. 'They can't take Hube! They can't!'

'There's nothing we can do for Hubert now, Nellie,' replied Mrs Wiggins. 'He's been a foolish young man.'

'But 'e din't do nuffin'!' she insisted. ''E couldn't've done. Hube's a good, kind, 'onest person. 'E wouldn't nick nuffin' from nobody! It's a lie! I tell yer, it's a lie.' She went right up to Mrs Wiggins and said defiantly, 'If they try ter pin it on Hube, I'll tell 'em 'e was wiv me all night. I will! I swear ter God I will!'

Mrs Wiggins shook her head slowly, then took hold of both Nellie's hands. 'You can't do that, Nellie. It would be wrong. You see, this is not the first time. Hubert's been in trouble before.'

Chapter 10

November was Monsieur Pierre's least favourite month of the year. The early winter mists played havoc with his bronchitis and it was also generally a rest month in the music hall before the onslaught of the Christmas panto season. Madame, however, rather enjoyed the respite, for it gave her the chance to catch up with all the household jobs she was unable to do while they were on tour, and also to be with Sid and Lenny who had to spend most of their schooldays staying with their grandparents in Hilldrop Crescent. But during this period, at least one of their regular treats remained untarnished: the daily morning trip to Beales Restaurant.

The place was quite full when they got there, which was just the way Monsieur liked it because there was always the chance that someone would recognise him and ask him for his autograph. For Madame, it was the smell of bread baking in the kitchen ovens and the heady aroma of Camp coffee that immediately made her feel at home.

'Mornin', sir! Mornin', madam! Can I take yer order, please?'

Monsieur and Madame turned with a start. The voice was unfamiliar. So was the face.

'Mornin', me dear,' replied Monsieur, both hands balanced on the top of his cane. 'An' where's Nellie terday?'

'Who, sir?' asked the girl, who was so young, she seemed hardly out of school. 'Oh, Nell. Nell's gone, sir.'

'Gone?' asked a surprised Madame.

'Yes, madam. She left a few weeks ago.'

Monsieur and Madame swung a startled look at each other.

After a moment's pause, Monsieur spoke. 'Young lady, be so good as ter ask your supervisor if she can spare me a moment of 'er time.'

The girl looked puzzled, and wondered if she'd done anything wrong. 'Very good, sir,' she said, and scuttled back to the kitchen.

Mrs Wiggins was already coming out of the kitchen, and making her way straight to Monsieur and Madame's table. 'Mr Beckwith. Mrs Beckwith.' She had a broad, welcoming smile on her face. 'How good to see you again. I do hope you had a successful tour.'

'Extremely so, fank yer, Mrs Wiggins,' replied Monsieur, nodding his head graciously.

Madame leaned forward, and with lowered voice asked, 'Wot's 'appened to our young Nellie?'

Mrs Wiggins' expression changed and she sighed before she answered. 'Yes, it's very sad, isn't it? She left us, I'm afraid. A few weeks back. We had – some problems here, and she decided, well, she didn't want to stay on.'

'Problems?' asked Monsieur suspiciously. 'What sorta problems?'

Madame lowered her voice even more. 'You didn't – I mean, she wasn't—'

'Oh no,' replied Mrs Wiggins immediately. 'Nellie was a lovely girl, very hard-working and conscientious.' Aware that some of the other customers were looking at her, she leaned closer to Madame. 'It was her own decision. I'm sure you'll understand that I can't really say any more than that. Staff matters are always confidential.'

Once again, Monsieur and Madame exchanged a

glance. Beales' homely atmosphere suddenly seemed less homely.

''Ave yer any idea where Nellie's gone?' asked Madame anxiously.

'I did hear that she's taken a cleaning job. A dentist's surgery up by Archway, I believe. It seems such a waste. Nellie's far too intelligent to be doing that kind of work.'

Soon after eight o'clock in the morning, Nellie drew back the blackout curtains. The nights were getting longer now and, like everyone else in war-weary London, she found it depressing to have to observe the strict blackout restrictions from five thirty in the evening to eight in the morning. She had already been at work for over an hour, cleaning by electric light, and in the confined space of the dental surgery, it wasn't so easy to see into the dark corners. However, by eight o'clock she had swept the faded carpet in the waiting room with a hard brush, dusted the receptionist's desk, and generally tidied the place. Now she had to start on the surgery itself. Mr Horrocks, the dentist, didn't arrive until just before nine, and by then the lino floor had to be swept, scrubbed spotless with carbolic soap, and then wiped clean and dry with a floor flannel. This part of the job she hated most, for it played havoc with her knees and always left them bruised and sore. It was not her job to touch any of the surgical instruments but she made sure that the leather dental chair was wiped clean, and never finished off her two hours' work without leaving the place absolutely spick-and-span.

The cleaning job was a poor substitute for Beales Restaurant. But once it was proved that Hubert had been responsible for breaking into Mrs Wiggins' office and stealing the money from her safe, and the management decided to press charges against him, Nellie decided that life there without the only true friend she had known was untenable. This was Hubert's third conviction for burglary, and as he had now turned twenty-one years of age, he was serving a six-month sentence in the horribly grim Pentonville Prison in Caledonian Road. Ever since it had happened, Nellie had lain awake at night thinking about him, wondering whether his criminal activity was in some way a revenge for what he saw as his own inadequacies, such as failing to get into the police force. She thought he was a fool, that all boys and men were fools for having this tendency to nick things from other people. And she thought about Toff and the vacs gang, and how stupid they were too.

The dental surgery was situated above a tobacconist's shop, and at about five minutes to nine, Nellie heard loud footsteps coming up the narrow stairs from the street door. She recognised them as Mr Horrocks'; he always made heavy weather of the morning ascent. She braced herself for his habitual effusive greeting.

'Hello there! And how's our little girl today?'

It never changed, every morning the same. There he was, a middle-aged man, dressed more like a City broker than a dentist, in his bowler hat, navy blue jacket and pinstriped trousers, a rolled umbrella over one arm, a copy of the *News Chronicle* under the other.

'Thought you'd be gone by now, young lady,' he said, taking off his bowler and hanging it on the waiting-room coat stand. He wasn't a bad looking man for his age, with dark bushy eyebrows and only a tinge of grey hair above the ears. But Nellie thought he had terrible teeth for a dentist. 'Mind you, I'm glad you're not,' he continued. 'Always glad to sit and have a little chat with our Nellie.'

Nellie had stacked away her cleaning utensils and was already putting on her hat and coat. ''Aven't got much time, sir,' she said quickly. 'Got ter get ter my uvver job by nine.'

'You're a good girl, Nellie.' Mr Horrocks took off his

jacket, placed it on a coat hanger and hung it on the same coat stand. 'In my newspaper today they're talking about the number of girls around town who are not doing their bit to help the war effort. They can't say that about you. Three jobs in one day. You certainly do your bit for your country.'

'Fank yer, sir,' Nellie said, making for the door.

But Mr Horrocks was there before her, blocking her way. 'By the way, Nellie,' he said, a bright gleam in his eyes. 'I was wondering whether you'd like to come out to dinner with me one evening, up West.' He lowered his voice. 'I know a little place where they do meals on the black market. Get anything you want – roast beef, chicken stew, fresh eggs, pork and dumplings . . .'

'Fanks all the same, sir,' Nellie replied, trying to open the door. 'I don't get much time ter meself.'

'Come now, Nellie,' said Mr Horrocks, voice low, holding his hand against the door. 'A young girl like you should *make* time.'

Nellie could hear the receptionist's footsteps coming up the stairs, so she felt brave enough to reply, 'But wot would yer wife say, sir?'

A few minutes later, Nellie was out on the street. It was pouring with rain and she hurried into the entrance of the Archway Underground Station, which was just a few yards from the dental surgery. There were plenty of people around, for it was still rush hour, with heavy traffic passing to and fro along Holloway Road to the south, Junction Road to the west, and Highgate Hill and the main arterial Archway Road to the north. Nellie watched the seething mass of humanity rushing here, there, and everywhere, puppets on a string dancing to a tune none of them could hear. She noticed how many more women and girls there were among that throng; the call-up to active service had taken its toll of the male population. Her mind became numbed by the thought of the humdrum existence these people, including herself, were leading. How could they live like this, making the same journey day in and day out, travelling on crowded buses and Tubes in the morning, returning at the same time every evening? Then she caught sight of the scrawled headline on a newsvendor's placard: 'ARK ROYAL SUNK: A HUMAN TRAGEDY'.

There was nothing humdrum about death, about war. Every one of these people she was watching was, in one way or another, a part of the tragedy.

''Ello, Nellie.'

Nellie hadn't really taken in the faces of the small group of people who, like herself, were sheltering from the rain in the Underground entrance. But when her eyes focused properly, she immediately recognised the woman who had spoken to her. It was Doris Beckwith – Madame. 'Mrs Pierre!' She could hardly believe her eyes.

Madame's face was partly hidden by the rainhood she was wearing. 'I saw yer come out of the dentist's,' she said, raindrops dripping from the end of her nose.

'I don't know wot ter say,' Nellie said, suddenly feeling self-conscious in her dowdy winter coat. But she was genuinely pleased to see Madame. 'Wot're yer doin' up 'ere?' she asked.

Madame smiled, and put her arm round Nellie's shoulder. 'S'pose we go an' 'ave a cuppa tea, an' I'll tell yer.'

A few minutes later they were in a dingy workmen's cafe in Junction Road. There was no waitress service, so Madame collected a tray and they both queued up for two chipped mugs of tea. They found seats at a table right in the middle of the cafe, which they had to share with two grubby looking elderly plasterers who were tucking in to plates of dried scrambled eggs and toast with a scrape of margarine.

'We was very upset ter 'ear yer'd left Beales,' said

Madame, taking off her rainhood and putting it on her lap. 'It was Mrs Wiggins who put me on ter comin' up 'ere. She told me about you workin' at the dentist's.'

Nellie lowered her eyes guiltily.

Madame leaned across and covered Nellie's hand with her own. 'She din't tell me *why* yer left,' she added.

For the next half an hour, Nellie tried her best to tell how she had felt after Hubert had been charged with the break-in at Mrs Wiggins' office. Madame listened sympathetically. After the two men had left the table, she got up and moved to the seat alongside Nellie. Just by them was a wood-burning stove which struggled to heat the place.

'You once told me an' Albert that yer never wanted ter leave Beales,' said Madame. ''Ow are yer managin'?'

Nellie shrugged her shoulders. 'Monday ter Friday I do three part-time jobs a day,' she said. 'Apart from the dentist's, I do cleanin' up the Mayfair picture 'ouse in Caledonian Road, and I scrub out a school 'all, up 'Ornsey Road.'

'An' yer make a livin' out of that?'

Nellie again shrugged her shoulders. 'I manage,' she replied, leaning across to the stove to warm her hands.

'But where're yer staying, Nellie?' asked Madame, taking a sip of her rapidly cooling tea.

'I found a room. It's not much, but it's all I need. It's over a pub, down 'Olloway Road.'

Madame shook her head despairingly. Around them, the cafe was gradually losing its breakfast customers and one of the assistants was clearing the tables and wiping them with a damp cloth.

'Look, Nellie,' Madame said, 'I've bin talkin' it over with Albert. We 'ave a suggestion ter make. Remember the last time we saw yer, back at the 'ouse in Tufnell Park? Remember wot Albert said about there always bein' a 'ome for yer there wiv us?'

Nellie quickly turned away, embarrassed. 'No, fanks all the same, Mrs Beckwiff,' she said.

'Why not? There's a room there. It's only goin' ter waste.'

Nellie shook her head. 'I couldn't do that, Mrs Beckwiff. You've bin marvellous ter me already. I'm not goin' ter be a stone round yer neck.'

Madame smiled. 'Don't be so silly, child,' she said. 'You'd never be a stone round my neck – nor anyone else's. Now look.' She stretched her hand forward and turned Nellie's face towards her. 'I'm sure yer must know by now that from the first time we saw yer, Albert an' me took a shine ter you. You're like the daughter I always wished I'd 'ad.' She took her hand away from Nellie's face, and the two of them were now staring straight into each other's eyes. 'We'd like ter do somefin' for yer – for you, an' fer us.'

'Wot d'yer mean?'

'I'm sayin' that I don't fink a girl of your age should be gettin' down on 'er 'ands an' knees scrubbin' floors. That's a job fer older people. Yer've got a good mind on yer, Nellie. Yer should be puttin' it ter better fings.'

'I 'ave ter earn me livin'.'

'There are better ways.'

Nellie suddenly felt uneasy. 'Dunno wot yer mean.'

The cafe assistant came up to their table and glanced down into their mugs. 'Finished?' she asked.

'Yes, fanks,' replied Madame, placing the two mugs on the assistant's tray.

'I want ter ask yer somefin', Nellie,' said Madame when the assistant had gone. 'That night you come up ter see Albert's act, at the Finsbury Park Empire. Did yer enjoy yerself?'

'Yer *know* I did!'

'Then 'ere's an idea for yer,' Madame continued quickly. 'Wot d'yer say to a job in the music 'all?'

Nellie stared at Madame in disbelief. 'The music 'all? *Me?*'

'Why not?' said Madame eagerly. 'It's a tough life, but a good'un, full of surprises and interestin' times. An' yer get ter meet lots of nice, warm-'earted people. Yer could come an' work wiv Albert and me. We'd look after yer, show yer the ropes.'

Nellie was dumbfounded. 'But I don't know nuffin' about the music 'all,' was all she could say.

Madame took hold of Nellie's cold hands and squeezed them. 'Yer don't 'ave ter know nuffin', Nellie,' she said reassuringly. 'There are plenty of jobs yer can do, far better than the rubbish you're doin' now. In fact, I know somefin' yer could do that yer'd really like, somefin' that's really werfwhile.'

Nellie, taken aback and nervous, shook her head.

Madame squeezed her hands tighter. 'Listen ter me, Nellie,' she pleaded. 'Yer deserve a chance in life. After all yer've gone through, yer deserve a chance ter get on an' 'ave a family who care for yer.' She leaned closer. 'Come an' live wiv us, Nellie. Come an' let us be yer family. I promise yer, yer can trust us. We'll take care of yer. Yer won't regret it, 'onest yer won't.'

Chapter 11

'Roses is red, violets is blue.'

''Ow d'yer know they're blue?'

''Cos I saw 'em 'angin' out on the washin' line this mornin'!'

The only person who ever laughed at Ruby Catmonk's jokes was Ruby herself. And when she laughed, the whole wardrobe room knew it, for it was such a chesty laugh, so hoarse, so coarse, it could deafen anyone at ten paces. But she was a good soul, remarkably well preserved for her seventy-odd years, with dyed bright ginger curls which were really an obstinate silver-grey straining to get out. She made no concessions to her weight, despite the fact that countless doctors had warned her that if she didn't knock something off her fourteen stone, she'd one day tumble over and fall right through the stage floor. Her great joys in life were fags and black market gin, and she was the best seamstress on the British music hall circuit.

Nellie and Ruby got on like a house on fire from the moment they met. Monsieur and Madame had introduced them in the tiny backstage room that was used for costume repairs at the Finsbury Park Empire, and in no time at all Nellie was learning the art of needlework. She even had some lessons on Ruby's ancient Singer sewing machine, and by the time she'd finished the week, she knew practically everything there was to know about running repairs to both male and female theatrical costumes. Madame was right. This certainly was a job that was worthwhile.

Since her meeting with Madame just two weeks before in the workmen's cafe up at Junction Road, Nellie's life had been transformed. Everything had happened so fast. That same day she gave in her notice at all three part-time jobs and left her digs over the pub in Holloway Road to move in with the Beckwith family at number 147A Tufnell Park Road. For Nellie, it was like a dream come true, for she had her own room with a window overlooking the back garden, pretty green floral curtains and wallpaper to match, a single bed and brass bedstead, covered with a huge beige eiderdown and two soft flock pillows. The moment she got there, she just had to throw herself on the bed and bounce up and down on it. She had her own dressing table, chest of drawers and a spacious built-in wardrobe that took up almost one whole wall of the room, although she had hardly any clothes to put in it. The other walls, like the rooms downstairs, were covered with framed photographs of music hall artistes. She hadn't the faintest idea who they were because she couldn't read their names.

Nellie's most exciting time had been the first day at her new job. When Madame suggested that she should become the personal dresser to Monsieur and herself, she was certain that she would never be able to cope with such a job. She didn't even know how to use a needle and cotton, so how could she be expected to keep them in good repair? But once she met up with Ruby Catmonk, all her doubts were dispelled.

It was now just three weeks before Christmas, and rehearsals for the annual panto were in full swing. This year it was to be *Babes In The Wood*, and the cast was headed by the favourite music hall and radio duo, 'Wee' Georgie Wood, who was playing Simple Simon, and his partner, Dolly Harmer, as his mother. Apart from his usual 'Illusionist Extraordinaire' act, Monsieur Pierre was cast as a foreign-sounding Baron Hardup. He had to wear a variety of colourful costumes which included silk robes, a turban, and a selection of exotic outsize hats.

Watching rehearsals from the empty stalls was a fascinating but in some ways unnerving experience for Nellie. There seemed to be so much frenzied activity everywhere, with performers walking around the stalls trying to memorise their lines, chorus girls and boys practising their musical scales, featured artistes singing snatches of songs, members of the orchestra tuning their musical instruments, dancers limbering up and stretching their bodies with alarming flexibility, 'speciality' acts such as Monsieur Pierre with Ange his assistant and Madame going through some of their new material, and the panto director constantly on the move as he shouted instructions to everyone, from lighting people to sound engineers. The atmosphere was often charged with tension, but the more the show took shape, the more excited Nellie became.

A couple of days before opening night, she was in the costume room ironing one of Monsieur's fancy shirts when the door was flung open by a highly irate Ange.

'Nell!' she growled indignantly. 'I fawt I told yer I wanted these two top buttons taken off the uniform. If you're goin' ter do this job, then fer Gord's sake do it properly.'

Nellie put down the hot flat iron and looked at the red military-style uniform jacket Ange was dangling before her. 'Sorry,' she answered, a bit taken aback. 'I was goin' ter take them off but Madame told me not to. She said she didn't want yer ter show too much cleavage.'

Ange was outraged. 'Bleedin' cheek!' she yapped. '*I'm* the one that's wearin' it, not 'er!'

'Well, yer'd better get yerself some tits first, gel,' sniffed Ruby as she bent to pick up her fag end from the floor where Ange's sudden entrance had sent it flying from the edge of the table she was working at. 'It's no use tryin' to show somefin' that's not there!'

Ruby's acid remark infuriated Ange. 'And we can do wivout your clever comments too, fank yer very much, Ruby Catmonk! Just remember somefin'. Albert Beckwiff's act ain't nuffin' wivout me.'

'Goes wivout sayin',' replied Ruby sarcastically, with only a passing glance at the girl over the top of her tortoiseshell specs as she tried to puff some life back into her battered fag end.

Ange glared at her, then threw the tunic on to Nellie's ironing board. 'Just do it!' she snapped, and stormed out of the room, slamming the door behind her.

'Pardon me fer breavin'!' snorted Nellie. 'Is she always like that?'

Ruby's only response was to laugh. 'Don't take no notice of our Ange,' she chortled. 'Nobody else do.' She took one last puff of her fag end before stubbing it out in the lid of an old Zube tin on her work table. 'Got ideas above 'er station, that one. Dunno wot ol' Albert sees in 'er – 'cept the obvious.'

Nellie took Ange's tunic and put it on a hanger alongside others that were marked 'The Great Pierre'. She felt like throwing it on the floor and trampling on it.

Ruby watched her over the top of her specs and grinned. 'I know 'ow yer feel, Nell,' she said sympathetically. 'But yer'll get used to it. There's plenty more of 'er kind around treadin' the boards.'

'I fawt they said people in showbusiness 'ad 'earts of gold,' Nellie said.

Ruby looked up from her sewing. 'Yeah,' she replied. 'Only sometimes the gold's really only brass.'

Ruby's comment brought a smile to Nellie's face, but it also made her think. Although the music hall was glamorous and exciting, it had an ugly side, just like anything else in life – except maybe Ruby. She was of the old school, a former chorus girl who had had to give up the bright lights after a dancing accident on stage when she was only nineteen years old. Every time Nellie looked at the tatty old posters of past shows peeling from the walls of Ruby's tiny domain, she knew where the old lady's true affections lay. 'So wot d'yer fink I should do, Rube?' she asked. 'Shall I take off 'er lousy buttons or shall I go an' ask Mrs Beckwiff?'

Ruby shot her a cautionary look. 'Take the bleedin' fings off,' she said firmly. 'Never play one against the uvver. She's a mischief-maker, that one. If she can put the knife in yer back, she'll do it.'

Nellie was puzzled. 'But why? Wot 'ave I done ter hurt 'er?'

'Yer ain't done nuffin', gel,' replied Ruby. 'She's jealous, that's all. To 'er, you're a threat. That one can't cope wiv competition.'

'Competition?'

Ruby took off her specs, rubbed her eyes, and looked at her. 'Albert an' Doris 'ave taken to yer, Nell. They're good people. If I know them, they'll take care of yer as if yer was one of their own.' She pointed her specs at Nellie to emphasise her words. 'But wotever yer do, keep out of that gel's way. She's a dose of poison, Nell, a real madam. If she takes agin yer, Gawd 'elp yer!'

Babes In The Wood opened just two nights before Christmas and was a huge success. The theatre was packed to capacity at every performance. Despite the depressing fact that, after the Japanese attack on Pearl Harbor just two weeks before, Britain and America had joined forces to declare war on Japan, the raucous atmosphere of the Finsbury Park panto raised everyone's spirits.

Living with the Beckwith family made Nellie realise how much joy and happiness life could bring. Her only problem was the two Beckwith boys, Sid and Lenny. From the moment she had moved in, they had made it clear that they resented her. They were full of sarcastic remarks about her height, and made her feel as though she had been dumped in an orphanage by a mum and dad who never really wanted her. Nellie tried to ignore their jibes, putting it down to jealousy because they were no longer the centre of their parents' attention. Their spite usually only surfaced when Monsieur and Madame were not present, and it was a matter of some concern to Nellie. She did her best to befriend the brothers, and make them take to her, but this proved difficult, and even harrowing, as she discovered during the Christmas festivities.

For Nellie, spending Christmas with her adopted family fulfilled all her dreams. Monsieur and Madame were both determined to make her a part of it all and she was swept along by the excitement of helping Madame do the shopping and wrap up presents for everyone. Then, on Christmas Eve, Madame asked Nellie to take the boys out to do their own personal shopping. Their first destination was the North London Drapery Stores in Seven Sisters Road.

'OK then,' Nellie said as Sid and Lenny dutifully followed her up the main staircase to the ladies' clothes department on the first floor. 'Who's got all the lolly?'

'Yer don't fink we're goin' ter tell you, do yer?' sneered Lenny, overtaking Nellie as he raced his brother up the stairs. 'It's our pocket money. We can do wot we want wiv it.'

'Course yer can do wot yer want wiv it,' Nellie said as she reached the top of the stairs. 'As long as yer know 'ow much yer've got ter spend on presents.'

'Wot yer talkin' about?' asked Sid. 'Who said anyfin' about buyin' any presents?'

Nellie did a double take. 'Well, wot we doin' 'ere then?

I fawt I was s'posed ter be 'elpin' yer to buy yer mum and dad's Christmas presents.'

'Give over!' squawked Lenny. 'Who d'yer fink we are?'

'We don't buy presents fer mum an' dad,' explained Sid.

'We don't buy presents fer no one,' added Lenny. 'Don't yer know it's Chrismas? It's a time fer kids, remember, not grown-ups.'

Nellie was taken aback by their comments. As she watched them hurrying off towards the children's department, she could hardly believe how little they cared for their parents.

There were plenty of shoppers milling around the rails of ladies' clothes. It was surprising really, for the garments seemed drab and unimaginative, dreary grey two-piece suits and pill-box hats, plain blouses and narrow, straight skirts, for to save labour and material, no pleating was allowed. Nellie wasn't impressed with anything she saw, and thought to herself that even if she had the money and ration coupons to spend, she certainly wouldn't use them here. But she had managed to save a little of her earnings and was determined to find a small present for Monsieur and Madame, and something for the two boys.

'Come an' see wot we've found, Nell.' Sid was tugging her arm and she allowed him to lead her into the children's department where Lenny was standing among a group of other boys watching an electric train race round a vast track. Pleased that she had been asked to join them, Nellie stood there watching with everyone else, happy to know that Sid at least was showing some sign of accepting her.

''Ow long you goin' ter stay wiv us, Nell?' Sid asked, quite suddenly.

Nellie was surprised by the question. 'Wot d'yer mean?' she asked.

Sid repeated the question. ''Ow long yer goin' ter stay? At our 'ouse, workin' wiv Mum an' Dad?'

'I dunno, Sid,' she said. 'I reckon it's up ter them.'

Sid kept his eyes on the model train. 'It's not the sorta place fer someone like you,' he said, his voice flat.

Before Nellie had a chance to respond, the air was pierced by the wail of an air-raid siren, which was soon joined by the deafening sound of the fire alarm inside the store itself.

Within moments, shoppers were streaming down the stairs. Some hurried out into the street, while others, including Nellie, Sid, and Lenny, made for the shelter in the store basement. It was the first air-raid alert for some weeks and no one was taking any chances.

After a quarter of an hour or so, the siren wailed again, this time for the All Clear. During that time there had been no sound of ack-ack gunfire, bombs, or panic. Nobody in the shelter knew quite what had caused the alert, only that this was a sinister reminder that the war was still on.

A few minutes later, Nellie left the store with Sid and Lenny, and all three made their way home along Seven Sisters Road. Sid didn't refer again to his conversation with Nellie in the store. And neither did Nellie.

On Christmas morning, Nellie woke up to the smell of a fifteen-pound turkey cooking in the kitchen oven downstairs. It was a wonderful smell, and a rare one, for in this time of acute meat rationing, finding any size turkey was an achievement. But Monsieur had his connections, and despite his patriotic fervour, he was quite prepared to use the black market for personal luxuries.

When Nellie looked at the small alarm clock on her bedside cabinet, she was surprised to see that it was still only eight o'clock in the morning. She and the family had not got to bed until two in the morning after a Christmas Eve party at the theatre.

In the kitchen downstairs, Madame was already hard at work preparing the potatoes, Brussels sprouts, parsnips, carrots, and cauliflower, and her homemade Christmas pud was bubbling away on the gas hob. Nellie adored watching Madame in the kitchen, for she was a wonderful cook, nothing fancy, but good, wholesome English food which her own mother had brought her up on in Stepney.

Monsieur was, as expected, the last to appear, and he didn't really come alive until after he'd coughed on his first Abdullah of the day. Sid and Lenny had been up for hours, pestering their mum to hurry up with the chores so that they could get down to what they considered the only important business of the day, namely, opening their Christmas presents.

After a sparse breakfast of tea and toast, Nellie helped to clear up, and at eleven o'clock on the dot, Monsieur's ancient parents arrived, together with his younger brother Louis, and Louis' wife Merle. Nellie liked them all, especially Monsieur's mum, Lillian, who was fat and cuddly and never stopped putting her two sons in their place. Her husband, Maurice, was a dear old thing; although he was bent over with back problems, he never stopped beaming at everything and everybody. Louis was quite unlike Monsieur – portly, with a bushy moustache which he constantly twitched and a full flock of light brown hair, and he stood a good six inches shorter than his elder brother. His work was very different too; he was a fitter for the Gas, Light, and Coke Company, and wouldn't say boo to a goose. Louis' wife Merle was a pretty little thing who only spoke when she was spoken to. She seemed a bit self-conscious of the fact that her accent betrayed that she came from a 'better class' of family up in Palmers Green.

While the women had a cup of tea, the men opened a quart bottle of brown ale, despite the fact that it was

153

still only mid-morning. A few minutes later, Madame's mother, a widow, arrived. Edna had a barbed tongue and treated everyone, including her son-in-law's family, with suspicion and resentment. Madame actually preferred her mum-in-law, and never felt at ease when the two families were together.

Just before midday, Sid and Lenny's great moment finally arrived. Everyone gathered round the six-foot Christmas tree in the living room where the presents, wrapped in brightly coloured paper, were piled high. Nellie loved the way everyone treated her as a member of the family, for they had all bought her something.

'It ain't much, dear,' said old Lillian as she watched Nellie open her gift, a small bottle of eau de cologne. 'But you're a pretty little fing, an' at least it'll make yer pong nice!'

Nellie joined in with the old lady's laughter. She was thrilled. To her, eau de cologne was the equivalent of getting the most expensive perfume in the world. Nellie was overwhelmed by the trouble everyone had gone to. She received real silk stockings from Monsieur and Madame, and a woollen scarf from Louis and Merle. Monsieur and Madame gave Louis and Merle two new cushions, and they had bought cigarettes for Monsieur and some new popular sheet music for Madame. Apart from practical presents to wear, Sid had additional carriages for his model train set, a game of Lotto, and a new cricket set. Lenny was swamped with comic annuals, a Meccano set, a chemistry set, and numerous puzzle games. Monsieur gave his wife some money to buy a new dress, and Madame gave her husband a pullover she had knitted herself, together with a bottle of whisky she had bought on the black market from a stagehand working at the Chiswick Empire. The only one who didn't fare too well was Edna, who seemed to receive much the same present from everyone: three pairs of gloves, two packets of hair curlers, and three potted chrysanthemum plants. But she accepted all her gifts graciously, particularly the two bars of Lifebuoy soap, for all soap was rationed and in very short supply. The most telling moment for Nellie came when Monsieur and Madame opened the presents that she had bought for them. Sid and Lenny had already opened theirs and dismissed them without so much as a thank you – a pack of playing cards for Sid, and a model of a Spitfire fighter plane for Lenny. Nellie had never had anyone to buy presents for until now and she was quite nervous.

'I know wot she got fer you, Dad!' Lenny proclaimed smugly.

'Ssh!' Madame scolded him. 'It's s'posed ter be a surprise.'

Lenny ignored his mum and continued, 'I was wiv 'er when she got it in the Drapery Stores. She paid three bob fer it. It's a fag case.'

There was an intake of breath from everyone present.

'Lenny!' Madame was furious.

'That weren't very nice, dear,' said Lillian, shaking her head.

'Wot difference does it make?' Lenny sniffed dismissively. 'It's only a present.' Then, to everyone's horror, he turned to his mum. 'She got *you* a new hand mirror.'

'No, Lenny!'

There were cries of protest from everyone.

Monsieur refused to take any notice of his son and carried on opening his small, carefully wrapped parcel. When he took out the modest tin cigarette case he found there, he let out a gasp of delight that made everyone feel as though it was made of pure gold. 'Nellie!' he said, looking up at her with a start. ''Ow did yer know? This is just wot I needed!' He went up to her and gave her a big kiss right in the middle of her forehead. 'Fank yer, gel!' he

155

said with a stony glance towards Lenny. 'This is the best present I've 'ad fer years.'

Nellie's distress turned to real delight.

Madame's reaction was much the same. 'Oh, Nell!' she exclaimed. 'Wot a beautiful mirror!' Then, after throwing her arms around Nellie and hugging her, she asked, ''Ow did yer know pink was my favourite colour?'

Nellie felt embarrassed. 'I knew yer wanted a new one. I 'eard yer say so, in the dressin' room at the Empire.'

Madame hugged her again. But, over Nellie's shoulder, she directed an icy look at Lenny.

Nellie thoroughly enjoyed the Christmas lunch. She had never seen so many people crowded round one table before. There were no formalities; once Monsieur had sliced the turkey, everyone tucked in and helped themselves to the vegetables, homemade blackcurrant jelly, and gravy, and while it was all going on, Monsieur, Louis and Maurice sank the best part of two bottles of brown ale, leaving the solitary bottle of red wine, left over from before the war, to the ladies. When it was time for the Christmas pudding, needless to say it was Lenny who discovered the traditional threepenny piece in the middle of his portion; everyone knew Madame had sneaked it in while she was serving it. Everyone pulled Christmas crackers and donned paper hats, and then collapsed back into their chairs, their stomachs full. Old Lillian was the only one who seemed to have any energy to make conversation.

'So, Nellie, dear,' she said, using a paper napkin to wipe the remains of Christmas pud from her lips. ''Ow d'yer like livin' wiv the Beckwiff family?'

A broad smile spread across Nellie's face. 'I fink they're the most won'erful people in the world,' she said, turning to look at Monsieur and Madame.

Everyone, except Sid and Lenny, used either their fingers or a piece of cutlery to tap on the table in agreement.

'I hear yer've now got your papers fru from that children's 'ome,' said Louis, always the practical one. 'Be able ter get yer identity card, I reckon.'

'And her ration card,' added Merle, who, on hearing the sound of her own voice, quickly shrivelled up again.

'It was no problem really,' explained Nellie. 'Miss Ackroyd, the woman in charge, she sent everyfin' fru. She said I was very lucky ter live wiv such a nice family.'

'We're the lucky ones,' said Madame, squeezing Nellie's hand.

Nellie smiled back at her.

'This is no ordinary family, yer know, Nell,' Louis snorted, after gulping down half a glass of beer. 'They're all exhibitionists. Even Mum an' Dad 'ere. Did yer know they used ter be a double act – "The Flying Equilibrists".'

'An' a great act we were too,' boasted Lillian. 'Weren't we, Dad?' she added, turning to her husband who was sitting at her side.

'The best!' he said modestly.

'So tell me, Lou,' said Monsieur, 'wot's so ordinary about you an' Merle?'

'We don't 'ave ter work evenin's,' Louis joked.

Everyone laughed, and there was a chorus of ''Ear! 'Ear! Yer can say that again!'

During the meal, Madame's mum, Edna, had said very little, preferring to eat her food and make the most of any alcohol that was going. Unlike her opposite number, Lillian Beckwith, she had never had anything to do with the music hall; she came from a family of bricklayers. But she loved singing popular songs, and when Doris was young, Edna had encouraged her to take up piano lessons. 'Nuffin' wrong wiv the music 'all,' she said now, on the verge of being a little tipsy. 'At least it 'elps yer ferget this bleedin' war.'

For a brief moment, her comment brought a hush to

the after-lunch chat. Until now, all talk of the horrors of the past two years had been carefully avoided.

'I'm not sure you're right, Edna,' said Lillian soberly. 'A lot 'as 'appened in these two years that some of us'll never ferget.'

Several pairs of eyes turned to look at Nellie.

Nellie tried hard not to react. The devastating experience of surviving the bomb explosion at Barratts' Orphanage was now behind her, and she had no wish to try to remember anything about it. But she did remember the Christmas she had spent with Toff and the vacs gang back in the gutted-out furniture store. In that split second, she could see Toff's flashing good looks smiling at her, wanting her. And she wanted him. She wanted him more than she had ever thought possible. But where was he now? Would she ever see him again?

'Best not ter look back, eh, Nell?' said Monsieur sympathetically. 'You're our little gel now.'

Sid and Lenny exchanged a strained look, then without saying a word they got up from the table and left the room.

On Christmas evening, several music hall friends of Monsieur and Madame turned up, and in no time at all there was a party. Practically every one of the friends did a turn, either a song or an impersonation of people like comics George Robey and Harry Bennett or popular music hall favourites such as Marie Lloyd, Randolph Sutton, Ella Shields. It was a very theatrical occasion, with everyone talking shop, and Nellie could understand what Louis had meant when he said this was no ordinary family. After a while the party turned into a knees-up, with Madame bashing out song after song on the piano, and the guests doing everything from the hokey-cokey to a spoof ensemble tango. Nellie loved it all, and joined in the laughter along with the rest of them. She was amazed by Madame's resilience and abounding energy – she was the only one who had had nothing alcoholic to drink. 'I've got nuffin' against it, dear,' she said. 'I just don't like it, that's all.'

During the course of the evening, Nellie and Merle went off to the kitchen to make some sandwiches from the leftovers of the midday meal. Nellie got on well with Merle, despite the fact that the two of them hardly spoke the same language. But once they were alone together, Merle was far more outgoing, and Nellie was able to talk to her more freely about the family.

'Hearts of gold?' said Merle, in response to a comment from Nellie. 'Oh yes, Doris and Albert've got that all right. In fact I can't imagine more generous people. They'd do anything for anyone. Except themselves, of course.'

'Wot d'yer mean?'

Merle shrugged her shoulders. 'Oh, I don't know. Sometimes I get the feeling that they're always on stage, always acting. I'm a good bit younger than Lou, and I notice these things.'

Nellie, cutting bread while Merle sliced the remains of the turkey, stopped briefly to look at her. 'Wot d'yer notice, Merle?' she asked.

Merle looked up. She was indeed younger than her husband; she had a lovely complexion and large brown eyes, with hair swept back behind her head. 'They don't know how to be themselves,' she replied.

Nellie thought hard about this for a moment, but she still didn't quite understand.

'Don't get me wrong,' continued Merle. 'I adore Albert and Doris. They're the best brother-in-law and sister-in-law you could ever have. But sometimes they exhaust me. Especially Albert. Always on the move, always playing to the gallery. I just wish sometimes they could be more of a husband and wife than an *act*.'

The sound of Madame playing the piano filtered through the open serving hatch. It was a lovely, poignant love song, 'Let the Rest of the World Go By', and when Nellie turned to look out through the hatch, she was enchanted to see Monsieur singing the words of the song, his arms lovingly folded round her neck and breasts. It was a wonderful picture, and in complete contrast to what Merle had just said. If this wasn't being a husband and wife, she thought to herself, what was?

Most of Monsieur and Madame's friends didn't leave until well after midnight. But as most of them lived within walking distance, there was no real problem about getting home. By the time the family finally said goodnight and went to bed, Nellie felt exhausted and exhilarated. Her mind was so full of all that had gone on during the day that she found it almost impossible to sleep, and for nearly an hour she lay awake reviewing all the images before her and asking herself over and over again what she had done to deserve the kindness of her new mum and dad.

Eventually she dropped off to sleep, but about three o'clock in the morning, her eyes flicked open. She had heard something, something downstairs, a movement.

Getting out of bed, Nellie put on the pale blue carpet slippers Madame had given her on the day she had arrived, then quietly left her room.

It was dark on the landing, but she could see a small chink of light coming from the kitchen downstairs. Carefully holding up her nightie, which was a little too long for her, she began to creep down the stairs. As she went, she could smell the remains of the cigars that Monsieur, Louis, and Maurice had been smoking in the living room earlier in the evening. The cigars had been given to Monsieur by a director of the Moss Empire circuit after the first night of the panto, and they had clearly been of a good quality, but the sweet-smelling tobacco smoke they produced was overpowering.

By the time she reached the bottom stair, she began to wonder if someone had merely left the light on in the kitchen, for there was no sound coming from there, and there was certainly no sign of life from the upstairs rooms.

She paused a moment, and listened. At first, no sound. But then she heard someone sniffing, as though they had a bad cold. As quiet as a mouse, she tiptoed slowly towards the kitchen door which was very slightly open. She put her head round the door, and the first thing she noticed was a strong smell of spirits.

Madame was sitting at the kitchen table, her back towards the door. The sniffing sound Nellie had heard turned into a sob. And on the table beside Madame was a bottle of gin, from which she poured what appeared to be a rather large measure.

Chapter 12

The grey stone walls of Pentonville Prison looked grim enough at the best of times, but against the dim winter light of a January afternoon, they looked positively soul-destroying. Most local residents hated the place, for it was a huge eyesore spread out along a great stretch of the Caledonian Road between Holloway and King's Cross, and there had often been complaints that it was neither ethical nor fair to have two prisons within the boundaries of the London Borough of Islington, Pentonville for men and, less than a mile away, Holloway for women. But there it stood, a monument to the horrors of modern-day life, housing both petty criminals and convicted murderers, a joyless place, particularly at the time of an execution when the black flag of death was raised and the gruesome chapel bell pealed its toll of doom.

This was the first time Nellie had come to visit Hubert in gaol. She had wanted to come soon after he had been put in there, but he had sent a message to say that he was too depressed to see anybody, even her. However, using Ruby Catmonk to write a letter for her, Nellie had managed to make contact with Hubert, and he had at last agreed to see her.

Nellie walked the mile or so to the prison. It was quite an easy journey from Tufnell Park Road, for she was able to take short cuts through Dalmeny Road, Camden Road, and Hillmarton Road, which eventually brought her out into Caledonian Road just a few hundred yards from the prison itself. She had deep forebodings about visiting such a place. And when she got there, her fears were justified.

Outside the main gates, a small group of visitors had already gathered, some of them quite rough-looking but most of them very ordinary people, their faces showing anguish more than anything. Once inside and signed in at the reception area, Nellie and the others were shown into the waiting room where they were allocated individual chairs positioned in front of a long counter which had a barrier of wire mesh down its length. Despite being just one of many visitors waiting to see a prisoner, Nellie felt very self-conscious, almost as though she was a criminal herself. No matter how she felt, however, nothing could have prepared her for her first glimpse of Hubert.

''Ello, Nell,' he said, as he sat down on a stool on the other side of the wire mesh. 'Fanks fer comin'.'

Nellie took a moment to focus on him. In just a few months, he had changed beyond recognition. 'Hube!' She had to lean close to the barrier for him to hear her clearly. 'I've missed yer so much.'

'Missed yer too, Nell.'

For a brief second, they just stared at one another.

Nellie tried hard to smile, but she was so distressed to see her old mate looking so emaciated. He had always been as skinny as a drumstick, but now he looked so ill, so pale and drawn. ''Ow they bin treatin' yer then?' was all she could ask.

Hubert's parched skin practically cracked with his wry smile. 'They keep me on me toes, Nell, that's fer sure.'

Nell's stomach churned over inside. She felt into her small shoulder bag and brought out two packets of his favourite Woodbines. 'Got these for yer,' she said. 'Lucky ter get them fru though. They searched me at reception.'

Hubert pulled the packets underneath the barrier. 'Yer

164

shouldn't 'ave, Nell,' he said. 'I got no right ter expect anyfin' from yer.'

There was an uneasy silence between them. There were so many questions Nell wanted to ask him, so many things she wanted to say that might help. Finally, Hubert broke the silence.

''Ow've yer bin, Nell?' he asked. 'Are yer 'appy wiv this family?'

Nell's faint smile broke the gloom. 'Oh Hube, I can't tell yer 'ow won'erful they are ter me. They couldn't treat me better if I was their own daughter.'

'Yer deserve it, Nell,' he said earnestly. 'If anyone deserves a bit of luck, it's you.'

Nell lowered her eyes awkwardly, then raised them again. 'Did yer know I'm learnin' ter read an' write?'

Hubert grinned. 'You?'

'It's this woman up the Empire,' replied Nellie with sudden enthusiasm. ''Er name's Ruby. Ruby Catmonk. Wot a name, eh! Anyway, I work wiv 'er, sewin' an' fings. An' she's givin' me lessons. Not official like, but a few words 'ere an' there. A'tually, I'm gettin' on really well. I could read the noticeboard outside. "H.M. Prison, Pentonville." Wot does the H.M. stand for?'

Hubert's grin broadened. 'His Majesty's.'

Nellie looked puzzled. ''Is Majesty's? Wot's this place got ter do wiv the King?'

'Good point, Nell,' Hubert replied. 'Good point.'

After her sudden burst of talking, Nellie sat back in her chair and there was another awkward pause. Then she again leaned forward. 'Why did yer do it, Hube? Why did yer 'ave ter get inter this mess?'

Hubert lowered his eyes in anguish.

The room was filled with the buzz of prisoners talking to their visitors. It was a strange sound, for their voices echoed round the green varnished walls. The smell of carbolic used to scrub the lino floors pervaded the place.

Hubert's eyes flicked up again and he stared at Nellie's face behind the wire mesh. 'It's a part of me, Nell,' he said candidly. 'I just can't 'elp meself.'

'But free times, Hube!' Nellie said, pressing forward so that her lips were almost touching the wire mesh. 'I can understand it 'appening on the spur of the moment, but free times. Why?'

Hubert thought for a moment before answering. ''Cos it's the only way ter get anyone ter take notice of me,' he replied. 'I'm fed up wiv bein' stopped from doin' all the fings in life I want ter do. When I left school, I 'ad plans, all kinds of plans. I wanted ter go in the army, then the police force. I wanted to find the right gel, save up, get married, 'ave me own family an' settle down. But every way I turned, it never 'appened. There was always somefink, someone ter stop me, someone ter tell me I was just a toerag who 'ad no right ter nuffink at all.' He paused only long enough to take a deep sigh. 'Well, maybe they was right – no, they *was* right. I *don't* 'ave the right to expect anyfin'.'

'You're right, Hube, yer don't.' Nellie's lips were now pressed right up against the wire mesh. 'But it doesn't mean yer 'ave ter stop tryin'.'

Shaking his head, Hubert leaned back in his chair.

'Listen ter me, Hube!' Nellie said fiercely. 'Just listen!'

A burly uniformed prison officer came forward and gently eased Nellie back from the mesh. 'Not so close, please, miss,' he said firmly but politely.

Nellie obeyed, waited for him to go, then resumed what she was saying. 'Look, Hube, just 'cos we find it 'ard tryin' ter get the fings we need most, doesn't mean that we 'ave ter go around breakin' inter uvver people's 'omes and offices. *I've* 'ad ter struggle too, Hube. I've never 'ad anyone ter stand up fer me an' fight my battles. But I'm not goin' ter give up tryin'. I'm not goin' ter keep takin' it out on uvver people. An' I'll tell yer this.' She leaned towards the wire mesh again, then remembered the prison officer watching her and sat back. 'I'll tell yer this,' she continued, her voice low, 'I won't give up tryin'. I won't give up tryin' ter get on wiv my life, in me own way, wivout 'urtin' everyone round me.'

As he listened to her, Hubert kept his head lowered. When she had finished, he looked up with a strained expression on his face. 'I asked yer ter come 'ere, Nell,' he said, with obvious anguish, ''cos I wanted ter say g'bye.'

Nellie immediately felt a sense of panic. 'Goodbye? Wot yer talkin' about?'

Hubert leaned forward as far as he dared, and looked along the line of other prisoners to make sure no one was listening. 'When I get out of 'ere, I'm goin' away, Nell.'

'Where?'

'It doesn't matter where. I'm just going, that's all.'

Nellie felt as though all the blood was draining from her body. 'But yer can't go anywhere, yer can't survive wivout a job. 'Ow yer goin' ter get a job after yer've bin in this place?'

Hubert sighed again. 'Let me worry about that, Nell.'

'Let me 'elp yer, Hube. I'll talk ter Mister Beckwiff. I'm sure if I talked ter 'im 'e'd 'elp find yer a job.'

Hubert was suddenly very firm with her. 'No, Nell! I said, let me worry about it.' Abruptly, he got up from his stool.

'Hube! Why are yer doin' this? Don't yer like me any more?'

Hubert felt his whole body tense. This was his supreme test. This was the moment he had been preparing for during the past few days while he had been rehearsing this meeting with Nellie. For a moment, he just stared at her. Then slowly he raised his hands and pressed the palms against the wire mesh. 'I like yer all right, Nell,' he said, his voice a croak. 'I could never stop likin' *you*.'

Nellie got up from her seat. She, too, raised her hands and placed her palms against his through the mesh.

After a brief moment, and without speaking another word, Hubert turned and quickly strode back to the door leading to the cells, where a prison officer let him through.

Nellie watched him go, cold and numb, and as the door slammed behind him, she shivered.

Nellie felt total despair. Making her way down the ramp from the main entrance of the prison, she hardly realised that she was back in Caledonian Road again. Her legs told her that it was too much to expect them to take her all the way back to Tufnell Park Road without help, so she crossed to the bus stop on the opposite side of the road. Within moments of her leaving the prison, huge hailstones began pelting down on to the pavement. There was no place to shelter at the bus stop, so she took cover beneath the railway bridge which spanned Caledonian Road. As far as the eye could see along the main road, hailstones thumped down, reducing visibility practically to nil. Nellie felt as though she was on an alien planet. After a moment, several other people ran to join her, but she paid no attention to them. All she could think about was Hubert, the torment he was enduring, and the cold hard fact that she might never see him again.

'Well, hello.'

Nellie barely heard the voice addressing her from behind, so she ignored it.

The gentle Irish-sounding voice was not deterred. 'I hope your taste in music's improved since we last met.'

Nellie turned with a start. Standing just behind her was the young bloke she had almost come to blows with in Saville's Record Shop in Holloway Road a few months before. Her lips pursed. 'Wot *you* doin' 'ere?' she asked sniffily.

'Much the same as you, I reckon,' the boy replied. 'I don't usually enjoy walkin' in a hailstorm.'

Nellie shrugged dismissively and diverted her gaze.

Looking at the back of Nellie's head, the boy smiled. He knew he was irritating her. 'It's still Spike Jones, is it?' he asked.

Nellie swung back to him. 'Wot d'yer say?' she asked tetchily.

'Spike Jones and his City Slickers. You know, your favourite type of music.'

Nellie knew he was getting at her, so she turned away again.

'Actually, I quite like them meself,' the boy said, his Irish accent now more pronounced. 'Not quite in the same class as Rachmaninoff, but pretty close.'

This caused Nellie to smile. After all, even she had to admit that the cacophonous sound of Spike Jones and his City Slickers was about as similar to classical music as Hitler was to Yorkshire pudding. 'Well, yer don't get many laughs from Rick Mani – whatever 'is name is!' she quipped.

This broke the ice, and both of them chuckled together.

'Patrick,' the boy said, offering his hand.

Nellie hesitated briefly, then shook it.

'Are you goin' to tell me yours? You do have one, I suppose.'

'Nellie.'

Patrick grinned. 'Pleased to know you, Nellie.'

The hail finally eased off, and the small group that had been sheltering beneath the railway bridge dispersed. The storm had left the air bitingly cold, and the hailstones covered the pavements, making them treacherous, but as Nellie and Patrick moved out into the street, the sun broke through and lit up the whole of Caledonian Road, transforming it into a much more attractive place than it

169

had been ten minutes ago. By the time the two of them had reached the bus stop, a rainbow arched across the sky, forming a multi-coloured backcloth to the silver barrage balloons that were bouncing up and down at the ends of their umbilical cables, their bulbous silver shapes glistening in the sunlight.

A long queue had formed at the bus stop, and it was obvious that they were in for quite a wait.

'So how far d'yer live?' Patrick asked, pulling the hood of his fawn-coloured duffel coat as tight as he could over his head.

'Not far from the Nag's Head,' she replied vaguely. She thought he had a bit of a nerve asking such a question on so short an acquaintance. Still, she had to admit he was really good-looking and he had a devastating smile. But it wasn't his looks or smile that fascinated her now, it was his gentle manner and soft-spoken accent, so different from the boys she had known so far. Different from Toff, with his direct, no-nonsense, plum-in-the-mouth delivery, and the boys in the vacs gang who, like herself, fractured the English language with their rough Cockney slang. Different also from Hubert, sitting back there in his prison cell, lighting up his beloved Woodbines.

'Looks like you've got company on the number fourteen then,' said Patrick, who kept on looking at Nellie's lips as he talked.

'Huh?' Nellie was miles away. 'I'm sorry, wot did yer say?'

'I said, d'yer mind if I join you on the bus? I live up Hornsey Rise way.'

Nellie shrugged her shoulders. 'It's a free country,' she said, briefly aware that she had made eye contact with him. Embarrassed, she quickly looked away to see if there was any sign of a bus approaching.

'My pals tell me I'm the shy sort,' said Patrick. 'What do you think, Nellie?'

Nellie turned back to him. 'I dunno,' she replied. 'D'you fink yer are?'

Now it was Patrick's turn to shrug his shoulders. 'Well, I suppose I've got a bit of a cheek to be chattin' you up. Especially after our last meeting.'

'Chattin' me up? *Are* yer chattin' me up?'

Patrick was still looking at her lips. 'Yes, I am. D'you mind?'

Nellie didn't know how to respond. She found it disconcerting the way he kept staring at her lips. 'Like I told yer,' she said, 'it's a free country.'

Patrick smiled and leaned towards her ear, whispering, 'Tell me something, Nellie. What d'you think of Paddys?'

'Paddys? Irish people, yer mean? Dunno. You're the first one I've met.'

'A lot of people think we're dubious.'

'Wot's that?'

'They don't trust us.'

This remark was a little louder than Patrick had intended, and it prompted an elderly woman standing just in front of them to turn round and glare at him.

'Every person's a diff'rent person,' Nellie said after a long moment's thought. 'What part of Ireland was yer born in then?' she asked, trying to sound as though she was only making casual conversation.

'Actually I was born in London, where I live now in Hornsey Rise. But me mam comes from County Donegal, and me dad's from Muswell Hill. He's in the Army. And by the way, would you care to have a drink with me some time?'

Nellie thought she hadn't heard right. One minute he was talking about his mum and dad, the next he was trying to date her. 'Wot d'yer mean?' she asked.

'I'm inviting you to have a drink with me. You know, in a pub. Any time you like. Tonight if you want.'

Nellie looked at him in disbelief. If this bloke was shy, then she was a Chinaman. 'I'm not allowed ter drink in pubs,' she replied. 'I'm under age.'

'You can drink a lemonade, can't you? Or even a shandy.'

'Are all Paddys like you?'

'Some of them,' Patrick answered, quick as a flash. Then with a broad grin and a mischievous twinkle in his eye he added, 'But none of them are as charming and tactful as me.'

For a brief moment, Nellie looked him over. Then she laughed.

The Theatre Royal in Drury Lane was one of London's oldest playhouses. Its origins went back as far as the year 1616, and during its long and distinguished history, its most celebrated patron had been Charles II. Some of the most famous actors in the land had appeared at the theatre, and although the building itself had had several incarnations, its colourful past had now become folklore.

Nellie had never been inside such a famous and beautiful theatre, and when she first entered the elegant cream and gold-leaf auditorium, with its red plush fauteuils, stalls, three circles and stage-side boxes, one of them with a royal crest proudly displayed above the canopy, she was overawed by the sheer grandeur of the place. One of the joys of working for Monsieur Pierre was experiencing moments like this, the chance to enter an empty auditorium with its rich galaxy of past artistes and audiences surrounding her. She could almost see the performers in their colourful costumes, and the audience in all their finery, laughing, applauding, gasping with horror or ecstasy.

But today Nellie's presence did not involve a live performance. Today Monsieur Pierre was giving the first audition he had given since he set out to become a music hall performer back in the early 1930s. He was prepared to do whatever was asked of him, for today he was auditioning for a place with the Entertainments National Service Association, or ENSA. There was no disgrace in auditioning for such an organisation, for what mattered was the chance to entertain the armed services.

The day had started early for Nellie. She had got up at six o'clock in the morning to make sure that Monsieur Pierre's stage costume was carefully ironed, his vast black cloak folded neatly and packed into his suitcase, his white gloves stretched, and his tall black top hat brushed, steamed, and free of every particle of dust. Madame's dress had also to be attended to. She would be wearing her long blue sequined gown which Ruby Catmonk had only recently restored to full glory after nearly nine years of continuous stage wear. The only panic was Madame's tall ostrich feather, which she always wore in the back of her hairpiece, and which overnight had become limp and obstinate. But with careful combing using a fine nailbrush, and some nail varnish to keep it in line, even the feather lived up to expectations. Needless to say, Monsieur's young assistant, Ange, left everything to Nellie, contributing nothing to the huge task of getting all the costumes and props on time to the theatre.

Nellie enjoyed the journey to Drury Lane, for it was the first time she had ever travelled in a taxi. On the way, Madame pointed out the sights, some of which Nellie had already seen when she and Hubert had strolled around Piccadilly Circus and Trafalgar Square together the previous August Bank Holiday Monday. Monsieur spent most of the time puffing on an Abdullah through his short, slender cigarette holder, silently miming the words of his act.

The dressing room allocated to Monsieur and Madame seemed to Nellie to be not much bigger than the one they occupied at the Finsbury Park Empire. But it was certainly better furnished, with an elegant chaise-longue covered in fine yellow brocade and a wrought-iron radiator that made the room warm and cosy. Nellie laid out Monsieur and Madame's costumes, then left the room while they got changed. She made her way to the stage where she helped a stagehand to identify the props belonging to Monsieur's act.

When Monsieur and Madame were fully costumed, Nellie checked to see that there were no hairs, or dust, or creases lurking on their garments.

'No sign of Ange, I s'pose,' said Madame, sounding as though she was used to the late appearance of Monsieur's stage assistant.

'I ain't seen 'er yet,' replied Nellie. 'If yer like, I'll go up an' see if she's in the supports' dressin' room.'

'I wouldn't bovver,' said Monsieur dismissively as he practised various dramatic poses in front of the dressing-table mirror. 'If I know 'er, she'll turn up just as we're goin' on.'

Nellie made her way back into the auditorium, and on the dot of eleven o'clock, the auditions began with a wonderful act by Billy Reid and his accordion band, who were already famous in the music hall and on the wireless. Nellie sat on her own at the back of the stalls and watched with huge enjoyment, quietly joining in with the songs. They were followed by a tap-dancer who juggled clubs and rubber balls at the same time, a comedian who told conversational jokes about his 'affairs', a pair of male acrobats who were so daring Nellie was convinced one of them was about to be catapulted into the front row of the fauteuils, and finally a female impersonating a singing soldier. Nellie had a wonderful time, and felt that the whole show was being put on just for her alone. But the proceedings were continually spoilt by the voice of a middle-aged man in Army uniform who was sitting in a seat three or four rows from the front, flanked by one male and one female assistant. Nellie was horrified by the way the man kept yelling at the artistes on the stage, 'Get on with it! How d'you think you're going to perform an act like that in the back of a lorry?' He sounded really nasty and Nellie only hoped that when it was time for Monsieur and Madame to come on stage, his manners would have improved.

'Wot d'yer fink of our Basil then?' It was Ange, speaking into Nellie's ear from the seat behind. ''Is name's Basil Dean. 'E's in charge of ENSA. A real charmer, that one. Most people'd like ter cut 'is bleedin' 'ead off!'

'I'm not surprised,' replied Nellie. 'I 'ope 'e's not like this durin' our act.'

'*Our* act?' Nellie could hear the indignation in Ange's voice. 'Since when 'as this act bin anyfin' ter do wiv you?'

Nellie could have bitten off her tongue. 'That's not wot I meant, Ange,' she said, almost apologetically. 'I just meant that I'd 'ate ter see that geezer down there talkin' ter Monsieur like that.'

'Don't you worry about that,' whispered Ange. 'Me an' the ol' man know 'ow ter take care of ourselves. Oh yes, an' 'ow!' Then she leaned closer, adding, 'As a matter of fact, me an' Albert can give as good as we take, if yer get my meanin'.'

'What the hell's going on back there?'

Nellie froze as Basil Dean's voice boomed out from the fauteuils.

'If I hear one more person chatting during my auditions, they're out! Do I make myself clear?'

Nellie shrank down in her seat. She imagined Ange had done the same. Only when the next act was called did she have the courage to sit up again. When she turned to look round, Ange had gone.

Basil Dean had the good sense not to talk to Monsieur

in the same way that he had addressed some of the other artistes. Monsieur was known for his sharp East End tongue, and one word out of place from Basil Dean would have unleashed a torrent of good old-fashioned costermonger fury. Nellie was amused when at the conclusion of Monsieur's act, the irascible producer even managed a compliment. 'Well done, Mr Beckwith,' he said. 'I'm sure you'll be a great asset to ENSA. The troops will love you.'

As Nellie set about packing up the props and costumes, Ange's lewd insinuations were far from her mind. But as she made her way back to the dressing room to collect the costume case and take it to the stage door, she came face to face with the reality behind Ange's words. There, partly concealed behind some scenery at the back of the now deserted stage, were Monsieur and Ange.

To her horror, Nellie realised that the Great Pierre and his young assistant were locked together in an intimate embrace.

Nellie told no one about what she had witnessed in the Theatre Royal, but during the following days it caused her a great deal of anxiety. Questions flooded her mind. Was this the reason why Madame had been so concerned about her husband going out so many times after the show, supposedly with either his agent or the theatre manager? Was this why Madame was a secret drinker? What was it about that little tramp, Ange, that attracted Monsieur to her? Was it really possible that he was having an affair with her, and that she was in a position to blackmail him? Nellie began to worry. She wanted to talk to Ruby about it, but the old lady was too close to everyone in the theatre, and she might dismiss her accusations as malice, motivated by her dislike of Ange. But she had to talk to someone. She just had to.

Nellie thought of Hubert. He understood her so well,

probably better than anyone else she knew. So, one afternoon a few days after the Drury Lane auditions, she made her way along Caledonian Road to that grim, grey building. She checked in at reception and asked to see Hubert. To her surprise, she was told that prisoner Hubert Pickering had been released on parole just forty-eight hours earlier – and prison regulations did not allow a forwarding address to be given.

Chapter 13

The spring of 1942 was a particularly good time for daffodils. At least, that's how it appeared in the back garden of 147A Tufnell Park Road, for the fifteen inches or so of soil that covered the top and sides of the corrugated iron Anderson shelter were a riot of yellow which positively gleamed in the light of the early morning sun. A few weeks earlier, white snowdrops had been the dominating feature, but during February they had been engulfed by a heavy fall of snow, and by the time the thaw finally came, all that remained were soggy limp stalks with none of the beautiful white petals that provided so much hope in the depths of a hard winter. In the past year, there had been relatively few visits from Field-Marshal Goering's Luftwaffe bombers, which meant that the Anderson had seen very little use. Just occasionally, however, Monsieur did use it as a retreat from his two sons, who distracted him when he was trying to work out new ideas for his stage act. The only problem was that the shelter was also a haven for stray cats who left the place stinking of urine.

Early in March, Monsieur, Madame, and Ange left on a three week ENSA tour of army bases around the United Kingdom, and the boys went to stay with their grandparents. Nellie was left on her own in the house, for with strict security regulations and small budgets, ENSA could not make provisions for artistes' personal staff. She was very disappointed, for she had never travelled outside London, but at least she wouldn't be lonely because she was now seeing the Irish boy, Patrick, on a fairly regular basis.

Despite his gentle, smooth manner, Patrick Duvall was quite a brash character, who used his irresistible smile to conquer anyone he talked to. Not that Nellie ever felt conquered by him. In fact, he puzzled her. She found it curious that he spoke with such a marked Irish accent when he had been born in London. The fact that his English dad was away in the Army didn't entirely explain why he should have picked up his Irish mum's way of talking to such an extent. Just how Irish Patrick really was intrigued her, and it was with a certain amount of trepidation that she agreed to go with him to 'Mulligan's Friday Night Out', an Irish evening at the Arcade Dance Hall, just opposite the Nag's Head in Holloway Road.

'Funny night ter 'ave a dance,' Nellie said as they made their way into the Arcade next door to the Marlborough Cinema.

'Ha!' laughed Patrick. 'Shows how much you know about Paddys. Friday night's pay night. Straight in the Nag's Head across the road, then over here for the dance. Anyway,' he added, holding Nellie firmly round the waist and kissing her quickly on the tip of her nose, 'it was my namesake's day last Tuesday. You don't think we're going to forget blessed Saint Patrick, do yer?'

The dance hall was crammed, for this part of Islington had a large population of Irish people. As it was a celebratory night, there was a good mixture of young and old, and the music was traditional, including the best of Irish jigs and folk songs. And Patrick was right, quite a few of the men had obviously come straight from the Nag's Head. Spirits were high but Nellie was impressed by the cordial atmosphere and laughed openly every time a complete stranger came up to her spluttering things like, 'Darlin'! Where have yer been all my life?'

'D'yer know all these people?' Nellie yelled over the

whoops of delight and clapping to the rhythmic Irish group dancing.

'You must be jokin'!' he replied. 'Looks as though half the Borough of Islington's in ternight!'

He grabbed Nellie round the waist and led her into the middle of the crowd who were doing what Nellie considered to be a mixture of 'Knees Up Mother Brown' and a Highland fling. About halfway through the dance, while she was in the middle of changing partners, Patrick signalled to her that he was going out for a couple of minutes. Nellie nodded back, and did her best to keep up with some rowdy young men who were now dragging her into what seemed to be an impromptu Irish tap dance. After the dance had finally come to an exhausting end, there was still no sign of Patrick.

As she edged her way slowly towards the exit door, to search for him, her tiny figure was swamped by the crowd and all she could really see were the light fittings dangling down from the ceiling above her. It wasn't an easy task getting out of the hall, for every young man Nellie tried to pass did his best to waylay her. By the time she did finally manage to reach the main door, the accordion band on stage was launching into its next group of songs, and the great sway of dancers started to swarm back on to the floor.

A bouncer was standing by the door, his hand on the blackout curtain.

''Scuse me,' Nellie said, 'd'yer know a bloke about this 'igh, brown eyes, dark wavy 'air? 'Is name's Patrick.'

The burly man burst into laughter. 'Patrick?' he chortled, in a thick Irish brogue. 'Now there's a new one if ever I heard it! Sorry, me darlin'. I've never heard a name like that in me whole blessed life!'

Nellie thought he was bonkers, and left.

It was quite chilly in the arcade just outside the dance hall, and as she hadn't brought her coat with her, Nellie didn't want to hang around there for too long. There were a few people around, most of them young couples snogging in the dark corners of the various shop doorways, but when she moved out further towards the street, the place seemed deserted. She decided to have a quick look out into Holloway Road before she went back to the hall, just in case Patrick was chatting up some bit of skirt she didn't know about. The sky was full of dark night clouds, and it was difficult to see anything clearly, but the main road, too, seemed deserted. It was quite late and most of the last buses and trams of the day had gone.

She was about to turn back into the arcade when she heard men's voices coming from a brick public shelter close to the side exit of the Marlborough Cinema. Even though she was some distance away from it, she was positive that one of the voices she could hear was Patrick's. She decided to investigate.

As she approached the shelter, the voices became more distinct, and it sounded to her as though a quarrel was going on. All the voices had a strong Irish accent. She was standing outside, shivering in the cold and wondering what to do next, when the door of the shelter was suddenly flung open and two men appeared. Neither of them saw Nellie, for she immediately ducked into the shadows. One of them turned back and called out, 'It's up ter you, Pat! This is the last time, so I'm warnin' yer!'

A third man came out of the shelter, and paused. Although it was pitch dark, Nellie knew at once that it was Patrick, for she recognised that well-scrubbed odour she had come to know so well. 'Enjoyin' yerself?' she asked.

Her voice coming out of the darkness took Patrick completely by surprise. He whirled round, grabbed hold of her and raised his fist.

'You lay yer 'ands on me, mate, an' it'll be the last fing yer ever do!'

'Nellie!' Patrick immediately released his grip on her. 'What are you doing out here?'

'I might ask you the same question,' she replied angrily. 'Am I mistaken, or did yer ask me out wiv yer ternight?'

'I'm sorry, Nellie, truly sorry. I – I had ter see these two blokes. It was business. I – I just had ter—' He stopped suddenly, and his voice hardened. 'How long were you standing out here?'

Nellie shrugged. She was shivering with cold. 'Long enough,' she replied. 'But don't worry. I din't 'ear nuffin'.'

'Not that it matters,' said Patrick dismissively. 'It was nothin' important.'

Nellie didn't believe a word of it, but she didn't say so.

Patrick suddenly noticed she was shivering. 'Yer poor thing,' he said, taking off his jacket. 'You're freezin'! Here.' He quickly placed the jacket round her shoulders. Then he leaned close to her. 'I'm sorry,' he said softly. 'Will yer forgive me?'

'Wot's there ter fergive?' There was more to Nellie's reply than her tone implied, but Patrick didn't realise it. He put his arms round her and hugged her tight. Then with one hand he raised her chin and kissed her full on the lips. Nellie didn't resist. They had kissed many times before, and she loved the feeling. As his lips pressed against her own, she let the tip of his tongue slide against her teeth.

'Let's go back to your place, Nellie,' he whispered. 'I want you so much.'

Nellie pulled away quickly. 'No, Patrick,' she said firmly. 'It wouldn't be right.'

'Don't you want me?'

'That's not what I meant.'

Gently he pulled her close again, his face against her cold cheek. 'I don't mind if it's your first time,' he whispered. 'I won't hurt you, Nellie. I'd never hurt you.'

'It wouldn't be right,' she insisted.

'But everyone's away,' he said, lovingly biting the lobe of her ear. 'Why wouldn't it be right?'

'Because . . .' Nellie desperately searched for a reason. 'Because it's not my house. Because, Monsieur and Madame – they trust me.'

'Then trust me too, Nellie,' he replied softly. 'I know how fond you are of your family, I know what they've done for you. But you're entitled to a life of your own, Nellie. You're not a kid any more. You're a woman.'

Nellie wanted to tell him that in the eyes of the world she was still a kid, for she was not yet eighteen. But the words wouldn't come. She just couldn't say what she knew she had to say. She was too aroused, too infatuated by this smooth-talking boy, too overwhelmed by the attention he was giving her. And he was right. She *was* a woman; at least, she felt like one, and she wanted to know what it was like to *be* a woman, to experience all the emotional and physical feelings of *being* a woman.

That night, Nellie slept with Patrick, in her own bed, in her own room at 147A Tufnell Park Road. It was her first time, and she was nervous, consumed with guilt. But Patrick kept his word. He was gentle – and kind – to her, and never once made her feel that what she was doing was wrong. But no matter what he said, in the aftermath of a night of love-making, she felt a sinking feeling of shame and despair, and that she had betrayed the trust Monsieur and Madame had placed in her.

Patrick left before daybreak. While they were together, she never once mentioned the two men she had heard him arguing with in the air-raid shelter. If he was in some kind of trouble, she didn't want to know. Not just yet anyway.

It was well after ten o'clock in the morning before Nellie got out of bed and raised the blackout curtains. As her room was on the second floor at the back of the house, she could look down on the row of small back gardens along the terrace. For as far as the eye could see, a profusion of stately daffodils swayed to and fro in the slight morning breeze, like groups of happy faces turning up towards the sun. Nellie felt a bit like them, for she, too, was in the springtime of her life, exploring, reaching out for all the things that until now had seemed so beyond her.

As the day wore on, however, her feelings of guilt and shame began to dominate. The more she thought about the night she had spent with Patrick, the more she felt she had betrayed the family who had embraced her. What could she do to put things right? For most of the morning, she just wandered aimlessly around the house, unable to concentrate on anything, not even the children's book Ruby Catmonk had given her to help her reading. What could she do? Oh God, what *should* she do? Should she own up and tell the truth, or should she just keep quiet about her one night of love with Patrick? For that's what it was, just one night, nothing more. She would never do such a thing again, never! In any case, as physically exciting as she had found the whole experience, Patrick lying in bed with her was just a body, a boy's body. It wasn't what she had really wanted. It wasn't Toff. Oh God, should she tell Madame? Surely she of all people wouldn't turn her back on her. After all, she had often told her to think of her as her own mum, so wasn't she the one person she could turn to for help and advice?

It was the middle of the day before Nellie made up her mind what to do. She didn't want to eat anything, but she was determined to be practical. She would do something positive for Madame and Monsieur. She would clean the house from top to bottom, so when the family came back in a couple of days' time, they would find everything spick-and-span and smelling of carbolic and furniture polish. This was the way to deal with things; she should stop fussing about what was right and wrong and show

185

Monsieur and Madame how much she loved them by letting them see how beautifully she had looked after the house while they were away.

She made herself a cup of tea, then set about cleaning the house. She started on the top floor with the two boys' room. Needless to say, it was in a disgusting state, for it never occurred to them to put anything away once they'd used it. But Nellie was determined to sort it out, for once Sid and Lenny got back from staying with their grandparents, the room would once again revert to looking like a rubbish dump. On the first floor, she swept the carpet in Monsieur and Madame's bedroom, and also the runner which ran along the landing. By the time she had scrubbed the bathroom floor and used Vim to clean out the washbasins, toilet pan, and bath, the place smelt like new. Downstairs, she swept out the conservatory, cleaned the inside of the windows, and watered all Madame's potted plants. The kitchen was the most difficult and obstinate of all; the gas stove in particular needed a great deal of elbow grease to get it clean. By four o'clock in the afternoon, she had achieved everything she had set out to do. But she was absolutely exhausted. She had made herself another cup of tea and a Spam sandwich, but as soon as she settled down on the settee in the freshly dusted sitting room, she just closed her eyes and went right off to sleep.

About half an hour later she was awoken by the slamming of the front door and the sound of someone rushing up the stairs. It took her a moment to focus, but when she did, she realised it must have been one of the boys, for no one else apart from her had door keys. She hurried out into the hall and shouted up the stairs, 'Sid? Lenny? Is that you?'

The only reply was the slamming of the boys' bedroom door on the top floor.

'Sid! Lenny!'

Nellie started to worry. The boys were not due back from their gran and grandad's until their parents returned in a couple of days' time. She hurried up the stairs to the top floor, and called again.

'Sid! Lenny!'

'Get out of it!' came a shrill, hysterical yell from Sid. 'It's nuffin' ter do wiv you!'

'Wot's up, Sid? Wot's wrong?'

'*Go away!*'

Nellie crossed the landing and went into Sid's room. 'Sid! Wot's up?'

Sid was lying face down on his bed. He was sobbing his heart out. 'Leave me alone, will yer!' His voice was barely audible for his mouth was pressed hard into the pillow. As Nellie drew closer, he turned round and growled at her, 'This is *my* room! Leave me alone!'

'Sid!' Nellie was shocked, for the boy's right eye was closed and swollen, and his nose and lower lip were bleeding. 'Wot's 'appened?' she asked anxiously, sitting on the edge of his bed. 'Who did this to yer?'

Sid recoiled from her like a scared animal, grabbing the blood-stained pillow and hugging it to his body as though trying to protect himself. 'Keep away from me!' he blurted. 'I don't like yer! I don't like yer!'

This irritated Nellie. 'No, mate! An' I don't like you neivver. But the least yer can do is tell me wot 'appened!'

Sid cowered away from her, which made her feel guilty, and sorry for him. She tried a more gentle approach. 'Tell me wot 'appened, mate,' she pleaded softly.

The boy sensed Nellie's concern, and after a moment's silence he responded to her. 'I 'ad a fight at school.'

'Who wiv?' Nellie asked, watching him carefully.

'This boy. 'E's always pokin' fun at me, always pickin' on me.'

'Why?'

''Cos 'e don't like me! 'E calls me a lump of East End shit.'

Nellie's eyes widened in anger. ''E wot?'

''E usually 'as a go at me in the playground durin' break. Pushes me around all over the place, showin' off ter the uvvers. After school terday 'e waited fer me outside the gates. Then 'e started again.'

'Wot 'appened?'

'I took a swipe at 'im.'

'Why?'

For a moment, the boy looked embarrassed, and diverted his gaze. ''E called Dad a music 'all pansy.'

Nellie was outraged. 'A *wot*?'

''E's always sayin' fings like that. 'E reckons all people who work in the music 'all are eivver pansies or layabouts. 'E tells everyone Dad's a cheat and don't know the first fing about doin' magic tricks.'

'Oh, 'e does, does 'e?' Nellie replied. 'So yer took a swipe at 'im, did yer?'

Again, Sid looked embarrassed. 'Well, it wasn't exactly a swipe. I just, well, pushed 'im away, that's all.'

Nellie was simmering, but she tried to contain her anger. She got up from the bed and went to look out of the window. She thought how stupid boys were, how all they ever wanted to do was to prove how tough they were, and to fight, and to cause as much upset to people as they possibly could. It made her think of Toff and the vacs gang, and how full of bravado they all were, living like street urchins instead of going back to their own homes and making peace with their mums and dads. It was all so pointless, such a waste of time and energy. Life should be about getting on with people, not about making enemies all the time. And this poor young quivering creature who had always treated her with such disdain was no different; he was like all the rest of them, all show, not a brain between his ears to work things out properly. But something had to be done about this pile of rubbish at the school, there was no doubt about that. Anyone who said the kind of things about Monsieur that that snipe-nosed little bag of wind had said needed to be taught a lesson.

'Tell me somefin', Sid,' she said, turning from the window. 'Wot would yer say ter givin' this pal of yours a bit of 'is own med'cine?'

Sid looked up with a start. 'Don't be a nark,' he replied. ''E's older than me. An' much taller.'

Nellie crossed her arms. 'So wot?' she replied defiantly.

''E towers above me!'

'The taller they are, the 'arder they fall.'

The boy punched the pillow he was still holding against his stomach. 'You don't know nuffin'. You're only a gel.'

Nellie gritted her teeth. This was not the first time this sort of thing had been said to her, and it got up her snout. 'Try me,' she said, with a fixed smile.

The boy looked at her warily. 'Wot d'yer mean?'

Nellie, arms still crossed, walked slowly back to him. 'I mean, why not see 'ow much a gel *really* knows?'

''Ow?'

She uncrossed her arms, moved closer to the bed, and sat on the edge of it. 'D'yer want ter get yer own back on this pal of yours?'

''E ain't my *pal*!' the boy snapped. 'An' anyway, I've told yer. Everyone's scared of 'im. 'E'd make mincemeat out of me.'

Nellie smiled wryly. 'Not after *I've* worked on yer,' she said with a gleam in her eye.

'Wot d'yer mean?' Sid asked suspiciously.

Nellie stood up. 'S'pose we get yer cleaned up first. Then I'll show yer.'

Chapter 14

Monsieur and Madame were absolutely exhausted. Although they had been told that touring army bases around the country with ENSA would be a tough assignment, nothing had prepared them for the long hours, late nights, and very basic working conditions. They were, in effect, on duty twenty-four hours a day. To the troops, the touring artistes were a link with their homes, and understandably they were very demanding.

'The best place though,' said Madame, removing a long hatpin, 'was the show we did in an aircraft 'angar, up near Newcastle. Must've been more than two thousand boys crammed in there – Army, marines, Air Force. They went wild. It was just like a football match.'

'Better crowd than the Sunderland Empire,' said Monsieur, who had flopped on to the settee, his feet resting on a footstool. 'An' that's on a good night.'

Nellie was thrilled to see them again. To her, the house had seemed so empty during the long three weeks they had been away, and now, suddenly, with their return, it had come to life. It was also good to see them getting on so well together. From the moment they first stepped into the house, Nellie had noticed how Monsieur had referred to his wife as 'me dear ol' dutch', and how Madame had responded with loving looks. The concerns Nellie had felt since she had unwittingly glimpsed Monsieur embracing Ange were thankfully dispelled. Whatever had been going on before, there was no doubt in her mind

now that Albert Beckwith was devoted to his beloved
wife Doris.

'I 'ope yer didn't get too lonely when we was away,' said
Madame, placing her arm round Nellie's shoulder affectionately. 'It's a big 'ouse ter sleep in all on yer own.'

'Oh no, Mum,' Nellie replied, heart in mouth.

'Weren't yer scared of sleepin' on yer own, wiv nobody
'ere?'

Nellie felt her heart racing. 'No, Mum,' she said, trying
to sound convincing. 'I just pretended you an' Dad were
in the next room.'

'I wish we 'ad been, Nellie dear,' Madame said wistfully. 'I do wish we 'ad been. You're so precious to us,
yer know. We 'ated goin' off an' leavin' you like that. But
it was worf doin' the tour. Yer should've seen the look on
those boys' faces. Gawd bless 'em.'

Nellie wanted to tell her. She wanted to tell her so
badly about her night with Patrick here in Monsieur and
Madame's own house. But she couldn't do it; the words
just wouldn't come. Not yet. Not now. Not until the right
moment.

She took a quick look at Monsieur to see if he had
noticed anything strange in her behaviour. Clearly he
hadn't; he was nodding off on the settee, his new day-wear
black toupee slowly shifting down towards his left ear.

The following day, Sid and Lenny didn't get home from
school until almost four thirty. Nellie was waiting for
Sid in his room. Lenny knew what had been going on
for the past couple of days, so he came too. Luckily,
Monsieur and Madame had gone up to Bond Street
to look for some new sheet music for the act, and they
were not expected back until after six. This left Nellie
clear to carry on with the lessons she had been giving
Sid.

'Now don't ferget wot I told yer,' she said, her two fists

positioned up in front of her in a classical prize-fighter's pose. 'Keep yer mitts up in front of yer, and never leave yer face unprotected fer one single minute. Got it?'

'Got it.' Sid, one foot in front of the other, both fists raised and clenched, was copying Nellie's pose as closely as he could.

Nellie waited for the right moment, then moved in a flash. 'Right! Let's go!'

She and Sid launched into a sparring match, darting back and forth, moving from one foot to the other with the grace of ballet dancers. Every so often Nellie would strike out towards Sid's face, and Sid would duck.

'Keep yer mitts up, Sid!' she commanded. 'Don't look at the floor! Keep yer eyes on me!'

Sid did as he was told, and took a crafty right-hander at Nellie.

Nellie ducked. 'That's it! That's it! Keep it light on yer 'eels, Sid. Light as a fevver, mate. Not so 'eavy.'

Sid did as he was told, and used his feet as though he was learning how to dance instead of learning how to box.

Lenny sat cross-legged on Sid's bed, watching in awed fascination. When his elder brother had told him that Nellie had been taught how to box by one of the vacs street kids, whose old man was once a pro, he quite literally fell about laughing. A pro was one thing, but a girl teaching a boy how to box was just plain stupid! If Sid was going to defend himself against Alfie Clipper, then in Lenny's opinion his brother was about to be annihilated. But as he watched Nellie dancing about barefoot, he couldn't believe his eyes. Time and again his big brother had nearly been laid out by this half-pint-sized girl who moved with the speed of a bullet and whose punch looked as deadly as the world heavyweight boxing champion's himself, Joe Louis. If either Sid or Lenny had ever doubted Nellie's claims that she had been taught how to box by some snotty-nosed runaway kid out on the streets, then those doubts were rapidly dispelled.

Nellie was teaching Sid how to box in as professional a way as she knew how. As far as she was concerned, the Alfie Clippers of this world were the amateurs, and they would always lose out to an opponent who used their brains rather than just their fists.

'Wake up, Sid!' Nellie yelled as strands of her hair swished across her face and eyes. 'If yer wanna teach that great big pile of 'orse manure a lesson, then yer'd better move yer arse!'

Listening to that kind of language, Lenny was absolutely convinced that Nellie was definitely not like any girl *he'd* ever known!

Nellie and Sid continued to spar, unaware that in Monsieur and Madame's bedroom directly beneath them, tiny particles of flaking paint were falling from the vibrating ceiling.

''Ang on a minute, Nell!' Sid shouted, panting heavily. ''Ang on!'

Nellie immediately came to a halt and lowered her fists. 'Wot's up now?' she asked, completely composed.

'I wanna ask a question,' said Sid, swallowing hard, sweat pouring down his forehead. All of a sudden he seemed to be all legs, thin and gangling. 'You said if I cover me face wiv me left fist, I should use me right ter do the strike.'

'Right,' replied Nellie. 'So why aren't yer doin' it?'

''Cos I'm so busy concentratin' on me left fist, I keep fergettin' about the uvver one.'

'Then don't!' growled Nellie. 'Yer 'ave ter co-ordinate.'

'Do wot?'

'Concentrate!' yelled Lenny.

Sid swung round to glare at his younger brother. 'Mind yer own business, Len!' he snapped.

'Watch me, Sid,' Nellie said, raising her fists again. 'Just watch me, then do exactly as I show yer. OK?'

'OK,' sighed Sid. 'But I don't fink I'm gettin' the 'ang of all this.'

'Up wiv yer mitts!' commanded Nellie.

Sid raised his rather pathetic little fists.

'Now, like this.' Nellie proceeded in slow motion, first covering her face with her left fist.

Sid copied her every move.

'An' like this.' Nellie slowly moved her right fist towards Sid's jaw. 'Cover yerself!' she yelled. 'Don't let me reach yer chin, yer berk!'

Sid immediately covered his chin and deflected Nellie's slow-motion blow.

'That's it! That's it!' Nellie was delighted as Sid pushed her blow away. 'Now fer Gawd's sake, do it like that *all* the time.' She raised her fists again. 'Right. So I'm Alfie Clipper, an' I'm coming after yer,' she said aggressively. 'So wot yer going ter do about it?'

Sid's face turned to stone and he immediately went on the attack with a left, then a right, then a left, and finally with a right upper cut which caught Nellie completely off guard, walloped her hard on the chin, and sent her flying to the floor.

This was greeted with wild applause from Lenny.

Sid was horrified. 'Nell!' he shrieked. He dropped to his knees and crouched beside her. She was lying flat on her back, eyes closed.

'Nell!' he shouted again, trying to shake some life back into her.

'Is she dead?' asked the ever cheerful Lenny.

'Nell!' spluttered Sid, pushing, shoving, digging Nellie, and fearing the worst. 'Say somefin' ter me, Nell! *Please* say somefin'!'

After a moment, Nellie's eyes opened. She felt quite dazed, and didn't even attempt to raise her head. 'Wot d'yer mean, say somefin', Nell! Yer bleedin' near killed me.'

Sid was distraught. 'I'm sorry, Nell! I'm really sorry.'

Nellie turned to look at him, and tried to focus. 'Wot d'yer mean, you're sorry, yer stupid berk! You just laid me out fer the count. Now yer can do the same ter Alfie bleedin' Clipper!'

'Jack and Jill . . . went up . . . the hill ter . . . ter fe-tch a pail of . . . water . . .'

It wasn't easy for Nellie to read. No matter that it was a children's book of nursery rhymes, it took a long time to understand letters and words, and how they were put together, and what they meant when they were put side by side. Being unable to read at the age of nearly eighteen was a major disadvantage for Nellie. The fact that she was now able to make at least some sense of written words was due entirely to Ruby's tireless patience. The old lady was a tower of strength to Nellie, and in just a few short months she had become more than just a friend; she was also her mentor.

Once or twice a week, Nellie went for her lessons to Ruby's tiny flat in Blackstock Road, which was just a few minutes' walk from the Finsbury Park Empire. The flat was situated above a funeral parlour which Nellie found disconcerting. It was a peculiar feeling to know that she was learning to read children's books and newspapers while a whole lot of dead people were being washed and laid out in the room directly beneath her. But Ruby was a good teacher in every way; she gave Nellie the confidence to read, and also the chance to confide in her.

'Fank Gawd I'm not Jack an' Jill!' Ruby sniffed as she peered over her specs at the nursery rhyme. 'The way you're readin' it, no wonder it took the poor buggers so long ter get up that bleedin' 'ill!'

Nellie laughed. She didn't take offence at anything

Ruby said, for she knew it was only meant to help her. 'I'm sorry, Rube,' she replied above the loud purring coming from a large ginger tom cat on Ruby's lap. 'Accordin' ter Miss Ackroyd from the orphanage, I never was no good at readin' an' writin'. Why can't I remember anyfin' about those days, Rube?'

'Maybe it's 'cos yer don't want to,' said Ruby, gently lifting Caesar the cat on to the floor to join his four pals who were all strays collected by Ruby. 'Sometimes the mind plays funny tricks wiv yer. It tries ter tell yer somefin', especially if it's got somefin' troublin' it.' She rested her arms on the table in front of her. ''Ave yer got somefin' troublin' yer, Nell?'

Nellie shrugged her shoulders and shook her head.

Ruby smiled. 'Sure?'

Nellie hesitated, and leaned back in her chair. It was difficult to keep anything from the old lady. Ruby was so shrewd, she was practically a witch. Nellie needed advice, she needed it badly, and who better to give it to her than Ruby? 'I'm worried about . . . Mum an' Dad,' she said eventually.

Ruby sat bolt upright in her chair. The movement dislodged a bright ginger curl of hair which flopped untidily over her forehead. 'Albert and Doris?' she said anxiously. 'Yer ain't fallen out wiv 'em, 'ave yer?'

Nellie quickly shook her head. 'No, Rube, nuffin' like that. Well, not yet, any rate.' She leaned across to Ruby, and looked directly into the old lady's face. And what a face it was. It was so heavily lined that Ruby herself had often remarked that a tram would have no trouble finding its way about. 'The fing is,' this was difficult, and Nellie hesitated again. 'The fing is, there's somefin' I 'aven't told 'em, somefin' I should've told 'em but I'm too worried that if I do, they'll want ter kick me out.'

'Who is 'e?' Ruby asked without a moment's hesitation.

Nellie gaped at her. 'Er, wot d'yer mean?'

'So yer've got boyfriend trouble,' Ruby said, stretching for her packet of Capstans.

'Ow'd yer know?' Nellie asked, eyes wide with amazement.

Ruby extracted a fag and laughed. 'I weren't born yesterday, yer know!' she roared. 'If a gel your age didn't 'ave some kind of boy trouble, I'd fink there was somefin' wrong wiv yer.' She stuck her fag between her lips and gave Nellie a measured look over the top of her specs. ''Asn't put one in the oven for yer, 'as 'e?'

'No, course not!' replied Nellie, embarrassed. Then she added, 'Well, I 'ope 'e 'asn't.'

Ruby lit her fag, then got up and went to the sideboard, where she picked up a bottle of gin. 'So who is 'e? Wot's it all about?'

Nellie took a deep breath before replying. ''Is name's Patrick. 'E's an Irish boy. I – slept wiv 'im one night last week.'

Ruby came back with the bottle of gin, unscrewed the top, and poured some into the cup of tea she had made a few minutes before. 'Where?' she asked uncompromisingly.

Nellie bit her lip anxiously. 'Back 'ome,' she replied. 'In my bedroom.'

Ruby raised her eyebrows, said nothing, then moved to pour some gin into Nellie's cup.

'No, Rube,' she said, covering the cup with her hand. 'I'm under age.'

'Yeah,' replied Ruby. 'So am I.' She pulled Nellie's hand away from the cup and poured a dash of gin into it. 'Go on,' she said.

'Nuffin' more ter say. The fing is, I shouldn't've done it, Rube. It wasn't right. I shouldn't've taken 'im back. Not to Mum an' Dad's 'ouse.'

Ruby took a gulp of her gin tea. 'Where else would yer take 'im? To a bleedin' graveyard?'

'Yer don't understand, Rube. Mum an' Dad trust me. They left me alone in the 'ouse – *their* 'ouse. I was supposed ter be lookin' after fings.' She sighed, and put her hands round her cup. 'I feel as though I've let them down.'

Ruby sat back in her chair and rocked with loud laughter. There was a flurry of different coloured moggies as they fled for cover under the table, the sideboard, and out into the kitchen.

Nellie looked hurt, and not a little surprised. 'Wot yer laughin' at?' she asked.

'People wiv guilt complexes always make me laugh,' the old lady replied. ''Onest, Nell, I don't know wot you're gettin' yerself all worked up about.' She leaned forward in her chair, cup of tea in one hand, and her fag in the other. 'Let's face it, gel, wot difference does it make *where* yer do it? The important fing is, did yer *want* ter do it?'

Nellie lowered her head.

'Well, did yer?'

Nellie nodded.

'So good luck to yer!'

'But wot about Mum an' Dad?'

'Wot about 'em?' Ruby asked. 'Albert an' Doris are broad-minded people. They come from the music 'all, from the feater. Yer can't survive long in this business, gel, unless you're broad-minded.'

Nellie wasn't convinced. 'But that doesn't mean wot I've done is right, does it?'

Ruby considered that for a moment, then thought that if she was honest, she would have to agree with the girl. She picked up her cup of gin tea, got up from her seat, and went to the window. 'I want ter tell yer somefin', Nell,' she said, finally emerging from her few moments of silence. 'I knew this feller once – oh, it was long before you was born, when I was still only a kid your age. I was in this variety show at the old Met, down Edgware Road, in the chorus.' She turned briefly to look at Nellie. 'I'm tellin' yer, I 'ad damned good legs.' She faced the window again. 'Anyway, he was a fiddler, played violin, in the pit. 'E was a year or so older than me, real knockout looks, the sort yer lie in bed only dreamin' about. I'd seen 'im lots of times durin' the run, but I only met 'im properly at the party on the last night of the show. But we sort of got tergevver, and I fell for 'im, 'ook, line an' sinker.

'One night,' Ruby continued, 'we met up an' went fer a drink at a pub up near the Angel, an' after chuckin' out time, 'e asked me ter go back wiv 'im to 'is digs up Liverpool Road way. I said I couldn't 'cos my mum was waitin' back 'ome an' she'd know wot I was up to.' She paused, waiting for a noisy lorry to pass in the busy Blackstock Road below. 'It wasn't the last time 'e asked me. Oh no. 'Alf a dozen times, I reckon. But every time I said no. The fact is, I knew it was wrong. Even though I wanted 'im more than anyfin' else in the 'ole wide world, I knew I 'ad no right ter . . .' She stopped to take a quick gulp of her gin tea and a puff of her fag. 'Ter cut a long story short, one night I said yes. 'E took me back, an', well, it was just wonderful. All I ever dreamed about, an' better. The only trouble was, me mum found out. Don't ask me 'ow – it must've been one of the gels in the chorus or somefin' – but she found out, an' she never talked ter me again. It was a cruel fing ter do. But yer see, I'd hurt 'er.' There was pain in her voice now. 'I always regret that I never told 'er. If I 'ad, I think she'd've respected me for it. The trouble was, I never told her nuffin'. I never asked 'er for advice, I never took 'er inter me confidence, I never once told 'er that she was any use ter me at all. But she was. No matter 'ow narrow-minded she was, she was still my mum. All I 'ad ter do was talk to 'er.'

Nellie got up from her seat at the table, went across to the old lady, and put both her arms round her waist.

'It's silly 'ow we let fings prey on our mind, ain't it, Nell?' said Ruby. 'But one mistake – 'cos that's wot it was – practically destroyed my life. When my mum died, we 'adn't so much as passed one single word ter each uvver fer over forty years.'

Nellie hugged her tightly.

'And the stupid fing is, I never saw me feller again after that one night of passionate love. Oh yes, 'e was off, mate, like a flash of lightnin'. I did 'ear that 'e copped 'is lot in the last war, in the navy, went down in a sub or somefin'. I din't shed no tears, though. Wot's the point? Anyway, there were plenty more where 'e come from, most of 'em from music 'alls up an' down the country.' She grinned briefly. 'All us ol' pros stick tergevver, yer know.'

For a few moments, Nellie stood there, her arms round the old lady's waist, her chin on her shoulder.

'Tell me somefin', Nell,' asked Ruby, softly. 'D'yer want ter go steady wiv this boyfriend of yours?'

Nellie shrugged her shoulders and sighed. 'I'm not sure, Rube.'

'Well, just remember, Nell,' Ruby said. 'Yer've got a mum an' dad of yer own now. Don't 'ide fings from them. It ain't worf it. They'll fink much better of yer if yer talk to 'em.'

As she spoke, there was a chorus of miaows from the moggies in the kitchen.

'All right! All right! Muvver's comin'!' Ruby called as she hurriedly made for the kitchen. 'I know it's yer bleedin' dinner time.' She paused briefly to say to Nellie, 'I tell yer, by the time I finish wiv this lot, I ain't got much ration left fer meself. They couldn't care less there's a war on!'

Nellie couldn't help laughing as she watched the old lady disappear into the kitchen. Then she looked around at the shabby surroundings where Ruby had spent so much of her life. She couldn't help wondering how someone so special had managed to survive in a place that was hardly big enough to swing a cat in, let alone five cats.

It was exactly four o'clock in the afternoon when young Sid Beckwith left Tollington Road Boys' School at the end of the day's lessons. A few minutes later, his brother Lenny came out of the building and they made their way across the playground towards the school gates. They had got halfway across when, as anticipated, they were confronted by a tall, well-built boy who looked about fourteen.

'So wot's all this then, Becky?'

Alfie Clipper had his own pet name for most of the boys in the school, including Sid Beckwith. He was a lumbering sort of boy, whose legs and arms seemed out of proportion to the rest of his thick-set build. If it hadn't been for his perpetual snide grin, he could have been quite a reasonable-looking boy.

'I was told yer wanted ter see me. Right?'

Sid pushed his younger brother to one side. 'Right,' he replied.

Alfie took one step towards him, and stared him out. 'If people *wish* ter see me, they *ask*,' he said. 'I take it you're *asking*.'

'No, Clipper,' Sid replied. 'I'm telling yer. I 'ave somefin' ter say to yer.'

Alfie was becoming irritated. He took a step closer. 'Then say it!'

Although a good proportion of the pupils had been evacuated, there was still a sizeable number of boys at the secondary school, and a small crowd of them started to gather, but not too close; they knew all about Alfie's ferocious temper.

'I want an apology, Clipper,' said Sid, with no apparent trace of fear.

'You wot?'

'You called my dad a pansy. I want you to apologise.'

Alfie could hardly believe his ears. For a moment he just stared at Sid in disbelief. He was already working out how he was going to knock the living daylights out of this gangling son of a music hall poof. 'An' wot d'yer intend ter do about it if I don't?' he asked in the silliest namby-pamby voice which was meant to amuse his spectators.

Sid beckoned to Lenny, and passed him his school satchel. Then he took off his black school cap with the white badge, and handed that to him as well. Last of all, he took off his black school uniform blazer. Then he turned back to Alfie and fixed him with an icy stare. 'Say you're sorry, Clipper,' he said firmly, 'or I'll knock yer head off.'

Alfie threw down his satchel and lunged at Sid.

Sid was ready for him. Up went his two clenched fists in the pose that Nellie had shown him, and as Alfie came at him, he covered his face with his left hand and with his right hand struck Alfie with a sharp upper cut to the jaw.

There was a great roar from Lenny and the other boys watching as Alfie staggered under the unexpected blow. But Alfie was quite a lump, and he quickly regained his balance, straightened up, and with a ferocious look on his face launched himself at Sid again.

But Sid was prancing around as light as a daisy, ducking and weaving, while Alfie lumbered after him like a bull in a china shop. When this got him nowhere, he tried to grab Sid round the neck and land a series of heavy blows on his face and stomach. Once again, Sid was ready for him. He ducked out of the way before Alfie could get anywhere near him. Then he swung round behind Alfie, tapped him on the shoulder, waited for him to turn, then punched him, once, twice, three times in quick succession, just as he had practised with Nellie.

Alfie started to reel, and a trickle of blood appeared on his lip.

'Say sorry, Clipper!' called Sid, twirling and curling round Alfie.

Alfie suddenly let out a huge roar, swung round, and aimed a heavy thump at Sid.

Sid ducked down, then immediately leapt up again and landed a really hard upper cut on Alfie's jaw, and then another blow to his left eye.

Heavy and cumbersome as he was, Alfie was knocked off balance and sat down hard on his rump.

The crowd, now swollen by many more boys from the school, went wild.

Dazed, Alfie shook his head and tried to focus.

'Say sorry, Clipper!' demanded Sid.

Alfie glared at him. 'Piss off!' He struggled to his feet. But the moment he managed to stand up, Sid thumped him one straight on the jaw again. Alfie went down on his knees then slumped to the ground.

Sid moved in for the kill. Placing his foot on Alfie's chest, he stooped down, his fist clenched menacingly a few inches away from Alfie's face. 'Say sorry, Clipper, or else!'

'Get off!' yelled Alfie in panic. 'All right, I'm sorry! Leave me alone, will yer! Leave me alone!'

Sid hesitated a moment, then withdrew his fist and his foot. 'I'm warnin' yer, Clipper,' he growled, pointing his finger menacingly at Alfie. 'You ever say fings like that about my dad again, an' I won't let yer off so lightly!' He swung to the crowd of boys who were watching in awed admiration. 'Somebody get this cry-baby out of 'ere!'

Sid coolly took his blazer and cap from his brother, and put them back on. Then he slung his school satchel over his shoulder and with Lenny at his side made his way to the school gates – where Nellie was waiting for him.

Chapter 15

Easter 1942 was a special time for the Beckwith family. It was the twentieth anniversary of Monsieur and Madame's wedding, and the first public holiday the whole family were able to spend together since the war had started. And to Nellie's delight, that included her.

Soon after eight o'clock on Good Friday morning, Sid and Lenny were bundled off to the baker's shop at the end of Tufnell Park Road to buy two bobs' worth of hot cross buns. And they were hot, steaming hot, straight out of the oven, smelling of delicious mixed spice and topped with the traditional marzipan Christian cross. It was a miracle that twenty-four of those buns ever managed to arrive home intact, but it helped that Nellie went with the boys.

The fact that Sid and Lenny had actually asked Nellie to go with them was in itself quite an achievement. Since Sid's crushing defeat of Alfie Clipper, in both brothers' eyes Nellie could do no wrong, and from that moment on she was the one they turned to for advice, sympathy and, more significantly, companionship. To them, Nellie was now truly one of the family, and they rarely went anywhere or did anything without consulting her first. They trusted her, not as a sister but as an elder brother. Nellie made it clear that just because she had taught them how to defend themselves, scrapping with people was not something they should do unless there was a real reason for it.

Nellie's only real worry now was her guilt about the night she had spent with Patrick while Monsieur and Madame were away. Ruby was right. Until she had talked it over with her adopted mum and dad, her mind would remain in torment. The only trouble was how and when to do it.

The opportunity came on Easter Monday, when Monsieur announced that he had managed to acquire enough petrol to take the family on a day's outing to the seaside. The chosen resort had to be reasonably close to London, for petrol was difficult to come by and if Monsieur's ancient Morris ran out of petrol en route, the chances of getting a fill-up would be remote. Clacton was top of the list, mainly because Monsieur and Madame had played there at the Hippodrome several times, and also because Clacton and Southend were the only two seaside resorts where Sid and Lenny could get their favourite Rossi's ice-cream cornets.

Mercifully, it was a bright and sunny Easter Monday morning. There was still quite a chill in the air, but not a cloud marred the azure blue sky. To ensure that the family could get away early, everyone was assigned a job. Madame and Nellie made the sardine and fish paste sandwiches, then packed them into a picnic basket together with some apples and pears, two flasks of tea, a bottle of brown ale for Monsieur, and a bottle of ginger beer for the two boys. In the street outside, Monsieur gave a last-minute polish to 'the old gel', his beloved Morris motor car. By the time he'd finished, he reckoned it could compete with Max Miller's prize Rolls-Royce. Luckily, he didn't notice the burn mark on the faded blue paintwork, which had been caused by hot cigarette ash dropping from the Abdullah wedged between his lips.

Action stations came at eight thirty on the dot. With Monsieur driving, Madame at his side, and Nellie squeezed between the two boys on the narrow back seat, the great trek east began. The illuminated indicator arm shot out to the right, and Daisy, as the Beckwith family car was known, moved proudly out into Tufnell Park Road.

By the time they reached the outskirts of London, Nellie felt as though she was encased in a block of ice. There was no heater in the car, and during the winter months passengers were obliged to keep warm by huddling beneath a blanket. Nellie also had a hot water bottle on her lap, but despite this her legs felt numb with cold and she seriously doubted she would ever be able to stand on her own two feet again.

Things got better once they reached the fringe of Epping Forest and the sun grew stronger, which also helped to clear the condensation from the inside of the car windows. Nellie could now concentrate on the scenery, and she craned her neck to look out of the window past Lenny's big head. She had never seen a large forest before, and she loved the way the sun kept popping up and down behind the leafless branches of the trees as the car hurried past. The fine Bank Holiday had brought out people from all parts of North and East London, and despite the mud after a few harsh weeks of spring rain, the damp forest picnic areas were already thronged with day-trippers.

'Yer know somefin'? Essex in't nearly as flat as I fawt.' Whenever he wanted to say anything, Monsieur had the disturbing habit of taking his eyes off the road and turning to look at Madame at his side. From the back seat it wasn't easy to hear what he was saying, for his teeth were firmly clamped on his cigarette holder, with the strong Abdullah smoke filling the car. He certainly looked the part; his brown and white checked jacket, plus-fours, flat cap, and white driving gloves were clearly the envy of every other motorist.

'Oh, I know, dear,' replied Madame, who had a happy smile on her face as she took in the rural scenery.

'Didn't you see that hill when we passed the uvver side of Braintree?'

'I saw two 'ills,' chimed in Lenny.

'I only saw one,' said Sid.

'That's 'cos yer was 'avin' a kip,' quipped Lenny.

'I must say, I'd love ter live out in the country,' sighed Madame wistfully. 'So much fresh air, and space. Wot d'yer reckon, Nellie?'

Nellie leaned forward to answer her. 'I love the country,' she replied. 'But I still love London. Specially Tufnell Park Road.'

Nellie's reply brought a warm smile to Madame's face, and she reached back to rest her hand on her shoulder. Nellie immediately responded by covering Madame's hand affectionately with her own.

'Well, I tell yer one fing,' Monsieur said. 'There's bin a good dozen cars or so on this road in the last ten minutes. Where do they all get their petrol coupons from? I'd like ter ask. Why don't people just stay at 'ome where they belong? Don't they know there's a war on?'

The authorities had relaxed regulations forbidding unnecessary travel to any of the south and east coast seaside resorts, and Clacton-on-Sea was pulsating with life. Not since before the war had so many day-trippers crammed into the town, despite the fact that most of the beach areas were sealed off with barbed wire. By midday, queues had formed outside every fish and chip shop along the promenade, and even the ever popular funfair, which had been closed since before the war, was partly operational again to cater for the surge of weekend visitors. Clacton bristled with pride and new-found confidence; its Edwardian and Victorian terraced shops and houses basked in the Easter sunshine, and even the landladies of the bed and breakfast mock-Tudor bungalows were able to display 'NO VACANCIES' notices at their lace-curtained windows.

The warm spring sunshine had induced some men to wear grey flannels and summer jackets, while a lot of young girls wore their brightest cotton dresses with a turban, and one or two had even opted for the only real fashion of the war, the one-piece siren suit. However, no one took the lull in aerial bombardment for granted, and many a day-tripper was vividly reminded of what had happened during the Blitz as they strolled past buildings that had been gutted by incendiary bombs or reduced to rubble by high-explosive bombs. Most people made a mental note of the exact location of the nearest air-raid shelter, but the hope was that for one Bank Holiday at least, the shelters would not be required.

Nellie was overcome with excitement. This was the first time she had seen the sea, and she couldn't believe how different its colour was to the sky. This was the east coast, where the water seemed grey and muddy but calm and inviting, although Monsieur had told her about the landmines that had been buried on the beach to deter enemy invasion. Yes, she said to herself as she stood alone for a few minutes on some stone steps over-looking the stretch of seafront, they *are* out there, those people who had brought so much death and destruc-tion to her home city. Just on the other side of that water, they were waiting for the day when they could march into the streets of this lovely old seaside resort, just as they had done in all the cities and towns of Europe.

'An' 'ere, my gel,' said Monsieur grandly after helping himself to a chip from his wife's three penn'orth which were smothered in salt and vinegar and wrapped up in a page of the *Daily Herald*, 'yer 'ave one of the great wonders of the world!' He raised his cane and flourished it towards the majestic if somewhat jaded edifice that was Clacton Pier.

'If God gave everyone birds and bees and grass and

209

trees,' Madame said to Nellie in a low voice, 'He also gave Albert this place!'

Nellie gazed at the fine old Victorian pier reaching far out over the water on its iron struts. Much of it was boarded up but the remains of an old billboard above the entrance announced a past summer season of variety shows starring a host of talented music hall performers. 'I fink I'd be scared sittin' in a feater watchin' a show wiv the sea rushing underneaf me,' Nellie said.

'Never!' objected Monsieur, with a grand gesture of his left hand which was still holding the now cold chip. 'Once that orchestra started ter play, the curtain rose, an' the dazzling bright lights tore into yer soul, the sea beneath yer din't exist. I tell yer, Nellie, there's nuffin' like a show by the seaside ter send people 'ome in the best of moods. As a matter of fact, I gave one of me best performances 'ere. Same bill as the great Randolph Sutton.'

Nellie turned to Madame for enlightenment.

'Wonderful singer, dear,' she explained, then launched into a few bars of his popular song, 'On Mother Kelly's Doorstep'.

'It didn't matter that we were paid peanuts fer a summer season,' continued Monsieur. 'It was the atmosphere. Just us on stage, an' the payin' customers. It was magic. Pure magic.' He looked at Nellie. 'It'll come back,' he said confidently. 'Get this ruddy war over, an' it'll come back.'

Madame wrapped her scarf round her head to keep her ears warm in the cool sea breeze. 'Let's 'ope so, dear,' she said. 'Let's 'ope so.'

Sid and Lenny managed to find a space on one of the promenade lawns overlooking the sea, and among the formal gardens of late daffodils and early tulips the family laid out their picnic. When they had eaten, Sid and Lenny became restless for both Rossi's ice cream and a trip to one of the two amusement arcades which had opened up for the Bank Holiday weekend, so Monsieur took the boys off, leaving Madame and Nellie to finish their cups of tea in peace.

Elated as she was at the prospect of her first day ever by the seaside, Nellie knew that this was her chance to talk to Madame in confidence. It was now or never. 'Yer've been so good ter me, Mum,' she began. 'I don't know what I'd've done wivout you an' Dad.'

Madame was sitting on a low canvas chair which she always took with her on outings. 'We're the one that should be fankin' you, Nellie dear,' she said, warming her hands round the cup of tea from her vacuum flask. 'Yer've given this family a new lease of life. Albert was only sayin' so the uvver day. An' as fer Sid and Lenny, well, it's a miracle.' She leaned across and smiled at Nellie. 'We know wot yer did fer young Sid. 'E told us everythin'.'

'Oh Mum,' Nellie sighed. ''E shouldn't've. I told 'im it was somefin' fer 'im an' me, an' not ter go worryin' you about it.'

'Yer taught 'im 'ow ter fight.'

'I showed 'im 'ow ter defend 'imself. There's a big diff'rence, Mum. That's why I wanted 'im to know 'ow ter fight in the proper way, not ter go in there like any uvver scrapper down the street.'

'Yer taught 'im more than that, Nell. Yer taught 'im all sorts of fings, about gettin' back 'is confidence and self-respect. You're a wonderful gel, Nell. We're all proud ter 'ave yer in the family.'

Nellie felt her insides churning over. 'Mum,' she said quickly, lowering her eyes and biting her lip, 'there's somefin' I've got ter tell yer . . .'

'An' there's somefin' I want ter tell you too, Nell.' Madame eased herself off her chair and squatted alongside Nellie on the picnic blanket. 'Albert an' I, we've been talkin' it over. We want ter adopt you – I mean official like.'

Nellie's eyes widened. 'Mum!'

Madame smiled, and took Nellie's hand. 'Yes, Nell. That's wot I want ter be, yer mum. Not yer real one, of course. There's no way we can put that right. But someone yer can talk ter, someone yer can feel belongs to yer. That goes fer Albert too. We want yer ter be our daughter. An' Sid an' Lenny want it too. They want yer ter be their sister.'

Nellie felt as though she was going to cry. But all this wonderful show of love and affection from Madame was only making it more difficult for her to say what she had to say.

Madame was watching Nellie carefully. She was worried by her silence and lack of response. 'Is there anyfin' wrong, Nell? D'yer not want us to adopt yer?'

Nellie looked up quickly. 'Oh, I do, Mum,' she said eagerly. 'I can't fink of anyfin' in the 'ole wide world I'd like more. You an' Dad are wot I've dreamt about, me own family, people I can care about and call me own.' She stopped abruptly and felt anguish rising up through her body. 'But I can't do it, I can't let you an' Dad do it until – until . . .'

'Wot is it, Nell?' asked Madame gently. 'I'm yer mum. Yer can tell me.'

Nellie waited a moment, then told Madame everything about her relationship with Patrick, and the night they had spent together in her bedroom. By the time she finished, she couldn't look Madame in the face. To make matters worse, Madame had listened to everything she had said in total silence, staring out to sea as though trying to pretend that what she was hearing was nothing more than a dream. Or at least, that's what Nellie thought. But when she ended with the words, 'I'm sorry, Mum. I'm truly sorry fer lettin' you down,' she was astonished to hear Madame roar with laughter.

'Oh, Nellie!' she said, throwing her arms round her.

'Why do yer even fink yer 'ave ter apologise ter *me*? It's all right, Nellie. It's perfectly all right.'

Nellie was bewildered. 'Yer mean – wot I did, it's all right?'

Madame looked her straight in the eye. 'No, Nell,' she said. 'It'd be wrong of me ter say it's all right ter do – wot yer did. All I'm sayin' is, it's somefin' that 'appens. As a matter of fact, the same fing 'appened ter me when I was your age.'

Nellie stared at her in disbelief.

Madame smiled, her voice becoming a touch more serious. 'Yes. It's a situation we all 'ave ter face up to at some time in our lives. When you're young, it's a big adventure, like knowin' you're doin' somefin' yer shouldn't do. But when it's all over, that's the time yer 'ave ter start askin' yerself questions.' She leaned closer again. 'Tell me, Nell. This boy, Patrick. D'yer love 'im? Is 'e the one yer want ter spend the rest of yer life wiv?'

Nellie paused a moment, then shook her head. 'I like 'im,' she said. 'I like 'im a lot. But I don't love 'im. I don't fink I ever could. I just don't know enough about 'im. 'E's just a mate – nuffin' more.'

'That's all right then. No 'arm in that.' Then she added tentatively, 'As long as there're no – complications?'

Nellie, embarrassed, shook her head and lowered her eyes.

With a reassuring smile, Madame put her hand under Nellie's chin and gently raised her head. 'Fanks fer tellin' me, Nell. After all, that's wot mums are for.'

Nellie and Madame sat on the seafront lawn and talked for over an hour. Nellie felt as though she had known this wonderful woman all her life, and thought to herself that she would rather have her for a mum than anyone else. And Doris Beckwith felt the same way about Nellie. She was truly someone she could talk to, share a laugh with, and get on with. Above all, Madame felt she had gained a daughter to whom she would one day be able to tell the truth about the heartache and suffering she was being subjected to.

It was mid-afternoon when Monsieur returned with the two boys, both of whom looked the worse for wear after consuming four Rossi's ice-cream cornets each, and two more bags of chips.

'My legs're gettin' cold!' griped Sid to his mum. 'Why can't I wear long trousers now? Most of the uvvers at school wear 'em. I'm too old fer shorts.'

'I've told yer, Sid, yer've got ter 'ang on fer anuvver year or so. The Government says there ain't enough material around ter put all boys your age in long'uns.'

Sid groaned. Lenny sniggered.

''E's bin moanin' on like this all afternoon,' complained a weary Monsieur. 'As if they boaf 'aven't cost me enough on those ruddy pin machines!'

'Somefin' tells me we'd better be on our way, dear,' replied Madame, helping Nellie to fold up the picnic blanket. 'By the time we get back 'ome, it'll be—'

A loud explosion drowned the rest of Madame's sentence. There were yells and screams from people everywhere, followed by a wild dash to the nearest air-raid shelters.

'Wot is it?' gasped Madame. 'Is there an air raid?'

Simultaneously, the air-raid alert sounded from the top of the police station a couple of streets away.

'Let's get out of 'ere!' shouted Monsieur.

'No, Dad!' yelled Sid. 'Look out there! Look!'

The family turned to where Sid was pointing. Far out to sea they could see a vessel under attack from a dive bomber. Above it, the sky was criss-crossed with vapour trails; a fierce dogfight was taking place between at least a dozen aircraft.

'My God!' gasped Monsieur, quickly focusing his binoculars. 'It's a warship! Jerry's tryin' ter bomb it! Oh my God!'

'Over 'ere, Nell!' yelled young Lenny who, with his brother, had climbed up on to a wooden bench overlooking the beach. 'Yer can get a smashin' view up 'ere!'

Both boys gave Nellie a bunk up, then huddled together to watch the action.

'No, please, let's get to the shelter,' begged Madame anxiously. 'They've sounded the alert. Jerry could start bombing over 'ere any minute . . .'

'Bravo!' cheered Monsieur, closely echoed by the crowd now watching along the promenade. 'They've got one of 'em! Our boy's 'ave got one of 'em! Look at 'im! 'E's on fire!'

'It's a Messerschmitt!' yelled Lenny, his knowledge based on his model aircraft kits.

'Down, yer bugger, down!' yelled Monsieur.

Nellie stared out at the incredible battle being fought out before their eyes. The cloudless, crisp blue sky was now streaked with dozens of thin white vapour trails, and as the blazing German fighter twisted and turned down into the sea, it left a trail of oily black smoke. Its pilot was clearly visible, holding on for grim death to the cords of his flickering white parachute which fluttered down helplessly, only opening just before it hit the water. One fighter plane chased another, and Nellie was sure they would collide as they twisted and turned, chasing, circling, diving, skimming the waves. She could see and hear the tracer guns as two enemy bombers dived towards their naval target. And the sound of fury, determination, and annihilation. No wonder it was called a dogfight. There were no rules, just a free-for-all.

'Stuka!' yelled Lenny, pointing out to sea and jumping up and down excitedly on the bench.

'It's a Heinkel!' came a yell from another young-ster nearby, hanging precariously from a promenade lamppost.

'Don't be daft!' Sid growled back. 'Anyone can see that's a Stuka dive bomber!'

''E's right!' Monsieur pronounced, his binoculars glued to his eyes. ''E's got a couple of sniffers on 'is tail!'

'Spitfires!' yelled the know-all.

''Urricanes!' replied Monsieur. 'They're 'eadin' this way!'

'Oh please, Albert!' pleaded Madame, starting to panic. 'Do let's get ter the shelter!'

Nellie could see the three fighters roaring in from the sea. 'Come on, you two,' she said urgently. 'Mum's right.'

She had hardly spoken when the German fighter bomber came twisting and turning in from the battle, hotly pursued by two RAF Hurricanes. And as the enemy plane approached, it made straight for the shoreline, its machine guns blazing, strafing the beach, the bullets sending up small funnels of sand on the way.

'Everyone down!' yelled Monsieur. He threw himself on to his wife, bringing her and himself to the ground, shielding her with his body. 'Down!'

Nellie grabbed both Sid and Lenny by their necks and shoved them to the ground beneath the bench they had been standing on.

Within seconds, one of the two Hurricanes had caught up with the intruder and filled his tailplane with machine-gun bullets. The enemy bomber banked straight out to sea, but before it had reached more than half a mile or so, there was a loud explosion and the entire aircraft disintegrated.

Some of the more daring onlookers on the promenade stood up and started cheering.

'He's down!' yelled an elderly woman whose basket-weave hat had been crushed in the excitement.

Then someone else, a teenage boy, yelled out. 'Look at that! There's nuffin' left of 'im!'

There was a huge cheer from everyone, and as Nellie turned to look, the promenade crowd threw caution to the wind and lined the seafront, waving and shouting, cheering and applauding. Monsieur helped Madame to her feet and as they both turned to look out to sea, he put his arm round her waist and hugged her.

Then an extraordinary thing happened. As the exultant cheers faded away, there followed a strange, unnatural silence. Nellie looked along the promenade at the quiet faces of all the people, now tinged with the red glow of the sun which had begun its downward journey towards that mystical line between sea and sky. No one spoke. No one even cleared their throat. It was as if every person there had been joined together by some unseen force. There was now no sound of battle either; the ferocious dogfight had come to an end, leaving the warship free to continue its journey and the remaining enemy bombers to retreat. Silence, but for a hungry seagull squawking for scraps as it swooped low over the heads of the crowd. Until finally one solitary voice began to sing, 'Oh, I do like to be beside the seaside . . .' Slowly, barely audible at first, it grew stronger and was joined by another voice, then another, and another. It built in a crescendo until the air along the Clacton-on-Sea promenade was filled with one of the most beautiful and stirring sounds Nellie had ever heard.

This was a Bank Holiday Monday that she, and everyone else, would remember for a very long time.

Chapter 16

Nellie hated Monsieur Pierre's latest addition to his act, which he called 'Biting the Bullet'. It involved a volunteer from the audience being asked to fire a handgun directly at Monsieur, who had first been blindfolded and had his hands tied behind his back. The intention was to shock, startle, and trick the audience into believing that Monsieur had caught the bullet between his teeth. The bullet in the gun was, in fact, a blank, and Monsieur would put a real cartridge in his mouth while the trick was being set up. But Nellie was intensely nervous of the idea, for two reasons. First was that the last person who had tried the stunt had been killed when a real bullet was accidentally inserted into the gun instead of a blank. Secondly, she thought Monsieur was tempting fate by trying out the idea at the Wood Green Empire where the earlier accident had taken place on the same stage in 1912. The artiste who was killed was called Chung Ling Soo, although he was no more Chinese than Monsieur was French.

For three weeks before the new illusion was to be shown for the first time, Monsieur spent a great deal of time with his old mate, Gus Maynard, who was a member of the local Home Guard unit and knew about handling guns. The rehearsals were carried out, like all Monsieur's 'illusions', under great secrecy, although Madame told Nellie that permission had been given to use a target range at an ammunitions factory somewhere in the East End. Both Madame and Nellie were relieved every time Monsieur arrived back home in one piece after a rehearsal; they dreaded the moment when the new act would be tried out on the first day of the Great Pierre's week's booking at the Wood Green Empire.

Top of the bill that week were Elsie and Doris Waters, better known by their stage names Gert and Daisy, two of the most loved Cockney performers of their time. Nellie got to meet them during music rehearsals, and they were so friendly and jolly she felt as though she had known them all her life. They had worked on the same bill as Monsieur many times before but they, too, were nervous about his new 'illusion'.

'You tell Bert Beckwiff from me, Nell,' said Elsie, the plump one of the two, ''e should keep away from guns and bullets an' things. Far safer wiv his Indian rope trick. Wot say you, Gert?'

'Yer can say that again, Daisy!' answered Doris, following her sister's lead and using the style of their stage act to convey her concern.

Elsie Waters could see the anxiety in Nellie's eyes. She dropped the Cockney persona and reverted to her everyday gentle suburban voice. 'Don't worry, dear,' she said reassuringly, 'old Bert's a survivor. He's always dreaming up one mad lark after another.'

'Tell him from us,' added Doris, 'he'd better get through the week if he wants to get paid on Saturday!'

Nellie felt cheered as she watched the two great artistes disappear down the corridor to their dressing room.

Before first house that evening, Nellie had to get in early to make sure that Monsieur's new jet-black wig was combed properly. It was one of the jobs that she didn't particularly relish, for she was sure the hair had been taken from a dead horse. For the act that week Madame had decided to wear a long burgundy chiffon dress, with a large vermilion sash over her left shoulder and an artificial rose pinned to the right side of her waist. Unfortunately, during a Sunday night performance at the Wigan Hippodrome the week before, the hemline of the dress had got caught under Madame's piano stool.

The torn material had been stitched up by the local theatre seamstress, but when Nellie checked over the dress before the morning rehearsal, she was none too pleased with the hasty repair. So one hour before the show began, she sat in Monsieur and Madame's dressing room and used the expertise she had learnt from Ruby to sew up the tear.

Monsieur and Madame arrived just a few minutes later, and Nellie immediately noticed the strained atmosphere between them. They said no more than was absolutely essential to each other, and Nellie's fears about tonight's act increased.

On the half, the time when all artistes were expected to be in the theatre, Nellie went upstairs to make sure that Ange had arrived. Monsieur's assistant was having to share a dressing room with two other girls who were not leading artistes, much to Ange's disdain. They were a tap-dancing duo called the Sisters Tapp who had been around the halls for quite some time and knew the ropes, and Ange soon found out that when it came to bitchy repartee she had met her match.

Nellie knocked on the dressing-room door only once before opening it and peering in. 'Monsieur says you're to watch yer timin' on the Magic Box bit ternight,' she called. ''E says 'e don't want yer smilin' too much till 'e brings out the glass of beer at the end.'

'Tell 'im ter get stuffed!' came Ange's reply.

Nellie took a step into the room. 'Wot did yer say?' she asked. She couldn't see where Ange was.

'I said, tell 'im ter get stuffed!'

One of the Sisters Tapp leaned back in her chair at the dressing table and nodded to the right of the door.

Nellie looked behind the door. Ange was stripped down to her knickers and bra, standing in the small washbasin, sponging down her legs with Lifebuoy soap and cold water. 'Ange!' she gasped, horrified. 'Wot yer doin'?'

Ange paused only long enough to swing her an icy glare. 'Wot d'yer fink I'm doin'? Catchin' up on me beauty sleep?'

'You'd 'ave a job!' quipped one of the Sisters Tapp in a broad Geordie accent. She and her sister sniggered.

'Yer shouldn't be doin' that, Ange,' Nellie scolded. She pointed to a notice pinned to the wall above the washbasin. 'Yer can see wot it says on this notice: "Standing in washbasins is strictly forbidden".'

'Oh, well done, yer clever gel!' sneered Ange. 'Didn't know yer could read anyfin' but kids' books.'

'Meee-oww!' squealed both Sisters Tapp.

'It's dangerous,' insisted Nellie. 'There've bin a lot of accidents. If that basin collapses, yer could hurt yerself bad.'

'Wishful finkin', Nell?' Ange turned off the water tap and climbed out of the sink. 'If it's *my* job you're after, ferget it. I'm a pro, mate.'

All this was too much for the Sisters Tapp, who exchanged a bored and impatient look and got up from the dressing table simultaneously.

'If you'll excuse us,' said the older of the two acidly, '*we* 'ave a show ter do.'

They checked their sailors' mini uniforms and fishnet

stockings in the long mirror, then turned off the electric lights framing their dressing-table mirror and left the room, the steel taps of their dancing shoes clip-clopping down the corridor.

Nellie closed the door behind them and turned angrily to Ange. 'Just exactly wot d'yer mean about me bein' after your job?'

Ange sat down at her dressing table to dry her feet and legs on a towel. 'You know wot I mean, lil' ol' Orphan Annie!' she said nastily. 'Can't wait ter step inter my shoes, can yer? Bright lights an' sweet music, an' yer fink you're a star. Well, yer got anuvver fink comin', Miss Blue-Eyed an' Innocent.' She was glaring at Nellie. 'I'm 'ere ter stay.'

'I don't want your job, Ange,' snapped Nellie. 'I like wot I'm doin', an' I'm grateful ter Monsieur an' Madame fer givin' it ter me.'

'Fer Chrissake cut out all that crap about Monsieur an' Madame. They're nuffin' more than Bert an' Doris Beckwiff from Stepney. Common as muck!'

'Ter me they're Mum an' Dad!' Nellie's voice was raised. 'They're the salt of the earth!'

'Ha!'

Ange's dismissive grunt infuriated Nellie. 'I love them fer wot they are, not *who* they are!'

'Oh, so do I,' replied Ange silkily. 'I love 'em boaf, specially Bert – oh, sorry, *Monsieur*.'

'An' wot's that s'posed ter mean?'

'You know very well,' replied Ange with a smirk on her face. She went back to the washbasin, wiped it round with her towel, then returned to her seat at the dressing table. 'I take good care of Monsieur, Nell, an' 'e takes good care of *me*.'

Nellie watched the reflection of both herself and Ange in the brightly illuminated mirror as they sized each other up. Ange started applying her make-up, using first her basic Five and Nine greasepaint sticks. 'Yer've got a lot ter learn about the feater, mate,' she said, rubbing the foundation into her cheeks. 'Specially wot goes on *after* the show.'

Nellie turned away and made for the door. The combination of the smell from Ange's greasepaint and the heat generated by the dozen or so electric lightbulbs round the dressing-table mirror was stifling her.

'Yer mustn't let it get yer down, Nell,' Ange called, using a deep red carmine stick on her lips and watching Nellie carefully in the mirror. 'We all 'ave ter get on in this world, don't we?'

Nellie paused at the door. 'You're right, Ange,' she said quietly. 'An' some of us like ter dream, don't we?'

They were interrupted by a banging on the door. 'Overture and beginners, please!' yelled the call boy's voice from the corridor outside.

The show – the real show – was about to begin.

First house Monday at Wood Green was full. The people of nearby Harringay, Turnpike Lane, Palmers Green and Stoke Newington knew what they liked, and with favourites like Gert and Daisy, the Great Pierre, the Flying Ellisons, and popular stand-up comedian Billy Bennett on the bill, there wasn't a seat to be had. Most regulars had their own particular evening for visiting their local music hall, but tonight they swarmed into the traditional red plush and gold auditorium because the word had got around that the Great Pierre was going to attempt something really daring this evening.

At six fifteen, the house lights dimmed and the conductor took his place in the centre of the orchestra pit. Nellie was in her usual place, standing on her own at the back of the stalls. There were five acts to go before

Monsieur took the stage but her stomach was already churning. She was also concerned that Patrick had not yet turned up, which irritated her after all the trouble she had gone to to get him a complimentary standing room only ticket. By the end of the overture, however, he crept in, and sneaked his arm round Nellie's waist.

'Where've yer bin?' Nellie whispered as the Sisters Tapp took the stage with a frenzied tap routine to the strains of 'I Got Rhythm'.

'Business,' replied Patrick, close to her ear.

'Wot kind of business?'

'I've just robbed a bank and nicked ten thousand pounds.'

Nellie chuckled at Patrick's flippant reply, but she was still curious to know what work he did. Although she had been seeing him for several weeks, she knew as little about him now as she did when they first met.

The Sisters Tapp left the stage to tumultuous applause, and everyone settled down to a thrilling high slack wire act, the Flying Ellisons, which was followed by what Nellie thought was one of the funniest stand-up comedians in the business. Billy Bennett, billed as 'Always a Gentleman', was a portly little man with a boozer's flushed face, blood-red nose, and a bushy brown moustache. He came on stage looking like everyone's favourite uncle, wearing a bowler hat, three-piece brown serge suit, and highly polished brown leather shoes. 'I'm 'ere to talk on behalf of the workin' class,' he opened, and for the next fifteen minutes he sent wave after wave of laughter through the audience as he passed comment on the world as he saw it, and recited from his own repertoire of humorous wartime poems.

Nellie and Patrick both rocked with laughter, and for those few minutes Nellie forgot about the ache in her stomach that kept telling her that there was only one more act to go before the Great Pierre took the stage. That act was the 'Novelty Juggler' Frank Marks with his lovely young assistant, Iris. At first, Nellie found little to interest her in the act which consisted of juggling with up to eight clubs at a time. But then she remembered what Madame had once told her about supporting acts like this being the very life and heart of the music hall, where people worked long hours to make a name for themselves and were often only there to keep the audience warm until the appearance of the top of the bill.

There was a gasp from the audience as the house lights dimmed and the act culminated with a dazzling array of wildly flashing clubs whirling high into the air, each one lit up by a tiny coloured light, and all to the rousing orchestral accompaniment of Johann Strauss's 'Thunder and Lightning Polka'.

Once again thunderous applause rocked the theatre, and as the secondary stage curtains swished gracefully together, Nellie felt her stomach rise up into her mouth. Patrick could feel the tension in her body. He knew the reason for it and gave her waist a reassuring squeeze.

At last the moment arrived. The house lights dimmed from stalls to gods, and the entire theatre was plunged into almost total darkness. Nellie could feel the current of excitement and anticipation running through the auditorium; there was dead silence, but for one young teenage girl who sniggered nervously. Then, from the orchestra pit, came the sound of a cymbal, quivering and hissing like a snake, and as it built in volume a bright white spotlight no larger than a tennis ball picked out the ghostly white face and thin black moustache of a figure dressed from head to foot in black, swirling round and round, arms outstretched, massive black cloak swirling through the air as if in slow motion.

Gradually the spotlight expanded to reveal the whole face until, quite suddenly, the hissing cymbal came to a loud climax, whereupon the figure froze, statue-like, in the centre of the stage, dark, pencil-lined eyes fixing the audience with a menacing stare.

'Ladies and gentlemen!' The auditorium echoed to the sound of the stage manager's voice booming out over the theatre's loudspeaker system. 'The Wood Green Empire is proud to present THE GREAT PIERRE!'

The theatre erupted with applause as Monsieur took a very theatrical bow. Simultaneously, the curtains behind him opened to reveal a sinister black backcloth with, on one side of the stage, Madame at the grand piano, only just visible in a subdued blue spotlight, and on the other side of the stage Ange, poised like a figure of death in a black hood and long black cloak that reached to the floor. Monsieur turned with a dramatic flourish of his white-gloved hands and the stage became bathed in green light, Madame started to play, and Ange let her cloak drop to reveal her scanty stage costume of glittering green sequins.

Nellie's eyes travelled over Madame's burgundy dress, checking that the repair she had made just a short time earlier was no longer visible. Satisfied that it wasn't, she turned her attention to the act.

First came the juggling with swords, which at times gave the impression that they were sliding in and out of Monsieur's body. That was followed by the Magic Box trick, in which Ange, orchestrated by Monsieur, had to pull a variety of unlikely objects out of the box – a white mouse which ran up Monsieur's arm and disappeared into his white-gloved hands, an electric lightbulb which flashed on and off without any sign of a connection, several kitchen utensils, a large ginger tom cat, and finally dozens of Union Jack pennants which, together with Madame's rousing accompaniment of patriotic piano music, brought a round of applause from the audience.

Then came the old favourites, such as sawing the lady (Ange) in half, the Indian rope trick, in which a length of rope coiled uncannily on its own out of a woven basket like some dangerous reptile, and the most extraordinary sight of all, the levitation of a human form (Ange again) which rose up from the stage like a laid-out corpse, lit only by a chilling red spotlight. It was all heady, mesmerising stuff, and Nellie never ceased to be amazed by the tricks. No one was allowed to know how they were done; Monsieur always insisted that during his act, nobody was allowed to watch from either the wings or the flies above. Even at home he worked on his tricks behind the locked door of his workroom on the top floor of the house and not even Madame was privy to the innermost secrets of the Great Pierre.

Finally, it was time for the climax of the act, the moment that Nellie and the entire audience had been waiting for. It was heralded by a roll of drums in the orchestra pit, and the melodramatic voice of the stage manager.

'Ladies and gentlemen!'

Roll of drums, terminated by the clash of a cymbal.

'Tonight, Monsieur Pierre will embark on the most dangerous, the most death-defying illusion of his entire career. Before your very eyes, a volunteer from the audience will be asked to fire a bullet from a handgun directly at Monsieur Pierre . . .'

Gasps from the audience.

'Monsieur will then attempt to *catch the bullet between his teeth* . . .'

More gasps from the audience.

Monsieur stepped into the bright white spotlight, bared his teeth and with one gloved finger pointed to where he intended to 'Bite the Bullet'. Then he quickly stepped back out of the spotlight.

'Ladies and gentlemen,' continued the booming voice of the stage manager, 'this illusion requires the utmost concentration by Monsieur Pierre. He therefore asks each and every one of you to be absolutely silent throughout the remarkable event you are about to witness. If you wish to clear your throat or blow your nose, please do so now.'

It seemed that the entire audience wished to do so; the auditorium was suddenly filled with the nervous sounds of throats being cleared and noses being blown.

Nellie did neither. Her blood had turned to ice, and she was so tense she could hardly breathe.

'And so, ladies and gentlemen,' continued the dramatic voice, 'we come to the moment of truth. First of all, we ask if we have a volunteer in the audience tonight who would like to fire the fatal bullet at this great and fearless artiste?'

There was a deathly hush. Ange, who had spent much of the act adopting various absurd poses and who always acknowledged the applause at the end of each turn as though it was all meant for her, shielded her eyes from the stage footlights and peered out into the audience to see if anyone was offering their services.

'Come now,' called the stage manager. 'One person, just one courageous person who is willing to put Monsieur to the test.'

'Over 'ere!' came a man's voice from the back stalls. 'I'll 'ave a go!'

The audience craned their heads as one to see who was volunteering.

With a spotlight covering her, Ange moved to the steps on the left-hand side of the stage and went down to meet the man who, to Nellie's relief, turned out to be Monsieur's old Home Guard mate, Gus Maynard.

'A volunteer!' proclaimed the stage manager's voice triumphantly. 'Let's give him a big hand, ladies and gentlemen.'

The audience was too wound up to demonstrate very much enthusiasm, so while Ange led Gus up on to the stage, Madame played some mood-setting music.

Nellie's heart was thumping. But, scared as she was, Ange's squeaky little voice started to echo through her mind: '*I take good care of Monsieur, Nell. An' 'e takes good care of me.*'

The audience watched with bated breath as Monsieur greeted his 'volunteer', gave him the handgun, and went through the motions of showing him how to use it, making quite sure while he did so that the barrel was kept pointed down towards the floor.

Once again, the house lights were turned off, leaving only two spotlights, one on Monsieur on one side of the stage, the other on the apparently courageous 'volunteer'.

A roll of the drums. A clash of the cymbal.

Monsieur raised his arms out from his sides and turned towards the 'volunteer', who raised the handgun and took aim.

'*Allez!*' called Monsieur, in very Cockney French. He rarely spoke during his act, but this was one of the few French words he had taken the trouble to learn. '*Un . . . deux . . . trois* . . . SHOOT!'

Nellie turned her head away and crunched up in terror as the shot was fired.

The audience gasped, squealed, shouted, and one or two women even screamed.

Nellie looked up. Monsieur had fallen to his knees, seemingly in pain as he covered his face with his white gloved hands.

'Oh Gawd!' howled Nellie, causing several people in the back stalls to turn round and look at her. ''E's bin 'it! 'E's bin 'it!'

The wave of horror that swept through the audience suggested that the tragedy of 1912 had just been repeated. But just when one or two people felt distressed enough to get up from their seats, Monsieur suddenly recovered himself, stood up, and with a flourish took his hands away from his face to reveal the bullet lodged firmly between his clenched teeth.

The conductor of the orchestra, who was just as relieved as the audience to know that Monsieur's illusion had worked, immediately prompted his musicians to give this dramatic climax to the act a triumphant orchestral flourish.

Nellie didn't know whether to laugh or cry; her relief and excitement were so great that she just threw her arms round Patrick and hugged him tight.

On stage, Monsieur took the bullet from between his teeth and held it up for all to see, while his adoring audience shouted, cheered, whistled, squealed, applauded, and stamped their feet in appreciation and admiration. As the main house curtain came down behind Monsieur, he took bow after bow on his own in the spotlight, until he was finally joined by Madame on one side and Ange on the other, and hand in hand they bowed and curtsied together.

It was yet another triumph for the Great Pierre.

After the second house show, Monsieur and Madame's dressing room was crammed with wellwishers. Monsieur, a glass of brown ale in one hand and the smoke from his Abdullah fag wafting up from the holder in his other hand, lapped up all the attention he was getting. Madame was pleased that her husband's new illusion had been both safe and successful, but she was less happy about the way Ange was standing alongside Monsieur, attempting to hog as much of the limelight as she could. Nellie had brought Patrick to meet her mum and dad and he, too, was full of praise for the way the act had held the audience absolutely spellbound. Monsieur graciously acknowledged the compliment and opened up the conversation with Patrick. ''Aven't 'eard from any of your boys just lately,' he said expansively while admiring himself in his dressing-table mirror over Patrick's shoulder.

Patrick exchanged a puzzled look with Nellie. 'I don't foller you, sir.'

'The IRA,' Monsieur said lightly. 'They seem ter be keepin' themselves ter themselves these days, fank the Lord.'

Patrick stiffened visibly. 'I don't know nothin' about the IRA, sir,' he said.

'But you're Irish, ain't yer?'

Madame was embarrassed. 'Don't be silly, dear,' she cut in quickly. 'Not all Irish people belong to the IRA.'

'Well, let's face it,' responded Monsieur, determined to continue with what he considered to be a bit of harmless fun, 'most of 'em ain't on our side in this war, are they? I mean, look wot they done in nineteen forty just before the Blitz – that bomb down Whiteley's store in Bayswater, and the one outside that 'otel in Park Lane. Not exactly an act of friendship, would yer say?'

'Patrick don't 'ave nuffin' ter do wiv politics, Dad,' Nellie interceded; she could see the tension rising in Patrick. 'That's right, ain't it, Patrick?' She turned to look at him, even though she was unsure she believed what she had just said.

'I doubt anyone in their right mind believes in politics,' said Madame, trying to defuse the atmosphere.

'There's no time for it durin' a war. We all 'ave ter stick tergevver.'

Monsieur was at last beginning to realise that perhaps he had gone too far. 'You're absolutely right, me dear,' he said, giving Patrick a friendly smile. 'No offence meant, Pat lad. As a matter of fact, some of me best pals are Paddys.'

Patrick looked at Nellie. His expression was thunderous. 'I'd better be goin',' he mumbled. 'Got an early call termorrow.'

'I'll see yer out,' said Nellie following him anxiously to the door.

'No need,' replied Patrick. 'I can find me way. G'night, Mr Beckwith, Mrs Beckwith. It was a grand act.' He quickly pecked Nellie on the cheek, then left.

Madame looked mortified. 'Go after 'im, Nell,' she said, very concerned. 'Tell 'im we didn't mean nuffin'.'

Nellie rushed out of the dressing room and caught up with Patrick just as he was leaving by the stage door. 'Patrick!' she called anxiously. 'Don't go. Yer mustn't take any notice of Dad. 'E's just excited, that's all. 'E din't mean wot 'e said.'

Patrick stopped and swung round. 'Oh, he didn't, didn't he?' he snapped angrily. 'Well, let me tell yer somethin'. That man is nothin' more than a pile of horseshit!'

Nellie immediately stiffened. 'Don't talk like that, please, Patrick. 'E's my farver!'

'Then go back ter 'im!'

'Fer Chrissake, wot's 'e said that's upset yer so much? Yer'd fink 'e'd stabbed yer in the back or somefin'!'

'As far as I'm concerned, he has!' Patrick turned and started to walk away from her.

'Wot's up wiv you?' Nellie barked. 'You got a guilt complex or somefin'?'

Patrick stopped and again swung round on her. 'And what's that supposed ter mean?'

'If yer've got nuffin' ter 'ide,' Nellie replied, 'I don't see wot you're gettin' so worked up about.'

'I have *nothing* ter hide!'

Although it was now late and dark, there were still a few people strolling home from the Silver Bullet pub just round the corner. Suspecting there was some kind of lovers' tiff going on, they gave Nellie and Patrick a wide berth.

'D'yer realise I know nuffin' about you, Patrick?' Nellie said, trying to lower her voice. 'Ever since I met yer, yer've never told me exactly where yer live, wot yer do, or anyfin' about yer folks. That's wot I call secretive.'

Patrick glared at her 'OK! OK! So tell me, wot d'yer want ter know?'

Nellie hesitated for a moment, then took the plunge. 'Who were those two blokes yer was wiv that night yer took me to the Irish dance at the arcade down the Nag's 'Ead? You was 'avin' a barney wiv two blokes in the air-raid shelter.'

Patrick froze. 'So that's it,' he said contemptuously. 'You *were* spying on me.'

'Don't be stupid!' Nellie shouted. 'Yer suddenly leave me all on me tod in the middle of a dance 'all, then 'cos I come lookin' fer yer, yer tell me I'm spyin' on yer!'

'Then how d'yer know we was arguing?'

''Cos I *heard* yer. I'm not deaf, dumb, an' blind, yer know!' She walked right up to him, kept her voice as low as possible, and challenged him. 'Who were they, Patrick? Are yer mixed up in somefin' – in the IRA?'

For a moment, there was no response from Patrick. He just stared at her in silence. Then he turned away and started to walk off.

Nellie wasn't having it and bellowed after him, 'Yer

can't just keep fings from me, Patrick! Sooner or later, yer'll 'ave ter tell me!'

Patrick swung round angrily. 'They're my brothers! My own family! We were discussing something personal. Is that good enough for yer, Nellie? Are you happy now?'

Nellie was at a loss for words. With mixed feelings, she watched Patrick stride off in the dark. As he disappeared out of sight round the corner into Seven Sisters Road, she was convinced that this was the last she would see of him.

Chapter 17

The number 14 bus took for ever, at least that's what it seemed like to Nellie. She had already had to endure a journey of half an hour, for the bus was early, and the driver was taking his time, despite the fact that Hornsey Rise was no more than ten minutes or so away at the most. Even before she got to the bus stop in Caledonian Road, she knew she would have to wait. There seemed to be something about London buses; they never came on time. They blamed it all on the war.

Nellie had no idea where Patrick lived. He had never given her the address, only that he lived with his parents in a house somewhere near a small park just off Hornsey Rise. She had to find him. No matter how long it took her, she had to find him and apologise for what she had said to him outside the Wood Green Empire the night before. Every time she thought about it her stomach turned over. Why did she have to assume that he was mixed up with a bunch of Irish spies just because she had overheard him having a row with two men that she hadn't even heard properly. If he said the row was personal, about family matters, then who was she to disbelieve him? She cringed at the thought of her behaviour but was determined to put things right. The only trouble was how to find him.

The bus finally limped to a halt at the junction of the busy main Hornsey Road and the rather posh-looking Hazelville Road. Nellie decided to get off so that she could stroll around a bit and make a few inquiries.

Luckily, she did not have to be at the theatre until first house that evening; it was only mid-morning now so she had plenty of time on her hands. But where to start?

First she searched for a park, but after looking around and asking several rather bemused passers-by, there didn't seem to be much on offer except a small area of grass close to where she had got off the bus. Like so many other parts of Islington, Hornsey Rise had had its share of bomb damage. There were the inevitable empty sites piled high with rubble, and gaps in the neat rows of Edwardian and Victorian terraced houses. Even so, this part of the borough seemed to Nellie to be more affluent than those small back streets behind the Nag's Head. There were more trees, and more space, and people walked with their heads up and seemed to know where they were going, unlike some of those in Seven Sisters Road, who appeared to be mesmerised by either the pavement or the shop windows when they walked.

Nellie reached the highest point of the 'Rise' after walking around for nearly an hour and a half. The view from the top wasn't the most exciting in the world, but she could see Holloway stretched out in the distance below, and behind her the leafy outskirts of Crouch Hill with a distant view of the radio mast on top of Alexandra Palace towards Wood Green. By this time, her feet were killing her, and as soon as she found a bench which overlooked Hornsey Road, she stopped to rest for a few minutes.

It was a lovely summer's day, and the sun was picking out colours magically, when under normal circumstances the same objects looked grey and drab. Even the single-decker buses climbing up Crouch Hill glowed a spectacular red in the midday sun, and Nellie thought that if she had been an artist, she would have liked to capture a scene that was at first glance so ordinary but also so alive. Then she thought of why she was here, and how futile and pointless it all was. How could she possibly find Patrick among all these streets and houses? It was like trying to find a needle in a haystack. As her eyes scanned the patchwork of rooftops laid out in the valley beneath her, her attention focused on the steeples of three churches. Surely they were worth a try. At least one of those churches would be Roman Catholic, and surely someone there would know an Irish family in the neighbourhood by the name of Duvall.

The Reverend Archie Scott at St Luke's was certainly the most likeable of the vicars Nellie called on during her trek round the three churches in Hornsey Rise. In fact, he couldn't have been nicer. Unfortunately he was a bit on the vague side and seemed more interested in telling Nellie about the night an oil bomb fell just behind the church and blew in their only stained-glass window. The fact of the matter was that he hadn't a clue who the Duvall family were, or where they could be found. Nellie didn't have much luck at St Thomas's either, for the vicar there was a ferocious Church of England Bible-puncher, and the mere mention of the words Roman Catholic was enough to give him palpitations. Finally, Nellie found her way to the Church of Our Lady, which was situated in a quiet back street between, rather appropriately, a pub and an undertaker's parlour. The only problem was that when she got there, a funeral Mass was in progress, and when it was over, Father Michael O'Halloran had little time to spare for Nellie. However, an elderly Irish nun named Sister Marie Louise came to the rescue.

'Duvall?' she asked, peering over the top of tiny rimless spectacles. 'Yer don't mean our little Patrick, do yer?'

Nellie's eyes lit up. 'Yeah, that's 'im!' she said eagerly. 'Patrick. Patrick Duvall. D'yer know 'im?'

'Know him? Ha! Little scoundrel! I've known him since he was nothin' but a glint in his mother's eyes. And his brothers too. They're all young scoundrels, all three of 'em!'

Nellie breathed a sigh of relief. She smiled at the old lady who was chuckling merrily to herself as though she was reliving her whole relationship with the Duvall boys. So it was true what Patrick had told her the previous night. He *did* have two brothers.

'Are you a friend of the family?' asked the old nun whose sunny smile was in complete contrast to her pallid complexion visible beneath her white coif.

'Sort of,' replied Nellie. 'Fing is, I've bin away a bit, an' I've lost their address.'

The old lady was still fondly thinking of the Duvall boys. 'They're good people, that's for sure,' she said, with a nod of the head. 'Those boys have stuck together through thick an' thin. I tell you, harm one an' yer harm the lot. Their mother an' father must be proud of them. An' so is our Lord God the Father.' She looked up towards the church ceiling, and with two fingers of her right hand, crossed herself. Nellie briefly lowered her eyes.

'Do all the bruvvers live tergevver then?' she asked.

'Mercy, no!' came the quick reply. 'Tom and Seamus are still at home with their parents. I'm afraid they'll both be called up in the next few months, God help us.'

Nellie was puzzled and wanted to ask more, but before she could do so the old lady was called silently away by one of the other sisters.

'Number Fourteen Winsford Place,' said the old nun quietly before she scurried off. 'It's a tiny little mews just off Hornsey Lane. Yer can't miss it. Give that rascal Patrick my love!'

Nellie watched her go, relieved to know that at least Patrick was held in such high regard.

An hour and a half later, Nellie at last found the elusive Winsford Place. The elderly nun had said it was just off

240

Hornsey Lane, but Hornsey Lane stretched for what seemed like a couple of miles from Crouch End Hill to Highgate High Street. Winsford Place turned out to be far scruffier than the name suggested. There were about two dozen small houses in all, facing each other on either side, and like most other properties in the borough they clearly needed a coat of paint and extensive renovation. Some of the windows were still boarded up from the Blitz two years before, and weeds were growing out of cracks in the stucco on the flat roofs. All the houses had just two floors, and it seemed to Nellie that it would be quite a crush for any fair-sized family to live in.

Number 14 was the last house on the right-hand side. It was joined to a large brick wall which seemed to form part of a junk yard full of old motorcar tyres. The small paved area in front of the house had three over-full dustbins, one of which was used for pig swill and was very smelly in the afternoon sun.

Nellie made her way to the front gate. The latch was broken and made a sharp grating sound when she opened it. The front door had both a doorbell and a rusty door knocker. Nellie chose the bell, but when she tried pushing it, it seemed to make no sound at all, so she banged on the door with the horseshoe-shaped door knocker. There was no response. When Nellie peered through one of the smoked glass door panels, she could see no sign of life at all. All the curtains at the ground-floor bay window were drawn, so she couldn't even get a glimpse of how the Duvall family kept their place. Eventually, she gave up, but as she turned away, she came face to face with a young woman not very much older than herself.

'Are yer lookin' fer someone?' she asked, with a slight Irish brogue.

'Oh, yes,' replied Nellie, a bit sheepish, and feeling as though she'd just been caught trying to break

241

in. 'I was wonderin' whevver the Duvall family lived 'ere.'

The girl's face relaxed. It was actually quite a sweet face, although rather tired and drawn. 'Yes, we do,' she replied. 'Can I help?'

'I'm lookin' fer Patrick,' said Nellie awkwardly. 'Is 'e at 'ome?'

''Fraid not,' replied the girl. 'He doesn't get back from the pub till after three.'

Nellie was puzzled. 'Pub?'

'The Hornsey Arms, it's just up the lane. He works behind the bar there.'

Nellie didn't say anything for a moment. There was nothing wrong with Patrick working in a pub, but it just hadn't occurred to her that someone like him would be doing such a run-of-the-mill job. 'But this is the right 'ouse?' she asked. 'This is where 'e lives wiv 'is mum an' dad?'

'His mum an' dad!' The girl roared with laughter. 'Over my dead body!'

Nellie was beginning to feel decidedly ill at ease. 'Can I ask,' she said, 'who are yer?'

The smile disappeared from the girl's face. 'I was about ter ask you the same question.'

The two girls stared briefly at each other in silence. 'I'm a friend of Patrick's.'

'My name's Bridget,' replied the girl, stony-faced. 'I'm Patrick's wife.'

Nellie felt her stomach turn inside out. She wanted to say something, but she didn't know what. All she could do was grab hold of the broken front gate and open it. 'I'm sorry ter 'ave bovvered yer,' she said.

The girl stood aside to let Nellie pass. Behind her was a baby's pushchair containing a beautiful child, a little boy. It started to grizzle as Nellie rushed off.

'Can I tell Patrick who called?' called the girl.

Nellie stopped only long enough to turn and say, 'I wouldn't bovver. If yer ask me, I reckon 'e's got quite enough on 'is plate.'

Ange was in one of her spiky moods. Nellie knew it the moment she got back to the house from Hornsey Rise, for she could hear Ange outside in the conservatory, ranting to Monsieur about the way she was being treated by the Wood Green Empire management. Nellie couldn't bear the sound of Ange's voice at the best of times, but today it was more shrill and ugly than ever. As she climbed the stairs to her bedroom, she could hear her shout, 'Yer couldn't do the act wivout me, an' yer know it! You keep that bloody woman's nose out of my business, or I'll tell 'er wot I *really* fink of 'er!' Even after she'd gone into her bedroom and shut the door, Nellie could hear that bossy, demanding little voice, and it nauseated her. Why did Monsieur keep bowing to her demands? What hold had that trumped-up, brassy little cow got over him?

She threw herself down on the bed and stared up at the ceiling. What a day it had been! Why couldn't life just be simple? Why couldn't people behave like civilised human beings and be grateful for what they had? How she hated Patrick for lying to her, for leading her on as though she was some cheap little pick-up from the street. And then she thought back to the night when they had slept together in the very same bed she was lying on now. Her flesh crept at the thought of how stupid she'd been. Men! They were nothing but liars and cheats. One of these days she'd get her own back. One of these days . . .

A few minutes later, Nellie heard the front door slam. She got up and made her way downstairs.

Monsieur was still in the conservatory. Nellie felt really sorry for him, for he was sitting bent forward on a wicker-work chair, his elbows on his knees and his head buried in his hands, looking as though he had the worries of the world on his shoulders. Which wasn't surprising after listening to Ange ranting on, thought Nellie. 'Anything wrong, Dad?' she asked tentatively.

Monsieur looked up with a start, clearly surprised. 'Nell,' he said anxiously. 'Din't know yer was 'ome.'

Nellie smiled warmly. 'I was listenin' ter the wireless up in my room,' she said, trying to allay his fears. Then she sat on another wickerwork chair beside him. 'Is everyfin' all right, Dad? I mean wiv Ange, an' all that?'

'Ange?' he replied brightly. 'Course there's nuffin' wrong. Wot gave yer that idea?'

'I just wondered, that's all,' replied Nellie. 'I saw yer talkin' to 'er when I came in.'

Monsieur was getting a little agitated. 'Oh, it was nuffin', nuffin' at all. We was just talkin' over the new act. You know our Ange. She's a bit 'ighly strung. Always gets 'er knickers in a twist when I 'ave ter change anyfin'.'

Nellie leaned across and put her arm round his shoulders. 'Yer mustn't let 'er bully yer, Dad,' she said gently. He was obviously under some pressure. 'It's your act, not 'ers.'

'Bully?' said Monsieur, quickly reaching for his packet of Abdullahs. 'Oh no, Nell. Yer've got it all wrong, gel. Ange ain't tryin' ter bully me. Oh no. She's just – finkin' of the good of the act, that's all.'

Nellie watched him carefully as he got up, looked for his cigarette holder, and wedged an Abdullah into it. In the background, a small imitation antique clock chimed the hour. Nellie turned to look outside the conservatory window, where a blue-tit was tapping for scraps of bread. Whilst she waited for Monsieur to light up his cigarette, only one thought dominated her mind after all she had been through that day. Why was it that men had to be so deceitful? Once they were married, they had the best of all worlds – a wife, kids, a good home, and yet it wasn't enough. They wanted adventure, to take risks with their marriage. Why did they do it? Was it because they wanted to stay young, or was it that they just had to prove something to themselves? Maybe it was the same thing. Deep down inside, she was in despair. After all she had learnt in so short a time, how could she ever love a man? But then she thought that maybe there was someone out there whom she could love.

Monsieur had lit his Abdullah and now started coughing. 'Why do I smoke these bloody fings!' he said angrily, pulling the cigarette holder out of his mouth and glaring at it. 'This is nuffin' ter do wiv me, Nell,' he spluttered in an outburst of pent-up frustration. 'This is part of my uvver self, somefin' that comes ter life just twice a night up on some stage somewhere.' He found the nearest ashtray and firmly stubbed out the Abdullah. Then he opened a small drawer in the wickerwork table and took out a packet of Woodbines, a much cheaper brand. 'This is what I'm all about, Nell,' he said, lighting up again. 'Bert Beckwiff from Stepney, not Monsieur Pierre from bloody Frogland.' He inhaled a lungful of smoke, then took the fag out of his mouth and smiled at it. 'Yes, Nell. This is wot I'm all about. This is no music 'all illusion.'

Nellie got up from her seat, went across to Monsieur, and lightly kissed him on the forehead. 'See yer later, Dad,' she said affectionately. Then she turned to go.

'Nell?'

Nellie stopped and looked back.

'I'm sorry fer the way I talked ter yer bloke last night,' he said awkwardly. 'I 'ad no right. Will yer fergive me?'

Nellie smiled weakly at him. 'Don't be silly, Dad,' she replied. 'I don't 'ave nuffin' ter fergive yer for. Anyway, yer was probably right. Paddys are all the same.'

Monsieur was watching her carefully. 'No, Nell,' he said, showing uncharacteristic sensitivity. 'All *people* are the same. We all 'ave faults, we all make mistakes. I know I've made a good few of 'em in my time, an' don't worry, you'll make quite a few yerself as time goes by. But it don't mean we're all bad. It just means we're weak. An' that's somefin' we all 'ave ter pay fer, one way or anuvver.'

A sharp summer thunderstorm cracked loudly over the Wood Green Empire just as the first house audience was arriving. The approach roads to the theatre were carpeted with a swaying mass of dark umbrellas, and by the time they reached the theatre itself, they looked like a vast field of mushrooms. Those without umbrellas had to sit through the performance in wet clothes.

There was quite a thunderstorm brewing inside dressing room number 5, too. Ange had accused Gladys, one of the Sisters Tapp, of nicking her bottle of wet white, a liquid powder used for covering blemishes. The row had become so fierce that Gladys, a tough Geordie who was known in the music hall business for her quick right hook, was very close to sending the 'little tart from Clapham Junction' on stage with a black eye. Nellie saved the situation by finding the precious bottle of wet white on top of the toilet cistern in the ladies' room next door, where Ange had apparently forgotten it.

During the first house performance, Nellie stayed in Monsieur and Madame's dressing room. The agony of watching someone firing a revolver at Monsieur every night was too much for her and as she had quite a lot of sewing to do, she decided to keep away from it all. Before they went on, Monsieur and Madame discussed the act, what changes should be made and how best they could improve things. Nellie was proud of how professional they both were, and listened to everything they said with interest. She had heard the act discussed so many times, she felt she knew it off by heart – apart from what Monsieur called 'the secrets of the trade'. Even Ange was only permitted to know what was absolutely essential to her part in the act.

There was always a long wait between their first and second house appearances. Usually, neither of them felt like eating until after the final curtain of the night, but tonight Monsieur's appetite was whetted by the smell of someone backstage eating chips; so Nellie volunteered to go out and get them all some fish and chips from the shop just round the corner in the High Road.

The thunderstorm had now given way to a less angry sky, and as Nellie left the stage door and made her way out on to the main road, the pavements were glistening in the short bursts of mid-evening sunshine. The storm had cleared the air, and Nellie felt relieved to get away for a few minutes from the clammy atmosphere of the backstage dressing room.

As usual, there was a long queue outside the fish and chip shop, and Nellie hoped that by the time she got to the counter, they would not have sold out. Fish and chips were, as Monsieur kept telling her, 'the poor person's slap-up meal', but as fish supplies were being hit hard by the war in both the North Sea and North Atlantic, fish was not as easy to come by as it used to be.

''Ow's me ol' mate doin' ternight then?' asked Gracie, the doyenne of Islington fish and chip shops. Gracie and her husband Mitch were great characters, the salt of the earth to their customers, Gracie always immaculate in clean apron and turban, and Mitch in his white jacket and straw boater hat. 'Tell 'im from me, 'e nearly give me a 'eart attack last night,' Gracie said, piling a scoopful of chips into an old copy of the *Daily Herald*.

''Onest ter Gawd, I fawt 'e'd copped 'is lot when that stupid geezer fired a shot at 'im on that stage!' added Mitch.

A few minutes later, Nellie was on her way back to the theatre, her string bag filled with generous pieces of cod and chips for Monsieur, Madame, and herself. As she turned into the small back alley where the stage door was located, she found her way barred.

'Hello, Nell.'

Nellie didn't even have to look up to know that it was Patrick. She didn't reply, merely tried to walk past him.

'Nell,' he said, placing himself right in front of her. 'Give me a chance to explain, please.'

Nellie couldn't bring herself to look at his face, so she kept her eyes lowered. 'There's nuffink to explain,' she replied coldly. Then she made another attempt to move round him.

Again, Patrick blocked her way.

'I should have told you, Nell,' he said, both hands clutching her shoulders. 'I had no right to – to . . .'

'You 'ad every right ter do wot yer like, Patrick,' Nellie said impassively. 'It's a free country.'

'I didn't want to deceive you, Nell. You've got to believe that.'

Nellie finally looked up at him. 'I believe yer, Patrick,' she said, without any feeling at all.

'I fell in love with you, Nell,' he continued, his voice anguished. 'I'm still in love with you. I don't want us to lose what we have.'

'Lose wot we 'ave?' Nellie asked. 'Wot do we 'ave, Patrick? Din't your mum, or your dad, or your bruvvers, or that good priest up your local church ever tell yer, it ain't possible ter love two people at the same time?'

'Oh, but it is, Nell! I love you, I love my wife, and I love my baby.'

'So wot yer goin' ter do, Patrick? Share us around a bit, one night fer me, one night fer 'er?'

Two stagehands approached, and Patrick waited until they had disappeared through the door before answering. 'You don't understand, Nell. I love all three of you, but I love you most of all.'

Nellie looked straight through him. 'Then yer've got a problem, ain't yer, mate?'

'I've been trying to summon up enough courage to tell you for weeks. That night you saw me quarrelling with my brothers. It was nothing to do with the IRA. I'm not a traitor, Nell. I love this country, and I'd never do anything to harm it. It was *you* we were quarrelling about. They wanted me to get rid of you. They told me my place was at home, with my wife and my child. They told me I should go to see Father O'Halloran, to confess my sins. They told me I was a disgrace to myself and all our family.'

'Is that a fact?' replied Nellie. 'Good ter know some people know wot's right an' wrong.'

'D'you feel nothin' for me, Nell? Nothin'? After all we've had together?'

Nellie paused a moment before answering. 'Yes, Patrick. I do feel somefin' for yer. I feel you've destroyed my confidence in all the fings I believe in most. I trusted you, Patrick. I trusted yer so much that I slept wiv yer, the first an' only time I've ever slept wiv any feller. I did that knowin' that I was betrayin' my family, my own family, the only ones who've ever meant anyfin' ter me.' She pushed him to one side. 'Wot kind of a person d'yer fink I am, Patrick Duvall?'

'Someone special, very special. Someone I truly love, and can't do without.'

Nellie looked at him just one last time. 'Sorry, mate,' she said, unsmiling, and without emotion. 'That's your problem, not mine.' With that she disappeared through the stage door.

At the conclusion of the second house show, Monsieur informed his wife that he had an important meeting with his agent, which meant that he wouldn't be able to come straight home with her and Nellie. Madame took this news in her stride, or appeared to; she had become used to these sudden 'important' meetings after the show and had long ago decided that it would be useless to complain. So as soon as Nellie had finished helping both Monsieur and herself to hang up their stage costumes, Madame suggested that they leave their usual taxi for Monsieur and take the bus.

Although it was now quite dark outside, there was still a wonderful glow in the midsummer air, which hung over the rooftops as if to suggest that it would not be many hours before it was light again. Both Madame and Nellie thought that the air was now so light and fresh that they would walk to the bus stop at Turnpike Lane, which was about ten to fifteen minutes further down the road.

'Yer know, Nellie,' Madame said as they strolled quietly along the High Road, watching the last of the theatre crowds making their way to their buses. 'Before the war, from down 'ere yer could see the light on top of the mast at the dear old Ally Pally.'

Nellie turned to look up in the direction Madame was indicating. But she could see no sign of that great glass exhibition hall called Alexandra Palace, high on top of the hill at Alexandra Park, for, like all other buildings throughout the capital, the war had extinguished all its lights.

'When we was young, Albert and I used ter go roller-skating up there.' The nostalgic smile on Madame's face was tinged with sadness. 'That was before we 'ad the kids, of course. They was good days. Me and Albert used ter share so much tergevver.'

Nellie was careful in her reply. 'D'yer wish it was like that now, Mum?'

Madame shrugged her shoulders. 'Fings can never be the same as they were at the beginning. After all, times move on. We all 'ave ter change, don't we? At least, that's wot people keep tellin' us, so it 'as ter be true, don't it?'

'I don't fink change means better,' replied Nellie. 'We shouldn't ferget fings as though they never existed.'

'Wot about you, Nellie?' asked Madame. 'Would you like ter remember the past? Your time at the children's 'ome an' all that?'

Nellie was surprised by the question. But it made her think. 'I sometimes fink about Miss Ackroyd,' she replied. 'She seemed a good woman. I'd like ter see 'er again one of these days.' She linked her arm through Madame's as they walked. 'But she couldn't mean as much ter me as you do. Nobody could.'

Madame smiled and gave her arm a squeeze.

'Mrs Beckwiff!'

Both women stopped and turned. Standing just behind them was Dandy, the younger of the two Sisters Tapp.

'Dandy!' Madame said. 'Wot's wrong, dear?'

Dandy was out of breath, having run the length of the road to catch up with them. 'You'd better come quick, Mrs Beckwiff,' she spluttered in her broad Geordie accent, clearly in some distress. 'Mr Beckwiff asked me to come after you. There's been an accident!'

Madame and Nellie hurried back to the theatre and made their way straight to dressing room number 5. A group of people were already there, gathered around a near hysterical Ange who was stretched out on the floor, screaming, her legs lacerated and bleeding.

'Dear God!' said Madame, immediately kneeling beside the girl. 'Wot's 'appened, Ange? Wot 'ave yer done to yerself?'

'We tried to tell her, Mrs Beckwiff,' said the distraught Dandy. 'We told her not to do it!'

'Told 'er not ter do wot?'

'What do yer think?' came the acerbic voice of Gladys, the other Sister Tapp. 'She was washin' 'erself, standin' in the washbasin.'

At this, Ange let out a piercing scream.

251

'Send for an ambulance!' called one of the stagehands. 'For Gawd's sake, somebody send for an ambulance!'

Madame leant over Ange, tried to comfort her, and use her handkerchief to mop up the blood on her legs. 'It's all right, Ange,' she said repeatedly. 'Everyfing's goin' ter be all right, I promise yer.'

This only sent Ange into another fit of sobbing.

Nellie looked around the room. Her eyes came to rest on the ashen, stunned face of the only member of the group who was standing well back.

It was Monsieur.

Chapter 18

Nellie had never been so scared in all her life. Only twenty-four hours before, she had been quite content to do her job as personal dresser to Monsieur and Madame. Now here she was, less than an hour before curtain up on the first house show, waiting anxiously to make her debut as the so-called glamorous assistant to the famous Illusionist Extraordinaire, the Great Pierre. Even to think about it made her feel faint.

Ange's accident in the washbasin had landed her in hospital. Both her legs and part of her back were so badly cut, she needed many stitches. No matter what Nellie felt about Monsieur's assistant, she would never have wished such a thing on her. It was a tragedy for Ange, and for Monsieur's act. The week's engagement was not even halfway through, but everyone kept saying that the show must go on. Why did it have to go on? Nellie asked. Why couldn't an announcement be made that 'owing to unforeseen circumstances' the Great Pierre would be appearing for the rest of the week without his usual young female assistant? But in her heart of hearts, Nellie knew it was wrong to think like that. In many ways, Ange had been right. Monsieur's celebrated stage act could not work without help, without someone to be sawn in half, or to disappear from a wooden cabinet, or climb up a piece of rope suspended from nowhere, or levitate like a dead body. Someone also had to coax a member of the audience up on to the stage, or appear to do so, like Monsieur's regular 'plant', old Gus Maynard. If only Ange hadn't been so stubborn and stupid.

Both Monsieur and Madame had pleaded with Nellie to take Ange's place in the show. It was an impossible position to be in. She hated the idea of going on stage. She felt self-conscious about her height, her skinny legs, and everything else about herself. But Monsieur and Madame were not only her employers, they were now her own mum and dad. They had done so much for her, and come to her rescue when she was at her lowest ebb; now it was her turn to help them.

The whole day had been one mad rush. It had started at six thirty in the morning, when Madame started fitting Nellie out in Ange's two costumes for the current act – the scarlet military-style uniform jacket with gold shoulder tassels, mini skirt, and silver boots, and the scanty green sequined dress with matching high-heeled shoes. The trouble was, Ange was three inches taller than Nellie, which meant that some pretty drastic alterations had to be made and rather fast. So, later in the morning, Ruby Catmonk was sent for, and she gladly got to work with her scissors, needle, and thread.

Most of the day, however, was taken up by a crash course in the basic art of assisting the Great Pierre. For the first hour or so, it was left to Madame to teach Nellie how to move on the stage, how to stand, how to pose, how to use all her feminine charms and how to react to the brilliant tricks as if she was seeing them for the first time. From late morning, the sitting room was cleared to make room to rehearse the act itself. From his private workroom at the top of the house, Monsieur produced various boxes, pieces of furniture, and other props that he used to practise on. For the levitation, Nellie merely had to learn how to lie like a corpse, covered from shoulders to feet with a large black sheet. Actual levitation could only take place on the stage. Nonetheless, lying absolutely still for several minutes at a time was not an easy task, despite Monsieur's somewhat sick suggestion that she should 'imagine yerself really dead, Nell'. The disappearing act was less arduous; the wooden cabinet in which the trick was performed was cunningly built to allow her to slip out of it at the rear without being noticed. 'Sawing the lady in half', however, was a nightmare. Crouching painfully inside the timber coffin, with only her head on show, she had to keep a fixed smile on her face while Monsieur began to saw and she could feel the sharp serrated blade brushing down past her knees inside. But how did he manage to show her feet, and then ask her to waggle her toes? 'Ah,' was all he would say. 'All in good time, gel, all in good time.'

When the time came for Nellie to leave for the theatre, she felt a nervous wreck. So much so that Ruby had to give her a good talking to.

'Take it in yer stride, Nell,' she said, peering over the top of her specs, her usual Capstan with all its ash intact dangling from her lips. 'But most of all, enjoy it! I mean, just look at yerself. Go on! Stop bein' so self-conscious!'

The old lady turned Nellie round so that they could both look at her in the full-length mirror.

'Don't, Rube,' Nellie protested, cringing with embarrassment at her reflection. 'I look awful!'

'Don't you believe it, gel!' scolded Ruby. 'Yer've got a neat little figure, slender 'ips, a bosom that makes Ange's look like table tennis balls, and as shapely a pair of legs as I've seen on any young gel since I was your age.'

'But I'm so small, Rube,' Nellie said with anguish. 'Just look at me, barely five feet two inches even in 'igh 'eels.'

Ruby quickly swivelled Nellie round towards her. 'Listen ter me, young lady,' she said firmly. 'Small's beautiful! Don't yer ever ferget that. Wot you've got in these five feet two inches is worf six foot to anyone wiv a bit of know-'ow. You're a good-lookin' kid, Nell, believe me. When you walk out on that stage at first 'ouse, Bert Beckwiff's goin' ter 'ave a job stoppin' every red-blooded feller in that audience from gawpin' at yer.'

Nellie turned back to look at herself in the mirror again. 'But I'm not a performer, Rube,' she said, her face screwed up in anxiety. 'I've never wanted ter be in front of the bright lights.'

Ruby watched Nellie's reflection in the mirror again, and smiled. 'Whevver yer want ter or not, gel,' she said with more than a tinge of pride, 'ternight is *your* night!'

The first house audience was filing in. Some were still downing their drinks in the bars, while upstairs in the gods many had brought their own sandwiches. Eager faces were pressed against the brass safety rail, peering down with fascination at the rich people below. Wednesday mid-week evening shows were not traditionally the most sought-after tickets, but once again there was a capacity audience and the usual air of anticipation.

Backstage, Ange's accident in the washbasin had made it necessary for the Sisters Tapp to be moved into an alternative dressing room, which they only too willingly shared with Nellie. The atmosphere in the room was friendly and cheerful as Gladys set about helping Nellie with her make-up, while Dandy worked on Nellie's hair.

'Take it from me, kiddo,' said Gladys, her Geordie accent at full throttle. 'Tonight you are going to be *the* number one sex bomb of Wood Green! Just wait till they get a whiff of you out there. There'll be a stampede to get at you!'

Both sisters laughed out loud, but not Nellie; she was too cold with terror even to smile. By the time the girls had finished with her, Nellie didn't recognise herself. Staring in the mirror, she reckoned she looked just like a tart. Thanks to the sticks of Five and Nine, she had a complexion that made her look more like Carmen

Miranda in *Down Argentine Way*, and Gladys had used the deep red carmine so liberally that Nellie's lips looked as though they were bleeding. But the two sisters thought differently.

'You're a knockout!' exclaimed Dandy.

Gladys agreed. 'If I could look like that, I'd sell my body to the highest bidder!'

For a brief moment, Nellie felt just a grain of confidence. But the moment the sisters were called on stage to do their opening number, Nellie's stomach ached with panic. Now alone, she sat at the dressing table, staring in disbelief at herself in the mirror. Why had she ever allowed herself to get into this crazy nightmare? Everything inside her was telling her that the moment she set foot on that stage, she would just seize up and most probably die of fear. She tried to remember all the things Monsieur had told her – stand like this, don't react to that, never allow yourself to look as though you know what's going to happen next, always show your teeth to the audience, smile, smile, smile! She tried to focus on the rehearsal she had had on stage with both Monsieur and Madame, and she knew that climbing that suspended rope was not going to work. It was an impossible task even for someone more experienced than herself. What on earth had possessed Monsieur to ask her to do such a thing? But it was too late now. She had to go ahead with it all, regardless of how much of a fool she was going to make of herself, not to mention the celebrated name of the Great Pierre.

She focused on her reflection in the mirror again, and squirmed at the sight of herself togged up in a scarlet military tunic with gold tassels and make-up that made her look like a toy doll. And what about all those technical names that the stagehands kept throwing at her during that final rehearsal? How would she ever remember things like the gantry, the wings, spot one and mirror spot, floods, flaps, backcloth, stage left, stage right, and stage centre? It was like trying to learn Chinese. It was madness!

'Dear Nellie. Yer look t'rrific!'

Nellie looked up with a start. Madame was peering round the door at her.

'I'm so proud of you, my dear,' she said as she came across to Nellie. 'I can't tell you how grateful your dad and I are. If it wasn't for you, we'd 'ave 'ad ter withdraw from the show. It would 'ave done yer dad a great deal of 'arm, specially with Moss Empires and the Stoll people. Word gets around so fast.'

'Mum.' Nellie swung round on her stool to face Madame. 'I want ter ask yer just one last time,' she said, with pleading eyes. 'Are yer sure I can do this? If I let yer down, I'll never fergive meself fer the rest of me life.'

Madame gave Nellie a reassuring smile, crouched down, and taking hold of her hands said, 'Yer could never let us down, Nellie. You're one of us now. You're a Beckwiff. We're a team. All yer can do is yer best. Nobody can ask fer more.'

Nellie tried a weak smile. Then her mind started racing again. 'Wot 'appens when Ange gets well again?' she asked delicately. 'She ain't goin' ter take kindly ter me takin' on 'er job.'

Madame lowered her eyes. 'Ange won't be coming back, Nellie,' she said. 'The doctor at the hospital says her legs are going to be severely scarred for the rest of her life. There's no way she could ever appear on the stage again.' She took a deep breath, and looked up. 'She's bin a very foolish gel, Nellie. In every way.'

Nellie didn't need an explanation. She understood Madame's remark perfectly.

By seven o'clock in the evening, Nellie had begun to wonder whether the Novelty Juggler's act would ever come to an end. For twenty-five minutes or so, she had been waiting in the wings, watching the acts as they came on. Although she had seen all of them now several times, somehow they all looked so different from the side of the stage, unreal, and larger than life. She didn't dare to take a peek at the audience through the spyhole in the flaps, for if she did, she knew she would probably be sick. A few minutes before she was due to take her place on the stage, Monsieur and Madame joined her, and all three of them stood in silence waiting for the juggler's final bow.

When the moment finally came, Madame leaned across and hugged Nellie. 'Good luck, dear Nellie,' she whispered.

Monsieur squeezed her hands affectionately. 'Don't worry about a fing, gel,' he said with a wink. 'Just remember, smile, smile, smile!'

The closing music of the juggler's act played him and his assistant off stage. As they went, both of them gave Nellie a thumbs-up before disappearing to their dressing rooms.

The auditorium was in darkness. It was time for Monsieur, Madame and Nellie to take their places on stage. This was it. This was the moment of truth, the moment that Nellie had prayed would never come. Shaking from head to foot, she picked her way carefully in the dim light behind the front of house curtain, finally reaching her position at stage right. She immediately took up her pose, arms upstretched and hands dangling delicately high above her head, and her teeth bared. If anyone had approached her they would have thought she was a savage dog. To Nellie, the next few seconds were a living hell.

And then came the quivering, hissing sound of that terrible cymbal, which heralded the appearance centre stage of Monsieur, suave and sinister as ever.

'Ladies and gentlemen!'

The sound of the stage manager's voice booming out

over the theatre's loudspeaker system sent a wave of panic through Nellie's body.

'The Wood Green Empire is proud to present THE GREAT PIERRE!'

As usual, the theatre erupted with applause and Monsieur bowed theatrically.

Gradually, the house curtains behind him opened to reveal Madame at her grand piano on one side of the stage, and Nellie on the other, both of them picked out in their own spotlights. Nellie was now ready to faint. The bright light was blinding her, and all she could think about was that beyond that light and all the other lights sat an audience of people who would now be watching every movement she made! Yes, she thought, the only solution was to faint. At least that was a legitimate way of getting out of this ordeal. But then she remembered what Monsieur had told her: 'Smile, Nellie! Smile, smile, smile!' Thankfully, Monsieur had changed the opening so that she did not have to appear as a figure of death, togged up in that ridiculous black hood and cloak, a device used by Ange to such effect.

Madame started to play, which was the signal for Nellie to drop her hands and arms – but not her fixed smile. The atmosphere on stage was stifling; the place was like a steam bath and it seemed as though the entire audience was smoking. But there were other smells too wafting in from the auditorium. Nellie couldn't identify them all, but she recognised cheap perfume, the familiar Zube cough sweets, cheese and pickled onions, and brown ale.

The first illusion involved the Magic Box, which Nellie had to collect, together with the small card table it was on, from the back of the stage. Although it was only a few steps from where she was standing, her legs felt like lumps of lead and she had no idea how she would get there. But somehow she managed to move and, with her fixed smile still beaming out brightly towards the audience, she placed the props over the chalk mark centre stage, where the spotlight picked it out. Then she moved to one side, followed by her own secondary spot.

As she did so, a chorus of wolf whistles and shouts of 'Cor!' echoed out from the auditorium. Nellie stopped dead and self-consciously looked down at herself, terrified that something was showing. Then she quickly glanced up at Monsieur, who had his back to the footlights, and she saw that he was grinning at her. The wolf whistles were clearly meant for her! Embarrassed, Nellie tried to slink back into the shadows, but the calls and wolf whistles from her male admirers in the audience continued, so she kept quite still and waited for the hubbub to subside. She was astonished. To think that, even for just a few seconds, she, Nellie, could be the centre of such attention! She couldn't believe that such a thing was happening to her. What was it Ruby had said to her? *'Listen ter me, young lady. Small's beautiful! Don't yer ever ferget that!'*

From that moment on, Nellie found the confidence she was so desperately lacking and was gradually able to shrug off her self-consciousness. She was proud of what she'd got, and if they wanted to look at her, then good luck to 'em! In fact, she even began to enjoy herself, and as she collected the objects Monseiur pulled out of the Magic Box, she smiled and smiled and smiled out at her adoring audience for all she was worth. She was a star! Not in the same league as the Great Pierre, of course, but she had established her presence, without shame, even if it had been with a great deal of fear. At the end of the Magic Box sequence, Nellie waved her hand towards Monsieur, inviting the audience to applaud him to the rafters. She felt good, oh so good, and she resolved that never again would she let stage fright get the better of her. But even as she stood there, basking in her new-found confidence, fate decided that it still had one or two unexpected tricks

261

up its sleeve. And the first appeared in the form of a howling wail which suddenly cut through the audience's cheers.

It was the sound of the air-raid siren.

The morning after the night before invariably brings the ring of truth, and more often shame. And so it was with Nellie. Lying in bed, exhausted by the ordeal of appearing on stage for the first time in her life, she felt nothing but shame, not only for those few exhilarating moments when she fantasised that she was a 'star', but also for the vanity of believing that she was more important during the act than the Great Pierre himself. How could she even think such a thing? she kept asking herself. She was no better than Ange. She cringed with embarrassment as she recalled herself during the first and second house performances. She hated the sight of herself, with that fixed, toothy smile, togged up in a scanty costume, with an artificial flower stuck behind her ear. It was shame-making, absolutely shame-making! She didn't want to be a 'star'. She never wanted to go on to a stage again as long as she lived, and she had every intention of begging Monsieur and Madame to find a replacement for Ange as soon as possible.

The air raid during the first house performance was the first such interruption the Wood Green Empire had had for some months, but the performance continued despite the threat of enemy action. The audience, given the choice of leaving the theatre or staying on to watch the show, decided to stay. In the event, two enemy raiders did manage to penetrate the defence system round the outskirts of London, but the only damage appeared to have been a stray bomb in Victoria Park, Hackney.

Nellie was never very good in the mornings, so she didn't get up until around eight thirty. She had a bath, got dressed, and went downstairs.

To her surprise, nobody was around. Sid and Lenny would have already gone off to school, but there was no sign of Monsieur or Madame either, although they were usually up good and early every morning. 'Mum! Dad! Anyone at home?' she called. Still no response. Monsieur and Madame must have gone off early somewhere. She made her way to the kitchen. The moment she entered, there was a shout of 'Congratulations!' from a crowd of people gathered there: Monsieur and Madame, Sid and Lenny, Ruby Catmonk, and even Monsieur's old Home Guard mate Gus Maynard.

Madame embraced her in a tight, warm hug. 'Oh, fank yer, dear Nellie!' she said, her voice cracking with emotion. 'We were so proud of yer last night. Where would we 'ave bin if it 'adn't been fer you?'

Then old Ruby hugged her. 'What'd I tell yer?' she said with a mischievous twinkle in the eye.

Nellie was too taken aback to reply. She wanted to say that it was the most painful experience of her life, but old Gus was enthusiastically shaking her hand. 'You're a trouper, Nell, a real trouper!' he said, his eyes gleaming with admiration. 'I'm tellin' yer, that audience took to yer the moment yer set foot on that stage. Marvellous, Nell! Absolutely blinkin' marvellous!'

Sid and Lenny grabbed her round the waist and tried to make her dance with them. 'Nellie's on the music 'all! Nellie's on the music 'all!' they sang triumphantly.

'Stop it, boys!' protested Madame, trying to restrain them. 'This poor girl's had a nerve-racking night. We've got ter give 'er a chance ter unwind.'

'Mum. Dad . . .'

'Come 'ere, Nell,' said Monsieur, beaming. He took her in his arms and hugged her gently. It was not something he did very often, for he very rarely showed emotion. But this morning was different. 'Wot can I say to yer, gel?' He held her out in front of him and gazed at her admiringly. 'Last night yer showed yerself ter be a true pro – one of the best. An' Bert Beckwiff don't say that ter many people.'

'Dad,' Nellie said, 'I shouldn't've done that last night. When yer asked me ter do it, I should've said no. I had no right ter make such a fool out of yer.'

There was an immediate howl of disbelief from everyone.

'It's not true, dear!' protested Madame, and old Ruby shook her head.

'Yer saved the day, Nell!' added Gus. 'It's as plain as a pike!'

Nellie shook her head vigorously.

'Nell,' said Monsieur, 'don't yer understand? I'd never've asked yer ter do it if I thought yer couldn't. But yer did. In just one day, yer learnt enough ter go on that stage and give me the support I needed. 'Onest ter God, I'd've bin a dead duck wivout yer.'

'Gert an' Daisy said *you* was the real star of the show!' proclaimed Lenny.

'So did Billy Bennett!' added Sid.

Nellie covered her face in embarrassment.

Monsieur gently removed Nellie's hands. 'Don't be embarrassed, Nell. Every time yer do it from now on, it'll get easier. We'll 'ave lots of rehearsals. By the time we've finished, you'll be the best support on the 'alls.'

Nellie shook her head. 'No, Dad,' she replied firmly. 'I can't go on wiv it, not for ever. I'll do me best though, just till yer can find someone else.'

Monsieur exchanged an anxious look, first with his wife and then with Ruby.

'The bright lights are not fer me, Dad,' insisted Nellie. 'I don't like meself enough.'

'Plenty of uvver people do though, Nell,' chimed in old Gus. 'Take a butchers at this.' He picked up a copy of the

Daily Sketch from the kitchen table. 'Just 'ere, down the bottom. See?'

Nellie took the newspaper.

Madame was uneasy. 'Nellie doesn't read proper yet, Gus,' she said. ''Ere, dear.' She stretched out to take the newspaper from her. 'Let me—'

'"Girl Saves Show."' Nellie was hanging on to the newspaper and reading out loud from it. '"Last night, a seventeen-year-old girl stepped in when the assistant to the Great Pierre stage act became involved in a backstage accident at the Wood Green Empire in Norf London."'

Monsieur and Madame exchanged a look of astonishment. Nellie was reading out loud, fluently, and without any help whatsoever.

'"Nellie Beckwiff,"' continued Nellie, '"who 'ad never before bin involved in featrical work, took over at twenty-four 'ours' notice, ter rapturous applause from an appreciative audience. A spokesman at the feater last night was quoted as sayin' that in everyone's opinion, Nellie's cool an' professional nerve 'ad saved the Great Pierre's act from disaster. There was no doubt that she was headin' for an 'ighly colourful career in the music 'all."'

Nellie lowered the newspaper and looked up at everyone. 'I've never 'eard such a lot of old cods in all me life!' she said.

'Nellie!' gasped Madame, hardly able to believe what she had just heard.

Nellie was bewildered to find everyone gawping at her. 'Wot's up?' she asked.

'Yer can read!' yelped Sid incredulously.

'All on yer own!' added young Lenny.

Nellie smiled. 'Ruby's bin teachin' me.'

'Try somefin' else, Nell,' said Monsieur, taking the newspaper from her and looking for another report for her to read. ''Ere! Try this.'

Nellie took the newspaper back from him, and after glancing at the report he was pointing to, slowly started to read out loud again: '"Berlin gets the jitters. Berliners are nightly awaitin' a raid by one thousand British bombers, as they believe their city ter be an inevitable target in the near future . . ."'

Ruby listened with quiet satisfaction as Nellie continued, her pace quickening the more she read.

'I can't believe it!' cried Madame. She threw her arms round Nellie, and hugged her. Everyone applauded, and patted Nellie on the back.

'It's not me that done it,' Nellie called to them all. 'There's the one that 'elped me,' she said, going across to Ruby, taking her hands and squeezing them. 'If it wasn't for Rube 'ere, I couldn't've done it. She's the best teacher anyone could ever 'ave.'

'Don't be silly, Nell,' said old Ruby, with a smile. 'I just gave yer a bit of a push, that's all. Yer've worked 'ard.'

'A few years ago, I couldn't do nuffink,' Nellie said, looking straight at her, 'I couldn't read or write, and accordin' to the Orphanage, I was 'opeless wiv all me school studies. I owe yer so much, Rube – so much.'

Madame was practically in tears. 'We all owe you, Rube,' she said, emotionally. 'Yer've given our Nellie a new lease of life. Now she can read, she can do anyfin' she wants.'

And from that time on, that is exactly what Nellie did. Between the first and second house shows at Wood Green, she read everything she could lay her hands on – newspapers, old magazines, the words on sheet music, even notices on the back of lavatory doors. Being able to read properly was like being born all over again, and once she was confident enough to read, with her mum's help, she even began to learn how to scrawl a few words. She was on her way. Thanks to Ruby Catmonk, there was no looking back.

Most rewarding of all, however, was the fact that Nellie was using her mind to the full. If learning to read and write had been one way to reach her lost memories, then losing her reluctance to talk to people about the war was another. Many a night she lay awake allowing memories of her past to come flooding back. Gradually, images appeared before her, and she could now visualise Barratts' Orphanage, and all the children and staff with whom she had shared her life.

But most of all, she remembered Miss Ackroyd. And she knew now that her life could never be fulfilled until she saw her again.

Chapter 19

Barratts' Orphanage had come up in the world. Its new premises, set in the middle of woodland just outside Harpenden in Hertfordshire, was an eighteenth-century manor house owned by an aristocratic local family. They had found the vast building too much to handle, let alone live in, so they had leased it to Hertfordshire County Council who in turn rented it to Barratts' for a minimum sum. After the stuffy, war-torn back streets of Islington, it was a veritable paradise for both children and staff. They relished the crisp, fresh air, the lush green fields and trees of every shape and size, with wonderful straggly branches that stretched up towards the sky.

Nellie reached the home after a journey from Holloway that took her the best part of three hours. She could have taken the train from Kings Cross, but as it was Sunday she decided to make a day of it and she took the Green Line bus from the Nag's Head to Barnet, a double-decker bus from there to St Albans, and a single-decker bus on to Harpenden town centre. From there, she still had a twenty-minute walk ahead of her, but it was such a glorious autumn day that she didn't mind a bit. The air was warm, and the trees and hedgerows were tinged with the most beautiful autumn hues.

As she made her way along an overgrown country lane and headed towards the big house on the other side of the fields, she was brimming with all kinds of emotions. It was well over two months now since her stage debut at the Wood Green Empire, and she had now accepted the fact that it was a way of life that she could embrace, as long as she kept her feet firmly on the ground and didn't make the same mistakes as Ange. There had only been four weekly bookings since then, which involved a tour on the Moss Empire's circuit in London and the provinces. In many ways it was quite fascinating, for she was seeing all sorts of new places and it was interesting how audiences reacted differently in different parts of the country. She was still getting wolf whistles from the men, but in one of the older music halls in Leeds a woman in the audience had shouted out that it was a sin for a young girl like her to show her bare legs in public.

Learning how to read and write had somehow triggered something in Nellie's memory. It had brought her past life into focus with uncanny detail. She remembered nearly every detail about the old Barratts' Orphanage in New North Road, about the staff, Mr and Mrs Driscoll, old Mrs Hare the cook, and Miss Ackroyd. Especially Miss Ackroyd. But she also remembered the children she had spent so much of her time with. Lucy, ten years old, with never a smile on her face; Jane, twelve years old, forever drawing pictures of everything and everyone she saw; 'Big' Ben, fourteen years old, always being teased about his height, which was why he was Nellie's favourite. And then there was Lizzie, fifteen years old, the biggest troublemaker on God's earth, and Nellie's sworn enemy. But why? Try as she might, she couldn't remember any reason for the enmity between them, only that it had always been like that.

By the time she reached the huge iron gates of the big house, Nellie felt a sense of deep apprehension, and she was beginning to wonder whether it was a mistake to have written to Miss Ackroyd suggesting this visit.

The driveway was nearly half a mile long, covered in small shingle and overshadowed by tall elm trees which had already lost their fresh summer look and were now gradually beginning to shed their finely veined serrated leaves. But when the driveway finally opened out on to a wide paved courtyard, Nellie was less impressed than she had expected, for the big house was in need of urgent repairs. Some of its exterior walls were covered over with pebbledash, which robbed the vast building of its former elegance. Nonetheless, it was still a great improvement on New North Road; the grounds extended to four acres, with room for a football field for the boys, and a rounders pitch for the girls.

'Vicky!'

The sound of old Mrs Hare's voice sent a warm glow to Nellie's cheeks. There she was, running down a wide flight of steps from the house as though she was half her age. And she was exactly as Nellie remembered her, her white hair tied back in a bun behind her head, a coloured pinny tied round her vast tummy, and eyes that were as welcoming as a sun-drenched morning, despite the fact that the last time they were together, the old girl had ranted and raved at her and called her a mouthy little troublemaker!

'Oh, Vicky!' she cried, virtually sprinting towards Nellie and embracing her in a huge hug. 'I thought I'd never see you again!' Then she stood back to look at her. 'Oh, goodness, I almost forgot! It's not Vicky any more, is it? And just look at yer! You're so grown-up!'

'It's good ter see yer again, Mrs 'Are. Yer 'aven't changed a bit!'

'Vicky!'

This time it was Martha Driscoll, hurrying across the courtyard with her husband Arthur. 'Oh Vicky!' she called. 'This is wonderful, wonderful!'

'Look at her!' observed Arthur as he joined the rapidly expanding group of staff who were gathering. 'Too damned skinny! Don't they feed you in the music hall?'

Laughter, tears, anxieties. Everyone wanted to see Nellie, and when some of the orphan children spotted her through the windows, she was soon in the centre of a jostling crowd. There they all were, a little older now but exactly as she remembered them – Lucy, now with a huge smile on her face, Jane, Big Ben, some of the younger kids from the upstairs dormitory, a bunch of boys she used to play football with. There were so many stories to exchange, and when Nellie first hugged Lucy, the poor girl burst into tears. It was all too much. But there was one face that Nellie was longing to see, and she didn't have to wait long. At the top of the long flight of stone steps stood Miss Ackroyd, tall and erect as ever, her short auburn hair shining in the midday autumn sun, her large soulful eyes brighter than Nellie remembered. And the moment their eyes met, they both broke out into a wide smile. Without another word, Nellie rushed through the crowd and quickly made her way up the stone steps to Miss Ackroyd.

'Hello, Nellie,' she said warmly. 'Welcome to Barratts'!'

It was a strange experience for Nellie, sitting down to Sunday lunch in Barratts' dining room with all the staff and orphans. It was as though time had stood still, as though everything was exactly the same as when she left. This time, however, she was sitting at the staff dining table, listening to that all too familiar sound of children eating their food and scraping their plates once they had finished. In some ways it was a rewarding sound, and it brought a smile to her face. As she looked up and down the trestle tables all around her, she could see herself sitting there, playing up with her mates Lucy and Jane while the staff were not looking. Subconsciously, she was also looking around to see if Lizzie Morris was amongst the faces along the trestle tables. But she wasn't there. And it made Nellie nervous. Luckily, the taste of Mrs Hare's

Yorkshire pudding soon distracted her attention, as did the inevitable treacle tart and custard that followed as sure as night follows day. It was such a comforting feeling to be here, but also sad, for the children were still without a home – a real home – and none of them had the benefit of a loving family to support them. But Miss Ackroyd and the staff did all they could, and Nellie wondered what would have happened to the children if there hadn't been people like them to step in and take care of them.

After lunch, most of the children went off to play football or rounders, or take an afternoon stroll down to the beautiful lake in the grounds. This gave Ethel Ackroyd the chance to show Nellie around the place, and to speak to her alone.

'They often talk about you,' she said as they made their way towards the stream in the field behind the big house. 'Sometimes I hear the girls talk about that night, the night of the bomb, the night you made them all believe you were dead.'

'Is that what you believed?' Nellie asked.

'Not for one single moment. There was absolutely no doubt in my mind whatsoever. And when Lizzie told me that she'd seen you in the audience at the Hackney Empire, I knew that I'd find you alive somewhere.'

They reached a small and rather rickety timber bridge which stretched across the narrow stream. Pausing half-way across, they could hear the sound of some of the orphans shouting and laughing in the distance on the football field. Then both of them stopped to gaze at the water in the stream below, as it trickled over a large stone in strange kaleidoscopic patterns.

'The last time we met,' Nellie began, 'yer said fings about me that – disturbed me. Yer said I knew 'ow ter 'urt you.' She turned to look at the older woman. 'Wot did yer mean?'

Ethel hesitated before answering. 'I meant that you

273

knew what I was going through. I've never had anyone to love me, Nellie,' she said, with difficulty. 'You knew that, but you wouldn't do anything to help.'

''Ow could I 'elp?' Nellie replied. 'I was only a kid. I din't know nuffin' about anyfin'.'

'Oh, but you did, Nellie,' insisted Ethel. 'You were always older than your years, more perceptive than anyone I've ever known. There were times when I felt I could talk to you as one woman to another, to tell you things about myself that I could never tell anyone else. But whenever I reached that point, you always shunned me and made me feel cheap.'

Nellie was consumed with guilt but she didn't know why. 'I made yer feel cheap? Me? But 'ow? Wot did I do?'

'You ignored me, Nellie.'

Nellie was at a loss for words.

'You see, I once had a baby of my own – a little girl. It was born out of wedlock. I hardly knew the father.' Ethel was staring into the stream. 'It was a long time ago now, several years before the war, before I took over Barratts'. I didn't tell my parents. I couldn't! And so there was no one I could turn to.' The sun was glistening in the water and reflecting straight back into her eyes. 'The only solution I had was to dispose of the baby.'

Nellie was horrified. 'Yer mean yer got rid of it?'

'Yes,' replied Ethel, fighting back her emotion. 'I had an abortion. It nearly killed me.' She looked up from the stream and met Nellie's eyes. 'That's why I eventually came to Barratts'. I hoped it would be a kind of therapy, but it didn't work.' Her face was filled with anguish. 'You see, Nellie, I was always so desperate to have a husband and children, a family I could call my own. But I never knew how to do it the way other people did it. Instead I chose the first person who looked at me. It was a tragic mistake.' She took a moment to compose herself, and then continued. 'The problem was, it ruined my life. I could never have a relationship with anyone ever again. I was incapable of it. And *you* knew, Nellie. You could tell, just by looking at me. That's why you called me an old hag.'

'Oh Jesus!' Nellie said, covering her face with her hands in horror. She remembered. Now she remembered *everything*.

'No, Nellie,' said Ethel, gently putting her hand on her arm. 'You were right. You have nothing to blame yourself for, absolutely nothing. I had no right to burden someone as young as you with my problems. It was just that you were always the only one I could trust, because you told me the truth.'

For a moment, Nellie was silent. 'I don't know what ter say,' she said, taking her hands away from her face.

'There's nothing *to* say,' said Ethel with a reassuring smile. 'But I had to tell you. You do understand that, don't you?'

Nellie paused a moment, then nodded.

Ethel smiled at Nellie again, put a comforting arm round her shoulders, and led her off the bridge. 'There is just one thing I want to ask you,' she said as they slowly moved on. 'Is it true that you wanted to run away from Barratts'?'

Nellie stopped with a start. 'Run away?' she gasped. 'Wotever d'yer mean?'

'That's what Lizzie Morris told me. She said that just a few days before the bomb explosion at Barratts', you told her that you were planning to get as far away from me as possible.'

Nellie suddenly became very angry. 'It's a lie!' she snapped. 'If she told yer that, it's a lousy, stinkin' lie!'

'But you did disappear.'

'That night,' replied Nellie, 'after the bomb dropped, I din't know nuffin'. I didn't know who I was, where I

275

come from or where I was goin' to. It all 'appened so quick, I din't know wot I was doin'. I never wanted ter run away from Barratts', Miss Ackroyd. I never wanted ter run away from you, nor anyone else. Yer've got ter believe me!'

They came to a halt. All around them was a vast landscape of rolling hills and green pastureland.

'I've always believed you, Nellie,' said Ethel, the faint tones of her Yorkshire background audible. She looked at the diminutive figure at her side. 'I also love you, and admire you. Nothing will ever change that.'

Soon after tea with Miss Ackroyd, Mrs Hare, Martha and Arthur Driscoll and the rest of the staff, Nellie took her leave and made her way back to Holloway. But she left Barratts' with a heavy heart, and as she made her way along the shingled driveway towards the main gates, she turned to look back over her shoulder several times at the group of staff and orphans who had gathered to wave her off.

Nellie's day had turned out to be a mixture of elation and trauma. It was as though all those sixteen years of life had come into focus again, and as she now began the first part of her journey towards maturity, she could at least know that the shadows had been cleared, and she knew who and what she was. She found it a rewarding experience to see all those freshly scrubbed faces watching her as she ate lunch with the staff in the dining room. There was so much hope there, hope that their lives would tread the same lucky path as hers had. She did consider herself lucky, for she had found people who wanted her, and cared for her, people who were not prepared to see her spend the rest of her days in the care of an institution. And then she thought about Miss Ackroyd, and the candid way she had taken her into her confidence. As Nellie hurried along, all the old emotions of her childhood days came flooding back. How she loved all her mates back there in the dormitory, the late-night giggles, the fights and quarrels, the sharing of news and gossip about the staff, and, most of all, the feeling of just being together. But then she thought of Lizzie Morris, that sly creature who knew of her special bond of friendship with Miss Ackroyd, and who had done everything in her power to drive a wedge between them. It was Lizzie who had lied to Miss Ackroyd that she planned to run away, Lizzie who had made up stories to the other teachers about the awful things she was supposed to have said about them. Why, oh why did she do it? Nellie kept asking herself. Her instinct was to hate Lizzie, but at the same time she felt sorry for her. After all, like most of the children at the orphanage, Lizzie did not know what it was like to be loved and cared for by a family.

Ten minutes later, Nellie reached the main gates. As she opened and closed them behind her, she heard someone calling to her.

'Vicky!'

Running down the driveway towards her was the slight figure of a teenage girl wearing a dazzling white ankle-length dress with hemline frills. Nellie didn't have to look twice to know who it was, for she immediately recognised that round, insipid, doll-like complexion, and that long auburn hair that was now tied back with a white ribbon. It was Lizzie Morris.

'Vicky! Don't go!' As Lizzie reached the gate, she pressed her face up against it.

Nellie watched her in silence, a look of revulsion on her face. Then she slowly moved towards her.

For a moment the two girls stared at each other. Then Lizzie pushed her hand between the iron bars of the gate and stretched her arm out as far as it would reach.

Nellie watched her impassively. She hated that face more than any other she knew. But as she drew closer, her only action was to take hold of Lizzie's hand and shake it.

Then, without saying a word, she calmly turned and walked off.

During the next few weeks, Nellie continued to work on her role as assistant to the Great Pierre, and, as Monsieur had promised, the more she practised, the easier it became. She had now got used to the nightly ritual of climbing a rope, disappearing from a wooden cabinet, and being sawn in half, but she was never comfortable watching Gus Maynard fire that revolver at Monsieur. In fact, once or twice Monsieur had had to scold her for anticipating the shot by flinching before the wretched thing had even been fired.

During the second week of September, Nellie had her eighteenth birthday. The act had been booked in for a week at the Metropolitan Music Hall in Edgware Road, so the usual two evening shows had to be got through on the day she turned eighteen but this did not deter Madame from organising some lavish celebrations for her newly adopted daughter. In the morning, Nellie came downstairs to be given her first ankle-length evening dress, made of navy blue velour and bought quite legitimately with Madame's own clothing coupons, with the advice and connivance of Ruby Catmonk. Monsieur's gift was a row of imitation pearls to go with the dress, and Sid and Lenny contributed to a black evening bag, made by Ruby, and decorated with small white shirt buttons. Her special treat of the day was to be taken to her old workplace, Beales, for lunch. A delicious three-course meal, including boiled scrag end of beef, had been secretly organised by Madame with Nellie's former boss, Mrs Wiggins, who was genuinely thrilled to see how Nellie was blooming into such a lovely, well-composed young lady.

The biggest treat of the day was yet to come, for after the

second house show in the evening an eighteenth birthday party had been arranged by Monsieur. Among the invited guests was the much-loved star of the show, the female impersonator from Lancashire, Norman Evans. Both he and all the show's supporting acts contributed a few bob towards a birthday present for Nellie, which turned out to be a framed poster of the week's theatre programme. She was thrilled, because her own name, Nellie Beckwith, had now been included in the billing beneath that of the Great Pierre and Madame. There was no cake, as the sugar ration did not stretch to such wartime luxuries, but once the front of house curtain had been raised, a table was set out on the stage containing sausage rolls, Spam, cheese, and sardine sandwiches, a large fruit trifle made by Madame, and plenty of quart bottles of brown and light ale, stout, Guinness, and R. White's lemonade and Tizer. There were also one or two bottles of gin and whisky, which had been bought from the theatre bar before the first house show.

When it came to the birthday toast, Monsieur had an important announcement to make.

'Ladies and gents,' he bellowed. 'I'd like yer all ter raise yer glasses ter one of the sweetest little gels that ever walked the stage of the good old Met. Our Nellie has bin in our family now fer the best part of a year, and I tell yer, me, Doris an' the two boys don't know 'ow we've done wivout 'er all this time.'

There were cries of ''Ear 'ear!'

Monsieur turned to Nellie and addressed her directly. 'No, but seriously, Nell, bringin' you inter the family was the best fing we ever done. Yer mum an' I are proud ter 'ave yer as our daughter, and young Sid and Lenny 'ere don't know their luck gettin' a sister who can box the daylights out of any bloke twice 'er size!'

He waited for the laughter to die down, then continued.

'An' so, everyone, I'd like yer ter raise yer glass to our daughter, Nell, on 'er birfday. 'Ere's to yer, Nell. 'Appy birfday, and Gawd bless yer!'

Everyone raised their glasses and said, ''Appy birfday, Nell!' Then they all joined in a rousing chorus of 'Happy Birthday to you' which echoed out into the empty auditorium.

'Oh, yes, an' before I ferget,' said Monsieur over the hubbub, 'I've got some good news for yer, Nell. Me an' yer mum 'ave got an ENSA tour booking. We're goin' up norf – somewhere your way, Norman. Wot's more, they've agreed ter let us take you along too, Nell!'

This brought a burst of applause from the guests.

'Me?' Nell gasped. 'Are yer sure, Dad? I mean, I fawt they didn't want yer takin' a gel assistant wiv yer round the army camps.'

'Well, they do now,' replied Monsieur.

'If I was you, Bert,' called Norman Evans in the same disapproving female voice that he used in his 'Over the Garden Wall' act, 'I'd keep that girl handcuffed to yer, mornin', noon, an' night!'

This brought howls of laughter, and one or two wolf whistles from some of the stagehands.

'It'll be lovely 'avin' yer wiv us, Nellie,' said Madame. 'It's really thrillin' fer yer dad an' me.'

'Can't do wivout yer, Nell,' added Monsieur. 'Let's face it, you're part of the act now.'

He had hardly spoken when a voice called from the wings, 'Now ain't that nice. All comfy an' cosy.'

Everyone turned. It was Monsieur's former assistant, Ange.

There was an immediate hush as everyone watched Ange limp across the stage, her legs covered in thick surgical stockings. She came to a halt directly in front of Monsieur. 'Got it all nice an' sewn up now, eh, Albert?' she said acidly, a nasty grin on her face. 'Congratulations!'

Then she moved towards Nellie. As she did so, the other guests made way for her to pass.

'An' you, little Miss Wide-Eyes,' she said stingingly. 'Got it made, ain't yer, mate? Just wot you wanted.' And with a chuckle she added, 'Well, we'll soon see about that, won't we?'

Chapter 20

Nellie's first experience as an ENSA artiste came during November and the first two weeks in December, when she toured with Monsieur and Madame around some of the army bases in the North of England. It was hardly an easy assignment, for although the Navy, Army, and Air Force Institutes (NAAFI) provided the transport for artistes, the journeys were often undertaken in cold, unheated vans.

Most of the shows were played in quite small venues such as NAAFI canteens, camp cinemas, or even the back of army lorries, so there was no room for the more elaborate stage props used in Monsieur's Great Pierre act. A far simpler routine and more moderate illusions had to be worked out, which included the disappearing white rabbit, strange electrical tricks, and even a 'second sight' item, which was a new and complicated routine. The ENSA revue they had joined for the tour was called 'Fickled Pink'. It was headed by a second-rate quick-fire comedian with the stage name 'Fickle Fred', whose act consisted mainly of an endless stream of jokes about his mother-in-law. Fred was always jealous of his supporting acts, and he was well-known for his wandering hands, so when Monsieur accepted his next six-week ENSA contract, he made quite sure it was not part of 'Fickle Fred's' company. As far as Monsieur was concerned, Nellie had quite enough lechers among the soldiers to cope with!

In March the following year, the Great Pierre road show was devised as a self-contained ENSA revue which used magic and mystery and song and dance in equal proportions. Monsieur was in charge of the show, and for support he took along the Sisters Tapp, a nimble-fingered accordion player called 'Maestro' Jack Pickle, and two rather po-faced balladeers named Ellington Manners and Millicent Withers. It turned out to be a winning combination; the armed services, which on this occasion included both RAF and army bases in southern England, lapped it up.

Having the Sisters Tapp in the company was a great comfort to Nellie. They had done much to help her overcome her stage fright before her terrifying debut at the Wood Green Empire only a few months before, and they had also shown her solid support when Ange had given her such a hard time while she was still Monsieur's assistant. Nellie had taken it for granted that after Ange's accident the Beckwith family would no longer be troubled by this vile-tempered troublemaker. But she was mistaken. Since the night Ange had appeared, uninvited, at her eighteenth birthday party, things had gone from bad to worse. Ange knew her stage career was over but she was determined that Monsieur was not going to get off so lightly. She wanted more from Monsieur than words of sympathy and a quick brush-off, and that meant just one thing – money. Nellie was not sure how much Madame knew about what was going on between Monsieur and Ange, but given the way in which Monsieur had been behaving since that ugly scene on stage at the old Met, Nellie feared the worst; she was convinced that her dad was being blackmailed by this troublemaking little bitch. However, until she found some way to help, all she could do was give as much love and support as she could to her newly adopted mum and dad.

During the last week of March, Nellie's life took an

unexpected turn. The show was due to appear at a small RAF airfield in Kent, near the south coast. The airfield was called Hawkinge, and had been one of the foremost Battle of Britain bases during the Blitz, but as visiting artistes were never allowed to reveal to anyone the location of camps where they performed, Nellie never asked where the show was taking place from one location to the next. What she did know was that on this occasion it would be performed in the NAAFI canteen before an audience of young airmen and women of all ranks.

As usual, they were a pretty rowdy lot, and the Sisters Tapp and Nellie both soon realised that the 'boys in blue' were no less licentious than members of the other armed services. But they were a courageous bunch of young people, many of them not much older than Nellie herself, who had been plunged into the thick of the fighting at a moment's notice, and been part of that immense effort to protect Britain's skies from the Luftwaffe. The show was a huge success including the accordion virtuoso 'Maestro' Jack Pickle, but also those endearing songsters, Ellington Manners and Millicent Withers, who, resplendent in full evening wear, launched into a fine rendition of 'songs old and new', which brought everyone joining in with them, despite the odd rowdy hoot, jeer, or whistle from one or two well-tanked-up young fighter pilots. However, as ever, the Great Pierre was the real hit of the show, involving the participation of some members of his blue tunic audience, whilst Madame clanged out background music on her well-battered upright piano. Needless to say, the most vocal reception was reserved for Nellie, who was wearing a brand new mini dress in pastel blue specially made for the road show by Ruby.

After the show, everyone who had taken part was invited to have drinks in the officers' mess, but at this stage of the tour Nellie was beginning to feel the strain of the daily routine of travelling from one base camp to another, doing a show, then being given hospitality by the same good-natured but repetitive kind of officers, so she declined.

Making her way back to her accommodation, which had been provided in the WAAF officers' quarters nearby, she paused for a moment on the parade ground between the NAAFI canteen and the building she was making for. It was a bitterly cold evening, and over her flimsy stage costume she wore a thick uniform topcoat, which she had been lent by a well-meaning squadron leader. The early spring moon was managing to show itself for only a few seconds at a time as it popped in and out of fast-moving clouds. The atmosphere inside the canteen had been unbearably stifling, for practically every serviceman and servicewoman seemed to be smoking. So, despite the cold, Nellie stood there briefly, taking in long, deep lungfuls of the crisp night air.

'Halt! Who goes there?'

Nellie nearly jumped out of her shoes with fright. Two dark silhouettes were standing right in front of her, shining a torch beam directly into her eyes.

'I say again,' said the deep male voice, 'who goes there?'

'It's me, Nellie,' she replied, teeth chattering with cold. 'Nellie Beckwiff.'

'ID card!' demanded a second male voice. 'On the double!'

Nellie's heart missed a beat. She had come out tonight without the green ENSA identification card that she had been instructed to carry on her at all times while on Government premises. 'I ain't got it wiv me,' she replied nervously. 'I left it back on me bed.'

'ID card number!' barked the second voice.

Nellie was now in a right two and eight. Surely these two idiots knew who she was. 'Don't be stupid! I can't remember me bleedin' number!' she protested. 'I've just come from the NAAFI. We've bin doin' the show—'

'You're under arrest!' growled the first voice.

'Wot?'

'At the double, intruder!' snarled the second voice.

'Intruder?' yelled Nellie. 'I'm not a bleedin' intruder. 'Ere, where yer takin' me?'

'To the guard room,' growled the first voice.

Before she had a chance to protest further, Nellie found her arms grabbed on either side by the two shadowy figures.

'Left, right, left, right, left!' bawled both men simultaneously as they frogmarched Nellie across the parade ground. 'Come on now! Get those feet up!'

'Lemme go! Lemme go!' spluttered Nellie, who had by now forgotten how cold she was. 'Wait till I tell your CO! 'Elp!'

A door was opened and Nellie found herself being shoved inside some kind of building. The door slammed shut behind her. She began to panic, for she knew that the guard house at the main gates was in a completely different direction to where she had been taken. Now, left alone in total darkness, she feared the worst. Was this some prank by a bunch of randy young airmen who had got carried away by the sight of a few scantily clad girls in the show they had just seen? Yes, she tried to convince herself. That's what this was all about. She was sure she'd heard about this kind of thing happening to showgirls before. But why should they be frustrated when they had all those girls in Air Force blue around the place? It just didn't make sense. She could feel warmth coming from somewhere but she was still shivering with fear and apprehension. 'Is anyone there?' she yelled. 'Can anyone 'ear me?'

There was a movement behind her and a light was suddenly switched on. She turned with a start, to find a shadowy figure in uniform, arms crossed, sizing her up from the other side of the room. She was in some kind of an office, blackout curtains drawn at the windows.

''Ere, you!' she snapped, trying her best to sound tough. 'Who d'yer fink yer are bringin' me 'ere like this! I know your CO. Just wait till I see ''im!'

There was no response from the shadowy figure.

'Did yer 'ear wot I said?' Nellie shouted.

'Honestly, Nell,' came the shadowy figure's voice, with a chuckle. 'You haven't changed a bit.'

Even before the figure stepped into the light, Nellie recognised that familiar, cultured voice. 'Toff!' she gasped. '*You!*' She lunged at him, spurting, 'Yer rotten sod! Yer set me up!' She didn't know whether to pummel him with her fists or to throw her arms round him. In the event, he solved the problem for her. He grabbed hold of her, pulled her to him, and hugged her tightly. In those few seconds, everything that had happened to her during those few eventful weeks with the vacs gang came flooding back – the dark, dingy nights down the air-raid shelter at the old furniture store, the endless jobs sniffing for food in people's homes, the constant danger of shrapnel, and above all the gang members themselves, living rough on the streets day after day, night after night, an utterly pointless existence. And then she thought of Rats and Bonkers, brought down in a hail of machine-gun bullets from an enemy aircraft as they tried to rescue a small kitten.

With her face pressed firmly against Toff's chest, she could smell the shaving cream he used and the Players No. 1 tobacco smoke on the rough serge of his blue uniform jacket. After a moment, she looked up at him. He was smiling that smile again, the same one that had always made her feel so helpless every time their eyes met. At that moment, she would not have protested if he had wanted to kiss her. But they had never actually kissed before, and the last time they were together had

been a deeply distressing experience. 'Wot're yer doin'
'ere then?' she asked. 'When d'yer get off the streets?'

'That was a long time ago, Nell,' he replied. 'A lifetime
ago.' He was staring straight into her eyes. 'After what
happened to Rats and Bonkers, none of us could face
living out on the streets any more.'

'All of you?'

Toff nodded. 'There was no point. I went back home.
It wasn't easy. My parents found it hard to forgive what
I'd done. But we got over it. As soon I was eighteen I got
my call-up papers. I joined the RAF.'

Nellie looked over his uniform to see if he had any flash
tags. 'Are yer an officer?'

Toff laughed. 'No, Nell. Just one of the boys. I work
here, in the Central Registry. We're not all flight crew.
Some of us have to do the office work.'

Nellie was surprised. With his posh voice and cultured
ways, she found it hard to believe that he was just a
pen-pusher.

'I missed you, Nell,' Toff said quietly. 'I never forgave
myself for the way I talked to you.'

He was stooping as he looked at her, and their lips were
very close.

Nellie lowered her eyes. 'It wasn't just you,' she replied.
'It was everyfin'. Wot 'appened ter Rats an' Bonkers was
more than I could take.'

Toff's mouth curved into an admiring smile. 'Well,
you seem to have made the right decision,' he said, his
eyes moving over her face and curled hair. 'You look
wonderful.'

Nellie suddenly remembered Patrick and felt uneasy.
She gently pulled away. 'A lot of water's passed under the
bridge since I last saw yer. The Great Pierre and his missus
are my mum an' dad now. They adopted me.'

'Yes, I know,' replied Toff.

'Yer know? 'Ow?'

Toff fumbled around on a desk for his cigarettes. 'I know everything that's happened to you since you left,' he said. 'Right back to your job at Beales Restaurant.'

'Wot?'

'It wasn't easy to let go of you, Nell,' he said. 'A lot of friends helped me keep track of you.'

Nellie took a long, hard look at him. He was as tall and thin as she remembered him, with the same slight slant to his eyes, and rich black hair. In the stark light of the single electric lightbulb, his skin looked almost olive coloured, and it was the first time she had noticed that his eyebrows were as dark as his hair. 'Yer knew where I was,' she said in a strained, incredulous voice, 'an' yet yer never come ter see me?'

'No, Nell,' replied Toff, lighting his cigarette. 'I felt I hadn't the right. I blamed you for what happened to Rats and Bonkers. I was wrong. I had no right to be part of your life.' He turned to look directly at her again. 'But I never stopped thinking about you, or wanting you.'

Nellie was embarrassed. 'It's bin good seein' yer again, Toff,' she said with an awkward smile. Then she turned to the door.

'No!' said Toff, hurrying to head her off. 'Don't go, please.'

'Look, Toff,' Nellie said, 'we ain't seen each uvver fer two years now. That's a long time. We ain't kids no more. Two years makes a big diff'rence. We begin ter see the future, ter know wot it's goin' ter mean one day, an' 'ow we'll cope wiv it. You say yer never stopped finkin' 'bout me.' She flicked her eyes down, then up again. 'Well, I fawt about you too, Toff. I used ter lie awake wonderin' where yer was each night, or whevver yer was even still alive. When I got me memory back, I was over the moon. I wanted ter tell yer 'bout it, but then I remembered 'ow yer looked at me that night when Rats an' Bonkers . . . Yer looked at me wiv such 'ate. I know we only knew each uvver fer a few munffs, but the only fing I could remember was that look. Yer should 'ave come after me, Toff. If yer knew where I was, yer should've come after me.'

She turned and opened the door. But the moment she did so, Toff slammed it closed again. And in one swift movement he pinned her against the door and kissed her. It was a hard, passionate kiss, and as Nellie felt the moisture on his lips mingling with her own, a wave of excitement swept through her body.

When Toff finally pulled away, he rested his chin on her shoulder. 'Nell,' he whispered in her ear, 'I want to tell you something. Those few months, the months we spent together, it was like I'd known you all my life. What you and I endured together during those few months would have been like a lifetime to anyone else. We grew up before our time, Nell. War makes savages out of innocent people. But we survived. We've got to go on surviving.'

He leaned down, and kissed her again. When their lips parted, he whispered, 'This time, I won't let you go, Nell. Whatever happens from now on, I'll never let you go.'

At the end of the six-week ENSA contract, Monsieur, Madame, and Nellie arrived home to some unnerving rumours that Hitler was about to renew his aerial onslaught on London and the Home Counties. During the past month, there had already been a series of hit-and-run air raids on targets in the south-east, and some of the Nazi bombers had even penetrated the Greater London area, where single-engined fighters and fighter bombers had machine-gunned streets, a hospital, and a railway station. At least a dozen people had been killed, which prompted the authorities to issue warnings to everyone to be prepared for further attacks. All this came as quite a blow to the Beckwith family, for during the lull in air raids over the past months, Monsieur in particular had assumed that life was now back to normal and that the music hall was at the centre of that life. Nellie did not take such a view, and the moment she got back to Tufnell Park Road, she, Sid, and Lenny set about pumping rainwater out of the old Anderson shelter, which, due to lack of use, had filled up over the past few months.

A stack of mail was waiting for Monsieur. Madame recognised Ange's handwriting on three of the envelopes, but didn't mention it when she handed them over to her husband. Nellie suspected what was going on, and she prayed that her mum knew nothing, for it would break the poor woman's heart. If it was true that Ange really was blackmailing Monsieur, Nellie was determined to do something about it. That little tart had to be put in her place once and for all.

Since her accident, Ange had been living in a basement flat in Harvest Road which was a quiet back street just off the main Hornsey Road. It was mid-afternoon when Nellie got there, and the first thing she noticed was that the blackout curtains at the front room windows were drawn, which was odd, since it was still a couple of hours before blackout time. After taking a deep breath, she opened the small iron gate, which squeaked mercilessly, and made her way down a few stone steps that were badly in need of repair. The small yard in front of the basement bow windows smelt of cat's pee, and there were tall weeds growing between the cracked paving stones which were littered with household rubbish. There was no bell or knocker, so she tapped on the door.

To her surprise, the door was opened immediately by Ange. She was wearing a long cotton dressing gown, a fag in her mouth. 'Well, if it ain't little Miss Wide-Eyes,' she snorted. 'Wot you doin' 'ere?'

'Come ter see yer, Ange,' replied Nellie, determined not to be provoked. ''Aven't seen yer since me birfday. I was wond'rin' 'ow you're gettin' on.'

292

''Ow very fawtful of yer,' Ange replied. 'Who sent yer? The boss, I 'ope.'

'No one sent me, Ange.'

Ange sized Nellie up for a moment. 'Yer'd better come in then.' She stood back to let her enter.

There were more smells in the small passage that led from the front door to the back yard. Nellie thought it smelt a bit like clothes that had just been ironed, and her guess was right, for when she followed Ange into the front room, an ironing board was set up there and a pile of clothes awaiting attention was heaped on a chair. It was quite dark with the blackout curtains drawn; the only light was provided by a battered looking standard lamp.

'Can't offer yer any tea, I'm afraid,' Ange said. 'Got no more ration coupons left till the weekend. But yer can sit down if yer like.'

'Fanks,' replied Nellie, trying to find somewhere that didn't have a pile of washing on it. She plumped for an armchair, after first allowing Ange to remove a soldier's army tunic that had been thrown there. 'So, 'ow's it goin', Ange?' she asked amicably. 'Legs 'ealed up OK?'

'You din't come 'ere ter talk about me legs,' said Ange abrasively. 'Wot d'yer want?'

Nellie paused a moment, then smiled. 'I fawt I'd ask you the same question, Ange. Wot's goin' on between you an' my dad?'

Ange roared with laughter. 'Yer *dad*! Ha! That's a good one, that is. Wanna know somefin', Nell?' she said, hands on hips, fag in mouth, leaning down at Nellie. 'Yer should've stayed at that kids' 'ome. Yer wouldn't 'ave ter worry about randy ol' buggers there.'

Nellie's face hardened. 'Yer've bin writin' 'im letters,' she said calmly but firmly. 'Wot about?'

'None of yer business. Not yet anyway.'

'Is 'e givin' yer money?'

'Better ask '*im*, 'adn't yer?'

293

Nellie didn't like this conversation but she was determined to get the truth out of this little cow. 'I bet 'e gave yer money ter 'elp yer recuperate after yer accident!'

Again, Ange was amused. 'Is that what 'e told yer? Well 'e's a liar. That's wot your dad is. 'E's a piss-achin' liar!'

Nellie was getting angry. 'Don't talk about my dad like that, Ange!'

'OK, OK,' replied Ange, the picture of fair play. 'If that's wot 'e told yer, then you go right ahead an' believe 'im.'

At that moment, Nellie suddenly caught a glimpse of someone sneaking along the corridor outside. It was a well-built young man, bare-chested, with tattoos on his upper and lower arms, and wearing army trousers. Her eyes flicked back to Ange. 'Are yer tryin' ter blackmail my dad, Ange?'

For some reason, the word blackmail infuriated Ange. 'Look, mate,' she snapped, 'I don't *blackmail* anybody! But if they take advantage of me, they 'ave ter pay fer it!'

'In wot way did 'e take advantage of yer?' Nellie asked, her voice calm and controlled.

Ange tried to stare Nellie down, then she grinned. 'I'll tell yer somefin', after wot your lovin' dad 'as done, I reckon 'e must really 'ave the 'ots fer me.'

Nellie sat there staring at Ange, her face quite impassive. She had nothing but disdain and loathing for this dirty little go-getter. The very room she was sitting in smelt of Ange, her ironing, the ashtrays that were overflowing with cigarette butts, the half-empty beer glasses that hadn't been washed. The windows probably hadn't been opened in months. She decided to call Ange's bluff. 'You're a liar, Ange,' she said boldly. 'You're a liar, and yer know it!'

Ange's face went taut. Without looking at Nellie, she went to one of the overflowing ashtrays and stubbed out her fag. Then she went to a built-in cupboard at the side

294

of the tiled fireplace. She found what she was looking for almost immediately. When she returned, she had a photo in her hand, which she held out to Nellie. 'Take a butchers at that,' she said triumphantly.

For a brief moment, Nellie kept her eyes on Ange's face. Then she took the photo and looked at it. It was of Monsieur, stretched out on some grass, lying in what appeared to be an uncompromising clinch with Ange.

'My friend yer just saw,' said Ange, ''e's a photographer in the army. Seein' 'ow the Great Pierre is so famous, seein' as 'ow 'e's always bein' written up as such a lovin' family man, my friend reckons that picture could be worf quite a bit ter the papers. Specially the *News of the World* or the *People*.' She leaned down closer to relish Nellie's reaction. 'Wot der *you* fink, Nell?'

Nellie was in despair. Lying in bed in the early hours of the morning, she had to face the fact that Monsieur really had been involved with that cow of a girl. It was deeply depressing. As she lay, tossing and turning in the dark, the sight of that repulsive photo was like a recurring nightmare. Although Ange's flat was no more than fifteen minutes away from Tufnell Park Road, Nellie had taken the longest route back, wandering aimlessly around the little back streets behind the Nag's Head, fearful of how she would appear when she saw her dad again. Luckily, however, when she got home, she discovered that Monsieur and Madame had gone out for the evening. Madame had left her a piece of home-cooked dried egg and sausage tart to heat up in the oven, but she left it on the table and went to bed soon after nine o'clock.

It turned out to be a sleepless night. She kept asking herself how her dad had got himself involved with a bit of trash like Ange. Surely it must have been obvious to him, as it was to everyone else, that Ange was only interested in using him to further her own ambitions. Madness! Sheer madness! But Ange was clever, there was no doubt about that. She had exploited Monsieur's middle-aged vanity and would now use it to destroy both his marriage and his career in the music hall. Nellie's heart ached for Madame, for her mum. She now suspected that Madame knew everything that had been going on between her husband and that girl; she had probably known since it first started. It was heartbreaking.

Eventually, Nellie got out of bed. If sleep wouldn't come, there was no point in fighting it. She crossed to the window and pulled back one of the blackout curtains. It was a dark night; the sky had been invaded by thick black clouds and there was no sign of either the moon or stars. Her attention suddenly focused on the back garden below. To her astonishment, she could see a chink of light coming from the tiny entrance to the Anderson shelter, which was a wartime offence and also a dangerous invitation to any enemy aircraft. Quickly replacing the blackout curtain, she put on her dressing gown and slippers, and hurried downstairs.

When Nellie got to the conservatory, she found the back garden door wide open, which alarmed her. She collected the spare torch which was always kept on the ledge above the flower pots and made her way out into the garden.

It was a typical April night outside, with a stiff, ice-cold breeze battering the small back gardens along Tufnell Park Road. Many of the early spring flowers were struggling to stay upright. Nellie pulled her dressing gown tightly round her.

As she approached the Anderson, she could see the protective blackout curtain which hung across the entrance flapping in the breeze, causing the light inside to be clearly visible. Obviously the Anderson door had been left open, which was odd. Peering in round the curtain, she was momentarily dazzled by the white glare of the paraffin lamp. There was an unpalatable smell of paraffin and gin. To her amazement, Madame was propped up in a canvas chair, her head lolling to one side. 'Mum!' she called, quickly climbing down the three steps into the stifling atmosphere of the shelter. 'Wot're yer doin' 'ere, Mum? Wotever are yer doin'?'

Madame's head suddenly straightened up, but she had difficulty focusing on Nellie.

'Mum, dear,' Nellie said gently, squatting beside her. She took the empty glass from Madame's hand. 'Wot're yer doin' down 'ere, all on yer own, in the cold? Come ter bed now, Mum. Come on . . .'

Madame's eyes opened enough to be able to see who was talking to her. And then she smiled. 'No point, Nell,' she muttered, only just comprehensible. 'It's 'er 'e wants, not me,' and her head toppled over to one side again.

As Nellie tried to hold her in her arms, the same words came spluttering out over and over again.

'It's 'er 'e wants, not me . . . not me . . .'

Chapter 21

The crisis that was looming within the Beckwith family seemed inevitable. Fortunately, Monsieur had been fast asleep in bed during Madame's agonised outburst in the Anderson shelter, but in the cool light of day, Nellie realised that the time had come for her to have a heart to heart chat with her mum. The opportunity didn't come until the following afternoon, when they were able to slip away and have afternoon tea in the cafe restaurant of the Gaumont Cinema on the corner of Tufnell Park Road. Decorated in Art Deco style, with potted palms and crystal chandeliers, the cafe was situated at the top of an ornate staircase which curved up to the mezzanine floor overlooking the spacious foyer below.

'I'm really sorry fer the way I be'aved last night, Nell,' said Madame with a pained expression. 'I've always tried ter keep this from the family, but just lately, well, it's all bin gettin' just too much fer me ter take.'

Nellie waited for the waitress to put down the tea tray, and then stretched across to hold Madame's hand. 'Yer shouldn't've kept it to yerself, Mum,' she said. 'Remember, I'm yer daughter. Yer can talk ter me about anyfin'.'

Madame tried hard to smile. But her eyes were still red from a night of tears and heavy drinking. 'I know, dear,' she said. 'I know.'

Nellie poured her a cup of tea. 'Right. Now tell me,' she said, being very practical. 'When did yer first find out about all this?'

Madame sat back in her chair, and sighed. 'Oh, a long time ago, Nell. It seems ages now – before you come inter the family. The funny part is, when yer dad was lookin' round fer a gel ter 'elp 'im in the act, I was the one who chose Ange. She seemed such a pretty little fing, so sweet an' considerate.'

Nellie pulled a face. This was hardly the way she would have described Ange.

'But then,' continued Madame, 'after she'd bin wiv us just a few weeks, I noticed the way she kept lookin' at Albert. It was – too intimate. But the funny fing was, Ange always made more of it when I was around, as though she wanted me ter notice.'

While they talked, cinema-goers were leaving the afternoon film, and slowly making their way up the grand staircase to the mezzanine.

'Anyway, the first time I knew somefin' was goin' on was when we was doin' a week's contract up norf, at the Liverpool Empire. I caught a glimpse of 'er wiv 'er arms round his neck, just be'ind the flats on stage before the show.'

'Was that the only time?' Nellie asked.

'Oh no,' replied Madame. 'I seen 'em doin' it lots of times since then – all over the place.'

'Wot about Dad?' Nellie asked. 'Does 'e know yer've seen all this goin' on?'

'I've no idea,' replied Madame, taking a sip of tea. 'But *she* does.'

Nellie's mind went back to that time at the Theatre Royal in Drury Lane when she had caught a glimpse of Monsieur and Ange together backstage. She remembered how Monsieur had had his back to her and might not have known that she was there. But Ange certainly did. 'Mum,' she asked, ''ave yer ever 'ad this out wiv Dad?'

Madame sighed again and shook her head.

'Why not? Wouldn't it've bin best to bring it all out in the open?'

'Yes,' replied Madame, rather primly, 'I've no doubt it would, Nell. But I 'ave the family ter consider. I don't want ter break up my family. They mean too much ter me.' She picked up her spoon and although there was no sugar in her tea, she began to stir it. 'Me only 'ope is that, in time, 'e'll feel the same way too.'

'I still think yer should talk ter 'im,' Nellie said, leaning across the table to her.

'You're very young, Nell,' she said with a faint smile. 'One day you'll know wot men feel when they're worried about gettin' older. They look fer change, fer somefin' new. When a younger woman comes along an' flatters 'em, they get restless, it reminds 'em of when they was young. I s'pose it's the same wiv some women too. When yer get ter a certain age, yer want love an' attention.' She stopped stirring her cup of tea and replaced the spoon in the saucer. 'It's easy ter fall in love, Nell, but it's much harder ter 'ang on ter it. As far as I'm concerned, if Bert wants ter rock the boat, then 'e must do so. But as long as I still love 'im, *I* never will.'

Nellie was upset. 'Dad *does* love yer, Mum,' she said firmly. 'Wotever yer do, yer must never fink uvverwise. Fer some reason or anuvver, Dad's got 'imself in a mess. An' between us, we're goin' ter find a way ter get 'im out of it.'

On Sunday morning, Nellie played football in Finsbury Park with Sid and Lenny's team, the Tufnell Tigers. It wasn't her ideal way of spending a Sunday morning, but her two young brothers had conned her into it several weeks before when they had discovered, quite accidentally, that she had a pretty nifty right foot which could spin a ball into the net past even the best goalie. At first, the other members of the Tufnell Tigers were sceptical that a girl could have any talent on a football field, but the moment they saw her in action, she was in. Every team they had played since had complained that it was against the rules for a girl to play in a boys' game, but when they realised that she could dribble and foul with the best of them, they grudgingly accepted her.

This week they were playing a team called the Enkel Warriors which was made up of boys from some of the back streets behind the Nag's Head. During the match, Nellie caused the referee to give her a warning – she had punched one of the players on the head with her fist for stamping on her foot with his studded boots. There were always injuries at every Sunday morning match; Sid invariably came home with either a gash on his leg or a black eye and, more recently, Lenny had lost a front tooth, which left a nasty gap. Lenny was a bit off colour during the match, and when he came off the field he had a hacking cough, so Nellie decided to get the two boys home as quickly as possible.

It was a twenty-minute walk from the park back to Tufnell Park Road, and on the journey along the busy Seven Sisters Road, Nellie thought she would sound out her two young brothers on what they knew, if anything, of the difficult situation that existed between their mum and dad. She felt that the two boys were old enough to talk sensibly about family matters, and if they were conscious of anything going on, she would do her best to reassure them. But when she carefully started to ask them oblique questions, the response was unexpected.

'Trouble wiv Mum is she boozes too much,' said Sid, bouncing the team's football as they strolled along.

Nellie was taken aback. 'Sid! That's not a nice fing ter say. Yer know Mum don't drink booze.'

Both boys laughed.

'Not much!' said Lenny, who was trying to control another fit of coughing.

302

'You should see 'er sometimes durin' the night,' added Sid. 'She can 'ardly stand up.'

Sid's comment sent a chill down Nellie's back. Even though she knew about Madame's drinking, she thought it best to sound surprised. 'Yer've seen Mum drinkin'?' she asked.

'Course,' said Sid. 'Lots of times. I was 'ungry once, an' I come downstairs fer somefin' ter eat. She was sittin' cross-legged on the floor in the kitchen wiv a bottle of gin.'

'Oh, well, I s'pose everyone 'as a nip of somefin' from time ter time,' she said dismissively. 'Specially people who work in the music 'all.'

'Dad don't like 'er bein' on the booze though,' Sid said. ''E told me so.'

''E told me too,' added Lenny, who had recovered from his coughing fit. ''E told me that if we saw Mum like that, we was ter leave 'er alone. 'E said she was only like that 'cos she was fed up.'

Nellie felt her heart racing. 'Did Dad tell yer *why* she was fed up?'

'Nope,' replied Lenny.

Lenny's blunt reply convinced Nellie that it would be unwise to pursue the topic. But for the rest of the walk along Seven Sisters Road, she felt uneasy about the effect this miserable business was having on the family. Sooner or later, something was going to give, and when it did, it would be nothing short of a tragedy. Deep down inside, she was beginning to feel a sense of disillusionment. All that time she had craved for a family of her own, and now she had one, there was a danger that it was disintegrating before her very eyes. The only comforting thoughts she had now were Toff's letters, which arrived regularly twice a week.

By the time they reached the Nag's Head and crossed Holloway Road, Nellie had decided that, even if it meant alienating herself from her own mum and dad, she just had to have it out with Monsieur.

When they got home, Lenny had another severe coughing fit, and Madame discovered that the boy had a high temperature. Concerned that he may be starting the flu, she made him some hot broth then duly packed him off to bed with a hot water bottle.

The following day, the Great Pierre was contracted to start a week's engagement at the Theatre Royal, Margate, in Kent. This meant that early on Monday morning, Monsieur, Madame, and Nellie had to travel down in a hired van which they needed to transport their rather cumbersome stage props. Madame was encouraged enough by young Lenny's condition to feel that she could undertake the engagement, so once she had ensured that Monsieur's parents, old Lillian and Maurice, were able to come and stay at the house to keep an eye on the boys, she left with the others.

Before the war, Margate had always been the ideal booking for any artiste appearing at the popular Theatre Royal. The white, sandy beaches were perfect for a day's picnic, and the seafront promenade was thronged with lovers and casual strollers who wandered from one fish and chip shop to another, queued up at the jellied eels van, or tried their luck in the dangerously addictive amusement arcades. Margate was, quite simply, a happy family resort, with an abundance of good bed and break-fast guesthouses, and countless select residential areas. Now it was wartime and the beaches were sealed off by barbed wire; it was also the end of April, which meant plenty of squalls and biting winds blowing in off the English Channel. But everyone found the tiny Theatre Royal a joy to play in despite the somewhat bleak conditions in the backstage dressing rooms, and Nellie soon made friends with some of the supporting cast, who included a trapeze act, an outsize xylophonist, a girl crooner, and a bird impersonator. Unfortunately, nobody got on too well with the rather tetchy orchestra conductor, called Reginald something or other, for he was a last-minute replacement for the regular conductor who was apparently down with laryngitis. The Great Pierre was top of the bill, and Nellie felt very grand when, for the first time ever, she was given her own dressing room, next door to Monsieur and Madame. And their digs, a lovely double-fronted Edwardian guesthouse overlooking the sea at Cliftonville, were a veritable palace compared to some of the places they had put up in.

The week's booking was an unqualified success, with the act being cheered to the rafters each evening, mainly by servicemen from the many surrounding army bases, who filled the small auditorium, often overflowing to the standing room only areas. For Nellie, it was a very happy experience. Lillian telephoned each day to report on Lenny, and the latest news was that he was now back at school. The thought of poor Grandma Beckwith using the ancient wall telephone at Tufnell Park Road tickled Nellie no end, for she knew the old lady was terrified of telephones and usually shouted into them as though the person she was talking to was at the other end of the garden.

As the week progressed, Nellie watched carefully for any signs of strain between Monsieur and Madame. If her dad knew about her mum's drinking, then surely he must also know that the poor woman suspected something? But they were professionals, both on and off the stage. They knew how to disguise anything that might disrupt their public or private lives. As Madame had confided to her, 'I don't want ter break up my family, Nell. They mean too much ter me.' So, for the time being, Nellie said nothing.

On Thursday, Nellie arrived at the stage door of the

theatre to find a message waiting for her. It was from Toff. He had telephoned to say that he had managed to get a twenty-four-hour pass, that he would be coming to Margate for the day on Saturday, and would she please meet him off the train from Canterbury, which arrived at nine fifteen in the morning. Nellie was over the moon, and on Friday night she didn't get a wink of sleep. In fact, on Saturday morning, she got to the railway station fifty minutes before the train arrived, and by the time she saw Toff hurrying towards her along the platform, she was so excited she just threw herself into his arms as though she hadn't seen him for years.

A short walk from the station they stopped to have a cup of tea and a toasted bun at a market stall. It went down a treat, for neither of them had had time to have any real breakfast before they set out. The market was brimming with shoppers and fruit and veg stallholders soliciting business with shouts of, 'Come on now, gels an' boys. Let yer eyes be yer guide!' and, to gales of laughter, 'Don't give in ter Jerry, missus. 'E don't like sausage an' mash!' The war was still on, but it certainly hadn't dented anyone's sense of humour.

After a while, Nellie and Toff found their way to a covered seaview shelter. Above them were Nellie's digs high on top of the cliffs, and spread out before them was the untouchable stretch of beach which extended far beyond Margate towards the Thames estuary in the west and Ramsgate to the south. Although the sun was popping in and out of scattered white clouds, there was still a cold breeze which sent ripples across the incoming tide.

'D'yer fink it'll ever 'appen?' Nellie asked as she snuggled up to Toff to keep warm. 'I mean, Jerry's only just on the uvver side of that water. D'yer reckon 'e'll try an' get over 'ere?'

Toff's eyes scanned the cold, grey expanse of the

English Channel. 'If you'd asked me that a year ago,' he replied, 'I'd have said yes. A lot has changed since then. A lot of good people have given their lives to make sure they can't get here.'

Nellie knew what he meant. If it hadn't been for the courage of a few young pilots during the Blitz, the German invasion would have taken place a long time ago.

'Most of the 'dromes around the coast took a real hammering,' Toff continued. 'There's a place called Sugar Loaf Hill, just between our place and the sea. It's a real landmark for our blokes trying to get back to base after an all-night raid. A sort of oasis in the middle of a desert, really,' he said. 'They say, when you get a view of Sugar Loaf, you're home and dry. Quite a few never make it.'

For a moment or so, they sat there, snuggled up together, just staring out to sea, listening to the breeze. Down on the beach below them, an armed soldier on patrol stopped briefly to adjust his tin helmet. He seemed such a slight figure against the full power of the incoming tide.

'Tell me about yer mum an' dad,' Nellie said out of the blue.

Toff, puzzled, turned to look at her. 'What on earth for?' he asked.

''Cos I'd like ter know,' she replied. 'After all, I've told yer all about *my* mum an' dad.'

'That's different,' replied Toff. 'Your parents are interesting. They do an interesting job.'

'They're just ordinary people, wiv ordinary problems – just like everyone else.'

Toff thought a moment, then reached into his overcoat pocket for his fags. He was in civvies, and to Nellie his clothes had style. He was wearing a chunky navy-blue overcoat, grey flannels, a white shirt with blue cravat, and a white V-neck tennis pullover. 'They didn't take too kindly to my going into the RAF.'

307

'Well, yer can't do much about that, can yer?' said Nellie. 'There's a war on. You was bound ter get called up sooner or later.'

'That's not what I mean,' replied Toff, lighting up. 'What they didn't like was that I didn't take a commission.'

'Commission? Wot's that?'

Toff smiled at her. 'If they had to have a son conscripted, they'd prefer him to be an officer.'

Nellie pulled a face. 'Well, yer've got the brains fer it,' she said. 'Why din't yer?'

Toff took in a lungful of smoke and exhaled over her head. 'Because I don't want to do what's expected of me,' he replied drily. 'And anyway, I had enough of being in charge back on the streets. And look what happened there.'

They were silent again. Nellie put one of her hands in his overcoat pocket to keep warm.

'Are yer goin' ter let them meet me some time?' Nellie asked.

'No way!'

Toff's response was a bit brusque for Nellie, and she looked up at him sharply. 'Why not?' she asked.

'Because I say so. Because you'd have nothing in common with them, nor they with you.'

Nellie straightened up. 'Who are yer ashamed of? Me or them?'

'Oh, don't be so bloody silly, Nell!' he snapped. 'Why do we have to talk about my parents? You know how I feel about them.'

Nellie was taken aback. 'Yes, I do know,' she said indignantly. 'I just wonder why, that's all.'

Toff was getting irritated. He stood up. So did Nellie.

'It's funny, in't it?' she said, arms crossed, staring aimlessly out at the sea. 'There's me, always longed fer a family of me own. An' now I've got one, suddenly it

308

don't seem real any more.' She hesitated, then linked her arm with his. 'An' then there's you. Good class family, well-ter-do, an' all yer want ter do is turn yer back on 'em.'

Toff threw his half-finished cigarette to the ground. 'Look, Nell,' he said intensely. 'My old man comes from good Jewish stock. He's a Jew, and wants to be nothing but a Jew. As far as he's concerned, his only son's a Jew too, and he expects me to behave like one. In his book, there's no room for compromise. D'you understand what I'm saying?'

Nellie's face was quite expressionless. 'Yes, Toff, I understand,' she said. 'So where does that leave me?'

Toff had no time to reply, for they were both distracted by the sound of someone calling to Nellie.

'Nell! Nell, up here!'

Nellie and Toff turned to look up towards the cliff path where Madame was shouting and waving frantically.

'Mum!' Nellie shouted back, at the same time rushing up to meet her. 'Wot's up? Wot's 'appened?'

They met halfway, with Toff following on behind.

Madame was fraught; she had not even had time to put on a coat. 'It's Lenny!' she cried. 'Grandma's just telephoned. They've taken 'im ter 'ospital.' She was fighting for breath and had difficulty getting her words out. ''E's . . . collapsed . . . they've . . . taken 'im . . . ter 'ospital. 'E's spittin' up blood, Nell. Spittin' up blood!'

Monsieur and Nellie took the last train of the day up to London from Margate. For both of them, it seemed an interminable journey, for it was a slow train which stopped at every station. And despite the fact that they were travelling first class, the compartment was unheated and filthy dirty with a layer of thick black soot from the steam engine all over the upholstered seats. Monsieur was also incensed that the strips of sticky protective paper on the windows were peeling off, and because there were no blackout blinds, the dim light available in the compartment had to be turned off. To make things worse, when they stopped at Maidstone, there was a routine security check. It seemed to take the two Special Constables for ever to check everyone's identity cards. Monsieur said he would write a letter of complaint to the railway company about it all, but by the time the train finally pulled into Charing Cross, he had forgotten all about the journey and was only interested in finding a taxi to take them to the Royal Northern Hospital in Holloway Road.

After the traumatic telephone call from Grandma Beckwith, Madame had withdrawn from the last two shows of the week in Margate and gone straight back to London. As the Great Pierre was top of the bill, it was decided that Monsieur and Nellie should finish off the last two shows of the week, with the help of the theatre orchestra's resident lady pianist.

If the news of Lenny's collapse distressed Monsieur, Nellie saw no sign of it. On the train he had said very little, preferring to sit in silence and stare out into the night, watching the distant dark shapes of the countryside fluttering in and out of the thick black engine smoke as the train sped by. It was the same in the taxi as it wound its way through the almost deserted streets of wartime London. No comment, nothing said. Only fear, hope, and prayers. Nellie had never known him to be so silent, and for so long. It told her quite a lot.

It was nearly half past one in the morning when they reached the ward where Lenny had been taken. Madame was waiting for them.

'It's pneumonia,' she whispered, her voice cracking and her eyes sore from crying. 'Apparently it was touch an' go. When they got 'im 'ere, 'e was coughin' 'is 'eart

310

up. 'E looks terrible! I blame meself. I should never've left 'im. I should never've gone down ter Margate.'

'Calm yerself, gel.' This was the first time Monsieur had really said anything since he and Nellie had left Charing Cross Station. 'We 'ad no idea this was goin' ter 'appen. There's nuffin' we can do. Len's in good 'ands.'

Madame's face crumpled and she started to sob quietly to herself.

Nellie put her arm round her and hugged her. 'It's all right, Mum,' she said comfortingly. 'Lenny's a tough little devil. 'E'll be OK, you'll see.' She wasn't sure she believed what she was saying. During the past month or so, she had noticed a subtle change in young Lenny's appearance. For a boy of thirteen, he was far too skinny. He had also lost his ruddy complexion and lacked bounce and energy when he was playing football with the Tufnell Tigers.

'You can go in now,' said the night nurse softly. 'He's fast asleep, so just a few minutes, please.'

Due to the seriousness of Lenny's condition, he had been put in a small room by himself. When Monsieur, Madame, and Nellie filed in, they found him with an oxygen mask strapped to his face, a huge cylinder at the side of the bed.

Nellie flinched at the sight of Lenny. He looked so small, lying flat on his back in a bed that seemed to be far too big for him, with the oxygen mask strap caught up in the straggly curls of his mop of blond hair. She couldn't bear to see him like this. This was Lenny, this was her own brother. Inside she wanted to cry, to shout out loud. She wanted to bend down, to take him in her arms and say, 'Don't do this to us, Lenny! There's nuffin' wrong wiv yer. We love yer. Don't yer know that? We love yer!'

She, Monsieur, and Madame stood in silence beside the delicate, motionless frame of the boy. The only sound was that of Lenny breathing through the oxygen mask.

It was an unnatural sound, a real struggle between life and death.

On one side of the bed, Madame gently covered Lenny's hand with her own. On the other side, Nellie did the same.

Monsieur remained silent, standing, watching. Then he put his arm on his wife's shoulder to comfort her. But she pulled away.

The house was empty when they arrived home, for with Lenny in hospital, Sid had gone to Grandma and Grandad Beckwith's for the night.

Nellie felt ill at ease. 'Why don't I make us all a cup of tea?' she suggested.

'Fanks, Nell,' said Monsieur, trying hard to put on a brave face. 'Good idea.'

'Mum?'

Madame said nothing. She just shook her head briskly, took off her coat and hat, and threw them carelessly on to a kitchen chair.

Nellie exchanged an anxious look with Monsieur as Madame went to a kitchen cabinet and took out a bottle of gin.

Monsieur quickly crossed to her and tried to take the bottle from her. 'No, Doris,' he said gently but firmly. 'It won't help.'

Madame wrenched the bottle back. 'Wot d'yer mean, it won't 'elp?' she growled angrily. 'Wot do *you* know about 'elp, *Monsieur*?' Her look cut straight through him, and her voice had a ferocity that Nellie had never heard before. 'If there's one fing I've learnt in life, Bert,' she continued, 'it's every woman fer 'erself!' She poured herself a half tumblerful of neat gin and took a gulp.

Monsieur and Nellie looked on helplessly.

'Please, Mum, don't,' Nellie pleaded, going to her.

Madame backed away from her, shaking her head

312

vigorously. 'It's not your fault, Nell. This was bound to 'appen sooner or later. That's why our boy's in 'ospital. We should've seen this comin' but we didn't!'

'That's not true, Doris,' said Monsieur, making a move towards her. 'You're gettin' everyfin' mixed up.'

Madame held fast, holding up her hands in front of her face as though trying to shield herself. 'Mixed up?' she shouted. 'Mixed up? Is that wot it is, Bert? I'm mixed up because I failed to notice that my own son – *our* own son – was comin' down wiv pneumonia?'

'It's somefin' that could 'appen ter anyone,' Monsieur said defensively. ''Ow're we ter know these fings?'

'By noticin' our kids, Bert!' blasted Madame. 'By bein' wiv 'em when they need us.' She took another gulp from her glass. 'That's the trouble wiv us, Bert. Our 'ole lives live an' breave the Great Pierre. They live an' breave 'ow the act goes, 'ow people are goin' ter like it, an' 'ow they're goin' ter like you!'

'That's not true, Doris,' he snapped. 'That's an unfair, untrue fing ter say.'

'Is it? Then why aren't yer there when your family need yer? Why do they always come last when yer 'ave one of your so-called important *appointments* to go to?'

Nellie was appalled by her mum's ferocious outburst. She had never seen her like this before. But as she stood there between them, deep in despair and disillusionment, a cold, hard fact was beginning to emerge. Even in the best of families, things were never exactly as they appeared. There would always be suspicion; mutual trust would always have to be worked for. Hard as it was to accept, nobody, not even her own mum and dad, was perfect.

Monsieur, clearly devastated, stood helplessly as Madame went out into the garden to her usual haunt, the Anderson shelter.

He turned to look at Nellie. ''Ow can she say those

fings, Nell?' he said, totally crushed. 'I love 'er. I love all me family – an' that includes you.'

Nellie, who was herself reeling from Madame's words, looked at her dad. His face was racked with anguish, and he seemed as vulnerable as poor Lenny lying in his hospital bed. This was the moment, she decided. This was the moment when she had to tell him the truth. It was now or never. He pulled back a kitchen chair and sat down, and she joined him at the table. With calm dignity she said the words she knew she had to say. 'She knows, Dad. She knows about you – and Ange.'

Monsieur slowly looked up. Despite his height, sitting at the kitchen table he looked small and bent. 'I don't know wot you're talkin' about, Nell,' he replied, a look of genuine bewilderment on his face.

'Mum knows you've been 'avin' an affair wiv Ange.'

Monsieur was thunderstruck. He quickly shook his head. 'No, Nell! It's not true. It wasn't like that. I swear ter God, it wasn't like that at all.'

Nellie's face crumpled up. 'Dad. Everyone knows. They've seen yer.'

'Everyone don't know nuffin'! OK, so I 'ad a kiss an' a cuddle wiv 'er a coupla times a while back. It was stupid but it ain't ever gone any furver than that. I swear ter God it ain't!'

Nellie lowered her head briefly, then quickly raised it again and stared him straight in the eyes. 'Dad,' she asked with pain and embarrassment, 'wot about that snapshot? You an' 'er bunked down tergevver on the grass?'

Monsieur's eyes widened with shock. 'Yer've seen *that*? 'Ow d'yer see it?'

'It don't matter 'ow or where I've seen it, Dad. The fact is, I've seen it.'

Monsieur quickly searched for his packet of Wood-bines, took one out and lit it. 'I was set up, Nell,' he said, inhaling deeply and trying to speak with a throat full of smoke. 'One day, before you ever come, she asked me ter meet 'er in Finsbury Park. She said she wanted ter talk over one or two fings she found difficult ter do in the act. It was all rubbish, of course. Anyway, we sat down on the grass, just up near the lake – there were plenty of people around. It 'appened just as I was askin' 'er wot the problem was. All of a sudden she fell against me, pinned me down, an' – an' kissed me, right on the lips. I pushed 'er away, told 'er not ter be so bloody silly. But she did it again, and kept tryin' it on. Next fing I knew, she slung 'er bloody 'ook an' left me like a lemon stretched out there. I fawt wot a silly little cow she was, goin' after a bloke over twice 'er age, an' I decided there an' then that I'd give 'er the boot, get 'er out of the act, out of my life fer good.' The smoke lingering in his throat made him cough, and it took him a moment or so to recover. 'Wot I din't know was while she was performin' 'er little act, she'd got one of 'er mates 'idin' be'ind a tree, takin' a few juicy snaps of us.' He finally summoned up enough courage to look directly at her. 'I was set up, Nell,' he said. 'Ange's a go-getter. She was only ever after all she could get from me. I knew that from the start.'

Nellie was unconvinced. 'Then why din't yer get rid of 'er?'

Monsieur drew hard on his fag and exhaled. It took him a moment to answer, and when he did, it was with difficulty. 'Nell, it's easy fer a man my age ter be flattered. I was a fool, a stupid, blind fool. I 'ad the gall ter fink that this gel, this good-lookin' gel really fancied me. By the time I knew the facts of life, it was too late. I was a fool, Nell. I admit it. I was a bloody fool!'

Nellie hesitated for a moment. 'Dad, I want ter ask yer a question. But please tell me the truth. I've seen yer kissin' Ange, back at Drury Lane. Was it fer real?'

Monsieur had a pained look. 'It weren't fer real, Nell,' he replied. 'But I was chuffed enough ter go along wiv it.'

Nellie sighed. 'Don't yer care about Mum any more?'

'Care?' Monsieur looked up, stubbed out his fag in a tin ashtray, and exhaled the last few remains of smoke. 'Let me tell yer somefin', Nell,' he said passionately. 'I care fer Doris more than anyone else in the 'ole wide world. I'd be lost wivout 'er.'

Nellie came back at him like a shot. 'Then why din't yer tell 'er about all this? If yer love Mum as much as yer say yer do, why couldn't yer 'ave trusted 'er enough ter tell 'er?'

Monsieur shook his head. 'She wouldn't believe me, Nell.'

Nellie was exasperated. 'Dad! 'Ow d'yer know if yer don't try?'

''Cos she's always bin the same. Every gel I've ever bin in contact wiv, she's always got it into her 'ead that I've bin after 'em.'

''Ave yer, Dad?' Nellie asked.

Nellie's cool response upset him. 'No, Nell,' he said with quiet emotion but avoiding her look. 'Wot 'appened wiv Ange was the first time. I swear ter God I'll never let it 'appen again.' He covered his face with his hands and broke down. It was an extraordinary and quite unexpected moment; Monsieur so rarely showed any emotion at all, Nellie had thought him incapable of crying.

''Ave yer any idea 'ow I felt, seein' that boy of mine lyin' in that 'ospital bed ternight?' he sobbed. 'I don't care about the bloody Great Pierre, Nell. I don't care if I never tread the boards again as long as I live.' He looked up at her, and with tears streaming down his face added, 'I'd sooner lose me arms an' legs than let one of my own go through anyfin' like that!'

Nellie knelt down in front of him, threw her arms round his neck, and held him. 'I believe yer, Dad,' she said

316

reassuringly. 'An' so will Mum, you'll see.' A determined, defiant look came to Nellie's face as she added, 'An' don't yer worry a fing about Ange. As a matter of fact, I know exactly 'ow ter take care of *'er*.'

Chapter 22

Sid Beckwith sat on the edge of his bed without saying a word. It wasn't his usual bed, for ever since his young brother had been taken ill, he couldn't bear being alone in the room that he shared with him so he slept in a small box room next to his mum and dad's bedroom on the first floor, where he spent most of his time after getting home from school in the evenings. Nellie did her best to be with him as much as she could; she had noticed the close bond between the two brothers, despite the fact that they often argued and quarrelled with each other. 'Is Len going to die, Nell?' was a question he frequently asked, and it revealed a great deal of the despair he was feeling.

Although young Lenny's condition had stabilised, he was still seriously ill. It was now almost a week since he had been rushed to hospital, but despite rest, medication, and constant supervision, his temperature remained stubbornly high, and his dry cough was also troubling him. He lacked all energy, and the only time he showed any interest at all was when Monsieur and Madame took Sid to visit him. This did not go unnoticed by Lenny's doctor, who was of the mind that the brothers' closeness was the younger boy's best means of recovery.

Lenny's illness had at least brought the crisis between Monsieur and Madame to a head. With Nellie's encouragement, Monsieur told his wife everything about his association with Ange, including the reason she had been blackmailing him. Although this cleared the air, it still left the problem of the snapshots. If Ange showed them to a newspaper, it would put his marriage to Madame under the public spotlight and also cause intense embarrassment in his career. However, Nellie had one or two ideas of her own.

'How d'yer find a soldier?' retorted Ruby Catmonk, in reply to Nellie's question. She let rip with a great chesty laugh. 'Go an' stand outside any army barracks and grab the first one that comes out!'

Nellie laughed with her. 'No, Rube,' she said, 'I din't say 'ow d'yer find a soldier. I asked 'ow d'yer find out about a soldier. I wanna find out about this feller I met. 'E's in the army – a photographer.'

Ruby scratched her head. Her dyed ginger hair was getting a bit thin on top. 'A photographer in the army? 'Aven't the foggiest! Why? Wot's all this about then?'

'I'm curious, that's all. I've got a 'unch about 'im.'

Ruby took a fag end from her lips and pressed it into her ashtray. Then she immediately lit up again. They were sitting in her sewing room at the Finsbury Park Empire, and they could hear the sound of the first house performance.

''Ave yer tried the War Office?' she asked, as she picked up a pair of scissors and started trimming her heavily painted fingernails.

''Aven't tried anywhere,' replied Nellie, who was leaning on Ruby's table, looking at her, arms crossed. 'I fawt you might know. You know everyfin', Rube. You're a genius.'

'Yes, I know I am,' agreed the old lady. 'That's why I'm sewin' costumes in the bleedin' Finsbury Park Empire.' She took off her specs and flung them down carelessly on the table. 'As a matter of fact, I do know someone. 'Aven't seen 'im fer a while though. I once 'ad a bit of a ding-dong wiv 'is old man.' Without removing her cigarette, she blew smoke out of the side of her mouth.

'If yer want ter know about this photographer, you'll 'ave ter tell me more about 'im, gel.'

Nellie thought a moment. "'E's got a tattoo,' she said.

'A tattoo?'

'One on each arm.'

Ruby looked across the table at Nellie, then actually took the fag out of her mouth. 'Piece of cake!' she said, taking the mickey. 'We should 'ave no trouble at all findin' a soldier in the British Army who 'as a tattoo on each arm!'

'Stop takin' the piss, Rube,' Nellie replied. 'It's all I've got – well, at the moment. But 'e's a photographer, remember. That narrows it down a bit, don't it?'

Ruby sighed and shook her head. 'Why, Nell?' she asked. 'Why d'yer want ter know about this bloke?'

Nellie lowered her eyes uneasily. 'Can't tell yer, Rube,' she said apologetically.

Ruby briefly put her hands in front of her, palms facing Nellie. 'Ask no questions, 'ear no lies,' she said. 'But I still need ter know *somefin*' about 'im.' She cleared the bits of sewing material from her table and found a pencil and piece of paper. 'Right,' she said. 'Where der we start?'

A week later, Monsieur and Madame were asked to call in to see Lenny's specialist. He was a man they hadn't seen before, and when they arrived at the hospital they found him waiting for them in the ward sister's office. His name was Mr Timothy Whetstone, and to Monsieur and Madame he looked old enough to be near retirement. But he had a pleasant face, even if, like so many other people in his profession, he found it difficult to offer anything more than the suggestion of a comforting smile.

'I wanted to talk to you personally,' he said, once Monsieur and Madame had sat down, 'mainly because there are one or two things about your son's condition that you ought to know.'

'Is 'e any worse?' asked Madame anxiously.

Mr Whetstone sighed and took off his reading spectacles. 'I can't be absolutely certain about that at the moment, I'm afraid, Mrs Beckwith,' he said, again trying a smile. 'We still have one or two more tests to do.'

'Does pneumonia usually take as long as this ter clear up?' asked Monsieur, the knuckles of his hands white as they rested on his walking cane.

'That's just the trouble, Mr Beckwith,' replied the specialist, sitting back in his chair. 'Your son's condition is not as we first thought. It's not pneumonia. It's primary tuberculosis.'

Madame gasped, and put her hand against her mouth.

Monsieur went visibly white. 'Tuberculosis? Yer mean TB?' he asked, in a state of shock.

'It's not as bad as it sounds,' continued Mr Whetstone. 'Not for the time being anyway.'

'But don't people die wiv that?' asked Monsieur, his voice cracking with anxiety.

'People die of all sorts of things, Mr Beckwith. And I won't disguise the fact that this disease can be a killer. But young Lenny does have a fighting chance. As I said, what he's suffering from is the primary stage. We weren't absolutely sure until we took some X-rays.'

Mr Whetstone stood up to switch on a screen on the wall showing Lenny's X-rays.

'If you'd like to come over here,' he said, 'I'll show you what I mean.'

Monsieur helped Madame up from her chair, and they both joined the specialist at the screen.

'As you can see,' said Mr Whetstone, using the tip of a pencil to point out the affected areas on Lenny's X-rays, 'there's a dark patch at the base of his left lung, here. And there's a smaller one just here. That's why he's been coughing so badly, and spitting up blood and pus-filled sputum. What has happened is that the bacteria has attacked his lungs, which is the usual case.'

'Is there anyfin' yer can do ter get rid of it?' asked Monsieur.

Mr Whetstone sighed, and continued staring into the bright light of the X-ray screen. 'Well,' he said, 'this phase of the disease usually lasts for several months. Hopefully, the body will resist it by using its own natural defences. But there's always the chance that the bacteria may spread into the bloodstream.'

Madame seemed to shrivel up in despair.

'However, that's not always the case,' continued Mr Whetstone as they went back to their chairs. 'In our experience, the disease quite often never develops beyond this primary stage. Especially in youngsters of your son's age.' He looked at his notes. 'But sometimes natural resistance cannot subdue the bacteria, and although the initial outbreak can be overcome, it could flare up again after a lapse of several years.' He looked up from his notes. This time he didn't even attempt a smile. 'This phase is much more serious.'

'What are Lenny's chances, sir?' asked Monsieur sombrely.

Mr Whetstone paused briefly before answering. 'I'll be perfectly frank with you, Mr Beckwith,' he replied. 'In someone whose natural resistance is abnormally low, primary tuberculosis spreads so quickly that it can be fatal unless it's treated very early. Your son, I'm afraid, has very low resistance.'

Madame felt the inside of her stomach collapse. 'But there must be somefin' yer can do,' she said, staring into the man's eyes, looking for just one ray of hope. 'There must be some kind of treatment yer can give 'im.'

'There are drugs, Mrs Beckwith,' replied Mr Whetstone. 'But they're not a cure, only a relief. The only effective treatment is the right kind of food and a prolonged period of rest. I'm afraid that, with this condition, it would be out of the question for Lenny to go back to school. We'll do all we can, but once we've got him on his feet again, it'll be up to you and your family to give him as much attention as you possibly can.'

While Monsieur and Madame were with the specialist, Nellie sat with Lenny in his room at the end of the ward. Although his breathing had improved enough for the oxygen mask to be removed, he was still lacking all energy and was too weak to engage in much conversation. Nellie couldn't bear to see her young brother like this, his face as white as the sheets covering him, and his eyes bulging out of their sockets. It was heartbreaking. It was so unfair.

'Yer better get out of 'ere soon, Len,' Nellie said in a soft, over-hearty voice. 'The Tigers've got quite a few big matches comin' up in yer school 'olidays. They need all the support they can get.' She knew that she sounded utterly false but she had to keep up the boy's morale somehow.

Lenny smiled, and Nellie detected just a trace of that old fanatical support for his team in his tired eyes.

Nellie moved her chair closer so that her legs were under the bed and she could talk to Lenny just a few inches from his face. 'Sid says when 'e comes in ter see yer on Sat'day afternoon, 'e's goin' ter bring yer that new Football Annual – you know, the one 'e got fer 'is birfday.'

Although he continued to stare at her, Lenny's reaction was silent and blank. He seemed so drugged, he was unable to focus. But at least the awful hacking cough had stopped, for the time being anyway.

Suddenly, Nellie noticed that he was trying to say something, so she leaned as close to him as she possibly could. 'Yes, Len?' she said eagerly. 'Wot d'yer say, mate?'

324

Lenny's voice was slow and precise, but it was clearly an effort to speak. 'Could yer . . .' he wheezed.

'Yes, Len,' Nellie replied, quickly. 'Tell me, mate.'

'Could yer . . . show me . . . 'ow ter do boxin' . . . like Sid?'

Nellie wanted to cry. She was so upset, and yet so happy that Lenny was showing interest in something. 'You bet yer life I'll show yer,' she said firmly, squeezing his hand.

The door opened quietly behind her and the ward sister came up to her. 'Could you come outside for a moment, please? Your mum would like to see you.'

In the corridor outside, Madame was in tears. 'It's TB,' was all she could say over and over again. ''Ow could 'e catch such a fing, Nell?' she asked, between sobs. 'We've never 'ad nuffin' like that on our side of the family, nor yer dad's.'

Nellie didn't know what to say. She had no idea what TB was, and when her mum told her about tuberculosis, she thought a disease like that was only ever connected to things like cows. But it sounded bad, and the whole business gave her a sinking feeling.

'I've got ter take care of 'im, Nell,' said Madame. 'I'm goin' ter give up the act, give up the 'alls. I'm never ever goin' ter leave that boy alone as long as I live!'

'*We'll* take care of 'im, Mum,' Nellie replied. 'I'm part of the family now, an' Len's me bruvver. We'll all stick tergevver, an' 'e'll pull fru, just yer wait an' see.'

Monsieur left the hospital in a daze. In fact, he was so shocked that he left his overcoat behind in the ward sister's office. But it didn't matter that it was freezing cold outside. Nothing mattered. What he had just heard from Mr Whetstone the specialist was, in Monsieur's opinion, more than anyone should have to bear. Tuberculosis? Damn the disease! Where did it come from? Who gave it to him? In a fit of illogical rage, Monsieur slammed his walking cane against a lamppost and it snapped in half. But he hardly noticed and kept on walking.

He had left the hospital alone. Sid would be getting back from school fairly soon and he would think that something was wrong if he arrived home and found no one there. But the walk back to Tufnell Park Road turned into a faltering crawl. It was only a short distance home from the Royal Northern Hospital in Manor Gardens but by the time Monsieur had got as far as the Gaumont Cinema, his body felt quite numb. He put his hands in his jacket pocket. Without realising it, he had come to a halt and was staring aimlessly along the street he had lived in for so many years with his darling Doris and the two boys. For some reason, it all looked so different, as though he hardly knew the place. And then he thought about what Doris had said to him. Yes, she was right, he hadn't cared enough about her and the boys. It was one thing to think in your mind how much you cared for someone, but it was quite another thing to tell them so, and to show it. He was tormented by so many thoughts. He was beginning to believe that he had wasted his life on trivia, acting the fool on a music hall stage. Real life was outside the theatre, in the street, in the home, in the lives of ordinary people like his own family. Yes, his life was nothing more than a make-believe world, and he deeply regretted what he had turned into. Oh God, he thought, if only I could live my life all over again.

'Dad.'

Monsieur came out of his trance to find Nellie at his side. 'Nell?' he spluttered, almost as though he didn't know her.

'It's not as bad as yer fink,' she said firmly. 'Yer've got ter take 'old of yerself.'

''E's goin' ter die, Nell,' Monsieur said, distraught. 'My boy's goin' ter die.'

326

Nellie grabbed hold of his arm and squeezed it. 'No, Dad! That's not goin' ter 'appen, an' yer mustn't carry on as if it is! Yes, Lenny's ill, 'e's very ill. But if 'e's looked after, 'e's goin' ter pull fru an' 'ave a perfectly normal life.'

Monsieur was shaking his head. He didn't believe her.

'Dad, listen ter me!' Nellie persisted. 'Please don't bury someone before they're dead! Lenny's only a kid. 'E's got plenty of fight in 'im, you'll see. But if 'e's goin' ter make it, 'e's goin' ter need all the love an' support yer can give 'im. So does Mum. Sid too. An' that means bein' strong, Dad, strong ter face up ter anyfin' that comes along.'

A queue was forming outside the Holloway Road side of the cinema; the current film was clearly very popular. Aware that she and her dad were attracting attention, Nellie took him gently by the arm and led him off slowly along the other side of the cinema, which was their own road. Daffodils, tulips, and other spring flowers in people's front gardens were dying off and gradually giving way to the pink and white blossom of cherry trees. Nellie was aware of this, and had often thought how touching it was that, despite the war, people in the city streets still tended their small gardens with such loving care.

'You're right, Nell,' said Monsieur, staring down at the pavement as he walked. 'I *ave* bin neglectin' my family. They need me as much as I need them.' He suddenly came to a halt and turned to look at her. 'I've made up me mind. I'm goin' ter give up the 'alls and spend more time at 'ome.'

'Dad!' protested Nellie. 'Yer've got it all wrong. That's not wot I'm sayin'. Yer don't 'ave ter give up everyfin' yer've ever worked for ter stay wiv yer family. The music 'all's yer life!'

'So are me wife an' kids,' insisted Monsieur. 'From now on, they come first.'

Nellie was frustrated that she wasn't getting through to

327

him, so, without thinking, she propped herself up on the narrow coping stone of a front garden wall. 'Let me ask yer somefin', Dad,' she said. 'If yer give up the act, give up all the good work yer've ever done on the 'alls, wot would yer do then?'

Monsieur shrugged his shoulders. 'I'd find somefin',' he replied.

Nellie looked up at him. He towered over her, so she grabbed his arm and forced him to sit down beside her. 'Would yer, Dad?' she asked. 'Would yer really be able to find somefin' ter replace wot yer 'ave in yer blood, the one fing that drives yer along every day of yer life?'

Monsieur's only response was to shrug his shoulders again.

'There's nuffin' wrong wiv the music 'all,' Nellie continued. 'It's a wonderful fing ter be a part of, givin' so much pleasure ter everyone. An' the people who tread the boards are pretty special people too. They're your friends, they're warm-'earted, they stick tergevver when you're in trouble, an' as long as there's someone ter come an' watch 'em, they'll keep on goin' till they drop. Wot der yer call 'em, Dad – troupers? Well, that's wot *you* are. You're a trouper, an' yer must never ferget it. You're one of the pillars of the music 'all. If everyone like you gave it all up, it'd all come crumbling down. An' fer wot?'

Monsieur was staring down at the pavement as he listened to her.

'Doin' wot you're doin' ain't responsible fer wot's 'appened ter Len, Dad,' Nellie continued, voice low. 'I din't know much about family life till I met you an' Mum. But wot I 'ave learnt since then is that bad times can come when yer least expect 'em. Yer can be up one day, an' down the next. Bein' ill is no one's fault. It just comes when it comes, an' yer just 'ave ter cope wiv it any way yer can.'

'Oy! You two!'

The shrill, angry yell coming from the house behind them caused Nellie and Monsieur to get up with a start.

A middle-aged woman with hair in curlers was leaning right out of her window, waving her hand and shouting at them. 'Who the bleedin' 'ell d'yer fink yer are?' she rasped. 'Ain't yer got no wall of yer own ter sit down on? Push off!'

Monsieur looked over the top of the hedge, took off his hat, and waved it at the woman. 'Sorry, Mrs Hoddle!' he called. 'We're just on our way.'

Mrs Hoddle looked horrified. 'Oh! It's you, Mr Beckwith,' she called, her voice immediately transformed into genteel sweetness and charm. 'I din't see it was you. You stay there as long as yer want, dear!'

Monsieur waved his hat once more then put it back on.

Nellie was grinning. 'See wot I mean?' she said, with a wry chuckle. 'Yer never know from one minute ter the next 'ow life's goin' ter treat yer.'

Monsieur's face lit up with a faint smile for the first time that day. Then he held out his arm for Nellie.

They moved on up the road and made for home. As they went, Monsieur was surprised to notice how tall his adopted daughter was. In fact, as far as he was concerned, she was much taller than he was.

Chapter 23

Summer was in full bloom, and during the first heat wave of the year, the streets were filled with people in their brightest summer clothes. In fact it was so hot that one or two teenagers tried frying an egg on the steps of the Marlborough Cinema in Holloway, but with disastrous effect. There was, however, a general malaise in the streets, for after a long lull enemy raiders were making two or three attacks on London and the south-east each week, which were officially described as tit-for-tat reprisals for Allied air raids on targets deep inside Germany, including Berlin itself. The people around the Nag's Head, Holloway, were not complacent but they did not rush straight out to the air-raid shelter as soon as the siren was heard. The Allied successes in North Africa were giving them renewed hope that the end of the war was in sight, and that feeling was reflected in the atmosphere of relaxed calm.

Several weeks had passed since Nellie had asked Ruby Catmonk to get her the information she required on the soldier photographer. Fortunately, apart from one-night appearances at a few Masonic dinners, the Great Pierre had, for the time being, no music hall engagements to fulfil. This suited Nellie, for, apart from spending as much time as she could with young Lenny, who was being lovingly cared for at home by Madame, she had some important business of her own to attend to.

During recent weeks, Nellie had spent a lot of time, usually in the afternoons, in and around Harvest Road.

She kept watch from a scruffy workmen's cafe in nearby Hornsey Road. The cafe was used by some of the local Civil Defence workers, such as Special Constables, ARP wardens, and firefighters from the fire station round the corner in Shelburne Road School, and after a while they regarded her as a regular. They gave her some useful but casual information about the young couple who lived in the house she was so interested in on the other side of Harvest Road. The cafe was a perfect place to keep out of sight, especially when either Ange or her army photographer boyfriend came out of the house, for at no time did they take even a passing glance at the window where Nellie sat slowly sipping her cup of tea.

Ruby's information was taking a long time to materialise because her contact in the War Office was away on a secret mission overseas, and until he returned there was no one else they could approach to sort out who Ange's boyfriend was. Nellie refused to give up hope; there was too much at stake. Moreover, she was sure she had seen the soldier with tattooed arms somewhere before. Her feeling was confirmed when Ruby came back with her startling information.

During her vigil inside the workmen's cafe and on the streets nearby, Nellie had discovered that Ange left the house every afternoon regularly at around three o'clock. This suggested that she had taken some kind of part-time job. Her mysterious boyfriend seemed to spend a lot of time in civvy street, for he rarely came out of the house except to tinker with his rather battered Hercules motorcycle. She never saw him in uniform, which seemed strange for a soldier during war – strange, that is, until Ruby provided her with the information she was looking for. It was on that basis that she set up her plan.

One Wednesday afternoon, she took the bold step of returning to the house in Harvest Road. Ange had already left. Nellie approached the front gate as quickly as she could and opened it without closing it behind her. She went straight down the stone steps to the basement area and knocked on the door. She concealed herself as much as possible in the porch so that anyone peering out through the bay window would not be able to see who their visitor was. She had to knock three times before the door was finally opened, and then only a crack. 'She's out.' The tattooed soldier was only just visible.

'It's you I've come ter see, not 'er,' replied Nellie with a small but mischievous smile.

The soldier didn't move. 'Got nothin' ter say to yer,' he growled. 'Come back in the mornin'.'

Nellie put her hand against the door, preventing him from closing it. 'I said it was you I've come ter see – Sergeant Fowler.'

The soldier glared at her, then opened the door fully. He was angry, unshaven, and wearing a threadbare white singlet and baggy khaki shorts. 'Wot d'yer want?' he asked, scowling.

'A little chat, mate, that's all.' She was feeling very unsure of herself but she was determined not to let it show. 'I fink yer might be int'rested in wot I've got ter say.'

The man hesitated then stood back to let her enter. 'This'd better be worf it,' he said, closing the door behind her.

Nellie didn't wait to be invited into the sitting room; she just marched straight in. The place was in exactly the same state as the last time she had been here, untidy, and, in the middle of the heat wave, Ange's ironing board smelt even more disgusting than ever.

'Right.' The soldier was standing in the sitting-room doorway, hands in his shorts pockets. ''Ow'd yer know me name?'

'I've come about the snapshots,' said Nellie, ignoring his question.

The soldier grinned. Nellie had to admit to herself that

he was a handsome young bloke; it was a seductive grin and he had eyes that seemed to see straight into her. 'Wot snapshots?' he asked.

'The snapshots of Ange and my dad,' she said firmly, refusing to be intimidated.

'Oh, *those* snapshots,' replied the soldier, apparently amused. He came into the room, retrieving a half-finished fag from behind his right ear. 'Wot about 'em?'

'I want 'em back. Every one of 'em. Includin' the negatives.'

The soldier turned to look at her. 'Do yer now?' he replied, playing the game with her. 'Well, I'm not sure Ange can 'elp yer wiv that. They're worf quite a bit, yer know.'

'It's you I'm talkin' to, mate, not Ange.'

The soldier moistened the end of his cigarette with his lips, then lit up. 'You're wastin' yer time.'

Nellie went and stood right in front of him. 'An' you're in danger of ruinin' a man's life,' she growled.

''E should've fawt 'bout that when 'e tried to lay a gel 'alf 'is age, dirty ol' sod!'

Nellie wasn't taking any of it. 'You set 'im up,' she snapped.

'I beg yer pardon?' replied the soldier indignantly.

'You set 'im up,' insisted Nellie. 'You an' that bitch. It was a real con job.'

'Nice gels don't say fings like that, *Miss* Beckwiff.'

'An' army deserters don't burn their fingers blackmailin' people,' retorted Nellie, adding, 'Do they, *Sergeant*?'

The lit match the soldier was still holding burnt his fingers and he quickly threw it into the empty fireplace. 'You better start talkin', darlin',' he rasped menacingly.

Nellie stood her ground. 'On the run, ain't yer, Sergeant? Yer've bin on the run since before Christmas – so my contacts tell me. Somefin' about nickin' cash from the NAAFI at some army camp up norf. My contact says you're AWOL. Apparently, in the army that means absent wivout leave. Is that right, Sarge?'

The soldier's face was like thunder.

'Stroke of luck, really,' continued Nellie, moving away from him and aimlessly picking up and looking at some of the clothes that were waiting to be ironed. 'Y'see, me an' my dad we get ter tour round the army camps doin' shows fer ENSA from time ter time. Well, one day, we was just checkin' in at the main gates of some barracks or somefin', which 'appened ter be in the guard 'ouse.' She paused and turned to look briefly at him. 'You know wot a guard 'ouse is, don't yer, Sarge? Sort of gaol or somefin', ain't it?'

The soldier did not respond. In the stifling atmosphere of the small room, his forehead and chest were saturated with sweat.

Nellie smiled at him, then continued, 'Well, while I was standin' there waitin' ter sign in, I suddenly caught a butchers of this noticeboard – sheer chance, really. Anyway, guess wot?' She walked up to him. 'Lo an' be'old, your picture was there.' She was eyeball to eyeball with him. 'It was your picture, wasn't it, Sarge? The one that said WANTED . . .'

The soldier flicked his fag butt into the fireplace and moved away from her.

Nellie's eyes followed him. 'Shows yer wot a good memory I've got fer faces, don't it, Sarge? It's a funny fing, but the moment I saw yer flittin' down that passage the last time I come 'ere, I knew I'd seen yer somewhere. I just 'ad ter put two an' two tergevver, an' get a little bit of 'elp from this pal of mine.'

'Wot d'yer want?' the soldier suddenly snarled.

'Yer know wot I want, Sarge,' Nellie shot back, utterly fearless. 'I want them snapshots, every single one of 'em.'

'An' if I don't give 'em to yer?'

Nellie chortled. 'As yer can see, Sarge, I've got friends in 'igh places.'

The soldier paused a moment, sizing her up. His lip curled up on one side in a slight suggestion of a smile. 'You're a real little firecracker, ain't yer?' he said.

Nellie smiled back at him. 'That's right, mate. Yer better watch out I don't blow up on yer.'

The sergeant waited a moment, then turned to look at himself in the mirror. Nellie watched him, fascinated, as he used his hand to rub the sweat from his chest. What a vain piece of shit, she thought. But she was only too aware that this lout had enough muscle power to make mincemeat of her.

Abruptly the sergeant stopped looking at himself in the mirror, went straight to the cupboard beside the fireplace, took out the snapshots, and held them out to her. 'Take the bloody fings!' he growled.

'No! Don't give 'em to 'er!'

Nellie swung round to find Ange standing in the doorway. She had not expected this, for only a short while ago she had seen Ange leave the house.

Ange rushed in and grabbed the photos from the sergeant. 'Don't listen to a word she says! It's bluff, all bluff!'

'It's your bloody fault!' the sergeant shouted at Ange. 'I told yer it wouldn't work! If she lets on, I'll 'ave that guard 'ouse brigade down on me like a ton of 'ot bricks!'

'It's *your* bloody fault,' Ange yelled back. 'I told yer ter keep out of sight when this little bitch was around!'

This was just what Nellie wanted, a real slanging match between them.

'Give 'er the bloody pictures!' rasped the sergeant.

'No!' shouted Ange, pulling the photographs out of his reach. 'There's nuffin' she can do, nuffin'!'

'Oh, I wouldn't be so sure, Ange,' interrupted Nellie. 'My pal assures me that blackmail ain't looked on too kindly by the law. Specially when yer've done it before – several times.'

The sergeant darted a rapid glance at Ange. 'Wot's this?'

'Don't bloody listen to 'er! She's makin' it up!' she said, her forehead streaked with sweat. 'She's makin' up the 'ole bloody fing!'

Ange was right, Nellie was making it all up, but it was a good way of getting Ange and her boyfriend at each other's throats. 'Oh, I can assure yer my contact knows a lot about you, Ange,' she said mischievously. 'All them poor ol' geezers yer've bin knockin' around wiv, tryin' ter squeeze every penny yer can out of 'em. My contact says the rozzers've got a file on you six books 'igh. Just wait till they hear 'bout you aidin' an' abettin' a deserter.'

The sergeant immediately turned on Ange. 'Yer silly little cow! Give 'er the pictures!' he shouted, trying to grab the snapshots out of her hand.

'No!' barked Ange, pulling away from him. 'She's tellin' an 'ole pack of lies!'

'I said give 'er the pictures!' The sergeant gripped Ange's wrist and prised the photographs out of her hand. ''Ere!' he yelled to Nellie, throwing them at her. 'Take the bloody fings an' get out of 'ere!'

Nellie was about to leave when there was a loud banging on the front door, followed by men's voices shouting, 'Open up! Police! Get this door open!'

The sergeant, in a cold panic, rushed to the window and peered out through the blackout curtains. Pushing against the front door were two uniformed military policemen. 'MPs!' he gasped as he made a dash out into the passage.

'Sorry,' Nellie said as he pushed her out of the way, 'I forgot ter mention they was comin'.'

The two MPs outside were getting impatient; they were thumping and pushing hard against the front door.

'Open up! If you don't open this door, we'll break it down!'

'Wait, Mick!' Ange bawled as she, too, tried to push Nellie out of the way. 'I'm comin' wiv yer!'

But Nellie momentarily blocked her path. Although she was nearly three inches shorter than Ange, she grabbed hold of her chin and held on to it with a vice-like grip. 'If I ever see this poxy face near my dad again,' she said icily, 'I won't be quite so fergivin'.'

Now that young Lenny Beckwith was being looked after at home, 147A Tufnell Park Road had acquired a lived-in appearance that it had never really enjoyed before. The room that the two brothers had shared on the top floor was now occupied solely by Sid, for Madame thought it safer to keep Lenny in the small room next to her and Monsieur's own bedroom.

Madame had kept her word. She had given up her place in the Great Pierre's act, and was now devoting her life to looking after her family, which meant cooking the right kind of nourishing food for Lenny to help him rebuild his sadly depleted constitution. Fortunately, special food ration coupons were available for someone with his condition; black market food was becoming difficult to obtain owing to the many recent prosecutions of the dealers involved. But no matter how hard she tried, Madame could not escape the fact that Lenny was still a chronically ill child, and looking after him at home was difficult.

By September, the hospital was suggesting that the boy would stand a better chance of recovery if he were to be placed in a sanatorium, where the right treatment and conditions would be available twenty-four hours a day. 'Never in a million years!' was Madame's adamant reply to that. 'My boy stays at 'ome, where 'e belongs!' Although her reasoning was well intentioned, it was a selfish attitude to take, for Lenny's hacking cough could be heard throughout the night, every night, and there was no doubt that professional help was the obvious solution.

After the return of Ange's revealing snapshots, Monsieur had taken on a new lease of life. With the withdrawal of Madame from the act, he set about reshaping the form and style of the show so that whatever orchestra they were working with at the time could provide the accompanying mood music.

Despite the glamour and excitement of the twice nightly shows, Nellie had never really taken to the bright lights of the music hall stage. For her, there was something embarrassing and superficial about keeping a huge smile on her face night after night, and once Madame had gone, 'Miss Nellie' as she was billed, was becoming something of a name in her own right. Nellie didn't like all the attention she was getting, especially the wolf whistles and suggestive remarks that were yelled at her from the gods. But when she tried to express her concerns to Monsieur, he urged her to try to enjoy the admiration audiences clearly had for her, for if she played her cards right, one day she might become a star. Nellie told him that she didn't want to be a star. To her, there was absolutely no point if she couldn't sing, dance, tell jokes, play a musical instrument, or walk a high wire. And even if she could have done any of those things, it still wouldn't have appealed to her. No. Being on stage turned her into something larger than life, the kind of person she just didn't want to be. All she wanted to be was plain Nell Beckwith, daughter of Mr and Mrs Albert Beckwith, of 147A Tufnell Park Road. But she assured Monsieur that as long as he needed her in the act, she would not fail him.

Fate had other ideas for Nellie, and they came in the shape of Monsieur's agent manager, Eddie Buxton.

Nellie had met him many times backstage at various theatres, and once or twice when he came to the house to discuss business with Monsieur. Eddie was a jovial little man, who always seemed to wear rather loud three-piece checked suits. But he was a shrewd negotiator and in many ways he had been the driving force behind the career of the Great Pierre. Right from the first time Nellie had joined the act, he had been impressed by the way the audience reacted to her. He finally made his feelings known one evening after a one-night performance during the Billy Cotton variety show at the majestic Astoria Cinema, Finsbury Park. The show played every Friday night between the supporting film and the main feature film. It was billed as a gala night, and audiences loved it so much that hours before the evening performance began queues would form outside the theatre, stretching right down Seven Sisters Road and Isledon Road on both sides of the massive white tiled cinema. When Nellie first stepped on to the stage and saw the three thousand faces of the audience staring at her, she felt as though her legs would collapse beneath her, but the shouts of approval from the male contingent in the audience soon dispelled her fears. By the time she had survived being levitated, climbed the Indian rope, and re-emerged in the audience after disappearing from the mystery cabinet, she got almost as big a round of applause as the star performers of the show, Billy Cotton and his band and singers, and Terry's Juveniles, a superb line-up of singing and dancing local youngsters.

'I won't mince my words, Nell,' said Eddie in Monsieur's dressing room after the show. 'You're dynamite out there. We've got to find you a piece of the action.'

Nellie hadn't the faintest idea what 'a piece of the action' meant. But she was worried about the suggestion all the same.

'They're crackers for you, Nell,' insisted Eddie, joining

340

Monsieur in a glass of best brown ale. 'It's obvious they want to see more of you.'

Nellie sighed. She knew that Monsieur had been talking to him. 'Please, Mr Buxton,' she replied. 'I can't do nuffin' 'cept stand out there. I don't want ter do anyfin' else.'

Eddie was not listening to her. 'We're talkin' about big money here, Nell,' he said. 'Those audiences out there, they have an instinct. They know when someone takes their fancy. It's a kind of love affair. They want you to be there with them all the time.'

'But I can't *do* nuffin', Mr Buxton!' Nellie repeated.

'How d'yer know?' Eddie replied quick as a flash.

Nellie shrugged her shoulders. 'I just know, that's all.'

'Can you sing?' Eddie persisted.

Nellie roared with laughter. ''Ave yer 'eard me?' she spluttered.

'I've 'eard yer.' The voice was young Sid's. He had sat in the audience that evening with Grandma and Grandad Beckwith, who were also in the room, listening intently to the conversation. 'I 'eard yer the uvver day,' continued Sid, 'when yer was tryin' ter get Lenny ter join in wiv yer.'

'Don't be a twerp, Sid!' Nellie retorted. 'That was diff'rent. Lenny's ill. I was only tryin' ter cheer 'im up.'

'She *can* sing, Mr Buxton,' Sid insisted.

'Yer should listen ter Eddie,' Monsieur told Nellie. ''E's bin in the business a long time. 'E knows wot 'e's talkin' about.'

With both hands, Eddie pulled Nellie up from the chair she was sitting on, placed her directly in front of him, then sat in the chair himself. 'Come on then. Sing something for me.'

'Oh no,' gasped Nellie. 'This is ridiculous.'

'Anything,' persisted Eddie. 'Anything you like.'

'I know, Nell,' suggested Monsieur eagerly. 'Wot about "Auld Lang Syne"?'

Nellie started to panic and tried to move away. 'I can't sing that.'

Eddie immediately got up and placed her back in position again. As he did so, Monsieur started to sing the song. 'Should auld acquaintance be fergot . . .'

Nellie was acutely embarrassed, but not wishing to hurt her dad's feelings, she reluctantly joined in with the song.

As soon as Nellie began to sing, everyone in the room stopped to listen. Lack of confidence made her sound amateurish and faltering, but her voice was clear and pleasant, and as she stood there, staring at the floor self-consciously, her singing was strangely poignant.

When she had finished, everyone, with the exception of Eddie Buxton, applauded. Nellie was relieved that it was over and Monsieur's agent could now forget about her as a music hall performer.

Everyone watched the agent closely as he got up from his chair, put his hands in his jacket pockets, and went to Monsieur's dressing table to collect his half-finished glass of brown ale. After taking a quick gulp, he turned to Nellie and said, 'You've got a voice there, all right, Nell. All we need now is someone to train it.'

Over the following few weeks, Nellie was sent to a retired singing teacher, a Mr Pikestaff, who specialised in coaxing popular songs out of even the most mundane voices. Nellie was against the idea, for she saw no point in it at all. But both Eddie Buxton and her dad had talked her into the notion that if the public wanted something, then they should have it. And if they were willing to pay for it, so much the better. What she found hard to believe was Eddie's insistence that it wasn't just her legs and sex appeal that the audiences were going for, it was her personality that endeared her to them. Reluctantly, Nellie went along with the idea, firmly convinced that sooner or later it would all end in disaster. Nonetheless, if this was what it needed to breathe new life into her dad's act, then she would go along with whatever they asked her to do.

And so Mr Pikestaff set about turning Nellie Beckwith into a music hall songstress. It wasn't an easy task, for Nellie couldn't read a note of music, which meant that she had to memorise each song she was being taught. And time and time again she got the giggles when she was asked to do some rather animated breathing exercises, which usually resulted in her exploding a lungful of air straight into Mr Pikestaff's face. It didn't help that the man who was teaching her had some very eccentric habits, such as sipping black tea and gargling with a mouthful before swallowing it. He always wore a Spanish troubadour's shirt, and while Nellie was struggling to sing 'As Time Goes By', he flounced around the room conducting every note she warbled. But after she had been working with him for less than six weeks, even she was surprised to realise how much she had learnt about volume and tone, rhythm and balance and, above all, pace and timing.

Ruby Catmonk was tickled pink by this new development in Nellie's life, and every time Nellie came to visit her, they roared with laughter at the antics that Nellie got up to with the prissy Mr Pikestaff. But Ruby did not go along with Nellie's dismissive assessment of her own potential.

'Go for it, gel,' said the old pro, as Nellie put some more coke on to the fire in the tiny fireplace in Ruby's flat. 'Yer know wot 'Etty King used ter say, Gawd bless 'er: take what's comin' to yer, an' get straight off.'

Like most of the artistes Ruby talked about, Nellie hadn't the faintest idea who Hetty King was, even though her act as a singing male impersonator was for years the sensation of music halls all over the country.

Since Ruby had helped her nail Ange and her army sergeant boyfriend, Nellie had grown more attached to the old woman than ever. Whenever the two of them got together, a lot of gossip passed between them about people they knew. Ruby was an astute old dear, and during her long life in the music hall, she had learnt a lot about human nature. 'I'll tell yer this much about some of 'em though,' she said, her usual Capstan cigarette dangling from her lips while she sat at the table painting her ancient fingernails bright red. 'There are those who fink they've got it, and those who fink they ain't. I know the ones I'd go fer.' She blew smoke out of the side of her mouth and peered at Nellie over the top of her specs. 'I reckon you could get anyfin' yer set out fer,' she said with a twinkle in the eye, 'if yer really want it.'

'That's the trouble, Rube,' said Nellie. 'I *don't* want it. In fact, I don't really know wot I want at all.'

'*I* do,' replied the old girl.

Nellie swung a look at her.

Ruby had a sly grin on her face. 'When's that bit of Air Force blue comin' 'ome on leave again? The Jewish one.'

Nellie couldn't help smiling at Ruby's shrewdness. But then she sighed. 'No idea,' she replied. ''E writes me plenty of letters, but they're usually censored. I don't know why, but I've got an uncomfortable feelin' inside. Somefin's goin' on at these camps that we don't know about.' She finished putting the last pieces of coke on the fire and went across to join Ruby at the table. 'The papers keep goin' on about all these dogfights wiv Jerry over the south coast of England,' she said anxiously. 'It scares the daylights out of me. I never know from one day ter the next if Toff's alive or dead.'

Ruby put the brush back into its bottle, then blew on her nails to dry them. 'I shouldn't worry too much about that if I was you. In my experience, they soon let yer know if anyfin' like that's 'appened.'

344

This was little comfort to Nellie. Toff's absence only made her yearn for him even more. 'I know it's stupid,' she said, 'but even though I've only known him properly these past few months, I don't fink I could cope if—'

'Oh, don't worry,' interrupted Ruby, 'you'd cope all right. We all do. I know *I* 'ad to.'

Nellie looked at her inquiringly.

'It 'appens to most of us at least once in a lifetime, Nell. I 'ad this stupid geezer once. Years ago – the last war. 'E was younger than me, bright-eyed, bright-arsed little sod. But I loved 'im – oh yes, all that. Loved me, too. When we got married, 'e said it was fer life.' She finished blowing on her nails, then took off her specs, put them on the table in front of her, and squinted at Nellie. 'Trouble is, 'e didn't tell me 'ow long that life was goin' ter be.' She paused only briefly. 'Got blown up by a shell on the Somme.'

Without her specs on, Nellie could see that the old lady's eyes had faded from their original dark brown. 'I didn't know yer was ever married,' Nellie said. 'I'm sorry, Rube.'

'No need ter be,' replied Ruby, rubbing her eyes before putting her specs back on again. 'I only tell yer 'cos we all 'ave ter make the best of fings whiles we've got 'em. But I want ter meet this lover boy of yours. 'E don't get *my* seal of approval till I know 'e's goin' ter be the right geezer fer me best pal.'

Nellie's face lit up. 'Hey, Rube,' she said brightly. '*Am* I yer best pal then?'

'Don't push yer luck, mate!' Ruby replied. 'As my ol' mate Charlie Chaplin said ter me when we was in the same show at the 'Olloway Empire, back in 1907 it must've bin, 'e said, "There's only one person that's better than a good mate, an' that's a lover!"'

Both of them roared with laughter.

'Did yer really know Charlie Chaplin, Rube?' Nellie asked.

'Don't be daft,' replied the old girl. 'Ruby Catmonk knows *everyone*.'

The two of them continued to laugh together.

Nellie hadn't noticed that where her elbow was resting on the table, Ruby had dreamily dropped some small blobs of red nail varnish on to the clean yellow tablecloth.

Chapter 24

The deafening barrage of ack-ack guns was the fiercest London had heard for many months. From twenty miles outside the city, the constant flashes of bursting shells could be seen lighting up the sky as ground artillery did their best to bring down the small party of raiding enemy aircraft that had broken through the tight ring of coastal defences. The attack was as sudden as it was unexpected, and as usual Islington did not escape the onslaught, which seemed to be part of a renewed campaign by the Luftwaffe since the start of the new year.

At 147A Tufnell Park Road, Madame, Sid, Lenny, and Nellie were all taking shelter in a large, empty cupboard under the stairs. Since Madame had got it into her head that the damp conditions inside the Anderson shelter were responsible for Lenny's illness, she had decided that the family should take its chances inside the house. The old cupboard was a tight squeeze, and did nothing to insulate them from the deafening sound of the ack-ack fire outside which was rocking the very foundations of the house.

'Who was it said nineteen forty-four's goin' ter be the last year of the war?' groaned Madame, who was cradling Lenny protectively on her lap. 'Listen ter all that up there,' she sighed, looking up at the roof of the cupboard. ''Itler's not finished yet, not by a long way. An' the war's bin on fer over four years!'

'It's 'is last fling, Mum,' said Nellie, trying to sound

reassuring. 'Once the invasion starts, there won't be any more of this.'

'Invasion, invasion!' replied Madame tetchily. 'That's all yer ever 'ear these days. If this General Eisen'ower bloke's s'posed ter be in charge, why don't 'e just get on wiv it?'

Nellie chuckled. ''E's only just got 'ere, Mum,' she said. 'Give 'im a chance.'

Another outburst of heavy gunfire caused Lenny to whimper and snuggle up tightly to his mum.

'It's all right, son, it's all right,' she said, smoothing his hair comfortingly with her hand. 'We're all 'ere. We won't let nuffin' 'appen to yer.'

'Mum,' whinged Sid, who was cramped up in a tiny space on the floor, covered with his own eiderdown, 'I want ter go back ter bed.'

'Don't be so silly, Sid,' Madame snapped. 'Just listen ter all that rumpus outside. It's not safe ter stay in bed.'

'Then why don't Dad come down?' Sid moaned.

Madame had no real answer to that. Ever since the war began, Monsieur had solidly refused to abandon his own bed for an air-raid shelter, and he certainly wasn't going to start now. 'You know as well as I do, Sid,' said Madame, 'if the 'ouse came down on top of yer dad, 'e still wouldn't give up 'is kip!'

Nellie laughed, and adjusted the blanket covering Lenny on Madame's lap.

'I don't like air raids,' said Lenny, whose voice was so much weaker since his illness. 'The noise scares me.'

'Nuffin' ter be scared of, Len,' Nellie said brightly. 'It's just a few stupid ol' Jerry planes tryin' ter scare us. But they ain't goin' to, so there!'

'I wanna go back ter bed.' Sid was grizzling again.

'Tell yer wot,' said Nellie, all perky. 'Why don't we all 'ave a sing-song? By the time we've finished, I bet yer we'll 'ear the All Clear. What d'yer say, Len?'

By the dim light of the torch propped up on the cupboard ledge, Nellie could just see Lenny nodding his head wearily.

'Right then,' she said, sitting up straight on the stool she was perched on. 'What'll it be? Any suggestions?'

'You're the singer in the family now, Nell,' replied Madame. 'Choose somefin'.'

Nellie's stomach turned over as she was reminded that within the next few days she would be singing a song in public for the first time, a song which Monsieur was going to incorporate into the act. But the mood in the cupboard under the stairs called for something quite different, so she launched straight into a rousing version of 'Don't Fence Me In' which was currently a great favourite, made popular on a gramophone record by Bing Crosby and the Andrews Sisters.

It took a moment or so for the others to join in, but when they did, their voices did much to drown the sound of the guns belting away outside. And what an inspiring sound the Beckwith family made – Madame, with her high-pitched soprano voice, Sid, wide awake now and bellowing his lungs out, and Nellie with her newly trained crooner's delivery. Frail as he was, even young Lenny raised enough energy to join in the chorus.

When the song was over, Nellie applauded loudly, even more so when she realised that the ack-ack guns had actually gone silent. 'See! Wot'd I tell yer?' she announced triumphantly. 'It's all over!'

No sooner had she spoken than the barrage of gunfire broke out once more.

Lenny quickly hugged up to Madame again, and Sid covered himself with his eiderdown. Undaunted, Nellie burst forth with a defiant rendition of 'Rule Britannia'. The others joined in with gusto, and the competition between the Beckwith family and the ack-ack outside became a battle of wills. But the singing became less and less vigorous as they turned their eyes towards the ceiling and listened to the drone of aeroplanes zooming down towards the rooftops overhead. Everyone tried very hard not to show how scared they were but gradually the singing stopped altogether and they just listened.

Out of the cacophony dominating the skies above them, there came a much more deadly sound, whistling down from the night clouds.

'Down! Down!' yelled Nellie.

The explosion rocked the house. Madame and Sid screamed out loud, glass shattered, plaster fell from the ceilings, and dogs barked in panic along the back gardens outside.

It seemed to take for ever before the terrifying sounds settled down, and when they did, Lenny was crying and nestling up as tight as he could against his mother's body. Everyone was covered in dust.

'Doris! Are yer all right!' Monsieur was hurrying down the stairs as fast as he could. 'Oh, Christ, Doris!' he called frantically. 'Are any of yer hurt?'

By the time he reached them, Nellie was already helping Madame and Lenny out of the cupboard. Then she pulled the dust-covered eiderdown off Sid and yanked him up on to his feet. 'Are yer OK, Sid?' she asked quickly, anxiously. 'Are yer?'

Sid's striped pyjamas were also covered in dust, but he seemed unhurt and calmly nodded his head.

'Are we 'it?' Madame spluttered, trying to spit out some of the dust. ''As it 'it the 'ouse?'

'No, fank Gawd,' replied Monsieur, taking Lenny from Madame's arms. 'We got the blast, that's all. It must 'ave come down up Junction Road somewhere.' Lenny was shaking, crying, and coughing in his arms. 'It's all right, son, it's all right,' he said, hugging the boy. 'The worst's over now.'

But the house was still being shaken by the gunfire

outside. They stood there helplessly, not knowing which way to turn.

'Wot're we goin' ter do, Dad?' said Nellie, rubbing the dust out of her eyes with the backs of her hands.

'It can't last much longer,' he replied, making for the kitchen door. 'Better get down the shelter.'

'No, Bert!' Madame rushed to pull Lenny out of her husband's arms. 'This boy's not goin' down that shelter. It'll kill 'im!'

Monsieur held on to the boy. 'Don't be ridiculous, Doris,' he said angrily. 'The raid's gettin' worse. We can't take no chances!'

Again Madame tried to pull Lenny out of Monsieur's arms, but he resisted, and it looked as though a tug-of-war was about to ensue. 'Leave 'im ter me, Albert?' she pleaded. 'There's nuffin' wrong wiv 'im. 'E'll be perfectly all right wiv me.'

Monsieur turned on her. 'Wot do you mean, there's nuffin' wrong wiv 'im? Just look at 'im, Doris. Go on, take a good look at 'im.' Lenny was deathly white and thin, and crying pitifully in between fits of coughing. 'Does this boy look as though 'e'll be all right, Doris? Does 'e?' Monsieur's face was stiff with tension and he had to shout to be heard above the barrage of ack-ack gunfire. 'When're you goin' ter listen to uvver people, Doris, when? Lenny shouldn't be 'ere in this 'ouse, any sensible person can see that. 'E should be where 'e can be taken care of, somewhere safe, away from all this, away from the bombs, the noise, the stress. Can't yer see 'e needs care an' attention? Attention that none of us 'ere can give 'im!'

He turned to go into the kitchen and Madame followed him. 'No, Bert,' she pleaded. 'I beg yer. For the love of God, please don't take 'im down that shelter!'

Monsieur stopped at the kitchen door and turned briefly. 'I'm sorry, gel, yer've got ter learn – we've boaf got ter learn – it's Lenny we 'ave ter fink of, not ourselves.'

With that, he turned away, kicked the kitchen door open with his foot, and made his way to the back garden door.

Nellie immediately went to comfort her mum who was in tears.

Neither of them noticed young Sid making his way back upstairs to his own room.

The trail of havoc and destruction caused by the previous night's lightning air raid galvanised the communities in and around the Nag's Head. The extensive blast damage to number 147A and other properties along Tufnell Park Road had been caused by a high-explosive bomb on a chemist's shop in Junction Road, as Monsieur had guessed, less than a mile away. Fortunately, there were no casualties, which was more than could be said for other parts of London, but the aftermath of the raid left people in a deep state of shock.

The immediate problem was getting the place cleared up. Tiles had been blown off roofs, windows shattered, and plaster dislodged from walls and ceilings in houses within a two-mile radius stretching from the Archway to Kentish Town. There was an immediate rush to find carpenters, glaziers, plasterers, and anyone who knew anything about building repair work. Monsieur, however, was no mean hand when it came to do-it-yourself jobs, and so, with Nellie and Sid to help him, he set about replacing the glass in his windows himself. The only trouble was that putty was in short supply, so he had to use his standing as a local celebrity to prise some out of Smith's the builders' merchant in Upper Holloway Road. Plastering was not his strong point but he made a good stab at it and by the end of the day he had managed to patch up holes in three of the top floor ceilings.

The previous night's tense exchange between Madame and Monsieur about young Lenny worried Nellie. She understood both their points of view, although in her heart of hearts she did think that Madame was being a little too possessive in keeping Lenny at home. He quite clearly needed the peace and tranquillity of care in some kind of convalescent home. But this was one area in which she could not interfere; Lenny's welfare could only be decided by reasonable discussion and mutual agreement between the boy's mum and dad. Nonetheless, as she swept up broken glass from the shattered stained-glass panels in the front door, she couldn't help feeling a bit depressed that things at the moment were not all they should be for the Beckwith family. She yearned for something nice to happen.

'Hello, Nell.'

Nellie's face lit up. 'Toff!'

They rushed into each other's arms and kissed passionately halfway along the garden path. It was several moments before they came up for air, during which time the neighbours not only had their money's worth, but also a timely distraction from their painful task of clearing up after the air raid.

'Why din't yer let me know yer was comin'?' Nellie said, her hands linked behind his neck. ''Ow long 'ave yer got?'

'Only a thirty-six hour, I'm afraid,' said Toff. He had come straight from Charing Cross Station, and was still in uniform, a rucksack over his shoulder. 'I have to be back by twenty-three hundred tomorrow night.'

Nellie hadn't the faintest idea what twenty-three hundred meant, but it sounded lousy. 'Yer should've let me know,' she said. 'I've missed yer, Toff.'

'I've missed you too, Nell.'

They both spent a full minute just staring into each other's eyes.

★   ★   ★

Alexandra Palace nestled majestically on top of a steep hill overlooking the wide open spaces of Alexandra Park below. It was a glorious building, much loved by the residents of Wood Green on one side and Muswell Hill on the other. The present palace, built in 1873, had never had any royal residents, for it had been built mainly to stage national exhibitions and symphony concerts, which set off the grandiose interior to perfection. The Ally Pally, as it was affectionately known, contained the very best of Victorian design, with marble floors, huge crystal chandeliers, and a glass dome which before the war had been magically lit up from inside and could be seen for miles around. The vast main hall, where many concerts had been held over the years, contained one of the largest and most beautiful pipe organs in England. The view from the main entrance steps outside the good old 'Ally Pally' had always been a favourite of Toff's. Whenever he wanted to get away from home in nearby Highgate, this was where he came.

'Before the war, I remember coming up here one Guy Fawkes night. There was a terrific fireworks display – bangers, Catherine wheels, sparklers, and rockets shooting right up into the sky over the park. You could see the rooftops over Hornsey and Crouch End in the distance changing colour every few minutes. It was magical.'

Toff was doing his best to pass on his enthusiasm to Nellie, but it wasn't easy. From where they were sitting now, the January evening view consisted of nothing more than total darkness, not a light to be seen in the bleak wilderness of the wartime blackout.

They crossed the road in front of the palace and made their way down into the park. 'Pity we can't turn back the clock,' she said. 'Everyfin' seemed ter be so much better.'

'If we turned back the clock,' replied Toff, 'we'd have to

go through this whole damn war again. No. It's the future I want. A new start.'

They picked their way in the dark by the dim light of Nellie's pocket torch. It was slippery under foot in the wet grass, and bitterly cold. And yet, as they strolled along with their arms around each other's waists, it seemed to make no difference at all that Toff towered above Nellie. In their own world, tall or small played no part at all.

Stretched out before them in the dark were the strange, twisting shapes of trees, and although they could hear the far distant rumbling sounds of traffic, they were surrounded by an eerie silence. They came to a halt and for a moment, neither said anything. Then Nellie felt Toff moving round in front of her and both his arms sliding round her waist. Almost at once, his lips searched for hers. When he found them, he kissed her hard and long.

'It's funny, isn't it?' he said softly. 'What a snotty-nosed little brat you were when we first met.'

'I beg yer pardon!' growled Nellie in mock indignation.

'It's true,' he said, teasing her. 'Brash, opinionated, full of yourself . . .'

'An' wot 'bout you?' she countered. 'Mister Smoothie of all time. Why d'yer fink the gang called yer Toff?'

Toff was silent for a while. When he spoke again, it was with some difficulty. 'They called me Toff because I was the only one who seemed to offer them some kind of hope. I was someone they could look up to, to follow, and make the decisions. They were wrong. I was no better than any of them.'

Not far away, they could hear young voices whispering to each other in the dark. This was a popular area for courting couples.

Toff leaned down and hugged Nellie, so that her head was resting against the rough serge of his Air Force greatcoat. 'I blame myself for what happened to Rats and Bonkers,' he said with quiet anguish. 'When the police and the ambulance turned up to collect them that night, me and the others just split up and got away as fast as we could. I've never seen any of them again from that day to this.'

'It wasn't your fault, Toff,' Nellie replied. 'Yer told them not ter go after that kitten, but they did. It wasn't your fault.'

He shook his head. 'I was the oldest one among them. I should have been a leader, a *real* leader. I should have told them to go home, to go back to their families. I blame myself. I'm not a leader. I could never be one.' He squeezed her tight. 'I don't want to be Toff any more, Nell,' he begged. 'I want to be me. I want to be Martin. I want to be just like anyone else.'

Nellie listened to him in silence. Pressed hard against his heavy coat, her mind began to dwell again on the events of that horrible night outside the old furniture store. It reminded her of how wrong she had been at the time to blame Toff for trying to prevent Rats and Bonkers from taking their life in their hands. Whatever he had just said, she firmly believed that if anyone had displayed qualities as a leader that night, it had been him.

She could hear Toff's heart beating. It was a firm, decisive beat, and it made her feel warm and secure. But what a strange, complicated boy he was. Since she had got to know him, she had discovered that if there was a right or a wrong way to work out a situation, then Toff would invariably choose the wrong one. And the way he constantly tore himself apart for no reason was absurd, and totally different to her own way of thinking. And yet she was drawn to him. At this moment she felt so deeply for him, she wanted him to throw caution to the wind and make love to her. But every time that idea came into her mind, she thought about Patrick Duvall, and how she would never be able to trust a man again. Nevertheless, all she knew now was that she wanted Toff, she wanted him so much, and try as she may, she just couldn't understand why he always held back from that one ultimate, inevitable act of true love.

'Martin.'

Toff was taken by surprise. Without moving he whispered, 'Nell? What did you say?'

Nellie looked up and whispered back, 'I said Martin.'

Martin reached down in the dark, found her lips again, and kissed her passionately. 'I love you, Nell,' he said, softly.

'Don't be stupid,' she replied. 'Yer don't even know me.'

'Oh, I *know* you, Nellie Beckwith,' he said with an affectionate smile in his voice. 'I know you very well indeed.' He kissed her again, longer this time. 'I want us to move in together,' he said quite unexpectedly.

Nellie looked up at him in surprise. 'Wot d'yer mean?'

'I love you, Nell,' he repeated. 'I want us to be together.'

Nellie took a moment to think this one out. 'But we're both under age. We'd 'ave ter 'ave permission ter get married.'

'I wasn't talking about getting married,' Martin replied. 'Not yet, anyway.'

Nellie gently pulled away from him. 'We can't live tergevver, Martin,' she said awkwardly.

'Why not?'

''Cos – 'cos it's not right fer people ter live tergevver until they get married. Nobody does fings like that.'

'Listen to me, Nell,' he said, drawing her close and lowering his voice again. 'We can do *anything* if we really want to. I love you. Stupid though it may sound, I really do love you.'

Nellie sighed. 'I love yer too, Martin,' she said, without

a suggestion of doubt in her voice. 'But let's do it the right way. We've got plenty of time.'

'No, Nell, we don't have plenty of time. You see, I won't be seeing you for quite a bit. Something's happening, something important – I can't tell you what. But when I come back, I want to know that you'll be there. I want to know that we'll be together, that we can make love, and that nobody can ever part us again.'

Nellie hated opening nights. To her, there were always hidden terrors in appearing for the first time in front of an audience that she had never worked before. Collins' Music Hall on Islington Green was considered in the business to be a number two hall, which meant that it rarely attracted star names, and audiences there, particularly in the gods, had the reputation of being rowdy. Monsieur had turned down a six-week booking on the number two tour, but he wanted to try out the new act and Collins seemed to be the ideal place to do it in.

The act was already beginning to cause some controversy; Monsieur had decided to change its staging completely and to cut down the length of the performance from sixteen to twelve minutes. Eddie Buxton had a hard time selling the new Great Pierre to potential managements, despite the fact that Nellie would make her debut as a singer during the act. 'Customers like what they're used to,' said one rather sceptical entrepreneur. 'Muck around with the goods and you've lost your profits.' In a sense, he was right, for during the past year there had been definite signs that variety on the halls was beginning to wane. During the war years, the music hall had done so much to boost people's morale, but despite the air raids of the previous few weeks, everyday talk now was of an impending Allied invasion in Europe, which was giving people the impression that the war was all but over.

'We've got ter face up ter the fact, Nell,' said Monsieur

gloomily. 'Fings're never goin' ter be wot they used ter be, not as long as people've got the pictures ter go to an' the wireless ter listen to.'

'You're right,' agreed Eddie. The three of them were mulling things over in Monsieur's dressing room after the morning rehearsal. 'An' I'll tell yer something else. When the war's over, there's going to be quite a lot of competition when they start up television again.'

'Television!' spluttered Monsieur dismissively. 'Television can't compete wiv the wireless and live stage shows. It's nuffin' but a box wiv a flickerin' light.'

'Mark my words, mate,' warned Eddie ominously. 'Just mark my words.'

Nellie listened to all this with calm detachment. She didn't care one bit if people stopped going to the music hall or stopped listening to the wireless. She didn't even care if they stopped going to the pictures. But she did care about the effect it would have on all the people like Monsieur, whose whole life had been dedicated to the bright lights.

'Anyway,' continued Eddie, 'tonight's going to be a turning point for the act. I think you've got some great new ideas, Bert. And as for Nell's song,' he gave her a huge smile, 'touch of genius!'

Nellie smiled back at him, weakly. She knew he was only saying that because it had been his suggestion.

Eddie got up and went to the door. 'Whatever happens,' he said, 'it's now or never. See you at first house, boys and girls.'

After he had gone, Monsieur sat deep in thought. 'Mustn't take too much notice of Ed,' he said to Nellie, trying to put a brave face on it. ''E's just nervous to know 'ow the new routines'll go ternight.'

'So am I,' replied Nellie. 'I just 'ope I don't let yer down, Dad.'

Monsieur, who was sitting at his minute dressing table,

swung round on his stool to look at her. 'You could never do that, Nell,' he said with a warm smile. 'Just be yerself, an' we can't fail.'

With the minutes ticking by before she went on stage, Nellie felt her mouth going as dry as a bone. She had already drunk two glasses of water, but there was not enough water in the whole world to quench her nerves. It was bad enough to be stuck in a dressing room that was no bigger than a broom cupboard, but to have to go halfway down the passage every time she wanted to go to the ladies made life even more difficult. And to make things worse, the girl she had to share the room with, who was part of an acrobatic dog act, could speak very little English and smelt a bit like some of the furry artistes she worked with.

The first house curtain was due up at six twenty-five, and for the final hour before the performance, Nellie must have looked at the wristwatch her mum and dad had given her at least a dozen times. She had plenty of reasons for doing so, for apart from the show itself, she knew that Martin was already well on his way back to camp. And the more she thought about that, the more depressed she became. Her only consolation was that she had at least been with him for those few last precious hours, and that, despite his complicated moods, she felt closer to him than ever. For Martin, meeting Monsieur and Madame had been a far more relaxing experience than he had anticipated, for music hall people had a reputation for being outgoing and demonstrative, which was something he had been dreading. But Nellie's mum and dad had been nothing but a joy to be with, and both Sid and young Lenny quickly treated him as one of the family. As she sat at her tiny dressing table, putting on her Five and Nine, Nellie mulled this over in her mind, and for one short moment it even brought a smile to her face.

Shortly after seven o'clock, Nellie joined Monsieur behind the flats at the back of the stage. The acrobatic dog act was in full swing, much to the approval of a full but fairly vocal audience. It had not escaped Nellie's notice that the Great Pierre act had lost its place as the climax at the end of the show's first half. Although Monseiur would never show his disappointment at such a decision, she knew it hurt him. 'Sign of the times, Nell,' he had said wistfully during the morning's rehearsals. 'That's life.'

At exactly five minutes past seven, the Great Pierre finally took the stage. But this time everything was different. There was no loudspeaker introduction, and the clash of the cymbal had been replaced by a far more formal opening, with the orchestra playing a selection of mood music specially chosen and arranged by Madame. Monsieur made his entrance quite simply, from behind a door cut into the black backcloth. Even his appearance was different. He was still dressed in black from head to foot, but to complement his white gloves he had used white make-up on his face, which gave him a droll, poignant look. His entrance provoked a few coarse whistles and remarks from some of the customers up in the gods but he was astute and professional enough to acknowledge them with a graceful bow, a flick of the wrist, and a silent snap of the fingers. This was to be the hallmark of the new Great Pierre.

As for the act itself, there was no longer any 'Sawing the Lady in Half' routine – Monsieur had decided that he would leave this trick to the traditional stage magicians. There was no climbing the rope either – this had been in the act since Monsieur first introduced it many years before. What he was now offering was a programme of *real* illusions, in which his audience would be offered deceptive impressions of the real thing. This he duly set out to do by skilfully mesmerising his audience into a state of unconscious *belief*: what they saw was not what they saw at all. Monsieur was, in every sense, a hypnotist, but he worked silently, using his hands and not his voice to speak the words. And as he worked, he spun round the stage with movements that were as light as a cat's; his eyes darted from the stalls up to the gods with lightning speed, he was never still for a single moment. His whole act was, in fact, an illusion in itself. And there to help him manifest it all was Nellie, getting the usual wolf whistles as soon as she appeared and still lusted after by every red-blooded male in the audience. But this time her sex appeal gave Monsieur's illusions the dream-like quality he was trying to project. Instead of posing endlessly to draw out the audience's applause, she was placed in a single spotlight at the side of the stage where, at the given time, she gracefully sang, unaccompanied, the poignant words of 'When I Grow Too Old to Dream'. Her voice, although not strong, was sweet and innocent, and helped to enhance the extraordinary atmosphere in the house. The audience were, quite simply, transported into an uplifting, trouble-free world of beauty.

When the curtains finally closed on the new act, it was for several moments greeted with total silence. But when Monsieur and Nellie came up front and joined hands to take their bow, the audience burst into life and applauded and cheered as they had never done before. Some people were so overwhelmed they had tears in their eyes. Even Monsieur's cynical agent, Eddie Buxton, couldn't believe that he was seeing the same artiste that he had represented for so many years. Shorter the act might be, but it was a sensation!

During the first and second house shows, the air-raid siren sounded the alert. But this did not deter the next house audience from filing into the theatre, for the management had immediately given a categorical assurance that the show would go on. And so it did, despite the fact that heavy ack-ack gunfire was heard from time to time, which caused the overhead chandelier to rock and sway in time to the carefully orchestrated songs everyone was invited to sing along with the top of the bill crooner Sam Browne. But shortly before the show finished there was consternation when the whole theatre vibrated to the sound of two heavy bomb explosions. They were a little too close for comfort.

In his dressing room after the show, Monsieur received the congratulations of endless visitors. Everyone was of the opinion that the Great Pierre had taken on a new lease of life and was, quite simply, a supreme artiste. But a great deal of the praise was reserved for Nellie, for it was obvious that her beautiful singing of that one song had enhanced the act to perfection. Madame hugged Nellie for all she had done to help restore Monsieur's confidence; she couldn't wait to get back to tell Lenny and Grandma and Grandad Beckwith all about it. But Sid couldn't see what all the fuss was about. He boasted that he still knew how all the tricks were done. The only person who seemed to be missing from the celebrations was Monsieur's agent, Eddie Buxton, who had not been seen since the final curtain came down nearly an hour earlier.

As Nellie, Monsieur, Madame, and Sid left the stage door, the air raid was gathering momentum. Ack-ack shells burst constantly in the sky above them, and fire-engine bells clanged all the way along Upper Street. There was no sign of any buses running and apart from a few people hurrying to the nearest shelters, the streets were practically deserted.

'Better get down the Tube,' called Monsieur. 'Let it calm down a bit before we try ter get 'ome. We can't take any risks wiv all this shrapnel comin' down!'

Madame was at first unwilling; this was the first time she had left young Lenny in the charge of Grandma and Grandad Beckwith since he had left hospital. But with pieces of sharp, jagged shrapnel from the ack-ack shells raining down on to the pavements all around them, she had no choice. Nellie put her arm round her waist and led her on quickly behind Monsieur, who was clutching Sid's hand and setting the pace towards the Angel Tube just down the road.

They had gone only a few yards when they heard someone calling to them.

'Bert! Doris! Wait!'

They turned to find Eddie Buxton hurrying out of a taxi.

'Thank God I've caught you,' he said, rushing to them where they were sheltering in a shop doorway.

'Wot is it?' asked Monsieur.

'Something terrible's happened, Bert,' Eddie replied. Even in the blacked-out street, they could see how distraught he was. 'There's a bomb come down. It's terrible! Just terrible!'

'Oh Christ!' gasped Madame. 'Not *our* place! Please don't say it's *our* place!'

'No, no,' replied Eddie, shaking his head vigorously. 'It's up Finsbury Park way. Just round the corner from the Empire. People killed. The whole place – terrible, terrible!'

Nellie felt a rush of panic. '*Where*, Mr Buxton?' she asked frantically. 'Where exactly 'as it come down?'

'Blackstock Road,' Eddie replied in utter despair. 'I went straight down there from the show. I've got friends there . . . they told me . . . they told me it was a direct hit on the Gas Board.'

'The Gas Board!' Nellie gasped, desperate with shock. 'That's next door ter the funeral parlour!' She was half-crazed with fear and anxiety. 'Oh Christ! Tell me, Mr Buxton, fer God's sake, tell me, wot's 'appened ter the funeral parlour?'

Eddie shook his head. He could hardly bring himself to

answer her. 'It's gone, Nell,' he said painfully. 'The whole bloody lot's gone.'

Nellie felt the blood drain from her body. All she could think about was the person who lived in the small flat above that funeral parlour, the best pal she had ever had in the whole wide world – that cunning, ginger-haired old cow Ruby Catmonk.

Chapter 25

The Finsbury Park Empire rarely offered matinee performances. But today was different. The fauteuils and stalls might not have been full to overflowing, but the people who were there had a very important part to play in these particular proceedings.

Ruby Catmonk's long association with the music hall, not just with Finsbury Park but with many of the other halls in London, had earned her a special place in the hearts of everyone who had ever had anything to do with live variety theatre. Ruby went back a long way, starting as a chorus girl in pantomime at the tender age of sixteen, but it was for her latter years that she would be remembered, for she had gained a reputation among artistes everywhere as 'the best needle and cotton in the business'. A special matinee tribute had been arranged for her, and a lot of her old friends, famous and not so famous, turned up to pay their last respects. It was what Ruby would have wanted most of all, for, although she was Jewish by birth, she had lived her life as an atheist, leaving instructions that on her death there should be no religious service at her funeral. Her wishes were duly carried out, and she was cremated with the minimum of fuss at Golders Green crematorium on a bright and sunny winter's afternoon at the beginning of February. Few people attended the event. Those who did included Monsieur, Madame, and Nellie. It was all over very quickly, and there were no flowers. 'Bleedin' waste of money,' Ruby often said. 'Wot's the use of leavin' a bunch of beautiful flowers to rot on top of a grave, or bein' chucked in a fire on top of a coffin!'

Ruby's death devastated Nellie. The night the bomb destroyed the old girl's tiny flat, Nellie had wanted to rush up there straight away to help the emergency services dig her out. But Monsieur absolutely forbade her to go, saying that the last thing Ruby would have wanted was for anyone to put themselves in danger because of her. Nellie couldn't understand his attitude. 'Ruby's my pal!' she bawled, tears streaming down her face. 'Ever since I've known 'er, she's 'elped me. I can't let 'er down now, I can't!' But Monsieur had his way, and it was not until the following morning that Nellie finally saw what was left of those two small rooms she had visited so many times. By then, Ruby's body had been recovered and removed from the pile of rubble which contained the remnants of the few possessions she had owned.

At the matinee tribute, Ruby's old mates Gert and Daisy performed a few minutes of Ruby's favourite double act, and then shared their memories of a 'dear and trusted friend'. The wonderful crooner, Anne Shelton, invited everyone to join her in a chorus of 'You Are My Lucky Star', a song Ruby had adored. This brought a few tears to the stalls, which, said Monsieur at the conclusion of the matinee, 'would have tickled the old girl no end'. Everyone had something to contribute, including the manager and the theatre orchestra. The box office staff came too, as did usherettes and backstage staff from several other London music halls. Ruby had been one of them, and her death in such tragic circumstances had touched the entire profession. And on the stage itself, artistes lined up to contribute either a bit of their own act, or a few words about incidents involving 'that shrewd old bag who never let any of us down'. Ruby was held in such high esteem that the much-loved Lancashire comedian, Frank Randle, had come down all the way from Manchester to do a 'bit of a laugh for the old girl', and also to add his own poignant farewell. And to make this memorial performance even more personal, many of the artistes who were appearing wore costumes that Ruby had either made or repaired on her battered old Singer sewing machine.

During the extraordinary hour-long performance, Nellie was too distressed to sit with the rest of the audience downstairs, preferring to spend the time watching from the front row of the gods, whose customers were, in Ruby's own words, 'the real bread an' butter of the 'alls'. It was a sad and desolate feeling to be sitting all alone in such a vast empty space, for the music hall was all about togetherness and having a good time. This was what Ruby had loved about it all, and the reason why she had wanted to be a part of it in some way or another for the whole of her life. What an extraordinary, sentimental lot of old softies they were down there, Nellie thought. Just look at them, sobbing their hearts out, when old Rube was probably watching from somewhere, coughing her lungs out on a Capstan and laughing her head off at the jokes. But then Nellie thought to herself, why shouldn't they be softies? After all, music hall folk had feelings just like anyone else. The only difference was that they found it difficult not to show how they felt.

At the conclusion of the show, a huge laugh went up when the stage manager asked everyone to stand and sing the song that Ruby was often heard lah-de-dahing to herself as she toiled away at her sewing machine. It was a good old Cockney song called 'Boiled Beef and Carrots'. Nellie stood up too, but while she joined in with the rest of the audience, her mind was on something quite different – the hand-written letter she had received two weeks before from the son of Ruby's old flame who worked at the War Office, the same officer who had provided the information about Ange's soldier boyfriend:

> Dear Miss Beckwith,
>
> I am a friend of the late Miss Ruby Catmonk.
>
> Some weeks ago she asked me, in the event of her passing, to let you have the enclosed.
>
> As you are probably aware, Miss Ruby possessed few personal belongings, and I fear that those that did survive are somewhat beyond repair. However, she asked me to pass on to you the warm feelings she had for you, and hoped that you would accept the modest gift, enclosed, as a token of her love and affection.
>
> In the absence of any legal representation, I am duly carrying out Miss Ruby's wishes as she instructed.
>
> Yours sincerely,
>
> Richard Jeffreys, Captn.   Enclosed: £5.

The raucous climax of 'Boiled Beef and Carrots' brought Ruby's tribute show to a conclusion, with everyone cheering and applauding wildly. They all hoped that the old girl had been able to hear them, and that if she did, she had joined in.

But up in the gods Nellie profoundly hoped that her old mate couldn't see her, for tears were streaming down her face.

The taxi arrived dead on time at 147A Tufnell Park Road. Sid was the first to see it as it approached from the Holloway end of the road, but when he ran into the house with an excited yell of 'It's 'ere! It's 'ere!' he was greeted with little enthusiasm. Especially from Madame.

'Go an' get yer coat on,' was all she could say as she solemnly put on her own hat and fixed it with a pin.

Monsieur came up behind her and put his arms round her waist. 'It's fer the best, Doris. It 'as ter be.'

Madame didn't know how to respond, for she had exhausted all the arguments she had had for trying to keep young Lenny at home. Over the past few weeks, his condition had clearly deteriorated. This had been obvious even before the blast from the Junction Road bomb had covered him with dust and ceiling plaster, which had got into his lungs and made him much worse. The boy was now too weak to be carried up and down the stairs, and Madame's excessive cleaning of the house to keep down the dust simply did not help his condition. The plain fact of the matter was that Lenny needed the sort of expert medical attention that he couldn't get at home. And so it was decided to send him to a sanatorium for tubercular patients near the sea, just outside Bristol in the West Country.

Nellie had been dreading this day ever since Monsieur had convinced Madame how necessary it was. From the moment it had been decided, Nellie spent a great deal of her time trying to excite Lenny about the wonderful place he was going to. She kept telling him to think of it as one long glorious holiday where he would be spoilt rotten by all sorts of people. But the greatest advantage, she insisted, was the certainty that he would fully recover there and be back home before he even realised that he had gone. Deep down inside, Nellie had as many misgivings as everyone else in the family, and it was not easy to stop an endlessly tearful Grandma Beckwith from conveying her fears to her grandson.

As usual, however, it was Sid who made his young brother's departure more easy to cope with. 'If yer want, yer can take some of my comics wiv yer,' he said as he watched his dad carry the frail boy in his arms down the stairs. 'I'll bring yer some of the uvvers when I come up ter visit yer.'

'Fanks,' replied Lenny weakly.

'Yer can't 'ave this week's *Film Fun* though,' Sid added. 'I 'aven't finished wiv it yet.'

'I din't ask for it, did I?' protested Lenny tetchily.

'I just fawt I'd mention it, that's all,' sniffed Sid.

This exchange between the two brothers made Nellie feel so much better; she was impressed that Sid had deliberately rejected any show of emotion in order to diminish the poignancy of the occasion.

'Better get in the taxi, son,' said Monsieur to his eldest boy. 'Don't wanna miss the train.'

Sid collected his school cap, wound his long woollen scarf round his neck, and hurried outside to the taxi.

For a last brief moment, Madame fussed over Lenny in Monsieur's arms, making sure that he was tucked up snugly beneath his blanket. Then she and Nellie followed them out.

'God fergive us if we're not doin' the right fing,' said Madame as she came out of the front door arm in arm with Nellie.

'You *are* doin' the right fing, Mum,' Nellie reassured her. 'It's the only fing ter do. When Lenny comes back 'ome all fit 'an strong again, you'll kick yerself fer not doin' this sooner.'

Madame turned briefly to her with an appreciative smile. 'I 'ope so, Nell,' she said. 'I 'ope so.'

Sid had already claimed his place on one of the pull-out seats in the taxi. As soon as Monsieur reached the vehicle with Lenny held firmly in his arms, the taxi driver hurried round to meet them.

Nellie left Madame for a moment to give Lenny a mock boxer's jab towards his chin. 'Gels don't kiss boxers,' she said with a mischievous grin. 'At least, not till they win.' Then she made another light jab at his nose. 'So 'urry up an' win, mate!'

Lenny managed to smile back at her. ''Bye, Nell.'

The taxi driver made sure that Monsieur and Lenny were comfortable in the back seat, then turned to help Madame get in.

'See you later, dear,' said Madame after kissing Nellie on the cheek. 'An' don't wait up fer us,' she added. 'We shan't be back till the last train. If yer need us, yer've got the telephone number. I've left it on the kitchen table.'

''Bye, Nell!' called Monsieur and Sid.

''Bye!' Nellie called back. 'Safe journey!'

She closed the taxi door and waited for the driver to get in. As the taxi moved off, the last thing she saw was young Sid waving madly and pulling rude faces at her through the window. She waved back.

And then they were gone.

Back inside the house, she closed the front door and paused a moment to look around. Suddenly, everything seemed so quiet, so lost and empty. She slowly made her way upstairs towards her room, but when she reached the first-floor landing, she saw that the door of Lenny's bedroom had been left open. She went across to close it. Before doing so, however, she peered inside. The room was pretty untidy, mainly because Sid had got up early in the morning to play a last game of Snakes and Ladders on the bed with his young brother. Nellie decided to go in and clear up.

Her spirits were too low to do much, so she merely picked up pieces from an unfinished Spitfire model aircraft that Sid had been working on with his brother right up to the previous evening. Then she collected a pillow that had been dumped on the floor and she tossed it on to the bed. Her attention was suddenly drawn to the walls of the room, which were crammed with newspaper pictures of footballers. Nellie hadn't any idea who most of them were, but she knew that Lenny did. In fact there was hardly a footballer in the country that he didn't know about. Talk about football mania. But a huge grin came to her face when she caught a glimpse of a very different type of photo, pinned to the wall right in the middle of a poster of the previous year's Cup Final winners team. It was a pin-up of a very sexy, very glamorous film star called Betty Grable, posing in a dazzling yellow one-piece bathing suit and high-heeled shoes. And scrawled right across it in black crayon in Lenny's hand-writing were the words: 'Yes, please!'

Nellie suddenly felt uplifted, and she laughed out loud. 'Fanks a lot, Betty!' she said, giving the pin-up a salute. 'I couldn't agree more!'

Yes. Lenny *was* going to survive. Of that, Nellie now had no doubt whatsoever.

For the next few weeks, Monsieur refused to take on any more music hall bookings. He and Madame had carefully worked out a plan which enabled them to visit Lenny at the sanatorium twice a week, on Wednesday and Saturday afternoons, and until they were confident enough that he was being looked after properly, work took a very second place. It was an expensive arrangement; it involved taking a train on the Great Western Line from Paddington Station to Bristol, and then a taxi to the sanatorium, which was nearly two miles away. The sanatorium itself was also very expensive, but Monsieur had saved well over the years, and where his son was concerned, money was no object. Occasionally Nellie went along too.

By the end of May, Lenny's condition was showing such improvement that Monsieur and Eddie Buxton felt confident enough to start planning the next tour for the new Great Pierre act. The first booking to be arranged was for a season in pantomime later that year at the

Ilford Hippodrome, which was a popular theatre on the fringes of London, in Essex. The panto was *Robinson Crusoe*, and the offer was for Monsieur to appear as a wizard, with Nellie as his assistant, which would give them ample opportunity to use some of their regular Great Pierre material. Although the booking was still a few months off, pantos had to be cast well in advance. Monsieur was cheered by the prospect of being in the same show as the Scottish star comedienne, Renee Houston, and her American husband, Donald Stewart, with whom he had worked several times before. Until then, Monsieur signed up to take the new act on a six-week tour of the Stoll Theatres circuit in and around London.

Before the tour commenced, worrying rumours were circulating in the newspapers of a new 'secret weapon' being developed by the Germans, who claimed that it was so powerful it would not only entirely destroy London, it would also bring a glorious victory to the German nation.

'Pilotless planes!' scoffed Monsieur after listening to Eddie Buxton reading out the latest newspaper speculation. 'Bloody lot of ol' rubbish! Wot der they fink they're goin' ter do wiv planes an' no pilots?'

'They say they can carry high-explosive bombs, Bert,' replied Eddie pessimistically. 'All they have to do is to head them our way, then use radio control to crash them anywhere they like.'

Nellie shuddered at the thought of it. 'That's wicked,' she said gloomily. ''Ow can they even fink of killin' innocent people fer no reason at all?'

'Oh, Jerry's got plenty of reasons, all right, Nell,' replied Eddie. 'Just think of the Jews. Hitler hates their guts. I tell you, if the Nazis ever got a hold on this country, they'd do the same to the Jews here as they've done all over Europe.'

Nellie immediately feared for Martin. She knew, because he had told her, that his own family had originally come to this country as refugees from Germany. If the Allies lost the war, there was no doubt that Martin and his entire family would be in grave danger. Deep in thought, she stared out anxiously through the conservatory window.

'Well, there's no way Jerry's goin' ter win this war now,' insisted Monsieur, quite unconcerned. 'Once the invasion comes, it'll all be over – pilotless planes or anyfin' else!'

Nellie didn't really hear what her dad had said. She was too busy thinking about Jews, and what made them, in the Germans' eyes, so different from anyone else. Was it the way they looked, or the way they spoke? And then it suddenly came to her how some of the kids back at the orphanage used to pick on a small bunch of Jewish kids. 'Big nose!' was the usual jibe, and it was a kind of teasing that Nellie had always hated. Martin didn't have a big nose, and even if he did, what difference would it make? And what about all the Jewish people in the music hall? There were plenty of them, and they were no different from Roman Catholics or tall people or short people or thin people or fat people. Nobody had the right to single anyone out because of who or what they were, because prejudice, even at the most simple level, could lead to what was happening in Hitler's Germany. It was all so nasty and vicious – and mindless. Oh God, Nellie begged in her own silent way, please start the invasion soon.

The Allied invasion of continental Europe began on Tuesday, 6 June. Nellie was standing in a queue at Liptons general food store at the time, desperate to get to the front before the latest arrival of fresh Cheddar cheese disappeared in the scramble.

'It's started!' yelled an excited woman from the open doorway. 'They've landed on the French coast!'

A great cheer went up, and suddenly the whole place burst into excited chatter, with everyone in a state of euphoria. Nellie cheered with them, although she didn't share some people's view that 'it'd all be over in a week'. The general excitement was so great that by the time she reached the front of the queue and handed over the family's four ration books, she got more than the one ounce of cheese per person per week everyone was allowed. In fact, the girl behind the counter was so emotional, she forgot to take any coupons from Nellie at all.

In Seven Sisters Road outside, news of the invasion spread like wildfire, and small groups of people started to gather everywhere. This was the news they had been waiting for, praying for. This was the beginning of the end for Hitler, a real sock in the eye! One rather large middle-aged woman was so overwhelmed with excitement that she started singing and dancing all by herself, shopping bags bulging with vegetables, and the curlers in her hair popping out one by one. The atmosphere was infectious, with cars, motorcycles, trucks, and bicycles stopping at the kerbside to find out what was going on. It was the culmination of years of frustration. Now, the tide had turned, and it couldn't be that long before the boys who had been taken away from home would return. But as Nellie listened to all the opinions, the hopes and dreams, and the speculation, she wondered how soon that return would be.

And then she remembered that she hadn't heard from Martin for over two months.

On the Monday evening following the Anglo-American invasion, the new Great Pierre act made its debut at the Wood Green Empire. For both Monsieur and Nellie it was a significant return engagement, for it was at

377

this same theatre that Ange had had her serious washbasin accident, and where Monsieur had first tried out the dangerous Biting the Bullet sequence. Mercifully for Nellie, Monsieur had now dropped that idea and replaced it with an act that was altogether more classy. But even as she took her place in the solo spotlight, twice nightly from Monday to Saturday, singing her song like an angel, she often mulled over why it was that Monsieur had ever decided to change the act so radically.

In many ways, this new act was a complete change of direction for Monsieur, for in place of a traditional, rather tricksy music hall act, to Nellie's way of thinking, he had devised something that was really quite beautiful, almost surreal, with a wonderful use of mime, light, and shadows. But then in some ways Monsieur himself was also changing. Young Lenny's illness had affected him far more deeply than he would admit; it had made him take a closer look at himself, and to question what his life was really all about. Since then, he had felt that the Great Pierre act had become tired, shallow, and pointless, and when the management of a number two music hall like Collins relegated him to a minor spot during the first half of the show, he knew it was time to change direction.

It had now been a week since the Allied invasion, and each day the wireless and newspapers reported on the stiff enemy opposition Allied ground troops were up against. Consequently, the wave of D-Day euphoria had been replaced by a more cautious air of hope and prayers, and this was clearly reflected in the audience at Wood Green, who greeted Monsieur's new act with dignified enthusiasm.

With no chorus girls, jugglers, or dog acts on the bill this week, Nellie was relieved to find that she had the luxury of her own dressing room. But it was an odd experience to be using the same room that Ange had shared with the Sisters Tapp. The shattered washbasin

378

had been replaced and a new, bolder warning notice stuck to the wall above it.

After the first house on Wednesday evening, Nellie usually went into Monsieur's dressing room where she shared some sandwiches which Madame always brought along. But to her surprise a knock on her door brought her two unexpected visitors.

'Hello, Nellie.'

Nellie looked at the tall, middle-aged woman, with dark brown hair, dark brown eyes, and a complexion like porcelain. She hadn't the faintest idea who she was. 'I'm sorry,' was all she could utter.

'I'm Marion Hecht,' said the woman with just the faint suggestion of an accent. 'And this is my husband, Jacob.'

The woman stood back so that Nellie could see the man at her side. He, too, was tall, with jet-black hair, a bushy moustache, and slanting dark eyes. 'Hello, Nellie,' he said, his voice also revealing a slight accent.

Nellie was confused. 'I'm very sorry,' she said. 'Do I know yer?'

The woman, elegant in a plain black dress with a single piece of jewellery pinned above her left breast, answered for both of them. 'We're Martin's parents,' she said.

'Oh my—!' Nellie spluttered. 'I'm so sorry! Come in! Come in!' She opened the door wide to let them enter. Still wearing her skimpy stage costume, she suddenly felt coarse and awkward. 'Yer'll 'ave ter fergive me,' she said, rushing to put on her dressing gown. 'They didn't tell me I 'ad visitors. Please, sit down.'

'No, no, my dear,' said Marion. 'We only came for a few moments. We saw your show tonight. Congratulations. It was so very beautiful.'

'Really?' Nellie was astounded, particularly as Martin had always given her the impression that his parents wouldn't take too kindly to seeing his girlfriend half-naked on a music hall stage. 'Fanks very much.'

'So different to what we expected,' Jacob said, nervously fingering the rim of a dark trilby hat he was rolling around in his hands. He looked very smart in a long, grey overcoat. 'We think you have a most delightful voice.'

Nellie blushed. It was something she rarely did, but the compliment sounded so genuine, she couldn't help it. 'Oh, by the way,' she put her hand out to shake hands with Marion. ''Ow d'yer do. Pleased ter meet yer!'

Both visitors smiled warmly at her, then Marion took Nellie by surprise and gently kissed her on both cheeks. Jacob shook her hand.

'We've heard so much about you,' said Marion.

Again Nellie was surprised. 'Yer 'ave?'

'Martin left out the most important part though,' said Jacob. 'He didn't tell us how pretty you are.'

Nellie was determined that if they carried on like this, she'd make them her friends for life. ''E never tells me nuffin' eivver,' she said. ''Ave yer 'eard from 'im lately?' she asked, trying to sound as casual as possible.

There was a difficult pause, during which their expressions changed from warm smiles to concern.

'No, Nellie,' said Jacob, exchanging an uneasy glance with his wife. 'We were wondering if you had heard from him.'

Nellie shrugged her shoulders. 'Not a word for over two months.' She looked from one face to the other, and as she looked at Jacob, she could see the resemblance between him and Martin, the same jet-black hair and dark slanting eyes. 'Is there anyfin' wrong?' she asked.

There was another moment of hesitation.

'There's been a lot of – trouble on the south coast, Nellie,' said Marion with some difficulty. 'Jacob knows a journalist – he's a war correspondent on the *News Chronicle*. You mustn't repeat this, but he says that just before the invasion last week, two enemy fighter planes attacked one of the Air Force stations in Kent. He didn't say which one – precisely.'

'Nellie,' said Jacob, taking over where his wife left off. 'There was an – incident – with an Air Force truck. It was on its way from the base to Folkestone. There was a huge build-up of troops all along the coast.'

'The truck was full of ammunition,' Marion said. 'It was hit by gunfire from an enemy fighter. There was an – an explosion. It – blew up.'

Nellie clasped her hand to her mouth, horrified. 'Oh Gawd, no,' she gasped. 'Yer don't mean—'

'At the moment, we know nothing, Nellie,' Jacob said. 'Absolutely nothing.'

Nellie didn't know what to say, or what to think. 'But 'e didn't 'ave anyfin' ter do wiv trucks. When I was down there that time, 'e told me 'e worked in this office.'

Marion was shaking her head.

'They were short of men, Nellie,' said Jacob, with a despondent sigh. 'They needed drivers urgently. With the invasion so close, there was pandemonium. Everyone had to do any job that was necessary.'

'But 'ow der we know that Martin . . .'

Marion took hold of Nellie's hands and held them tightly. 'Our friend told us that there are quite a few men unaccounted for,' she said anxiously. 'He says the authorities have refused to release the names of casualties until the invasion is well on its way.'

'Until then, Nellie,' said Jacob, grave-faced, 'we shan't know if Martin is one of them.'

Chapter 26

The war was entering a decisive stage. In North Africa and Italy, the Allies were pushing forward on all fronts, and now that the Anglo-American invasion had secured a foothold on the Normandy beaches in France, there was a feeling throughout the country that the German war machine had at last been halted. But, once again, Prime Minister Winston Churchill warned the nation not to be complacent. The Luftwaffe were still capable of launching reprisals for the massive Anglo-American air raids on Berlin and other German cities, and these could come at any moment, without warning.

In the early hours of the morning following the second house show at the Wood Green Empire, two pilotless planes exploded within about ten minutes of each other. One came down on a vegetable allotment in Gravesend, Kent, and the other destroyed a railway bridge in Grove Road, Bow. Most of the Beckwith family were in bed and fast asleep at the time, but Nellie woke up immediately and rushed to her window. There had been no air-raid alert, so she assumed it was either a hit-and-run attack by a stray enemy aircraft or an explosion caused by something other than an air raid. However, whatever it was seemed to be some way away, and after scanning the sky for several minutes, Nellie thought no more about it and went back to bed.

It was a somewhat different story a couple of evenings later when Monsieur, Madame, and Nellie were in

Monsieur's dressing room, tucking into the dried egg and sausage flan that Madame had made for supper. The final turn of the first house show was still on stage, and over the loudspeaker in their room they could hear the audience rocking with laughter at the comic aristocratic capers of 'Britain's premier radio personality', Mr Gillie Potter. The Squire of Hogsnorton, as he called himself, was no more than five minutes into his witty tales of country life when the entire theatre suddenly became aware of a loud, piercing, shuddering noise. Everyone backstage, on stage, and in the audience turned their eyes up towards the ceiling, as though the noise was somehow being manipulated from the roof. But then there was relief as the sound went as quickly as it had come. But before the star performer had managed to improvise a gag about what they had all just heard, a tremendous explosion rocked the theatre.

The stage manager rushed on to the stage, and with Mr Potter staring on in disbelief called through the microphone: 'Ladies and gentlemen, please stay calm. The performance will continue.'

But the performance did not continue, for the audience rose almost as one and filed out in orderly procession through every exit.

In Monsieur's dressing room, as in the auditorium itself, small pieces of plaster fluttered down from walls and ceilings, and the contents of the dressing table either toppled over or went crashing to the floor.

'Outside!' barked Monsieur, rushing to open the door for Madame and Nellie. 'Quick as yer can, gels!'

In the back alley outside, a group of stagehands had gathered. Most of them were staring up at the sky, for it was a fine summer's evening and the air was crystal clear. By the time Monsieur, Madame, and Nellie got there, they were quickly joined by other turns from the show, including Gillie Potter himself.

384

'What is it?' asked the star performer. 'I didn't hear the alert.'

'There wasn't one,' replied one of the backstage electricians.

'Looks like it's over Stoke Newington way,' added the stage manager who was drawing everyone's attention to a great cloud of thick black smoke in the distance.

Nellie put a comforting arm round her mum who was shaking like a leaf. 'Must've bin a one-off,' she said, having to shout above the clanging of fire engine and ambulance bells, and the sound of general mayhem echoing out from the High Road nearby.

While the group was standing there, bewildered and confused, someone shouted, 'Look out! Anuvver one!'

'Oh my God!' gasped Madame as she, Nellie, and Monsieur flicked their eyes up towards the sky.

They could hear the sinister drone of what had already been described in one newspaper as a 'robot' plane approaching at high speed, drowning every other sound in the vicinity. It was a terrifying, menacing sound as it chugged and spluttered across the sky, and when it finally came into sight, it looked like a small black rocket, with clipped wings, a light in the nose, and a fierce red flame burning from the tail.

'What the hell is *that* thing?' asked Gillie Potter, his assumed upper-class voice thoroughly outraged and indignant.

'Looks like its arse is on fire,' called one of the stage-hands.

Nobody laughed. They were all mesmerised by this extraordinary new weapon.

As the pilotless plane sped across the sky, leaving a trail of thick black smoke in its wake, fascination turned to fear when the sound of the machine cut out and the flame from its tail disappeared.

'It's diving!' yelled the stage door keeper.

Somebody else yelled, 'Take cover!'

Automatically, everyone crowding around the stage door threw themselves to the ground. Monsieur did his best to cover Madame and Nellie with his own body.

The eerie silence from the robot machine seemed to last for ever. When the explosion finally came, it was deafening, and closely followed by the sound of glass shattering. Someone on the corner of the road nearby shouted, 'Christ Almighty!' In a shop doorway, a woman was stretched out on the ground, desperately trying to shield her two young children.

For the next few moments, nobody moved. But as the second robot plane seemed to be the last, eventually everyone felt confident enough to get up on their feet again.

'It's all over, dear,' said Monsieur, cool as a cucumber as he helped his wife up. 'That's the last one.'

Frantic with worry, Madame said, 'Bert, I've got ter get back ter Sid. Oh God, I shouldn't've left 'im on 'is own. Ternight of all nights!'

'Don't be silly, Mum,' said Nellie, holding on to her. 'Sid's perfectly all right wiv Grandma and Grandad. They're probably all tucked up nice and safe in their Morrison shelter.'

'Damn 'em!' shouted Madame, angrily shaking her fist up at the trail of black smoke that still streaked the sky. 'Who was it said this bloody war was all over?'

'So wot 'appens about second 'ouse, everyone?' called the harassed stage manager from the back of the group. 'Do we pull it fer the night?'

'Pull it?' Gillie Potter was outraged by the suggestion. 'The customers have paid good money to see this show. For God's sake, don't let's hand it on a plate to Herr Hitler. Let's get back on stage and get on with it.'

Everyone stood aside to let the star performer get back into the theatre, then they followed him in, including Monsieur, Madame, and Nellie.

During the course of the second house show, three more robot planes droned mercilessly across the darkening evening sky.

Then they cut out, dived into the middle of whatever populated area they happened to be above, and exploded with a devastating roar. Fortunately, the Wood Green Empire did not sustain any damage, and although the theatre rattled and shook, the show continued without interruption.

There was no doubt that the customers on this extra-ordinary night certainly got their money's worth.

Nellie thought that Marion Hecht was one of the most beautiful women she had ever seen. She had almost classical features, a delicate complexion, and wore just a suggestion of lipstick, no other make-up; it was hard to believe that she was old enough to be Martin's mother. Even the way she brushed her dark wavy hair, so that it was held behind her ears with brown oyster-shell combs, had such style, Nellie thought she was glamorous enough to be in the pictures. Her husband, Jacob, was a wonderful match for her, for he had distinguished features, kindly eyes, and a full moustache, which exactly complemented the slightly greying hair above his ears. They both towered above Nellie, but as all three of them sat together over tea in the Hechts' ornate lounge, Nellie didn't feel at all ill at ease, especially after Jacob made a light-hearted joke about how he, his wife, and his son were often compared to a family of lampposts.

After all the bitter things Martin had said about his parents, Nellie had had many preconceptions of what they would be like. But when they had so unexpectedly turned up in her dressing room at Wood Green just a couple of weeks before, they couldn't have been more different from what she had imagined. There was still no news about Martin's fate after the enemy attack on the RAF lorry he might have been driving, and sitting here in his home in Highgate with his parents, Nellie was all too conscious of the fact that Martin, for some reason, had not wanted her to meet his family.

'Isn't it strange,' said Marion, sitting alongside Nellie on a large velour settee, 'we've only known each other for a short time, and yet I feel as though I've known you for years.' She looked across at her husband who was in one of the chairs of the matching suite. 'Isn't that so, Jacob?'

He shrugged his shoulders. 'Absolutely,' he replied, putting down his fine bone china teacup and saucer on the coffee table.

Nellie, who was wearing her Sunday best, a pastel yellow cotton dress she had bought on the clothes ration while she was working at Beales Restaurant, nodded her head in agreement. 'I feel the same way about you,' she replied. 'I don't understand why Martin always kept so cagey about 'is 'ome life.'

Marion exchanged a pointed look with her husband. 'When you've known Martin as long as we have, my dear,' she said with a sad frown, 'you'll know what a complicated boy he is.'

Jacob Hecht leaned forward in his chair. 'I can assure you, Nellie,' he said, 'he talks an awful lot about you. I think he wants to make us jealous.'

'Oh, that's not fair, Jacob,' scolded his wife. 'Martin's just like any boy of his age. When he has somebody he cares for, he wants to boast a little.' She turned to Nellie, smiled, and briefly clutched her hand. 'And I don't blame him one little bit!'

Nellie's eyes were discreetly scanning the room. It was much bigger than she was used to, even in Tufnell Park Road. Behind the blackout blinds, there were expensive floor to ceiling brocade curtains, antique furniture, a Persian carpet covering most of the floor, and a lamb's wool rug in front of a big, open fireplace with a brass fender and companion set. Surrounded by so much comfort and style, she found it difficult to understand why Martin had once chosen to roam the war-torn streets of North London.

As if knowing what was going through Nellie's mind, Marion got up from the settee and picked up one of the large collection of framed family photographs on the mantelpiece. 'This is Martin soon after his Bar Mitzvah,' she said, handing Nellie the photograph. 'He was thirteen when that was taken.'

Nellie smiled at the picture. It showed Martin in a smart navy-blue suit with short trousers, an open neck white shirt, and a plain black yarmulke skullcap trimmed with white brocade on his head.

'Bar Mitzvah marks a Jewish boy's assumption of his religious obligations,' Marion said, watching Nellie closely as she looked at the photograph. 'You did know Martin is a Jewish boy?' she asked carefully, her face a little taut.

'Oh yes,' replied Nellie, nodding her head.

'It doesn't concern you?'

Nellie was puzzled to be asked such a question. 'Course not. Why should it?'

Marion relaxed. 'To some people it does,' she replied. 'Especially Martin.'

Nellie was confused. 'Wot d'yer mean?'

Marion took the photograph back from Nellie and replaced it on the mantelpiece. 'You know, Nellie, Martin's father and I have never tried to force religion down his throat. For reasons that only Martin himself understands, he has problems with being – what he is.'

Nellie shrugged her shoulders. 'Yer can't 'elp wot yer come from.'

'I know, I know,' Marion replied. 'But Martin has always felt that fingers point at him. He feels that he can be pinpointed in a crowd, wherever he goes. And it repulses him.' She sat back in the settee, crossed her arms, and stared out aimlessly through the large windows on the other side of the room. 'I think it had something to do with his grandmother's Yahrzeit, the anniversary of her death. He was very fond of her. They used to play card games together, and laugh a lot. But when he went to light a candle in her memory, he just couldn't bring himself to recite the holy Kaddish – our prayer of mourning. We said it didn't matter, but in his strange mixed-up way, he blamed us – Jacob and me. He said she would never have died if we had looked after her more.'

'It was rubbish, of course,' said Jacob bitterly. 'I loved my mother just as much as he did, but she was old, she was at the end of her time.'

'What I'm trying to say, Nellie, is that although Jacob and I actively pursue our own religious faith, we have never expected Martin to do the same. We love him. He's our son. If anything has happened to him . . .' Her face began to crumple. 'But we don't want to own him,' she insisted, fighting back her distress. 'He will be alive long after we are gone. He must make his own decisions.' She took out a small, lace handkerchief and dabbed her nose with it. 'The only thing that we find hard to accept is that he should be ashamed of who and what he is. When he was an evacuee, it took him a long time to come back to us after he had run away. It hurt us. It hurt us deeply.'

'It's because he's an only child,' added Jacob. 'I blame myself. We should have had more.'

Marion immediately swung him an anxious glance. 'Please, Jacob, one guilt complex is enough for any family.'

Nellie listened in silence. Remembering all the odd things Martin had said about his parents, about their not wanting him to go into the services without a commission, and about his father not wanting to be anything but a Jew, she was fascinated to hear the other side of the story. But who to believe? Who to trust?

'You know, Nellie,' Marion continued, 'when Martin first started talking about you, I felt so good. I felt that, for the first time in his life, he was not taking everything so seriously, that he had found someone who could love him, and be his equal.' She looked directly into Nellie's eyes. 'You do love him, don't you, Nellie?'

Nellie suddenly felt that a great weight had been placed on her shoulders. But then she thought about the possibility that none of them might ever see Martin alive again. And although there was something inside her which slightly resented being asked so personal a question, a question that concerned only Martin and herself, her heart told her that there was only one reply she could give.

'Oh yes. I love 'im all right.'

Towards the end of August, Monsieur and Madame took a momentous decision. Despite the Allied advance on all fronts in Europe, hordes of robot planes, now nicknamed buzz bombs or doodlebugs, were streaming over London day and night. The destruction caused by these terrifying machines was awesome, and the loss of life was mounting relentlessly. Everyone somewhere had a relative or friend whose house had been either hit or caught in the blast; there seemed to be no escape from the rain of terror pelting down on the rooftops of thousands of innocent civilians. The military came under increasing pressure to shoot down the buzz bombs before they had the chance to reach London, and this they did with a certain amount of success but there were still far too many of the deadly bug-like machines getting through, and the last straw for Monsieur and Madame came during the second week of August when a flying bomb smashed through the roof of the huge Gaumont

Cinema on the corner of Tufnell Park and Holloway Roads.

Now temporarily recovered from the primary stage of his tuberculosis, young Lenny had only been home for a couple of weeks when his father decided to evacuate Madame and both their sons to the safety of Aunt Ethel's house in Somerset. Madame was reluctant to agree to her husband's wishes, but the danger posed by the flying bombs and the talk of an even more deadly rocket weapon being tested by the Germans forced her to comply. Nellie was asked to go too, but as she and Monsieur were still on the road with the Great Pierre act, she insisted that she stay behind and continue to support him.

After the family had gone, the house in Tufnell Park Road seemed like a mausoleum. On the few nights that Monsieur and Nellie were there, there was little hope of any sleep, for the air was constantly fractured by the thunderous sounds of ack-ack gunfire trying to bring down the pilotless raiders over the least populated areas. After a hazardous week of appearances at the few music halls in and around London that had remained open, Nellie persuaded her dad that it would be safer to spend at least part of the nights in the Anderson shelter. In the event, this was only possible once Nellie had helped Monsieur with the back-breaking job of pumping out three feet of rainwater, using an officially provided stirrup pump. Even then the place was not habitable, for it needed at least fourteen hours to dry out.

With the family away, Monsieur's morale was very low. 'I just don't see the point in carryin' on wiv a show when the 'ouse is only 'alf full,' he said to Nellie as they endured yet another grim night in the Anderson.

It was true, of course. The 'new Blitz', as the V-1 was being called, was driving people out of London in their thousands, and this inevitably had an effect on audience numbers in theatres and cinemas all over London, most of which were playing to no more than a handful of sturdy regulars. Even business in the pubs was down, and the streets looked empty.

'I don't see wot else they can do, Dad,' replied Nellie, propped up in a wicker chair, wrapped in a blanket, only half awake. 'They 'ave ter keep the 'alls open somehow.'

'Why?' snapped Monsieur. 'Why should we risk our lives just fer the sake of uvver people? D'yer realise that one night you an' me could be up there on that stage and – boom! All of a sudden we could cop our lot. These bloody buzz bombs don't tell yer they're comin', yer know.'

'Come on now, Dad, this isn't like you. Our chances of bein' 'it are no more than if we was down the Tube.'

'At least down the Tube we'd 'ave a couple a tons of earth ter protect us.' By the dim light of the hurricane lamp, Nellie could see him shaking his head. 'No, Nell,' he said gloomily. 'I can't take much more of this. I don't like bein' parted from my family. It's not natural.'

Nellie leaned across and tried to calm him. 'Don't give in, Dad,' she said. 'It won't be long now. The war's nearly over. Just yer wait an' see, we'll soon 'ave Mum and the boys back 'ome wiv us.'

Monsieur was not convinced. He leaned his head back in the chair and tried to settle down. But his eyes remained wide open, staring up despondently at the curved, cold steel roof of the tiny shelter. This was not what life was all about. This was life in hell.

'Try an' get some sleep, Dad,' Nellie said, yawning and closing her eyes. 'It'll all be over soon . . .'

Even as she spoke, the night was pierced by the sound of yet another flying bomb as it ground its way across the sky above. Nellie's eyes sprang open. Eventually, but quite suddenly, that most feared of all wartime sounds cut out. It was almost as though a switch had been turned off.

In the heart-stopping silence that followed, Nellie and Monsieur waited tensely.

'Please, dear God,' she prayed silently. 'Don't let it be us.'

Mercifully, Nellie's prayer was answered.

By the end of August, most of the launching sites for the V-1 flying bombs at the Pas de Calais on the French coast had been overrun by Allied forces. The number of raids gradually diminished, and those people who had fled from London at the height of the new Blitz, including thousands of children, started to return. The music halls that had closed reopened but Monsieur and his fellow artistes were still playing to half-empty houses.

Madame, Sid, and young Lenny returned home from their evacuation in Somerset to a rapturous welcome from both Monsieur and Nellie. It had been the first time Monsieur and Madame had been apart for so long, and their reunion was very emotional. On their first evening at home, Nellie surprised them all by cooking the evening meal, which she had carefully planned all week. When she first came to live with the family, she had no idea about cooking, but having watched Madame so many times, she had picked up quite a few ideas. For her welcome home meal she gave them sausage meat with fresh breadcrumbs and chopped fresh parsley, well-seasoned, shaped into patties, and fried. With this she served mashed potatoes, fresh beans and carrots which she had bought that morning at Hicks the greengrocers in Seven Sisters Road. The trifle that followed was delicious, and was a particular favourite with both Sid and Lenny, for it was full of tinned fruit, topped with strawberry jelly, and finished off with a strawberry blancmange made with dried milk. Everyone made short work of the meal. Nellie was thrilled to see Lenny looking so much more like his former self, with colour in his cheeks and a little more flesh on his bony limbs. The family reunion was a joy. All that was wanting now was the end of the war.

But in the early hours of the morning, a new type of rocket bomb came down on a populated area in Chiswick, West London.

Nellie's hopes of seeing Martin alive again were fading fast. It had been over two months since his parents had told her about the attack on the RAF lorry in Kent, and since then there had been a security clampdown. The Allied invasion was now being consolidated, and the last thing the Government wanted at this delicate stage in the campaign was for the general public to feel that there had been any kind of setbacks. But for those who lived in hope for even the barest minimum of news, it was a heartbreaking ordeal.

Life, however, had to go on, and two weeks after the first rocket bomb fell on Chiswick, Monsieur accepted an invitation to take part in an all-star benefit show at the Chiswick Empire, which was being held to raise funds for the victims of the devastating tragedy. Nellie was thrilled to be there, for it gave her the chance to be among some of the greatest names in the music hall. The turn she was most excited to see was by the famous stage and radio comic Rob Wilton. His sketch, 'The Day War Broke Out', had boosted the morale of so many of his radio listeners and audiences since the darkest days of the Blitz. But despite the fact that there were so many great names on the bill, including the Western Brothers, Jeanne de Casalis ('Mrs Feather'), Wilson, Keppel and Betty, Arthur Askey and Richard 'Stinker' Murdoch, Will Fyffe, Flanagan and Allen, Gertie Gitana, and G.H. Elliott ('The Chocolate-Coloured Coon'), Monsieur and Nellie more than held their own. In fact, while Nellie was singing her 'When I Grow Too Old to Dream' number, the entire celebrity-packed audience joined in.

For this once only performance, Nellie had to share a dressing room with some of the Tiller Girls who were just about the best line-up of chorus dancers in the business. But during the interval, she joined her dad and mum in the dressing room Monsieur was sharing with Arthur Askey and 'Stinker' Murdoch. The laughs came fast and furious, but although Nellie adored being with the man whose catchphrase 'I thank you!' was a national favourite, she found that he, like so many comedians, was far more quiet and serious than she had imagined.

The finale of the show had been arranged as a patriotic sing-song for the company and audience combined. Nellie was placed right at the end of the line, nearest to the wings. During the first song, 'Two Lovely Black Eyes', Nellie noticed one of the young stagehands signalling to her. She edged her way discreetly towards him.

'Telephone call! Urgent!'

'Don't be daft,' spluttered Nellie in disbelief. 'Not now, yer idiot! Tell 'em ter phone back!'

'It's urgent!' insisted the stagehand. 'She must speak to yer *now*!'

Nellie thought the young bloke had gone stark, staring mad. 'Who is it?'

'She says she's Martin's muvver!'

Nellie left the stage running and pelted down the small passage that led to the stage door where the keeper was holding out the telephone receiver to her.

'Mrs 'Echt!' she said breathlessly. 'It's me, Nellie.'

The following morning, Nellie could hardly get up to Highgate fast enough. It wasn't easy, for although there were normally plenty of trolley buses running up to the Archway, for the past two weeks there had been regular V-2 rocket attacks and transport was even more unreliable than usual. Eventually she managed to get a bus which dropped her outside the Tube station. From there she had quite a walk up the hill to Highgate Village.

On the way, she felt as if she'd been born all over

again. The telephone call from Martin's mother had left her feeling exhilarated. Martin's home! He's alive! All through the night, she hadn't had a wink of sleep, and every fifteen minutes or so, she had switched on the light to look at the time. It was too wonderful for words. Martin's home! He's alive! The only thing was why hadn't he called her himself? His mother had explained how he was still recovering from his injuries, but surely, surely he could have come to the phone to talk to her, somehow.

The Hechts' double-fronted house was set well back from the leafy lane where it snuggled comfortably between other similar grand houses. The driveway was paved with York stone, which was badly cracked and in need of replacing. But as she rushed up to the front door of the large imitation Tudor house, the only thing she could see in her mind's eye was Martin.

Marion Hecht was already opening the front door before Nellie reached it. As usual, she looked as immaculate as ever, except that she seemed somewhat drained and tired. 'Thank you for coming, Nellie,' she said wearily. 'I'm so grateful.'

Nellie's expression changed immediately. She found Marion's greeting curious. 'Thank you for coming, Nellie.' Why was she thanking her?

Marion took her into the farmhouse-style kitchen where Jacob was sitting at the kitchen table, his head buried in his hands. As Nellie entered the room, he got up to greet her. His face was pale and drawn. 'Nellie, my dear,' he said, trying to smile. 'Thank you for coming.'

Nellie was taken aback. What was wrong with them both? 'Thank you for coming, thank you for coming.' What were they going on about?

'Martin's in the garden,' Marion said softly, nodding her head towards the window.

Nellie briefly looked out through the small leaded glass windows; she could just see Martin at the far end of the lawn, sitting in a wheelchair with his back to her. 'Is he – all right?' she asked tentatively.

Marion exchanged a brief, strained glance with her husband. 'There's something you should know, Nellie,' she said, with obvious difficulty. 'Martin doesn't know you're here. He didn't want me to tell you that he's home.'

Nellie was devastated. 'Why not?'

Marion took hold of Nellie's hands and held them tightly. 'His injuries were – far more serious than I told you on the telephone last night. You see . . .' It was too much. She had to stop.

Jacob took over. 'There was a fire, Nellie. The lorry he was driving . . . it was a bad fire . . .'

Nellie wanted to hear no more. She pulled her hands from Marion's grasp and made for the door.

'Nellie!' Marion called.

Nellie stopped and turned to look at her.

Marion wanted to say something to her, but she found it impossible. So she merely shook her head and turned away.

It had been a beautiful sunny September so far. As Nellie hurried out into the garden, she felt the warmth on her face, and smelt the faint, sweet scent of late-flowering roses. The garden was so big, Martin appeared quite lost in it, such a tiny figure in the distance, sitting at the side of an ornamental pond.

She decided not to rush. She slowly paced her way along the narrow stone path that led first to a central round flowerbed, then on to the pond at the far end of the garden. As she drew closer, she could see more clearly the wheelchair Martin was sitting in, and even though his back was turned towards her, she could see that he was still in his dressing gown. She also saw that he had a large bandage round his head.

Martin didn't hear her approach, and for a moment

or two she just stood there, looking down at him from behind.

Finally, she plucked up enough courage to say quietly, 'Martin.'

Martin stiffened but didn't turn.

'Oh, Martin,' she said, putting her arms gently round his shoulders, and kissing the top of his head. 'You're alive. Fank God you're alive.'

Martin still didn't respond. So she calmly moved round in front of him. As she did so, she saw that his head was bent forward. 'Martin?' she said, with growing concern.

Martin slowly raised his head to look at her. His face was white and drawn, and his eyes stared straight through her.

Chapter 27

It had been a harrowing experience. Nellie spent almost an hour and a half with Martin, crouched on the grass beside him, holding his hand, talking to him quietly, just letting him know that she was there, that she cared for him, and that she loved him. Martin was in deep shock; he'd been like that ever since the RAF lorry he was driving came under attack from two enemy fighters just before D-Day. It had left him in a serious condition: a broken left ankle, and second-degree burns down the left side of his body. Some of his black hair had been burnt off, and if it hadn't been for the quick action of his mates, his scalp would have been in one hell of a mess. On top of that, the choking smoke from the fire had practically asphyxiated him. The shock had been so great, he found it difficult to use his vocal chords. Mercifully, his hair was now growing again, and every so often he would say a few words. Martin had been one of the lucky ones. Three of his mates travelling with him in the lorry at the time had been killed outright. It was a miracle that Martin had survived.

Nellie didn't unwind until she got back home to Tufnell Park Road. By then, the shock of seeing Martin in such a condition caught up with her, and the moment she reached her own bedroom, she threw herself down on to the bed and bawled her eyes out. When her mum came in to find out what was wrong, Nellie found it difficult to hold back all the pent-up emotions she had felt inside since her first sight of Martin sitting in his wheelchair at the end of the Hechts' garden.

'At least 'e's alive, fank Gawd,' said Madame, holding Nellie in her arms and trying to comfort her. 'It could've been worse, Nell. Don't ever ferget that.'

'Oh, I know, Mum,' Nellie sobbed. 'But it's so unfair. Martin 'ad so much goin' for 'im. 'E was such a good-lookin' feller, an' 'e 'ad so many brains . . .'

'You're talkin' about 'im as though 'e's dead, Nell. 'E's not dead. 'E's alive, an' there's no reason why in a few munffs' time 'e shouldn't be back on 'is feet again, doin' all the fings you an' 'im want ter do. Now listen ter me, child,' Madame continued, stroking Nellie's hair as she talked. 'If you love your boy as much as I fink yer do, then you can be the one ter get 'im back on 'is feet again. D'you know wot I'm sayin'?'

Nellie nodded, and used her knuckles to wipe the tears from her eyes.

'I know yer, Nell,' Madame said. 'I know wot you can do fer people, 'cos yer've done it fer me and yer dad, yer've done it fer Sid and Lenny. You 'ave so much love in yer, you'll never fail in anyfin' yer want ter do. An' d'yer know why?' She leaned down closer. 'Because yer know what it's like ter survive, Nell. Yer've 'ad ter do it, since the day yer was born.'

Nellie thought carefully about what Madame was saying to her. In fact it made her think back over her entire life – those early years without a mum or dad to call her own, her time in Barratts' Orphanage with Miss Ackroyd, the bomb and the debris of the orphanage all piled up on top of her. And yet she had survived it all. But how? Why was she singled out to be the one who crawled out of all that carnage, to walk the streets without name or direction? Her life could have ended right there and then, but it didn't. But most of all she thought about Toff and the vacs gang, Shortso, and Nutty, and Rats and Bonkers. In her mind's eye, she could see them all as if they were standing in front of her right now. Yes, Madame was right, she *was* a survivor. Her whole life was a testament to it.

'Let me ask yer somefin', Nell.'

Nellie blinked, to find Madame still holding her.

'When yer dad an' I first saw yer waitin' on tables in Beales wiv yer neat little cap an' apron – remember? Yer told us about all that time when yer lost yer memory. Yer couldn't remember one single fing, right? Not even yer name.'

Nellie nodded.

'Wot did it feel like, Nell, not knowin' who yer were, or where yer came from?'

Nellie thought for a moment. 'It's 'ard ter tell,' she replied. 'All I can remember is that everyfin' was blank, as though a big wall was shutting me out from who I really was.'

'An' yet it never stopped yer from gettin' on wiv a new kind of life.'

Nellie shook her head. 'No,' she replied. 'When you an' dad asked me ter come an' live wiv yer, it was like bein' born all over again.'

Madame smiled. 'Well, 'as it occurred ter you that perhaps it's the same wiv Martin? P'r'aps 'e needs some 'elp ter do exactly the same fing.'

Nellie turned and looked up at her.

Madame nodded. 'Yes, Nell,' she said. 'An' you're probably the one person who can 'elp 'im do it.'

During October, the V-2 rocket bomb attacks increased, and at the beginning of November one of them came down in Upper Holloway, almost completely destroying a whole street of working-class terraced houses. The number of casualties ran into hundreds, including many deaths, and the blast was felt up to two miles away.

At the time of the explosion, Nellie and Martin were

having Sunday tea with the Beckwith family in Tufnell Park Road, which was less than a mile away from where the rocket had come down. The blast ripped off quite a lot of tiles from the roof, and the chimney pot, like many others in the area, tilted at a dangerous angle. A few minutes earlier, the family had been out in the back yard letting off fireworks. It was, after all, 5 November 1944, Guy Fawkes night.

In the six weeks since he had come home on indefinite sick leave, Martin, with Nellie's help, had made slow but significant progress. Within ten days or so, Nellie had revived his confidence so much that he had discarded his wheelchair, which she had insisted was totally unnecessary for the injury he had sustained to his ankle. Her first task was to get him mobile again, and with the initial aid of a pair of crutches, he was soon getting around without the help of either Nellie or his parents. Every week he had to go to the burns unit at the Charing Cross Hospital in the West End of London. The burns all down the left-hand side of his upper body, thigh and leg were kept under strict supervision, and treated with the most up-to-date lotions, creams, and drugs that were available. Ignoring his protests, Nellie always accompanied him to the hospital, and waited in the corridor outside until he was allowed to go home again. Her presence helped his morale, for the burns took longer to heal than he had anticipated. Eventually even they started to improve, and when the prospect of some skin grafts for the worst areas was suggested, his full recovery was in sight.

Martin's psychological scars were quite a different matter, however, and despite Nellie's sensitive and loving care, he found it difficult to readjust. This was never made more obvious than the few moments immediately following the Guy Fawkes V-2 explosion, which left him shaking from head to foot and unable to speak coherently for nearly an hour.

Towards the end of the month, Nellie took a bold decision. She had thought about it for some time, in fact every time she accompanied Martin to the hospital. The burns he had received on his body had left him highly sensitive to anyone, other than the hospital staff, seeing his scars. Especially Nellie. Whenever they met, he made quite sure he was wearing a polo-neck pullover that covered his neck, and he never took the risk of letting her see him without a shirt. It was a tragic situation, and Nellie knew that unless Martin could be persuaded to overcome this traumatic revulsion for his own body, their relationship would never flourish.

Her opportunity came one afternoon late in November. Martin's injured foot, which had been in plaster for so many weeks, was now fully healed, and he was able to walk a little more each day. Usually Nellie would go up to Highgate to collect him and they would take a slow stroll together around the quiet back lanes where many of the rich and famous of pre-war days had bought opulent houses overlooking smart golf courses. Hampstead Heath was only a few minutes' walk away. Nellie loved the heath best in winter, for it seemed to have a peace and tranquillity that was often lacking during the summer months, when a huge fairground was the centrepiece of most Bank Holidays.

The sky was heavy with dark grey clouds as they wound their way along Hampstead Lane, past the old Spaniards Inn and into Spaniards Road where two mobile anti-aircraft gun units mounted on army lorries were parked. At Jack Straw's Castle pub, they paused to buy two cups of tea from a stall, joining several soldiers and Civil Defence workers who were discussing the number of V-1s and V-2s they had brought down during the previous twenty-four hours.

The grass on the West Heath was long and damp, and Nellie and Martin were both glad that they were wearing wellington boots. It was hard going, for over the past few days it had snowed quite a lot, and in places it was five or six inches deep. On the way, they passed children tobogganing on boards down a steep slope. Their shouts and laughter echoed around the leafless trees whose dark branches were highlighted with snow. When they reached the Leg of Mutton pond, they found it covered with a thin layer of ice and snow. A notice warned: 'DANGEROUS. KEEP OFF.' For several minutes they stood at the edge of the pond, just staring down at it. The clouds permitted a thin ray of sun to break through, and its narrow beam settled on the surface of the pond, transforming it into a dazzling array of tiny snow crystals. But no sooner had the ray of sunlight come than it disappeared back behind the grey clouds.

Nellie slipped her arm round Martin's waist and leaned her head against him. 'D'yer know wot I was finkin' about last night?' she said.

Martin shook his head. 'No,' he replied, putting his arm round her shoulders.

'That church. D'yer remember it? That Catholic place you, Rats and Bonkers found me in.' She looked up at him. 'It was the first time I set eyes on yer.'

'You looked half dead when I saw you,' he said, still struggling to regain his normal pace of speech.

'I *was* 'alf dead. If it hadn't been fer you, I'd never've survived.'

Martin grinned down at her. 'Don't you believe it. You're tougher than you think.'

Nellie paused a moment, then asked him a question. 'Martin, wot did yer fink when yer first saw me?'

'I thought, if she was a couple of years older, I could go for her.'

Quick as a flash, Nellie retorted, 'Well, I *am* a coupla years older. So wot d'yer fink now?'

He didn't answer. She could feel him stiffen.

'Martin?' she asked uncertainly.

He broke away from her and moved a few paces closer to the pond.

Nellie joined him. 'Did I say somefin' wrong?'

'It's not going to work, Nell,' Martin said, staring aimlessly down into the pond. 'Not now. Everything's changed.'

'Yer mean yer don't go for me any more?'

Martin swung round. 'No, Nell,' he said firmly. 'That's not what I mean. I've never met anybody in my whole life like you. When I was lying in that hospital bed back at the base, it was your face I could see, night after night. It kept me going, Nell. It was the only thing that kept me going. But I'm not the same person I was. What happened in that lorry has changed my whole life, changed the way I think, changed the way I *feel*.'

'An' it's the same wiv me, is that it, Martin? Yer just don't feel the same way terwards me any more.'

'Please don't say things like that to me, Nell. It isn't true. I'll always feel that way towards you. What I'm trying to say is . . .' He was talking with such difficulty, he turned away from her again. 'I can't expect you to spend the rest of your life with me.'

'A few munffs ago yer was sayin' yer'd never let me go,' she reminded him. 'Yer said yer wanted us ter live tergevver fer the rest of our lives.'

'That was before, Nell,' he replied, his back still turned towards her. 'Not now. Not the way I am now. I don't have the right.'

Nellie took a pace towards him and used both her hands to turn him round to face her. '*I* 'ave a few rights too, yer know, Martin,' she said. 'Don't *I* get a say in the matter?'

For a brief moment, he looked her in the eyes. It was the first time he had done so for a long time. 'Nell,' he said, raising his voice above the sound of some ducks having a heated argument on the other side of the pond, 'would you really want to spend the rest of your life with someone who's been through what I've been through? Would you?'

Nellie decided that she would no longer listen to him feeling sorry for himself. 'You're not the only one in the 'ole world that's suffered, Martin. As a matter of fact, I've 'ad my share too. So 'ave a lot of people.'

It did the trick, for Martin immediately leaned down and hugged her. 'Oh, Nell,' he said guiltily. 'What's wrong with me? What the hell is wrong with me? It's not what I meant. You've been so good to me. I couldn't have got through these past few weeks without you. What I'm trying to tell you is that I can't bear the thought of your seeing me like this. I'm just not the same person I was when we first first met inside that church.'

'Neiver am I, Martin,' Nellie replied, her voice muffled against his thick duffel coat. But when she looked up at him again, he heard her loud and clear. 'But it don't make no difference, mate,' she said with a cheeky look. ''Cos I still fancy yer!'

Behind them, two ducks swooped down from the sky and skidded boisterously across the surface of the pond. High in the sky above, a long, thin vapour trail cut in and out of the dark clouds, indicating that another V-2 was on its way to yet another target.

And then it started to snow.

By the time Nellie and Martin got back to Highgate, the snow flurries had turned into a blizzard. The snow was drifting heavily in the biting wind, making it difficult to struggle against.

When they got into the house, Martin told Nellie that he felt a bit like Scott of the Antarctic, and he was glad he had built up the fire in the drawing room before they set off on their walk. A few minutes later, his mother telephoned to say that she and his father had been caught in the blizzard at his grandmother's home in Hertfordshire, where they had spent the day, and wouldn't attempt to get home until it had cleared.

Once Martin had got the fire going, they sat for a few moments warming themselves in front of it. Then he suggested that if she would like to have a hot bath, she could use his mother's bathroom upstairs, and he would have one in his own bathroom. Nellie was impressed. Two bathrooms in one house! So this was how rich people lived. No signs of water rationing here, she thought to herself. But she was grateful for Martin's suggestion. He laid out one of his mother's dressing gowns for her, then he left her for his own bedroom upstairs.

Nellie enjoyed the luxury of her bath, and it certainly warmed her up as she lay there, soaking in the maximum amount of hot water permitted under Home Office war regulations. The wooden ledges round the bath were covered with Marion's cosmetics, and there were also two soft cotton flannels in different colours. Jacob's toiletries were more modest, and included a shaving stick and brush in a small bowl, and on the ledge above the sink, a lethal looking safety razor which looked anything but safe. Outside, the gale-force wind was blasting the windows with snow, which gave the bathroom a bright white glow.

When she had finished her bath, Nellie dried herself on what was definitely the largest bath towel she had ever seen, let alone used. She wrapped herself up in Marion's dressing gown, which almost touched the floor, and left the bathroom.

Martin had suggested that when she finished her bath, she might like to make them both a cup of tea, so she started to make her way to the kitchen which was on the other side of the stairs. She could hear Martin splashing about in his bath upstairs. She stopped and listened for a moment. In a carefully considered change of mind, she turned round and slowly made her way up the stairs.

Despite the fact that his injuries were now virtually healed, Martin still had to be careful as he got out of the bath. As he began to dry himself, he took a long, lingering look at his reflection in the full-length mirror. He hated what he saw, for although his black, wavy hair was now full and thick again, the burn marks down the side of his body still looked red and patchy, and no matter how hard he tried, he just couldn't dismiss his feelings of despair. As he averted his eyes from the sight, he was shocked to see someone else's reflection in the mirror, standing in the open doorway. It was Nellie.

'No, Nell!' he gasped, quickly covering himself with his towel.

Nellie didn't respond. After staring at him for a moment, she closed the door behind her and moved slowly across to him.

Martin backed away, agonised, shaking his head, trying to cover himself. 'No, Nell, please, I beg you, there's no way . . .'

Nellie ignored his protests, loosened the cord round her dressing gown, and let it fall to the floor.

Feeling traumatised and threatened, his face crumpled in anguish, Martin shook his head. But gradually his eyes could no longer resist the delicate white curves of Nellie's smooth, naked body.

She slowly moved forward and stood directly in front of him. Then she stretched out and with one hand removed his towel.

For one brief moment, they just stood there, staring into each other's eyes. Nellie took hold of both his hands and kissed them. Martin watched her, as if in a daze. Then Nellie moved to the side of his body that had been burnt. And in one, gentle, touching movement, she started to kiss the scars delicately, one at a time, until she had

410

tenderly caressed and kissed every one of them she could find. When she had finished, she looked up into Martin's eyes. They looked angry. But then Nellie smiled. Slowly, he smiled back.

He threw his arms round her, embraced her tightly, and kissed her passionately.

For the rest of the afternoon, they made love.

Monsieur and Madame were aware that Nellie was at last beginning to find the happiness that had eluded her for so long. She didn't have to tell them anything. They could see it in her eyes, in the way she got up in the mornings, and in the way she talked and looked. It was wonderful to see, for they knew how hard she had worked to help Martin regain his confidence and self-respect.

With young Lenny now on the road to recovery and back at school, times were at last improving at 147A Tufnell Park Road. Both Monsieur and Madame had put behind them the ugly events surrounding Ange and her so-called revealing snapshots, and they were now closer in their married life than they had been for many years. Nellie made quite sure that whenever there was an opportunity, her mum and dad should spend time together on their own. After all the years they had worked as a stage partnership, they needed to rebuild their life as husband and wife. Times were also changing for Sid. As he approached his seventeenth birthday, he acquired his first girlfriend; he was becoming more independent, and spent a lot of time with his friends.

At the beginning of December, Monsieur and Nellie started rehearsals for their panto season at the Ilford Hippodrome in Essex. Although the theatre was only just outside London, the journey there and back each day proved to be more of a hardship than they had expected, for it was already turning out to be one of the most severe winters for several years. The other problem was the V-1s and V-2s. Although the number of attacks was now considerably down from the height of the campaign a few weeks before, the Germans, in a last desperate attempt to stem the tide of the war against them, were launching V-1 flying bombs from regular heavy bomber planes. A considerable number, however, were caught in the lethal barrage balloon wires, and many more were shot down by the determined efforts of anti-aircraft gun crews. Much more sinister and worrying were the V-2 rocket bombs which came without warning, leaving the most horrific devastation in their wake.

Before the first read-through of *Robinson Crusoe* at Ilford, Monsieur had more or less decided to pull out of the show, insisting that he hadn't the right to put Nellie's life at risk by taking her into what he considered a danger zone. It was true that the eastern side of London was, at this time, more susceptible than anywhere else because the launching sites for the V-2s were based in Holland, but Nellie wouldn't hear of him pulling them out of the show. 'This is 'Itler's last fling,' she said. 'We mustn't let 'im ruin the kids' enjoyment. Not now, not after all we've bin fru.' Monsieur reluctantly agreed to go ahead with the show, but in order to prevent a hazardous journey by train to and from Ilford each day, he booked them into bed and breakfast digs just behind the theatre.

When Nellie arrived at the Ilford Hippodrome, she fell in love with the old music hall at first sight. Situated right on the main Ilford Broadway facing the clock tower, she thought it looked just like a large house, with three tall windows above the foyer entrance, a red and grey brick facing wall, and a tiled roof. Just beneath the huge words ILFORD HIPPODROME were four small sculptures in stone, like cupid's faces, and the impressive entrance below had no less than six polished timber doors. To Nellie, this was the ideal music hall, the perfect setting for a pantomime.

The theatre was equally impressive inside. The auditorium was a delight, with fauteuils, stalls, a grand circle and an upper circle, all in gilt and red plush like so many other music hall theatres. The orchestra pit seemed to be so small, however, that Nellie wondered if there was enough room down there for any musicians.

Meeting the cast was an extraordinary event because there were so many of them. Apart from the featured artistes, there were hordes of young teenagers in the singing and dancing chorus, some of them as young as thirteen and fourteen. Nellie wondered how all of them were going to fit into the few available dressing rooms.

The moment the cast got together, it was as though they had known each other all their lives. When Monsieur introduced Nellie to the stars of the show, Renee Houston and Donald Stewart, she knew at once that this was going to be a panto season that she would not forget. 'I tell ye,' muttered Miss Houston in her broad Scottish brogue, 'if I can squeeze into that sailor's costume, it'll be a downright miracle!' It was easy to see why she was not entirely comfortable playing the leading boy, for she was a lady of fairly ample proportions. Her American husband, Donald Stewart, who seemed to tower over her, just smiled affectionately at everything she said. He was clearly madly in love with her.

The first day's get-together was not entirely successful as far as Monsieur was concerned. It started soon after the read-through of the script, when the panto's energetic manager, Rex Mervyn, told Monsieur that, owing to the fact that the show was playing to three houses daily, Monsieur's regular Great Pierre act would have to be reduced to no more than a few minutes, which meant that both he and Nellie would have to concentrate more on ensemble work within the company. Monsieur was not at all pleased, but Nellie reminded him that it was, after all, only panto, so perhaps the best thing they

413

could do was to just get on with the show and enjoy themselves.

Three days before Christmas, Martin told Nellie that he had now been declared fit enough to return to his unit.

On their final day together, Nellie asked him if he would marry her.

Chapter 28

'*You* asked '*im* ter marry yer!'

'Yes.'

'You're round the loop! Gels don't ask fellers. Fellers ask gels.'

'Oh, don't be so old-fashioned, Sid. Why shouldn't a gel ask as much as a feller? It's the same fing.'

Nellie's exchange with Sid brought the Beckwiths' New Year's Eve party to an astonished halt. Even Madame was a bit taken aback. 'Yer 'ave ter admit, it is a bit unusual, dear,' she said tentatively.

'Oh, I don't know, Doris,' said Monsieur. 'I wouldn't've minded if you'd proposed ter me.'

'Not a hope!' replied Madame to gales of laughter from the other guests. Grandma and Grandad Beckwith were there, Monsieur's brother Louis and sister-in-law Merle, Madame's mum, and quite a few of Monsieur and Madame's music hall chums.

'The important fing is,' said Grandad Beckwith, 'wot answer did 'e give?'

Nellie was thoroughly enjoying the excitement she was causing, so she delayed her reply while she scanned the expectant faces of the party guests. ''E said – yes.'

There was a roar of approval, delight, cheers, and applause.

Madame threw her arms round Nellie and hugged her. 'Oh, Nell!' she said, quite overcome. 'I'm so 'appy for yer.'

415

'Not so fast, Mum,' said Nellie, taking a good, hard look at her. 'I'm still under age, remember. As your legally adopted daughter, I 'ave ter get yer permission first.' Then she turned to Monsieur. 'Yours – an' Dad's.'

Monsieur had a broad, happy grin on his face. 'Well, the answer's – no!'

There were groans and protests all round.

'Yer've only bin our daughter fer five minutes, an' you're goin' ter let some young bloke take yer away from us.' Then, after exchanging a mischievous look with Nellie, he opened his arms wide for her. 'Come 'ere, you!'

Nellie left her mum and went straight to her dad for a hug.

''E'd better treat yer right,' said Monsieur quietly into Nellie's ear. 'Or 'e'll 'ave me ter deal wiv.'

With the final hour of 1944 ticking away, Monsieur and Madame's party now had even more to celebrate. In many ways, it had been a grim Christmas, for not only was the winter turning out to be the worst many people could ever remember, with temperatures consistently below freezing, there was also a shortage of just about everything – fuel, turkeys, meat, vegetables, dairy products, sugar, basic toiletries such as soap, toothpaste, and corn pads, and even Christmas trees and paper decorations. Despite all these hardships, however, everyone at Monsieur and Madame's party had made up their minds that this was the last time they would have to celebrate the start of a New Year during wartime.

As most of Monsieur and Madame's pals were from the music hall, everyone, as usual, was expected to do their party piece. This meant a song or a stand-up comic routine or, once the sitting-room carpet had been rolled back, a soft shoe shuffle. There were plenty of old favourites, including ballads like 'I'll Get By', 'You'll

Never Know', and 'The White Cliffs of Dover', and good old rousing knees-up songs such as 'Any Old Iron', 'She'll Be Coming Round the Mountain', and 'Daisy Belle'. There were lots of impersonations of great artistes like Marie Lloyd, Randolph Sutton, Vesta Tilley and, of course, George Formby. Perhaps the most poignant duet of the evening, however, came from Grandma and Grandad Beckwith who, accompanied by Madame on the piano, sang unfalteringly 'My Old Dutch'. Nonetheless, final honours went to Nellie who, to thunderous applause, gave a flawless and utterly charming rendition of the song that was now so closely associated with her, 'When I Grow Too Old to Dream'.

At about ten minutes to twelve, Monsieur said his few traditional words to round off the year. 'When it come ter December thirty-first,' he said, 'most of us 'ere are convinced that the New Year's goin' ter be diff'rent to any year we've ever 'ad, an' in our case that means a few good bookin's an' 'opefully a summer season that goes on right fru till winter!'

Although Monsieur's comment brought laughter and applause, it was tinged with a certain amount of fore-boding, for there was no doubt in most of the guests' minds that once the war had ended, variety shows were going to have a hard struggle to survive.

'But I tell yer this much, me friends,' continued Monsieur, 'when Jerry's finally bin licked once an' fer all, you lot 'ere, an' all our mates up 'an down the country, well, I reckon we can 'old our 'eads up 'igh.'

Murmurs of ''Ear, 'ear!' from the others.

'The war this time round 'asn't only bin wiv our boys out on the battlefields, it's also bin right 'ere, amongst ordinary people, in the back streets, the pubs, the factories – in every walk of life. An' where they've bin, our lot 'as bin too, keepin' up their spirits, no matter wot it took. Like everyone else, we've risked our lives over an' over again – yes, an' we'd do it again if we 'ad ter.'

Calls of 'Absolutely!' and 'We would!' from the others.

'Wot I'm sayin' to yer, mates, is that as we come ter the end of this bleedin' war, our lot 'ave got quite a lot ter be proud of. Oh yes, they can call us show-offs but when we tread those boards, we at least bring a smile ter people's faces. It may not be much, but it's done its bit ter end this war.'

Nellie joined in enthusiastically with the chorus of approval.

'The uvver day,' continued Monsieur, 'I 'eard some-one on the wireless say that 'e fawt music 'all folk've got 'earts of gold. Well, maybe 'e's right, I dunno. But one fing I do know is that in years ter come, wherever you and me an' all our mates may be, I 'ope people won't ferget us, ferget wot we done in this war, an' not only in the war. 'Cos it's the good old music 'alls themselves that's given us our 'earts of gold. Make 'em sing, make 'em laugh, make 'em 'appy. That's our motto, it's always bin our motto. Whatever nineteen forty-five brings, no one can say that we didn't try. Gawd bless, an' 'Appy New Year to yer all!'

Everyone responded with a combined, ''Appy New Year, Bert! 'Appy New Year, Doris!'

'It's time!' yelled Lenny as he turned up the volume on the wireless.

The solemn chimes of Big Ben ushered in the New Year, and everyone joined hands to sing 'Auld Lang Syne'.

By one o'clock in the morning, Monsieur had drunk so much brown ale that he was packed off to bed. It was left to Madame and Nellie to see the remaining guests off at the front gate. It was bitingly cold outside, and the two or three inches of snow that had fallen during

418

the previous few days had turned to ice. There wasn't a cloud in the sky, and Nellie thought that the moon was so bright, it looked like a huge theatre spotlight picking her and Madame out on a vast white stage. Despite the cold, for a moment or so the two of them stood at the gate, staring up at the magnificent sky with its great universe of stars flickering down at them.

'Nuffin' seems to 'ave changed, does it?' said Madame, her arms crossed to keep warm. 'Them stars up there. They don't look any different ter last year. An' that was only an hour ago.'

Nellie put her arm round her mum's waist and leaned her head against her. 'They look just as beautiful,' she said, the warmth from her breath mixing with the cold night air and quickly disappearing into the stark white moonlight.

For a moment, they said nothing, their faces bathed in the incandescent glow.

'Goin' ter be quite a change fer all of us though, this year,' said Madame, soft and reflective. 'The end of the war. You married.' She sighed wistfully. 'We're goin' ter miss yer, Nell. In yer own way, yer've changed all our lives.'

Nellie hugged her tight. 'Yer won't get rid of me that fast, Mum. In fact, yer'll *never* get rid of me.' She raised her head and looked up at Madame. 'I'm a Beckwiff, remember. Us Beckwiffs 'ave got a rosy future ahead of us.'

High above them, a shooting star shot across the cold dark sky. It reflected in both women's eyes.

Nellie didn't say what was in her mind. That the shooting star reminded her a bit of a V-2 rocket.

Robinson Crusoe opened at the Ilford Hippodrome on Monday, 8 January. Once again it was freezing cold outside, but the first house three o'clock matinee was a resounding success. Nellie loved the way everyone mucked in with each other. Even the stars of the show, Renee Houston and Donald Stewart, moved scenery around when something didn't go quite right, and there were an awful lot of giggles among the cast. Monsieur soon got over his resentment at being given so little to do in the panto, and during the long periods that he was not required on stage, he either put his feet up in the dressing room he shared with some other male members of the cast or took the opportunity to pop out and have a quick half-pint at the nearby Black Horse pub.

Nellie found being in a panto three times a day quite hard work. But the atmosphere, both in front and behind the footlights, was quite unlike anything she had ever experienced. It was mainly because of the excitement generated by the audience themselves, and especially the kids. The look of awe on their small faces as they saw Robinson Crusoe come to the edge of the stage to talk directly to them was a sight to behold. The excitement was infectious, so much so that the cast forgot how exhausted they were after two or three weeks of rehearsals. Nellie herself was astonished at the things she had learnt to do. For this show, she was joining in the popular songs of the day, dancing, and at one point even taking part in a fantasy scene involving Kirby's famous flying ballet. But she didn't mind what she was asked to do, and by the time she and Monsieur launched into a condensed version of the Great Pierre act, she felt like an all-round trouper.

Between those Monday first night shows, Nellie decided to write a letter to Martin. To her delight, he had already written one to her, even though it had been less than a fortnight since she last saw him. She had no idea where the letter had been posted, and it had clearly been heavily censored, but as she read the words she had been allowed to read, she felt a warm glow, as though she was snuggled up right there in his arms:

420

New Year's Day   Somewhere
(Can't tell you where!)

My Dearest Nell,

It's the first day of 1945, and here I am in XXXXX where it's so cold, I can't even feel my toes! Worst of all, I miss you like hell. Every time I get depressed, I look at that snapshot you gave me, and I suddenly remember that I'm the luckiest bloke alive. I love you, Nell. If you don't know that by now, then you're just as crazy as I am. I want to marry you. I want us to have a place of our own. I want us to have kids. I want us to have more kids. I want us to have *even* more kids. Oh, and by the way, I'm not going to put you through the ordeal of being converted (to a Jew!). I think you already know my feelings on that matter. In fact, I've told my mother and father that when you and me get married (*soon!!!*), we can do it in a register office, no problems, no worries, no upsetting anyone. I hope you agree? Yes?

Sorry. Got to go. Please keep away from V-1s, V-2s, anything that Jerry can still send over. Oh, and by the way, keep away from any other bloke, because if you don't, I might commit murder.

I love you, Nell. Oh God, I can't tell you how much I do love you.

Your Toff (Martin to you!) X X X

Although she had only received the letter two days before, Nellie had read it so many times, it was getting Five and Nine make-up all over it. The problem was, how to reply to a letter like that, so full of love and determination? Nellie had sighed to herself many times since she first read it. If only she had Martin's brains and was capable of telling him all the things she wanted to tell him.

421

With three performances of the panto each day, Nellie was relieved that Monsieur had booked them into a lodgings just behind the theatre. The digs, in a terrace of small cottages, were fairly modest, but at least they were clean and, thankfully, quiet. Nellie particularly loved the breakfasts, which were cooked by the elderly landlady and her husband. She never bothered to ask where they managed to get the fresh farm eggs from, nor what seemed to be an endless supply of bacon, tomatoes, and even baked beans.

When Nellie and Monsieur returned to the cottage after the third house show on the fourth day of what was to be a two-week season, Nellie was surprised to find Monsieur going into the tiny downstairs sitting room instead of straight to his own room, as he usually did. 'Got somefin' ter tell yer, Nell,' he said, kicking off his shoes and flopping down into a comfortable easy chair.

Nellie knew something was brewing; she had sensed it ever since opening night a few days before. She curled up on the settee opposite him. 'Wot's wrong, Dad?' she asked.

'Nuffin' wrong,' replied Monsieur. 'In fact, I feel better than I've felt fer a long time. Can see fings straight,' he said, lighting up a Woodbine fag without using the holder. Nellie had noticed that he had stopped smoking his Abdullahs. 'Now I've made me decision, I feel marvellous.'

Nellie was puzzled. 'Decision?'

'I'm callin' it a day, Nell,' he said. 'I'm turnin' it in.'

'Wot d'yer mean?'

'I've 'ad enough treadin' the boards. It's time ter move on.'

'Dad!'

'It's nuffin' ter worry about, Nell,' he insisted. 'Me

422

an' Doris've bin talkin' it over fer a long time. I just feel I've done all I can wiv this act. I don't want ter go on till the customers start peltin' me wiv tomarters or somefink. Every pro knows when it's time ter call it a day. We can't go on fer ever.'

'That's not true, Dad!' Upset, Nellie sat up straight on the settee. 'Yer mustn't give up just because they 'aven't given yer full time in the panto.'

Monsieur was shaking his head. 'It's got nuffin' ter do wiv the panto, Nell,' he said. 'I've bin wantin' ter do this fer a long time. I want ter live the rest of me life wiv me family. I want ter be part of 'em. I want them ter be a part of me.' He leaned forward in his chair. 'In a few years' time, Nell, there won't be such a fing as music 'all any more. When the war's over, we'll be on the scrap 'eap, just like anyone who's bin around fer too long.'

Nellie stared at him with incredulity. 'But the 'alls've bin your 'ole life, Dad. Wot're yer goin' ter do wivout 'em?'

'I'm goin' inter partnership with Eddie, my agent. We're goin' ter set up an office down the West End, bookin' acts for revues and clubs, that sorta fing. Believe me, Nell, it's goin' ter be big business.'

Nellie slumped back on to the settee again.

Monsieur could see Nellie's concern, and immediately sought to reassure her. 'Don't you worry about a fing, Nell,' he said eagerly. 'Eddie and me've got big ideas fer you. We reckon we could get you into the new revue at the London 'Ippodrome wiv no trouble at all. They say Vic Oliver's goin' ter do somefin' really big there, and—'

'Dad. I don't want ter be in the feater. Not wivout you. Not wivout the people I care for most. I joined the Great Pierre by accident, remember. If it 'adn't bin fer Ange an' all that, I'd still be sewin' away backstage, just like Ruby taught me.'

'But, Nell,' protested Monsieur, 'you're a natural. The customers love yer. Yer can really go to the top if yer set yer mind to it.'

'I don't want ter go ter the top, Dad,' replied Nellie, taking his hands and holding them. 'I told yer once before, the bright lights ain't fer me. When you've frown yer 'at in, the only fing I want ter do is ter get married ter Martin.'

Monsieur paused a moment, looking deep into Nellie's eyes. 'D'yer mean that, Nell?' he asked. 'D'yer *really* mean it?'

Nellie took a deep breath. 'I've never meant anyfin' so much in me 'ole life.'

'It's a big decision ter take, Nell,' he replied, after another pause. 'Marriage is fer life. Yer 'ave ter work 'ard at it. You're still only young, gel. Yer 'ave ter be sure you're makin' the right decision.'

Nellie had a resolute look on her face. 'I *am* makin' the right decision, Dad. Believe me.'

'It won't be easy 'itchin' up ter someone from a strict religious upbringin'. A lot of me mates 'round the 'alls are Jews, Nell. They don't all take kindly to their kids gettin' mixed up wiv people from uvver religions.'

'Dad,' said Nellie, 'Martin and me ain't marryin' our mums an' dads. We ain't marryin' our diff'rent religions. We're marryin' each uvver. Trust me.'

Monsieur squeezed her hands. 'I trust yer, Nell,' he replied, moved by her candour. 'I trust yer more than anyone else in the 'ole wide world.'

The matinee performance on Friday was a real pig. It had something to do with the kids being too overawed by the occasion. Some of them cried when the pirates threatened Robinson Crusoe, and for some reason or another they just wouldn't join in with the traditional sing-song at the end. It was hard going for most of the cast, and good-natured as she was about the young panto customers, even Renee Houston was so exhausted she was heard to exclaim as she came off stage, 'Aye. Well, I know what I'd like to do with *that* little lot!'

Fortunately, the second house customers were totally different. From the gods to the fauteuils, they filed to their seats laughing and joking, calling excitedly to each other, and staring hard at the front of house curtains as though they couldn't wait for them to open to reveal a whole world of fun, mystery, and magic. Which was exactly what they were about to do.

Backstage in the dressing room that Nellie was sharing with some of the younger chorus girls in the show, the call boy had already called the 'five', which meant that the overture would be starting in five minutes, and that opening performers should be ready to go on stage. Monsieur had nothing to do in the show for twenty-five minutes or so, but Nellie was already togged up in her sailor costume to take part in the opening ensemble number.

The audience was now in its usual high state of excitement and anticipation, and by the time the orchestra had finished playing a medley of popular tunes for the overture, the cast was in position for the opening number.

Exactly on cue, up went the main front curtain to the strains of 'The Fleet's In', to reveal the entire stage filled with pantomime sailors in white uniforms. Within a few moments, Robinson Crusoe, in the person of Renee Houston, came strutting on to the stage in true nautical style. It was a typical star entrance, and the star played it up for all she was worth. As she launched into the song, the whole stage, with its backcloth of a sailing ship, came to life, with singers and dancers, including Nellie, and all the show's supporting artistes, swaying in time to the music. It was a glorious, colourful spectacle, which thrilled the family audience who joined in with the song, waved, and clapped their hands and tapped their feet in time to the music. This second house audience could not have been more different from the dour matinee crowd. Even the leading man, Donald Stewart, who was waiting to go on, told the stage manager that this was the sort of audience that all performers loved playing to.

During the opening number of each show, Renee Houston would stop the music, lean over the footlights, and talk to the children who were nearest the stage. This was the part of the show that Nellie liked best, for the faces of the small children were an absolute picture as they watched Robinson Crusoe actually talking to them. Tonight, the theatre was packed to the rafters, and when the music stopped, Nellie was certain that she could hear every little heart in the theatre pounding with excitement.

'Hello, children!' called Robinson Crusoe to all his young crew out there in the audience. But before there was time for their response, the show came to a dramatic halt as a loud explosion suddenly shook the entire building. There were screams from all parts of the house as scenery came crashing down on to the performers, with the star of the show knocked off balance and thrown heavily into the orchestra pit. In the wings, the leading man was struck hard on the head by a falling beam, and soon everything and everybody was covered in dust and masonry from the collapsing walls round the stage. Nellie was blown off her feet by the force of the explosion, and before she had the chance to recover, the huge sailing ship backcloth came hurtling down on top of her. The orchestra had immediately stopped playing, and the sound of young teenage chorus girls screaming out in terror seemed louder than ever. Meanwhile, the audience, who were so far unhurt, looked on in horrified astonishment as the entire stage area seemed to disintegrate before their very eyes.

Dazed, and covered in dust and plaster, the stage manager struggled on to the stage and grabbed hold of the microphone in a desperate appeal to the audience. 'Keep calm, everyone,' he called. 'Please, keep calm.'

The audience made their way in an orderly retreat to the nearest exits. Cut, bruised, and in a state of shock, Renee Houston was helped back on to the stage, where she immediately joined in the rescue operation. Whilst this was going on, the orchestra's conductor, who had himself been cut by falling debris, raised his baton, and got his musicians to start playing again. The departing audience were astonished to hear music booming out from the orchestra pit, and turned back to applaud and cheer this amazing display of courage.

On stage, there was pandemonium, with everyone searching for friends and fellow artistes buried beneath the rubble.

'Sylve! Where are yer, Sylve?'

'Over here! Please, somebody, over here!'

'Give us a hand, someone!'

'Watch that beam!'

'Get back! Get back!'

The frenzied calls for help were in danger of being overwhelmed by the sound of 'Daisy Belle' belting out from the orchestra pit. Scenery and masonry was still crashing down everywhere, and it seemed as though the whole stage would cave in at any moment.

Adding to all the mayhem, a special effects machine high above the stage started to spray everyone with water. 'Bloody thing!' shouted one of the backstage staff who was desperately trying to remove a steel girder which had pinned one of the chorus girls under a heap of rubble. Then several girls started to scream as sections of one of the upper stage boxes came crashing down.

427

Someone else was yelling out hysterically after a large pane of glass had dropped straight down on to her foot, almost severing it, and one of the stage electricians was struggling to free himself from some lighting equipment which had toppled over, sending huge blue sparks across the mass of smoking cables. Cut and bleeding, Renee Houston finally reached her husband, Donald Stewart, who had been injured by falling timber and masonry and was being helped off stage by the stage manager.

Mercifully, Nellie had missed the worst of the falling debris. All around her, young teenage chorus girls were wandering about, dazed and sobbing, trying to come to terms with the chaos around them. The smell of gunpowder was everywhere, giving the only real clue to the source of the blast.

Struggling through the wreckage backstage, Nellie finally managed to reach the stairs leading up to the dressing rooms, where she found scenes of horror. As most of the lighting system had been demolished, the place was in darkness and she had to pick her way carefully over the debris. There were shouts of panic and confusion everywhere, and by the light of the few available torch beams, Nellie could see that some walls were bulging dangerously, others had simply collapsed, and inside the dressing rooms window frames had been blown out completely, glass shattered, and dressing table mirrors and electric lightbulbs fragmented. In her own dressing room, she immediately set about helping some of the stagehands who were using their bare hands to try to free two teenage chorus girls who were trapped under a pile of rubble, screaming their heads off. The young girls' injuries were terrible, including severe cuts and facial injuries. One of them had an eye that was bleeding profusely, and another had lost several front teeth. 'It's all right,' Nellie said, over and over again, trying to comfort and reassure both girls who were sobbing hysterically. 'They'll soon 'ave yer out. It's all right. Just 'old on.' The look of terror on their innocent young faces upset Nellie deeply. It was something she would remember for the rest of her life.

Once the girls had been freed from the rubble, Nellie went off to find her dad. 'Bert Beckwiff!' she yelled at every person who passed her in the dark. 'The Great Pierre! 'Ave yer seen 'im?' There was too much going on all around for anyone to help her very much. She picked her way over the rubble to the dressing room her dad had been sharing with three other performers. When she got there, she was horrified to find that all that was left of the room was a pile of rubble.

'Nellie? Nellie Beckwiff? Is that you?'

Nellie turned with a start to find someone pointing a torch beam directly into her face. 'Yes!' she answered, unable to see who was talking to her. 'Me dad. Wot's 'appened ter me dad?'

''E went back ter the cottage, Nellie,' replied the shadowy figure. ''E said 'e was goin' ter wait there till 'e was due on – before the show started.'

Nellie gasped and clenched her hands together in relief. 'Oh, fank God!' she said. 'Fank God!' But as she started to rush off, the shadowy figure called out to her.

'Nellie!'

Nellie stopped and turned. The torch was shining into her face again.

'The cottages, Nellie. The rocket, the V-2. It came down on the cottages at the back of the theatre. It was a direct hit.'

Nellie had to fight her way through the audience hurrying out of the theatre. Everyone was in a state of shock and seemed too dazed to get out of the way to allow the Civil Defence and other emergency services to get through. The street itself was nothing less than sheer chaos, for hardly a building had escaped the V-2 explosion. Shops, houses, a cinema and various pubs, including Monsieur's favourite, the Black Horse, looked as though they had taken a tremendous hammering. Windows were blown, chimney pots and roofs were down, and customers were wandering about in a daze, blood streaming from face and hand wounds. Nearby, a trolley bus had clearly had a miraculous escape, despite the fact that all its windows had been blown in. Its poles had become detached from the overhead electric cables and were producing dangerous blue flashes as they dangled about perilously. The noise was indescribable, for apart from the constant clanging of fire, police and ambulance bells, every person in the entire street seemed to be shouting in desperation.

For Nellie, the worst part of the nightmare was still to come, for when she finally reached the cottage where she and her dad had been lodging, she found that, like other houses in the same terrace, there was nothing left but a heap of rubble. As the Civil Defence started to move in searchlights to begin rescue operations, Nellie's mind was torn by images of her own escape from Barratts' Orphanage just a few years before. 'Dad!' she yelled at the rubble, her hands tearing through her hair in despair and tears welling up in her eyes. 'Don't do this ter me, Dad! Don't do it!'

The searchlights were turned on and the whole area was immediately transformed into a sea of glaring white. Within seconds, special sniffer dogs arrived and were soon scrambling all over the debris, in a race against time to find survivors.

Nellie stood there, her face still covered in stage make-up but now smeared with dust and soot and blood from a gash on her forehead. Her carefully permed hair was full of small particles of glass and plaster dust, and her white sailor's costume and stockings were grey and torn. For one brief moment as she stood there, with the glare of the searchlights on her agonised face, she felt as though she was back on stage again with her dad, facing those bright lights with the Great Pierre. With tears now streaming down her face, and the noise of the frenzied, desperate rescue operation going on all around her, she slowly started to sing to herself, 'When I Grow Too Old to Dream'. Until finally she sank down on to her knees, covered her face with her hands, and dissolved into tears.

'Nell.'

At first she didn't hear who was talking to her. Then she felt a pair of arms round her shoulders. Her eyes glistening with tears, she slowly looked up. 'Dad!' She leapt to her feet and hugged him. 'Oh Dad!' she sobbed. 'I fawt yer was gone. I fawt yer was gone!'

Monsieur held on to her tightly. 'No, Nell, not me,' he replied, his own voice cracking with emotion. 'They don't call me the Great Pierre fer nuffin', yer know.'

Chapter 29

Nellie was becoming a little worried about her eldest daughter, Vicky. It wasn't that she was a bad girl, far from it. In fact, she often did things that surprised both her mum and her dad, like clearing the table after a meal or taking the dog for a walk, and occasionally helping to bath her newly arrived little sister Esther. The trouble was that Vicky was at a difficult age, when kids sometimes start getting a bit cheeky and independent, like her mum had been at the same age. Nellie and Martin, however, had begun to notice that Vicky, at eleven years old, and the eldest child, was beginning to show some resentment of the way her parents were, in her mind, showing too much attention to the younger members of the family, her brother Abraham, who was four years old, and baby Esther. That was the main reason why Nellie had suggested a day out, for it gave all the family a chance to be together and to show that there were no favourites.

Of course, it helped that Grandma and Grandad Beckwith were with them. After all, a day at the seaside wouldn't be the same without them, especially as the old folk would be able to keep an eye on the kids if Nellie and Martin should want to go off and spend a little time on their own. There was certainly enough room in the car, for now that Martin had a secure job as a senior floor manager at Woolworth's department store in Holloway Road, he had been able to put enough money aside to rent a decent two up, two down semi in a quiet back street up near the Archway. He also had a good enough credit rating to put a down payment on a second-hand Ford Anglia car which Nellie washed and polished so regularly, it was a wonder any of its green paint was left intact.

'I wouldn't mind an 'alf-crown fer every time we've done this journey, eh, gel?' Monsieur said to his wife who was sitting at his side in the back seat, with young Vicky squeezed up by the window and Abraham perched on his grandad's lap.

Madame sighed, then turned and gave him a wistful smile.

'I must say, I was amazed yer wanted ter go ter Soufend again, Dad,' said Nellie from the front seat, cradling little Esther in her arms. 'I fawt yer'd be bored stiff wiv the place by now.'

'Bored stiff?' spluttered Monsieur indignantly. '*Me* bored stiff wiv Soufend? Yer got ter be jokin'! Soufend can knock spots off the French Riviera any time!'

'We've 'ad some of our 'appiest days there, that's fer sure,' said Madame. 'Specially wiv you, Nell. An' Sid – an' our dear young Len.'

Nellie didn't have to see her mum's face to know how she was feeling. Young Lenny's death from secondary TB a couple of years after the war had devastated the whole family. It was a loss that none of them had ever really got over. In her mind's eye, she could see his face before her now, reflected in the windscreen in front of her, so lively, so cheeky, so curious about life, and living. Lenny's death at such a young age was a tragedy. He had so much to live for.

Madame leaned forward slightly so that Nellie could hear her. 'Remember that first outing you ever came on wiv us?' she asked. 'We went ter Clacton, that Easter Monday, 'bout 'forty-two it must've bin.'

Nellie half turned and said over her shoulder, 'Don't be silly, Mum. Course I remember!'

Oh, Nellie remembered all right. She remembered every single day she had ever spent with her family, not only the trips to the seaside. She remembered every Christmas and New Year, the parties with Monsieur and Madame's music hall pals, and the chin-wags with her mum every time they went out shopping down Seven Sisters Road together. She remembered those days when she first met her future mum and dad, when she waited on them at Beales Restaurant, and Monsieur relished the fact that some of the other customers recognised him. And she remembered her brother Sid, oh, long before he got married, then divorced, then married for a second time. What a lot of water had passed under the bridge since those days when she taught him how to box and to stand up for his rights against Alfie Clipper, the school bully. Fifteen years ago! It hardly seemed possible. But most of all, Nellie remembered what it had felt like to be part of a family, a real family, with all its ups and downs, all the bad things as well as the good, the crises, the disagreements, the sulks, the moods, the tensions. On the day God was dishing out luck, she thought to herself, she must have been in His good books.

'Are you sure you want to go via Ilford?'

Martin's voice snapped Nellie out of her thoughts. 'Sorry, love,' she said. 'Wot did yer say?'

'Ilford. We have to turn off at the next junction if you want to stop off there.'

'All right, Dad? Shall we do it?'

'All right wiv me,' replied Monsieur. Even as he said it, he wasn't sure that it was all right. But it was something that had to be done. He knew that.

In fact, both he and Nellie knew that this was their last chance to do something they should have done a long time ago.

Martin drew the car to a halt outside a chemist's shop at the far end of Ilford Broadway. Everything looked very different

435

from how it was during that traumatic time in the last year of the war. A lot more people were around, building was going on everywhere, there was more traffic, and a lot more in the shop windows than there ever was during the war. But this was, after all, 1957, and the world had moved on. Not necessarily for the better, Nellie often thought, with the Russians invading Hungary, and the British and French seizing the Suez Canal. It seemed as though no one had learnt anything from all the horrors of the last war.

Once everyone had got out of the car, Martin retrieved little Esther's pushchair from the car boot and helped Nellie to strap her into it.

'Where's the sea, Grandad?' asked Abraham as he held firmly on to Monsieur's hand.

'Don't be so stupid, Abe!' snapped Vicky. 'Ilford's not by the sea. Everyone knows that!'

Madame was the only one who really understood why her granddaughter was always so spiky towards her kid brother, so she put a reassuring arm round her and walked along with her.

Nellie and Martin moved off first, with Martin pushing little Esther, and Grandma and Grandad following on behind with Vicky and Abraham. 'Are you sure you're going to be able to cope with this?' Martin asked Nellie as they went.

Nellie turned a brief, weak smile towards him and nodded her head. 'I want ter see it just this once before they start pullin' it down,' she said. 'Then I can put it all be'ind me. It's best fer Dad too.'

Martin put his arm round her waist and pushed Esther's chair with one hand. As they slowly wandered along the Broadway, she leaned her head against him, and if it hadn't been for Esther in her pushchair, passers-by would have taken them for any young lovers. To Nellie, however, her Toff had been so much more than a lover. Ever since the V-2 explosion had nearly killed her and her dad on that cold January evening twelve years before, Martin had been a tower of love and support, not only to her but to the entire Beckwith family. The thought that he might have lost her for ever had been too much for him, and as soon as he was told what had happened, the only thing he wanted was to take Nellie and hold on to her for the rest of his life. That time came on a rainswept morning in August, soon after Martin was demobbed from the RAF and just a month before Nellie's twenty-first birthday, when they got themselves, in her brother Sid's words, 'well and truly hitched' at the register office at Islington Town Hall. And despite Martin's concerns about his parents' religious objections to the marriage, they and other members of his family turned up in force on the day, and got on like a house on fire with everyone on Nellie's side.

It was only a short stroll to the old Hippodrome, and when they heard the sound of pneumatic drills, they knew they were drawing close. The old music hall, or what was left of it, was due for demolition. Nellie knew it was bound to happen one day, but she still felt a sense of loss and grief that it was actually going to disappear for ever.

The whole family was now standing on the pavement which had at one time been the entrance to the theatre. All they could see now was a mass of fallen, twisted steel girders, the shell of a once beautiful auditorium, and mountains of rubble over what had once been the stage. It was a sad and poignant sight.

'Is *this* a music 'all, Mum?' asked Vicky, who was clearly not going to grow any taller than Nellie had been at her age.

'It was, darlin',' Nellie replied. 'A long time ago.'

'Don't you believe it,' said Monsieur. 'It's still a music 'all. Can't yer 'ear it?'

A blank, quizzical look came over Vicky's face. She was trying to listen really hard. 'I can't 'ear nuffin',' she said.

'It's there,' insisted her grandad, putting his arm round her. 'Listen to 'em, Vicks, listen! People laughin', singin'.' He drew close to her and lowered his voice. 'Now they're tap-dancin'. Can yer 'ear 'em tap-dancin'? An' the band. Can yer 'ear the band?'

Again, the child listened carefully, then shook her head. All she could hear was the sound of building workers with their pneumatic drills.

'Yer 'ave ter listen real 'ard, Vicks,' said Grandad. 'You ask yer mum.'

Nellie exchanged a knowing, affectionate smile with her dad. She didn't have to listen hard, for she could hear everything. She could see it too. In fact, in the middle of all that rubble, the dust, and burning timbers, she could see not only the beautiful old Ilford Hippodrome but every one of those magnificent music halls she had ever been inside. Empires, Hippodromes, Metropolitans, Grands, Alhambras – they were all there. Wood Green, Chiswick, Shepherd's Bush, all those wonderful boards up and down the country, and of course her beloved Finsbury Park Empire. And as she raised her eyes to look up at what had once been the old Hippodrome gods, the sun on her face felt just like a bright spotlight, picking her out on stage. But there were no bright lights for Nellie now, and there never would be again. The only lights she wanted, had ever wanted, were her own family, and all those she would never stop loving – the brightest lights of all.

'Not much point in 'angin' 'round 'ere, eh, Dad?' said Nellie, linking arms with him. 'Bit too noisy fer me.'

It wasn't too noisy for Monsieur. He wasn't aware of the sound of pneumatic drills or falling masonry and steel girders. No. As he and his small family group slowly turned and moved off, the only sound the Great Pierre could hear was that of a girl's pure young voice singing 'When I Grow Too Old to Dream'.

Goodnight Amy

Victor Pemberton

'G'night, Amy. G'night.'

Those were the last words Amy Dodds heard her mum say. That night, Agnes Dodds walked out of the family home in Islington and disappeared into the streets of a London devastated by the Blitz.

For Amy, struggling to hold the family together, there is no time to feel sorry. With no mum, and a dad who proves himself useless, Amy sees little hope for the future until she meets Tim Gudgeon. Tim, who has secretly always loved Amy, fills her with the determination to find Agnes and discover why she left. But Agnes took a dark secret with her – one that Amy may wish she had never heard . . .

Praise for Victor Pemberton

'A vivid story of a community surviving some of the darkest days in our history . . . warm-herated' *Bolton Evening News*

'A real treat' *Peterborough Evening Telegraph*

'Warm and entertaining . . . brimming with the atmosphere of wartime London' *Coventry Evening Telegraph*

0 7472 6125 3

headline

Leo's Girl

Victor Pemberton

Some decisions can change you forever. For Peggy Thornton it is the decision to become a clippie to help with the war effort. It is a brave choice. She faces opposition from her family, who think the job is beneath her, and from her new work colleagues, who are suspicious of the nice, middle-class girl from Highgate Hill.

Peggy finds consolation in her blossoming relationship with Leo, one of the mechanics. But can they survive their parents' constant attempts to split them up? Especially when Peggy and Leo both doubt whether it's right to turn your back on everything you know for love. It isn't until the Blitz itself strikes that differences are finally set aside in the desperate struggle to save lives although, for some, it may be too late . . .

Praise for Victor Pemberton:

'A wonderfully detailed and involving study of a community surviving the destruction of war' Barry Forshaw, Amazon

'A vivid story of a community surviving some of the darkest days in our history . . . warm-hearted' *Bolton Evening News*

'A real treat' *Peterborough Evening Telegraph*

'Warm and entertaining . . . brimming with the atmosphere of wartime London' *Coventry Evening Telegraph*

0 7472 6652 2

headline

A Perfect Stranger

Victor Pemberton

The advent of the Second World War changes everything. So, when Tom, home on leave, asks Ruth to marry him, she agrees. After all, once Tom returns to the front, who knows if they'll ever see each other again? But months go by and Tom's letters dry up. Ruth is forced to get on with her life and starts to enjoy the attentions of another man. It is this temptation which will alter her life for ever. And when the war is finally over she will find the battle for her own personal freedom and safety has just begun . . .

A Perfect Stranger is a deeply emotional, evocative and gripping account of the difficult decisions facing women left on their own.

Praise for Victor Pemberton's wartime sagas

'A wonderfully detailed and involving study of a community surviving the destruction of war' Barry Forshaw, *Amazon*

'A potent mix of passion and suspense' *Evening Herald*

'A vivid story of a community surviving some of the darkest days in our history . . . warm-hearted' *Bolton Evening News*

'A real treat' *Peterborough Evening Telegraph*

'Warm and entertaining . . . brimming with the atmosphere of wartime London' *Coventry Evening Telegraph*

0 7472 6653 0

headline